Box Set collection contains:

Sexy Beast (Book 1)

Just one taste... And I'll wrap myself around you're heart

Layla Eden

He's forbidden and everything I should loathe in a man. Arrogant, foul-mouthed, inked, a bare-knuckle fighter, thinks he's God's gift to women, and yet ... one look into his magnetic eyes and I am doing crazy things I've never imagined doing.

I tell myself just one taste -- what harm can it do?

But what happens if one taste is not enough...

Billy Joe Pilkington

She's the hottest girl I know, and I've been lusting for her since I was old enough to fuck, but she's also a spoiled little fucking princess who swoons about the place like she's something special.

She wasn't so high and mighty after her first lesson on my knees.

Well I've got news for her -- I'm gonna kick down her walls, strip away the façade, and take what I want. And this time I'll keep what's mine...

Wounded Beast (Book 2)

What happens when the good girl meets a hard, ripped and dominant bad boy?

Ella

The first time I met Dominic his magnetic arrogance took my breath away. He was everything I'd never expected to have. Inked and Dangerous, a real Alpha bad boy.
But it was my job that led me into his path and he hit me like a freight train that I never saw coming. Suddenly this complicated man beast has erased the staleness of my terribly dull life and replaced it with a lust for the excitement, danger and knowledge he brings to my life.
The longer I'm with him, the more I need him.
His touch answers needs I never knew my body had.
Now, all I want is him.
Everything is perfect, well almost. Except there's the parts of him that I cannot reach. The parts he keeps locked away. The parts he wont let me explore...

Dominic

I've been dead for years. I wasn't looking for anything other than meaningless sex. But Ella had something that intrigued and enticed me. From the moment we locked eyes she got my attention.
Fuck it. I should have let her go.
But I can't. Instead, I lose myself in her body.
She thinks she can fix the pain. Save me.

But not even her incredible magic can conjurr up a potion to remedy that. Or can it ?

Beautiful Beast (Book 3)

He's determined to make her his... No matter the cost.

Snow:
If only he hadn't wrapped his strong hand around my wrist and caused me to look into those wickedly intoxicating eyes. But he did. Now I can't get this sexy alpha bad boy out of my head. There's just one obstacle. I belong to someone else. Though I don't love him, I'm a possession he's willing to kill for...

Shane:
If only she hadn't come into my club, and turned my head. But she did.
Now I'll risk it all to have this fairytale beauty in my bed. There's just one obstacle. She's indebted to him and forbidden to me. But I don't care. .
I'll die before I let him keep her...

ALSO BY GEORGIA

The Billionaire Banker Series

Owned

42 Days

Besotted

Seduce Me

Love's Sacrifice

Masquerade

Pretty Wicked (Novella)

Disfigured Love

Crystal Jake

Sexy Beast

Wounded Beast

Beautiful Beast

Dirty Aristocrat

Click on the link below to receive news of my latest releases.

http://bit.ly/1Oe9WdE

BAD BOYS OF LONDON

Published by Georgia Le Carre
Copyright © 2016 by Georgia Le Carre

ISBN: 978-1-910575-29-1

You can discover more information about Georgia Le Carre and future
releases here.

https://www.facebook.com/georgia.lecarre
https://twitter.com/georgiaLeCarre
http://www.goodreads.com/GeorgiaLeCarre

Dedication

Thank you Joseph Murray from 3rdplanetpublishing.com

for your skilled formatting services.

A Bad Boy
Romance

SEXY BEAST

International Bestselling Author

GEORGIA LE CARRE

SEXY BEAST

GEORGIA LE CARRE

Cover Designer: http://www.bookcoverbydesign.co.uk/
Editor: http:// jlynnemorrison@hotmail.com/
Proofreader: http:// http://nicolarheadediting.com/

Sexy Beast

Published by Georgia Le Carre
Copyright © 2015 by Georgia Le Carre

ISBN: 978-1-910575-13-0

The Mouse On The Bar Room Floor

Some Guinness was spilt on the bar room floor
When the pub was shut for the night.
Out of his hole crept a wee brown mouse
And, in the pale moonlight,
He lapped up the frothy brew from the floor,
Then back on his haunches he sat.
And all night long you could hear him roar,
'Bring on the goddamn cat!'

—An Irish Tall Tale

ONE

Layla

Love is when a girl puts on perfume and a boy puts on shaving cologne and they go out and smell each other.

—Karl, Age 5

'What are you standing there for? Go use the upstairs bathroom,' Ria says when she spots me at the end of the queue for the downstairs bathroom.

She is right. The queue *is* long. 'I'll just use the portaloo outside,' I reply.

'Don't be so silly. There's a humongous queue there, too.'

I bite my lip. Ria is BJ Pilkington's second cousin and we are in his house, Silver Lee, a cavernous mansion built in the art deco style with massive windows that wrapped all the way around the front and sides. BJ threw this party for my brother, Jake, and his new wife, Lily. And while I like and socialize with Ria, BJ and I share a stinging mutual dislike for each other.

In fact, I hadn't even wanted to come, but my mother forced me to. 'It's in your brother's honor,' she said in that displeased tone I knew not to disobey. 'It'd be ignorant not to, and God help me, I didn't bring you up to be ignorant.'

'Are you really sure it'll be OK?' I ask, looking doubtfully up the long, curving, dark wood staircase. Nobody else seemed to be going up it. It is understood that the party is restricted to the four reception rooms downstairs.

'Of course,' she insists confidently.

I give it one last attempt. 'I don't even know where it is, and I don't really want to go wandering around by myself.'

'Come on, I'll show you,' she says and, taking my hand, makes for the stairs.

'Thanks, Ria,' I concede, following her meekly. I do need the bathroom rather badly. At the top of the stairs I look down and see all the beautiful people dressed in their absolute finest. That's the thing about us travelers. We love our color. Peacocks, all of us. There isn't a plain black gown in sight. Ria takes me down a corridor and half-opens a door to a blue and white bathroom.

'See you downstairs,' she calls cheerfully and walks away.

I use the toilet, then wash my hands and stand in front of the mirror. My deep auburn hair comes down to the tips of my breasts. My eyebrows are straight and my eyes are dark blue. My nose is narrow, my lips are generous, and my jaw is well defined.

I am wearing a duck egg blue taffeta dress that I designed and sewed myself. It has a tight bodice and a wide bow at the base of my spine, the ends of which trail lower than the hem of my mid-thigh, Honey Boo Boo-style skirt. Underneath are layers upon layers of gathered electric blue tulle and lace petticoats. Crinolines, my grandma used to call them.

2

I fluff them up. I love petticoats. In my opinion, life is way too short not to wear petticoats that stick out from under your skirt. I reapply my lipstick, press my lips, and leave the bathroom.

The corridor outside is deserted. Faint sounds of the party downstairs float up. As I walk down the carpeted passage I am suddenly and very strangely overcome by an irresistible curiosity. I want to open a door, just one, and see how BJ lives. I don't know why, since I think him an arrogant beast. But just for those seconds, I want to see more than what everyone downstairs will see.

Oh! What the hell, just a quick look.

I open a door. The interior is plain; it's obviously just a spare bedroom. I close it and open another. It, too, has an unlived-in appearance. Again, very plain. I try another door. It is locked. Okay, one last door and I'm out of here. I stop before another door handle and turn it.

Whoa!

BJ!

I take a step forward, close the door behind me, and lean against it. And fuckin' stare. Two rooms must have been merged into one to make such a massive space. The walls are black and the words 'No Fear' are painted in white using a large calligraphy font. They glow in the light from a real fire roaring in the fireplace. It's been a long time since I've seen real logs.

A large chandelier hangs from an iron hook in the ceiling; it looks more like a meat hook than a decorative accent. The bed is a huge, wrought iron four-poster, obviously custom, with deep red fleur-de-lis patterned brocade curtains that have been gathered and held together by thick gold and black ties. On the bedside tables that flank it are elaborate candelabras with real candles that have dripped wax onto the gilt handles.

Wow! So this is what lies inside BJ. His cold, cold eyes hide the soul of a seventeenth-century lord. It is dark and dangerous but I am strangely drawn to it. With some shock I realize that there is something irresistibly seductive about my discovery. It's like walking into BJ's private world or looking into his soul.

I try to imagine the room with the candelabras lit. The candlelight dancing off the walls. My eyes move to the bed and I see me naked and crushed under BJ's large, powerful body, the light making his muscles gleam. The image is so erotic; it is at once thrilling and disturbing. I feel a flutter in my tummy.

I frown. I hate the man. And that is putting it politely.

And yet, here I am in his bedroom. A place I should never be. But, still unwilling to leave, I walk to the middle of the room, my petticoats rustling, the heels of my shoes loud and echoing on the hardwood floor. The fire crackles. It feels as if I am in a different world. Like Alice in her wonderland.

As if pulled by invisible hands, I head toward an antique, dark oak dresser. In a trance I stroke the metal handle. It is cool, smooth, full of all the events it has seen for hundreds of years, the squabbles, the trysts. A frisson of strange excitement runs over my skin. I pull at the metal handle. The drawer glides open with a whisper, smoothly, like it is on roller blades.

I stare wide-eyed at the contents.

Velvet boxes. Piled on top of one another. So many secrets. BJ's secrets. I take one and open it. A tiepin with a blue stone glitters up at me. I open another. A tiepin with a black panther, obviously old. I open another box and freeze. A gold tiepin that reads 'Layla' in cursive writing lays there. It ends with a small diamond at the end of it. I lift my head and look at the mirror above the dresser. I look different, strange, shocked. I shouldn't be here. This is wrong. I look into my eyes.

What the fuck are you doing, Layla?

But I don't turn away and run out of the room like any sane person would. Instead, I do a truly strange thing. Something I have *never* done before. I feel the blood pounding in my ears. So loud I cannot hear the logs crackling anymore. I take the tiepin out of its box, open my purse, and... oops... it falls in. Freaking strange that! I am a good girl, brought up as a proper Catholic. I don't take what's not mine. But my fingers snap my purse shut. The sound is loud and makes me jump. I can hear other sounds now, the merry fire and, faintly, the sounds of the party downstairs.

Slowly, almost afraid of what I will see, I raise my head and look at my reflection again. What I see there is far more frightening than a thief. My reflection is no longer alone in the mirror. BJ is standing in the doorway. His huge, muscular body fills it entirely.

Oh God!

TWO

Layla

Cold fear races down my spine. My pulse accelerates wildly while my mind jerks into overdrive. Maybe he didn't see me lift his tiepin. Perhaps I could just slip past him. I could pretend I am lost and that I didn't realize I was in his *bedroom*. Maybe. Just maybe. Very deliberately, I place my forefinger on the edge of the drawer, shunt it closed, and turn around to face him. Some men have looks, others have charm. BJ has presence. An edgy, almost menacing presence. The moment he appears in a room he owns it. He changes the atmosphere the way a grizzly coming into a room does.

He is wearing a silver hoop in his right ear, a black T-shirt, army surplus camouflage trousers, and combat boots. He is half-pirate, half-smuggler. He remains perfectly still. Danger and power ooze out of him. My heart starts to hammer inside my chest. *I can do this*, I think defiantly. *I'm not scared of you. I'm an Eden. Edens eat Pilkingtons for breakfast.*

Straightening my back and keeping my expression cool, I begin to walk toward him. I pray he cannot see my legs wobbling.

When I am five feet away I see his eyes. They are pools of gleaming black tar. No light there. They are flat and utterly impenetrable. For a fraction of a second I have the strangest impression of sexual tension. But of course, that is a trick of my overwhelmed emotions. His mouth is set in a forbidding line. I have seen it stretched in laughter, but never full on. Always from afar, by accident, and only from the corners of my eyes.

A foot away from his looming form I stop. He really is so damn huge. The scar on the top of his left cheek appears alive in the firelight. I swear no man has ever looked more inhospitable, or made me feel more intimidated.

'Sorry,' I say tightly. 'I got lost and wandered in here by mistake. I guess I better get back to the party.'

He does not step aside to let me through. He is so big, so meaty. He is like a predatory animal.

I clench my handbag tensely. 'Will you please move?'

'You want to pass? Squeeze past,' he suggests mildly, his face devoid of any expression.

'How dare you? I'll call my brother,' I threaten. Attack is always the best form of defense.

Something flashes in his eyes. I know then that I've made a mistake. I should have been more humble. It would have made my escape easier. He slips his large hand into his trouser pocket and produces a phone.

'That's a good idea.' His voice is silky with warning. 'Call him. Last time I looked he was with his pregnant wife. I believe your mother was sitting nearby, too. They can all rush up here to *my* bedroom and save their precious little princess.'

'What the hell is wrong with you?' I ask contemptuously.

His eyebrows rise. 'What the hell is wrong with me? You're a thief, Layla Eden.'

My cheeks flame, but I am not giving up so easily. 'I'm not,' I cry hotly.

'Then you have nothing to fear. Call your brother,' he invites.

I bite my lip. 'Look. I'm sorry I was in your bedroom. I'll just go downstairs and we won't spoil anybody else's night, OK?'

'OK.'

My mouth drops open at my effortless victory. I close it shut. 'Thank you,' I say softly and add a smile of gratitude.

'After you admit that you stole and … I've punished you.'

A bark of incredulity explodes out of my mouth. 'What?'

'It's only fair. You make a mistake, you pay for it.'

My eyes narrow suspiciously. I knew it. I've always known it. He is no friend of our family. This is the proof I have been looking for—that he is just low, low, low. He has always been low and he will always be low. Enough even to blackmail me! Perhaps he wants me to reveal some of Jake's business secrets. 'What kind of punishment are you talking about?'

'You should have what you've never had … a spanking.' His tone is terrifyingly pleasant.

I stare at him in disbelief. The idea is too ridiculous to contemplate. I laugh.

He doesn't. 'I fail to see the comedy.'

The laugh dies in my throat. 'You can't seriously mean to spank me?' I ask incredulously. I feel a chill invade my body.

He raises a challenging eyebrow.

'You seriously mean to spank me.' I repeat stupidly.

'The problem with you, Layla Eden, is that you were spoiled when you were young. Your Da and Jake were much too much in love with you to exercise any kind of discipline over you. As a consequence, you've grown up an unruly weed,' he explains patiently.

'How dare you—?' I begin.

But he interrupts me coldly. 'This is getting boring. The choice is simple: you apologize and submit to a spanking or we call your brother—or, if you prefer, your mother.'

Jake? My mother? My pseudo fury drains out of me like water from a sink plug. I worry my bottom lip and imagine my mother's eyes dimming with humiliation, Jake staring at me without comprehension. He has given me the best of everything. When we were young and poor, my mother says Jake would always forgo his share of something if I wanted it.

My actions are inexcusable. I have thoroughly disgraced and dishonored my family. I walked into a Pilkington's bedroom and stole something from it like a common thief. Worse of all, I have no idea why I did it. I've never done anything like this before. It is the stupidest, maddest thing I have ever done.

My gaze slides to his hands. They are as large as spades! My eyes jerk up to his tanned face. 'Why do you want to do this?'

He shrugs, nonchalantly, his face giving nothing away.

'There's nothing in it for you,' I insist desperately.

He smiles, an action devoid of any amusement. 'How do you know what's in it for me?'

My stomach sinks. I look at the space between his legs. It would be undignified, but I could try diving through it. I think I could make it, but it is almost certain that he will catch me, and that would be worse.

'Look,' I try to reason. 'I'm really, really sorry I came in here. It was wrong of me to intrude on your privacy, but if you let me go now I promise I won't tell a soul about any of this.' I wave my hand at the room. 'It'll be our secret.'

'That's a very kind offer, but I'm afraid there are only two ways you're leaving this room. With a spanking or,' he holds out his mobile phone in the middle of a baseball-mitt sized palm, 'or in your brother's company.'

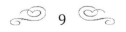

I stare at the plain black phone. Physical punishment for me, or mental anguish for both Ma and Jake. Not much of a choice. I swallow hard and meet his eyes. 'I'll,' I whisper, 'take the … punishment.'

'Great,' he says softly, slipping his mobile into his trouser pocket and taking a step forward. Suddenly the room seems so much smaller. Instinctively, I take a corresponding step backwards. He kicks the door shut with his heel.

'How do we do this?' My voice is clear and matter-of-fact. I have to assert some sort of control.

'I'll sit on the bed and you will position yourself on my lap. I will raise your skirt and spank you. Eight times.'

Raise my skirt! My eyes stray to his right hand. God! I feel heat creep over my body. Oh, the shame of it. And yet, to my absolute horror, there is something else sizzling in my core, something dark and hot. Something I'd never dreamed would happen to me. How could I be turned on by such a depraved, dreadful prospect? I look into his eyes. They are blank mirrors. There is nothing to see, only what I am. A thief.

But as I stare into his eyes, I see a flash of something old.

And suddenly I know. This humiliation is not punishment because I came into his bedroom and stole his tiepin. It is because of what happened when I was thirteen years old, when I tripped over a tree root and fell down. My skirt flew up and my panties showed. I can remember them even now, white cotton with red polka dots. All the other kids and BJ saw them. I hated everyone seeing them. I wanted to jump up, but I was too winded to move. Utterly humiliated and ashamed, I remained sprawled on the ground, an object of ridicule.

Some of the kids laughed. I knew them. They were afraid of Jake and they would never have dared laugh if BJ hadn't been there. At that time our families—BJ's and mine—were in a bitter generational feud. It is only recently that Jake and BJ had uprooted the barbed fences between our families. Since everybody knew about the bad blood, they thought they could ingratiate themselves with BJ by laughing at me.

But in a flash, BJ came to me and pulled me up easily. Even then he was a big lad. The other kids immediately ceased laughing. They were scared of him.

'Are you all right?' he'd asked.

But I was so mortally embarrassed that he had witnessed my humiliation, I lashed out ungratefully. 'Take your dirty hands off me, you filthy Pilkington, you,' I spat.

He had a mohawk then and it looked strange when he flushed bright red. He jerked his hand away from me.

I turned on my heel huffily, and limped away on my twisted ankle, my nose held high. I knew he was watching me but I didn't give him the satisfaction of turning back to look. After that we became enemies. And now he had caught me in his bedroom.

Finally, he can exact his revenge.

He takes a step towards me and I nearly cower, but he only strides past me. Alarm plucking at my belly, I watch him sit on his enormous bed, slap his thigh and say, 'Ready when you are.'

'Where force is necessary, there it must be applied boldly, decisively and completely. But one must know the limitation of force; one must know when to blend force with a maneuver, a blow with an agreement.'

—Leon Trotsky 1879 -1940

THREE

Layla

He holds a hand out to me. Dazed with disbelief, I walk up to him. Even now, I still can't believe he means to go through with it. This surely must be the part where he admits it has all been a brutish Pilkington joke. My eyes plead frantically with him.

'Lie across my lap,' he instructs politely.

Oh dear God! For a moment I cannot move, my mind unable to accept that he really expects me to submit to such humiliation.

Unaffected by my silent pleas, he cocks a dark eyebrow and nods meaningfully at his lap. 'No need to be shy. I've seen it all before, remember?' he taunts.

Our eyes lock. I flush furiously. Then my pride kicks in. *No, you despicable, disgusting, insufferable man, you haven't seen it all. So much has changed since you last looked.*

My bottom is naked, but for three bits of string and the smallest triangle of black lace. It's a far cry from the polka dot underwear he once saw. Only this morning, I had exfoliated my entire body until it was silky smooth, then rubbed Golden Brown Level 3 fake tan over every inch. I have nothing to be ashamed of. I am glowing!

I lift my chin and stare down at him with a mixture of contempt and stiff hatred. His reaction is to twist his lips with amusement.

I drop my purse to the floor and, gritting my teeth, I put my hand into his and gingerly lower myself onto his lap. I flinch when my skin makes contact with the steel-like muscles of his thighs. I turn in his hard lap and bend forward, laying my palms flat on the floor to steady myself. In order to keep my legs firmly together, my knees are straight and stiff. The tips of my toes don't touch the floor and hot blood floods into my head. The position is awkward and unsteady. My nose is less than a foot away from the dark floor and I can see the grain in the naked wood as it glows purple in the firelight.

'Are you ready?'

Hell would have to freeze over before I agree that I am.

Glad that my hair is hiding my burning face, I close my eyes with impotent fury and shame. He grasps the many layers of my skirt and flips them over my lower back ... and becomes completely still. So still it affects even the air in the room. A mad thrill runs through me. *You haven't seen it all have you, big guy?* Another thought: he's not immune.

I hear him inhale sharply before a large callused palm rests on the cheeks of my bottom. I know he can see the string of my panties between my pussy lips. Resentment races down my spine, but I am suddenly conscious that I am inexplicably wet. His palm is still resting on my skin. I feel it move slightly, almost a caress but not quite and I feel myself begin to tremble.

BJ

Who'd have fuckin' thought?

Layla Eden's damn near naked ass laid out like an eat-as-much-as-you-want banquet in *my* lap. I gaze down at my rough palm resting peacefully on her silky smooth skin in astonishment. Freaking unbelievable! How is this even possible? My cock gets busy inside my pants and I'm suddenly harder than I've been in my whole life. A state I'm clearly entitled to given the exceptional circumstances—I am, after all, looking down at Layla Eden's golden bottom sprawled across my fuckin' lap.

You got the peaches, I got the cream, babe.

The desire to caress the pert, round shape is so powerful, its pull catches me off guard. Lightly, almost against my will, my hand brushes the smooth center of the twin globes of firm flesh. That almost imperceptible action makes her body jerk. A shocked 'oh' tumbles out of her full lips and her right arm lifts off the floor, sinking her balance. Suddenly it's panic at all stations, her body tilts precariously and her deliciously long legs start flailing.

With pleasure, my other hand wraps firmly around her waist. She has a wasp-like waist. I could span it with my

hands. She returns her palm back to the floor and some semblance of order is restored.

I gaze down at my catch.

Her ass is a coy little thing, prudishly hiding her anus. Originally, there'd only been just enough of a gap underneath her cheeks to show off a tantalizing triangle of lace-curtained pussy, however since the pointless panic episode, her legs have moved further apart, and she is now quite brazenly exposing a fair bit of her fruitcake. Which, I must say, for a thin girl is surprisingly plump and ripe looking. Between the fat, pink lips, the black G-string of her panties is stretched tight and cutting rather cruelly into her flesh. Update: wet flesh. Someone is getting a little excited for her punishment, methinks.

It really is the most perfect sight.

Almost an open invitation.

My fingers itch to push aside the ridiculous string and enter her pussy. What would she do? Scream blue murder, no doubt. And that wouldn't be a bad thing. Hell, I'd love to fuck this woman spitting and hissing. I don't think I've ever been with such a haughty bitch before. Even the thought has me salivating, but I've got to pretend that this is about chastisement and not pleasure.

'You will count the blows or they will not register,' I tell her, my voice dead detached.

She freezes and around my palm gooseflesh begins to form on her perfect skin.

'Get on with it,' she grates.

I smile to myself. *Ah, Layla, you're so fuckin' transparent, so perfectly predictable.* She is determined to get through this unpleasant business as soon as possible and never give me the satisfaction of hearing her cry out.

No can do, baby.

I open my fingers on her butt and she tightens her cheeks with anticipation. I can't help it. My fingers curl and I squeeze the firm flesh. She moans and the unmistakable scent of her arousal hits me like a call during mating season. It's the kind of smell that can drive a man—well, me anyway—crazy. Heavy, suffocating, insistent. I want to answer it.

Layla Eden may be a snooty, spoilt bitch, but l want to fuck her so bad I'm like those dogs that jump fences and break their legs just because a bitch in heat is passing by on the other side. Hers is the kind of body that I can spend all night, every night, diving into. I want to pick her up like the doll she is, open her legs wide, and suck until her flavor runs over my tongue and coats my throat. Hours later, when she is passed out cold, I want to be able to swirl my tongue and taste her in my mouth all over again.

A voice in my head urges, *Jump the fence then. Break a leg. It'll heal. She bloody well asked for it. Didn't she come into your bedroom of her own freewill?* But another sane voice is already warning. *Even this is madness. What the fuck do you think you're doing with Jake's fuckin' sister?* I listen to the sane voice. I have resisted the call of her delicious body off and on over the years. I can do it again.

I could never really decide if I wanted to spank her saucy ass until it was scarlet or fuck her senseless. Now appears both impulses come from the same place. I watch her body. Frozen in place. Tense. Waiting for the flat of my hand.

I *will* hit her hard, hard enough to successfully convince her that this is a punishment and not the sexual encounter it is. I will be methodical. Each slap will land on a different spot. One cheek, then the other. Under the cups of flesh, and finally, where her thighs meet her body.

I rest the forearm of my left hand across her back and watch her toes curl. A delightfully involuntary response. I raise my hand and hold it suspended high above my head. Ms. Eden's butt trembles helplessly.

Oh! Yes ...

FOUR

Layla

I have never been smacked or beaten in my life. By anyone. Ever. And as soon as the heat from his palm leaves my skin I experience a wild second of pure, unadulterated panic. With my heart pounding like a war drum, I squeeze my eyes shut and prepare myself for the blow, but nothing happens.

What seems like an age passes.

Just as I think he has changed his mind after all, and relief starts pouring into my body, I feel him pull away slightly and a subtle disturbance in the air above me as his palm hurtles through it.

Thwack! His hand, heavy and hard, lands on my flesh.

I make no sound at all. First, I am absolutely determined not to give this vile beast of a man the satisfaction of a reaction. Second, the blow does not immediately register as painful. But a moment later I feel the effect. My eyes widen and my mouth opens in a silent O. By God, that really hurt! Tears of mortification well up in my eyes. I have to squeeze my eyes closed to try and prevent them from dropping.

He pauses. 'I'm waiting for a number,' he reminds me casually.

A number? What a sadistic bastard. He has no heart, this man. A hot needle of hatred for my tormentor stabs through me. I open my mouth. Shockingly nothing comes out. I try again. A totally unrecognizable shallow gasp exits.

'One.'

Almost immediately his hand crashes again onto my skin, but this time I feel the searing pain straight away. Bravely, I suck in my breath. Other than calling out in a trembling voice, 'Two,' I make no sound to express the fiery agony I am in. I have never suffered such pain in my entire sheltered life.

Another blow slams down and I bite back a scream. Even though each stroke has hit a different place, they all serve to build on the existing burn. My bottom feels like it is on fire. I press my palms so hard into the floor to refrain from wriggling and squirming or covering my bottom that my knuckles show bone white.

'Three,' I croak hoarsely. I *hate, hate, hate* him. I never thought it was possible to hate someone this much. I am getting closer and closer to unstoppable tears.

The pitiless thrashing continues. The pain is now so intense I barely manage to call out, 'Four.' My butt screaming, I take shallow breaths. My hate has grown in direct proportion to the shame and pain he is forcing me to endure. Halfway there, I tell myself. And the thought is so disheartening I want to bawl my eyes out.

The fifth falls on the tender, fiery skin of the curve of my bottom and I feel as if I will die of pain. The sting is unbelievable. To my eternal humiliation, a howl slips out.

'Ooooowww.' At this point tears are freely running down my face; I am like a baby. I can't talk. I can't breathe.

'Call it out.'

'Five, you asshole, five,' I sob, all pretense and pride shattered.

BJ

The last imprint of my hand shows white for a second before it reddens to a deep pink to match the rest of her ass. There are still three strikes to go, but her defenses are already broken. She is sobbing openly, and I know that the next blow will elicit a full scream.

But that's not what I want.

Not at all.

My pelvis is brushing her beautifully reddened ass and my nose is filled with the smell of her. I am hot. My dick is like a hunk of wood straining against the zipper of my pants. I want to fuck her so bad. My hands itch to grab her by the hair, spread her thighs, and rip into her slippery little cunt so deep she hisses with pain and pleasure as her muscles flutter like crazy around my dick. I want to empty my balls into her while she sees stars. Fuck, yeah.

But, of course, I don't.

This is Jake Eden's baby sister.

Instead ... I allow my little finger to spread out a little so it almost makes contact with her inner thighs, her sex. I rest my palm for a few seconds on her skin, my pinkie almost touching the glistening, salmon-colored flesh. The next time I raise my hand I will spank her pussy. Slowly, I lift my hand and let it hover in the air. Her tender skin is damp and glowing with sweat. Then I let the next wicked swing loose.

She shudders with shock and white-hot lust.

My little finger comes away wet. I smile with satisfaction. She freezes, her breathing shallow. I want to see her face. Very deliberately, I put both my hands on the bed on either side of me. Coldly, I say, 'I'm done.'

Immediately she scrambles to the floor and, crawling away, crouches like a cornered animal. She looks up at me with big, wet eyes full of hatred. Tears sparkle on her eyelashes. Her mouth quivers with temper. The princess exterior has been stripped away. Only the raw and helplessly sexual animal inside every human remains. Just as I know her buttocks must be humming, I know she will never admit that she is more turned on than she has ever been.

'Are you satisfied now, you sick bastard?' she spits. She is so furious her voice shakes.

'Fix your clothes and return to the party,' I tell her callously.

Using her palms to lever herself up, she springs to her feet and pulls her multi-layered skirts down over her stinging skin so roughly it makes her wince. She glares at me.

'I hate you,' she whispers.

'Join the queue.'

'I know now why they call you the bat. You're a fucking vampire, living in this ridiculous black dungeon.'

I shrug and look at her without expression. Sticks and stones maybe. Words? Forget it.

'I hope I never lay eyes on you again,' she hurls bitterly at me.

I watch her snatch her purse from the floor, and start walking towards the door.

'Layla.' My voice is a like whip. Even in her state she didn't dare disobey it.

She turns around and stares defiantly at me.

'My tiepin.'

She is so furious she very nearly breaks the clasp of her purse as she wrenches it open. She digs around, finds my tiepin, and violently flings it at my face.

I catch it easily in one hand. 'Enjoy the party,' I advise calmly.

'Pervert,' she snarls and slams the door shut on my mocking laughter. Sure, I get it: hers is the tale of the Princess and the Pea in reverse. She didn't enjoy being confronted with the animal inside her. Me, I am irredeemably base and animalistic, making me beyond excited to be acquainted with a newly created creature in my bedroom.

FIVE

Layla

The sounds of the party float up to me as I stand shocked and frozen in the hallway. Then it hits me: any moment now he could open the door and come out. With a panicked sob, I turn left and run for the bathroom. I lock the door with shaking fingers, and lean back against it, panting hard.

Why, oh why, did I ever go into his bedroom? Now *everything* is messed up. I look in the mirror. A red-faced stranger with smeared make-up, a gaping mouth, and crazy eyes stares back. Anger and hate sparkle in my eyes, but there is something else too. Something more primal.

I drop my gaze hurriedly and turn on the tap, splashing cold water on my face. I feel hot, confused, angry, and ashamed. My bum is stinging like mad, but ... God, I feel alive, in a way I have never felt. And ... I am wet. So wet.

The primal look in my eyes is pure arousal.

Sexual excitement.

Jesus! Oh sweet Jesus. What the fuck is wrong with me? I cannot understand why I am aroused. I hate that son of a bitch. I've always hated him. He is a callous, uncouth man-whore. A sleazy, bag of shit who regularly sleeps with strippers and makes his money running sex clubs. He's practically a criminal. I abhor men like him. Even through the tears that had filled my eyes, I had seen the satisfaction and gloating triumph on his face.

I should be livid.

I *am* livid. The memory of his large palm, full of calluses landing on my bare buttocks fills my head. With that last strike he had deliberately slapped my, my unmentionables. He had allowed his dirty fingers to touch my sex! How dare he? Bastard!

I turn around, lift my skirt, and look back at my throbbing bottom in the mirror. It is lobster red. I feel the fury bubbling in my veins, but another sensation more powerful than anger intrudes. I don't want to examine or address it. Taking deep, calming breaths, I repair my make-up with trembling hands, then open the door and stick my head outside.

The hallway is deserted.

I start walking down it, but as I pass his bedroom door I start running. At the top of the stairs I stop and walk down the steps slowly. No one has missed me or seen anything. Everything is exactly as I left it and yet I'm entirely different. My hands won't stop trembling and there is a tight knot of tension in my stomach. All I want to do is run away. I will die if I have to see him again in the state I am in. I walk quickly towards the main room, my eyes darting around fearfully. Fortunately I spot my brother, Jake, standing head and shoulders above the crowd. The sight of him makes me want to start bawling. Squaring my shoulders I push through the crowd and go to him. He is looking down at Lily with a lovesick expression on his face.

'Jake,' I call, my voice tremulous.

His head whips around, his body is immediately tense and his eyes narrow dangerously. 'What is it?' he asks.

'I don't feel well. I want to go home. Can you call me a taxi?'

He takes a step towards me, his body relaxing with relief. He is over-protective I can't even begin to imagine what utter havoc would ensue if he knew what BJ has done to me.

He puts an arm around my shoulder lovingly. 'What's wrong, little bear?'

I want to throw my arms around him and cry my eyes out, but I don't. I bite back my tears and lean against his strong, warm body. 'I think I ate something that didn't agree with me. I've just been sick in the toilet,' I lie miserably.

'Come on, we'll take you home. Shane can give Ma a ride when she's ready to go.'

Lily comes forward, her eyes are concerned and she is playing along, but she is a woman and she does not believe my fairy tale.

'I'll go find BJ. I should tell him we are leaving.'

I clutch his hand with both of mine and look up at him pleadingly. 'Can't you just call him from the car and tell him?'

He looks as if he is about to say something, but thinks better of it, and nods. Then the three of us make our way to a smiling girl in a Playboy bunny costume who takes our tickets and gives us our coats. It is only when we get outside that I am able to breathe properly again. I hardly hear when Jake gets on the phone with BJ and then Shane to arrange Ma's ride home.

I am too bruised and shaken.

SIX

BJ

I stand at the curving windows with my back to the party and watch her leave, Jake's arm curved protectively around her narrow back. Something within the darkest recesses of me whirls loose and flaps noisily in the wind. I had managed to ignore it for this long, but I know I cannot secure it back the way it was. You could say that the old hand is back, knocking at the old door.

I don't open the door.

My fists clench tight. I'll find release in another body. It was only a base animalistic reaction. There is nothing special about her. I'll find a body more suited to my taste and fuck it. A lush, full-figured woman. A pair of hips I can grab while I am ramming into her. Someone who won't look at me as if I have crawled out of the sewers, as if I make her feel itchy and unclean.

Yet my behavior was rotten. I shouldn't have given in to my crazy impulse. So unlike me and so fuckin' foolish.

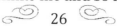

I turn away from the window. The party is still in full swing, but it is as if all flavor has been sucked out of it. A hand lands on my arm. I look down at it. Oval-shaped nails painted pearlescent, good skin. I let my eyes flow upwards.

Mmmm ... tight, yellow dress clinging onto breasts like planets. Well, big enough to feed a small African tribe anyway. I like that. Abundance. That's what stuck-up, spoilt Layla lacks.

And blonde. Yeah. I'm *very* partial to blonde pussy.

My eyes rise higher up to a plump, slightly sulky mouth. Perfect for sucking cock.

By the time I reach her eyes, it's a done deal. Cornflower blue, of course. As pretty as flowers and no hint that she sees anything unclean or itchy about the view in front of her.

I vaguely recognize her. The memory is fuzzy, but I think she's candy from one of Shane's clubs. I sort of remember flirting with her at the party Jake threw to celebrate the reopening of Eden. However, if I remember correctly, I ended up leaving with another dancer. It occurs to me that I had seen Layla that night too, and she had been rude to me then too. Bitch.

'Hello,' Blondie drawls. 'You went home with the South American dancer the last time.'

I smile, letting it reach all the way up to my eyes. 'I might have been a bit drunk and my cock might have been waylaid around the corner from you.'

She leans closer. 'You're not drunk tonight, are you?'

'As sober as a saint.'

'Good. Cause my pussy's been aching for that great fuck you promised ever since.'

My smile widens. I could do with a dose of random cunt. There is comfort, immense comfort in anonymous curves. 'I remember you now. You're the one who can suck cock for days.'

She smiles with satisfaction that I have remembered her. 'That's right. I can suck cock like you can't believe.'

I grab Blondie and, swinging her around, walk her backwards until her back presses against the wall, and she is hidden from the room by my bulk. I slide my hand under her dress and she helpfully spreads her legs. She is not wearing panties. Perfect. My kind of girl. She moans as my fingers part her slippery folds. She is so wet, even I am impressed.

'What's this?' I ask.

'Tug it and see,' she suggests.

I tug at the metal stud in her pieced labia.

She wriggles and tilts her pelvis towards me.

I insert a finger into her and slowly fuck her with it.

'Harder,' she urges throatily.

I fit another two fingers in and pump her so roughly her body jerks.

'Yes, yes,' she encourages fiercely, her eyes glazed with lust.

She's great, but she won't be enough. Not tonight. Not when I am this wired. I've got too much energy to burn. She'll be out cold before I'm finished.

'Listen cupcake, I'm looking for a threesome tonight,' I whisper in her ear.

'I have a friend,' she gasps immediately.

'Good. Go get her.' I take my fingers out of her pussy and hold them in front of her mouth. She tilts her head forward and sucks them greedily the way she would a dick, while staring boldly into my eyes. Yup, *definitely* my kind of girl.

My fingers exit her mouth with a wet pop.

I step sideways to let her pass, and watch her truly round and wonderful ass samba as she goes off in search of another body for me. I feel rather pleased with myself. It's gonna be a goooooood night, after all.

I bring my hand up to my nose and smell it, but she has sucked away the smell of her pussy. All that is left is Layla's scent, lingering like a rare perfume from a lost garden.

Damn you, Layla Eden. Just damn you.

Her friend is a Rita Hayward look alike, but with flaming copper hair. Obviously another dancer; I can always tell by the confident way they move. Unlike women who don't use their bodies to earn money, dancers get that their physical form gives them immense power over mere men. She slides up to me sinuously. I swear I have never seen a woman to walk in such a serpentine fashion before. It is actually fascinating to watch. My cock twitches with interest.

'I have a thing for men with gleaming raven hair,' she says, stopping less than six inches away from me. The tips of her perky breasts almost touch my abs.

'Oh yeah?' Her obvious attraction is a balm after Layla's unconcealed contempt and disgust.

A knowing smile stretches across her scarlet lips. 'Yeah. Is it true what they say about you?'

'I don't know, what do they say?'

She lays her palms on my chest, stands on tiptoe, and whispers into the side of my neck. 'That your mama gave you a horse cock.'

I grin slowly.

She puts her hand on my hardening dick, rubs along the length of it through the material and slowly opens her mouth as if she is becoming unbearably sexually stimulated. It is a practiced but highly effective move.

'Oh! That's no horse cock. That's a whole python you have there in your jeans, Mister,' she teases with a sly smile.

Yeah, she'll do.

SEVEN

BJ

The party is still going strong but I know my housekeeper, Marcel, will see to throwing everybody out when he starts to miss his bed. With a hand resting lightly on the small of each girl's back, I herd them away from the party and up to the Green Room.

I throw open the door and they enter like frisky lambs to the slaughter. I close the door, hit a switch, and a rotating disco ball with hundreds of colored LEDs comes on. Multi-colored light scatters around the room. I flick another switch and rap music throbs to life, Jason Derulo and Snoop Dogg go, 'Wiggle, wiggle, wiggle.'

The Green Room is the ultimate in bad taste. It has a mirrored ceiling, the largest bed in Britain dressed up with black satin sheets, red embossed wallpaper, a glass-fronted fridge with all manner of drink, and an Aladdin's showcase of sexual toys. The girls squeal with delight. They know that when something is this fucking bad it has to be good.

'Want something to drink?' I ask.

'No thanks,' Rita says and Blondie giggles.

'Get naked then.'

They waste no time. Quickly and expertly they shimmy off the few garments they're wearing. Blondie has the better body, but Rita's ass makes my jaw hang. Her flaming copper pubes are trimmed into a heart over the top of her pussy and Blondie is freshly shaven, which kinda makes me think she isn't a real blonde. In my experience, real blondes generally leave something behind as their badge of authenticity.

As if one mind, the girls gambol over to the showcase of toys. Both know exactly what they want. Rita gets a strap on dildo and Blondie chooses a vibrator and a long leather belt. They walk over to the huge bed with their toys and crawl to the middle of it. Getting on their knees, they face each other. Dappled light flows over their bodies, like they're creatures from an eighties porn flick.

Blondie leans in and pushes her tongue into Rita's mouth, her golden flesh pressing against Rita's pale skin as they deepen their kiss. Then Rita, obviously the stronger character of the two takes over. She breaks the kiss and with a coy glance at me, bends her head and begins sucking Blondie's red-tinted nipples. Blondie moans. Her hand moves downwards to finger Rita's pussy.

It's a cute show. Real cute. My cock hardens, but my heart remains utterly unmoved and cold. I stroll over to the fridge and get a bottle of beer, uncap it on the side of the fridge, take a swig, and turn around to watch the girls.

Rita falls away from Blondie. She lands on the bed on her back and spreads open her creamy alabaster thighs. Blondie immediately dives face first into her flaming muff and starts licking her out. Rita's pussy must be a juicy thing. From where

I stand I can hear the wet sounds of Blondie slurping and licking while Rita mews with pleasure.

I concentrate on Blondie's beautiful ass. She has it stuck high in the air in a deliberately provocative way with her legs stretched far enough apart to give me a graphic view of her pussy. It's fucking beautiful. All baby pink and luscious. The stud catches the light and glitters. She bobs her hips suggestively to make it obvious that she is inviting me to fuck her.

I smile inwardly. As if I need an invitation. This is my show, babe.

Then, all of a sudden, unexpectedly and for no good reason I can think of, a black string rudely separating Layla's salmon-colored folds flashes into my mind. And I remember the heady private smell of her that made me fantasize about grabbing her by the waist and dropping her on my upright dick. The craving to see her securely impaled on my dick had been almost overpowering. Not even Blondie and Rita together could bring forth such an overpowering desire. The thought irritates me.

I'm fucking invincible. I have no chinks in my armor. None.

And I don't need no stuck-up princess in my life.

I put the bottle on the top of the fridge, undress and stroke my throbbing length as I walk over to the side table. I take out a condom and roll it over my length. I see both Blondie's and Rita's eyes excitedly swivel in their heads to watch my inked body and my horse cock.

I kneel on the bed, grab Blondie by her full round hips and fucking bury myself so deep inside her, her head pulls back violently and her shocked mouth emits a strangled cry. Rita's hands grab Blondie by the hair to guide her mouth back onto her shiny pussy.

I pause. 'Too hard?'

'No. She likes it rough,' Rita says quickly.

Full of Rita's pussy, Blondie nods her agreement.

That is all I need.

Like a jackhammer I pump my cock balls-deep into Blondie. Her whole body jerks with the force of my thrusts even if her cries are muffled against Rita's snatch. We keep this up even while Rita climaxes with a howl to wake up the dead. Blondie's job is clear. It's licking up Rita's juices until Rita says otherwise.

One final slam and I explode with a great roar.

I pull out of Blondie's swollen, thoroughly fucked pussy and immediately Rita's voice rings out, 'Suck him.'

No rest for the wicked.

Blondie immediately makes a hundred and eighty degree turn on her hands and knees, her pendulous breasts bouncing. With admirable expertise she peels the condom off my dick with her lips and tongue. Opening her mouth, she takes my semi-hard cock deep into her warm velvety mouth. As she begins the task of sucking it into a full erection, I knot the used rubber and fling it over my shoulder.

Meanwhile, Rita ties on the strap on dildo and roughly plunges it into Blondie. Rita is so brutal I almost feel sorry for Blondie. Although, to give Blondie her due, she never complains or attempts to dislodge my growing dick from her mouth. The bigger I become, the more impressed I become with Blondie's dedication and skill. Fuck, with Rita slamming into her, I am so deep inside her throat my balls are pressed into her chin, but the girl doesn't even exhibit a gag reflex.

Instead, incredibly, she is not only moving back and forth along my length, she is also slowly moving her tongue from side to side underneath my dick. It's like a deeply satisfying and completely sensuous massage. Frothy white streams of pre-cum and spit gather at the corners of her mouth and dribble down her neck.

I throw my head back and look up at the mirror.

It's fun to watch my dick disappear so completely into a pretty face and I dig the sight our bodies make in the mirror overhead. I am face-fucking Blondie while Rita batters Blondie's poor pussy. With a grunt of satisfaction I shoot my load directly into Blondie's stomach.

EIGHT

BJ

I withdraw from her mouth and walk over to the fridge. After a swig of flat beer, I turn back to watch them. Rita is relentlessly hammering into Blondie. Sure looks like Blondie has picked the short straw. Rita has climaxed, I have come twice, and Blondie has had nothing. I walk over to the bed to pull Blondie off the dildo and open her legs. Shit, her pussy is really red and swollen. I lick it gently.

'Don't let her come,' Rita says.

Blondie's eyes become huge. 'Let me come. Please.'

'You can come whenever you want to,' I tell her, with an edge to my voice.

I put my lips around her clit and suck gently. She comes explosively almost immediately.

Sucking her has made me hard again. I lie on my back and Rita, who has discarded her strap on, fits a condom on my dick and climbs on top of me. Angling my cock to her core she pushes herself down. Her pussy is tighter than Blondie's and it closes around me like a perfectly-fitted glove. I groan from the heat and snugness.

'Fuck,' she groans. 'You're so big it's like fucking a bloody baguette.'

That said, she begins to ride me slowly and deliberately. As soon as she judges that she can comfortably take all of me she begins to slam herself down on my cock. Her orgasm comes quickly, but it lasts a long time. Panting hard she rises off me and Blondie gets on.

'I want to suck your tits,' I tell her and immediately she pushes her full breasts forward. I grasp them both in my hands, squeezing them together so I can suck both her nipples at the same time.

'Harder,' she begs.

Now I know why Rita was being deliberately rough with her. Blondie gets off on pain. I bite her nipples until she cries out.

'Want me to stop?' I ask.

'No,' she moans. 'Suck me until I am so swollen and raw even wearing my dress again will be painful.'

And that is exactly what I do. I suck them hard enough for her to be in constant pain while she fucks herself on me and brings herself to another orgasm.

'Demi loves to have her ass spanked … hard,' Rita tells me with that sly, almost evil smile of hers, her lips still glossy with my cum.

I look at Blondie/Demi. Her eyes are shining eagerly.

My mind flashes to Layla. This is turning to be a strange night. Fuck, the last thing I want to do is spank anyone else. Still…

'Use your belt,' Rita urges.

Blondie scrambles out of bed and brings the belt to me. 'Let me have it,' she begs. I take the belt from Blondie and she quickly goes and buries her face between Rita's legs while her ass hovers tantalizingly in the air.

'She'll suck me while you punish her,' she says excitedly.

I hold the belt in my fist and take the first swing. An angry red stripe blooms right across the middle of Blondie's fair skin. She grunts, but carries on slurping Rita's pussy. Rita nods in approval and wraps her legs around Blondie's head.

Blondie wriggles her bum to indicate her approval of the situation. So I let her have some more. Her plump bottom and the backs of her thighs turn a brilliant scarlet and Rita groans with pleasure, but suddenly, I find myself starting to tire of their game. I want to bring it to a close.

'Widen your legs,' I order.

Blondie rushes to obey.

I swing the leather right on her clit. She screams and climaxes instantly. Totally spent, she falls to one side. She is already snoring gently when I grab Rita and shove my never-ending erection into her mouth. She sucks on it willingly and voraciously, but it is not enough. For some reason I feel angry. With her. With myself. With the entire world. I grab a fistful of her hair and holding her head still, fuck her mouth hard and fast, but it is still not enough.

I pull out of her and push her so she is flat on her back.

I order her to raise her hips and she obeys immediately. While pinching her nipple I shove a finger into her ass. As I finger fuck her ass I tell her to do the same to her pussy. She does two things. She squeezes my finger with her ass and plunges two fingers into her gaping hole again and again until she squirts all over her own hand. Drops of dew glisten on her coppery, heart-shaped pubic hair.

'I cannot tell you how much I enjoyed your performance,' she whispers, her eyes sultry, her forefinger delicately tracing the ink on my forearm. She looks at me with a wheedling expression. God, I detest women who pretend to be weak in order to control men.

I immediately start moving away from her.

'Fuck Demi in the ass before you go,' she says suddenly, her voice hard as pebbles.

I turn around and look at her. She is smiling, but her eyes are fathomless pits of shadows. For an extraordinary moment something shimmers between us, her cruelty, my coldness.

My cock stirs to life.

I turn my head to look at the sleeping girl. She is lying on her side with her knees curled. Poor thing can't sleep on her front because her nipples are so raw they are twice their natural size. Can't sleep on her back because her ass is so angry. Even her pussy has been so battered it juts out like a peeled plum from between her thighs. It actually looks as sore as hell.

I turn back to Rita and her eyes are an open door into the darkness in her soul. At that moment I see into her. And suddenly I pity her ... and myself.

Is this it for us?

Is this all, we who save ourselves above everyone else, and thrive at the expense of others, will ever have?

Anonymous, meaningless fucks with other damaged creatures of the night. Where there is no guilt because it is too dark to see the willful damage we leave behind. At moments like this, does a little part of my soul crumble into dust, and fly away? The secret to the labyrinth is always at the beginning. Before you enter. Once you do it is too late. The thought makes me feel empty and depressed.

'Breakfast is included,' I say coldly, as I vault off the bed.

'Is sausage on the menu?' she calls.

I don't answer her. Naked, I head for the shower. My hands are not clean. My greatest enemy is myself.

NINE

Layla

I walk into my local supermarket, pick up a basket, and head towards the milk section, where I grab a carton. I then quickly make for the yogurt shelves. I haven't told anyone, not even Madison, my best friend, about the disgraceful thing I did in BJ's bedroom two weeks ago, or the way he retaliated. It is a combination of confusion and shame. Specifically, my reaction to the punishment I received. Sometimes, at night when I am in bed, it pops into my mind and I quickly kick it away without examining it.

It seems to fit in with the tawdry mess that my life has disintegrated into. Only a month ago my life seemed perfect. I had a gorgeous boyfriend, I was training as an apprentice at a top interior design firm in Milan (a post Jake had secured for me), and I was feeling strong and independent. Then last month I walked out of my job without telling anyone and ran back home with my tail between my legs. It all began when I opened a little email that began with

You are fucking MY boyfriend!

When it's in Italian it sounds a lot worse. She had attached hundreds of photos going back five years, which indeed proved that I was fucking her boyfriend. They had celebrated birthdays, barbeques, parties, and countless occasions in the company of a whole crowd of friends, none of whom I had met, of course.

I sat at my desk utterly shocked and sick to my stomach.

But he told me I was the most beautiful woman he had ever met. That no one was more beautiful than me. And he was going to take me to meet his parents next week!

I stayed over in his apartment. There had been nothing to tell me that he was cheating and so blatantly. There wasn't even a case of lipstick in his bathroom cupboard. The magnitude of his deception was inconceivable. Unbelievable.

I looked at his handsome face in the pictures laughing, happy, and utterly devoted to the pretty, olive-skinned woman at his side. I hadn't known him at all. Or was it simply that I was more naïve that even my brothers believed? I felt so stupid. So cheated. So hurt. I didn't want anyone to know that I had been the victim of such an elaborate charade and I *never* wanted to see the slick bastard again. All I wanted to do was run home to my mother's house and lick my wounds in private.

Since he was one of the top designers in the firm, I simply dropped my belongings into a plastic bag and left without telling anyone. I went back to my apartment, packed my bags, and caught a business flight back to London.

I remember the guy next me on the plane, oily and expensively suited, who had tried to pick me up. The bubble of poisonous, unreasonable hate I had felt simply because he was Italian made me turn on him with so much revulsion that he shrank back with surprise. But even before we landed in Heathrow I knew I was not broken hearted. It was only my pride that was bruised.

I was not in love with Lupo. I had never allowed myself to be.

He was the most handsome man I knew, other than my brother, Shane, of course. He said all the right things. But he had always revealed his true self in bed. Especially at the beginning of our sexual relationship, when we had sex he would shout out *puttana* as he came. Prostitute. Even after I had asked him not to, he would sometimes slip up. And when I got mad, he apologized and told me it didn't mean anything. It was the same as someone else screaming "Oh God!" during their orgasm. Nevertheless it had never sat well with me. And how right I had been.

After I got back to my mother's house everyone wanted to know why I had left Milan so suddenly.

'Did anyone upset you?'

'Are you ill?'

'Do you no longer want to be an interior designer?'

I never told anyone, especially my second brother, Dominic. Knowing him, he would have taken the first flight out to Milan, beat the shit out of Lupo, and calmly taken the next plane back as if nothing untoward had happened. As far as everyone was concerned, except Maddy, of course, I had come back because I was terribly, terribly homesick.

Now I am determined to start anew in London. On my own. Without any help from my family. I'll get a job like everyone else. Jake told me I could have a try at cutting it on my own, but I had to live in one of his properties. So I moved into one of his London apartments. I was happy because I was only five tube stops away from the apartment Madison shared with her boyfriend.

Absently, I pick up a tub of Greek yogurt from the shelf and place it into my basket. Turning away, I bump into Ria.

She screams with delight. She is wearing a grey blouse, brown leather jacket, faded blue jeans, and purple and orange sneakers. I don't think I have ever seen her look so casual.

'Hi,' I greet and laugh at her infectious joy at bumping into me.

'Just the person I wanted to see,' she exclaims with a huge grin. 'I was going to call you to invite you to come to my birthday party on Saturday. I know it's a bit last minute and all, but it is a last minute plan.'

I smile. 'Twenty-four, right?'

'Yeah, but after this year I'm freezing my age. I'm gonna be twenty-four now until I am fifty, then I will commence the count again.' She laughs her machine gun laugh.

I laugh with her.

'Will you come then?'

'What kind of party is it?' With Ria you have to ask. She's totally unpredictable.

'Dancing and drinking. Nothing big. Just some of my closest friends and family.'

Ria's idea of big is not mine. 'How many people is that?'

'About a hundred,' she says airily.

'You have a hundred close friends?'

'Don't you?' she asks curiously.

I struggle to keep a straight face. 'No, Ria. I don't.'

'Oh!'

'So, where're you having it then?'

'Laissez-faire.'

A warning tinge swirls up my spine. 'Isn't that one of BJ's clubs?'

'Yup. Free drinks all night! Until last week I was going to keep it family only and have a party at my mum's house, but then BJ offered his club and I couldn't believe it.'

'Look Ria. I didn't realize that your birthday was going to be held in London. I am spending the weekend at my Ma's.'

Ria waves my objection aside. 'No problem. BJ has already agreed to pay for cabs for all my single girlfriends.'

I feel trapped. I can't very well tell her I can't go now after I have already agreed. 'Um ... will BJ be there?'

'Well, he promised to drop in, but he said he won't be able to stay for long.'

I breathe a sigh of relief. 'What time?'

'People are going to start arriving around nine but the party will really only get going about ten.'

'OK.'

'When you get to the club just tell them you are there for Ria's party. Oh! And for ID you have to wear red shoes or a red hat.'

'Got it.'

'So what're you up today then?' she asks with a smile.

I shrug. 'Not much. Unsuccessfully looking for a job.'

She frowns. 'Why? Can't one of your brothers give you one?'

'They can but I want to make it on my own.'

'What for?'

'Just to try.'

She looks at me as if I am stupid so I quickly change the subject. 'And where are you off to dressed like that?'

'I'm off to a watch a bit of bare-knuckle fighting.'

'Who's fighting?' I ask, even though it's not too hard to guess.

'I'm putting a hundred quid on BJ,' she says with a cheeky grin.

'What are the odds of him winning?'

"BJ's never lost so the money will be shit. I'm just gonna bet on the amount of punches he has to throw or the minutes the other guy will last. That sort of thing.'

'Sounds exciting,' I say carefully, even though an underground fight where the opponents go on battering each other until one of them can't take it anymore is not my idea of fun. 'And where is it being held?'

'Some godforsaken barn in the sticks. Patrick's taking me. You remember Patrick, my second cousin, don't you?'

'Yes, vaguely,' I say politely. Then words I never intended appear on my tongue. 'Can I come?'

She looks at me sideways. 'Will your brothers be all right with it?'

I know Jake won't be okay with it. Lily told me how he wouldn't even let her watch him fight BJ. But after my humiliating experience in Italy, I've decided that it's time for me to grow up and experience things for myself. Take a few knocks if necessary. I don't want to be the sheltered baby of the family for the rest of my life. I want to see what a bare-knuckle fight looks like. Besides, I'll be with Ria. What can possibly happen to me?

'I won't tell them if you won't,' I tell her.

She giggles conspiratorially. 'My lips are sealed.'

'When are you going?'

'Now.'

I look at my shopping basket. A carton of milk and a pot of Greek yogurt. I take the basket to the check-out counter and give it to the cashier. 'I've changed my mind. Could you please ask someone to put them back on the shelves?'

'Ready?' Ria asks.

'Yeah. I'm ready.'

At that time I am just glad for a new experience. It has not yet occurred to me to do any mischief.

TEN

Layla

In the middle of someone's farm we find a barn that is alive with music and people. We pay our entrance fee and enter. Inside, I gaze around in surprise. The barn is packed to the rafters with far more people than there are cars outside. At a guess, I would say there are at least 300 people. Mostly men, but women of all ages too. Ria tugs my hand.

'Let's place our bets then get a drink. I want to be up front.'

I nod and follow her as she pushes her way through the crowd.

A man in a green sweatshirt and two missing teeth grins at her. 'What'll you have, love?'

'How much will I get if I put a hundred for BJ 'The Bat" Pilkington to win in less than 2 minutes?'

'A hundred and one pounds.'

'One pound profit? For a hundred quid? That's nothing!'

He shrugs. 'The Bat has won 92 fights and drawn once. You're talking about a favorite, a machine that renders men unconscious, love.'

Ria rubs the back of her neck. 'How much for him winning in less than one minute?'

'Twenty.'

'That's just crap. Less than thirty seconds?'

'I'll give you fifty for that.'

She looks at him doubtfully, and then makes her decision. 'All right, I'll just take less than a minute.'

She gives him five twenty pound notes and he passes it to another young man standing behind him, and writes something in his tatty notebook.

He turns to me. 'What about you, young lady?'

'Me? I'm not...' I pause. Why shouldn't I? Why shouldn't I bet like Ria? It's just for fun. 'What would give me a really good payout?'

He grins. 'The Bat to lose.'

'Other than that?'

'That The Devil's Hammer lands a swing on The Bat's face.'

I frown. 'Why's that?'

'Because except for his fight with Jake Eden, The Bat has never been hit in the face.'

'How much will I get for my hundred?'

'Two grand.'

'Wow! That's huge.'

'Yeah, right. The payout's so damn good, because it's never gonna happen. Don't do it, Layla. You might as well burn your money,' Ria advises with a frown.

'I like to live dangerously,' I say with a grin and hold out my money. The bookie secretes it away in single hand movement. Like oil pouring from a drum. A smooth, effortless miracle of nature.

He jots my bet down in his little book and we move away towards the bar. The bar is a collection of huge metal drums filled with beer bottles, ice, and water. We each order a bottle of beer, drinking straight from the bottle since there are no glasses available. I am strangely excited. The mood of the crowd has affected me. There is anticipation in the air.

We go right to the front of the pit, a small area cordoned off with bales of hay, and find ourselves a spot where we have a good view of the fight. In minutes the first fight starts. Two young men, who seem evenly matched to me, start walking towards the pit. One of them takes a step into the pit and establishes his jab straight away. Moving his head from side to side and jogging around. Suddenly, without warning, his clenched fist shoots out. Bang, a body shot that leaves his opponent reeling backwards into the hay. The fight is over in seconds as the aggressor then lunges forwards and knocks him out in one punch.

'Wow,' I say to Ria. 'He's brutal.'

'Wait 'til you see BJ.'

The next fight lasts a lot longer and is astonishingly violent.

I see it then for what it truly is, a festival of physical abuse. Men going for it, egged on by a baying crowd. There is no holding back. It's in their blood. To decide who is the hardest of them all. The sport of legend, guts, honor, and heart.

Both men are bloodied and in bad shape when one of them spits out his mouth guard and falls to his knees. His friends have to carry him away. My heart is pounding hard. That had been too brutal. I hadn't enjoyed it, but all around me the crowd has woken up. A thrill runs through them. An air expectancy hovers over us like that crackle in the air before a thunderstorm.

'BJ is next,' Ria says.

'Now for the fight you have all been waiting for,' the MC announces excitedly. 'Tony "The Devil's Hammer" Radley versus Billy Joe "The Bat" Pilkington.'

The crowd cheers and whistles.

'Tony "The Devil's Hammer" Radley,' the announcer screams over the whistles and calls. Queen's *We Are the Champions* fills the air and BJ's opponent, a huge, bearded man appears. He lifts his hands high over his head in acknowledgement and runs energetically towards the pit.

'And now for the undefeated champion, Billy Joe "The Bat" Pilkington.'

Meatloaf's *Bat Out of Hell* blares out and BJ walks out to the pit. The crowd goes absolutely crazy, clapping and cheering, banging their bottles on the wooden surfaces in the barn. There is no doubting the crowd's favorite.

He is wearing a plain black t-shirt and khaki trousers. As he walks into the pit, I notice that everything about him is different. His eyebrows are drawn straight, his eyes are pitiless, chips of black ice, and his face is devoid of any expression. It is like looking at a cold-blooded psychopath or a heartless machine. I try to imagine this cold, cold monster fighting warm, kind-hearted Jake and feel a tight knot of fear inside. No wonder Jake didn't want Lily to see the fight. This man is exactly what the bookie called him – a machine that renders men unconscious. He is here for one reason and one reason alone: to completely decimate the other man.

He is so different than the BJ I know, I am actually shocked.

The way he angles his head forward combined with his shoulders rounded and his hands slightly curled at the elbows reminds me of a charging bull. At that moment he is the most coldly aggressive man I have seen in my life. He doesn't look at the crowd. He has eyes only for his opponent. My gaze skitters over to The Devil's Hammer. He is holding his hands up in readiness and jabbing the air while jumping around with quick nimble steps, but in his eyes, I see fear. In his head he has already lost. The only question left is how badly he's going to lose.

BJ steps into the pit and ... and like a bull rushes towards him. It is an ambush, clear and simple. Blows rain on the unprepared man's body so quickly and so relentlessly he is overwhelmed by the ferocity of the attack. The Devil's Hammer flails uselessly. One power punch catches him flush on the chin and he flies backwards, landing on one of the hay bales. The crowds bays its approval. But The Devil's Hammer is not beat. There is life in him yet. He pulls himself up painfully, and lunges unsteadily towards BJ.

BJ stands still. Like a bull readying itself for a matador. He doesn't move a muscle. And suddenly I know what he is going to do. It's the oddest thing, but I do. He is going to land the punch that puts The Devil's Hammer to sleep. At the exact moment, as The Devil's Hammer prepares to throw his own punch, I open my mouth, and with all the power in my lungs, scream BJ's name.

'BILLY JOE PILKINGTON.'

Every person in the barn turns startled eyes in my direction. But my eyes are on BJ. He has turned towards my voice, an expression of total incomprehension on his face. I am the last person in the world he expects to see. His eyes find me and he looks as if he has seen a ghost. The Devil's Hammer's punch lands. It socks him in the face. A direct hit. The momentum causes BJ to stagger back slightly. His eyes rush away from me. When he straightens, he is an avenging angel.

He is so furious he looks as if he wants to tear the other man's head off. BJ pummels his opponent with such barbaric brutality that I have to close my eyes. I hear the dull thud of the man falling, then the crowd going crazy. I feel hot and claustrophobic. My heart is beating too fast. I turn towards Ria.

She looks at me strangely. 'Congratulations,' she says. 'You won your bet.'

I nod. People are giving me sidelong glances. I've made a spectacle of myself, but I don't feel embarrassed. In fact, I feel oddly detached. I think I am shocked at myself. At the harm I have caused to another. I have never harmed another human being before. I even hate it when I accidentally snap an insect or a frog in the garden with my hoe.

'Can I borrow a cigarette?' I ask Ria.

'Sure.' She gives me a packet. 'The lighter is inside,' she says.

'Thanks,' I say with a tense smile, and pushing my way out of the barn, go outside. It is freezing. I don't normally smoke, but I feel jittery. Even my hands are shaking. I walk to the side of the barn and light a cigarette. I have taken only one puff when I feel the air around me change. Become thicker. I turn my head slowly. Our eyes touch.

'Are we quits now?' BJ asks.

His left cheekbone is badly swollen and starting to discolor. I turn away from his cold, cold eyes. I feel raw. 'Yeah, we're quits.'

'Can I have one?'

I fit my cigarette between my lips and hold open the cigarette packet. He takes one. There is blood on his hand.

'Does it hurt?' I ask.

'No.'

'Why not?'

'I'm buzzing.'

I flick open the lighter and hold the flame up to him. My hand is shaking. His other hand comes up to cup the flame. In the intimate glow, I see the heat rise from his skin like steam. And I smell the sweat and the trace of endorphins and adrenaline radiating from it. Our eyes meet again and we stare at each other. Yes, I am shocked, and yes, I am shaken, but there is something else struggling to show its face. He inhales, the cigarette burns orange, and I kill the flame with a click.

I turn away, dropping the lighter back into the packet. I return my forefinger and middle finger back on either side of my cigarette and inhale a lungful of warm smoke. It makes me feel light-headed. I exhale it out slowly and put my hand down to the side of my body. There is a foot between us, and an unmistakable element of danger. Like being on one of those roller coasters that inverts you. You are scared to death and unbelievably excited at the same time.

I grasp that I'm not only aroused by the violence I witnessed in the pit, I am excited by the tightly packed, rippling muscles of his body. He is giving off vibes that are calling to me. My life-long hatred of him seems to belong to another place and time. By a strange trick of the light it has morphed into an intense desire to meld my body with his. Shocked by that realization and super aware of him, I carry on staring out into the empty frozen fields.

He doesn't say a word and neither do I. There is nothing to say. Words are superfluous in the wake of the thick, sexual tension crackling like electricity between our bodies.

Suddenly Ria is calling me. 'There you are. I've been looking for you.'

I let the butt of my cigarette drop to the ground and grind it with my foot. I hand her the packet. 'Thanks.'

BJ flicks the end of his cigarette away from him.

'Hey Ria,' he says quietly.

'That was a great fight,' Ria says.

'Thanks,' he says devoid of any emotion. As if he is totally unaffected by her compliment.

My phone rings. I take it out of my purse. Shit. It is my mother. I consider not taking the call, but I know what she's like. She will persist and persist until she gets me.

'Hi Ma.' My eyes flick over to BJ. He is watching me intently.

'Where are you?' she asks.

I gaze down at the frozen ground. 'I'm with Ria,' I reply. I don't dare tell her where I am. I know she won't approve. She'll probably tell Jake and he'll go mad.

'Right. Can you be home in an hour?'

'I guess so. Why?'

'Shane's coming around to your place. I've sent some food for you.'

'Oh, OK.'

'Call me when you get home, OK?'

'Will do.'

'But call Shane first,' she says, and rings off.

I put my phone back into my purse and look up at Ria imploringly. 'I'm sorry, but I've got to get home. My ma is sending my brother around to my place in an hour.'

'Blimey,' Ria says, widening her eyes. 'You better call him and make it an hour and a half.' She turns towards BJ. 'I'll see you this weekend then.'

He nods and looks at me.

'Bye,' I say awkwardly.

Then we are hurrying back into the barn in search of the guy we placed our bets with.

ELEVEN

Layla

Saturday. It takes forever to come, but when it does it brings a hard, tight knot into my stomach.

I know Ria and all her mates will dress to kill, so I take a long time getting ready. I soak in the bath for almost an hour with my mother's secret homemade masque recipe on my face and another of her concoctions in my hair. She claims it's guaranteed to make my hair shine. My mother's potions do a good job, my skin is glowing and my hair glossy and shiny.

I wear my white mini dress. It is sleeveless with a high Nehru collar, but what makes it daring without being slutty is a five-inch long oval cutout in the middle of the dress that reveals my nicely tanned torso and belly button. I stick a red beret on my head and slide into a pair of knee length, white suede peep-toe boots that were all the rage a few months ago in Italy.

I stand in front of the mirror and I know I look good. My thoughts go to that moment when BJ bent his head to me and we shared a flame. Unconsciously, my finger slowly circles my bare belly.

Laissez-faire is a cavernous, totally modern nightclub with under-flooring lights that flash blue and white and gleaming metal structures on the walls and pillars. Ria is having her party in the VIP area upstairs. As soon as I enter the cordoned off area, she runs towards me.

'Oh! My! God!' she screams. 'You look awesome, babe. I LOVE your boots.'

She looks glamorous in a red cowboy hat with a rhinestone band, a tight red and black striped dress, and the highest boots I have seen outside of a fashion magazine. The lights pick up the glitter on her lovely brown skin.

'Well, you look absolutely stunning yourself,' I tell her sincerely.

She flicks her long, summer-streaked hair. 'You bet I do.'

I smile. None of that false modesty for Ria. I hold out her present, a pretty chain belt I bought in Milan. 'Happy Birthday, Ria.'

She takes it, beaming. 'Thanks. Come on. Let's get you a drink.' She winks at me. 'We're drinking champagne. BJ said we could have anything we wanted, so we ordered bubbly, but we didn't go overboard and get the really expensive stuff though,' she tells me chattily as we cross the room for the bar.

We are halfway there when Ria's favorite song, Justin Timberlake's *Sexy Back,* comes on. With a shout of pure joy she puts her present on the floor, and gyrates provocatively around me. With a laugh I give in. We start bumping hips, twerking comically, and dancing around my present like two demented teenagers. Soon her other friends come onto the floor to join us.

When the song is over, Ria takes my hand and we attempt to continue our journey to the bar, but *All About That Bass* comes on and I love that song. I swing her around and we are at it again.

Laughing and breathless, we reach the bar five songs later. No sooner have we had a sip of our champagne than another of my favorite tracks comes on. Five of us girls rush off to the dance floor and give it all we've got.

The hours pass fast. The music is good and Ria is a great laugh.

It's almost midnight. I know because the girl next to me is whispering that there is a surprise cake to be cut at the exact stroke of twelve. I am sitting at the table with Ria, feeling relaxed and merry when the air shifts. I look up and BJ is standing over us, looming even bigger and broader than I remember. He is wearing a khaki t-shirt tight enough to show off his impressive muscles and the V of his torso. His jeans hang low on his hips.

But he is with a woman!

It takes a few seconds for that to sink in. But when it does—fucking hell!—I feel like the biggest fool this side of the equator. There was nothing between us after all. It was all in my imagination. I was wrong again. Just as I was wrong about Lupo. Without looking directly into his eyes, my eyes slide away to her.

She is voluptuous and hauntingly exotic with creamy skin, blue-black hair, either green or hazel eyes (it's impossible to tell under the club's lights), and high cheekbones that give her a feline appearance. She is wearing a short black dress that can barely contain her curves, and she has her hand possessively curved around BJ's arm. Her nails are long and red and she is running them lightly along the inside of his forearm in a way that is profoundly sexual. I find the sight so disturbing I have to drop my head and stare into my drink.

'Layla,' BJ says by way of greeting.

'Hi,' I reply brightly, looking up, but not letting my eyes rise past his mouth. He has a sexy mouth. The lower lip is so deliciously plump it makes you want to nibble it. Jeez. How much champagne have I had? I return my eyes to my drink. Five glasses.

To my horror Ria invites BJ to sit with us. She slides closer to me, and motions for me to scoot up further along the seat. The space she's freeing up does not seem big enough for him. Fortunately, he tells us that he's not staying. I look up with relief.

Big mistake.

He is staring at me and I am suddenly caught in his stare, unable to look away. I suck my bottom lip into my mouth. There is a curse word stuck behind my teeth. My skin comes alive and my heart dances in my chest.

'Layla. Isn't that an Arabic name that means the dark of the night?' the woman he is with asks with a fake-ass smile.

Before I can answer BJ speaks up. 'No, the real Arabic translation of Layla means that light, giddy feeling one has after the first drink of the night. Not drunk but on the way to being there. It is the beginning of intoxication.'

My breath catches in my throat. I stare at him shocked. The way he said Layla had been a sultry caress.

The woman laughs, a hostile, angry sound. 'Well, Arabic names on non-Arabs is a bit silly, really.'

'I can't imagine a more suitable name for her,' BJ says, his coal black eyes never leaving mine.

Flustered by the look in his eyes, I stand up in a rush. His gaze drops to my navel. His lust is so blatant, fiery heat rushes up my neck and into my face.

'Excuse me. I need to nip over to the ladies,' I tell the girls as I slide out of the banquette seat.

I feel his eyes burning into my back as I leave the sectioned-off area.

I stand in front of the mirror and stare at myself. There are two spots of high color on my cheeks, my hair is an untidy mess, and my beret is no longer set at its jaunty angle. Someone has stepped on the side of one of my beautiful new boots and there is a brown mark on it. I pull out some paper towels from the dispenser, wet them, and try to clean it off, but I have to give up without much success.

The weird thing is, I am doing all these things on autopilot. Some part of my brain is going crazy. *He came with another woman.* It rankles. But then he goes on about my name and *looks* at me as if he wants to eat me. What's he playing at? Is there or isn't there something between us

I run my fingers through my hair, apply a new layer of lip gloss and exit the toilets. As I walk along the frosted glass corridor a large hand reaches out from the darkness and slams me against an unyielding body.

TWELVE

Layla

What if we kiss? What then?

My breasts are crushed against his hard muscles, but I don't attempt to struggle. I have grown up with three brothers so I know how useless it is to fight with people who are bigger and stronger than you are. Instead I fix him with a venom-filled glare. *He brought a fucking woman with him.*

'Let go of me.'

'Scared?' he taunts, his voice rich and smooth.

'Of you?' I scoff sarcastically, as if even the idea is incredible.

He laughs. It comes from somewhere deep inside him, a wicked rumble. But I like it. I like it a lot.

'Yeah me,' he says. 'I like to tie girls up and suck their pussies until they scream.'

I feel my belly contract. How different this laughing man is from the one who shared a flame with me outside the barn. 'Oh, you are disgusting.'

He holds me at arm's length and lets his eyes travel down, deliberately lingering on my breasts before coming to a stop at my bare belly.

'Will you freaking stop staring at me like that?'

He grins and a dimple pops up in his chin. It makes him look edible. 'If you don't want men to look at you like that, why do you dress like that?'

'You're an asshole, you know?' I huff.

'And you're seriously fuckin' hot.'

My eyes widen. 'Are you fucking serious?' I gasp.

'My balls are already aching.'

'I don't believe this.'

'What sounds do you make when you come?'

'What?' I sputter. This is too much. It's outrageous. He's flirting with me and he has a woman waiting for him upstairs. What an arrogant bastard. 'How dare you?'

He smiles slowly. The slowest smile I've seen in my entire life. 'If you don't tell me, I'm gonna assume you want me to find out for myself.'

My palm swings upwards furiously, but his hand shoots out and catches it. Bending my fingers inwards he lifts my knuckles up to his lips. I try to jerk my wrist away, but it doesn't move at all. My breathing is erratic and my lips are trembling.

He smiles down at me, his eyes black and frighteningly unknowable.

'You want to expend some energy, wildcat? Give me your address and I'll come around later.'

My chest puffs out. My blood is pounding with fury and lust. I feel as if I am about to explode in his face. I don't know why this man can get me in this state with just the lift of an eyebrow. I shake my head. 'I can't decide if you are thick or just plain stupid. Read my lips. I. Don't. Want. You.'

'My, my, what a little liar you are. That's not at all what your delectable body is telling mine.' He runs a callused finger along the bare skin of my arm. It is not a particularly intimate or sexy move, but the way he does it makes me shiver. I freeze and hold my breath. When he reaches my wrist, he catches it and brings it up to his nose.

'You've never changed your perfume, have you?' His voice is quiet, reflective, but there are black fires burning in his eyes.

My breath comes out in a whoosh. He noticed! I don't tell him that this perfume was the last gift from my father. I had come back from a day of horse riding and my father had given me the box and said, 'A flower shouldn't smell like a donkey.'

'It suits you,' he says, looking at me as if he is drinking me in. I stare up at him stupidly. I am very tall but even in my high-heeled boots he still makes me feel tiny.

The music changes. Chris Isaak's sex anthem, *Wicked Game*, comes on.

'They're playing our song, Layla,' he says in a smoky drawl.

'We don't have a song,' I tell him, but my voice is weak

His eyes gleam with amusement. He bends his head and I jerk back. 'Who told you that?' he whispers, so close to my ear I feel his breath hot and smelling of mints.

Deftly, he whirls me around twice so I am suddenly thrust onto the edge of the dance floor. Isaak's yearning vocals fill the air and I feel something melt inside me. The pulsating bodies around us melt away and we are inside the sexy black-and-white Herb Ritts video. A dreamy place where everything happens in slow motion and I am frolicking with the most gorgeous man on earth.

When Isaak's voice slithers, *'What a wicked game you played to make me feel this way.'* I feel as if BJ is singing it to me. His arms envelop my body tightly, we fit together perfectly. We stare into each other's eyes. Lost in the dream world he has created, I lace my fingers around the back of BJ's powerful neck. The thick muscles contract under my hands. My fingers sweep and tangle in his hair.

'I'd never dreamed I'd love somebody like you'.

I rest my cheek on his chest and listen to the swaggering, strut-worthy tempo of his heart. Everything about him is so macho. Even his heartbeat has attitude. I close my eyes. His intentions are delicious and unapologetically impolite. I don't want to admit it, but some part of me aches for him.

'No IIIIIII don't want to fall in love... with you.'

He lifts me by my waist. I don't scream or yelp. My brothers have been doing it to me for years. When my throat is at his mouth level, he kisses it and I throw my head back and shudder at the warmth. He carries me higher still. I place my palms on his massive shoulders and look down on him. He stares at me, his eyes black and voracious. Slowly he twirls me. Round and round. Our eyes lock on each other. Then he moves his head forward and licks my belly button, like an animal. The carnality of the gesture makes me gasp.

Around us the music begins to slow down.

Isaak says, *'Nobody loves no one.'*

'I've tasted you and you are a meal I wish to devour,' he growls in my ear on my journey back to the ground. My feet touch the ground and my knees feel shaky. This is not a dance. This is a seduction, a kind I have never experienced. Primitive, raw, irresistible.

Dazed with hypnotic lust and mesmerized by his eyes, I gaze wordlessly up into his harsh face. A seduction is a promise of pleasure and release. I'm waiting. I guess I'm waiting for him to deliver. His head swoops down and his mouth captures mine. He kisses like a bandit. A time thieving bandit. Time slips away from me. The kiss goes on and on. I never want it to end. How long I stand within the circle of his arms while his mouth plunders mine I don't know.

Heat and fire flood my belly.

My entire body is a river of sensations. Nothing in my life has ever felt so good. With his hand on the small of my back he presses me even closer into his body as if he wants to meld me into him. As if he wants to completely crush and dominate me.

It is as if there is something inside both of us that is fighting to get to the other. My hips thrust into his thick hardness and I lust for him. The craving for him is like a fever. When he raises his head, I am such a mess I can do no more than blink stupidly.

Fall Out Boy's *Centuries* comes on around us and Patrick Stump is screaming, *'Remember me ... for centuries.'*

He lets go of me, his eyes narrowed. As ever, a sense of danger, something taboo, lingers around him. 'Meet me tomorrow,' he says. There is a thread of urgency in his voice.

The burn of his kiss lingers, and his scent is clinging to my skin like a touch. Nobody has ever kissed me like that. 'I can't. I'm going back to London tomorrow night.'

'Come for dinner on Monday.'

'Dinner,' I repeat stupidly.

'At Pigeon's Pie.'

Pigeon's Pie is one of his pubs. I hesitate.

'You can bring Ria with you,' he urges persuasively.

I shake my head and start backing away from him. 'No,' I whisper. I don't want to be another girl he's fucked and kicked to the curb. It would kill me.

'I'll be waiting for you,' he says.

I turn around and run into the crowd of people.

Up on his high station the DJ yells, 'Show some fucking mercy. Put your hands up,' and starts playing my most favorite song in the whole wide world. *Are you with me?*

BJ

I watch her run away in those crazy boots, boots that make me want to suck her cute little princess toes. I bet they smell like flowers. 'You can run little Sapphire Eyes, but you can't hide.'

This is the most exposed, terrified, and exhilarated I've ever been. It feels as if all the blood has drained from my head and gone into my cock. Across the crowd I spot my manager and walk over to him.

'Hey BJ,' he greets politely.

I nod curtly. He's good at his job, but I keep the demarcation clear at all times. We're not friends. He works for me. I'm his boss. This way nobody oversteps the mark.

'There's a girl with a red beret, white suede boots, and a white dress who is here for Ria's party. Find her and watch her like a hawk. Anyone that tries to chat her up, throw them out.'

His eyes bulge. He has never received an instruction like that from me before.

'Got that?' I ask, a little more aggressively than I had intended.

'Yeah, yeah, I got that,' he replies quickly, his hands coming up defensively.

'Good. Did you see the woman I came in with?'

'Yeah,' he admits warily.

'Call her a taxi when she's ready to go home.'

'Okay,' he says, with a smile of relief.

'Any problems with red beret call me on my mobile regardless of the time.'

'Got it.'

'Good. Have a good night.'

'Goodnight and thank you, BJ.'

I turn around. 'Oh, one other thing, make sure you escort red beret to her taxi.'

THIRTEEN

Layla

By the time I wake up light is filtering in all around the edges of the curtains. I peer at my bedside clock and see with surprise that it is almost eleven. I must have been more tired than I realized. Strange my mother didn't come to wake me up. I'd told her I wanted to help prepare Sunday lunch. I stretch luxuriously in the dim coolness of my childhood bed. And then the memory comes rushing back and my hand reaches for my mouth.

He kissed me!

A smile creeps onto my lips. I sit up and grab the teddy bear sitting on the shelf over my bed. I slide back under the warmth of the duvet, hugging my bear tightly. His name is Graystone and he is nearly 20 years old, but he has been well cared for and looks exceptional for his age. He smells of lavender. Once a month my mother opens his neck and stuffs him with sachets of dried lavender flowers. When I was very young, I used to have conversations with my bear and I honestly believed he would reply.

'Don't tell anyone, Graystone,' I whisper into his sweet-smelling head. 'But it was mind-blowingly hot, like nothing I have ever experienced. It almost made me dizzy.'

Graystone stays silent.

I sigh softly. 'I know. I know. He made it abundantly clear that it's just sex he's after, but so what?'

Last night I was a bit tipsy and had persuaded myself that I didn't want to be just another notch on his bedpost, but in the cold light of day, why not? This is the new, adventurous me. Besides there's always been this thing between us. Why not give in and just let it burn itself out. I'm not in any danger. It's just a physical thing. I *know* I won't fall in love with him or anything crazy like that. I mean I don't really even like the man.

I replay the dance, the kiss, the extraordinary way he had licked me as if he was claiming his territory. I touch my belly button and feel an immediate reaction between my legs. Wetness! It was never like this with Lupo or anyone before him.

I put Graystone back on the shelf and roll out of bed, determined not think of BJ until tomorrow when I'll decide whether or not to turn up at Pigeon's Pie. I open my bedroom door and hear the sounds of my brothers' voices downstairs. Still in my pajamas and without going to the bathroom first or making myself look presentable, I run down the stairs and into the living room. My mother is sitting in her armchair and my three brothers are sitting on the long sofa talking to her.

They all turn towards me.

'Sleeping Beauty is awake,' Shane says.

'Hello, sleepyhead,' Jake greets. I go over to the sofa and standing at the armrest, let myself fall like a felled tree into my brothers' laps. Just like I have been doing since I was a child.

'Timber,' Dominic calls and they catch me, laughing.

'Layla, you're not a little girl anymore. You're far too old to be doing such unladylike things,' my mother disapproves.

'No, she's not,' Shane rushes to my defense.

'Stop spoiling her,' my mother scolds him, but her voice lacks any real conviction. Secretly, she is proud of how close her family is. 'She's old enough to be a mother herself,' she adds grumpily.

'Perish the thought. She's still just a baby herself,' Jake says lazily, gently sweeping hair out of my face.

'She's never going to be too old for this even when she is 90,' adds Dominic, who is sitting in the middle. With a growl he begins to tickle my belly. Suddenly all of them have gotten into the act and there are hands everywhere, in my armpits, my ribs, my belly. With a yelp I try to wriggle and evade their roaming hands, but their grip is steel-like and there are too many hands coming from all sides. Helpless, I laugh until I am gasping for air and my stomach hurts.

'I haven't been to the toilet yet. I'm gonna wee on you,' I splutter desperately.

It works instantly. They stop immediately and I worm off them and land on the floor on my back, breathless and panting.

My brothers look down at me indulgently, but my mother is tutting away. I turn my head towards my mother's upside down face.

'I thought you were going to wake me up and let me help you with lunch.'

'I heard you stumbling around at two in the morning. I wanted you to have a good rest. You look better for it. Anyway, everything is done. Go and make yourself presentable. Lunch is in an hour.'

'Thanks, Ma.' I grin at her, then I turn my head back towards Jake. 'Where is Lily?'

'She was feeling a bit tired. She's lying down in Ma's room.'

I frown. I really like Lily. There is something so delicate and sweet about her. 'She's okay, right?'

'Yeah, she's fine.'

I sit up. 'OK, I'm going to go say hello. See you guys after I have peed.'

I run up the stairs towards my mother's room. Outside her door I knock softly and call, 'Lily?'

'Come in,' she says instantly.

I open the door and she is trying to sit up. She is already eight months pregnant and her belly is quite big for her tiny frame.

'Don't sit up,' I tell her and she lies back down.

I go up to her. 'Can I listen?'

She smiles.

I crouch next to the bed, put my ear against her stomach, and listen to my niece. For a few seconds everything is quiet. Then I distinctively hear a noise.

'What can you hear?' Lily asks.

'I think she just hiccupped,' I tell her.

Lily laughs. 'You're as bad as your brother. He swears he can hear her laugh.'

I look at her incredulously. 'Really?'

She looks at me and shakes her head. 'Through amniotic fluid? Very doubtful. But, to be fair, when he puts his head on my stomach she will shift around excitedly and kick hard. As if she recognizes her father.'

I look at her in wonder. 'Wow, how amazing is that?'

She chuckles softly. 'It is when you think about it.'

I sit cross-legged on the floor with an elbow resting at the edge of my right knee and my chin in my palm. 'Tell me about the day when you found out you were pregnant. I want to know everything. How you told Jake. And then what he said and did.'

She smiles with the memory. 'Well, I guess I knew I was pregnant two days after I missed my period. I'm like clockwork. So I bought a couple of pregnancy tests and both were positive. The funny thing is, it was one day before the first anniversary of the day we met, so I decided not to tell him until our anniversary night. We were going to spend it in Paris and I wanted to tell him at the hotel before we went to dinner.'

She looks away from me, a dreamy, far-away look in her eyes.

'He had booked us this beautiful hotel suite in Paris. It had one of those impossibly glamorous interiors, you know, the ones you see in movies. With tall, gilded ceilings, wall paneling, antique wooden floors, and a massive, intricately-carved gold bed. It had a three balconies and palm trees in Chinese pots. That's where I told him.'

She pauses and there are tears in her eyes.

'Oh Lily, you are crying.'

She shakes his head. 'It was just so beautiful. I had bought these little yellow shoes. They were the tiniest pair of knitted shoes you ever saw. They came in a white cardboard box and I had asked the girl in the shop to gift-wrap them. I still remember the wrapping. Yellow with red balloons. So just before we left for dinner I put the box into his hand. "For you," I said. He frowned, holding the small box in his hand as if it was the most precious thing in the world. "For me?" he asked as he did not quite believe it. You see, until then I had never given him anything. What could I give him? He was the man who had everything.'

She smiles, a glowing secret smile.

'He opened the box. For a while he simply stared at them incredulously and then he fished them out between his thumb and forefinger and looked at me. Oh Layla, you should have seen the expression on his face. It gives me goosebumps even now. He was so happy, but he didn't dare believe it, just in case it was a stupid joke or it meant something different. "Are you trying to tell me what I think you're trying to tell me?" he whispered.'

'I just nodded and watched as he carefully put the shoes back into the box, and put the box on the side table. Then, with a crazy, small boy whoop of pure joy, he lifted me up into the air and whirled me round and round until I was quite, quite dizzy.'

'Oh Lily,' I breathe. 'What a lovely story.'

'It *was* an unforgettable night,' she says softly, and strokes her belly with a contented sigh.

'I don't know if I'll ever find the kind of love you have.'

She looks me in the eye. 'Sometimes the man for you is closer than you think.'

BJ's face flashes into my mind. How would such an obviously cold and hard man react to the news he is going to be a father?

'One day you'll be pregnant and when you tell your man you're carrying his child you will know exactly what I mean. A light, a special light, comes into his eyes.'

For a while we stop speaking. Each of us lost in our own thoughts. Then Lily breaks the silence. 'Your mum said you went to a party at Laissez-faire last night.'

'Yeah,' I admit. 'It was Ria's birthday party.' I briefly consider telling her about BJ, about that slow-motion, sex-drenched dance and the drug-like kiss afterwards. Then I decide not to. Nothing has happened yet. Nothing will if I don't make it to Pigeon's Pie.

'Was it good?'

I grin. 'It was brilliant. The music was great and we danced all night, but there was a big fight at the end. A guy almost crashed into me, but I was lucky. The manager of the club appeared out of nowhere and pulled me out of harm's way. He immediately called a taxi and insisted on putting me into it. Very decent of him, I thought.'

Lily's eyes have an oddly knowing glint and she looks as if she is about to say something, but at that moment Jake enters the room, and I run off to the toilet. After I brush my teeth and hair, I dress in a pair of old jeans and a huge, comfy jumper. Then I run downstairs to join my family.

Lunch is fun. It always is when my brothers are around. Jake is the oldest and he took on the role of breadwinner when my father died, making him the lucky one I run to when I am in trouble. Then there's Dominic. He is a hothead with a hair-trigger temper, but he has a soft spot for me, so I can generally get away with murder with him. He's the one I go to when I've done something I shouldn't have and need to be forgiven.

Shane is only a year older than me. He's the coolest of my brothers, I can totally relax with him and say and do anything I want. He is also the most classically handsome Eden brother and the playboy of the family. He's got girls everywhere. When we go out together I get a ton of venomous and jealous looks from women. I almost pity the woman he will end up with. It must be hell to be with such a player.

Shane catches my eye and taps the handle of his knife so it hits the table surface and expertly flicks a pea in my direction. I open my mouth and in it goes.

'Stop it, both of you.' My mother looks at Shane sternly. 'Layla is *not* a child.'

Both of us erupt into irrepressible laughter.

My mother turns to me. 'By the time I was your age I was married with four children.'

'Shane started it,' I say.

'This is not proper behavior for a lady. Do you want people to think I raised a hooligan?' my mother asks.

I cast my eyes down.

'Let her be, Ma,' Dominic, ever the gallant, comes to my rescue. 'When she was away you were always moaning that it was like the life and soul of this family went away. All our meals were proper and dull. Now she's back and you won't let her have a bit of fun. She doesn't behave like this when we are out. This is our family meal. Let her have her fun.'

I look at Dominic with astonishment. My mum said that.

To my surprise Jake cuts in. 'It's true that we spoil Layla rotten, but she hasn't turned out so bad. She knows right from wrong. She's never ever mean to anyone. She's generous to a fault. She wouldn't hurt a fly. She's not stubborn or selfish or bossy or bitchy. Quite frankly, she makes me proud of her.'

'And she knows how to catch flying peas in her mouth,' Shane adds with a grin.

Everybody laughs. Even my mother smiles.

I gaze around the table at all their faces, even the latest addition, Lily, and my heart brims over with love. At that moment I think I am the most blessed person in the entire world

'How's the job search coming along, Bear?' Jake asks.

'I've got an interview on Wednesday. Fingers crossed,' I say and stuff a chunk of roasted potato into my mouth so that he can't ask where it is. Jake is such a control freak, he actually paid the people living in the flat next to me in Milan to keep an eye on me and make sure I was all right! God knows what he will do if I tell him where my interview is.

'Mmmm ... delicious, Ma,' I say around my food.

My mother makes the best roasted potatoes ever. Her secret is twofold. She strains the potatoes and gives them a good hard shake in a closed lid pot after they have been cooked to break up their edges. Then she drops them on a baking tray of very hot goose fat. Hot enough to make the potatoes sizzle. The result: crispy on the outside, billowy on the inside.

After lunch Jake and Lily offer me a lift back to London, a suggestion I quickly accept.

FOURTEEN

Layla

The journey is pleasant. The conversation is light and easy and it is only when Jake and Lily start talking about attending a wedding of a family friend that I kind of put my foot in it.

'Do you want to go, Bear?' my brother asks.

'Will BJ be there?' I reply.

Jake meets my eyes in the rearview mirror. He is frowning. 'Why do you want to know?'

I shrug. 'Just curious.'

'Stay away from BJ, Layla,' he warns in a steely voice.

I am immediately curious. 'Why? I thought the feud is over and we are best friends with the Pilkingtons now.'

'We're not best friends. We're friends,' he corrects.

'Ma said he saved your life.'

'Yes, he did and I'll be forever grateful for that, but I don't want him anywhere near my sister. He's a junkyard dog. He'll fuck anything in a skirt.'

'Oh, I don't know,' Lily says. 'I think BJ can be tamed. He is a bit of a beast, but a very seductive beast,' she says and flashes a wink in my direction.

The car suddenly stops.

'Out of the car, you,' Jake tells Lily. His voice is deadly quiet.

She raises her eyebrows at him, then flicks her eyes in my direction, as if asking, *You want to do this with you sister here?*

'I'm waiting,' he says.

'Are you serious?' she asks incredulously.

I look from one to the other curiously.

Jake doesn't reply. Instead he gets out of the car. As I watch totally bemused, he comes around to her side, opens Lily's door, and takes her hand to pull her out and lead her around the back of the car. For a few moments I don't turn around to look but then, oh fuck it, I have to know. I glance back, and my mouth drops open.

Whoa, Jake!

Lily is being crushed in Jake's arms. He is kissing the shit out of her. The domination and forcefulness of his embrace is astonishing. I didn't know he had it in him to be so intensely jealous and possessive. I swivel my head back quickly, not wanting to be caught staring like a half-wit at my brother eating his wife's face by the roadside. I needn't have worried though. It's a good few minutes before he settles Lily back in the passenger seat. Her cheeks are bright red. And no wonder.

He gets into his seat and turns around to face me.

'You've been warned. BJ saved my life. So I owe him big time, but if he hurts even a hair on your head I'll have to break his fucking legs, and I really don't want to do that. We've just made up with the Pilkingtons after centuries of pointless feuding. If you don't want to start an all-out war again between our families, stay away from him. Can you do that?'

I nod slowly.

'Good. He's not the only man in the world. There are millions of good guys out there for you. You don't need to pick a drug dealer.' He pauses. 'He's a criminal, Layla. Don't ever mistake him for anything else. You deserve better than him. Much better.'

'Ok,' I whisper.

He turns around and starts the car. We drive the rest of the way in complete silence.

'Thanks for the ride, Jake. Bye, Lily,' I say, opening the car door.

'No problem. I'll wait until you get in,' Jake says.

'You don't have to, Jake. What can possibly happen to me in broad daylight?'

'Layla,' he sighs wearily.

'OK, OK,' I say and, slipping out of the car and shutting the door, I run up the steps to my front door. I love my family to death and all, but sometimes they are so overprotective I feel stifled. I close my front door and I hear Jake's car drive away. My flat is quiet and still. So much so I jump when my phone rings. It's Madison.

'Hey, Maddy. How's it going?'

'Same old, same old,' she says, sounding bored. 'How was your party last night?'

I take a deep breath. 'I kissed … someone.'

'Wait one moment,' she says and I hear her moving around, doing something. 'Right. I'm back.'

'What were you doing?' I ask.

'Getting a tub of ice cream out of the freezer. So … who, what, where, when? Spit it out,' she demands bossily.

So I tell her.

'No fucking way!' she screams so loudly I have to hold the phone away from my ear.

I open the freezer and take out a carton of chocolate-chip ice cream and open it on the granite countertop.

'Are you kidding me?' she asks incredulously.

'Nope,' I say, getting a spoon out of a drawer and shutting it with my hip.

'But you hate him!'

I sigh, plonking myself on a stool and stabbing my spoon into the ice cream. 'I know.'

'What do you mean you know? Is this like some sort of a hate fuck?'

'I'm not sure I'm taking it any further than dinner.'

'Liar,' she accuses.

I slide the spoon into my mouth and let the ice cream melt on my tongue. Maddy is right. In my heart of hearts I know I'm not walking away.

'So what are you going to wear tomorrow then?' she asks.

'I don't know yet.'

'Wear your red dress.'

'No way. That's a summer dress.'

'You won't be wearing it for long, anyway.'

'Even if I do decide to go further, I'm not planning on sleeping with him tomorrow.'

'Of course, you're not. You're just practically salivating through the phone and into my ear,' she says with her mouth full.

I scoop more ice cream. 'Want to bet I don't sleep with him tomorrow?'

'To be really frank, I'd sleep with him.'

The spoon halts mid-way. 'What?'

'Wouldn't be the saddest day of my life.'

I lick the spoon. 'Really?'

'Yeah, he has badditude and that intense, laser stare going on.'

I grin. Badditude and a laser stare. That's one description for BJ.

'I like the way he fills out his jeans from the back too,' she adds.

I laugh outright.

'Oh! And I suspect he'll be very good in bed. He looks like he gets laid often.'

That observation shouldn't have troubled me, but it does. Which is strange because after Jake's warning I am of the mind that even if I do sleep with him it will only be the once or twice.

'So come on, what are you going to wear?'

'Something subtle. Maybe a white shirt and my dark green trousers.'

'Isn't that what you were planning to wear for your job interview?'

'No, I was going to wear my black trousers to the interview. I just don't want to give the impression that I'm a slut.'

She laughs. 'You? A slut? Pleeeease. You've got 'Don't Touch' written across your forehead.'

'I do not.'

'All right, I'm wrong. You've got Don't Fucking Touch Or I'll Call The Police blazing from your forehead.'

'Don't exaggerate, Maddie.' I sigh. 'Actually, I'm a bit confused.'

'About what?' she demands.

'I think I'm torn between excitement and panic,' I reveal.

'I get the excitement bit, but why the panic?'

'Because I know it's a bad idea.'

'Why?'

'Well to start with, Jake has threatened me off in no uncertain terms. Absolutely don't go there stuff. Forbidden in

capital letters. Huge family feud stuff. Jake actually called him a drug dealer and criminal. And he didn't say it just for effect. He really believes BJ is a massive gangster.'

'Ooook. You said to start with. What are the other reasons?'

'I sometimes get the uneasy feeling that I am standing at the edge of a cliff and about to jump in when I'm with BJ. There's this feeling of doing something deliciously destructive, but there is also the prospect of oblivion forever.'

'Man, only you can make a simple fuck sound so dramatic.'

FIFTEEN

Layla

If a girl will walk stark-naked by the light of the full moon
round a field or a house, and cast behind her at every step a
handful of salt, she will get the lover whom she desires.

Old Gypsy Magic

The moment Ria called to ask if I wanted to go to dinner
with her at Pigeon's Pie I knew. I was always going to say yes.
So I did. Ria and I agreed to meet at a wine bar in Waterloo
first for one drink and then take a taxi to Pigeon's Pie.

I arrive first. Nervously I order a glass of white wine and
find us a table. Ria is dressed in a skin-tight leopard print crop
top and leather trousers. She looks sexy and carefree.
Suddenly I wish I had taken Maddy's advice, and not dressed

so stuffily. We drink a glass of wine and chat about the people we know, then Ria looks at her wristwatch.

'We should go. We don't want to be late for dinner,' she says with a smile.

'No, we don't want to be late,' I agree nervously.

The taxi drops us across the road from Pigeon's Pie. From outside it looks like an old fashioned pub; a place with fruit machines, patterned carpets, dark wood furniture, and horrible pub food.

'You okay?' Ria asks.

'Totally,' I reply and follow her through the double doors. Inside it is exactly as I had envisioned. Only it is surprisingly full of elegantly dressed, well-heeled people.

'Come on,' Ria says and leads me to a back room. She opens the door to a wood paneled room, and—oh my God!— It's like I have been transported into an old gangster movie. This is the proverbial backroom where shady deals get struck. It even has another door, presumably a quick, back way escape door. BJ is sitting at a wooden table and there is a half-drunk pint of Guinness in front of him.

BJ

Forswear it sight! For I ne'er saw true beauty till tonight.

Oh Layla. Look at you. Dressed as if you're going to a job interview at a bank. A pink and white striped shirt, a tailored, almost masculine black jacket, and the unsexiest article of clothing I've ever had the misfortune to come across: a below the knee, wrap around skirt in gunmetal grey.

Still, it's shocking how relieved I am to see her. Some part of my brain can't believe she came. Of her own free will. I rise to my feet.

'Hey BJ,' Ria calls out with a big, friendly smile.

'Hey Wild Cat,' I reply easily.

She pouts prettily and lifts her face up to kiss me on the cheek. While her lips are stuck to my face, I shift my gaze to Layla. Her teeth are sunk into her bottom lip. Fuck! What a great mouth. And there's another inch in my pants. Ria dislodges herself with a wet sound.

'Layla.' My eyes take a lazy trip down her body. Jesus! I am crazy-lusting after her.

Color creeps up her cheeks, but her voice is cool. 'BJ.'

'Have a seat,' I invite. 'What do you girls want to drink?'

A waitress has already entered the room and is hovering nervously in the background.

'Champagne,' Ria says, perching delicately at the end of the chair opposite me.

I raise an eyebrow at Layla. 'The same?'

She shrugs. 'OK,' she agrees and slips into the chair next to Ria.

'Bring us a Bollinger,' I tell the waitress.

She nods and scurries away as if I bite. I sit down and lean back, curling my hand loosely around my pint glass.

'Do you still have Bertie?' Ria asks.

'Of course. She's a dead woman if she leaves me.'

Layla's eyes open wide.

Ria laughs. 'Yeah right. You're dead if she leaves you, you mean.'

Ria turns to Layla. 'Bertie was a housecleaner in Florida and came here to visit her niece who was going out with BJ. The niece invited BJ to their home, Bertie cooked him a meal, and the rest is history. She's amazing. She takes American comfort food and fuses it with European, Mexican, and Asian recipes. You won't believe how good they come out. Hard to imagine, but all those posh people out there, they could go to the best restaurants in London, instead they come here for Bertie the housecleaner's food.'

'Wow.'

She turns to me. 'But you prefer the plain comfort food though, don't ya?'

'Give me a plate of fried chicken and I'm a happy man,' I say lightly.

Ria laughs. 'I love coming here.'

The champagne arrives, gets poured, and the girls take their polite little sips.

There is the sound of birds tweeting. It has Ria reaching into her purse for her phone. She looks at the screen, frowns, and says, 'Sorry, I have to take this.'

'Of course,' Layla says.

I gaze at her expressionlessly.

'Oh no,' she exclaims dramatically. 'Noooo. Really? Do you want me to come over?'

I turn my attention to Layla. She is staring at Ria worriedly.

'Don't worry. I'll take a cab. I'll be with you in 20 minutes at the most. No, no, of course not. No, they won't mind.'

She ends the call and looks at me then Layla. 'I'm so sorry, but a friend of mine has just gotten some bad news. I've got to go and be with her. I hope you guys don't mind.'

I shake my head.

Layla says nothing. Just stares at Ria.

Ria turns to me. 'You will give Layla a ride back home, won't you?'

'Sure, I'll give Layla a ride,' I say.

SIXTEEN

Layla

One corner of his mouth crooks up. I love his mouth. The way he says ride is slow and sexy. I bet he can give me a ride. Silently, I watch Ria glug her champagne down as fast as is humanly possible. Her eyes drift longingly to the bottle, but she stands and comes towards me. I allow her to hurriedly air peck both my cheeks and watch while she does the same to BJ. Then she is gone.

And I meet his eyes. 'There's no emergency is there?'

Utterly unperturbed he grins. 'Of course not.'

I stand up.

He looks up at me. His eyes are no longer lazy, and tame. They are unblinking and burning with a fire-like intensity. 'You're all grown up now, Layla. You don't really need a chaperone, do you?'

'No, but I don't appreciate being manipulated.'

'Would you have come on your own?'

I pause. 'I guess not.'

'Do you want me to call Ria back?' he asks gently.

My shoulders sag. Of course I don't. I know what I'm here for. My anger is totally irrational, a result of nervous energy.

'Sit down,' he says softly. 'I promise it'll be the best fried chicken you'll ever eat.'

I take a deep breath and reoccupy the chair I'd vacated. He smiles.

There is something about this man .... Even when he was 15 and I had convinced myself that I thoroughly disliked him, he was still that tough insouciant who stared at me. Now that he's all grown up and forbidden to me, his magnetism whispers and beckons irresistibly. I want him. I want him more than I've wanted anything else in my life. I want him so much it's an ache somewhere deep inside me.

'Are you hungry?' he asks casually, the tone totally at odds with what I see in his eyes.

The reptilian brain lurking inside my head is not in the mood for pillow talk or cuddles or food. It wants what it wants. And what it wants is a fuck. A mindless fuck of epic proportions.

I shake my head and stare at his sexy mouth hungrily.

He lifts his eyebrows. 'You're radiating sex right now.'

My breath comes faster. 'Oh yeah?'

His nostrils flare. 'Yeah. You're giving me a raging hard-on.'

God that was delivered deep and sexy. Strange, my family made me believe I was made of sugar and spice and everything nice, and I have turned out to be made of an inner itching that makes me lewd and lusting.

I stand up and walk over to the door to turn the lock.

He stands up. 'Come and show me how wet you are.'

I walk towards him. When I am about three feet away, I leap up on him, loop my arms around his neck, and curl my legs around his hips, making sure to rub my damp panties against the hard bulge in his jeans.

His large hands curl around my thighs. 'Now you're talking, Princess.'

I lick my lower lip slowly.

He groans. 'Holy shit, Layla.'

I lean closer to his ear, my breath hot. 'What about the fried chicken?'

'Fuck the fried chicken.'

I look up at him from under my lashes. 'How about that ride then?'

'Time you were in my bed, young lady,' he growls and carries me with my wet pussy stuck to the fierce erection in his jeans. We go through a second door in the room that leads to a dim, narrow corridor lit only by an emergency light. I clasp my fingers tightly around his neck and feel like a tick hanging on to the neck of a huge beast.

His skin is warm and he smells wild, like the sea when it is stormy or the forest at night. And ale, I get a whiff of that too. I lay my cheek on his chest and hear his heart beating fast and loud under his clothes. The corridor leads to another emergency door that opens out to the cold night.

Snowflakes fall on his cheeks. I reach up and lick one. His skin feels hot. He leans imperceptibly closer. There is naked need in his eyes. I stare up at him and watch as his breath frosts before it reaches my face.

'When I find something I want to keep, I never let go,' he says quietly.

I smile.

He lifts my shirt and puts his fingertips on my belly.

I shudder. 'Cold.' But I don't jerk away. I don't want him to take his hand away.

He stops in front of a massive, souped up four-wheel drive. More lorry than car. He opens the passenger door and deposits me inside as if I weigh no more than a child. He closes the door, gets into the driver's seat, turns on the noisy engine, and we hurtle through the cold streets of London.

'Where are we going?'

He glances at me before returning his eyes to the road. 'Do you really care?'

He's right. I don't. We don't say a word after that. Sometimes I look sideways at him, but he has his head turned towards the traffic and his profile is stern, his jaw clenched tight. When he briefly looks at me his eyes are glittering and as cold as that of a serpent.

I wonder what he is thinking. I don't ask. It feels like this is what we were meant to do. Always. The dislike was a temporary cover for this volcano of passion and lust.

When we reach his house, he turns to me. In the light of the street lamp, his eyebrows are a straight line under which pools of blackness have gathered. The scar on his face seems alive. He is the most intimidating and magnetic man I have ever met.

'Last chance to back out,' he warns. In the strange shadows his entire body seems to be crouched, tense and waiting. The potty-mouthed bastard is gone. I've never seen him look so grim or so apprehensive. At that moment I know that this is one of those times when I hold all the cards. When my decision will change everything forever.

Both of us know this cannot and will never be just a one-night stand. There will be no going back from this. It will be messy. Other people will get involved. And the inevitable break-up will be heartbreaking. My family will be hurt. I blank out the implications even as Jake's face swims into my consciousness. *Make no mistake. He is a criminal.* This is a guy who gets laid a lot. I close my eyes. It can be a secret. It can be our secret. No one else needs to know. When it burns out, only I will suffer.

'No thanks,' I whisper.

His body becomes slack with relief. He got the girl again. He nods. 'Thank God,' he says savagely triumphant. 'My balls are aching like they've been sucker punched. I need to have my cock in your hot little cunt as soon as possible.'

He hauls open the door on my side, scoops me into his arms, and carries me off to his lair. I look up into his face. Who'd have thought?

Him and me.

SEVENTEEN

Layla

He kicks the front door shut behind him. The house is semi-dark and his footsteps echo. He obviously doesn't use this place much. There is a lamp lit in one of the rooms, its light spilling out into the hallway. He takes me up the stairs, opens a door, and lays me down on a very large bed. Silently, he moves to the fireplace and lights it. A gas fire throws up dancing flames and the sparse room becomes full of shadows.

He turns to me, an odd expression on his face, as if he is stunned to find me in his living space. There is almost an animal-like quality about him. Like a wolf that is crouched and tense, ready to spring on its prey. I drink him in, mesmerized by how large he is, how desperately I want him. He hesitates, as if his next move matters, then walks up to me and says, 'Play with yourself until you are wet and hot.'

'I'm already wet and hot,' I gasp.

'I want to see your pussy dripping. I want to be able to smell you from here. Can you do that for me?'

He emits heat like a radiator. I feel his power flow from his skin and envelop me like a mist. I don't know why, but I do not feel the slightest bit shy. I lift my skirt so he will have a clear view and, spreading my legs, slowly slip my hand into my panties and over my mound. I look up at him and deliberately push my finger deep into my slick channel. My sex is so swollen and engorged with lust that a moan oozes out of me. The sound is thick and so full of need that it is a revelation even to me.

He stands very still, a stranger, watching me avidly. As if this is the first time a woman has ever opened her legs for him.

'I'm dripping,' I groan, my legs squirming. I've never been so hot or so wet before.

'Show me.'

The ache is so strong it feels as if I am bruised between my thighs. I slide my panties over my legs and feet.

He catches me by my ankles, pulls my legs apart, and looks down at me. No man has ever looked at me the way he is looking. As if he is looking at the most beautiful thing he has ever seen in his life. Possessively and with pure, unadulterated yearning. It is addictive. I feel as high as I did that time I had a puff of weed behind the bicycle shed with Willow and her boyfriend. The knots in the thick muscles of his shoulders tell me how much control he is exerting over himself.

His gaze travels back to my face and our eyes lock. His are deliberately hooded, the half-moons holding a force that seems unsuitable for a junkyard dog willing to mate with anything in a skirt. It's more like something you would encounter in a slow-moving, achingly beautiful dream. I want him to enter me so bad my entire body feels like one exposed raw nerve.

'Take off your top,' he growls.

I pull it roughly over my head.

'Lose the bra.'

That went the way of the top pretty damn quick.

He grasps me by my waist as if I am a doll of little consequence or weight and turns me on my face. I hear him unzip my skirt and pull it down my legs. He turns me back around.

'I want to see you play with your nipples.'

I rub my fingers in circles and then catch them between my thumb and forefinger and roll them. His eyes widen.

He kneels down and a shock of black hair falls onto his forehead. My body rises off the bed as my hand moves helplessly to it. I claw my hand through his hair. He remains still, silent, powerful. *I like to tie girls up and suck their pussies until they scream.*

'Make me scream,' I whisper.

'Thought you'd never ask,' he says and slips his palms under my buttocks turning my crotch into a sort of plate or bowl and brings me to his mouth. For a second he looks like a beast about to devour me. And that aura of dominance turns me to mush. I cream. Slickness runs down the insides of my thighs. He extends his hot tongue, swipes it along the crack, and swirls the tip over my plumped, engorged folds.

There is not an inch he does not explore, tease, or brush. Down one side, up the other, this way, that way, a poke here, a brush there ... until my pussy is on fire and I am out of my mind with need, squirming and begging for release.

He sucks my clit and the molten heat of his mouth is such a shock to my system it makes my whole body shake. I come so fucking hard I scream. He doesn't take his huge head away from my oversensitive, pulsating clit and the orgasm goes on and on. The muscle contractions come and come until my head spins. It is raw, primal, and violent, unlike anything I have ever experienced.

'Whoa, that was amazing,' I whisper, in my stupor.

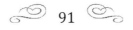

'Good. Because I'm ready to fuck.'

He pulls his t-shirt over his head and I gape. Holy shit! He is covered in tats. My brothers have them, but not like this. I let my eyes rove over them. Angels, demons, patterns, and the words No Fear blazing across his chest. He unbuttons his fly and his trousers hit the floor. He pulls down his underwear and his cock springs out. My eyes widen. Holy shit fuck! That is the biggest, angriest cock I have ever seen in my life. Swollen and decorated with throbbing veins it is literally jerking with aggression and animal vigor.

'So this is what all the fuss is about,' I say wonderingly. Now I know why he wanted me to be dripping wet.

'Don't fret, hun. Just spread your legs a bit wider,' he advises as he rolls a condom over the massive shaft.

Eagerly I splay my legs as far as they will go. He lifts both my wrists over my head and traps them under his large hand. Staring in my eyes he slowly sinks his massive cockhead into me, forcing my pussy to accommodate him. He is so big my mouth opens in a silent cry of shock. I've never been so stretched before or so damn full.

'Fuck, your cunt is incredibly tight,' he rumbles deep in his throat.

Unable to talk, I take a shallow breath, and he uses that opportunity to push himself even deeper into me.

Oh God. Yes.

'You like having a big dick inside you, Princess Layla?'

Vulnerable and totally exposed, I nod.

He pushes again. And he is balls-deep inside.

I expel the breath I was holding.

'You took it all like a good girl,' he growls and, bringing his mouth to my nipple, bites it.

'You fucking animal,' I curse and it is like playing with fire. The beast inside him takes over. He withdraws from my pussy and slams back in so hard my breasts quake, and my whole body shunts upwards. I feel the jolt in my bones. It is like being drilled into. I grunt.

He rams into me again, but this time I am ready for him and I enjoy it.

'Is that all you got?' I goad, squeezing the splendid thickness inside me.

It isn't. He turns my insides into molten lava. I think my clit is alive and will burst into flames. Trapped under this giant, I fucking lose it. Ferociously, I jam my hips upwards, tangle my legs around his ass, and scream like a foghorn as he continues to thrust into me.

When it is over, I gaze up at him mistily. His cock is buried so deep inside me I think I own it. It must be mine. It is a shock when he pulls out of me suddenly. He releases my hands and falls on his back on the bed.

'Now ride me,' he orders.

I cannot wait to fulfill that command. I crawl to him, greedily lower myself onto the glorious pillar of hard meat and lock my muscles around the throbbing goodness. Impaled on his cock, my body sighs with possessive pleasure. This man was made for me. I lean forward to balance myself and begin to move on his thick shaft. Each hard slam makes him shoot deeper into me.

'That's it. Ride me hard.'

He comes like a raging bull, his body heaving, his head thrown back, his lips curled back in a snarl, and his eyes glazed and unseeing. I ride him through it all. When he stops exploding and becomes still, I can see the wavy heat rising from our joined flesh. I rub my pussy on him restlessly. I don't want his cock out of my body.

'You want more, Princess?'

'I do,' I say, but in fact, I feel completely drained and sleepy.

He holds me and rolls himself so we are both lying on our sides facing each other. Slowly, he slips out of me. My legs feel cramped and stiff and I straighten them with a sigh.

He touches my hair. 'So silky,' he mutters.

My eyes droop closed for a second before I realize that I am falling asleep. I force them open and look at him. It is astonishing how awake and alert he seems to be.

'Aren't you sleepy?' I ask.

'Nope. I have a high metabolic rate. I don't tire fast. In fact, I hardly ever sleep.' He eases off the condom, ties it, and chucks it over the edge of the bed.

'Really? That's amazing.'

'It's not all it's cracked up to be. I spend too many nights when everyone else is asleep wandering around like some night creature.'

'Is that why they call you The Bat? Because you're up all night.'

He gives me an odd look, as if he is deciding what to tell me. 'No, that's not why.'

I get up on my elbow and look at him curiously. 'Why then?'

In one smooth move he is on his haunches and has pulled me upright on the bed. We stand facing each other. 'Because when I was 15 I didn't know how to control my rage or my power and that made me fierce and vicious. This is how I fought then.'

He tucks his chin down to his chest, rounds his shoulders, and moves his fists as if he is throwing punches to the sides of my body. They only touch my body, but I get a measure of how lightning-fast his delivery is, and how impossible it must be to try and evade them if he was doing it for real. In seconds, I feel disorientated and I don't resist when he grabs my shoulders, swooping down to touch his open mouth to the side of my neck. He lifts his head and stares at me.

'I bit them hard enough to draw blood. At the end of every fight, my mouth was always dripping with their blood and sometimes I even spat out flesh.'

I stand frozen with shock. 'Why were you so angry?'

Something flashes in his eyes. Something that hurt him badly. It shocks me to see him so vulnerable. And then a veil comes over his eyes. He had accidently revealed too much. 'I didn't bring you here to talk. You're here to fuck and to suck cock,' he says, pushing my shoulders downwards.

I get on my knees. His cock is already rock hard, but just a moment ago I saw something in his eyes. Some terrible pain.

'It's a nice cock. I'll enjoy sucking it,' I say, softly looking up at him.

I lean forward and lick the smooth head. He rakes his fingers through my hair, fists them, and fucks my mouth as if I am a prostitute he picked up on a street corner. But I understood, even when I was getting on my knees, that it is the hurt, the terrible hurt that I reminded him of that is driving him.

He comes in my mouth without asking if he can.

I get it. He has just made me submit. Made me swallow his cum. He has owned me. I look up at him, my mouth still full of his softening flesh. His shoulders heave. He pulls out of me, crouches down, and we stare at each other. And I know that something has changed.

'I have to leave,' I say.

'Stay the night.'

'I can't. Dominic is taking me out to breakfast.'

'Sorry, I can't let you go just yet. I haven't had enough of you yet.'

'I'm too sore, BJ.'

'I know,' he says softly, his voice husky. 'I won't hurt you.'

I feel my stomach lift.

He puts me on my back, pins me to the bed with his body, and kisses my eyes. What he does afterwards can only be called a worship of my body with his tongue and mouth. He covers every inch of me kissing, sucking, licking, nipping, biting. Neck, hands, fingers, legs, toes, breasts, nipples, stomach, hips, back, buttocks, asshole, and—finally, finally when I am shivering with arousal —clit.

The result of so much attention is an orgasm like I've never had. The kind where there are stars at the back of your eyelids and you really think you are going to pass out, or perhaps you even actually pass out. No wonder the French call it *la petite mort*, the little death. It is so consuming and powerful I feel almost melancholy and tears slip out of my eyes.

He looks at them curiously, bending his head to lick them.

The gesture is so innocent, so without guile that it makes me feel unreal. At that surreal moment I believe myself to be merely a reflection on a shiny surface or part of a dream. It is in the play of light from the flames in the fireplace on his face that pulls me back. I see him for what he really is. A totally misunderstood, half-man, half-beast, hiding a suffering heart. And I feel as protective over him as a mother bear of her cubs. I could never let anyone hurt him. And I know, in this moment, that I must never, never bring harm to him. I must guard him from the wrath of my family.

I touch his scar and he flinches.

'What happened?'

'Someone bit me,' he says quietly, but I know it was not just anyone. The scar is still alive in his mind. And sometimes when I look at him, it even seems so to me.

'A scar is a special thing. It means you were stronger than whatever tried to hurt you.'

His eyes widen. He stares at me in wonder.

'What?'

He shakes his head. 'You're just different than what I thought you would be.'

I smile. 'What did you think I'd be?'

He shakes his head again and looks away. 'Not like this.' He sits up. 'Are you hungry?'

'Starving actually.'

'Come on. I'll feed you and then take you home.'

We dress quickly as if we are leaving the scene of a crime. I have a great desire to stroke his cheek and make it better. But what am I making better? We have nothing but sex between us. There can be nothing between us, but secret passion. He looks at me, his stance, waiting, watching, patient.

I tie my skirt over my shirt, shrug on my jacket, and slip into my shoes. 'Ready,' I declare.

He takes me to a Chinese restaurant, one of these places that stays open all night. He orders what seems to be the entire menu.

'Are you really going to eat all that?'

'I burned a lot of calories tonight,' he says with a grin.

The food starts arriving almost immediately. He has ordered all kinds of food, but I feel full after a helping of Kung Po chicken and ginger prawns on half a bowl of rice. It is actually too late to eat.

Feeling lethargic and satiated and happy, I lean my chin on my hand and watch with sleepy detachment as he goes through the pile of food. In the car, I yawn and lean my head back against the head rest. He turns towards me.

'Meet me for dinner tomorrow?'

'I can't. I have to be in bed early. I have a job interview on Wednesday.'

'I'll call you and we'll meet for lunch instead,' he suggests.

The feeling of contentment disappears. 'Let me call you,' I say quickly.

'Why?'

I bite my lip. 'Jake doesn't approve of me dating you.'

He leans away from me, his eyes grim. 'I'm not going to sneak around behind anyone's back.'

I feel the happiness ebbing away. 'I was using the word approve euphemistically. He promised all-out war.'

He runs his hand through his hair. 'Let me talk to him.'

'No, don't. Please. Don't. It's better if you don't.'

'I'm not afraid of Jake, Layla. I'll fight anybody for what's mine.'

I stare at him in shock as a flare of pure joy zings through my body. 'I'm yours?'

'Yeah, you're fucking mine. And I don't take kindly to anyone standing between me and my woman.'

'He thinks you're a drug dealer and he wants better for me.'

'Too fucking bad. I don't tell him how to live his life. If I want you, I'll fucking have you.'

'Maybe if you weren't dealing in drugs, Jake wouldn't be so against our relationship?'

He looks at me. 'I do what I do because this is what I am. This is what I know and this is what I am good at. I won't change for Jake.'

I sigh. 'But what you're doing is dangerous. It's only a matter of time before you end up behind bars.

He shakes his head. 'You have to trust me. I deal only in class 3 grass where the sentence is light and I have set it up in such a way that it never passes through my hands.'

I feel suddenly heavy hearted and tearful. Jake is right. What future is there for me with someone like him? He won't change.

I drop my face. 'Anyway, what we have might burn out quickly and we would have upset everyone for nothing.'

He grabs my chin. 'You don't get it. I don't give a shit about upsetting everyone else. You're mine and the sooner everyone knows it the better.'

'Don't push me, BJ. I love my family and I don't want to hurt them. I'll tell Jake when the time is right. You have to trust me that I know my brother better than you.'

His jaw is set hard. A pulse throbs in it like a heart. 'Don't delay it too long, or I'll have to take it into my own hands.'

EIGHTEEN

Layla

'**D**id you sleep last night?' Dominic asks.

I flush. 'Why do you ask?' I question defensively. We are standing outside my flat in the weak morning sunshine.

'You always have blue shadows under your eyes when you don't sleep well.'

'Oh! Yeah, I didn't sleep too well last night. Just a bit worried about my interview tomorrow, I guess,' I lie.

'If that asshole doesn't give you the job, just let me know and I'll send a couple of boys around to smash up his offices.'

I give him a dirty look and he grins.

'That might have been funny if it had come from Shane. From you it's just downright scary,' I say, getting into his brand new BMW i8.

He laughs and I join in. I love it when Dominic laughs. It changes his whole face.

The car is filled with the scent of new leather and the strawberry air freshener that hangs from the rearview mirror. The engine roars aggressively to life and I settle back to enjoy a wild ride. My brother drives like a mad man.

He says he wants to try out his new chef, so he takes me to breakfast at a wine bar he has recently acquired. It's an old railway station that has been converted for commercial purposes. It still has the metal finials and a platform in the middle. He has named it Applegate Station. The décor is a cross between eclectic and sophisticated with a painted piano, French farmhouse style rustic accessories, chintz upholstery with peacocks and bright foliage, and dark wooden floors. The overall effect is effortless chic.

'What do you want to eat?'

He orders scrambled eggs with smoked salmon and I tell the waiter to double the order.

People are terrified of Dominic because he has such a ready and explosive temper, but I know he is the only one who can stand up to Jake if necessary. So I decide to very gently put out some feelers.

'I was out with Ria last night,' I say stirring sugar into my coffee, 'and I was curious. What was the feud with the Pilkingtons actually about?'

'I don't know. I don't think anyone knows. It was centuries ago. These things start for small matters and carry on through the generations. Each generation hating each other without knowing why.'

'I see. So now our families are friends?'

He takes a sip of orange juice and studies me over his glass. 'I guess so.'

I have to be careful. Dominic is a hot head but he is very intelligent. Very quick to catch on.

'Do we do business with the Pilkingtons?'

'Not really. We have our territories clearly drawn up so there are no misunderstandings. BJ doesn't mess with us and we don't mess with him.'

'So why did Jake and BJ fight then?'

'It was a misunderstanding.'

'Right.' I pause. 'So technically there's no reason why our families shouldn't do business or socialize?'

'Technically? No.' His voice has become still and his face watchful.

'Well, I think you've done a fine job with this place. It's beautiful. Ah… and here comes the food.'

The waiter puts the food on the table. After a flurry of questions about whether we want black pepper or more drinks, we are alone again. I pick up my knife and fork. '*Bon appetito*,' I wish heartily.

'Layla.' Dominic's voice is too quiet.

I put my fork and knife down and slowly lift my eyes up to his.

He is staring at me with disbelief. 'Who did you really go out with last night?'

I lean back against the bright peacock and foliage upholstered chair. 'BJ,' I admit quietly.

His hand comes crashing down on the table. The cutlery and plates jump. I jump. I have never seen Dominic get angry with me.

My hand covers my mouth.

'Fuck!' he swears loudly.

I stare at him. He puts his palm over one eye. 'What the fuck, Layla?'

'Please,' I beg. 'Please don't tell Jake.'

At the mention of Jake's name, Dominic erupts into another litany of loud curses. Fortunately, the place is not yet open to the public. I can hear the staff in the bar scurrying out to the back.

I sit it out until he gets a hold of himself. 'How far has the relationship gone?'

'I've only met him a few times. It's not really a relationship. It's just a sex thing.'

'Don't fucking tell me that! I'm your fucking brother.'

'Sorry,' I apologize quickly.

'BJ! Why? Why on earth did you have to choose him? He's such a fucking dog. He's gone through *all* the women in Shane's club.' He stares at me. 'Every fucking one.'

I look down. I know I should be ashamed. I should be mortified that I've given myself to a man who is so obviously a man-whore, but I'm not. And that thought gives me sudden strength. I won't sit here and let my brother abuse BJ. I have something with BJ and I don't want to be disloyal to that thing, whatever it is. I reach out my hand and place it on my brother's arm. It pulls him out of his rage.

'He's not like what you think.'

My brother groans. 'How can you even say that? He's got you going behind all our backs and lying! Shit! He's havin' a laugh at our family's expense. I thought he was more honorable than that!'

I flush to the roots of my hair. 'It's not his fault. He wanted to confront Jake, but I begged him not to. It's the wrong time. Jake is so happy at the moment. In less than a month he is going to be a dad. I don't want to spoil it for him.'

I see Dominic's expression change and I press my advantage. 'Besides, if BJ is the dog you say he is, it will all be over in the next couple of weeks. Why worry and upset Jake unnecessarily?'

'You deserve better than that barbarian, Layla.' He looks sad when he says it.

'It's just an experience, Dom. I'm not planning to marry him or have a family with him. I'm all grown up now and I'm just spreading my wings, living my life.'

'If he fucking hurts you ...'

'I am not going to get hurt. I'm going in with my eyes wide open. But if I do get hurt, then I'll pick myself up, dust myself off, and I'll be wiser for it. I won't shame our family.'

'I'll give you until the baby is born. If you're not finished spreading your wings by then I'm telling Jake,' he says sternly.

'Thank you. I know it will have died away by then.'

'It better fucking have,' he says morosely.

After that we eat our breakfast, but my news has put Dominic in a foul mood and by the time he drops me off I too have been affected by it.

I call BJ.

He answers on the first ring. There is tension in his voice. 'Hi. Everything OK?'

'Not really. I stupidly asked Dom a few questions about the feud and you, and he immediately guessed. So I had to tell him. He didn't react very well, but he did promise not to interfere and to let me tell Jake when I'm ready.'

'Want to do lunch?'

'Yeah, but let's go somewhere no one knows us.'

NINETEEN

Layla

I have my stockinged feet up on the radiator and the radio is on as we drive away from London to BJ's country house. Outside, the rain is lashing down in sheets making visibility poor. It makes me feel we are in a bubble. *Lost Frequencies* comes on.

'This is my most favorite song in the whole wide world,' I tell him and turn it up as loud as it will go.

He smiles.

My lips are painted red and I feel happy. The kind of happy that makes you feel like you can jump up and touch the ceiling. When you think you love the whole world and everyone in it because you are so happy.

The electric gates open and we drive into Silver Lee. It is only two o'clock, but it is already dark and all the lights have been lit. BJ opens the door and I precede him.

'Is no one in?'

'No, I asked my housekeeper to make himself scarce until later tonight.'

I grin. 'So we are totally alone?'

'Not quite. There is someone I have to introduce you to.'

I raise my eyebrows.

'He's a bit of an old fart and doesn't like people, but he's kind of important to me so let's see what you make of each other.'

'OK.'

We walk down through the house with its curving glass frontage. A storm is raging outside. He pauses by a door. 'He can be quite foul mouthed,' he warns.

Then he opens the door and a nasal voice screeches, 'Did you fuck him?' My mouth drops open. BJ makes an after-you gesture with his hand. 'Bitch, better have my money. Bitch better. Bitch better. Pay me what you owe me.' I enter the room and there is no one in there. There's just a grey parrot with a red tail.

'Meet Jeremy Thomas,' BJ says walking towards the bird. He holds his hand under it. 'Step up,' he says and the bird climbs on to his hand and looks at me with its head cocked to one side. 'Cunt.'

I laugh. 'Did your bird just call me a cunt?'

'Yeah, I forgot to say he's a bit of a misogynist. My mother hates him.'

'Has he called her one too?'

'I'm afraid so. He used to belong to a Jamaican pimp so he generally has a very bad opinion of women and he's always asking them for money.'

'Give Jeremy a nut. Give Jeremy a nut,' the bird squawks.

'What kind of a bird is he?'

'An African Grey.'

'And how on earth did you get him?'

'His owner owed me money and had to leave the country in a hurry. So I took the bird.'

Jeremy fixes me with a belligerent eye and flaps his wings. 'You're wet.'

I gasp.

BJ turns to me with a glimmer of laughter in his eyes. 'It's not what you think. He just wants a bath.'

I laugh.

'Want a cookie.'

BJ gives him something from his pocket and the bird holds it in his claws and eats it.

'Oh BJ. I think he's gorgeous.'

BJ grins happily and there is nothing to outshine his smile. I about melt into a puddle right there and then.

'God only knows why I care so much for this stupid bird,' he says.

'You're a wimp,' Jeremy says and begins to laugh like a human.

It is funny and we both laugh.

'Kiss. Oops, bad birdie. Bite the dog. Bad dog.'

'How old is he?'

'Not sure, but older than you and me. He's maybe 40.'

'Wow. Can he fly?'

'Give me the money, bitch,' the bird squawks.

'Yup, he can fly.'

'Do you take him outside?'

'I have in the past, but he doesn't really seem to like it.'

I watch Jeremy get a bath. It's the cutest thing ever. It is fun and we both laugh. I look at BJ with his bird and I can hardly believe that this is the same aggressive fighting monster I saw in the pit.

I offer Jeremy a nut. He takes it from me and quickly flutters away screeching, 'Where's my money, bitch.'

I laugh and BJ catches me by the waist. I look up at him, tall and broad-shouldered, and the laughter dies in my throat.

'Time my cock was inside you,' he says.

I hop on to his body and wrap my legs around his hips. 'Carry me to your bed and ravish me then,' I whisper daringly.

We go up the stairs and he opens the door to the bedroom where I had received my spanking. He puts me at the edge of the bed. Outside the wind howls. Inside we are absolutely silent. I cannot even hear my own heartbeat. The only sound is the fire crackling in the fireplace.

He starts off by kissing me. By the time he raises his mouth I am totally nude.

'That's a clever trick. Now show me my cock,' I whisper hoarsely.

He throws aside his t-shirt and unbuttons his trousers. I drink in the inked, tanned skin, the barely leashed strength in his coiled muscles and follow the line of straight black hair on its epic journey down to his crotch. The last scrap of cloth slides to the floor and I fix my gaze on his cock. Have me with a side order of caviar, or a maraschino cherry and two scoops of ice cream, or just me on my own, but fucking eat me, it screams aggressively.

I *love* his raging cock.

I grab his hips and slowly slide my puckered mouth over the thick roll of meat. He groans with pleasure. The heat of his lust flows from him onto my skin. I love sucking his cock. I'll make all the other women who have taken him into their mouths a memory that never was. It is a lazy, dreamlike thought.

Outside the storm passes. The sky becomes milky white, shadows move, but I do not stop. Every time he is about to come, I pause, I change my rhythm. He hisses with frustration. I understand. It's annoying. But there is a point to it all. My lips grow as numb, but I do not stop. As if sucking his cock is an old tradition that can bring bad luck if broken.

But he has other ideas.

He seizes my head, fully determined that I will no longer have the reins, and starts thrusting lustily towards his climax. I taste the salt in my mouth and jerk my head back so his cum sprays onto my face, my open mouth, my chin, and my throat. There is nothing he has done to another woman that he cannot do to me. When the last drop has been squeezed onto me I slip my tongue out of my mouth and slowly lick his cum from my lips.

He smears the rest on my face, neck and breasts.

Then he pushes me onto my back and presses his naked flank into my softness, crushing it beautifully, and thrusts into my body as it arches up to receive him. The sensation is magic. My loins ache. My insides feel raw. A gasp. A cry. A stiffening. His muscles strain and ripple urgently. We move together, slick and sliding against each other. My breath comes faster as his cock swells inside me. The whole time his gaze never leaves mine, his eyes smoldering and rapt. The moments lengthen into technicolor dreams: rich like wine. I sigh at his gentle hands, his velvet mouth.

Afterwards, I slip on his t-shirt and we drink apple mojitos. He is funny. I laugh. We have sex on the floor. Then we drink more mojitos and eat cold chicken and popcorn. I feel myself become lazily drunk.

'You up for a fuck?' I ask. There is a definite slur in my voice. An elongation of the vowels.

'Is Fukushima leaking radiation?'

I fling off his t-shirt and hair trailing down my naked back, crawl around the food towards him.

He puts a dark hand on my pale exposed shoulder.

I push him to the ground and climb atop him. His strong hands curl around my ribs to keep my body steady as I impale myself on his cock. I know I'm tipsy and without a steady rhythm. Despite that, we come quickly. I lie on his body and listen to the dull beat of his heart. I love simply having him inside me.

'I could fall asleep like this,' I whisper.

'Get on your hands and knees, woman.'

Hours later, the fire has burned down to embers and ashes. I lie weary and trembling beside him in the dark. I reach out a hand and touch him, a gesture that is both a question and reverent. My eyes are wide and filled with a strange new perspective, an awareness, an impossible intensity, as if I have never been truly or fully alive before.

'I have to get back to London soon.'

He turns towards me, his face drugged and slack with desire. 'Not yet. I've not had enough of you.'

'Ahhhhh,' I gasp, my juices splashing into his mouth.

TWENTY

Layla

'**I** got the job,' I crow into the phone.

He laughs. A good sound.

'You are now talking to a member of Vincent & Prestige's Studio's team of interior designers. I start my first design and fit-out assignment on Monday!'

'Want to celebrate over lunch?'

I feel the disappointment inside my body, like a wave passing through. 'I can't. I'm going shopping with my sister-in-law. We're buying baby stuff.'

'How's Lily?'

'She's quietly freaking out after convincing Jake that she should have a totally natural childbirth in their bathtub. She's actually going to give birth without an epidural! Apparently she's going to be sucking on sugar pills the whole time. I told her I think she's bananas. When I have a baby I want to be put out. And I don't mean just an epidural. I mean general anesthetic. I don't want to know nothing! Nada. I want to wake up to my husband holding a pink baby all clean and wrapped up in blankets.'

The silence on the other end is so thick you could have spread it on a slice of bread. Then it hits me how I must sound to him. A crazy woman banging on about babies three days after having sex with him. And with him being a player—yeah, even then I resisted the words junkyard dog.

'Thank God it will be at least ten years before I am in such a position,' I rush into the treacle of silence.

'We should celebrate your job offer,' he says evenly.

I breathe a sigh of relief. 'Yeah, we should,' I agree.

'Where do you want to go?' he asks.

My response is immediate. No need to think about it. 'Silver Lee.'

'Don't you want to go somewhere nice? It's a celebration, after all.'

'Nope. I still haven't had a proper tour of your house, remember?'

Strike two. I hear his reluctance, like sandpaper on my skin. He doesn't want to give me a tour. Why on earth not? 'If you don't want to it's OK.' Oh my God! I am becoming a doormat.

There is a pause. Then. 'All right. I'll show you around. Pick you up at 3:00?'

'See you then.'

I slip into the passenger seat of BJ's carbon-edition Aston Martin, close the door, and turn toward him. Wow! He's rocking a sexy five o'clock shadow, which makes him look all

moody and brooding. His eyes graze over me slowly, but being so dark they give nothing away.

'Hi,' I greet breathlessly.

He leans over and kisses me. I'll say this for him: the man can kiss. In seconds I want to throw my arms around his neck, curl my fingers in his hair, and climb over to his side of the car to lower myself on to his thick cock. My skin tingles. My head starts buzzing. My hand strays to his hard chest.

'What was that for?' I whisper, when he breaks away.

His eyes are smoky with desire. He places his finger on my lower lip and drags it along my skin. His voice drops to a faux whisper that caresses my skin. 'Because you're so damn beautiful.'

I drop my eyes and go all hot and red with sheer happiness.

He places a finger under my chin and lifts my face. 'Isn't that what all the boys who aren't afraid of your brother tell you?'

My stomach flips. 'I think there are more boys afraid of my brother than you think.'

'Since I'm not in the firing line yet, let me tell you, Layla. You're one hell of a beauty.'

'You're not so bad looking yourself,' I say shyly.

'Me? I'm an ugly mug. You, you're another matter. You truly are the beginning of intoxication.'

'That reminds me, how is it you know so much about my name. Even I thought Layla meant of the night in Arabic.'

'Because I researched it, Princess.'

'Is that why you bought a tiepin with the word Layla on it?'

His face closes over.

I frown. 'What?'

'Nothing.' He turns away and starts the engine. 'So Lily is having a homebirth. When?'

'Well,' I say settling myself into the seat. 'The baby is not due for another three weeks.'

'And Jake is OK with a homebirth?'

'Oh, he didn't like it one bit at first, but being the total control freak that he is, he went out and offered the best midwife in England so much money she is going to uproot her entire family, 3 kids no less, to go and stay at his house two weeks before the baby is due. From what I understand, the poor woman will be virtually a prisoner until the baby is born. Of course he's also hired a whole medical team to be on standby just in case there's any kind of complication.'

He laughs. 'That sounds more like him.' He sobers suddenly. 'When do you plan to tell him about us?'

It is my turn to sober up. 'I want to tell him, but he's so happy at the moment. In fact, I don't think I've ever seen him so full of laughter. Can you believe he sings to his baby?'

He turns to look at me briefly, his eyebrows raised.

'I just don't want to spoil this time for him. I'll tell him after the baby is born.' I pause for a second. Then, I don't know why, perhaps I am testing him, I add, 'If we are still together by then.'

His face registers no change, but his hands tighten on the wheel. 'OK,' he says tightly. 'We wait until after the baby is born, but if I am in a position where he asks me outright I'm not going to lie.'

'That's fair enough.'

After that we talk of things outside of us. Some of it is light and easy and I laugh a lot, but I come to realize quickly that BJ sees everything from a totally different perspective than me. A much darker, more cynical perspective. He is my total opposite in every way. We disagree on almost all the important aspects of life. He seems to be without the usual social pretensions that normal people indulge in. To start with, he doesn't have a Facebook page. He thinks all social media is narcissism gone berserk. He is of the opinion that only birds should tweet. Having 865 Internet friends is ludicrous. And wait for it ... he has never taken a selfie!

He says he will go back to church again when someone explains where black people came from since Adam and Eve were both lily white. He believes that people should not be trusted since the strongest human traits—greed, jealousy, envy, cruelty—are inborn and already active even in children. Humans have to be taught kindness, generosity, patience, and goodness. BJ believes those traits can only be a thin veneer for the real truth, a cauldron of negative emotions.

'So you don't trust me?' I ask him, my voice is light, my manner is flirtatious, but in fact I am really curious as to what he will say.

He throws a brief glance at me. 'Where does your mother think you are now?'

'With Maddy,' I say slowly.

'Have I answered your question?'

'Is there no one you trust?'

'Jeremy. I trust him.'

'That's sad, BJ.'

He shrugs carelessly. 'Save your sympathy. I set it up like this because I like it this way.'

'BJ, isn't your mother alive?'

'Yeah.'

'And you don't trust your own mother?'

'Don't get me wrong. I love my mother. I'd do anything for her but no, she hasn't done much to inspire my trust.'

'My God. What kind of childhood did you have?'

He gives me a sideways glance. 'It wasn't like yours.'

'So you've never trusted anyone in your life?'

'I trusted my father.'

'Why?'

'Because he always showed me his real face. At all times I knew exactly what he was and what I could expect from him.'

Then he is turning into Silver Lee. We go into the house and it is silent, but an amazing lunch has been set out on the dining table. It is almost like being in a fairy tale. Like in Beauty and the Beast when the father finds the deserted palace and a table set with a princely meal.

There is a note on the table. BJ picks it up and reads it.

I am so caught up in the Beauty and the Beast scenario I think that the note might be important. 'What does it say?' I ask curiously.

He passes it to me.

There is a tall jug of mojitos
waiting in the fridge.
Marcel

He looks at me, sexy smile on his face. 'Well, what do you want to do first? Eat or fuck?'

If any other man had said that I'd have slapped him and called him a coarse jerk. But BJ, he's the shining hero in the movie I'm directing, producing, and starring in.

And God! I want him.

'Fuck,' I say with half-closed, sultry eyes. Turning, I begin to walk away while undressing at the same time. The dark green top goes over my head and on the floor. My bra follows. I turn around and he is just behind me, staring at my breasts possessively. The desire to press my naked body against him is astonishingly strong, white-knuckle strong.

I lie on a long lilac couch and shimmy out of my skirt and panties. I am suddenly almost feverish with need. Daringly I open my legs wide. He gets down on his haunches and slides his hand up my leg, towards my distended, swollen clitoris. With precise, knowing strokes he rubs the flesh around it. His carnal expertise is irresistible.

I squirm and whimper.

It has never crossed my mind that I would ever be so wild for a man.

116

He brings his head closer and I prepare for his tongue. Instead a flow of warm air hits my exposed sex.

'Ah,' I cry at the exquisitely delicate sensation. Like a fine wine or the faint earthy flavor of truffle shavings on a plate of buttery pasta. My eyes close to fully savor it. When his silky tongue touches my clit it is unexpected and shockingly intense. My body arches like a bow. He licks the pulsing flesh like a kitten. He slides his fingers deeper inside me and pumps them furiously. My body heats up and sweat dampens my skin. I grasp his hair and curl my legs around his large body, the way he taught me to.

'Please,' I beg.

He lifts his head and unlocking my legs, opens me wide. He stands and looks down at me splayed and ready for him. With heavy-lidded eyes he starts to undress. He discards his pants and my gaze moves to the well-defined, hard bulge in his white briefs. The thick mushroom head is already poking out of the top of his underwear. He stops. My eyes move up to his and hot blood rushes up my throat to be caught looking at his erection so hungrily. I have never stared at a man like this. Not ever.

He fits a rubber on himself and, putting his hands on either side of me, mounts me. He pounds me hard a few times. There is something frenzied and electric about the urgency of his thrusts. I know then that he cannot wait any longer. I milk the cream of his body with my own and he explodes, his head thrown back and utterly silent.

For seconds his face is buried in my breasts. He might even have gently sucked my nipple, I am in a daze of contentment. Then he rouses himself and, looking into my eyes, brings me to climax.

'You're beautiful when you come,' he whispers. His face is flushed and his eyes are the softest black.

Afterwards, we eat, but I find I have hardly any appetite. Every time his eyes rest on me, I feel my lack of underwear, how wet I am, and how much I long to have him back inside me.

Maddy's call interrupts our total absorption with each other. She tells me my mother is looking for me. I didn't hear my phone while we were having sex. I look up at BJ. His eyes are expressionless. He listens to me call my mother and lie about where I am and what I am doing since I am not with Maddy after all. It is easy to lie to Ma. She isn't expecting me to. I end the call and face him.

'I'll get the mojitos,' he says and walks away. Strange. He is the criminal and yet he is the more honorable of us.

TWENTY-ONE

BJ

When I come back with the drinks she has slipped into my t-shirt and is seated in a recess of one of the tall windows. Twelve feet of pale yellow glow from the wintry evening sun falls on her wonderful, thick hair and tinges it with a light that I have only seen in paintings from the great Dutch masters. Perhaps a Rembrandt.

A living spectacle.

She turns to look at me and smiles a smile that nearly knocks me backwards. I have been with countless women, all of them beautiful, vibrant and sexy. But she makes them all pale into insignificance. The thought is terrifying and beautiful. Never again will I be with a woman who can satisfy me the way she does.

I stand over her and hold out the drink. She takes it with both hands. She is the first woman who has persuaded me to drink a mojito. And now I fucking like it!

'You promised me a tour,' she says. There is a hint of laughter in her voice. I love that about her. Only children and the truly innocent have that. I don't really want to show her my sex room, but she stands and holds out her hand. So we go through the entire house until we get to the sex room. I open the door and she goes in, flicks the switch, and the disco lights come on. She touches the switch beside it and Kanye West's *Gold Digger* fills the room. For a few seconds she says nothing.

Fuck. Fuck. Fuck.

I see what I have never seen before. I see how bad it really is. How stupid and vulgar and truly ugly and cringingly embarrassing it is. What was I thinking bringing her here? She is too grand for this gaudiness. I want to usher her out immediately and rip it all up.

Slowly she turns to look up at me and I swear I stop breathing. Her shoulders come up as she is about to be sick, but instead of being sick, her mouth trembles. I'll be damned. She is trying not to laugh! I don't know what is worse. That she should think it hideous or laughable.

'Come on, let's go,' I say brusquely.

She grabs my arm. 'No, no, I think it's great. Really.'

I look at her curiously. Is she serious?

She gestures around her. 'Everything all at once like this. I've just never seen it before. That's all.' She becomes serious. 'But in fact, I should have expected it. It's you. You say it like it is. There's no pretense. No veneer of what is socially acceptable. It is what it is. A room for sex. If someone gets brought here, they'll know without any doubt what you want from them.'

She walks into the room, heads for the bed, and sits on the edge. She pats the space next to her and strangely I don't feel my cock rise to the occasion. Instead I feel a horrible feeling in my gut that even just sitting on that bed would somehow contaminate her.

She pats it again and smiles slowly.

I walk over and sit next to her. She climbs into my lap. My cock forgets its reservations and stirs to life.

'I was thinking of dismantling this room,' I say.

'Why? I like it. We can have funny sex here.'

'Funny sex?'

She draws away from me. 'Yeah, like when you bang your head on the headboard, laugh, and then have sex anyway.'

'Right.'

'You've *never* had funny sex?' she asks incredulously.

'I guess not.' And judging from her description it's not something I'm going to rush to try either.

She tilts her head to one side and I feel something inside me melt. Shit, I'm done for. This woman has me all tied up in knots. She tries to tickle my midriff. I'm not ticklish. Her fingers move to my armpits. I shrug. 'Sorry.'

'You're really not ticklish?'

Her expression of incredulity is adorable and I laugh.

'There you go,' she says laughing and pushes me backwards towards the bed. She puts her palms on either side of my face and brings her open mouth to mine. Ah, the kiss. This is not me kissing her. This is her kissing me. Soft. Her mouth is so soft and sweet. Smelling of mojitos and sugar and Layla. My Layla.

It seems that I like funny sex after all.

What part of her flesh have I not tasted? Her smell adheres to my hands and nails.

TWENTY-TWO

Layla

'**C**ongratulate me. I'm an aunt,' I shout excitedly into the phone.

'Brilliant. How's the mother?' BJ asks.

'She's fine. Now ask me how the father is.'

He laughs. 'How's Jake?'

'Freaking out. You should see him. He's so crazy about his baby he won't even let anyone else carry her. I had to elbow him out of the way to even look at her.'

'So everyone is happy.'

'Yeah, everyone is really happy. I'll send you a picture of her. She's got hairy ears, but ma says even I had hairy ears when I was born and it will fall off.'

'You still have hairy ears.'

'Quit it or I'll send you the pictures where she still has cottage cheese all over her body.'

He bursts out laughing.

'Layla,' my mother calls from behind me.

'Got to go, Maddie, I'll speak to you later, OK?' I say and quickly cut the connection.

'Are you staying for dinner?' my mother asks. She is so happy she is glowing like it's Christmas morning. This is her first grandchild and an event she has been praying for ever since Jake turned 21.

I touch her hand. 'Might not be a good idea, Ma. I have to work tomorrow. I'll come back on the weekend.'

'Are you leaving now then?'

'Yeah, before the traffic gets heavy.'

'Do you want me to make you a sandwich before you go?'

'No, I'll go and say goodbye to Jake and Lily and be off.'

'Lily is sleeping. Poor thing is exhausted.'

'Fine. I'll just go say goodbye to my brother and my niece then.'

'Come and see me in the kitchen before you go. I've made some food for you to take back.'

'OK,' I say and run up the stairs of Jake's house. I stand at the door of the nursery transfixed by the sight of Jake bent over Liliana's cradle.

'Hey,' I say softly and he looks up, his expression soft.

'Hey,' he whispers.

I walk up to the cot. He is gently stroking her cheek with his finger.

'Congratulations, Jake. Other than the hairy ears she's beautiful.'

He looks up at me, a huge, stupid grin on his face. 'She is, isn't she.'

Suddenly I feel an overwhelming wave of love for my brother. All these years he never had anything for himself. To call his own. Always he was fighting all our battles. I blink back the tears.

His eyes narrow. 'What's wrong?'

'Nothing's wrong. Everything's just perfect.'

He nods. 'Are you going back to London now?'

'Yeah. The traffic won't be so bad now.'

'Why don't you stay a bit longer and let Shane drive you back?'

I shake my head. 'Then you'll just have the hassle of sending my car back to me.'

He frowns. 'It's no trouble.'

I smile softly. 'No, it is trouble for you. I'll be back for the weekend.'

'All right. Drive safely.'

'I will.'

That's the thing about Jake. Even at a time like this he is worrying about me. I hug him tightly and go down to the kitchen. My mother is putting together plastic containers of food into two carrier bags. The containers are labeled so I know exactly what's in them. Dom is sitting at the table finishing off a massive bacon and sausage sandwich.

'Are you off?' he asks me.

'Yeah.'

'Didn't you have something else you had to do?' He puts the last bit of the sandwich into his mouth and raises his eyebrows meaningfully.

I glance at my mother, but she is busy washing her hands.

'I'm not doing it today. I'll be back this weekend, I'll do it then.'

My brother wipes his mouth and stands up. 'I'm off then. See you at dinnertime, Ma.' As he passes me he whispers, 'I wouldn't wait beyond the weekend if I were you.'

I watch my brother leave with a heavy heart.

'Put this bag into the fridge and consume it today, tomorrow at the latest,' my mother says. I turn back to her. 'And the other bag, you can freeze it and eat on Thursday and Friday. You'll be back here on Saturday, won't you?'

'Yeah. Thanks.'

'Do you want to take some cake for Maddie too?' my mother asks.

'No, I'll share what I've got with her.'

'All right then,' she says moving towards the fridge.

'Ma,' I say sinking into a chair.

'What?'

'Did you ever think we'd all turn out like this?'

She looks at me. 'Never.'

'What did you think we'd become?'

'I didn't know. I didn't dare dream anything like this. I thought we'd always be struggling,' she says softly.

'You're really proud of Jake, aren't you?'

She is so choked up she can't even speak. Just nods violently, her body clenched tight.

'Me too,' I say.

She comes outside with me, and waves as I drive away. I watch her become smaller in the mirror and I get a horrible cold feeling in my stomach. When I am far enough away, I pull over by the side of the road and call BJ.

'What's up?' he asks immediately.

'Oh, BJ. I don't know how I can ever tell Jake about us.' My voice is shaking.

There is a tense pause. 'Where are you now?' he asks urgently.

'About a mile away from Jake's house.'

'Look, I can be at Silver Lee in about an hour. Do you want to go there and wait for me?'

With all the excitement about the baby, no one will notice my absence so I could even spend the night there and leave very early in the morning for London. 'But what about Marcel?'

'I'll ask him to leave the French doors open for you.'

'OK, I'll see you there in about an hour,' I say.

'Layla.'

'Yeah.'

'We'll figure it out, OK.'

'OK.'

'BJ.'

'Yeah?'

'Nothing. I'll talk to you when I see you.'

I sever the connection and stare at my phone. It seems impossible that I once thought my relationship with BJ would diminish with time. That I had actually told Dom that it was just a sex thing. It's far from just a sex thing. My feelings have grown and grown.

I know BJ likes me. Maybe a lot, but I also know that I can't base my future on that alone. He owns clubs full of beautiful women who are constantly throwing themselves at him. When I am not with him, I sometimes worry. All kinds of thoughts plague me. We haven't promised to be exclusive with each other. Our relationship is like a dirty secret. We never go any place where we could be recognized. No one in his life knows. Even Marcel has never seen me. At least in my life, Maddy and Dominic know. Now that Lily has given birth, I might even tell her and ask her advice.

With a sigh I put my phone back into my purse and start the car. I reach Silver Lee in about 40 minutes. The gates are wide open and I drive through. It is the beginning of spring and there are daffodils all along the road up to the house. It looks beautiful. And somehow that makes me feel sadder. Will I see them next year or the year after? I park my car and walk along the side of the house. One of the French doors is open and I slip in and lock it.

I know Marcel would have taken Jeremy and the house feels silent and totally empty without BJ. My heels are loud on the floor. I go to the kitchen and open the fridge and smile. Marcel made a jar of mojitos before he left. I pour myself a tumbler and go into the vast, open living room. I sit on the long lilac sofa and gaze out into the countryside.

I'm surprised to hear BJ's car roar up the driveway a few minutes later. I put my drink on a nearby table and go to the front door. He opens it as I get there. The moment is rare. I've never opened a door to him before. It's nice. It makes me feel like we are a normal couple.

'You got here fast,' I say softly.

His eyes are dark and searching. 'I drove fast.'

I take a step towards him. He pulls me hard into his arms and kisses me.

'Come on. Marcel has made us mojitos,' I say breathlessly.

He looks down at me and nods.

We go to the kitchen where I pour a glass for him and we walk out together to the sofa. We chink glasses.

'Here's to the new aunt,' he says.

I smile. 'And the new baby.'

'And that,' he adds.

We both take a sip. He eyes me over the rim of his glass. 'My poor Layla,' he says quietly.

'I'm sorry I'm being such a baby, but I can't bear the thought of disappointing them all, especially Jake.'

'He has to know, Layla. Sooner or later. We can't carry on like this.'

'I know. I know. I will.' I drop my face into my hands. 'I just don't want him to hate me.'

'He's not going to hate you. This is your life. Nothing would have stood in the way of him being with Lily. He has no right to stop you from seeing anyone you want to. You're a grown woman.'

'It's just feels as if I have betrayed him.'

'The longer you leave it, the worse the betrayal will be.'

"Maybe I'll tell him after Ella's wedding. You're going too, aren't you?'

He grins. 'Only to look at you.'

I blush. 'Really?'

'Abso-fucking-lutely.'

'Anyway,' I say, suddenly feeling all shy and awkward. 'I'll be staying over at my mother's that night and I'll break it to all of them at the same time.'

'Do you want me to be there?'

'No.' I shiver at the thought. 'Definitely not.'

'OK.' For a moment we are both silent. He takes a sip of his drink. 'Have you heard the story of Layla and Majnun by Nizami?'

I shake my head.

'It's about a moon-princess who was married off by her father to someone other than the man who was desperately in love with her. It resulted in his madness.'

I bow my head. It would be all so different if he wasn't a criminal.

TWENTY-THREE

BJ

'I know so little about you, BJ,' Layla complains as she locks her arms around my waist and angles her head back to catch my eyes.

God, she's so fucking sexy, I just want to fuck her every time she comes near me. She's got about ten minutes before I fill that honey mouth of hers full of cock.

'What'd you want to know, Princess?'

'Tell me why you became a criminal?' she asks.

I shrug carelessly. 'Why does anyone?'

She gazes up at me, her beautiful blue eyes narrowed. 'Is it for all the power and respect you command: men shaking in their boots, women worshiping at your feet?'

'I followed in my father's footsteps, Layla,' I tell her. An early memory of my father floats into my mind. He is sitting on a barstool flexing and unflexing his bulging arm muscles just before a fight. There is loud music in the background and on the table in front of him, two pints of Guinness are lined up.

'Your father?' she says softly. 'He must have been quite a character. Your mother showed me her wedding photograph and he looked very handsome. It was so sweet to hear her describe him as a "rakishly dreamy charmer".'

I remember Lenny Pilkington differently. The charm was long gone by the time I knew him, and my young self saw only a giant of a man, with a flattened, boxer's nose, shrewd eyes, and a savage temper. My jaw stiffens unconsciously.

'What's wrong?" Layla frowns.

I block the thoughts immediately. 'Nothing.'

Her eyes narrow suspiciously. 'Did he force you to become a criminal, BJ?' she demands.

I let my facial muscles relax. 'Of course not. I desperately wanted to follow in my father's and my uncles' footsteps. I guess I was impressed by their big, flashy cars and their jacked-up pick-up trucks.'

'So how old were you when you joined them?'

'Eleven.'

Her eyes become saucers. 'Eleven? I was still playing with my dolls when I was eleven.'

Seems so long ago and yet the day I accompanied them on my first job is as vivid as if it happened yesterday.

'You were just a kid. What did they make you do?'

I laugh at her belligerent expression. 'Relax. All I had to do was stand casually outside the gates of an industrial site and hoot twice like an owl if anyone, especially the pigs happened along while my father and two of my uncles filled their truck with scrap metal.'

'I still think you were far too young to be involved in something like that,' she says, her voice full of disapproval. In her world fathers protected their sons.

Strange, even after all these years I still feel the burning need to defend my father. 'The truth is, Layla, it felt fucking great. From that first time I was hooked on the mix of adrenaline and excitement that pumped through my body.'

'What did you guys do with the scrap metal?'

'Dropped it off at my uncle's yard.'

'And after?'

'Afterwards, we drove to the local pub. It was a winter's night and I sat in the beer garden and froze my ass off while my father went in and bought me my first pint of ale. It was fucking terrible, but I drank it all up. I can still remember putting my hands into my armpits and in a drunken haze soaking up their tall tales.

'So the little gangster learned quickly?' she says sadly, dropping her head.

I put my finger under her chin and lift it up. 'Why so sad? My father and uncles prepared me well for a life in the underbelly of society. They taught me to see the world the way it really is. As a sort of jungle where the human race can be divided into three categories: gazelles, lions, and hyenas.'

She looks at me curiously.

'The gazelle is the food of both the lions and hyenas. However, contrary to perceived wisdom, it is not the hyena that steals from the lion, but the lion that will snatch from the mouth of the hyena its hard-won kill. In every place where the lion dominates, the hyena must hunt in packs and use its cunning—or perish all together.

'Am I a gazelle in your world, BJ?'

I shake my head slowly.

'What am I then? Explain the inhabitants of your jungle to me, BJ.'

'The lions are the captains of industry, the bankers, the politicians, the landowners. They wear the mask of nobility. Normal society is represented by the gazelle. They register their births, work all their lives to pay countless taxes, obey even the most idiotic laws, and exist purely to fatten the predator lions. But we Gypsies, you and me, are different. We are the hyenas. Meekness and slavery are not for us. We have, and always will, survive and prosper on our own terms, using our specific talents and wits.

'Now, you sound like Jake. He is always going on about greedy bankers and lying politicians too.'

'That's because he sees through the illusion. And that's why we, Gypsies, have travelled incessantly through the centuries never stopping long enough to put roots. We did it so no one could count us, corral us, educate us, tame us, or enslave us.

She frowns. 'But your father sent you to school?'

'My father was a very shrewd man. He understood the changing times meant we would soon be forced to play their game, anyway. He decided that I would be the first one of us who would have two educations, ours and theirs. So by the time I left school I could read and write as well as the next boy, but my true specialty was numbers. I excelled at them. I didn't even have to try. They just came naturally.'

She smiles for the first time. 'Yeah?'

'Yeah. I was so fucking good I could walk into a scrap yard and in less than thirty seconds, I would have picked out everything of value. I knew where it was going and exactly what it all was worth.'

'You make it sound easy.'

'It was. Money poured in. By the time I was eighteen I got my first shiny new car. A glorious Aston Martin. Paid for in cash.' Those were the days when no one frowned on you for paying in cash. Even now I can feel that rush of pride and possession I felt when I drove that beauty off the forecourt.

'I wish I had been your girl-friend then,' she says softly, and presses her face into my chest.

I don't tell her that was the point in my life when I got into the business of grass. Selling grass to the gazelles.

TWENTY-FOUR

Layla

I wake up early in my bed at my mother's house. The house is quiet. I pull Graystone from his shelf and bury my face against his fur. Today is the day I promised BJ and Dom I will break the news to Jake. And today is also the day I break my great secret to BJ. With a heavy sigh, I get out of bed and open my bedroom door.

'Is that you, Layla?' my mother calls from the kitchen.

'Morning,' I yell back from the top of the stairs.

'Brush your teeth and come down for breakfast. Your ride will be here in an hour.'

Even the thought of breakfast makes me feel sick. 'I don't want breakfast, Ma.'

I hear her footsteps come from the kitchen. Her face appears at the bottom of the stairs. 'Are you sick? Why don't you want breakfast?'

'I just don't feel like it, Ma. I think I'm nervous about today.'

My mother frowns. 'Nervous about today? Why? You've been bridesmaid loads of time. Besides, it's your cousin Ella.'

'Yeah, you're right,' I concede.

'Hurry up then. I'm making you pancakes.'

I get ready and go downstairs. My mother puts a plate with two warm buttery pancakes in front of me. I spread Nutella on one and eat it slowly. It settles like a heavy stone in my stomach. The car arrives and I am borne away to my cousin's house. Fortunately, her house is in such a flurry of hectic activity that I quickly forget my worries and morph into the role of bridesmaid. The flower girls make me laugh. They've overdosed on spray tan and they all look as if they have been thoroughly shaken inside a Doritos bag.

Soon it is time for Ella to get into her wedding dress. It is a monster meringue affair, weighing a staggering 90 pounds. There are 520 Swarovski crystals on the bodice and more than 100 rings to puff the skirt out to over eight feet in diameter. Someone fits the veil on her head and she turns to us with shining eyes.

'You look like a fairy tale princess,' I tell her. She really does.

'I feel like Cinderella, Sleeping Beauty, and Snow White all rolled into one,' she says with a catch in her voice.

At that moment I feel a faint sensation of unease. Will I ever be such a happy bride? And then it is time to pick up her 20-foot long train. It takes us more than an hour to stuff her and her dress into the white limo.

Somehow we make it to the church on time.

It is not until later at the church that I spot BJ. He's standing at the back wearing a white shirt, a dove grey jacket, and black trousers. He doesn't smile and neither do I, but my breath catches. I quickly look away from his seductively dangerous eyes.

Sweet Jesus. I'm in love with the guy.

The wedding goes without a hitch. Of course, I don't catch the bridal bouquet even though Ella deliberately aims it in my direction. A woman I don't know lunges in front of me and catches it. She seems so excited, I can't even be annoyed with her.

Afterwards, when we are taking photographs, I manage to catch Jake.

'Where's Lily?' I ask him.

He tells me that she is observing the Chinese confinement tradition that doesn't allow her to leave the house for a whole month.

'Really?'

'Yes, really. She has to be on a special bland diet of soups and rice. And there is whole list of forbidden foods: raw fruit, vegetables, coffee, seafood, or anything cold.'

'Oh my God!'

'You think that's bad,' Jake says. 'Poor thing is not even allowed to bathe. All that's allowed is wipe-downs twice a week using washcloths steeped in smelly herbal medicine.'

'Well, she's made of sterner stuff than me then,' I say.

With a sigh Jake tells me that her grandmother, a woman that he describes as "formidable," is staying at the house overseeing to the torture. After the possessive kiss I saw Jake give Lily, I can only imagine how happy he will be once the 31 days are up.

'Can I speak to you later tonight at Ma's?' I ask casually.

'Is anything wrong?'

'Not really.'

He frowns. 'Do you want to talk about it now?'

'No, no, it can definitely wait.'

The reception is held in a large banquet room at the same venue. There are speeches and toasts. BJ is only a table away, but Jake is at the same table as me, so I dare not even look at him. Then the couple stands up to have their first dance. I turn my head towards the door and freeze.

Lupo is standing there.

He is browner than everybody else in the room and he is staring at me. I stand up as inconspicuously as possible and casually head towards him.

'What the hell are you doing here?' I whisper fiercely.

'I've come for you, Bella.'

'What?'

'I realize now what a big mistake I made, what a *stronzo* I have been, so I have come for you. I'm in love with you, Layla.'

My mouth drops open. And then I remember where I am. I grab his arm and drag him down the corridor. I open the first door we come across. It is a slightly smaller reception room with red carpets, rows of stacked chairs, and a musty smell.

I close the door, putting some distance between us, and look at his handsome face. I didn't notice it before, but he looks a lot like Enrique Iglesias. But what is really surprising is that I feel nothing. Not even rage. In fact, I am shocked that I ever thought he was worth climbing into bed with. Other than his looks, he has nothing. There is not even sexual attraction.

'How did you find me?'

He shrugs. 'I asked your mother, no?'

'You went to my ma's house?' I wail in dismay.

'Of course. Don't worry. I told her I was your friend.'

I breathe a sigh of relief. 'I'm sorry you've come all this way, but I'm not in love with you,' I say coldly. I need to get rid of him as soon as possible.

'No, you are just saying that because of what Gabriella told you. It's not true, you know. I was never in love with her.'

'I found someone else.'

'Who?' he demands angrily, his chest puffing up like a fighting cockerel's.

'Does it matter?'

'Yes, it matters. You are my girl. Who is this man?'

He takes a step forward and tries to put his arm around me. I pull away and he tightens his hold.

'Let go of me,' I say with gritted teeth.

'Don't be like that,' he cajoles and moves his face forward. I am just about to knee him in the balls when the door crashes open and BJ stands there, rigid with fury. His face is a thundercloud. His eyes are dangerously narrowed and cold, the whites laced with red. A muscle in his face twitches madly. I have never seen him in such a state. Not even in the pit.

He snarls more than speaks. 'Take your hand off her.'

Lupo shrivels before him. He looks like a man about to vomit. He looks at me and back to BJ and the penny drops. He starts backing away with his hands raised in the air. 'I want no trouble,' he mumbles. What a coward.

When he is closer BJ leans forward slightly and, perfectly composed, utters, 'Don't ever come back.'

The door closes and we stare at each other. Then he walks towards me and pulls me into his solid muscles.

'What the fuck was my woman doing with that spineless little cunt?'

I look up at him. I can feel the aggression radiating off him. 'He's my ex.'

I twine my fingers in his hair, rising up on my tiptoes to gently place my lips on his. His hand snakes around my body and his mouth claims me. It is a demanding, aggressive, passionate kiss. I get so lost in it I don't even hear the door open until Jake's voice is upon us like the crack of a whip.

'What the fuck?'

I pull away from BJ's lips and still in his embrace, turn towards Jake. He is staring at me in disbelief. I feel the blood drain from my face. I open my mouth.

'Step away from him,' he says clearly, staring at BJ with murderous fury.

For a second I think about disobeying him, but I know that I need him on my side. I quickly squeeze BJ's hand and move aside.

'I can explain everyth—'

It goes down so fast, I don't actually see how it happens. One moment Jake is looming in the corridor, the next he is flying towards BJ. I am so shocked to see my brother attacking BJ, I can't even scream. For several seconds I stand and watch Jake swing his arm into BJ. I know BJ is not fighting back, just avoiding the blows. The first two hits don't catch. The third lands and BJ staggers back slightly and knocks a table. A glass vase full of fake flowers falls to the ground. Flowers go flying. The sight of it somehow galvanizes me.

'Stop it. Stop it,' I scream.

But neither man stops. I run towards them and both men look at me and growl for me to stay out.

'I'm pregnant,' I sob. 'I'm pregnant.'

For a shocked second everyone freezes.

Then all hell breaks loose.

TWENTY-FIVE

Layla

'**Y**ou fucking crazy son of a bitch. You didn't even use a fucking condom! That's my sister, you fucking dog,' Jake roars and swings out hard. BJ, still shell-shocked by my announcement, stumbles back against a pile of stacked chairs. The chairs go crashing and BJ falls over with them.

Both men are on the floor. Jake has BJ by the throat and he is choking him to death. Pure, uncontrollable panic surges through me. I run screaming towards them and drop to my knees beside them. 'Please, Jake,' I beg desperately, my hand uselessly trying to pull his away from BJ's throat. 'Please. Please don't. I love him,' I plead.

BJ swivels incredulous eyes towards me. Jake stiffens, but his hands are still frozen around BJ's throat.

I am sobbing hard now. 'He's the only one for me. If you love me please, please, I beg you, don't hurt him.'

Suddenly BJ chokes out, 'What're you going to do? Kill me? You can't fucking control everything in your world. I wanted to tell you, out of respect, man to man, but the fact is, your sister is all grown up and she wanted to tell you herself. But since you've ruined that possibility for her, here's how it's going down. I fucking love her, man. I've loved her since I was 14.'

I hold my face in the palms of my hands and stare incredulously at BJ. Jake sits back, his hands falling to his sides, his chest heaving. He stares at BJ coldly. 'If you cause her to shed one single tear, I swear, I'll make you cry blood. Then, I *will* fucking kill you.'

There is a trickle of crimson flowing from the side of BJ's mouth. He wipes it with the back of his hand. His shirtfront is smeared red.

'I won't,' he says clearly.

Jake gets to his feet, straightens himself, and sighs. He sounds defeated. He looks at me, and his eyes are sad. He wanted better for me. 'I'll see you at my home, later tonight?'

Unable to speak, I nod. Jake closes the door softly behind him and I run to BJ.

I touch the swelling on his jaw. 'Oh my God. It must hurt like hell.'

'Can't feel a thing. Too wired up.'

'I'm so sorry, BJ. This is the second time you've taken a hit for me.'

'Third time,' he corrects softly.

I frown. 'Third?'

'First time was when I fought Jake. He's a strong fighter, but I'm trained and he's not. I could have taken him, but I didn't.'

I remember that I had to look away at the ferocity with which he dispatched The Devil's Hammer. 'Why didn't you?'

'Why doesn't Batman kill the Joker?'

'I don't know. Why?'

 141

'I wasn't being magnanimous or a hero when I drank a couple of cans of stout and allowed myself to fight loose and stupid. It was because of you. At the heart of my mercy was self-interest. I didn't want to vanquish Layla's brother and turn him into an unforgiving foe. Sometimes, your rival today becomes a vehicle for your legacy tomorrow. I wanted us to be equals. Sure I like Jake, but I've gone out of my way to maneuver myself into a place where he owes me one.'

Shocked by his confession, I sit back and stare at him. 'Were you really telling the truth when you told Jake that you love me?'

He expels the air in his chest in a rush. 'Love you? You're like a hundred flashbulbs in my face, Layla. You blind me. You always have. Ever since you trooped into church with your brothers, all of you wearing the old curtains my grandmother had donated to the charity shop. My mother sniggered, but my heart swelled just to look at you. Just to know that such beauty existed in this world. I tried to fight it. I even pretended to myself that you were a spoilt little brat. All these years.' He shook his head. 'Every conceivable type of woman. But none would ever do. My heart was taken."

I feel almost euphoric. 'So that's why you have the Layla tiepin.'

He flushes, the area above his cheekbones becoming dark red. 'Yeah I bought that when I was 15. One day, I promised myself, I'm going to walk down the aisle with that girl and I'm gonna wear it. But then you fell and when I went to help you up, you treated me as if I was a lump of dog shit. I realized you were too grand for me. So I killed the love in my heart. Or rather I thought I had, but I was just kidding myself.'

'I love you, BJ,' I whisper.

He swallows hard.

'It's not a death sentence,' I joke weakly.

He looks down. 'You don't understand. I thought you'd never say it. I thought …. You don't know how long I have waited to hear you say that,' he mutters close to my ear, his voice raspy and broken.

And suddenly I see the sweetness of this beautiful man. 'I love you so much I could die,' I say softly.

He lifts his head, his dark eyes shining. 'Say it again,' he commands.

'I love you so much I could die.'

'Again.'

This time the words roll out of me like a river breaking a dam.

He carefully wipes all expression off his face. 'Were you telling the truth? About the pregnancy? Or was it just to stop Jake from beating the shit out of me?' he asks lightly, but I know him well now. His whole body is tense.

I grin happily. 'Clearblue digital confirmed last night that we just contributed to the world's overpopulation problem.'

He stares at me with wide eyes. 'Fuck woman. Just for once can't you be like your brother's wife and give me a pair of baby shoes instead of this insensitive, sassy bullshit,' he croaks.

I look around the room, locate my purse a few feet away, and reach out for it. I take out a little box of baby shoes and shove it into his chest. 'There you go,' I cry triumphantly.

To my shock, tears fill his eyes.

I feel my eyes prickling too. 'Jesus, BJ. If I'd known it was that easy to make you cry I'd have got pregnant sooner.'

'I hate clichés, but fucking hell, Layla. This is the best day of my goddamn life.' He grins and I can feel the happiness pouring out of him. He stands suddenly, grabs my waist, and lifts me up as high as his arms can reach, whirling me round and round. I know he is doing it because I had told him about Lily's experience and how special I thought it was.

I start laughing. 'You're making me dizzy.'

'I know,' he laughs. 'That was the plan. You're always quiet when you're dizzy.'

'Why don't you use your usual way?' I tease.

He puts me down. 'I was saving that for last,' he says and covers my mouth with his own.

When he lifts his head, my insides are all gooey and melted. 'We're going to rule the world, aren't we?' I say dreamily.

He grins. 'Absolutely. I'll be the king and you'll be my queen.'

'And we'll sit on gold thrones.'

He touches my face. 'Oh Layla. You're the dream I didn't even dare have.'

I can't stop smiling. 'I've always wanted to be the dream someone didn't dare have.'

'I guess you'll have to marry me now, and in a hurry too, won't you?'

'Is that your idea of a proposal, BJ Pilkington?'

'No, I'll do a proper job, later, when I'm between your legs.'

'Oh my!'

'Come on. Let's get out of here.'

'Yes, lets,' I say drunk with love. Unable to believe where my day has ended. I was worried about telling Jake about BJ and telling BJ about the baby. And now everything has just fallen into place in the most extraordinary way. I know Jake *will* come around. BJ is happy about the baby. And everything is just so, so, so perfect.

TWENTY-SIX

Layla

It is 8:00 by the time I make it to Jake's house. All the lights are on and in one of the upstairs windows I can see the silhouette of Lily's grandmother cradling my niece in her arms. Anxiously, I go in through the kitchen hoping to meet my mother first. Shane is sitting with his legs up on a chair and eating a strawberry trifle.

'Hey, Bear,' he says, licking the spoon.

'Good you are in time for dinner,' Ma says, not looking up from chopping vegetables.

'How come he gets to eat dessert before dinner?' I ask.

'Because I'm not staying for dinner,' Shane says.

'Shane, I need to talk to Ma,' I tell him pointedly.

'Don't mind me,' he says, not moving from his chair.

My mother looks up. 'What do you want to tell your old mother? That you've got a man.'

I stare at her shocked. 'Yes, how did you know?'

'Do you think I'm stupid, Layla?'

'I'll be damned,' Shane says, grinning and slapping his thigh. 'Who's the poor sod?'

'Of course, I know,' my mother says. 'You've been walking around with your head in the clouds for at least a month now. So I checked with Queenie and she told me he is a good boy. One of ours. And I have been patiently waiting for you to tell me all about it. Sit down then.'

Bemused and pleasantly surprised at how easy all of this is turning out to be, I sit down and tell them that it's BJ.

'What? BJ!' Shane exclaims with a frown. 'Shit, Layla, he must be the worst man-whore in all of England and Scotland.'

'You're a fine one to talk,' I snap at my brother, glancing worriedly at my mother.

But my mother is not worried at all. 'Billy Joe is a good lad,' she defends. 'He'll be good to you. He's always had a soft spot for you.'

'You knew he had a soft spot for me?' I ask dazed.

'Of course. You could see it a mile off. He used to stare so intently at you in church I thought his eyes would pop out.'

I grin. The way my mother exaggerates anyone would think I was some great beauty. 'Really?'

'Him and half the boys in the congregation,' Shane adds.

'Yes, poor Jake always had his hands full giving them all dirty looks,' my mother says.

'So you think I made a good choice?' I ask my mother happily.

'I fucking don't,' Shane says.

But Ma is unshakeable in her convictions. 'I do. But it's Jake you'll have to convince. He's in the library. Go on and talk to him before dinner.'

'Uh, Ma. I've got something else to tell you.'

She stops chopping. Her mouth drops open. 'Oh, Layla. You're not.'

I bite my lip. 'I am.'

'What?' Shane asks looking from me to Ma and back to me with confusion. 'You're what?'

'I'm pregnant.'

Shane's eyes widen. 'Poor BJ!'

'Come here,' my mother says. From her face I can tell she is fighting hard to keep from crying.

I go and crouch next to her. Up close, I see all the fine lines that fan out from her eyes. My mother is getting old. The idea is distressing. I don't want my mother to grow old. I don't ever want to lose her. She holds my face between her work-worn palms and kisses my forehead. 'My mother was right. It is never the wild ones that get knocked up. It's always the good girls. How far along are you?'

'Just about four weeks.'

She nods.

'I'm sorry, Ma.'

She takes her hands away from my face. 'Don't be sorry. He's a good boy. He'll do right by you. Now go and talk to your brother.'

I grasp my mother's hands and kiss them. 'I love you, Ma.'

'I love you too, Layla,' she says and tears glimmer in her eyes.

On my way out, I punch Shane hard on the shoulder.

'Did you see what she did?' I hear him ask.

I don't hear her reply. I walk along the corridor and knock nervously on my brother's door.

'Come in, Layla,' Jake says.

Taking a deep breath, I enter. My brother is sitting behind his desk. He leans back in his chair and looks at me expressionlessly.

'Look, first of all I want to say I'm really sorry that I didn't tell you sooner, but you were so excited and happy about Lilliana's arrival that I just didn't want to spoil it.'

My brother nods. 'So you're in love with him.'

'Yes. Very much.'

He sighs. 'I wanted better for you.'

'I know you did, but BJ is my destiny, like Lily is yours.'

'I know. But all said and done, he's in the drug trade, Layla. He'll make a mistake one day and he'll go to prison. Are you prepared for that?'

'No.'

'Then use that great love he has for you to make him give it up. It's not like he needs to do it. He already has more money than he knows what to do with. He's got his clubs and pubs and all his properties.'

I move deeper into the room. Jake is right. BJ is going to be a dad. He doesn't need to be involved in the drug business.

'Now is your best opportunity, Layla. Before you get married. Lay down your terms. You'll be a mother soon. Think of your children.'

'OK, I will.'

'I want you to be happy. You know that, don't you?'

I walk around the chair and touch his cheek. 'I know that. I didn't want to disobey you. It just happened.'

He smiles sadly. 'Just remember, no matter what happens, I am always here for you.'

'Thank you.'

'How many weeks gone are you?'

'Four.'

'Are you happy?'

'It's all so perfect I couldn't have planned it better.'

He grins. 'I'm proud of you, Layla.'

I grin back. 'Can you believe it? I'm gonna be somebody's mummy.'

'You'll be a good mother, Layla. I can feel it in my bones.'

-All of me loves all of you-

TWENTY-SEVEN

Layla

Ki shan i Romani - Adoi san' i chov'hani.
Wherever gypsies go - there the witches are, we know.

I clasp my hands together and fix my gaze on his face. 'BJ, what will happen to me and our baby if something happens to you? Like you get caught by the police.'

'I won't get caught. I told you nothing passes through my hands.'

'There's no such thing as never. There are always people who will betray you to save their own skin or mistakes or an envious friend.'

His face closes over. 'What do you want me to say, Layla?'

'I want you to give it up. I want you to give it up, because if you don't, I will never, ever feel secure.'

'It's what I am, Layla.'

'No, it's not what you are. It's what you do.'

He covers his face with his hands, rubbing them upwards towards his head. 'What if I say I can't stop? Will you leave me?'

I drop my head, because I don't want him to see how crushed and disappointed I am. If he had asked for something that was important to him, I would have moved heaven and earth to give it to him. It means all his words are empty and meaningless. He doesn't truly love me. Not the way I do.

'Well?' he prompts.

I clear my face of the pain I am feeling and look up. 'No,' I say dully. 'I won't leave you.'

'What if I said that I've already taken steps to get out of that business?'

I hardly dare believe it. 'You have?'

He nods. 'Don't you know? I'd do anything for you. Anything.'

The joy I feel is what I imagine being hit by very mild lightning must be like. I feel my skin tingle and my entire body wants to shake, jump, and dance around. 'You can't imagine how crushed and sad I was when you said you couldn't do it.'

'Good,' he says and laughs, and I decide that now is the best time to give a little of my bad news.

'By the way,' I say as casually as I can, 'Jake wants us to have a commitment ceremony.'

'A fucking what?'

I nod, trying to keep the amusement from my face. 'You heard correctly.'

'You better be kidding me ...'

I shake my head slowly, not daring to say another word, laughter bubbling inside me.

'The paranoid motherfucker.'

The laugher spews forth.

'You're enjoying this aren't you?' he accuses.

'I have to drink the brew too, you know.'

'So what are you laughing about, then?'

'If you could see your face.'

'When does he want this ceremony to take place?'

'Tomorrow night. It's a full moon. Good for spells.'

'Oh for fuck's sake. I don't believe this shit. Did he have one with Lily?'

'That's exactly what I asked him.'

'And what did he say?'

'He said Lily isn't his sister, but if she was he would have insisted on it.'

He shakes his head in wonder. 'Let me see if I've got this right. We sit inside a circle at some outdoor location and make promises to each other in front of some shaman.'

'And drink a potion.'

His eyes narrow suspiciously. 'Exactly what's in the brew?'

I chew my lower lip. 'I think articles of our used clothing, animal lung of some sort, definitely liver, fat, and probably salt. It's usually put into love charms to ensure the duration of the attachment.'

He folds his arms. 'All right. If it makes you happy and you're OK with it, then I am too.'

I laugh. 'Actually, Jake says since I am pregnant I only need to have a very small sip. A taste were his exact words. You'll have to drink most of it.'

'I knew it,' he bursts out. 'This is to punish me, isn't it?'

I'm dying to laugh. 'A bit.'

'Other men get a stag night with booze and strippers from their brother-in-law-to-be and I get this!'

'We can get some strippers for the ceremony if you want.'

'You find this all very funny, don't you, Miss Eden?'

And I can no longer hold back the laughter. Eventually he laughs too. When we stop, he looks into my eyes and his voice is very serious. 'Jake knows nothing. I'd walk over hot coals for you. Drinking fat, liver, and lung, I could do it every day for the rest of my life if it means having you.'

'I love you, BJ Pilkington. I really, really do.'

'By the way, can they make that article of clothing one of your used panties? It might make the lung, liver, and fat a bit more palatable.'

'Oh, you disgusting man, Mr. Pilkington,' I scold, but I am laughing and so crazy in love with him, I could pop him between two slices of bread and eat him for lunch.

Despite the fact that Jake glowers all through the commitment ceremony, it turns out to be something different and more precious than I imagined it to be. One day I will tell my grandchildren about it. BJ's mother gives me an antique shawl. My mother gives me a gold chain with a sapphire pendant.

It's a cold night and we all dress in warm clothing. The moon is very bright, hanging like a lantern in the sky as we drive out to a wooded area and walk to a clearing.

The shaman is already waiting for us.

God only knows where Jake found her. She is an ancient creature, straight out of the witches' scene in Macbeth. Hunched underneath an old, black cloak, her face in the moonlight is craggy with deep grooves and her skin is mottled with coffee-colored spots. Her hair is silvery and surprisingly thick. One eye is completely white, the pupil covered over with cataract, and the other is jet-black and alive with an animal-like alertness. She wears a red rose tucked behind her ear.

Her body is thin and pitiful, but her movements are as stubborn and headstrong as that of a wild boar. When she extends a withered hand from the inky folds of her cloak, I see that every one of her bony fingers is heavy with an assortment

of large and intricate rings. There are ancient symbols carved into the stones.

She tells BJ and me to take off our shoes, pull our prayer shawls over our heads, and sit cross-legged inside the circle that she draws with a chalky stone. Then she half-squats on a low, four-legged stool and surrounds herself with the tools of her trade. Feathers, a fan, shells, and red and black candles, which she lights and shades with glass coverings. She unrolls a long ribbon and ties an end to both our wrists.

'Are you ready?' she croaks.

We nod.

She starts by inviting and welcoming helping spirits and the spirits of deceased loved ones. She looks at me directly. There is something enchanted and mysterious about her dark, bottomless eye. Her mystique is bewitching. I have the impression that I am staring into the eye of an ancient mystic feline. Timeless and weightless. That my spirit has intertwined with hers in an invisible sublime dance.

'Think of them, all the ones who have left you and they will come.'

I think of Father and call him to come.

Her black eye fixes on me again. 'It is always as forecast and necessary,' she says intriguingly.

Then she begins to sing in a language I do not understand, plaintively, as if she is calling to a lost love. Her voice echoes through the night. Afterwards, she burns some sweet herbs and offers rice to the spirits who have come to witness the ceremony.

BJ and I exchange bracelets made of twine with each other. Afterwards, we make our vows of fidelity and loyalty to each other. First to go is BJ. By the light of the candles, he recites the vows we have both chosen to make.

'I, Billy Joe Pilkington, by the life that courses within my blood and the love that resides within my heart, take thee Layla Eden to my hand, my heart, and my spirit to be my chosen one. To desire thee and be desired by thee. To possess thee and be possessed by thee without sin or shame, for naught can exist in the purity of my love for thee. I promise to love thee wholly and completely without restraint, in sickness and in health, in plenty and in poverty, in life and beyond, where we shall meet, remember, and love again. I shall not seek to change thee in any way. I shall respect thee, thy beliefs, thy people, and thy ways as I respect myself.'

Staring into his eyes, I repeat the same vow and it feels as if my heart will burst with the love I have for him.

Then it is time to drink the thick brown brew. It is truly disgusting. Even the tiny little sip I consume coats my tongue and makes me feel downright queasy. BJ is the real hero of the piece though. He drinks it all without fuss.

Later he whispers in my ear. 'I'm gonna need to forget this taste. Get ready to have your pussy in my mouth for a very long time.'

I try to suppress the giggles, but I am not very successful. I feel a great wave of love wash over me for this wonderful man.

'Jeez, Layla, don't look at me like that unless you want me to drag you behind some bushes and rape you.'

'Do you ever wonder what would have happened if I hadn't gone into your bedroom and tried to take your tiepin?'

He shudders. 'No.'

TWENTY-EIGHT

Layla

After the ceremony my life becomes a whirl of frantic activity. There are so many things to decide: locations, bridesmaid dresses, shoes, music, caterers, invitations, photographer, the cake, videographer, invitations, stationery, rings, favors, transportation, and, of course, my dress. BJ hires a wedding planner. She is so brilliant that I can't even imagine doing it without her. It's a great comfort to simply call her if I have a query or worry and know that she is already on top of it.

My mother makes an appointment with Thelma Madine, the dress designer. Thelma Madine is exactly how she is on TV. Warm, talented, and a practical businesswoman to the core. She would have made a good gypsy.

'How big do you want your dress to be?' she asks.

'Big,' my mother says. 'She's my only girl. My Princess.'

'Oh, Ma,' I say. 'It's a shotgun wedding. I was thinking of a simple mermaid dress.'

'Simple!' my mother explodes. 'Where's the fun in that?' She throws her hands up animatedly. 'This is a once-in-a-lifetime event. Who are you to deny yourself the best and most beautiful wedding dress possible on your big day?'

My mother is right. A wedding should be fun. Every gypsy wedding that I have attended, even the tackiest, most over-the-top ones with white stretch-limos and chocolate fountains have been far more enjoyable, exciting, and dramatic than any of the elegant, color-coordinated, chair-covered, non-gypsy ones. And when I think back, a sedate wedding is classy and admirable, but it is the big gypsy weddings that are unforgettable.

I look at Thelma. 'You know what, I will have that big ball gown after all.'

But Thelma is not the queen of the gypsy bridal dress for nothing. 'I can do you a mermaid wedding dress and make your mother happy too,' she declares confidently.

'Really?'

'Yes, really.'

And she is as good as her word. The very next day she comes back with two sketches. Ma and me agree on a fit-and-flare design with a sweetheart neckline, pearls on the bodice, and hundreds and hundreds of taffeta handkerchiefs sewn together to make the billowing skirt and train. It comes with a little bolero for the church. The whole ensemble is in shades of oyster.

In a week Thelma calls me for my first fitting. The three of us drive over to her shop. It is exciting and frightening. I'm not sure if she can really pull of a big mermaid dress.

'Come in,' she says. I can tell she is eager to show us her creation. She takes us quickly to the back of the shop. In a move that is pure drama, she pauses in front of a closed door, and with her hand on the handle, turns to us and asks, 'Are you ready for this?'

My mother, Maddy, and I nod. While butterflies flutter in my stomach, she theatrically flings open the door.

The dress is on a stand, its train of thousands of taffeta squares spread out like an enormous fish tail behind it. I gasp and stare in amazement. My mother squeals like a young girl and Maddy claps her hands with delight. Any fears I had that it would be tacky or too My Big Fat Gypsy Wedding are laid to rest forever. The dress is amazing. Totally and utterly spectacular. It is a masterpiece, pure and simple.

The days pass in a blur of hectic activity and excitement. Only moments shine through with full HD clarity. Those rare moments I look at in amazed wonder, sometimes disbelief. So this is my life. A week before the wedding, I give up my apartment, transport most of my stuff into BJ's home, and move into my mother's house. At this point BJ and I are no longer able to see each other alone and the separation is pure torture.

But suddenly, before I know it, my wedding day is upon me. I wake up early, a bundle of nerves, and lie very quietly in the dark. Already, I can hear my mother and aunts moving about the house. I put my hand on my stomach. It's still flat, but my baby is growing inside.

'We're getting married today,' I whisper, and a thrill of excitement runs through me.

Maddy is the first to arrive and we eat breakfast in my bedroom together. We speak in whispers and giggle quietly as if we are children on a midnight adventure.

The hairdresser arrives at seven. Ma makes her a cup of coffee and she sets about separating my hair into two parts, gathering the top half into a bun at the back of my head and putting corkscrew curls into the lower half and leaving them trailing down my back and shoulders. She fits a princess tiara over my head, and the make-up artist takes me on. She spends an hour on my face, painting, dabbing, drawing, brushing, and then gluing on individual spikes of false eyelashes.

By now the house is crowded with friends and relatives bringing presents. Gypsies are generous gift givers and the pile of presents soon fills the dining table and spills onto the floor, and still more well-wishers are flooding through the doors. Ma breaks into the stack of champagne cases and the house heaves as if it is a party.

Then the dress arrives.

From my window I watch Thelma and her two assistants carefully carry it into the house. They bring it upstairs to my room and Thelma and her assistants help me into it. My heart is racing with nerves.

'Oh, oh, oh,' exclaims a delighted Maddie. 'You look stunning.'

When I have been laced into the dress and the veil fixed into place, I walk over to the mirror with bated breath.

And ... almost do not recognize the person in the mirror. I look like I have stepped out of a page of a fairytale. Ma, who has changed into a pretty grey-blue dress, has tears in her eyes. She dabs them away carefully with the edge of a tissue.

'You look absolutely beautiful, Layla,' she says.

'You were right, Ma. The dress is perfect.'

My mother smiles through her tears.

Thelma and her assistants pick up the train and hem of the skirt as I go through the door, preventing me from stepping on it and falling headlong down the stairs. They carry the train as I go down the stairs in my pearl-encrusted slippers.

And then I am standing in front of Jake. He looks gorgeous in his grey morning suit. His eyes are so bright and full of pride.

'Oh! Layla. If only Da could see you. You're the princess he always said you were,' he says.

Lily smiles. The confinement thing has really worked. She is glowing and beautiful. 'I always knew he would get you.'

'You did?'

She nods. 'He's a good guy. I'll never forget what he did for Jake and me. I'm so happy for you. Be happy always, Layla.'

Then Dominic and Shane come to kiss me. They look incredibly handsome in their new suits. Dominic nods approvingly, and even Shane forgets to be a smartass. 'You look truly beautiful,' he says sincerely.

As I walk to the front door, everybody takes pictures and videos.

Gingerly, I step out of my mother's house and scream. I can't believe it. I don't know whether it is Jake or BJ who has arranged it, but it is the last thing I am expecting. A glass carriage is waiting on the road. It is dainty and ornate and quite simply magical, something you would see in a Disney movie. It has two grooms in livery and two white steeds with plumed headdresses.

'BJ insisted on it,' Jake says.

Jake gets in first and then Thelma helps me into the carriage so that I am sitting opposite him and my train is coiled between us. The door closes and we are off, with passing cars tooting their horns at us all the way to the church. Complete strangers hang their heads out of their cars, smile, wave, and wish me well.

By the time we get to the church, we are 30 minutes late and the bridesmaids and flower girls are all lined up and waiting. Maddy winks at me. Jake reaches over and squeezes my hand.

'Thank you, Jake. Thank you for everything,' I say. My voice sounds shaky.

'Never mind that. Don't ruin your mascara,' he says, his voice is gruff.

Thelma and her assistants help me out of the carriage. I step out into the sunshine. It is a beautiful, still spring day. There are strangers gathered all around watching the wedding procession. And suddenly I have an attack of nerves. I turn blindly to Jake. I've been doing that since I was child. Always Jake. Fighting all my battles.

'I'm with you every step of the way,' he says, holding his hand out.

I take it, and just like that I am no longer nervous that I will trip, fall, or make a mistake. I am excited by the future that awaits me in the church. We walk up the steps to the church, my fingers resting lightly on his forearm. The sound of the wedding march floats out the double doors.

We make our way to the entrance, instantly I see my bridegroom. All in white. So broad and tall and wonderful. In the periphery of my vision I can see my mother, my brothers, my friends, acquaintances, and even strangers lining the back pews. In a flash of white, BJ turns and everyone else disappears. Our eyes meet and we're alone in the church. Only him and me.

'Wow,' he mouths silently, his eyes blazing possessively.

Then my brother is moving forward and my legs follow his lead. I can feel the heavy train trailing for yards behind me, hear the swishing of the taffeta, smell the sweet perfume of the bouquets, and sense the solid muscles of my brother's arm under my hand, but I am in a total daze. My eyes never leave BJ.

My brother takes his arm away and I look at him stupidly. He smiles and I turn my face back to BJ. He puts out a hand and gently pulls me towards him. He is so big and beautiful, I cannot believe that he is really mine. The tiepin that had started everything glints on his cravat, catching my eye. It doesn't match and yet is perfect.

The vicar begins to recite our vows and I follow, repeating every word carefully, in awe of the sounds that leave my lips. For they come directly from some deep, unknown place inside my being.

'I do,' I say.

BJ slips the ring onto my finger and the vicar pronounces us man and wife. He doesn't have time to give BJ permission to kiss the bride. BJ has already leaned over the yards and yards of material separating us and found my mouth. The congregation erupts: cheering, clapping, and whistling. We are a rowdy bunch, us gypsies.

Thelma leads me to a small room at the side of the church. Carefully, she removes the veil and the bolero. The hairdresser touches up my hair and they help me out of the door. I stand for a moment at the entrance of the church. Then I see a brilliant flash of white and the crowds part to let him through. BJ stops in front of me and stares transfixed, his eyes devouring me. The dress has been laced up too tight to take a deep calming breath so I take quick shallow breaths through my mouth. He takes my hand.

'You ordered one princess?' I whisper.

'I did. And you ordered one love-sick husband?'

'Husband,' I repeat. The word lands onto my tongue as light as a butterfly. I find it to be a familiar word that brings peace to my entire body. As if I was always meant to be Mrs. Billy Joe Pilkington.

TWENTY-NINE

Layla

After my ultimate wish-upon-a-star, fairytale wedding, BJ whisks me off to Tuscany for our honeymoon. We stay in a magnificent palazzo near Maremma's woodlands. For four passion-drenched, slothful days we do nothing but explore each other. Once we wake up at dawn we ride into the outstandingly beautiful and wild countryside.

BJ is a strong rider, but so am I and it is exhilarating. When we stop we are both flushed and aroused. In the clear fresh morning air, we tear each other's clothes off and indulge in the delight of outdoor sex. At the end of it, I'm startled by an audience. A pair of beautiful roe deer wearing their reddish summer coats are looking at us curiously. We freeze, BJ still deep inside me, and stay still until they amble away.

'Wasn't that beautiful?' I whisper.

'Everything with you is,' he says.

Everyday we discover new things about each other. I now know that BJ doesn't have breakfast. He has eight raw eggs blended with a banana and some milk. And he knows that I like a selection of warm pastries from the village woman. And that I'll quite happily drink chilled, raw goat's milk with them.

In the afternoon, when it is too hot to do anything, we swim lazily consuming countless ice lollies by the pool. At night, we eat thin-crust pizza cooked in a traditional wood oven, or even barbeque fish we bought from the outdoor market on the terrace. Once BJ makes us a pasta pomodoro with steak. I discover he's not a bad cook.

'Did your mother teach you?' I ask.

'No, it's Bertie's recipe.'

Tonight, he's taking me to a famous restaurant a few miles away. The man who cleans the pool tells us that one has not lived until you've tried Il Cinghiale Nero's signature dish of wild boar and porcini mushrooms.

I soak in the bath inside the high-ceilinged, pink marble bathroom until he scoops me out and carries me, still dripping with soapsuds, to our enormous bedroom. He throws me on the bed and dives in after me. He has his own way of drying me. It doesn't involve a towel, but it does feature a great deal of effort on his part, and wet sheets. Afterwards, as I lay on my back satiated, he grasps my ankle in his hand and brings it to his mouth.

'It's amazing how brown you have become in four days.'

I look into his love-drunk eyes. 'Wait until you see me at the end of the week.'

He leans back on the pillows, eyes half-mast, and watches me slip into a sultry, red knee-length dress with a daring décolleté. I slip on exotic, toe-ring sandals with straps embellished with turquoise stones. I brush my hair, apply mascara and lip-gloss, and dab perfume on to my pulse points.

'Come here,' he says.

I cross my arms across my chest. 'Nope, I'm not having you ruin my primping. You can have me after you feed me.'

He bounds up suddenly, sending me screaming out of the bedroom and through the tall corridor with its gilded panels and oil paintings, then down the grand marble staircase. I stand at the foot of the stairs looking up, laughing and gasping for breath, and ready to bolt outside if he decides to come down after me, but he stands leaning on the banister.

'There'll be hell to pay if you keep it for later,' he calls out.

'Is that a threat?'

He grins. 'Consider it an invitation.'

I grin back. 'In that case, I accept.'

He nods and disappears back down the corridor.

The pool cleaner is right. It has to be the one of the best meals I've eaten in my life. It's when we're ordering dessert that our trouble starts.

I turn to BJ after ordering my sweet from the waiter, and he is scowling at me.

'What?' I ask.

'Stop fucking flirting with that waiter, or he'll find his pepper mill sticking out of his fucking ass.'

'Are you kidding me?'

'Does it look like I am?'

'I wasn't flirting.'

'No?'

'No,' I say very empathically.

'So what the hell was all that hair flicking and the "*si, si, sei troppo gentile*" all about, then?' he asks changing his voice to a mocking falsetto to imitate mine.

'That was me being polite,' I say, getting a bit irritated myself.

'How would you like it if I did that with the waitress?'

'I wouldn't mind at all. Go ahead. Be my guest,' I tell him.

A look crosses his face. 'All right. Just remember you started this.'

He looks around and catches the eye of the most attractive waitress in the restaurant and lifts his eyebrow. When she comes to him he gives her a slow smile and asks if she could bring a bottle of their best champagne.

She trots off and he smiles pleasantly at me. I am determined not to react so I smile back.

When she returns, totally ignoring me, he blatantly begins to flirt and laugh with her, blatantly. My blood begins to boil. Yes, it's true I did flirt with the waiter, but only lightly. He, on the other hand, was almost stripping her naked with his eyes.

At first I try my best not to show how furious I am. I tell myself that he's doing it deliberately. It's not like he truly wants her. He's just punishing me. I briefly toy with the idea of calling the waiter back and flirting in exactly the same way with him. See who cracks first. But I don't actually want to seriously flirt with another man on my honeymoon.

I could have held on and sat it out with my frozen smile if the quick-eyed slut had not given me a look that was at once pitying and triumphant. A look that said, *hey, you're a fool. Can't you see what your man is doing? How totally into me he is?*

Humiliated, I stand up. I don't have the car keys. Not that it matters. I wouldn't dare drive the powerful Maserati he has rented, especially on unfamiliar roads. Fuck him, I would rather walk the five miles back to the palazzo than stay here another second. Both of them turn to look at me. She seems glad that I might be leaving.

'Going somewhere, babe?' BJ asks sweetly.

'Nowhere that concerns you,' I answer with equal sweetness, and walk out of the restaurant.

Outside, I pause for a moment at the entrance. I am so angry I want to scream. How dare he behave like that on our honeymoon. I start walking fast in the direction we had come from. Fortunately, I am wearing flat sandals. I must have gone 20 yards before I hear the Maserati's engine idling along beside me.

'Need a lift somewhere?'

'What? Not taking your tart back with you?' I say huffily.

'Well, well, look who's all jealous?' His voice is rich with laughter.

His mirth irritates me. 'There is a difference between what I was doing and what you were engaging in! I was being polite and you were fucking her with your eyes.'

He laughs. His laughter is like smoke and silk. 'It'll take us forever to reach the palazzo at this rate.'

Even though the forecast called for a thunderstorm tonight, I am not prepared for the downpour that begins with large drops of hot rain that smells of dust. A couple fall on my head.

'Get in, Layla,' BJ says, his voice silky.

This time I open the door and get in, but I am determined to make him suffer for the humiliation he caused at the restaurant. I am going to give him the silent treatment.

THIRTY

BJ

I steal a sidelong glance at her. She was cute in the restaurant when she was acting all unconcerned while she was burning up with fury inside, but now that she is radiating waves of don't-touch-me she's smoking hot. It reminds me of what she used to be like. Having it inside this car with the smell of the thunderstorm raging outside, it's as sexy as hell.

I need to fuck my new wife.

Through the lashing rain I suddenly see it coming up ahead, a forest. This is it, real freedom, a centuries' old, living, breathing, magical wonderment. *Sometimes we need to let go of life's shackles and find oneness with nature.* Feeling reckless, my dick steering the vehicle, I veer off the motorway and head down a winding country lane. I don't need to look at Layla to know she is staring at me with narrowed eyes.

'Why the hell have you left the motorway?' she asks with a scowl.

'There's something I've always wanted to do,' I reply.

She stares at the rain lashing down on the windshield, the continuous streak left by the wipers. 'Well, whatever it is, count me out. I'm not going out in that rain.' she says in her best Ice Queen tone.

Excitement surges through my veins. I say nothing. Just stop the car, then make my way around to Layla's window.

I stand outside for moment, eyes focused on her. The gesticulation of her hands and exaggerated facial expression clearly indicate that she thinks I'm a raving fucking lunatic.

'It's bloody pouring,' she shouts, her voice barely audible.

I swipe at the water streaming down my face. Yeah, *like I hadn't fucking noticed.*

'If you don't get out now, I'll drag you the fuck out."

Her mouth drops open. A look flares through her eyes. I know that look too well. She's going to fucking lock me out. Before she has time to react, my hand is on the handle and the door is open. I grab her and haul her out while she struggles like a wildcat.

'What the fuck has gotten into you?' she yells in my face.

Her fury is pure bliss against the backdrop of the thunderstorm. It makes my blood sing for her. I let go of her.

And she takes a step back. I watch the rain drench her, her dress becomes transparent. She's not wearing a bra. Her chest is heaving. Her nipples are as hard as stone. God! My wife is so beautiful. Sometimes I can't believe she is mine. My cock starts straining for release as if it is a loaded missile zeroing in on its target.

Her mouth drops open as it dawns on her exactly what's on my mind. 'If you think I'm going to have sex out here in the middle of nowhere after the stunt you pulled in the restaurant as well, you better think again.'

I start to laugh.

'What's so bloody funny?'

'You babe.'

'You have a sick sense of humor. Letting your pregnant wife freeze to death in the rain,' she shouts.

'You're not freezing. On a hot steamy night like this, rain is lovely.' I grab her arms and pull her body tight against me. 'We,' I growl in her ear, 'are going to fuck like we've never fucked before.'

'You HAVE got to be kidding!' Rain splatters onto her face and flows in her gorgeous mouth.

'I don't kid around about how, when, and where I fuck my wife.'

'I'm not rolling around in the mud while an avalanche of rain is being dumped on me from the heavens,' she snaps.

'Why the hell not? What could be more perfect? There's no one around for miles. It's hot and steamy. The rain beating down on us will be kinda sexy.'

'Quite frankly, because you don't bloody deserve it. How dare you flirt like that in front of me? I was humiliated,' she spits at me furiously.

'Next time remember that before you start giving other men the come-on.'

'Oh!' She stamps her foot in frustration. 'I was not giving him the come-on.'

'Well, in future bear in mind that we have different ideas about what equates to a come-on.'

'So you're not going to apologize?'

'What do you think?'

'I think you should.'

'I think we should have sex.'

'What about our clothes? How will we get them dried? How will we drive back in this condition?'

I grin. 'We'll turn up the temperature in the car and drive home nude,' I tell her.

'Oh BJ, this is really crazy.'

'No, this is exactly what we need.'

Layla raises her eyebrows disdainfully, but she's not fooling me. Her true resistance is actually gone. She, too, wants to have her hormone-loaded little pussy filled in the rainstorm. 'I've always imagined what it might be like to have wild, animalistic, outdoor sex in a steamy climate. OK, maybe it was without the rain, but right now, that just adds to the fantasy.'

There is a burst of thunder and it startles her. She jumps against me. I take that moment to grab her hand and pull her to the front of the car.

In the glare of the headlights she looks even more fuckable.

Her long hair is plastered to her body, and the outline of her hardened nipples, aching to be free from that dress, is even more pronounced. Naked, spread-eagle, and trapped under me is how I want her.

I move closer to press my rock hard cock into her pubic bone and pull her hair backwards, until she is arched across the hood. For a second I simply stop and look at her, spread out, the rain exploding like liquid bullets on her body. Mist, the steam rising from the hood of the car, surrounds us.

She is a work of art.

Leaning over my Princess, I run a hungry tongue along her slender neck, tracing the stretched muscles. She tilts her head back even further, and looking up at the sky, exhales deeply. Just like that I know she's ready. It's surrender, pure and simple.

I use my knees to spread her legs, then trace my hand up the inside of her leg under her dress and rip off her panties in a single action. The tearing sound mingles with the drumming of the rain on the hood of the car. Her body clenches in anticipation. I get a good feel of her pussy quivering and sweet with honey.

Using both my hands I tear her dress open and expose the firm, tanned flesh underneath. For a moment I lift my bulk backwards and delight in the sight of her magnificence, her naked breasts glistening in the rain and her pale stomach just beginning to swell writhing against mine. I place my lips against hers, undo my jeans and yank the clinging material away. Her rain-soaked mouth is sugar. *Ah! Layla. Layla. Layla. It was always only you.*

How could you be jealous of any other woman?

I move my mouth down to her right nipple, flicking and teasing while I roll the left nipple between my fingers squeezing intermittently. Ever since she became pregnant her nipples have become even more sensitive. The slightest touch is enough to get her going. She groans helplessly while I suck and run the edge of my teeth and tongue across the hard buds. I let my fingers play with the inviting softness of her slickly swollen pussy. She responds by involuntarily raising her head and chest.

I push her downwards to the metal again, spread her thighs wider and put my left arm under her shoulders so I can control her body. I insert two fingers into her honeyed pussy.

'Yes,' she moans.

But I don't give her what she wants. She wants speed, thickness. I deny her both. I keep my fingers moving slowly and using my thumb work her clit, feeling the frustration mounting in her body.

She thrusts her pubic area restlessly towards my hand.

Just as she's about to climax, I stop and withdraw my fingers from her begging pussy. Rearing back, I swipe the water from my eyes and wrap my mouth around one of her erect nipples. Sucking hard, I plunge my throbbing cock into her depths.

'Oh. My. God. BJ!" she screams, her body arching like a pulled bow.

I swoop down on her other nipple and bite it. She screams again. I lift my head and watch the rain flow over the bitten nipple. I move closer and her whole body tenses as I trail my tongue on the other nipple. She trembles with anticipation.

She raises her head and looks at me, water running down her slack features.

'Were you flirting with that waiter?'

'No.' She swallows.

I slide my hands along her wet thighs.

'Are you sure?'

She nods.

'Don't lie to me, Layla. We can't move from here until you tell me the truth.'

She licks her lips. 'All right. Yes, I did it to make you jealous.'

I squeeze her thighs and ram my blood-filled dick deep into her.

'Ahh...'

'You like that?'

'Yes.'

'Do you know what is going to happen to you if you do that again?'

She shakes her head.

'I'm going to fuck you for days. I will fill your belly with my cum and have it running out of every orifice. Do you understand?'

She nods.

'I didn't hear you.'

'Yes. I understand,' she mutters.

'Good,' I say and bite her other nipple. Her mouth opens in a scream and I cover it with mine. I plunge my tongue into her warmth, hook her tongue into my mouth, and suck it hard as I thrust into her.

I feel her pulse change and her muscles tighten around the base of my shaft. I release her tongue. She digs her fingers into my ass cheeks as the erratic spasms of pleasure erupt deep within her body.

'Oh God,' she cries, 'I'm coming.'

I feel her nails embed themselves into my ass, but I don't give a fuck. I'm oblivious to any pain as I hear her cry out in ecstasy as her orgasm rips through her body.

My cock pulsates and throbs and I drive to the hilt one last time. With a jerk I start filling her pretty little pink pussy with my hot cum. Wrapping her legs tightly around my waist she milks my body expertly.

-You are the color of my blood-

THIRTY-ONE

Layla

My mother says I must have been born under a lucky star: I've not experienced any morning sickness. I wanted to carry on working until the baby was due, but neither my family or BJ will stand for it. *What's the point if you are planning on giving it up after the baby is born anyway?* I suppose they have a point. Still, I would have preferred it to be my decision.

I stand in the shower, water sluicing down my shoulders onto my braided hair and dripping over my growing belly. In the fast-moving water, my growing mound looks like an eyeball. I imagine his tiny transparent fingers clutching and unclutching at nothing. An animal instinct makes me curve my hands around my belly protectively.

It is a constant source of wonder for me, knowing that a human being resides inside me. I think of his tiny little heart beating, his mouth opening and gulping amniotic fluid.

During the ultrasound, it showed as a black bubble in his stomach. But the miracle that makes me smile the most is the thought that every half an hour or so his tiny bladder is emptying. My rude son is peeing inside me!

I wonder what he will smell like, how his story will unfold.

BJ wants to call him Tommy. Over my dead body, I informed him in no uncertain terms. I want my boy to be called Oliver or one of those really cool American cowboy names like Sundance or Texas Jack. At the very least, something proper like Charles or Phillip.

But Tommy is a proper Irish name, BJ insisted.

I love my husband to death, but Tommy? Ugh. No. Never. Like I said, over my dead body. I get out of the shower and rub rich coca butter on my tummy and hips before I get dressed. BJ is in the gym. A one-hour loop of Lost Frequencies *Are You With Me* is playing in the background. I listen to it so often I am sure my son will be born humming this tune.

The phone rings. It's the hospital.

'Mrs. Pilkington?'

'Yes.'

'This is St. James Hospital. This is Nurse Mary Varenne.'

'Hello.'

'Dr. Freedman would like to see you and your husband as soon as possible.'

Alarm bells start ringing in my head. I clutch the receiver with both hands. 'Why?' My voice is a frightened whisper.

'I'm afraid I'm not at liberty to say. But it is urgent that both your husband and you attend his surgery immediately.'

'What's wrong with my baby?'

'I'm sorry, Mrs. Pilkington, but I am just passing on a message. I have two appointment slots available.'

'Give me the first one.'

'Can you make it at two o'clock today?'

I swallow. Today! They want me to come in today! Shit! How urgent is this situation? I feel cold inside. 'Yes. My husband is busy all day. Can I come alone?'

'I'm afraid you have to come with your husband,' she insists.

'All right, we'll come in together.' My voice is a scared, foreign whisper.

'Good. I'll book you in.'

I don't run straight away to tell BJ. No, no, I won't frighten him unnecessarily. Suddenly I feel protective of him. He is so big and powerful, but I know that, on the inside, he would suffer far more than me. Mentally and emotionally, I am the stronger one. I will not show him my fear. Maybe it is nothing. Or maybe it is just a little thing.

She had sounded so serious though.

I touch my belly. Whatever it is, we will see it through. I walk into the kitchen and look around me. Everything looks the same. But it's as bewildering as a dream landscape. Perhaps I am still asleep. I blink and take a large breath. My hand flies up to my mouth to shut off the scream that wants to escape.

I walk to the island and I have the distinct sensation of weightlessness, as if I can float away like a helium balloon. I grab hold of the edge of the granite counter. I am gripping it so hard my knuckles show white. I stare at them with fascination. I am in such a state of shock I can't actually think. My mind is a complete blank. I take another deep breath and exhale noisily. It could be a mistake. That must be it. It happens all the time. I cling to the thought.

'It's most probably a mistake,' I whisper to myself.

I walk to the phone and dial Jake's number. He's always solved all my problems for me. I listen to the blurred sound of the rings in a daze. I terminate the call at the third ring and put the phone back down on the table. It's silly to call him. I'll call him when I know more.

'Oh God!'

Did they detect an abnormality during the scan? I wrap my arms around my stomach. Tears gather in my eyes and spill down my cheeks. 'I love you. I don't care if you are disabled or anything. I'm here for you. You chose me and I chose you. No matter what, you are coming into this fucked up world.'

A smile comes to my face.

'You're coming into this family, boy,' I say fiercely. Strange how loud and strong my voice has become. 'Nothing. Nothing is going to stop you from being born. I'll protect you with my dying breath,' I promise.

I go to the mirror and wipe my eyes. I smile at my reflection.

'Are you with me?' the melodious voice of Lost Frequencies asks.

Yeah, I'm with you. I'm your mother. I'll always be with you no matter what. Come, let's go tell Daddy that you are super special.'

I walk along the corridor and stop in front of the gym. I pause and compose myself. When I open the door, BJ turns to look at me. His face is instantly concerned. I never disturb him while he is training. He puts the dumb bells he is working with down.

'What's up?'

I start walking towards him and immediately his large strides eat the distance between us and he envelops me in his arms.

'What's wrong?' he asks with a frown.

I attempt to smile, but from the expression on his face, I don't think I pull it off. 'The hospital called. There might be something wrong with our ...,' I take a deep breath and, though I try to hold the tears back, my eyes fill up, '...baby.'

'What?' He stares at me, his eyes wide and blank with horror.

I start to babble, the words hurried and stumbling over each other. 'It's all right. I think I'm all right with it. He's come to the right home. You and I will love him more than any other mummy or daddy, right?'

'What the fuck are you talking about?' he asks. He is white under his tan and he is staring at me as if he has never looked at me properly before.

The tears start running freely down my face. 'There's something wrong with our baby.'

'No,' he snarls and pulls me into his arms. He holds me so tight I make a strangled sound. He lets go of me instantly. 'Sorry, I didn't mean to hurt you,' he whispers.

'You didn't.'

He stares at me in shock and disbelief. 'Could they have made a mistake?'

You cannot imagine how much hope that hopeless question gives me. I throw my arms around him and hug him tightly. 'I was thinking exactly the same thing.'

We hold each other for I don't know how long. Both unwilling to look the other in the eye, and stop pretending that it is all a huge mistake. Eventually, I know it will have to be me. I know that this tiny little life is mine to steer. I pull away.

'I was counting back the other day and I know we conceived him on our very first night together. Whether they are wrong or right, we're having this baby, right? He chose us to be his parents, right?' I sniff.

He pulls me close to him and groans, 'Oh, Layla. Of course, we are. He's ours no matter what.'

We drive to the doctor's in complete silence, both of us terrified of what awaits us at the hospital. A nurse shows us to Dr. Freedman's office. We walk into his room hand-in-hand

behind her. Dr. Freedman is a tall, bespectacled man. He looks up and smiles tightly. He is ill at ease.

'Mr. and Mrs. Pilkington. Please, have a seat,' he says politely indicating a set of blue chairs opposite him and letting his eyes slide away to some papers on his desk.

It is a surreal moment. I don't fear. I know in my DNA that, no matter what, I will protect my baby. I'm so aware of this moment that I can actually feel and experience everything. I sense the doctor's discomfort. I feel BJ's fear seeping out of his pores like something alive and tangible. I hear the faint sounds of people walking down the corridor. For them, it's a normal day. But for me, I can taste the disinfectant that the doctor used after the patient before us.

I can do this. I sit down and turn my head to watch BJ take the seat next to me. It hits me that this is a much bigger deal for him. I am clear in my head. No one. No one. No one can shake me. I turn to face the doctor.

The doctor's eyes are weary. He has done this too many times and is clearly dreading the task at hand. I smell his abhorrence of what he is about to say. Wordlessly, he pushes a box of tissues towards me.

I frown and look at BJ. His beautiful mouth opens and closes. And we realize that something is not just wrong. It is horribly wrong. It is worse, far worse than what I have imagined. Oh no.

NO. NO. NO

My darling BJ. So powerful and yet at this moment, felled. I reach my hand out and he envelops it in his own. I smile at him. He does not smile back.

'What's wrong with my baby?' I ask.

Dr. Freedman coughs and clears his throat. Behind him, I can see a poster of a skinless human body with all its veins showing.

'There's nothing wrong with your baby,' he says. 'It's you.' He says this gently and neutrally, but the room swings wildly.

THIRTY-TWO

Layla

'There's no easy way to say this. The ultrasound you had on the 15th showed that you either have endometrial cancer or hyperplasia that will likely rapidly progress to cancer. I'm so sorry.'

The unexpectedness of what he says is so great that I don't react at all. I feel myself go blank and numb. The big C? Me? Impossible. I'm born under a lucky star. I've been so spoilt. So sheltered. So fortunate. It's just not possible.

'What the fuck are you talking about? Can you fucking talk English?' BJ erupts aggressively.

Dr. Freedman shifts uncomfortably in his chair. It's obvious that he is not used to being spoken to so rudely. It is only BJ's size or pity that keeps him for retaliating. 'Your wife has a large mass in her uterus. It surrounds the baby on the top and sides. The rapid growth from total absence at the

183

dating scan to what it was yesterday, makes me strongly suspect that it is certainly malignant and aggressively so. You should have been told at the ultrasound session yesterday, but the sonographer wanted to run the scans by me before making such a drastic diagnosis.'

'You're saying my wife has cancer?' BJ asks in disbelief.

'Yes.'

BJ jumps up so suddenly and with such force that his chair crashes to the ground. He slams his hand on the desk, his black eyes boring into the doctor's, and shouts, 'No, this a fucking mistake. How do you know the test results haven't been mislabeled? You do those fucking tests again.'

'Please, Mr. Pilkington. Sit down and calm down. This outburst is not going to help your wife.'

I reach out blindly for BJ's hand. His hand closes over mine. I look up at him. 'Please, BJ,' I whisper. For a second he doesn't respond. 'Please,' I beg again.

He picks the chair off the floor, rights it, and sits down. I notice that his hands are shaking. He fists his right hand and covers it with his left hand.

'The treatment for cancer and hyperplasia to the extent I saw on the ultrasound,' the doctor continues, 'is immediate hysterectomy to stage and figure out the prognosis.'

'A hysterectomy?' I gasp.

The doctor shifts uncomfortably. 'I'm afraid so.'

'You want to take her womb out?' BJ repeats in disbelief. 'What the fuck! She's 23 years old, for the love of God!'

'I'm sorry,' the doctor says lamely.

BJ lunges forward suddenly. 'If you say you're sorry one more fucking time, I swear, I'll give you something to be sorry about. This is a mistake, pure and simple.'

The doctor's eyes bulge with fear. He leans backwards and places his hands on the armrests of his chair, as if he is getting ready to bolt. 'I know you are very upset, but I have personally gone through all the results and I can assure you, Mr. Pilkington, that there is no mistake.'

I glance at BJ and I see by his crushed expression that he knows the doctor is telling the truth. BJ has used violence to solve every problem in his life. He has never encountered a scenario that he couldn't win using brute force alone. But for the first time his fists are of no use. He is totally helpless. And it scares him.

'Is there another way? A way to save the baby?' I whisper.

'I'm very sor—.' The doctor stops mid-word and glances nervously at BJ. 'I'm afraid there is no way to save your baby. I must recommend immediate termination of the pregnancy.'

'What happens if I don't do anything?'

BJ has fallen eerily silent. He is cradling his head in his hands.

The doctor frowns. 'First of all you will be greatly endangering your own life. It's not a risk that's worth taking since the lack of room will mean your placenta will be on your cervix. With the weight of the baby and the tumor, you would be at a high risk for a placental abruption.'

I exhale the breath I was holding. 'What is that?' I ask.

'It's when the placenta peels away from the inner wall of the uterus before delivery. It deprives the baby of oxygen and causes heavy bleeding in the mother. It can be fatal to both mother and child.'

'I still want a second opinion,' BJ says with a deadly calm that's more frightening than his furious outburst before.

The doctor nods calmly. 'I have already arranged for your wife to see the head of OB and a maternal fetal specialist at 9:00 the day after tomorrow. They'll do another ultrasound with better equipment and they will also perform an ultrasound biopsy.'

'Is the ultrasound biopsy safe for my baby?' I ask.

The doctor looks pained. 'They will be able to stay away from the baby and the sac, but the chances for a spontaneous miscarriage afterwards exist. I would recommend an immediate termination.'

I stand up abruptly. 'All right. Thank you, doctor,' I say, and look down at BJ.

He gazes up at me. He looks so confused and lost I want to take him to my breast. He stands slowly. It's obvious he is not ready to leave, as if discussing it further could change anything.

We walk out of the doctor's office and cross the car park like two survivors of a war. Hanging on to each other. Seeing nothing around us. Shell-shocked. Devastated. BJ unlocks the car and opens the passenger door for me. I slide into the seat in silence. He gets in, closes the door, and puts the keys in the ignition, but does not start the engine.

I turn to him. He looks as dazed and bewildered as the moths that fly into light bulbs and fall to the floor, lying on their backs, they slowly wheel their legs into the arms of death.

'Can you believe it?' I ask.

'Oh, baby,' he croaks. 'I think I just need to hold you for a second.'

I throw myself at him and sob my heart out in the bleak hospital car park.

We drive home in heavy silence, both of us locked in our own pain. When we reach our home, I stare ahead of me blankly. I simply cannot summon the energy to open the car door and go into the house.

He opens my door and holds his hand out to me. With a sigh I put my hand in his and let him haul me upright.

Mrs. Roberts from next door meets us on the pavement.

'Are you all right, dear?'

I nod automatically. 'Thank you. Yes.'

She stares at us with a baffled expression as BJ helps me up the steps. He opens the door and we enter our silent home.

'Do you want to lie down for a bit, babe?' he asks me.

I nod. 'Yes, that's a good idea. But can I have a glass of water first?'

'Of course.' He seems glad to be of use. I watch him stride away towards the kitchen. Thank god it is Nora's, my housekeeper, day off. I couldn't bear to see anyone else. BJ comes back with a glass of water and I drink it all and give him the empty glass. He puts it on the nearest surface and comes back to me.

We climb the stairs together. When we reach the bed a great exhaustion swamps me and I sit heavily on the mattress. He crouches down and gently takes my shoes off. I look down at him, at the way his luxurious eyelashes sweep down to his cheeks, and a crazy, totally inappropriate thought pops into my head. I want to have sex with him. For a second there is intense guilt and then the consoling thought. It's not crazy. It's just instinct. My body has no intellect of its own. Every time it's near him, it just wants to copulate.

I close my eyes and let the instinct slink away in shame. Tenderly he kisses my palms and closed eyelids. Then he stands up and I lie down. Quietly, he covers my body with the duvet.

'Thank you,' I say.

He nods gravely, draws the curtains closed and leaves the room, closing the door behind him. I hear him hesitate outside the door, then take a few steps, stop, come back to the door. But, after a pause, he goes downstairs.

I lie on the bed and stare at the ceiling in disbelief. My mind turns round and round desperately, like a rat in cage, trying to find a way out. There must be another way. Slowly my hands cup my belly. I hear BJ climb the stairs. I put my hands down and turn to my side, facing away from the door, and close my eyes.

He comes in and stands over me.

He knows I am awake. I feel him sit on the bed. 'I love you, Layla. Whatever happens I love only you. You're my life. Without you nothing else matters.' His voice breaks, but I don't open my eyes. Tears slip out of my closed eyelids.

'I'm going out now. There are things I need to sort out, but I'll be back in an hour. Just rest, OK?'

He kisses my head and then I hear his footsteps run down the stairs. I know then that he has made his decision, and he can live it. And now he is doing everything in his power to facilitate that decision. I wait until I hear the front door close before I get up. I walk out of our bedroom and turn right, heading to the nursery.

I open the door, seeing the cot that Lily and I bought, and the full horror of my situation hits me. My knees give way and I slump to the ground outside my baby's room. My arms pull tight across my body, as if I am cold. I realize that I am actually in a strange, dreaming state. It feels as if my heartbeat has slowed down.

In that oddly still moment, I remember my mother taking me to a tarot reader as a small child. As if it had happened yesterday, I clearly and distinctly remember her telling my mother, 'I cannot read her cards now, Mara. Her destiny is special. A great sacrifice will be asked of her. If I am still alive then, I will read her cards for her.'

Even as a small girl I had picked up her sense of unease and dread, reverberating on a level beyond language, beyond what is cognitive. I didn't even need to understand her to feel it.

'What do you mean?' my ma had asked.

But she would say no more.

I stumble down the stairs and find my purse. I root around in it with trembling hands and find my mobile phone. Taking a deep breath, I call my mother.

'Ma,' I say into the phone. It is shocking how level and even I manage to keep my voice. A few hours ago, I wouldn't have understood how anyone could appear unmoved when they are dying inside. Now I know. The cold, hard part of me has detached itself enough to be able to function without the rest of me. Appearing unmoved is the price you pay for being able to speak at all.

'Ah, I was just about to call you,' my mother says cheerfully.

'Why?'

'I'm in a shop and I've seen the cutest little coats you've ever seen. I'm getting a pink one for our Liliana. Shall I get a blue one for Tommy as well?'

It is like a body blow. The only way to deal with it is talk about something crazy. 'Why are you calling him Tommy, Ma?'

'BJ told me that both of you had decided on that name.'

An involuntary smile escapes my stiff features. Oh, BJ. How sly you are.

'Have you changed your mind then?' my mother asks.

'No. No, we haven't. We are going with Tommy. Yeah, get the blue coat for him,' I tell her.

'All right, I will. What did you call me for?'

'I wanted the phone number of that tarot card reader you always go to. I've forgotten her name.'

'Queenie, you mean?'

'Yeah, that's the one.'

'I'll text her number to you. Do you want to go and see her then?'

'Yes.'

'We can go together if you want.'

'No, Ma. I was planning on seeing her today.'

'Is anything wrong?'

'No. Nothing is wrong. Just wanted to ask her something.'

'She should be free now. She doesn't work on Mondays. Too quiet on the pier. I'll text her number to you now. Speak to you later tonight.'

'Thanks, Ma.'

The text comes through and I call Queenie and make an appointment to see her in an hour and a half. Then I send BJ a text message.

Got 2 run an errand.
Will go directly 2 Silver
Lee after that. Call u
when I get there. xx

I switch off my mobile, input Queenie's address into my GPS, and drive my car to her trailer park. I'm there in less than an hour. I get out of the car and begin to walk.

The body remembers what the mind will not. My legs move confidently forward. My muscles and sinew know exactly where she lives. They always knew that one day I would be returning again to see the woman who could look into the future. She opens the door in her flowery housecoat. She is so small and shrunken. She is nothing like I remember.

'Poor child. So soon you have been asked for your sacrifice,' she says sadly.

My chin begins to tremble.

She steps aside and I enter her trailer. She bids me to sit.

'What do you want of me?' she asks.

'Read my cards.'

THIRTY-THREE

Layla

Frogs in my belly devour what is bad.
Frogs in my belly show the evil the way out!
                                    - Old gypsy witches' chant

By the time I arrive at Silver Lee, BJ's car is already parked in the forecourt. He comes tearing out to meet me, his hair tousled as if he has been running his hands through it and his eyes stormy with worry.

'Where have you been?' he demands.

I should feel guilty but I don't. The cold, hard part of me is still in charge. 'I went to see a friend of my mother.'

He stares at me in disbelief. 'What the fuck, Layla? I've been so worried. You switched off your phone. I didn't know how to reach you.'

'I'm sorry. I just needed a bit of time to think.'

'We need to talk.'

I put my hand out, the palm facing him. 'Not today.'

He opens his mouth to object and I say, 'Please, BJ. Tomorrow. We'll talk tomorrow.'

He looks at me warily. 'We *have* to talk. It's not going to go away, Layla.'

'One more day is not going to a make a difference,' I cry.

'All right. All right. Tomorrow. But it cannot be any later than tomorrow.'

'Thank you, BJ.' I look down at myself. 'I feel a bit grubby. I think I'll just have a shower first.'

He looks at me intently, but I ignore the look, I walk up to him and standing on tip-toes kiss him gently on the mouth before I go into the house. He stands where I have left him, staring after me with confusion.

'Hello, Layla,' Marcel calls cheerfully from the kitchen.

'Hey, Marcel,' I greet and go up the stairs.

I shower quickly, dress, and go downstairs. BJ is standing with his back to me looking out of the open windows. In one hand he is holding a glass of something amber, in the other a cigarette. An open bottle of Scotch is standing on the table. Its top is carelessly tossed on the table. I am wearing flat, soft-soled slippers and he has not heard me come down. For a moment I watch him. He's totally lost in thought, his powerful shoulders hunched forward and tense.

'I've never seen you drink Scotch before.'

He whirls around, his eyes narrowed, and running over me like water. 'Yeah, I needed something for my nerves.' He takes a long drag of his cigarette and kills it in the ashtray sitting on the window ledge. He straightens and looks at me. 'Do you want a glass of something?' he asks slowly.

I blink. There is a sharp pain in my heart. I haven't even had a sip of anything alcoholic since I found out I was pregnant and he has never offered before today.

We stare at each other.

'I'll have a glass of white wine,' I say softly.

He goes to the bar, selects a bottle from the fridge and pours me a glass.

I take it. Our hands touch, a spark runs through me.

Watching him over the rim of the wineglass, I take a sip. It feels cold on my tongue, but it doesn't taste too good. Perhaps I am not in the mood for it.

He picks up his own glass, taking a swallow, and looks at me with deliberately blank eyes. 'Want to tell me what you did this afternoon?'

I sit down on the sofa behind me. 'I went to see my mother's tarot reader.'

'Right,' he says carefully. 'What did she tell you?'

'Not much. Nothing that would help, anyway.' I stare down at the floor

'We'll have other children, Layla. I promise.'

My head shoots up and my eyes are stern. 'I don't want to discuss it today. Please, BJ.'

'Fine.' There is a note of frustration in his voice.

I put my glass of wine down on the coffee table and clasp my hands.

'Shall we go for a walk?' BJ asks.

'Yes, let's.'

We don't walk far. Both of us turning back as soon as we reach the end of the lane that leads into the forest. When we come back, dinner is ready and we eat it—well, push it around our plates—on the roof terrace in strained silence. Afterwards, we go upstairs, fuck like animals, and fall asleep entwined in each other's arms.

The last thing I hear is his voice whispering in my ear, 'God, if anything ever happened to you.'

I wake up in the early hours of the morning. One of the windows is open and a light breeze is coming in. Very quietly I get out of bed, slipping my nightgown over my head as I head for the nursery. The curtains are open and it's bathed in moonlight. I open one of the tall windows and sit on the deep ledge with my legs dangling out. Down below the rose bushes are in full bloom. Their heads are so big they look like cabbages in the dark. In the distance the enormous weeping willow is very still. Its sad branches trailing on the ground.

I hear a noise behind me. I don't turn around.

'Can't sleep?' he asks.

I shake my head. He comes and stands behind me and I feel the heat from his body.

'I don't think I like you sitting on the ledge like that. You could fall.'

I look up at him. In the moonlight his face looks like it is carved out of mahogany.

'I won't,' I tell him quietly.

He sits next to me, but faces the room. I turn my head and look into his eyes.

'It's already tomorrow. We need to talk, Layla.'

'OK, let's talk.'

'We need a second opinion. I've made an appointment tomorrow afternoon with a specialist, an oncologist. He's the best in England.'

'I see.'

'If he confirms the diagnosis then we'll go ahead with the termination immediately and begin your treatment.'

I drop my head.

'Layla?'

I look up. 'And you're all right with us never having children?'

He does not hesitate. 'Yes.' His voice is very clear.

'I'm not,' I say.

'Then we will adopt. There are enough children around crying out for a good home.'

He has everything figured out. I touch his dear face. 'I'm not terminating the baby, BJ.'

THIRTY-FOUR

Layla

He becomes still under my hand. 'What the fuck are you talking about?'

I take my hand away from his face and hug myself. 'I'm not giving up my baby. He's perfectly healthy and it's not fair that he should lose his life just because I am ill.'

He stands suddenly and begins to pace. I retract my legs and turn to face him. He stops in front of me. His face is pale. There's a white line around his lips. He is furious. He looks like he wants to shake me.

'You don't seem to get it. If you have this baby you're going to die, Layla.'

'Could die,' I correct.

He throws his hands up in disbelief. 'Were you not in the doctor's office with me? Did you not hear the terminology he used? Aggressively malignant. A risk not worth taking. Placental abruption. Pregnancy will not survive.'

'Then let it terminate on its own. Murdering my own child goes against every instinct and belief I have. I couldn't do that and carry on living.'

He is so shocked he takes a step back. 'Jesus, Layla. This is not murder. It's a fetus, yet unborn. It has no concept of being alive. It only exists. You on the other hand are alive and loved by so many people, living a charmed life.'

'Are you telling me that life can go on being charmed for me after I kill my child? Can you promise that I won't wake up in a cold sweat in the middle of the night because I've heard my baby crying? Or that for the rest of my life I won't be wondering what he would have grown up to be?'

He stares at me in open-mouthed horror.

'How will I ever stop mourning for my innocent child if I am the one who caused his death? It will be a bloody stain on my soul.'

'In that case, you don't need to make this decision. I will. Let it be a stain on my soul.'

I stand up and walk to him. 'This baby belongs to us, but at this moment it is in my body, and I'll defend it to my last breath.'

'Do you really believe that this child will grow up happy knowing that it killed its own mother?'

'No, he will grow up feeling that his mother loved him so much she gave up her life so that he could live. What a beautiful thought to carry through life. What richness!'

'I cannot believe what you are saying. You're really are just a spoilt child who wants what she wants, after all. Damn the consequences for everyone else,' he accuses brutally.

I shake my head. 'Yes, it's true that all my life, I've been spoilt and given everything I've ever wanted. All I had to do was ask for it and it appeared. And I lived like a princess, untouched by suffering, never giving more than a passing thought to all the misery in this world: the starving children in Africa, the wretched Palestinians in the Gaza strip, the pitiful child slaves in China who make my fashionable trainers, and the countless abuses that goes on in this big, unfair world. But, you see, I've never been asked to make a difference. I never even thought I could. This is the first time I am being asked. I know it's a big ask, but I'm up to it.'

'Who do you think you are now? Fucking Buddha?'

'I don't think that. I just know this baby came to me. And I'm not killing it.'

'So you're going to let it kill you instead?' he asks.

'It's not written in stone that I'll die if I have this baby. Doctors can be wrong. I'm going to do everything in my power to be well.'

'And how are you going to do that?' he snaps.

'I'm going to take all the holistic measures I can to keep the cancer at bay until the baby is big enough to survive outside my body. While Lily was pregnant I found out a lot from her about eating well and how the right foods and herbs can cure and keep at bay so many diseases. And during Lily's confinement period, I learned even more from her grandmother.'

'This is pure madness. You're talking about using herbs to fight cancer!'

'Don't twist my words. My plan is more far reaching than you are making it out to be.'

'I won't let you, Layla.'

'You can't stop me, BJ. No one can. My mind's made up.'

'What if this was happening to me? How would you feel then?'

I frown. I had not given it a thought. 'To be honest, I would probably react the way you are, but the thing is, I'm not you. I'm me, Layla. The only person this baby has fighting its corner. He chose me to be his mother. To live inside me until he is able to survive in this world on his own, and I'm not turning my back on him.'

'I don't want this baby without you,' he snarls suddenly.

Both my hands rush to cover my stomach protectively, as if he has administered a blow to my unborn child.

He shakes his head sadly. 'I couldn't love him, Layla. Not if he kills you. Every time I'd see him, I'd know you're not here because of him.'

I smile. 'You know what, I'm not afraid you won't love him. You will. Because he is a part of you and me.'

He closes his eyes. When he opens them they are pained. 'I'm sorry, but I can't do this, Layla. Other men may be able to do it because they don't love their wives the way I love you. I just can't. I can't stand by and watch you throw your life away, not even my own child. I can't choose him over you. I can't. I just can't. And you can't fucking ask me to.'

'All we have to do is hold on for another three months. Actually, it's not even three months. It's only 77 days before he will be 25 weeks and can be safely delivered via cesarean section.'

'You don't have three months. Don't you get what aggressively malignant means? It would have eaten into you by then. You need to cut it out now or it will be too late.'

'I *know* I can hold on for 77 days. We'll make a calendar and cross the days off together, OK?'

He looks up to the ceiling and exhales. 'Don't try and pacify me, Layla. You can't. I feel all torn up. I couldn't care for this child ... not without you. You'll be giving birth to an orphan.'

I put my finger on his lips. 'Shhh ... don't speak anymore. I want to call our baby Tommy.'

He buries his head in his hands and I put my hand on his head running my fingers through the silky black hair.

'I hope he has black hair,' I whisper.

He says nothing.

'I hope he looks like you.'

His body jerks.

'I love you, BJ.'

He looks up at me bitterly. 'Fuck you, Layla.'

'I love you, BJ.'

'With a love like yours, I don't need enemies,' he cries in an anguished voice, and strides out of the room.

I hear him run down the steps, then the front door slams. I turn to the window and see him rush towards his car. He opens his car door and suddenly looks up at me. We stare at each other. He drags his eyes away, slamming his car door and speeding away, the wheels spinning on the gravel.

I sit on the windowsill to wait for him.

It seems as if ages pass. I am sitting with my head leaning against the glass when I hear the powerful roar of his car. He parks, looks up to the window, sees me, and begins to run. I hear him take the steps three maybe four at time. He bursts through the door and crossing the room takes me into his arms.

'You're freezing,' he says. His voice throbs with emotion.

'I was waiting for you.'

'What did that tarot reader say to you?'

I lift my face away from his chest. 'She said I was born holding three lives in my hand. Mine, the baby's, and yours.'

'I love you more than life itself, so I am telling you now, I'll do everything in my power to stop you from having this baby.'

THIRTY-FIVE

Layla

'Layla, of course, we're all utterly and completely torn up about the baby, but we simply can't let you do this. You can't expect us to. We love you. You can't do this to us, to BJ,' Jake says gently.

I look at them one by one: my mother, Jake, Dominic, and Shane. For the last hour and a half they have taken turns, alternately shouting, coaxing, wheedling, and threatening to force me to change my mind. At different times, they have all looked at me as if I have gone completely crazy. Maybe I am crazy. All I know is that Tommy came to me, and asked me to be his mother. I agreed and I'm not going back on my word.

'I'm not changing my mind. You can either help me by finding out all the ways I can naturally hold the cancer at bay for the next 76 days or you can just stand by and watch me do it alone,' I repeat my stand again.

I look at them all calmly.

Jake shakes his head in disbelief, throwing his arms up into the air and striding off angrily. I know he will be back. Jake doesn't give up easy, but I *have* won this round.

As ever, it is soft-hearted Dominic who cracks first. 'All right. I will help you. Tell me what you want me to do and I'll do it.'

Gratefully, I rush to him and hug him tightly. 'Thank you. Thank you so much, Dom. You don't know what this means to me,' I say, tears stinging my eyes.

Next to capitulate is Shane. I squeeze both his hands. But my mother just sits there like a statue, tears pouring down her face.

'Leave me for a bit with Ma,' I tell my brothers. They leave the room silently and close the door.

I don't talk to my mother. I go and sit next to her, hold her hands, and look into her eyes. And suddenly we start crying. Both of us just weeping.

'How could this happen to you?' she sobs. 'You're my baby. Without you there is no joy in this family.'

'Then help me beat this,' I choke back.

'How?'

I wipe my eyes. 'I've already done a bit of research on the net this morning, but I'm going to do more. The plan is to keep myself so healthy that the cancer cannot advance at any great speed. I only have to keep it at bay for 76 days,' I tell her passionately.

I see a trembling ray of hope shine into my mother's eyes. '76 days?'

I nod. 'Just 76 days, Ma. That's not much to give up for a whole baby, is it?'

My mother covers her mouth with her hand and shakes her head.

I sigh with relief.

She uncovers her mouth. 'I'm so proud of you, Layla. You've really grown up good.'

I could have gone home and done my research there on my on laptop, but I want to include her, so we go upstairs to the desktop computer that she never uses and pour over cancer research together. We stay clear of allopathic treatments or websites that don't have any endorsement by serious doctors or researchers. In two hours, we've printed reams and reams of research material. We split the papers into two piles. Ma takes one and I take the other.

It is nearly lunchtime when I lift my head from the article I am studying. BJ is waiting for me at home. For as long as I can remember, my mother has always stood in the kitchen surrounded by food when I left the house. Today, she is wearing her reading glasses and the kitchen table is full of papers.

I look at my mother and I feel a great sadness. I pull myself together. I cannot afford, even for a second, to reflect on or question my decision. It will bring fear into my body and sap away my strength.

'Bye, Ma,' I say, kissing the top of her head.

She grabs me, hugs me tightly, and follows me out of the house. Her forlorn figure waves to me from the front door.

THIRTY-SIX

Layla

"Let food be thy medicine and medicine be thy food."
— Hippocrates, recognized as
the father of modern medicine

I arrive home and find BJ up on the roof terrace. He glances at me and carries on staring out at the landscape.

'Hey,' I say and sit beside him.

'Hey yourself,' he replies. There is something in his voice that makes me turn and look at him closely.

'What have you been up to?' I ask.

He kicks at something by his feet and an empty bottle of Scotch rolls out and hits the table leg.

'I see.'

'I've confirmed the appointment for the scan and biopsy tomorrow at nine in the morning,' he says.

'I'm not going.'

'Yeah? Why not?' His voice is vaguely aggressive, as if he is just getting started.

'Because there is no point, is there? All that will happen is they'll confirm what Dr. Freedman said and increase the chances of the pregnancy terminating.'

'Jesus, this just gets worse and worse,' he mutters furiously.

I touch his arm. 'BJ? Remember when you said you'd do anything for me?'

He closes his eyes, the anger dying out of him.

'I really need you to do something for me now.'

He opens his eyes. They are so black they are like holes in his sad face. 'I want to tell you something,' he says quietly.

'OK.'

He looks at me, his face twisted with bitterness. 'It's not going to be pretty.'

I don't speak. It is as if the air is made of the most delicate glass, cold and breakable. I feel scared. There is already so much on my plate and I am afraid I will not be able to cope with whatever he is going to tell me. My head inclines so slightly it's almost not perceptible.

'I've never told anyone. I don't even allow myself to think it.'

I stare at him, hardly daring to breathe.

'Do you want to know why I fight? Why I used to be so goddamn crazy in the pit that I almost killed a man once?'

I remember the way he had attacked his opponent in the pit. It was vicious and merciless. A light breeze ruffles his hair and drops it to his forehead. His eyes are vulnerable and defenseless. Yes, I can handle anything about him. Anything. I nod.

'At my birth, my mother was incorrectly told to push before she was fully dilated. It ruptured her cervix and she lost the ability to ever again carry a child to full term. After that, she lost four children: A boy at 18 weeks, a set of twins—a boy and a girl—at 22 weeks, and another girl at 21 weeks. There were others that fell out as lumps of blood in the toilet. It ruined her life.'

I shiver at the thought.

'My father had a smile identical to mine. Everybody thought so. They also thought he was the perfect father. No one knew that he blamed me for the deaths of my siblings, or that he often battered me senseless.'

I stare at him in shock.

He smiles bitterly. 'Yup. He had hands like raw meaty hunks. Broke my jaw twice, he did. He claimed he was toughening me up, but I think he enjoyed it. Abusing me was entertainment for him. I understood what he wanted early on. He wanted to see me cry. I'd be screaming inside, but I never cried. I kept it all inside. All the rage. All the pain. All the hurt.'

'Oh, BJ,' I gasp.

'From the time I was fifteen, I'd walk around looking for a fight. I'd walk into a bar or a club, and all it took for the rage to take over, for me to send a guy to the hospital, was a wrong look. Any provocation, no matter how small or insignificant, was enough to fill my guts with fury. I was a ticking time bomb.

'It poisoned my bloodstream. Every once in a while I had to let it out in a safe environment. Like a bloodletting. Stress relief. Every victory in the pit was a victory of my vulnerable, younger self over my father.'

I frown with confusion. 'Then why did you tell me you trusted your father?'

'I did. I trusted him to hurt me. He showed me the face that no one else saw.'

'And your mother. Did she know?'

'She knew. There was nothing she could do, but pretend. We both pretended.'

'What happened to you is absolutely horrific, but why do I sense that you're linking it with our child?'

'I'm the spitting image of my father. I'm gonna batter that boy, Layla. I'm not going to be able to help it.'

I freeze. 'You're *not* your father,' I whisper.

'You don't know that. Even I don't know what's inside me. His brutality created a monster.'

'Oh my great, big hero, my heart, my love, you're not your father. You'll never be him. I don't have even a second of worry that you'll batter our Tommy. Not for one second. Your father was a monster. I know you're not.'

He drops his gaze. 'I don't love this life enough to stay on without you. If you go, I want to go with you.'

I crouch in front of him. 'Listen to me. I don't plan to go anywhere. I really think I can do it. Other people have. I've been on the Internet all morning with Ma doing research. I've found out that people are fighting their cancers by all kinds of methods.'

He looks at me and I see how much he wants to believe me, but he is afraid to take the risk. He wants to take the riskless path.

'Cancer is not a disease I caught from dirty water or someone else. My own body made it. So even if they cut it all out, if I live in exactly the same way I have been doing until now, my body is going to make it again.'

'I feel so fucking helpless.'

I smile softly. 'Well, you're not as helpless as you think.'

He looks at me curiously.

'This is going to make you laugh, but you know how I said I wanted you to get out of the drug business? Well, looks like I'm going to need you to get back into it. I need you to supply me with marijuana.'

His eyes widen.

'I need the fresh leaves and buds. And I need loads.'

He frowns. 'For what?'

'Apparently the marijuana leaf is a highly medicinal substance. Besides being antioxidant, anti-inflammatory, and neuro-protective, it possesses an anti-cancer nutrient compound known as cannabinoid. Cannabinoid is capable of many wonders, but the most exciting thing about it, is its ability to normalize cell communication within the body. It bridges the gap of neurotransmission in the central nervous system and brain by providing a two-way system of communication, a positive feedback loop. So for people like me, whose systems are compromised by rogue cancer cells, a positive feedback loop can be established.'

'So you're going to be high the whole time.'

I shake my head. 'No, heat is needed to convert the THCA element of raw cannabis into THC, which creates the high. I'm going to juice raw marijuana leaves and buds and eat salads of hemp sprouts.'

'I really want to believe that raw cannabis is going to cure you, but I have to say, it sounds really far-fetched.'

'First off, marijuana is only one of the things in a whole host of measures that I will be taking. Cancer cells need an acidic environment to grow. So I'm also going to keep my system alkaline. And I'm going to cut out GMOs and pesticides, go vegetarian, completely cut out stress, etcetera. Here, look at this.' I open my bag, flicking through the papers to find the article I am looking for and put it into his hand. He looks at it eagerly.

'Check this out,' I say. 'Even though US federal government officials consistently deny that marijuana has any medical benefits, the government actually holds patents since October 2003 for 26 methods using cannabinoids as antioxidants and neuroprotectants.' I point my finger at the paper and say, 'See, US Patent 6630507?'

He looks up at me, almost believing, but not quite.

I grab both his hands. 'You have to believe me. I can do this.'

He sighs heavily.

'Even people suffering from end-stage cancer have benefited,' I say.

'OK, Layla. OK. I'll get the marijuana for you.' He stares at me. 'And I'll join you in your new diet.'

'Oh, my darling. You don't have to do that. You'll hate it. My diet will be filled with alfalfa grass, sprouts, kefir, and all manner of horrible stuff.'

'What the hell is kefir?'

'It's an organism that you put in milk to sour it and turn it into a probiotic food.'

He winces at the thought.

I laugh. 'Hey. I don't need you to go on the diet with me. I need you to eat what you want and be happy. When you are happy, I feel happy. And when I'm happy my body is happy.'

'So. You're gonna cook separately for me?'

'Why not? My food is going to be mostly raw anyway.'

'But you'll have to smell my food.'

'So what?'

He nods slowly. 'No. I wanna do the diet with you.'

'It won't make any difference to me.'

'It'll make a difference to me. We eat the same or I don't eat at all.'

'OK.' And I have to blink back the tears.

THIRTY-SEVEN

BJ

This morning I watched her tick the box on our calendar that held the sacred information: 60 days left. She turned to me bright and so full of hope. So I went to work. I called her a few times. She seemed fine. But when I return home at 7:00, she is in bed.

I rush to her. 'What's wrong?'

'It's nothing. Just a twinge.'

'What kind of a twinge?'

'It's normal. Even Lily used to get little twinges and stuff. Don't worry, the baby is OK,' she reassures.

I lose it then. She mistakes my expression of blind rage for fear. 'Don't worry, darling. There'll probably be many more such days.'

'What the fuck is the matter with you?' I roar. 'How can you do this to yourself?'

Taken aback by my fury, she tries to fluff over the utter madness of what she is doing. 'Darling,' she says. 'I'm all right. Really. I'm only lying in bed to ease the stress on my cervix.'

'Of course you are. Obviously, you don't want to go to the hospital and get a real doctor's opinion.'

She shifts. 'No, I don't.'

'That's just great,' I throw at her. In complete despair, I leave the house. I hear her call out to me, but what's the fucking point? She's just going to explode my head with more nonsense.

I get into the car, start the engine, and drive blindly. In the end, I find myself driving to one of Dominic's clubs. The valet jumps into my car and radios the staff in the reception. They wave me through. At reception there are more wide smiles, and of course, there is no entrance fee for me to pay. A pretty girl lifts the curtain and I enter Heat Exchange. The housemother comes towards me with a large smile.

'We haven't seen you for a while,' she says softly. 'We've had a really nice blonde girl join us. Anastasia is Russian. Beautiful body.'

I nod and she leads me towards a booth. It is early and there is hardly anybody in it. A girl is on stage gyrating. She has long dark hair. Something about her reminds me of Layla. I quickly look away.

I sit in the booth. A waitress comes. 'The usual?' she asks.

'No. Get me a bottle of rum.'

'Of course.'

A blonde girl, obviously Anastasia, sashays towards me. She is bite-your-arm-off beautiful and there is only one way to describe her body. Roger Rabbit's girlfriend's statuesque. She stops in front me and strikes a pose to show her body to its full advantage.

'Hey, big boy,' she says throatily.

'Hello.'

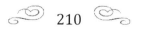

'You want a dance?'

'Sure,' I say and put a twenty pound note on the table and push it a few inches away from me.

She smiles, takes it, and pushes it into her garter. And then she starts dancing. At first keeping her distance and then getting closer and closer until her breasts are either a hair's breath away from me or accidentally brushing me. She times her five minutes with precision.

'Do you want to buy me a drink?'

'Why not?' I signal for the waitress.

'A glass of champagne,' she tells the waitress and turns her glance back to me.

'So, you have a clubs of your own?'

I nod.

'If I need a job, I can come to you?'

'No. I don't deal with that side of the business.'

'Of course. You are too busy.'

I find I can't be bothered to talk. I let my eyes travel down her body. She gets it straight away. 'You want to go to the VIP room?' she asks.

'Sure,' I tell her. We walk to the VIP room together, Roger Rabbit's girlfriend and me, but inside I am dying.

Layla

I dream that I am bleeding, that blood is gushing out of me. I try to staunch the flow with my hand and it oozes between my fingers. I feel myself become lighter and lighter and I float out of my body. I look down at myself, a corpse. I want to reach out and touch my own body. In my dream I think, *this is what I will look like when I die.* Then I wake up. I look at the alarm clock. It is almost midnight and BJ is not home. I call his phone, but it is switched off. I leave a message and call his manager. He has not been there all night. I try all the other places he could be. No luck. So I call Jake.

'Am I disturbing you?' I ask softly.

'No. What is it?' There is a wire of panic in his voice. In the background I can hear music.

'I can't find BJ. Is he there?'

I hear the relief in his voice. 'He's not here.'

'I'm worried about him. We ... we argued. He stormed out.'

There is a moment of silence. Then Jake's voice comes on. It is calm and business like. 'I take it you've already tried all his restaurants and clubs.'

'Yes,' I reply holding the phone with both my hands.

'I think I know where he is. Don't worry. It'll be all right. I'll call you a bit later. Get some rest, OK?'

Jake Eden

I end the call and look at my phone.

'What's wrong?' Lily asks worriedly.

I turn towards her voice gratefully. God, I cannot imagine what it must be like for BJ. If it was Lily I'd have to ... I walk up to her and kiss her. 'That was Layla. BJ is MIA and she's worried, but I think I know where he is. I don't know how long this will take so don't wait up for me, OK?

'I will wait up for you.'

I smile. 'Wear something special for me.'

'You bet.'

'Right, I'm off.'

'Give him a big kiss from me,' Lily says.

'You've always liked him, haven't you?'

'Yes, I've never forgotten that he saved your life.'

I don't say anything, but memories flood back into my mind.

There is no traffic on the roads and it takes me less than an hour to drive down to the coast to where the old smuggler's network of caves are. I know BJ used to go there many years ago. Once I stumbled upon him. We were still enemies then, but he was very drunk and he offered me a drink. We shared a bottle, but he was so plastered I don't think he has any memory of that night. If he has, he's never referred to it.

As soon as I turn off the road and drive down the dirt track, I spot his vehicle. I stop the car and text Layla.

Found him. All is well. Will make sure he gets home safe.

My poor sister must have been watching the phone like a hawk. She texts back almost instantly.

Thank u from the bottom of my heart. xxxx

I take my torchlight out of my car's glove compartment and go into the mouth of the cave. It is dark and dry. My shoes sink into the soft sand. After a while, the soft sand gives way to rock and I start to hear the sound of water dripping. A few yards later I come to the flooded area of the cave. I take my shoes and socks off and rollup my pants, then wade through the water.

When I reach dry stone, I put my socks and shoes back on and walk for another ten minutes or so through the twisting tunnel. It opens out to sheer drop into the sea. BJ is sitting at the end of it. He's so heavily slumped he looks like a rock in the darkness. He has an oil lamp beside him. I switch off my torch. As far as the eye can see is the ocean. In the moonlight, it glistens like a black, oily mass. Arching over it, the sky is a blanket of stars.

I notice that he's barefoot. He must not have bothered to put his shoes back on. I sit at the edge beside him and let my feet dangle down. He is holding a bottle of rum.

'Layla was worried about you,' I say.

He passes the bottle over to me. I take a swallow and return it. He takes a swig and wedges it between his thighs.

'It's funny, isn't it? There was a time I wished I knew what it was like to be with her, even for a moment. I guess I got my fucking wish. So I can't complain too much.'

I take the bottle of rum from him and take a huge mouthful.

He turns towards me. 'If you carry on like this you won't be able to drive me back to her. That's what you're here for, isn't it?'

'That's true. That's what she wanted from me.'

'And what Layla wants, Layla gets,' he says bitterly.

I frown. 'At first I, too, wanted her to terminate the pregnancy, but now I understand that she is making a moral decision. And that is her right. I can't force her. She wants to do the right thing, the thing that she can be proud of. I didn't realize my sister was such a little hero.'

He takes another swig and stares at me bleary-eyed. 'Yeah. I know. I want to support our little hero and everything, but I can't. You see, I only ever wanted her. I cannot ever remember a time when I've wanted another. All my life, I was waiting for her. And now she wants me to give her the OK to go and risk her life for a fetus that has a high probability of spontaneously miscarrying anyway. How the hell can I be expected to support that?'

'What will happen if you don't support her and ... something happens?'

He makes a sound. A grunt of deep pain. 'Something? Define something.'

I remain silent. It's impossible to say the words.

'Here's a question for you, then. What if it was Lily this was happening to?'

I grab the bottle and glug down so fast I have a coughing fit. BJ thumps me on the back. 'Well, that's no way to answer the question.'

I look him in the eye. 'At first, I thought I'd rather tear that baby with my own hands than let it destroy Lily. But a baby is a miracle, BJ. And if Lily wanted it, even if it killed me, I'd support her. I'd do whatever it took to ensure that she got the best holistic support. I'd have the best doctors in the world waiting in the wings, weeks in advance, to pull that baby out of her.'

'Ah yes, pain is inevitable. Suffering is optional. Smile through da pain.'

'You've got to get your shit together man. Layla needs you like never before.'

'Never in a million years did I ever think I would be in this situation. I feel like a mastodon dying from hundreds of crude spears in my flesh.'

'Come on. Let's get you back.'

He stands and sways slightly before righting himself against the wall of the cave, then turns to go.

'BJ,' I call.

He turns to face me. He's so broken. He looks nothing like the great fighter I once faced. At that moment I realize that he might not be able to survive without Layla. I had been wrong about him. He truly loves my sister.

'I'm sorry I made you have the commitment ceremony,' I say.

'I didn't do it for you.'

He picks up the lamp and starts moving into the dark passage. With a sigh, I follow him.

THIRTY-EIGHT

Layla

Maddie asks me to lunch and we arrange to meet in an Italian restaurant half-way between both our workplaces. I arrive first and am sitting with a bottle of mineral water when she walks through the door. She does not smile when her eyes meet mine. Not even as she slips into the chair opposite me.

'How are you?' she asks.

'I'm fine,' I say, surprised by her unfriendly demeanor.

'Yeah?' Her jaw is clenched, and her tone is an inch away from downright hostility.

I don't react to it. 'Yeah. I'm all right. I'm not in pain or anything like that.'

'Really?'

'Yes, really,' I say, knowing that she is brewing towards some kind of confrontation.

'Well, you're the lucky one, then. Because I'm in pain, and I bet you've got poor BJ bleeding his heart out.'

I stare at her in astonishment.

Her eyes stab at me angrily. 'I never thought I'd say this but you're so cruel, Layla. How could you do this to all of us?' She takes a shuddering breath before carrying on. 'We love you so much, and there you are giving it all up for a … a … fucking fetus. It doesn't love you like we do. Fuck, it doesn't even feel.'

I sense myself start to crumble inside. My defenses are weak. Everyday I am fighting to keep it all together when all I want to do is weep. Because I'm the one who could lose everything.

Blindly, I reach for a packet of breadsticks and tear it open. All around us are the civilized, muted sounds of cutlery against plates, conversation, laughter, and piped music.

Don't cry, Layla. Just don't do it.

I pull a stick out and bring it to my mouth, but my body doesn't want it. One part of me says it is full of preservatives another part simply feels too sad to even pretend to eat. No one truly understands. Not Ma, not Jake, not BJ, and now, not even Maddie. Tears are stinging at the backs of my eyes. I blink them away, and place the breadstick back on the pristine tablecloth so it is almost perfectly aligned with the knife.

'Cruel,' I whisper, my eyes fixed on the knife.

'Yes, cruel,' Maddie repeats vehemently. Her voice is strong, indignant, and throbbing with moral righteousness.

I raise my eyes. 'I'm not cruel, Maddie. You know what is cruel? This world is cruel. Fate is cruel. The God that decided that I should have a malignant cancer growing in my womb at the same time as my baby is cruel. And I'll tell you what else is cruel. Asking me to kill my own baby is cruel.'

But Maddie is unmoved. 'We all have to make horrible decisions. Our politicians kill hundreds of totally innocent people everyday in the Middle East and just call it collateral damage. A fetus is not even a proper person,' she cries passionately.

'Is it right? Shall I do it just because they do it?'

'No.' She stops a moment to change tack. 'Doesn't your great love for BJ count for more than this unborn fetus?'

'Love is love. You don't understand. It's the little and unimportant things that give a person away. They call it the waitress test. You can always tell a person by the way he or she treats a waitress. And that's because the waitress stands for someone who has no future value to you. If I claim to love this baby, then what I do to it will ultimately decide how I will love and treat BJ. How much I will be willing to sacrifice for him if he needed me to?'

'I don't want you to die,' she wails suddenly, her eyes suddenly brimming with tears.

'Oh Maddie,' I sigh, and reach out for her hand. Her hand is cold and limp. I grasp it strongly. 'This is not a death sentence. I am taking a calculated risk. Something we take everyday without knowing we are. I could get struck by lightning while I am sleeping in my bed, or get run over while I am crossing the road, or get shot while I am in a cinema by a man who is drugged up to his eyeballs with psychotic drugs.'

Maddie sniffs but she is listening intently to me.

'It may sound like I am being careless, but I am not. I promise you, I'm not. I am going by the findings of the Nobel prize winner, Sir MacFarlene Burnet, who said cancer cells are not foreign bodies. They are defective, mutated cells produced in the hundreds by our bodies. In a normal immune system they are naturally and quickly destroyed. The problem arises when our immune system is compromised, and does not trigger an attack on these rogue cells. So a tumor is not a problem, but a symptom of a failing immune system.'

I take a deep breath. This explanation is as important for me as it is for her.

'Therefore, I'm going to the source of problem. I am going to fix my immune system so it will do the job that it is designed to do. I truly believe the body has powerful healing abilities of its own.'

I gently stroke Maddie's hand and smile sadly at her. 'I love you Maddie. Always.'

Tears start flowing from her eyes. She doesn't attempt to wipe them away.

'Besides Maddie, you know me, I won't roll over and let anybody tell me that this is how it is, and I can never change it. The statistics are clear. Less people die of cancer than of cancer treatments.'

'I was so sad, I could not sleep last night, Layla.'

I bite my lip trying to think of something I can say to make it better. 'Remember that time when we were kids and that really good-looking guy, what's his name again? Oh yes, Marcus, invited us to that party?'

She frowns. 'Yeah.'

'Remember you wanted to go.'

'Yeah.'

'And I didn't because my gut told me something was wrong.'

'And you were right because that party got raided and all those kids got into big trouble,' she finished slowly,

'That same instinct is telling me now to stay away from the doctor's office.'

A new look of understanding comes into Maddie's kind, dear face.

THIRTY-NINE

Layla

I look at the calendar and smile with satisfaction. I have made it to four and a half months. There are only 40 days left. The baby's heartbeat is strong, my skin is glowing, and I have more energy than I have ever had.

At times like this, I feel as if everything happens for a reason. Because this happened to me, Jake bought an organic farm and now the whole family has organic vegetables all year round.

My mother and I have learned so much about things we would never have thought to even think about. We no longer eat wheat or processed foods or anything with preservatives in it. At first it was difficult. But my mother is a culinary genius. Now she even makes ice cream using organic ingredients.

I take out the marijuana leaves that have been soaking for five minutes in water, and put them into the centrifugal juicer and switch it on. For the fifth time today I drink the concoction. I follow it with a spoonful of organic bicarbonate soda mixed in with maple syrup. It is Nora's day off and I am cooking. It's nearly time for BJ to return.

Ever since that night Jake found him in the caves and drove him home he is a completely different man. I remember I went out into the living room to meet him when I heard the car and I saw him stumble like a drunk over the threshold. But when he saw me, he took me in his arms and, as sober as a judge said, 'I love you, Layla. Use me as the rock you lean on.'

After that he was unshakeable in his support. He did everything in his power to assist me, care for me and protect me. Sometimes though, I'd catch him looking at me with a yearning expression. Then he would smile almost sadly and say, 'Sometimes I can't believe how beautiful you are.'

I have a surprise for him today. He insists on eating the same food as me, but today I have brought him a lovely steak from a grass-fed, free-range cow. I called Bertie earlier and she gave me his favorite recipe. 'Make sure you put a knob of butter at the very end. It gives a beautiful rich taste to the meat.'

When I hear his car drive up, I heat the skillet and add a drop of oil. I drain the water from the potatoes and begin to mash them. I lay the meat on the hot metal. The sizzle is terrific. I add butter and milk and lightly mix them into the mashed potatoes as BJ walks through the door.

'Wow! Something smells good,' BJ says coming towards me. He nuzzles my neck. 'And that's not even taking the steak into the mix.'

I laugh.

'So what's with the steak?'

'It's for you,' I say simply.

'I told you. We're both eating the same food.'

'Just this once. I've gone to all the trouble.' I untangle myself from his arms, go to turn the meat and drop in some crushed garlic in the potatoes.

He watches me with folded arms.

'Go on. Sit down.' He sits at the table. It's set with salad and his drink. He takes a sip. I put the knob of butter into the pan and shake it slightly. My mouth actually begins to water. I haven't had meat in so long. I pull the pan off the fire to let the meat rest and begin to plate up. The mashed potatoes go underneath, with the sliced steak resting on top. I carry the plate to the table and put it in front of BJ.

I sit next to him. '*Bon appetito*.'

He watches me pick up my fork and dip it into my salad of greens, sprouts, seeds, avocado, and tomatoes. Then he sets half his meat onto my plate.

I look up at him. I am so tempted. I can smell it and my stomach is growling. 'I'm not really supposed to,' I say.

'It's just a tiny bit. It won't hurt you. You can have an extra helping of vitamin C or whatever tonight.'

I smile. 'OK. It is grass fed and organic. So it can't be that bad.'

We both cut a piece of meat and put it into our mouths at the same time. It melts in my mouth.

'This,' BJ says, 'is the most delicious piece of meat I have ever tasted. Other than your pussy, of course.'

I laugh, but he is right. We savor it slowly. Afterwards, we walk into the forest. In late summer it is cool and beautiful. It is quiet now, but in the bushes and undergrowth there are badgers and foxes and deer. We follow the little path towards the clearing where BJ's gardener has made a gazebo that he has covered with climbing roses. At this time of the year the roses are on their last showing. The area around it is full of petals giving off the last of their dying scent. We enter the gazebo and sit down.

It is so peaceful. For a long time we say nothing.

But there is something I want to confront him with. Something I must make BJ face. Ever since we found out about the cancer, BJ has never touched my stomach. Even when we are making love, he will avoid touching my belly. I unbutton my shirt from the bottom up and taking his hand, guide it towards my exposed belly. I feel the resistance and rigidity of his hand and look up to him beseechingly.

'Please,'

He relents and allows me to put his hand on my stomach. On contact his eyes darken. We stare into each other's eyes. Kick, Tommy, kick, I pray. There is no one else in the world but he and I. And then a kick. A hard one. We both feel it. Someone else has just entered into our world. We smile at each other. Our eyes filled with wonder.

'He's saying hello,' I say.

'Oh God!' BJ mutters suddenly.

'That's our Tommy,' I say.

'That's our Tommy,' BJ repeats, his voice choked with emotion.

He pulls the edges of my shirt across the bulge of my stomach and carefully drags the buttons through the holes.

'Come on, Princess. Let's get you and little fella home.

FORTY

Layla

"Life should be lived to the point of tears."

—Albert Camus

There are only 20 days left on my calendar. It's still dark as I descend the villa's staircase, holding on to the rough, tree trunk banisters. I cross the beautifully decorated space. It has a stunningly sculpted dining table, giant seashells hanging from the ceiling, a simple but elegant arrangement of tiles and stones and wood seals on the open windows. Soundless on my bare feet I make for the sliding doors. This is a holiday villa in Tulum, Mexico that BJ has brought me to. It used to belong to the drug lord, Pablo Escobar.

'Why Mexico?' I asked excitedly in the plane.

'It's a surprise,' he said with a smile.

And at midnight I found out. He had hired people to hang strings of blue lanterns all over the beach and a Mariachi band to play. There was a jug of non-alcoholic Margaritas on a mat on the beach.

'Don't you recognize it?' he asked.

And it hit me then. Of course, he was making my favorite song come alive. Drinking Margaritas by a string of blue lights under the Mexican sky while listening to the Mariachi playing at midnight. *Are you with me?*

I cried then.

As I walk on the white sand it flows up through my toes. I stand at the water's edge holding my belly. 'Look where we are, Tommy.' The cool morning breeze blows my hair from my face. I let the water rush up my toes and blanket my feet. It is incredibly sensuous. I am still standing there with my eyes closed when BJ comes to stand next to me. I look up at him. His eyebrows are drawn in a straight line making his face full of dark pools of shadow.

'You looked like a mermaid from the window. Something so beautiful I couldn't fathom touching,' he says softly.

I smile at him. 'Come and sit with me. It's so peaceful here.'

We walk away from the water's edge, sit on the white sand, and in perfect silence watch the sunrise together. Things are so different now. Every minute we spend together is like a precious gift. We were among the living. We had to do this. So we did it.

Red. Orange. Yellow. The sky becomes an amazing kaleidoscope of color. Next to us, there is a discarded Coke can. That, too, is life. I turn towards BJ. His face is golden, some shades of red.

'I love you, BJ.'

He leans down as if he wants to see who I am and looks deeply into my eyes.

'What is it?' I ask him.

'I was remembering that first night I found you in my bedroom.'

I grin. 'When you spanked me?'

'When you became wet?'

'You never told me. Were you hard?'

'Like a fucking rock.'

I laugh. 'Why did you come up to your room?'

'I followed you. I saw you go up with Ria. When you didn't come down, I knew that you must have found my bedroom.'

'What did you think when you saw me?'

'When I saw you stealing my tiepin?'

'Mmmm.'

'I could not believe my eyes. Layla Eden in my bedroom. And taking what didn't belong to her. All my Christmases rolled up into one.'

I shrug nonchalantly. 'I wasn't really stealing. It was mine. It had my name on it. Just like you have it across your dick.'

He laughs. 'It's fucking branded on.'

I pick up a handful of sand and let it flow through my fingers.

'Sometimes I wonder what would have happened if Ria had not asked me to use the upstairs bathroom. Would we never have got together?'

He takes my hand in his. His touch is soothing. 'I always dreamed of what it would be like to be with you. We didn't hook up by accident. I was always looking for a way to make you notice me. You had me from the day you lifted your skirt and showed me your polka dot panties.'

'I didn't lift it and show it to you,' I protest indignantly. 'I fell down.'

'That's what they all say.'

'Oh you are big-headed.'

'That's what they all say.'

'Oh!' I slap him around the head and he pushes me on the sand. The sex is gentle. The sea. The sand. The orange sky.

They were all witnesses. They would keep the memory of my love for this man if by chance I am not able. Inside my belly, Tommy kicks lustily.

Take care of Daddy, if I am not around.

FORTY-ONE

BJ

I buy her flowers and watch her stroke them as if they are hurt children she is soothing. Since that night in the caves with Jake, I don't tell her anymore how much everyday hurts. She is dying right before my eyes and there is not one damn thing I can do about it. I want to bellow. I want to howl. But it would frighten her. She looks at the calendar with joy. She is another day closer to her goal. I look at it with terror. I am another day to closer to finding out how much of her the cancer has eaten.

How much is left.

She hides things from me. I know she has written letters for Tommy. Eighteen. To be given to him on his birthdays. She gave them to her mother. I accidentally overheard her conversation. The intolerable pain of that discovery is impossible to describe. I wanted to go and fight ten men. I wanted to hurt someone the way I was hurting. I went into the bathroom and made a hole in the wall. It hurt like a mother. But it dulled the other pain.

Sometimes, when I have to share her with her family, I feel resentful. I feel as if they are stealing my time. What little is left.

I don't know how much more I can take of any of these feelings.

Everyday she makes me touch her belly. But I don't know how I feel about Tommy. He's my flesh and blood. He's mine and there is a connection, but there is no love in my heart. There is no place for him. For me there is only Layla.

I cannot love anyone else.

Not now.

Not yet.

Maybe because my heart has been ripped open and I'm bleeding. Maybe that's it.

After that night at Heat Exchange, I've never gone to a club or a strip joint. We entered the VIP room. She got out of her little dress, opened her legs wide, showed me her pussy, and asked if I wanted to touch it outside of work, and I felt nothing. Just disgust at myself. My dick was limp. I paid her and left. I knew when I walked out of that door that I had gone to the wrong place. What I was looking for could not be found in a bar or a strip club. Instead I retreated to a place where I'd found solace in the past. Somewhere I could not be found. In the darkness of the old smugglers' caves.

Bob Marley is singing, *No Woman No Cry*. The calendar reads Ten Days More. And oh yeah, its got a drawing of a happy face next to it.

FORTY-TWO

Layla

Tomorrow is the big day. Because I opted out of a biopsy that could cause me to miscarry, it will be like opening Pandora's box. They will do a biopsy on everything in my uterus to assess how bad the situation is. Immediately after, they will operate to remove the baby and perform the hysterectomy.

They don't know how long I will be out. The cesarean will only take 45 to 60 minutes. It's what needs doing after that's the unknown factor. I think I am too numb to feel afraid.

My bag is packed. It is an optimistic bag. There is chewing gum to help speed the process of bowel function returning to normal after a cesarean birth, compression stockings, sanitary towels, and a pair of champagne glasses.

How strange, then, that it feels as if I am packing never to return.

We have a quiet dinner early, as I am not allowed to eat after 8pm. I eat lightly and BJ doesn't eat at all. We talk a little. We stare at each other a lot. As if we are never going to see each other again. We end up in the bedroom. That afternoon I had taken the time to scent the place with aromatherapy oils, scented candles, and made the bed with silk sheets that I ordered from the Internet. By the bed there was tray of fruit and a big beautiful box of chocolates.

'Do you know?' he whispers to me. 'The sexual texts from The Ming dynasty regarded a woman's sexual organs as a crucible or a stove from which a man could cultivate vitality.'

'Oh, yeah,' I say biting my lower lip.

'Yeah. Want to try something Ming?' For a moment the old BJ glitters in the candlelight. Tonight he is strong and powerful and I am putty in his hands.

'OK.'

'Get totally naked, then shake your whole body; your legs, your head, and your sweet ass. Afterwards, sit down cross-legged on the bed and invite me into your body.'

So I shake my entire body, sit down, and ask him to come into me. He takes off his clothes, muscles rippling across every part of his body, and his cock standing to attention like a good soldier. He comes to sit in front of me.

'When I exhale, you inhale and vice versa. Pretend that you are able to take that breath you inhaled from me down to your sex organs.'

As he breathes out, I find myself breathing his breath into my body and down to my sex. Up so close he nearly takes my breath away. He is such a magnificent specimen.

Slowly, I become conscious that I am sharing all of me with him and he is doing the same. The realization makes my skin super sensitive, as if an electric current is running through my body.

He stares into my eyes. 'Now kiss me and share your breath with me.'

So we kiss and kiss and kiss and the strangest thing happens. I don't believe woo-woo stuff but suddenly, amongst the scent of the candles and aromatherapy oils and the silk sheet under us, we become one person. And I'm not even talking about BJ and I. I'm talking about BJ, Tommy, and I. Suddenly we are joined in a kind of magic circle. All of us linked forever. No matter what happens after tonight, we will always be together.

And then I am back in my physical body, on my hands and knees, reveling in the muscular caress of his shaft. He is like he was in the old days, before the cancer. Raw and unbelievably passionate. I feel his large hands on my body. Touching, claiming, branding. It is as it was on our very first night.

The orgasm when it comes is so shattering, so incredible, so crazy I can't even scream.

'Wow! That was so ... mind blowing,' I pant breathlessly.

He turns his raven eyes to me. 'You're mind blowing.'

'So are you going to honey talk me now?' I tease with a smile

'Why not? You are everything I could have dreamed of. You're a cool, cool girl, Layla.'

I look into his beautiful eyes. How I love this man. I take his warm, rough hands in my own. 'No matter what happens tomorrow, you know, I'll always love you.'

Something sad and dark crosses his face, but he hides it as quickly as it showed itself.

'Are you ready for your goodnight kiss?' he asks lightly.

As he has done from the day we got married, he opens my legs and lingeringly kisses me right in the middle of my sex.

'Good night, my darling,' he whispers softly into my core.

"Jump into the angry abyss with a smile on your face.
This how magic has always been created."

—Shamans

FORTY-THREE

BJ

Her eyes look like they are lit up from within and her skin is actually glowing. I remember something that scares me out of my wits. My grandmother once told me that a few hours before death the person always glows. You think they are getting better, but they are really just preparing for the final journey.

We are at the hospital. Her family is gathered outside. They have said their well wishes and now it's my turn. Only I can't say anything. I am too afraid I will break down. I can feel my insides sloshing hotly. I have never been so frightened in all my life.

'You will tell Tommy that I love him and I always will,' she says. There is slight tremor to her voice and fear in her eyes. She is just as terrified as I am.

Fuck, I can't do this. 'Fucking tell him yourself,' I say.

'Say something nice to me,' she says softly.

But I can't. If I stop being a son of a bitch I'm going to howl my eyes out. 'When you get out of here, I'm gonna fuck you so hard you're gonna need stitches.'

'I said say something nice.'

'It's hard to say something nice when you are bleeding out.'

'Oh darling.'

The nurse comes in. 'It's time,' she says.

I grab Layla's hand.

'Don't be afraid,' she whispers. 'I'm not.'

I want to cry. I want to envelop her in my arms and not let them take her away, but I let go of her hand and watch them wheel her through the swing doors. I stand there, lost and frightened in the empty room. I am so fucking frightened my breath comes out in a huge heave through my body. I feel a hand touch me. I turn around

'Come with me,' Jake says. His voice is firm and authoritative. And like a lost child I follow him outside. I feel hollow and emasculated. I let her go. She could die on the operating table.

I should have told her that she is one in a billion.

EPILOGUE

BJ

"Not to dream boldly may turn out to be irresponsible"
—George Leonard

There are fresh flowers on the grave. My mother must have visited earlier. I stand by the headstone and I feel a sense of serenity. For the first time in my life I feel at peace. There is no hate, no anger, no pain, no hurt.

All the lost jigsaw pieces of my life have come together in a brilliantly beautiful mosaic. Only now, I can see why that red piece happened, or why that blackness had to be right there, where I thought it should not be.

Now I see how perfect it all is.

There is a small ladybug on the black marble of my father's gravestone. I get down on my haunches and watch it. A gust of wind comes and it flies away. I touch the stone. It is warm from the morning sun.

I never thought the day would come when I would forgive my father. It reminds me of what a man once told me. He was a heroin addict.

'I am not to be reviled. I'm to be pitied. You have to walk in a man's shoes before you judge him,' he said.

I didn't understand him then, but I do now. I know that given the right circumstances, I could have been my father. Maybe I wouldn't have battered Tommy, but I wouldn't have loved him. Without Layla, I would have been dead inside the way my father was.

He was not to be reviled, he was to be pitied.

I turn away from the grave and walk towards the car. I have to stop by the local store and get a carton of organic milk for Layla. I haven't told you what happened, have I? They wheeled her into the operating theater to do the biopsy, only to find no tumor during the ultrasound. It had shrunk to nothing. They couldn't believe it. They probably still can't. They didn't even have to perform a Cesarean. Layla had been right all along. She never stopped believing. She made the miracle happen.

Layla carried our baby to full term.

Tommy was born a healthy, lusty baby weighing 8lb and 2 ounces. A bundle of joy.

It's a beautiful day, so I park the car and walk down the road to the corner shop.

'Coming for your milk, Mr. Pilkington?' Mr. Singh calls.

'Yup,' I say picking up a carton.

'Tell your wife, organic yogurt coming next week.'

I grin. 'That'll make her day.'

'Yes, yes, your wife very interested in organic things. She always looking for seeds. I tell her, I bring from India for her.'

'Thanks, Mr. Singh.'

'No problem.'

The bell jangles when I close the door. I light a cigarette and smoke it on the walk home. I kill it outside the front steps and chuck it into the bushes. I fit the key into the lock, open the door, and step inside.

Layla is coming down the stairs. She breaks into a smile.

'Hey,' she calls gaily and runs down the rest of the way.

I watch her approach, a sunburst in my heart. 'You look good enough to eat.'

'Never mind that now. I've got a secret to tell you,' she whispers.

'What is it?' I ask.

She giggles. 'It involves adding to the world's overpopulation problem.'

My eyes widen. I feel ten feet tall. I put the bag of milk on the floor and move closer. She smells of milk and baby powder. She starts laughing as I pick her up by her waist and whisk her into the air and whirl her. Round and round we go until we are both dizzy.

'You made me dizzy,' she says laughing.

Love is just a word until someone comes along and gives it meaning.

She. She is the meaning.

-The End –

This book is dedicated to
Gianna Beretta Molla.
Took the same decision as Layla, but did not survive.
Gianna was canonized as a saint of the Roman Catholic
Church in 2004.

"Lord, keep your grace in my heart. Live in me so your grace
be mine.
Make that I may bear everyday some flowers and new fruit."
—   Gianna Beretta Molla, 1922-1962

For the reader who is interested, here is some research to support the actions the characters in this book took to deal with cancer:

http://www.collective-evolution.com/2013/04/11/study-shows-chemotherapy-does-not-work-97-of-the-time/

http://healthland.time.com/2013/06/26/no-more-chemo-doctors-say-its-not-so-far-fetched/
http://healthland.time.com/2013/03/05/self-sabotage-why-cancer-vaccines-dont-work/

http://www.thedoctorwithin.com/cancer/to-the-cancer-patient/

http://www.bibliotecapleyades.net/salud/salud_defeatcancer.htm#Chemotherapy

Instances of people who have cured their cancers with a change in lifestyle as Layla did.

http://www.collective-evolution.com/2013/08/23/20-medical-studies-that-prove-cannabis-can-cure-cancer/

http://www.cancer.org/treatment/treatmentsandsideeffects/physicalsideeffects/chemotherapyeffects/marijuana-and-cancer

http://www.chrisbeatcancer.com/why-i-didnt-do-chemo/

Using cannabis:

http://jeffreydachmd.com/2014/04/cannabis-oil-brain-tumor-remission-jeffrey-dach-md/

https://patients4medicalmarijuana.wordpress.com/2013/04/21/24-yr-old-rejects-chemo-curing-brain-cancer-with-cannabis-oil/

http://www.dailymail.co.uk/health/article-2699875/I-cured-cancer-CANNABIS-OIL.html

Why Layla went on a pesticide free diet?

http://www.cancer.ca/en/prevention-and-screening/be-aware/harmful-substances-and-environmental-risks/pesticides/?region=on

http://www.canceractive.com/cancer-active-page-link.aspx?n=1253&Title=Pesticides%20and%20their%20links%20to%20Cancer

Why Layla juiced cannabis?

http://www.thesleuthjournal.com/20-medical-studies-proving-cannabis-cures-cancer-woman-replaced-40-medications-raw-cannabis-juice/

Why Layla went on an organic, GMO free diet?

http://www.collective-evolution.com/2014/07/15/new-study-links-gmos-to-cancer-liverkidney-damage-severe-hormonal-disruption/

https://en.wikipedia.org/wiki/Pusztai_affair

Why Layla went on an alkaline diet?

http://www.cancerisafungus.com/

http://www.canceractive.com/cancer-active-page-link.aspx?n=2719&Title=Cancer%20is%20a%20fungus

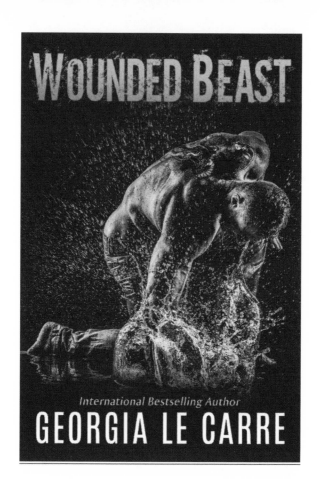

International Bestselling Author

GEORGIA LE CARRE

Wounded

Beast

Georgia Le Carre

Wounded Beast

Published by Georgia Le Carre
Copyright © 2015 by Georgia Le Carre

ISBN: 978-1-910575-17-8

ONE

Dom

Memories …
Why do you come back?
—Amit Singh, Poet

Sometimes you read a book or watch a movie and you get to that point in the story when everything is about to change forever. At this point the characters could escape and go on with their life as if nothing had happened. The moment when the hero or heroine stands in front of a closed door and decides whether to go in and face the unknown, or walk away. Once, I thought I stood at that door.

But in real life there is often more than one door.

If I hadn't called my accountant that morning, or if I had called him five minutes later when I was already in the one-way traffic system and it was impossible to turn around and go back, I would never have come across that door. But I did call him, just before I reached the point where the traffic system would have made the door disappear.

'Hey, Dom,' he says briskly.

'What time is your appointment with the parasites today?'

'They're already at the restaurant. I'm driving there right now, but I'll probably be another twenty minutes. I hope they don't start talking to the staff or snooping around.' He sounds apprehensive.

'Where are you meeting them?' I ask.

'Lady Marmalade.'

'I'm less than five minutes away. I'll go and keep the fuckers company while they wait for you,' I offer.

'No!' he shouts suddenly, so loudly it makes my eardrum vibrate like a tuning fork.

'What the fuck, Nigel!' I swear, tearing the phone away from my ear.

He calms down double quick. 'Sorry, didn't mean to shout. But please, whatever you do, don't go there.'

'Why not?'

'It's just better.'

'You think I'm scared of those pug-ugly inspectors?'

'No, no, no, I don't think that at all. I'd just really appreciate it if you didn't confront them.'

'I'm not going to confront them. I'll just pass by and offer them a cappuccino.'

I hear him take a deep breath. 'Dom. In my professional capacity I have to advise you not to make contact with them. They're dangerous. Anything you say could lead them to deepen their investigation. I know how to handle them. You don't.'

'Look. I'm already turning in to the restaurant. Tell me their names. I'll be the perfect host, I promise.'

I hear him sigh dramatically. 'It's Mr. Robert Hunter and Miss Ella Savage.'

'A woman?' I ask surprised as I switch off the ignition, open the door and step into the light summer rain.

'You don't want to underestimate her. Savage by name and savage by nature,' Nigel cautions immediately. 'She's like the Snow Queen. Beautiful and ruthless. You definitely don't want to hit on her.'

I laugh. Nigel always amuses me. I own strip clubs full of beautiful, willing women with hardly any clothes on. I'm hardly desperate enough or foolish enough to try to chat up the tax officer who has come to break my balls. Although, I kinda like the idea of taking a snooty cow down a peg or two. 'Don't mistake me for Shane,' I tell him. My younger brother Shane is the playboy of the family.

'Look, all I'm saying is don't rock the boat in any way,' he urges in frustration.

The back door of the restaurant is open, and some of my staff are lounging around smoking cigarettes under the canopy. 'Morning, boss,' they greet cheerfully, and I raise a finger in acknowledgment.

'Hang on, Nigel,' I say into the receiver and turn toward my boys. 'Are the tax officers inside?'

They nod. 'Yes, boss. Maria has already offered them coffee. They looked a bit pissed off that there was no management here to meet them. The bloke's gone to the toilet—he's been in there for the last five minutes—and the woman's waiting in the restaurant.'

I thank them and step into the washing up area of the restaurant. The dishwashers are running and it is noisy. I wait until I get to the kitchen area before I put the phone back to my ear.

'Right, Nigel, I'll see you in about fifteen minutes.'

'I'd really prefer it if you did not meet them, Dom,' he says, barely able to mask his anxiety.

'I know. You said.'

'Whatever you do, don't antagonize them,' he pleads.

'I won't.'

'Right. Just remember: the less said, the better. Don't let her manipulate you into revealing anything.'

'There's nothing to reveal, Nigel,' I say and kill the connection.

I nod at my chef, Sebastiano. He's standing over a hunk of meat laid out on the stainless steel table. In his right hand he's holding a knife, and with his left hand he's stroking the meat as if it's alive to locate the juiciest, most tender part so it can be precisely carved out and presented as tonight's Chef's Special. Cutting meat properly is a skill as old as hunting itself.

I walk past the fridges and the tables with the heating lamps suspended over them before reaching the swing door to the restaurant. Before I go in I stop and look through the round glass hole in the door. The restaurant is mostly in darkness. Only one section is lit. My eyes fall on the woman sitting under the light. At that moment she lifts her head from a file she is studying and I see her face.

FUCK! FUCK! FUCK!

I jerk away from the glass in shock and disbelief and lean against the cold tiles of the wall. Air is no longer reaching my lungs. My heart feels constricted, as if steel hands have reached inside my body and are squeezing it like a lump of fucking dough. I gasp for breath. How can fate be so fucking cruel to play such a trick on me? Why?

Something deep inside me starts screaming.

And suddenly, I'm not standing outside the door to my restaurant anymore. I'm in freezing, black water. All around me is pitch-dark. My legs are still kicking, but feebly. Far away in the distance I can see the headlights of the boat. Jake is coming.

I want to scream, but I can't.

My skin feels too fucking tight. Like the animal in the cage that chews at its own bloody tail in horror at its loss. In my peripheral vision, Sebastiano is holding the knife at the perfect angle as he slices into the muscle and fiber. That meat is dead. It will not feel the sharp steel cutting into it. I too am dead. I will not feel the pain.

Ah, it's that fucking door again. But I can walk away, and nothing in my life will change. I can remain dead.

I take a deep breath. I can still walk away. I should walk away.

But I don't.

I open the door and enter the restaurant.

And Ella Savage turns her head and stares coldly at me.

TWO

Ella

The first sensation I have at the sight of him is one of pure disquiet. Like stroking a cat against the lie of its fur. Something perfectly silky and smooth has become ruffled. It neither feels nor looks right.

My brain processes what my eyes see in disjointed bits.

Tall, broad, flat stomach, narrow hips. Serious swagger. Fit, but not gym fit: combat fit. A fighter. The long, prowling strides with which he is eating the distance between us gives the impression of coiled tension. A slowly stalking animal about to spring on its prey.

As he moves out of the gloom, his face catches the light.

His hair is damp from the rain and longer than in the photographs I found on the net. It curls around the collar of his leather jacket. And his face is ruggedly beautiful with the kind of tense jaw and five o'clock shadow that must leave delicious burns on a woman's inner thighs. Whoa! Where the hell did that come from? I suck in a harsh breath. A word I hardly ever use pops into my mind: rideable.

Not a good word, Ella.

Not a good word.

Oozing aggression and male strut, he comes to a stop in front of the table I'm sitting at and stares down at me. The sheer height and breadth of him is so overpowering, it actually makes me feel oddly shaky. *What the hell is Rob still doing in the toilet?* My skin tingles. Masking my unease, I return the angry alpha's stare coolly.

The light is directly above him so I cannot be certain of the color of his eyes, but they are light, and as fierce and intense as an eagle's. His chin tilts a fraction higher, and I see the gleam of his irises between his hooded lids.

They are blue: hot blue.

As if the sun had shone onto the ocean's surface and made it sparkle with reflected light. The unblinking orbs work their way over my face, lingering on my mouth, then sliding down my neck, and coming to rest on my breasts. I take a shocked lungful of air at the blatant arrogance.

His lips twist cynically at the rise and fall of my chest.

Even though I'm wearing my customary cotton shirt and a buttoned-up jacket, and only the suggestion of the shape underneath is on show, I flush deeply. His eyes sweep upward back to my scarlet face.

'Miss Savage, I presume,' he intones. His voice is deep and sexy. It feels like something warm melting down my back.

I straighten my spine and try to look unaffected. 'And you are?'

'Let's not play games, Miss Savage. You know exactly who I am.'

'I'm not playing games,' I reply calmly. 'I'm trained not to make assumptions.'

He doesn't smile. 'Except one?' His voice is acid.

I raise a coldly disdainful eyebrow. 'I beg your pardon?'

'You operate under the assumption that there is always an underlying intention to cheat.'

'If I'm involved there usually is.'

The shockingly blue eyes flash with temper, but his voice is tightly controlled. 'If you're implying what I think you are, Miss Savage ...'

I let the corners of my lips twitch upwards in a deliberately fake smile. 'If you have done nothing wrong then you have nothing to fear, Mr. Eden.'

'I wasn't aware I had anything to fear. I thought you were investigating the restaurant. I'm just an employee of the company that owns this restaurant.'

'Just an employee?' I repeat disbelievingly.

'Just an employee,' he insists softly.

I look at him steadily. 'In that case, you are not qualified to give me the information I require. Where is Mr. Broadstreet? This meeting is supposed to be with him.'

'Nigel has been delayed. Trust me when I say I *am* qualified to give you the information you require,' he informs, and begins to remove his leather jacket.

Underneath the blue shirt—*Is that silk? He definitely didn't get that off a store rack. It screams custom*—all kinds of eye-wateringly lovely muscles are rippling up and down his torso and upper arms. I watch him fit the jacket over the back of a chair and start rolling up his shirtsleeve. His forearm is brown, thick, and populated by silky, dark hairs.

My heart skips a beat; then begins to race. There is something incredibly erotic about being alone in an empty restaurant while a full-on, hundred percent certified alpha strips down under a pool of golden light. I catch my wandering thoughts and concentrate on the gold watch on his wrist. Of course, a Rolex. Just an employee, huh? A dishonest, lying, cheating dirtbag, more like.

He slides into the chair opposite me, and suddenly he is too damn close, the smell of his cologne punching me in the middle of my chest. The moment becomes charged. Somehow strangely filled with ... oh fuck ... sexual tension! Last thing in the world I need. *Where the bloody hell is Rob?*

Feeling flustered and awkward, I drop my gaze to the file in front of me. I'm a tough cookie. I'm here to do a job. I'm here on behalf of the Queen and country.

Resisting the impulse to turn around and look for him and so betray my intense discomfort, I take a deep breath and meet Dominic Eden full on, at close quarters.

And Oh! My! God!

The sexiest man in the entire fucking world is staring straight at me with *hunger* in his eyes. My mouth falls open. His eyes zero in on my lips. The air around us becomes electrified.

Whoa! What the ...!

I want this man to fuck me raw right here on this table in the middle of this darkened restaurant. The sensation vibrates down my spine and ends in a dull ache between my legs. The intensity of my desire for him shocks me. Doing this job, I've gone to a lot of trouble to hide, and even deny my sexuality, but it has always been there, lying in wait. Waiting for the right man to awaken it.

Knowing that doesn't make my reaction or my unprofessional behavior any less embarrassing. I have to pull myself together. Dominic Eden cannot know how affected I am by him. Taking a deep breath I raise my eyes and look into his. It's like a zebra trying to outstare a lion.

From the shadows comes the sound of a door opening. Someone is approaching us. I swallow hard unable to pull my eyes away from his, but before whoever it is can come up to our table, Dominic Eden breaks our stare, lifts his hand and holds his thumb and forefinger in the way that you would do if you wanted to show someone the measurement of an inch. I have been investigating restaurants long enough to know that the gesture means espresso, short.

The waitress goes away silently.

I cough. 'Er ... When do you expect Mr. Broadstreet to join us?'

'Fifteen minutes or thereabouts,' he murmurs and nonchalantly leans forward. I can't help it I flinch back as if avoiding a bullet, my hands grasping the edge of the table, and my heart galloping madly.

At that moment the waitress comes back. I look up at her, grateful for the distraction. On her tray is not a small espresso but a small liquor glass of some colorless liquid. Neat alcohol for breakfast? Wow!

She puts the glass on the table and immediately slinks back into the dim of the unlit restaurant. He leans back, completely relaxed, his forearms resting on the table. His eyes never leaving me, he reaches for the glass and downs the liquid in one swallow. He places the glass back on the table and smiles, the smile of a shark.

Not a shark smiling at a human, but a shark smiling at another shark.

It's a 'come out and play' smile from one predator to another.

Freaked out by my unexpectedly strange and intense reaction to him, I clear my throat. 'Shall we ... um ... start?' I stammer. I desperately need to regain some control over this situation. In a strange reversal of roles we are reading from the wrong scripts. It is he who should be fearful and respectful, and it is I who should be playing the part with all the power and authority. I am the tax inspector. He is the tax cheat.

'By all means,' he says, his eyes plenty hostile.

'Look, Mr. Eden, we need to collaborate, work together on a cooperative, non-adversarial basis in order to resolve this situation.'

'Non-adversarial? Is there a way to diplomatically throw someone under a bus?'

'I'm not here to throw you under a bus.'

'No? Aren't you here to screw as much money as possible out of this company?' A cold menace is in his voice.

'No,' I say firmly.

'You'll be telling me next I can eat a shit sandwich and not have brown teeth,' he says rudely.

But I refuse to rise to the bait. I am too professional for that. 'We are here to establish whether this restaurant is paying the correct amount of tax that is due.'

He hits the flats of his palms on the table and makes a hissing sound of disbelief. 'Do *you* even believe that bullshit?'

I jump, and for a millisecond I experience a sense of searing shame. He's absolutely right: I am here to squeeze every last drop of money possible. In fact, I wouldn't even be here if we had not already assessed that a substantial sum can be gleaned from this establishment. And the moment we find a flaw we'll be piling on interest charges and fines on top of any amount deemed to be owed to cover the cost of our involvement.

Then I remember my honest, hardworking parents. How proud they were that they paid their fair share even though all around them people were gaming the system. And yet now that they've both stopped working because my father is ill and my mother is his primary caregiver, their combined pensions are barely enough to get them through the month. And the reason there isn't enough is because of people like him. People who refuse to pay their fair share. Corrupt, devious people who get away with it just because they have expensive lawyers and accountants who arrange all kinds of sweet schemes for them.

Well, I took this job with Her Majesty's Revenue and Customs (HMRC) because I believe in the good we do and I'm here to make the world a fairer place.

I meet his eyes head on. 'If it transpires that you've paid the correct amount of tax, we will not harass you in any way.'

Before he can answer, the restaurant door opens and Rob comes in. We turn to watch his progress across the room. As soon as the light hits him, I see that he looks a sickly shade of green. I raise my eyebrows enquiringly at him. He shakes his head imperceptibly at me, and turns toward Dominic Eden.

'Sorry about that. I think I've picked up some kind of stomach bug. Can we reschedule this meeting for another day?'

'Of course, Mr. Hunter,' Eden says. There's a taunting smile in his voice.

I gather up my files, stand, and take a couple of steps forward so Rob's body is between him and me. Eden unfurls himself and stands, towering over Rob and me. Rob extends his hand, but he refuses to shake it, and Rob retracts his hand awkwardly.

'Right,' Rob says. 'We'll be in touch to make another appointment.' He turns around and starts walking toward the door.

Eden turns to me.

I nod and quickly follow Rob without looking back, even though I can feel Eden's stare like a dagger in my back. Rob holds open the door and I step out into the entrance foyer. My heart is racing. What happened in that empty restaurant was so crazy and so unlike anything I have ever encountered that I can't even think straight.

I look at Rob as he enters the foyer and closes the door behind him. There's a pinched look about his mouth, and his chubby face is shiny with perspiration. I must admit he doesn't look too well.

'Rude cunt,' he mutters disgustedly.

My eyebrows shoot up. Rob is never so crude. He must be feeling really unwell—or Dominic Eden rubbed him up the wrong way.

'Are you all right?' I ask cautiously.

'No, I feel bloody awful, but I'll survive. I just need to get home. Will you drive?'

'Sure,' I say, opening the street door. Outside it is still raining steadily.

Rob turns toward me. 'Damn, I left my umbrella in the restaurant. Will you be good enough to get it for me?'

I look at him in dismay. 'Me?'

'I'd go myself, but I'm not well, Ella,' he says irritably.

I continue staring at him. I really don't want to go back into that restaurant alone.

'Can't you see that I'm suffering?' he asks through clenched teeth.

'Yes, yes, of course.'

'It's by the table. Hurry, please. I'm afraid I'll have to rush to the toilet again.'

Without a word I go back into the foyer and, after crossing the small space, open the door of the restaurant.

THREE

T he first thing I see is the muscular bulk of Dominic Eden sitting at the table. He's hunched over with his forehead resting on his fist. At the sound of my entrance his head jerks up. His eyes are brimming with tears and the expression on his face is shocking.

He looks utterly tormented!

In fact, it appears to me that I have interrupted him in a moment of such extreme suffering that it seems impossible he is the same hostile, high-octane, sexual man I left a few minutes ago. This man could have just walked off a battlefield, the cries of the dying still ringing in his ears.

Horrified by the intensely private moment of grief I have accidentally stumbled upon, I begin to babble nonsense. 'I'm sorry, I didn't mean to ... Rob forgot his umbrella. I've come ...' My voice dies away at the change in his face.

It's an expression that is raw and primal and impossible for me to understand. The closest I could come to describing it is to say that it's almost a look of desperate yearning. As if I've taken something of great importance from him and he is silently begging me to return it, and yet ... how could it be?

We just met in antagonistic circumstances. I have not taken anything from him. Not yet, anyway. It doesn't make any sense.

Outside this closed, deserted restaurant, the world revolves inexorably: Rob waits with irritation, I have a two o'clock appointment I have to cancel, my mother will be cleaning the bathroom and waiting for my call to tell her what time I'm planning to pick her up tomorrow, my best friend Anna will have presented her dreaded sales report and be wanting to tell me all about it.

But in this strange world, I can do nothing except gaze at Dominic Eden in a daze. His suffering moves me more deeply than I care to admit and the part of me that I never allow out when I am at work, the part that gets angry when people are cruel to animals, propels me towards him. My hand reaches out and my finger lightly brushes his face. It is meant to be an expression of sympathy, but a small spark rushes up my arm.

The tax dodger and I stare at each other in shock.

We are connected at such a deep level it is even beyond attraction, desire or lust. I don't know how long I would have stood there if not for the expression of fury that suddenly crosses his face. He jerks away from my finger. The rejection is like a slap in the face.

He blinks away the tears, and I unlock my frozen muscles and force my hand down. I turn away from him blindly, my mind blank with shock. I'm here for Rob's black umbrella. I start looking around and spot it tucked under the table close to his leg. Yes, that's what I came for. I bend, grab it and quickly straighten.

'Well, I'll be off then,' I say awkwardly.

Without looking him in the eye again, I begin to hurry toward the door. I place my hand on the door handle and turn it.

'Will you have dinner with me, tonight?' His voice rings out and wraps around me like a cloak.

Dinner with him?

I take a deep breath. Oh my! It's shocking how much I want to agree. I turn around slowly. 'I'm sorry, I can't. It wouldn't be appropriate,' I say quietly.

'Why not?'

'You're under investigation and I'm the investigating officer. It would be wrong.'

'I thought it was the restaurant you were investigating.'

'You know it's the same thing,' I answer more truthfully than I normally would have done.

'Don't you think you'd find out more about me and the restaurant over dinner than you would pouring through dull reports from your central computer.' His voice is soft and persuasive.

Desire clings to my ankles like the waves that suck at your feet when you're standing at the shoreline. 'I don't think that would be very ethical.'

'Spare me the crap, Ella. They'll fucking hang a medal on you if you bring in a rope of information to hang me with.'

'Look, Mr. Eden—'

'Dom,' he corrects softly.

I bite my lower lip and hover uncertainly by the door. I have never been so confused or conflicted before. He gets to his feet and starts walking toward me. Instantly I feel a flare of panic. He comes within two feet of me before stopping. Too close. Way too close. His face is no longer in the light, but deeply shadowed, the outlines faint. Only his eyes shine with lust.

The damp curls caressing his powerful neck make me itch to push the fingers of both my hands into them. I even imagine myself sluttishly dragging my fingers up his scalp. As if he has heard my thoughts he leans closer. His scent invades my nostrils and my breath hitches. Staring up into his eyes, I feel my body slowly inching toward him. There is no doubt in my mind that he is dangerous for my sanity. That I should say no.

That I *must* say no.

'Will you come?' His deep voice seduces in the dark.

I really want to say no. I really, really do. It's the right thing to do. The most professional thing to do. But I remember again how we stared into each other's eyes and I felt as if our souls were touching.

And there is this attraction: irrational, crazy and unlike anything I have ever experienced. My mouth is watering to taste him and it is beyond words or explanations.

Am I just behaving in this reckless way because he's so drop-dead gorgeous? Or is it because I saw something I shouldn't have seen? Or is it because beyond my professional pride, my life is pretty dreary, and he is one of those shining things that come by once, if you're very lucky, in a lifetime?

Whatever it is, it makes me feel like an iron filing helpless in the pull of a giant magnet. This *thing* between us is unlike anything I have ever experienced and it is blatantly clear that I am not going to be able to think of anything but him for weeks. Either with regret that I succumbed to temptation, or with regret that I did not reach out and take what I wanted so badly. It is so hard to say no to someone your body craves, but say no I must.

Two throaty words tumble out. 'All right.'

'Good,' he mutters, and I'm startled to hear the same conflict in his voice that I heard in my head. He doesn't want to want me! It's just as inconvenient for him.

'I'll pick you up at seven?' he murmurs.

I nod.

'Where from?' he asks.

'7, Latimer Avenue.'

'Give me your phone,' he commands.

I hesitate a moment. Every brain cell that I have painstakingly trained over the many years to be independent, strong and take no bullshit from anyone cries out HELL NO, and every untrained, uninhibited, natural cell in my body screams FUCK YES.

It's just once in a lifetime.

I hand over my phone and watch him input his number into it and press call. A sound vibrates from his jacket. He ends the call and gives my phone back to me. The tips of our fingers graze and that brief, impersonal touch steals the wind from my lungs. The spark is undeniable. It lights up my body and makes my mind reel with images of us twisted together, our mouths fused, our sweaty bodies joined. I almost want to purr like a needy kitten. It's a far cry from the woman who strode into this restaurant like a consul less than an hour ago.

My fingers are tingling as I raise my eyes to search his. 'Why do you want to take me out to dinner?'

'Do you really want me to answer that?'

Our mouths are only a heartbeat away. I shake my head.

The answer is throbbing between us. I have never met a man I wanted the way I want him. But what shocks me is that a man like him should want me in the same way. Yes, I'm good-looking, but he has access to the most beautiful women.

Sex. Sex. Sex. And so what?

'Seven OK with you?'

'Yes.'

FOUR

I make it out of the restaurant and drive Rob back to his flat.

Then I get back to the office and try hard to be interested in a piece of gossip the receptionist has for me. I smile and nod at my colleagues as they walk by. I go to my floor and get myself a mug of coffee. Sitting at my desk, I put away the file marked 'Dominic Eden', and call my mother. She's a terrible worrier, and she is quietly relieved to hear from me. I tell her I will pick her up at twelve tomorrow. With that arrangement made, I ask after my father.

My mother drops her voice to a whisper. 'I think he's feeling a bit down, love. His prostate is playing up. It keeps him awake at night.'

'Let's all do lunch tomorrow,' I suggest brightly.

She seems pleased with the idea.

Almost as soon as I ring off, Anna's call comes through. Even by the tone of her voice, I can tell that her meeting went badly.

'I think I'm going to be fired,' she wails.

'They'd be mad to fire you. You're the best salesperson they have,' I say reassuringly. And that's no lie, either. Anna can close a deal like no one else I know.

'I kinda fucked up, Ella. I slept with my sales manager.'

'What?' I exclaim, shocked. 'Tony's disgusting!'

'I was drunk,' she says glumly.

'Oh my God! And he's married as well.'

'Tell me something I don't know,' she says sourly.

'When did this happen?'

'Last Friday.'

'And you're just telling me now?'

'It meant nothing. I was, like, really drunk,' she explains.

'Oh, Anna.'

'I'd already put it behind me, but now he's acting all weird. I think he's trying to get rid of me.'

Note to self: NEVER mix business with pleasure. Oh, DAMN.

After my conversation with Anna, I have a salmon and cucumber sandwich and some dark chocolate for lunch. That afternoon I get through an impressive pile of paperwork, answer the phone, and liaise with my workmates, but all the time my insides are clenched, and between my legs my cunt is fat with anticipation.

Before the clock strikes five, I am already crossing the reception concourse. Stepping outside into the hot evening, I walk down to the Underground station and take the Tube back to my apartment building. Ignoring the slow, smelly lift, I run up the three flights of stairs and let myself into my matchbox-sized, one bedroom flat. Yeah, it's tiny, but it's all mine—well, at least as long as I pay my rent.

I run to the mirror and look in it.

Unbelievable.

I still look the same. I pulled it off. No one knew.

My living room is west facing and it's like a sauna in my home, so I quickly open all the windows, switch on the fans and go into my bedroom. Even though it's very small, I've made it look pretty and cozy with blue and white vertical stripe wallpaper, an old-fashioned chrome bed and a painted French dressing table. It's my sanctuary. So far only one man has been in here, but he turned out to be a giant jerk. I quickly banish all thoughts of him and open more windows. The sounds from the street below float up as I start stripping the bed. I put on fresh sheets and stuff the soiled ones into the washing machine. I don't turn the machine on, because I don't want to come home to a crumpled wet mess.

I tidy up, dust all the surfaces and run the vacuum cleaner quickly around the place. By now I'm hot and sweaty. I glance at the clock: five past six. I stick a green apple scented refill into the plug-in air freshener and go into the bathroom. There I do what I've not done in months.

I trim down my bush and shave my legs. No nicks. Yay! I step into the shower and wash my hair. With a towel wrapped around my head and body, I come back into the bedroom and pad over to my closet.

It's been a long time since I cared this much about looking good. There are all kinds of options I can go for: sexy, or casual, or elegant, or professional. In the end I decide to go for subtle. A black lace shirt that my mother bought for my birthday teamed with a red pencil skirt that I got in a seventy percent off sale. I guess there's not too much demand for red pencil skirts. But the nice thing about the skirt is the slit up the back. Modest, but an invitation all the same.

You're not on a date, I tell myself even as I'm slipping into little bits of sexy underwear. Standing in my bra and panties, I dry my hair and, brushing it back, draw on a black velvet band. I go for smoky eyes and nude lip gloss. My cheeks are already tinged with pink so I skip the blusher.

From the back of my closet I take out my most extravagant purchase yet. I saved up for weeks to buy them. I open the box and take out my big investment: a pair of zebra patterned court shoes with red heels almost the same color as my skirt. I step into them and ... they are worth every penny.

Feeling like a million dollars, I dab on perfume and stand in front of the mirror on the closet door. I turn around and look at the back view.

'Not too bad,' I reassure myself.

I stuff my lip gloss, a twenty-pound note just in case it gets nasty and I need to get a taxi home, and a credit card into my evening purse. With one last look at my appearance, I go into the living room. It smells of apples. Satisfied that everything looks the way it should, I glance at the time.

I still have ten minutes to kill.

Until this moment all the activity has kept me going and in control. Now I'm suddenly a bundle of nerves. I feel as if I'm about to walk into an exam hall to take a test that I'm totally unprepared for. I walk into my kitchen and take a bottle of vodka out of my fridge. I pour two fingers worth of alcohol into a glass and down it neat into my empty stomach. It burns my throat, but the alcohol is good. Its warmth radiates quickly through me, warming my body, stirring my blood. I switch on the TV for some noise, and try to concentrate on the sounds and pictures on the screen.

The doorbell makes me jump like a startled cat at two minutes to seven.

The man is punctual!

I smooth my skirt and, taking a deep breath, open the door. And ... oh wow! If he looked good before, he is devastatingly dashing now in a snowy white silk shirt that contrasts amazingly with his tanned skin, a beautifully cut gunmetal gray evening suit, and black shoes polished to a mirror shine. Is that jaw for real? Freshly shaved, his jaw seems to me to have been chiseled to perfection by the gods themselves. As Anna would say, 'Gurllll! I'ma gonna have to call you back.'

'Hi,' I say awkwardly.

Silently, he holds out what looks like a box of very expensive, handmade chocolates. Wow, I certainly didn't expect that from a twenty-eight-year-old gypsy tax dodger. I take the box and finger the dark blue ribbon.

'How ... courtly. Thank you,' I say softly. My mother used to say any charm offensive that begins with handmade chocolates is bound to take effect eventually. I wonder when eventually will be.

He shrugs, his hot blue eyes pouring over me, taking in my face, my hairband, my lace top, my red skirt, and resting a shade longer on my zebra shoes.

He brings his eyes back to my face. 'Are you ready to go?'

'Yes,' I say, taking a step back to leave the box of chocolates on the little table by the door. I turn around to find his eyes scanning the interior of my tiny flat. When his gaze meets mine it is polite and deliberately neutral.

Stepping out, I close the door and we walk down the corridor to the lift without any conversation. He presses the button and still there are no words exchanged. His silence is unnerving, and I feel compelled to break it before the lift comes.

'Where are we going?'

He glances sideways at me. 'The Rubik's Cube.'

The lift doors open and we step in. The smell of piss hits me hard. 'The Rubik's Cube? It's not one of yours, is it?'

He looks at me sardonically. 'Take you to one of mine and have you accuse me of enjoying untaxed perks?'

'Right,' I say, as the lift slowly and jerkily bears us down.

His car, a model I recognize immediately as it's my father's dream car, is a brand new Maserati GranCabrio Sport bearing a price ticket of over a hundred thousand pounds. It's parked on double yellow lines right outside the building entrance.

'This road's notorious for parking tickets,' I warn, my eyes skimming the muscular lines of the sleek black machine.

'I know,' he says carelessly.

He unlocks the car remotely and opens the passenger door for me. I slip in and he shuts it. Alone in the luxurious space, I inhale deeply the smell of leather and immerse myself in the high-tech beauty and fabulous comfort of the interior. I stroke the door handle. Wow! I've never been in such a car. The dashboard, door and seats are all in soft burgundy leather with stitching in a matching color.

He slides into the driver's seat, retracts the roof, pushes a little button next to the column marked 'Sport', and what must be the loudest car in the world snarls, roars and with a sonic boom comes to life.

He turns to me. 'Ready?'

'Should I be scared?'

'Nah, you'll love it.'

I'd planned to play it cool, but a wild, unintended whoop escapes my thick wall of disapproval of him and ill-gotten wealth of all kinds when he hits the gas pedal, and the car takes off so suddenly it throws me back against the seat.

When I first saw the roof disappearing from above my head, I did worry about what kind of mess my hair would be in by the time we arrived at the restaurant, but the car has been built in such a way that my hair remains impressively unruffled. And the V8 engine is so brilliantly noisy with pops and bangs on the overrun that there's no need for conversation at all as we speed down empty back roads.

The noise also means that we're constantly the center of attention everywhere we go. It's a lovely summer evening and people are sitting outside restaurants, pubs and bars eating and drinking—so that makes for a lot of attention. And when we make a traffic light stop, excited tourists lift their phones and film the car.

He drives up to the Rubik's Cube's pillared entrance, gets out, and opens my door. Putting his hand lightly on the small of my back, he throws the keys to the parking jockey who catches them neatly. Even though his hand is barely touching me, I'm conscious of it as he guides me up the glossy granite steps. The imposing entrance has an air of intimidation about it, as if one runs the risk of being challenged by the staff with the question, 'Are you rich enough to be here?' The answer to which in my case is clearly no.

But apparently Dom is.

The doormen are impressively enthusiastic in their welcome, and it's instantly obvious that not only is he a regular here, but he must also be a tipper of massive proportions.

The restaurant is on the first floor, and we climb a sweeping, black-carpeted staircase. Upstairs, the interior of the restaurant is breathtakingly sumptuous with über-classy black and white velvet walls and huge arrangements of lush, exotic flowers at the front desk and in the middle of the restaurant. All the chair frames are made of some matt silver metal and the thickly padded seats and backs are covered in multicolored velour: orange, gold, red, green, blue, brown.

We're shown to what seems to be the best table in the place: an elevated platform next to a super-modern cascade fountain piece. Waiters swarm around our table pulling out chairs, bowing, scraping, smiling, nodding. Next to me, a waiter lifts the napkin from the charger plate, gently unfolds it, and courteously lays it across my lap. Bemused, I thank him. He nods solemnly in acknowledgment.

Another jacketed man flourishes menus at us. A complimentary, pink-tinged champagne cocktail appears magically on my right, but I notice that a glass of amber liquid is being offered to Dom. A young man of Middle Eastern descent smiles sweetly when I thank him.

A man oozing obsequiousness in a black suit materializes at Dom's elbow. The display of excessive servitude is quite frankly startling, but Dom seems accustomed to it.

'Would you like me to choose the wines to complement the dishes, Mr. Eden?' the man asks ingratiatingly. Ah, a sommelier. Well, well, I've never been to a restaurant that was swanky enough to hire a sommelier!

'Pair them with the lady's meal,' Dom says. 'And just my usual.'

'Very good, sir,' he says with a nod and a quick glance in my direction, and exits the scene.

I turn my attention to the menu. The combinations of ingredients are unusual and fascinating. I look up once and Dom is watching me. For a moment we stare at each other then I feel myself start to color and have to drop my eyes back to the menu. When Dom lays his menu down I do the same. Almost instantly the headwaiter is at my side. We place our orders and he diplomatically compliments us on our excellent choices.

A small plate of beautifully colorful miniature amuse-bouches is placed in the middle of the table. The waiter who brought it explains what the little titbits are, but his French accent is so thick I catch only the words 'black radish', 'fromage frais' and 'steamed mussels with pickle and Guinness'. He disappears as silently as he had arrived.

I pick up one of the ceramic tasting spoons holding a little cube made from three brightly colored, unrecognizable ingredients, sitting in a pool of soy sauce, and slip it into my mouth. There's a delicate burst from the green base of avocado, the rich meaty taste of tuna tartare and a complete texture and taste change with the rice crispies and deep fried shallots on the top.

'Good?' Dom asks.

'Very,' I reply sincerely.

He pops one of the smoked salmon shells between his lips and suddenly I find myself hungrily watching his incredibly sexy mouth. I drag my gaze away quickly and cast it around the opulent room.

If his intention is to dazzle me then yes, I'm dazzled—the suit, the car, the impossible to miss deference of the waiting staff toward him, the splendor of the restaurant, the five star excellence of the food—but it doesn't mean a damn thing.

That strange look we shared in his empty restaurant is worth more to me than one thousand nights in the lap of unrivaled luxury. I know that moment is gone forever. The man in front of me is wearing a mask and he has no intention of ever letting me see underneath the mask again.

He is either with me now because he wants to take me to bed or he is trying to get some information out of me. Most likely a bit of both. I won't give him any information, but I also know I can't be the one to hurt him either. Not after what I saw this afternoon.

Tomorrow, I will tell Rob that I want to be taken off this case. He'll ask why, and I'll tell him that I don't feel comfortable around Mr. Dominic Eden. That is tomorrow. Tonight belongs to me and the man in the mask.

I take a sip of the delicious champagne cocktail and meet his gaze. 'I notice you don't have a Facebook page?'

FIVE

He stares at me. 'Is that a crime?'

'No,' I concede. 'But it is rather unusual.'

'Why?' he demands.

I shrug. 'Everybody uses some form of social media. Twitter, FB, MySpace, Picasa, Tsu, Instagram, Plaxo, Xing, Ning ... You can't be found on any platform.'

He bares his teeth suddenly in a pirate grin. And ooh ... devilishly attractive. My heart flutters a bit.

'Can it be,' he mocks softly, 'that HMRC's latest and most formidable weapon, the eighty million pound super-computer Connect, needs me to supply it with data so it can effectively spot signs of potential non-compliance from me?'

'Hardly,' I reply. 'Connect holds over a billion pieces of data collected from hundreds of sources. As it happens, a lack of participation on social media is also "data". It indicates a desire to conceal suspicious activity.'

He raises one straight, raven-black eyebrow. 'Really?'

'Yes, *really*,' I say with emphasis.

At that precise moment, the sommelier appears with a bottle and tries to display the label to Dom, but Dom doesn't take his eyes off me. Not willing to be outdone, I stare back. When the bottle is uncorked, he makes a slight motion with his hand to indicate that he wants to dispense with the business of tasting the wine. The sommelier comes around to my side and fills my glass. When he goes around to Dom's glass, Dom gives a slight shake of his head. Quietly, the man slips the bottle back into the ice bucket and disappears.

I take a sip of wine. It is so smooth and ripe with different and distinct flavors that it makes every type of wine I have ever consumed seem like bootlegged versions of squashed grapes and vinegar.

'Just out of interest,' Dom says, 'what information does Connect hold about me?'

'And there I was thinking I was here to learn more about your business and not the other way around.'

'Touché.' He chuckles good-naturedly.

I smile faintly.

'So, what would you like to know about me?' he offers with a reckless smile.

I slip a steamed mussel into my mouth. It is so tender it melts on my tongue. I let it slide down my throat and wipe my lips on the napkin before I answer. 'I'd like to know why you aren't on social media.'

The broad shoulders lift, an almost Italian gesture. 'We're gypsies,' he says, as if that answers everything.

'And?' I prompt.

'By nature we distrust any form of surveillance, and as you've just confirmed, all forms of social media are Greeks bearing gifts.' A teasing quality slips into his voice. 'See, gypsies wouldn't have towed the Trojan horse into their city.'

'I don't want to be stereotypical or anything, but I honestly thought gypsies have always been rather brilliant horse thieves.'

His crystalline blue eyes twinkle with mischief. 'Ah yes. Perhaps it would have been a different matter if the horse had been real, or made of scrap metal. But being wooden ...'

I really want to laugh with him, but I suppress the urge. I'm *not* on a date. I cannot allow myself to like him. I'll just end up getting hurt.

We're interrupted by the arrival of our starters. My order of goat's cheese with roasted beet looks like a white and magenta millefeuille. I gaze at it with awe. Just as the amuse-bouches before, it is a precisely arranged work of art. Almost too beautiful to eat. Dom has seared scallops and walnuts served with a dinky pot of Parmesan brûlée

I cut into my millefeuille and fork a small piece into my mouth. It is so delicious I'm immediately struck by how much I'd love to be able to afford to bring my parents here, instead of all the cheap restaurants my tight budget forces me to take them to. I *know* they would never have tasted anything so refined and luscious, and it suddenly and painfully hits home that they probably never will. And just like that I no longer need to stop myself from liking him. That resentment for 'people like him' comes back into my gut. I welcome it like an old friend. It's better this way. I am too affected by him already.

'Why are you so afraid of surveillance if you're doing nothing wrong?' I ask.

'Why do you have curtains in your bedroom windows? Are you doing something wrong?' he shoots back.

'It's not the same thing,' I argue.

'Why isn't it? I don't want the government, its agents and a whole slew of marketers to have access to my private data. That's my business alone, and I take steps to keep it so. Why is that concept so foreign to you?'

'You'll be pleased to know that Connect holds very little information on you, or,' I continue, 'your brothers.'

He smiles a slow, satisfied smile.

Smile he should. Guarding his privacy has worked. He is a closed door to Connect's tentacles. All it managed to dig up was that at twenty-eight years old he has never made a benefit claim. He doesn't own or co-own any property or business. Needless to say, I don't believe that for a second. Him not financially tied with anyone? As if! He has two bank accounts that show a pathetic amount of activity, mostly direct debits for utility bills. No overdraft. He has a credit card, but he won't even use it to pay for petrol. He hasn't flown with a commercial airline for as long as Connect has been running. One look at that tan tells me he didn't acquire it in London. Which only signifies he's leaving the country using other, private means.

I flash him a fake smile. 'It would appear that you've fooled the super-computer into believing that you're a rather uninteresting employee.'

He lifts his glass of whiskey. 'I don't know how you meant that to come out, but I have to say it kinda looks bad when you give the impression that you believe you're better than a super-computer.'

I smile through my irritation. 'Connect is an amazing invention. At the touch of a button it can show an incredibly detailed picture about a person that would have taken months of research before, but it has no intuitive powers. The department relies on investigators and analysts like me to validate the data and pick up unnatural patterns.'

'Unnatural patterns? Like what?' he asks, fishing for information.

Well, he's not getting anything but the obvious from me. 'Like *everything* I've seen tonight. Like the clothes, the car, this restaurant.'

'So, you noticed my clothes,' he notes cheekily. It's hard to imagine that this is the same tormented man from this afternoon.

'One can hardly fail to notice that they're not off a department store's rack.' My voice is mild.

He widens his eyes innocently. 'I saved up for years to buy these clothes. The car belongs to the company, and I only come to this restaurant when I'm feeling particularly flush or on a really big date.'

'It's all a big joke to you, isn't it?' I accuse. I can feel myself losing my cool.

'It's not just a job for you, is it?' he asks curiously.

'No, it's not. It's a personal crusade.' I lean back as the waiting staff move in to efficiently and quickly clear away our plates. My wine is replenished and a fresh glass of whiskey is placed before Dom. I notice that he's not drinking any wine at all, which means that he ordered the bottle solely for me.

'So, you must hate people like me.'

'Hate might be too strong a word. Detest might be a bit closer.'

He looks at me with a perplexed expression as if he's trying to figure out a three-headed, ten-limbed, purple-striped creature. 'Why do you care so much what tax I pay? I couldn't give a rat's ass whether you pay yours or not.'

'Because people like you play the legal game and screw the country,' I accuse hotly.

'Trying to avoid paying more tax than you have to is not *screwing the country*. On the contrary, it's doing one's best to avoid being screwed by people like *you*. I'm paying the right amount of tax within the rules. Only a sanctimonious, pompous zealot would criticize someone for seeking every *legal* means possible to reduce their tax bill. Tax avoidance isn't wrong. It's perfectly sensible behavior.'

'Wow,' I gasp. 'This is a turn-up for the books. The tax dodger decides to take the moral high ground!'

He shrugs nonchalantly. 'Let not he who is houseless pull down the house of another, but let him labor diligently and build one for himself, thus by example assuring that his own shall be safe from violence when built—Abraham Lincoln.' He leans back, a smug smile on his face.

My main course—Dorset crab and black quinoa with tomato and Meyer lemon sauce—is put before me. It's a world-class visual treat, but I find I've completely lost my appetite.

'Bon appétit,' Dom says when we're alone again, and digs with relish into his Ahi tuna topped with caviar. It is lined with slices of zucchini that are so thinly sliced they're almost transparent.

I fold my arms over my chest. 'So, you think that you have a perfect right to pay little or even no tax if possible, because you're wealthy enough to have access to devious accountants, slick lawyers, corrupt bankers and tax havens while the rest of us subsidize your operations by paying for the education and health care of your workforce, the roads you and your companies use, and the police deployed to guard your restaurants and nightclubs from trouble.'

He leans forward, his eyes glittering dangerously. 'If you truly feel that way then why don't you do something about the really big tax avoiders like Google, Starbucks, Microsoft and Apple?'

I sit up straighter in my chair. 'My mandate does not cover multinational companies.'

He raises one mocking eyebrow. 'Your mandate doesn't cover multinationals? How fucking convenient.'

'Another department deals with them,' I defend tensely.

He bursts into a sarcastic, cynical laugh.

I stare at him furiously. How dare he make out that I'm in some insidious way complicit in the wrongdoings of the multinational companies?

'Since you seem completely clueless, let me tell you how your department for policing the multinationals dealt with the big boys last year. Starbucks had sales of four hundred million pounds in the UK last year, but paid no corporation tax at all. It transferred some money to a Dutch sister company in a royalty payment, bought coffee beans from Switzerland (hey! who knew Switzerland produces coffee beans, but there you go), and paid high interest rates to borrow from other parts of the business.' He pauses. 'Want to hear how they dealt with Amazon?'

I say nothing.

'I thought not. But here's the deal anyway. With sales in the UK of four-point-three billion last year, it reported a tax expense of just four-point-two million pounds. What percentage is that, Ella? Could that possibly be just nought-point-one percent?'

I know everything he's said is true, but I've always told myself that it's not my remit. If I do my job well then I've done my bit to make my country a better place. His arguments do not shake my foundations at all. I clamp my mouth shut and refuse to be drawn into an issue that has nothing to do with his tax situation—or me.

'Why so quiet, hmm? Is it because you already know that the same story is repeated with Google and Apple and every massive multinational? The obvious question that arises in any rational person's mind would be why should I not make my tax disappear too?'

I jut my jaw out aggressively. 'How about because it's morally wrong? Or because you care for the people of this country? Because your taxes will keep schools and hospitals from closing their doors? Because you don't have to do something wrong just because others are doing it?'

He shakes his head. 'You know what you are, Ella?'

'You're obviously dying to tell me,' I say dryly.

'You're someone's attack dog. The question is whose? You've obviously been fooled into thinking you're the attack dog for the poor and oppressed, but answer this: Every year you collect more and more taxes, so, how is it then that every year there's less and less for public services?'

I scowl, but he's touched a raw nerve.

He sees my second of hesitation and presses his advantage. 'Did you know that since 2007 our government has committed to spending over a trillion pounds to bail out banks? What does it say about their priorities if they're able to find the money to save the banks, bomb Afghanistan, bomb Iraq, bomb Libya, and now they're wanting to start a fresh war in Syria, but cannot find the funds for schools and hospitals?'

I stare at him in dismay.

'The truth is there are billions to be gained by going after the big boys, but no one's doing it. On the day our government acts to squeeze these massive tax cheats you're welcome to break my balls about the morality of my tax avoidance schemes and lecture me about your utopian ideals of wealth redistribution. Until then, give me a fucking break.'

I pick up my glass of wine and drain it. I put it back on the table slowly. It's possible that without realizing it I've drunk far too much. My head feels foggy. In my incapacitated state, I'm unable to come up with a single suitable argument to support my cause. My heart knows that even though his argument seems logical, it's not right. It can't be.

He looks at me almost sadly. 'You remind me of that old Led Zepplin classic, *Stairway to Heaven*. You're the woman who believes that everything that glitters is gold and that you're buying a stairway to heaven. But your stairway is whispering in the wind, Ella.'

SIX

The strings of a lute are alone
Though they quiver with the same music.
—Khalil Gibran

Unable to meet his eyes, I stare blankly at a waiter refilling my glass. When he straightens the bottle I'm shocked to realize that I've drunk more than half of it. That on top of the vodka and the champagne cocktail! No wonder he's running rings around me with his flawed 'I'll pay if they pay' reasoning.

He moves closer. 'Are you drunk yet?' he whispers.

Up close and suddenly he seems wild and full of dirty promises. I lean toward him like a moth to a flame. 'Were you deliberately trying to get me drunk?'

'Wouldn't you if you were me?'

My mind chases its own tail. 'Why do you want me to be drunk?'

'Can you handle the truth?' His eyes are hooded.

'Of course.'

'Because you're the kind of inhibited woman who needs to be intoxicated before she can explore her deepest desires. This way, you don't have to be responsible for your actions. "I was so drunk," you can say to your best friend tomorrow morning.'

It's a far cry from the truth—I'd sleep with him without even a whiff of alcohol—but I'll be damned before I tell him that. 'Very confident of yourself, aren't you?'

'I like playing with fire, Miss Savage.'

His phone must have vibrated in his pocket because he takes it out and looks at it. 'Do you mind?' he asks.

I shake my head.

'Hey, Ma,' he says, and listens while she tells him something. 'She did?' he says, and smiles, and it is a genuine smile. A soft, warm smile. I stare at him in surprise. I don't want to know that he has a mother whom he obviously adores. And I realize I can't go through with my plan of sleeping with him for one crazy night. I know having sex with him will open a door and what comes through I might not be able to control. He has the capacity to hurt me. I am too affected by him. I feel things that I have never felt before.

His eyes lift up, meet mine, and the smile freezes. 'I've got to go, Ma, but I'll pass by tomorrow. Give it to me then? OK. Bye.' He puts his phone away.

I look him in the eye. 'I can't have sex with you.'

'Why not?' he asks huskily.

I lean back against the chair, the alcohol buzzing in my veins. There's a pulsing in my temples. Telling him the real truth is out of the question. The half-truth is the only option. 'Because you're a crook.'

His eyes flash with real fury. All that urbane and polite stuff before was just a façade. This is the real Dominic Eden. The hothead who can be exploited by the right person. Maybe even me.

'On what evidence are you basing your accusation?' he asks coldly.

'Instinct.'

'That won't hold up anywhere. Until you find some evidence to support your "instinct", I suggest you refrain from making such wild accusations.'

'I'll find it,' I say, knowing it is an empty threat. Tomorrow I walk away from him and this case forever. For now I'll pretend that I'm the big, tough tax investigator.

'I'm sure you'll try.'

'Don't underestimate me.' My voice actually sounds harsh.

He smiles: a megawatt smile. It takes my breath away, lights up the room and registers as another warning in my heated brain.

I let my eyes travel down to his brown throat. It's not fair that a man should be this gorgeous. My eyes slide back upwards to those firm, kiss me slow lips, and up to his eyes. They are heavy-lidded. The eyelashes thick and stubby, the blue of his irises so intense they're piercing. To my horror, my alcohol-fueled body responds. My nipples tighten and harden.

'I need to go home,' I choke.

He lifts his hand. A waiter brings the check in a leather book. He opens it, glances at it, and leaves a wad of notes between the leather.

I play my part. 'Cash?' I taunt.

'Every fucking time.' His eyes suck me in.

I resist the pull. 'Why's that?'

'I like the smell of money.'

'People with things to hide pay with cash.'

'At the risk of repeating myself, people who don't want their bank and every fucking government surveillance agency in the world to have access to their entire fucking lives do, too. You ready to go?'

I nod and stand, swaying slightly.

His brows knit. It makes him all dark and brooding. Like my favorite hero of all time, Heathcliff. 'You all right?' he asks.

'Absolutely,' I say, and, straightening my shoulders, precede him out of the restaurant. We go back down the stairs. A man is coming up and he stares at me with barefaced interest. As he passes us, Dom stops, puts his hands on either side of the man's head, and turns his face so that it's pointing straight ahead instead of at me. The man's eyes bulge with shock and fear. He's only a head shorter than Dom, but he looks like a scared rabbit in the jaws of a tiger.

I watch Dom pat the man's cheek condescendingly before he turns to me and we carry on down the stairs. I glance back and the man is walking on up, his head stiffly held forward, too frightened to turn around and look at either of us. Fuck! That was like a scene from a Mafia movie.

I turn toward Dom. 'What did you do that for?'

'Asshole was lucky. I was in a good mood. He was looking to get his head fucking kicked in.'

'Because?'

'Because he fucking looked at my woman, that's why.'

A totally inappropriate but powerful thrill flashes through me, lighting up cells that have never seen light in their sad little lives. For that second I want to be his woman, I want him to speak so possessively about me. But that second passes as fast as it made its unexpected visit, and an odd sense of loss replaces it. I never suspected that inside me was such a needy being. What the hell is the matter with me! I'm so mentally unhinged by my own pathetic reaction that the words that leave my mouth are like cold, hard bullets.

'I'm not your woman.'

He glances at me, unembarrassed, unfazed, and without missing a beat says, 'He doesn't know that. I'd never disrespect another man by looking at the woman he's with like that.'

There's no more to be said after that.

Dom

She bends her head, and honey-blonde, silky hair tumbles over her shoulder. Something jerks inside me. Jesus, I can't do this. It's too fucking painful. She looks up at me, her eyes as large and enquiring as a child's.

'What's the matter?' she asks.

The look scorches me. 'Nothing.' My voice is harsh. I had not intended that.

She stiffens, her eyes becoming more distant.

I crack a smile and pretend to be the polite gentleman I've been all night long even though it kills me inside. I do it because I need her in my bed. I want to run my fingers along the wet seam of her pussy lips and I want to see how fierce and wild she'll be when my cock plunges into her.

Maybe she can stop the pain.

Ella

When he opens the passenger door our hands accidentally touch and both of us draw back as if we've been burnt.

'Sorry,' I mumble.

He inhales sharply and says nothing.

I slide in and he closes the door for me. When he gets in I glance covertly at his long, strong body. It's as tense as a coiled spring. Then the car guns into action and we're speeding through the cool night air.

The car stops outside my little flat. I turn toward him. 'Thank you for dinner. I really—'

'I'll walk you to your door,' he says, cutting me short.

'I'll be fine,' I say, but he's already opened his door and slipped out of the car. I shut my mouth and stare straight ahead. I think I'm a bit petrified about what might happen next.

He opens the passenger door. I put my hand in his outstretched palm and, placing my legs together, I swing them out as gracefully as I can and he heaves me out. He holds open the entrance door of my building and we walk together toward the lift. He presses the button to call it and it makes a clanking sound. It's stopped working again.

I turn to him. 'It's broke.'

'Thank God,' he mutters. 'I don't think I can bear the smell of piss at this time of night.'

I wave a hand in the air. 'Don't worry, you can go. I'll be fine. I always use the stairs, anyway.'

He looks down at me expressionlessly. 'I took the stairs when I came up to get you. I can't do bad smells. I only used the lift on the way down because of your high heels.'

'Oh!' I exclaim, blinking fast enough to have a seizure. 'All right, if you're sure,' I say airily, and, turning away from him, start walking toward the stairs.

We walk up three flights of stairs without saying much. Outside my door I bend my head and rummage around in my purse for my key. I fish it out and hold it up.

'Goodnight and thank—' I begin brightly and then I come to a dead stop.

He's staring at me in a way that should be outlawed. No man has *ever* looked at me like that. As if he's starving and I'm triple-seared rib-eye steak. I feel the breath rush out of me and I don't think I can remember how to take the next one. I'm still staring into his eyes with my mouth open when he takes the key out of my nerveless hand.

'This is a grave mistake,' I whisper.

'I need it, and you want it,' he says harshly.

He fits the key into the keyhole. I shake my head. 'It's wrong. We'll regret it.'

He opens the door and walks me backward through it. 'You might, I won't.'

He kicks the door shut. I take a deep breath and his eyes drop to my heaving chest.

'Dom,' I breathe.

He backs me up to wall, his mouth inches away from mine. His energy is like a force field that is pressing me to the wall. A soft growl rumbles in his throat. It's electrifying. My body responds by freezing. Blood rushes in my ears, deafening me, and every thought, sane or otherwise, flies out of my stunned brain. He cups the back of my head while his other hand comes around my waist like a band of steel and slams me into his hard body, crushing my breasts. It's a good thing he's holding me because my body feels boneless, as if I could melt and disappear into him.

I feel his breath waft over my face. It smells sweetish, like maraschino cherries soaked in alcohol. I've never felt so alive, or so vibrant, or so precious. I could have climbed mountains, flown to the stars, melted the sun. It's as if he's my secret dream. Something I've dreamed of and never known. I gasp with a mixture of shock and desire, and he clamps his lips onto my open mouth.

It's like falling into a giant tidal wave.

And drowning. I don't see him produce the condom, tear the foil, or even feel him fit the rubber. It's all done while I'm sinking deeper and deeper. He snatches his mouth away. I gasp for air. Grabbing the edges of the slit in my red skirt, he rips it right up to the waist. My panties are flung, wet and torn, to the floor. His hands run down my back and over my ass, cupping and lifting me until I'm dangling off the ground at almost eye level with him. Slowly he grinds his erection against me.

Then he points his cock at my entrance and rams into me, hard. Enormous ... Foreign ... Dominating. The shock of the sheer size of him makes me grunt. My muscles convulse to accommodate the unexpected intrusion.

'Does this feel wrong?' he snarls.

I curl my legs around his thighs. 'Fuck you,' I spit, and squeeze his cock tight.

'Yesssss, do that. Just like that,' he approves hoarsely.

He withdraws and thrusts up into me, so forcefully that my body climbs the wall behind me.

'Argh,' I cry out, but in fact it feels fabulous. This is the way it was always meant to be.

'Want it harder?' he asks, his voice raspy.

'Yeah,' I whimper.

He slams into me again and I start to quake: Oh fuck! I'm ready to come apart—right here—right now. Electric volts shoot through my system. My body begins to tense and contract. My heart pounds so loudly I hear it from the edges of consciousness. I try to push against it, but I'm standing in the way of a juggernaut. I climax with my head thrown back and screaming. He carries on thrusting through my orgasm until with a roar he, too, climaxes. I'm still panting hard when his eyes meet mine.

We stare at each other. Enemies again.

He pulls out of me and I feel a pang. Loss. Having him inside me felt right. Without him inside me I can think rationally again, and I'm suddenly ashamed and angry with myself. What an idiot I am.

He allows me to slide down his body, but when I try to wriggle away, his grip is steely. I quickly push the flaps of my skirt down over my throbbing sex and trembling thighs.

'Don't be expecting a repeat of that,' I say through gritted teeth.

He loses the condom, zips up, and fixes his eyes on me. His voice is unyielding. 'Don't kid yourself, baby girl. I'll have a repeat whenever I please.'

'Don't bet on it,' I snap.

'I'll bet my last tax dollar on it,' he says. He takes my chin in his hand. It's a hard man's hand, the fingers long and square. He pulls my face up and gazes down at me, his eyes deliberately veiled. I stare up at him resentfully.

'I'll pick you up at seven tomorrow night,' he says with a frown.

'I have another appointment,' I lie.

Something dangerous flashes in his eyes. 'Cancel it,' he says brutally.

I open my mouth to argue, but he catches the hair at the back of my neck in his fist and covers my mouth with his palm. I stare up at him with wide, half-fearful, half-excited eyes.

'I haven't even scratched the surface of what I fucking want to do to you,' he growls.

Then he's gone, shutting the door quietly behind him.

My chest heaves as if I've just run a marathon.

'It's just a physical thing. Just sex,' I whisper to the empty air.

I, stalker

I stand on the street and stare up at her bedroom window. For a long time I don't see anything. Then ... her shadow passes ... fleetingly. I behold the momentary vision eagerly. She is wearing something diaphanous and white, and her hair

swims down her back and catches the light in such a way that each silky lock seems to be individually illuminated. It gives her a wild look, as if her very soul is untamed and free. She moves away.

I wait another hour, but she never again appears at the window. I stare up at the window even after the light goes out. What a thrill it used to be to watch her while she was unaware. I spent hours imagining her in bed, her beautiful hair spread across her pillow, wondering which duvet set she was using that day. But today there is no joy at all even in the mind fuck of imagining her masturbating, climaxing, and falling asleep with her thighs wide open, her pussy wet and ready for me.

Hatred bursts into my gut like burning lava. Even though he had stayed for a short time I know he fucked her. He had the air of man who had shot his load. Proud, satisfied, disheveled.

I never thought she would betray me in this way. I feel like rushing up to her apartment. What a fucking shock she'd get. My feet start to move and then I catch myself.

Patience. Patience.

She will be mine...

SEVEN

Ella

I knock on Rob's door.

'Come in,' he calls.

I enter. 'You wanted to see me?'

He beckons me over to his desk with his finger. 'Have you made another appointment with the wanker's accountant?'

I know exactly to whom he's referring, but I feign ignorance. 'Which wanker?'

He looks at me with unconcealed irritation. 'How many wankers are we dealing with? That Eden wanker, obviously.'

'Er ... not yet. I didn't know when you would be coming back to work. How are you today?'

'Fine,' he dismisses curtly. 'Check my diary and make another appointment as soon as possible.'

I shift my weight from one foot to the other with the realization that apparently Dominic Eden is personal for both Rob and me. Me because I crossed the line last night and probably will again tonight, and Rob because Dom snubbed him by refusing to shake his hand, so he's decided to show him who the real 'boss' in this scenario is. Before yesterday he was just doing his job. Today he's out for blood.

Unfortunately this puts an end to my plans to exit gracefully. A) In this frame of mind, Rob wouldn't 'get' my reason. And B) I can't walk away and allow Rob to misuse his power and destroy Dom. I've seen him in this mode before, when people rub him up the wrong way, and I know just how vindictive he can be. Once he gets like this, he always demands the maximum penalties. Prison, if possible.

I close the door and walk into his room. 'Sir, do you ever wonder if what we're doing is right?'

His eyes fly up to meet mine. 'No.' He pauses and leans back in his chair. 'What's up with you, Savage?'

My face flames. God! If he knew what I did yesterday.

'Nothing,' I reply, keeping my tone light and easy. 'I was just wondering how it is that we always go after the middle and upper middle classes. We never seem to target the truly big corporations and the truly rich one percent who should be paying billions in taxes but don't.'

He looks at me as if I'm stupid. 'Because that's not our job. Our mandate is to go after the middle and upper middle classes. Going after the big boys is somebody else's job.'

'Whose job is it?'

'How would I know?' he says with a shake of his head.

'From what I can see, nobody's going after them.'

'Are you surprised?'

'What do you mean?'

He sighs. 'The best description of taxation I've ever heard was from one of our ex-Prime Ministers, Denis Healey. He, very sensibly, compared it to plucking a live goose: the aim is to extract the maximum number of feathers with the minimum amount of hissing. Plucking the corporations would create the kind of hissing we're unprepared to handle. They have the best lawyers and the most talented accountants who'd run rings around us. We're never going to get anything out of them. It would just be a pointless exercise.'

'So we go after the small and medium-sized fish because we can't catch the big white sharks and the killer whales?'

'Got it in one.'

'But that's so wrong.'

'No, it's not. Every year we recover billions from these slimy bastards.'

'And do what with that money?'

He looks at me with a sneer. 'Our shakedown pays for schools, hospitals, roads, people to collect your rubbish, police, fire services. Need I go on?'

'But it's still unfair,' I say softly.

He leans forward and steeples his fingers. 'Life *is* unfair, Savage. Is it fair that one child is born the great-grandson of the Queen of England with a golden spoon in his mouth, and another child, through no fault of its own, is born to starve in Africa?' He pauses to look at me with an expectant expression. When I say nothing, he adds, 'Now, go make that appointment with the wanker's accountant, will you? That's one goose I want to see plucked and cooked until crisp.'

I bite my lip. 'I don't know about his account, Rob. The computer flagged the tax return because there was one incorrect figure, but you and I know it's probably just a simple accounting error. If that one figure is adjusted as his accountant proposes there's no reason at all to suspect there's any tax fraud going on.'

His eyes narrow. A mean look comes into them. 'What's the matter with you today, Savage? Have you gone soft in the head?'

I take an involuntary step back. There's something cruel about Rob. I'd hate to be on the receiving end of his fury.

He goes on coldly. 'It's as obvious as the nose on my face that this restaurant is not paying the correct amount of tax. They never are. Dig hard enough and there's always something to be found. At the very least I expect to extract a massive penalty and interest for our time and effort.'

'Right. I'll go and make that appointment now,' I say, and quickly exit his office before he deduces more than he already has about my stance on the matter.

I go back to my desk and lean my forehead against my palm. What a bloody mess. Nigel Broadstreet has already called twice to speak to me and left his mobile number. I dial it and he answers the call.

'Mr. Broadstreet? Ella Savage, HMRC, here.'

'Good morning, Miss Savage.'

'Yes, I'm calling to reschedule our appointment.'

'Yes, of course. When would be convenient for you?'

I look at the computer screen showing both Rob's diary and mine. 'How about Monday, ten a.m.?'

'Excellent. Same place?'

'That will be fine.'

'I'll see you there, then.'

'Um ... Will Mr. Eden be attending, too?'

He pauses as if surprised. 'No,' he says very firmly. 'Mr. Eden is an employee who has very little information about the accounting side of things. As I explained before, and will prove during our appointment, this whole situation is an error made by a trainee, which can be rectified quite easily.'

'Fine. I'll see you Monday. Please don't be late.'

He coughs uncomfortably. 'Of course.'

'Goodbye, Mr. Broadstreet.'

'Goodbye, Miss Savage.'

I end the call and schedule the appointment into our diaries. Afterwards, I call my mother and confirm that I'll be picking her and my father up at twelve. Then I call down to John to remind him that I'll need to borrow the 'official business' car at eleven thirty. I lean back in my chair. Dom will not be at the meeting. Thank God. I honestly don't think I could act normal if he was there watching me with those eyes, knowing he's been inside me.

As planned, I pick my parents up at twelve and we have lunch at a local pub. The food tastes like what it costs—£5.99 for two courses and £9.99 for three—but my father seems to be glad of the change of scenery, and my mother's in a good mood. So, it's a nice, easy lunch.

After that, we all troop back into the car and I drive to Tesco to do the weekly big shop for my parents. Because I felt bad yesterday that I could never take them to a place like the Rubik's Cube, I start picking up stuff that's more expensive than I'd normally choose and place it in the trolley.

My mother touches my arm. She looks worried. 'That's too expensive for us, darling. Just the economy version will do,' she says.

'No,' I say with sadness in my heart. 'I want to treat you and Dad to something better than economy this week.'

'But, darling,' my mother whispers, 'you'll leave yourself short.'

I smile at her. 'It's only this one week, Mum. Next week we'll go back to the economy stuff, OK?'

I fill the trolley with fine ham, expensive cheeses, two good cuts of sirloin, some of Tesco's finest desserts, a lovely boxed Tesco's Finest carrot cake, all butter croissants, branded ice cream, two duck breasts and organic walnut bread. The bill, when it's rung up, is shocking. It's almost double what I usually spend shopping for economy stuff. My mother gives me a 'let's put it all back' look, but, ignoring her, I slide my credit card into the reader and key in my PIN.

I return to work at two p.m. to find a large brown box inside an Argos plastic bag. For one second I think my mother has sent me a gift. She does buy stuff from there, but then why would it arrive on my desk when I've just returned from spending time with her?

I walk toward the bag with a frown on my face. I take the brown box out of the bag and open it. Inside, there's another box, only this box is from an expensive boutique. I quickly drop it back into the brown box and put everything back into the Argos bag. My face feels hot and my heart is beating fast in my chest.

Now I know exactly who the package is from. I stuff the bag under my table, switch on my computer, and stare blankly at the screen. It occurs to me that whoever he got to send the box to me went to a lot of trouble to make it seem as if I was just receiving some cheap thing from Argos. For that I'm grateful. The last thing I need is my work colleagues thinking I'm being bribed by tax evaders.

Lena, from down the hall, puts her head around my door. 'You got your package then?'

'Um ... yeah.'

She comes in. 'So what's in it?' she asks nosily.

'Oh, just my mother sending me something for the flat. Probably crockery.'

'Oh.' She scrunches up her face as if to say, 'Nothing interesting, then.'

I shrug as if replying, 'That's life, what can you do?'

She brightens. 'Do you want to come with us for a drink tonight?'

'Uh ... No. Not tonight. I'm a bit tired.'

'Oh, come on. It's Friday.'

'I know, but I'm too tired.'

'You sure?'

'Yeah. You have fun, though.'

The first thing I do when I get home is open the brown box and take out the expensive box. There's an envelope attached to it. I pull it off and extract the card.

To replace the one I ruined.
Dom

His handwriting is bold and not the prettiest, but like him it oozes power and confidence. I open the box. Tucked amid white tissue paper is something red. I take it out and gasp. Wow!

It's the most beautiful dress I've ever seen. It has a slit at the back and even looks like it's my size. In a daze I run my fingers over the soft material. I've never owned anything so fine in my life.

Carefully, I hang the dress on a hanger and hook it on the door handle of my closet. Then, lying on the bed, I open the box of handmade chocolates, and, while eating them, admire the dress. The chocolates are delicious. The dress is fabulous. But I don't like how confused I am about things I used to be so sure of.

In one hour Dom will be here.

EIGHT

Dom

I step up to the shower, turn it on, and the jet of hot water cascades down my body, relaxing my tightly wound muscles. I close my eyes and she fills my thoughts like an exotic perfume. Her eyes, blue and Bratz-doll enormous, flash into my mind. All day I've been haunted by their damn beauty. I know I'm being reckless, but I don't care.

I'm gonna have her and fuck the consequences.

So many women have lain in my bed. They come, they go. They taste like fucking dry bread and tap water. A man needs to eat, so I filled my belly, but all the time I wanted honey and sweet flesh. A body that begs me to take it even when its owner doesn't want me to.

Ella.

Ella of the zebra shoes, sexy calves and the perfect ass. Oh, that ass! What I could do with such an ass. So, yeah, I'm gonna fucking risk it again today, just for that adrenalin rush of opening her thighs and ramming my dick straight into her wet, tight pussy while she sucks my tongue.

My mind replays the moment I threw her against the wall and fucked her as her mouth hung slack and a rush that I'd forgotten I could feel pulsed into my cock, engorging it, making it ache. I clutch it in my hand and it hums ... for her creamy body.

Soon, my friend. Soon.

I close my eyes and clear my head. Sometimes it feels as if I'm plunging off a cliff into the deep blue ocean. Maybe there are rocks under the surface. Maybe I won't survive. Maybe she won't take away the pain. Maybe she'll stand on the cliff edge and watch me bleed to death instead, but so be it. I can't stay away from her, even if it means my own destruction. I must see her soft hands lift her dress up and willingly offer me *everything*.

I must taste her honey again.

I keep my bedroom windows open, and when I hear the distinctive growl of the Maserati's V8 engine I lean out of the window and call down to him as soon as he cuts the noise. He looks up, surprised, and as darkly beautiful as an avenging angel.

'Don't come up, there's a parking attendant up the road. I'll come down,' I holler down to him.

'Well, hurry up then,' he shouts up.

I take one last look at myself in my pretty yellow sundress before running out of my flat and skipping down the three flights of stairs. As I step out into the street I see that Dom has come out of his car and is leaning his butt against it. My heart does a little dance. He looks super-edible in a black T-shirt, blue jeans and pristine Timberland boots. His arms are crossed, and my eyes greedily rove over the thick muscle cords. His eyes are as bright as gems and are focused on me. Hit by an unnatural attack of shyness (What? Me, shy?) I pause uncertainly by the entrance door.

'Hey, sexy,' he drawls.

'There's a parking attendant walking toward us with a very determined expression on his face,' I say as nonchalantly as I can.

He replies by opening the passenger door with a flourish. I walk toward him with a smile.

He grabs my arm. 'You're one incredibly beautiful woman, you know,' he says.

The compliment goes straight to my head and makes my skin burn. I have to pretend to look down at my shoes to hide my flustered face. He lets go of my arm and I slip into the seat. I turn my head to watch his fine ass go around the back of the car. He gets into the driver's seat and closes the door.

'Thanks for the dress. It's beautiful,' I say quickly, 'but I can't accept it. It's too expensive.'

He frowns down at me. 'It's just a replacement. I ripped your skirt yesterday.'

'Well, it's too expensive.'

'Well, I was *very* sorry,' he says with a glint in his eyes.

'It could be deemed a bribe.'

'Let me tell you how tonight and every night that we spend together is going to go down. We are never discussing my tax situation, or my finances, or any of that shit we talked about last night. You want that kind of information, you'll have to talk to Nigel. We are just going to eat, talk, fuck and have fun.'

'Rob and I have an appointment to see your accountant next week,' I inform him quickly. 'I'm saying this up front so there's no misunderstanding about the investigation. We are going ahead with it.'

'Good,' he says casually.

'You don't sound worried.'

'That's probably because I'm not.'

I look at him curiously. 'Why not? Most people in your shoes would be.'

'Why should I be? I haven't done anything wrong, and Nigel will finally get to do what he's paid a shitload to do.'

'Look, we won't ever talk about your tax situation again, but I have to warn you that you really pissed Rob off the other day when you refused to shake his hand. He took it as a personal insult, and I think he's going for maximum damage.'

A soft look comes into his eyes. 'Thank you for the warning. It means something to me.' Then he grins. 'But it's totally unnecessary. I meant to piss that asshole off. He's like a little bully on a power trip. In school he would have been one of those boys who joined a gang to terrorize all those smaller and weaker than them.'

It's startling how you can spend weeks and months with someone and be totally blind to their true personality. In one sentence Dom has described Rob's entire MO. Something I'd shut my mind to because I truly believed we were doing it for the greater good. But now I'm not so sure anymore.

Are Rob and I bullies? We threaten ordinary, hardworking people who've salted away something for their old age, so they don't have to depend on their children to buy them the necessaries the way my poor parents do, with prison sentences and force them to pay up. When possible, we even go into their bank accounts and help ourselves to their hard-earned money. We do it all because we can. And yet the multinationals, the super rich, the old money families who already have everything tied up in untouchable trust funds, we allow to get away with paying laughable amounts of tax or no tax at all.

Yeah. I guess the hard truth is, we are shameless bullies.

The idea disturbs me greatly, but I don't share my thoughts with Dom. Instead, I shrug slightly and say, 'Just ask Nigel to be careful. Rob can be really vindictive.'

'You know those hotshot accountants the multinationals use?'

My ears prick up. 'Yeah ...'

'We stole Nigel from them. Let Rob pit himself against Nigel. It'll be interesting to see if my accountant is actually worth his huge salary.'

I don't get to answer him because the parking attendant is standing outside the car next to me. To my surprise, he doesn't berate Dom the way he does other drivers with lesser cars. Instead, he asks in a totally awed voice, 'How fast can this beauty go?'

'I never took her over a hundred and fifty mph,' Dom says.

The man shakes his head admiringly and lets his eyes caress the smooth lines of the car. 'She's a beauty, man. I'd exchange my wife for a car like this.'

Dom laughs, kisses the pad of his thumb, and guns the car. The attendant watches us take off with a wistful expression.

'Where are we going?' I scream over the noise.

'My place,' he says.

We park in an underground car park beneath a posh building in Chelsea and get into a lift smelling of disinfectant. Both of us face the gleaming doors as we're silently and quickly whisked up to the top floor. His apartment is one of two on the top floor. As soon as he opens the front door, I say, 'Wow!' Most of the walls are made of glass and the view is breathtaking.

'Oh my God! You can see across the river for miles out.'

He chucks his keys onto a metal container shaped like a leaf on the sideboard while I look around in amazement. The way homes in designer magazines look. Spotless, not a scratch or mark anywhere, fabulous furniture, everything color-coordinated with one or two bold splashes here and there, the floors shining with polish, and a bowl of fruit on a statement coffee table.

'Does anyone actually live here?'

He looks at me strangely. 'I live here.'

'Wow, then you must have a shit-hot cleaner.'

'I'll tell Maria you said that,' he says with a grin.

I grin back foolishly.

'Come on. I'll show you the balcony,' he says and we cross the vast open-plan space. Our footsteps echo in the ultra-modern emptiness of the place. He opens the tall glass doors and I step outside.

'This is amazing,' I exclaim looking at the city bathed in the glow of the evening sun.

'Yeah, it is, isn't it? When you live somewhere for some time you start forgetting how beautiful you once thought it was.'

'You're very lucky,' I say sincerely.

His face closes over. 'It's still too early to say,' he says cryptically.

'No, you're already luckier than all the children who live in rubbish dumps in the Philippines and all the slave workers in China and India and all the homeless people in London.'

He looks down at me, and for a long time he doesn't say anything. Then he raises his finger and pushes away a skein of hair that the wind has undone from my face. His fingers feel hard and warm against my skin. I have to resist the impulse to rub my face against his hand like some needy puppy. Thank God, he takes his hand away before I do something I'll forever regret.

'Sometimes you can be happier on a rubbish dump than in a palace,' he says.

'Do you really believe that?'

'I don't believe it, I know it. Growing up my family was dirt poor and yet we were happy. Fiercely happy.'

I stare up at him. In the sunlight his eyes are like blue crystals with silver flares, the pupils seeming too large for a man.

'People don't understand what wealth does. Wealth makes you more dissatisfied. You buy a house, you fill it with the best, then you buy another, you fill that with the best; you buy a yacht, then a plane; you buy a vineyard and then you buy a bigger yacht, and a bigger plane. Then you start a luxury car collection. And you never ever come to a place where you think, "That's enough now. Why earn any more? I couldn't spend it all in my lifetime even if I tried. I'll just stop working and relax, enjoy all I have." No, you just keep on pushing yourself, constantly expanding the business. It's why billionaires in their eighties put in eighteen hour days.'

I think of my parents. They're poor, yes, but they're happy in their small world outside the rat race. And except for my resentment of the people who don't pay their taxes, I love my little matchbox flat and my little life.

'Are you hungry?' he asks suddenly, jerking me away from my thoughts.

'Ravenous,' I admit.

And he laughs. 'Good. There's plenty of food.'

I hear his laugh inside my chest. 'What're we having? A takeaway?'

'Sort of.'

His idea of a sort of takeaway and mine are worlds apart. Mine is a small pepperoni pizza with garlic bread, or chicken biryani and poppadoms, or a quarter crispy duck and special fried noodles from one of the takeaway joints inside the five-mile free delivery radius. His is a three-course meal from one of his restaurants.

The food—well, the raw ingredients—is brought by a man in a chef's uniform whom Dom introduces as Franco. Franco then proceeds to cook and serve us as we sit at the dining table. I take a careful sip from my glass of wine. I woke up with a massive hangover this morning and I don't want to repeat the experience tomorrow.

'So, you can't cook,' I say, cutting into my perfectly baked leg of milk-fed lamb.

'Nope.' Holding his food at the side of his mouth, he says, 'My brother Shane can, though.'

'He's the youngest, isn't he?'

'No, my sister Layla is. He's the second youngest.'

I pick up a dab of artichoke and pearl barley mash at the end of my knife. 'Ah, yes. I forgot. He's the youngest boy. Being a stay-at-home mother, your sister didn't quite make it on to our radar. But she's married to a rather ... um ... interesting character, isn't she?'

He leans back and looks at me expressionlessly. 'He may be a rather ... um ... interesting character, but outside of my brothers I'd rather have BJ guard my back than I would any other man on earth. He's a totally straight and loyal guy. Maybe one day you'll meet him.' He smiles. 'He might not like you too much, though. As you've probably figured out, us gypsies have no love for tax collectors.'

'And yet here I am.'

He takes a sip of his whiskey and puts it down on the table, then remarks almost to himself, 'Yes, yet here you are. Real enough to touch.'

Whatever the thought was that passed through his head, it made him suddenly pensive.

'Why are you doing this?' I blurt out.

He looks up at me, one sooty eyebrow raised. 'Doing what?'

'Fraternizing with the hated tax collector.'

He gives my question serious consideration and then says the most unexpected thing. 'It is a lucky man who finds an enemy who is so intoxicating.'

I frown. Hearing him say that is surprisingly wounding. 'We're not enemies,' I say softly.

His eyes narrow until they are dark slits. 'Ah, but we are, sweet Ella. We just find each other physically irresistible. That is all. *Never* make the mistake of thinking otherwise.'

NINE

We're having sweet grapes and cheese from Hervé Mons on the balcony when Franco comes out to say that he's leaving.

'Thank you for a really delicious meal. I'd never tasted Sauternes jelly until tonight,' I say with a smile.

He bows. 'I'm glad. Maybe I will cook for you again,' he says, and then shoots a wary look at Dom.

'I'll look forward to that,' I say.

'Ciao, bella.'

'Ciao, Franco,' I say, surprised at how normal my voice sounds. Quite frankly, I'm more than a little tipsy. From the moment Dom made that statement about us being enemies who find each other sexually irresistible, everything changed for me. Until then, I'd allowed myself to fall into a ridiculous fantasy that I was dating the most gorgeous man on earth. I was actually drifting through my evening in a cloud of naive happiness, dreaming of a life together with him. A slice of heaven with two kids and a demented puppy. How stupid. As if someone like him would end up with someone like me.

I think I might even know the exact moment I got caught up in the fairy tale. When I was lying in bed looking at the red dress he sent me. It was so special, and I've never been given anything so splendid by anyone—ever. In fact, no one I know can even afford to buy such expensive items. I guess I got totally sucked into my outlandish piece of fiction when I tried on the dress and it fit me like a dream.

But really, who can blame me? It was such a delicious fantasy.

When I was a girl, I always, always wanted to be Cinderella. I wanted to go to the ball all dressed up in a glittery blue gown and have a handsome prince fall in love with me. At midnight I'd drop my glass slipper and my prince would come looking for me. He would search high and low, and no one else would do. The slipper was mine. The man was mine. Dom is the prince I've always dreamed of, and subconsciously I was acting out my childhood dream.

It was the throbbing emptiness inside me that made me forget my good decision to drink carefully, and I became stupidly reckless. I think I've consumed more than half a bottle of wine on my own. Again. Dom never comments, just watches, and silently refills my glass. He doesn't even seem to care that I've gone strange and our conversation has become stilted. The harsh comment was designed to keep me at a distance. I guess he didn't want to lead me up the garden path. He wanted me to have no illusions. We're having sex and we're having fun.

Yay! What fun.

Dom uncurls his long frame and walks Franco to the door. Their voices roll through me as they cross the apartment. Feeling restless, I stand up. Whoa. Why is the floor moving? I put a foot in front of me, and another, and another, and I'm leaning on the railing. The city glitters like a bed of lights below. I hear the front door close and then Dom is back on the balcony. I turn around slowly. A wind has risen and it whips my hair into my eyes. I use both my hands to hold it in place.

He doesn't come closer. He just stands there watching me. I can't see his expression because the light is behind him, but his body is tense and taut. I think of how he pounced on me yesterday. I think of how shamelessly I responded.

'I think I'd like another drink,' I slur to him.

'Sure. What d'you want?' His voice is cool and distant. He really doesn't give a shit about me.

'I'll have that thing I saw Franco swigging from the freezer.'

I can't be sure, but I think he smiles. 'OK. Do you want to come in? It's getting a bit cold.'

'So, what do you care?'

He walks up to me and threads his fingers through mine. 'To be honest, you look like you're about to fall over the railing, and I'd feel a lot better if we went in.'

'Yeah?'

He sighs. 'Christ, you're so drunk.'

'I thought you liked me drunk.'

'Come on. Let's get you some grappa.'

We go into his kitchen and I sit on the counter while he opens the freezer.

'Is that ice cream I see in there?' I ask interestedly.

He pulls the carton out.

'Let me see that. Gin and tonic ice cream! Where on earth did you get this from?' I exclaim enthusiastically.

'My sister buys it. She loves the stuff, but she's on this strict organic diet, so she keeps a tub here so the only time she can have it is when she's here. But I believe there might be a tub at Shane's, Jake's, and my mum's, too.' His face softens while he's talking about his sister, and suddenly I feel sad. I want this beautiful, beautiful man for myself, but he doesn't want me. Yeah, he wants me to have sex with, but not all of me in sickness and in health, till death do us part.

He looks at me with amusement. 'Would you rather have the ice cream instead of the grappa?'

I have to think this one out. 'Can I have the grappa poured over the ice cream?' I ask.

He makes a face. 'Seriously?'

'Seriously,' I insist.

I pop myself on a high chrome stool—and, believe me, that's some feat when you're feeling the way I am—and I put my elbows on the gleaming surface of the island and watch him scoop the ice cream out. Gosh, the way he scoops ice cream is so yummy, I want to pour the melted stuff down his body and lick it off him. He picks up the bottle of grappa and looks at me.

'You sure about this?'

I wave my hand to indicate that he should continue with the task of pouring.

He pours the ice-cold grappa over the ice cream and places it in front of me. He opens a drawer, finds a spoon and lays it beside the bowl. Actually, it looks quite delicious. I might have found a winning combination here.

I take the spoon, dig it into the concoction and put it into my mouth. Ooooh! My eyes widen and my mouth starts moving sideways. Oh!

His reaction is admirable. He shoves the bowl under my chin just as I spit it out.

'Sorry,' I apologize.

'It was a vile combination,' he concedes, handing me a paper towel.

I wipe my mouth and tongue. 'Oh dear, that was not very sexy, was it?' I say weakly. How was I to know that gin and tonic ice cream with grappa poured over it would be so evil?

'Actually,' he says, his irises growing, 'everything you do is sexy, sweet Ella. Can't you tell? I've been wanting to fuck you for hours.' He tilts his head. 'My bedroom is that way.' Slowly, I turn my head in the direction he's indicated.

'Get naked and sit on the edge of the bed,' he commands.

TEN

Dom

Her eyes flash with surprise, but she obeys me without a word. Desire is like the burning heat of a midday Sicilian sun on my skin as I watch her take swaying steps toward my bed. She stops at the bedroom door and looks around the room. A sigh escapes her. It is the wistful sigh of poor people the world over. Even though I have only stood at her front door and scanned the interior of her home, I know that my bedroom is bigger than her entire flat.

If she weren't so proud, I'd take her for my mistress. Set her up in a swanky apartment and shower her with gifts. Then I'd never have to feel guilty about using her.

She goes into the dimly lit room and I wait a few minutes. I have something to do before I follow her. I walk up to the doorway to my bedroom and halt.

The bright light coming in from behind me falls on her naked body. There are two kinds of women: the very slim woman who looks better in clothes, and her more rounded counterpart who looks better, much better, naked. She is the latter.

She's a waking dream.

Just like those great beauties that my granddad used to perve over. Even their names evoke a lost time—Brigitte Bardot, Marilyn Monroe, Raquel Welch.

Ella Savage is curvy and creamy white. Her breasts are not the perfect silicone planets I'm used to, but they are deliciously full and round. The areolae are sweet pink, barely darker than her skin, upon which her nipples protrude like swollen buds. My gaze moves down to the wasp-waist and the gorgeously rounded hips. Her pubic bush, the same dark blonde as her hair, is neatly trimmed.

I take a deep breath. The moment is surreal with silence and anticipation. It is as if I'm not part of it, but watching it happen on a movie screen.

'Lean back and rest your weight on your hands,' I order. Even to my ears my voice sounds harsh. Strange, because I don't feel harsh at all. Inside, I'm melting like a marshmallow over a flame.

I watch her arch her body back sensuously, her chest pushing out and up. Even so, she's not flaunting it. She simply sits there and allows me to look at her.

'Open your legs.'

I watch her spread them, but it's only a shy-open. There's more to go. A lot more. Between the intriguing paleness of her thighs, full, luscious lips beg for a tongue to part them open. Taste them. Suck them. Fuck them. The desire to crawl up to her and eat her out fills me.

'Put your feet up on the bed.'

Another woman would have scooted up the bed for more space, but she doesn't. She simply obeys the command exactly as it has been given. Her breathing increases as she moves to obey. A graceless, almost vulgar movement, but I actually like that, it's more real. She plants both her feet on the bed so her knees press up against her breasts.

I walk toward the liquid dripping from her pink seam like a man in a trance. I grab her hips and swipe my tongue along the swollen, succulent flesh. My body shudders. I was right. *Honey.* She's pure honey. She throws her head back and moans. With that un-doctored sound of ecstasy, the whole world ceases to exist for me. There is only my tongue and her sweet pussy.

'I want you to watch me eat you,' I tell her.

She brings her head forward and we stare at each other in wonder while I eat her until she comes rocking, arching, shrieking, and squirting shamelessly into my mouth.

My breath hasn't even returned to normal and already his dark shape is hovering above me, his palm gliding over my nipples, fingers trailing on my collarbone. All my senses heighten and my sex aches for his touch. In the shadows that envelop us I can hear his heart pounding hard. Only one side of his face is illuminated, and it is an expression of fierce concentration, as though I'm something so exquisitely fragile that the least wrong move could break me. He raises his eyes and meets mine. His are gleaming pools of *hunger*.

His mouth swoops down and covers a nipple. It's hot and rough, as if he's trying to brand me with his mouth. Shock flares in my veins.

'Oh!' I gasp, my whole body trembling with sexual intoxication.

Watching me intently he takes the nipple between his teeth and pulls. I whimper. But the glimmer of momentary pain is a tease from a master seducer. He starts sucking the way you would if you wanted to give someone a hickey. The sensation is electrifying.

It feels as if my intoxicated mind is playing tricks on me. There is no doubt about the expertise of his technique. A burning desire rises within me as every muscle in my body

stretches and tightens. I clench my hands helplessly. The hot mouth leaves as his other hand arrives between my legs.

'Open up,' he purrs. His breath is sweet as it dances between our lips.

I splay my legs open and he pushes a long finger into me.

'More,' I moan.

'Patience, Ella,' he whispers and withdraws even that finger.

I look up at him with begging eyes. He cannot know how much I want him, but I'm past caring. I want to stay forever in this world where there's no one else but us. He slides his hands under my ass cheeks and smiles. There's something mysterious and wild in that smile. I fix my eyes shut.

'Look at me,' he instructs.

I snap them open and watch completely spellbound as his mouth draws closer and closer.

Oh, my sweet baby Jesus! Another! In which dimension does a woman get two face cakes in one go?

His hot, velvety tongue laps at the warm juice dripping from my pussy. He drinks it as if it is the finest nectar. Lost in the exhilarating pull of his technique, I look deep into his eyes as shudders ripple through my body. He plunges his tongue deep into me and I shake violently. His tongue, a muscular, practised thing, goes for the kill. His mouth encircles my swollen clit while it sucks!

Fuck! How it sucks. Why do Americans say it sucks when bad times hit them? It's fucking great when it sucks.

His fingers slip inside. Two, or is it three? Rough as his kisses had been. I'm too lost in the throes of a building orgasm to know or care.

'I'm coming,' I shout.

'Not yet,' he growls, but there's no way I can hold it any longer.

My thighs are already trembling uncontrollably. Every inch of me is tingling. I try to slither away, but it's too late. I prepared myself, but I could NEVER have imagined the explosion that the second eat-out brings.

It is indescribably beautiful. Only she who has experienced it can know what it is. Words are inadequate. Words are silly. How can you explain true ecstasy? Shaking and convulsing, I finally find out what a pussy is really for!

He is shirtless and yanking off his jeans when the waves ebb away. For a few seconds I simply lie there enjoying the show. He has an incredibly fit body. There is a beautiful tattoo on his left breast of a roaring tiger's face and a coiled snake on one of his biceps. I would have looked at them more closely, run my tongue over them, but he pulls his boxers off and his dick springs out.

'Wow!' I exclaim, my eyes wide and an awed grin on my face. 'Huge and straight and beautiful.'

'It's all for you, babe,' he says cockily.

My heart lurches. 'Fuck me,' I whisper.

His eyebrows lift. 'I fucking intend to. For hours!'

'So, what you waiting for then?' I invite cheekily.

A slow, devastatingly sexy smile spreads across his face. He puts his knee on the mattress and comes toward me on his hands and knees. He has held back for much longer than I would have done, and now he is coming to claim his reward.

I lift my leg and rest the sole of my foot in the middle of his approaching chest. He freezes, a new flash of excitement in his eyes. He thought I was shy. But I'm not. I'll be the wild temptress he could never have suspected.

'My turn,' I say. 'My rules.'

I lift my body upwards and place my finger in the dimple made by the meeting of muscles in his shoulders. Without warning I grab his forearms and he lets me tackle him to the mattress. I push him down hard and sit astride his thighs.

Taking his erect cock in my hand, I toy with it, enjoying the way it jerks and pulsates in my palm. It has its own musky scent that steals deep into my mind, infuses itself as a memory that will never be forgotten. Actually, it is a scent that drives me quite mad.

Like a feral animal, I bend my head and, taking him in my mouth, I suck the warm, satiny skin sensually and deeply. He growls, a low hum deep in his chest. The sound is erotic. I love blowing him. I lift my eyes and watch him watching his dick disappear into my face.

I slip the middle finger of my left hand into the slickness between my legs and sneak the finger between his legs up to his butthole. Michael, I remember clearly, absolutely adored it. I probe the entrance gently. A bundle of firm muscles pushes back. Nope, no one else has been in there.

Suddenly, a strong hand curls around my wrist and yanks it away. 'I ain't no pretty boy, baby. In my bed it's always going to be your ass that gets fucked.'

Right. Message received loud and clear.

And that, it seems, is the end of the 'my turn, my rules' episode. He fists his hand in my hair and thrusts his dick deep into my throat. Only once has a man ever done that to me and I was so shocked and offended I bit him. But with this god of a man, I'm not annoyed. Not even a bit. I let him take total control. He fucks my mouth forcefully. There's almost a desperation to his movements, a sentiment that I understand and welcome. It's good to know that at least on a physical level I'm as necessary to him as he is to me.

He reaches for something on the bedside table. I hear the sound of foil tearing. He passes the rubber to me. 'Climb on top of me,' he orders.

I roll the condom over his cock and hold myself poised over the massive throbbing shaft. The moment feels achingly sweet. The yearning to be totally filled is white hot. At a torturous snail's pace I allow his thick hardness to pierce into the wet heat between my legs and stretch me as I've never been before.

I stop the slow glide and hold myself suspended above him to accustom myself to his girth.

'An inch too far?' he growls.

'No, I can take it all. I know I can.' And I push myself down. Whoa! A shocked sound escapes and he smiles with satisfaction. As if it gives him pleasure to ruin me for all other men.

Our flesh slaps with a dull, wet sound while I impale myself on him over and over again. The faster I drop my sweat-slicked body over his shaft, the more heat collects between my legs.

'Harder,' he spurs me on, and lifts my body to speed me up.

My sex feels plump and tender with the pounding he is giving it. 'Damn your devil penis magic. I won't be able to walk for a week,' I gasp.

With muscles clenched, and the very devil in his eyes, he climaxes. Fascinated, I stare at him. He is a magnificent sight of pure maleness. He digs his fingers into my hips and, grabbing handfuls of flesh, he slides me on his body, agitating my clit until my juices flow over his cock and pool between us, and I break apart for the third time.

This orgasm is like brute force. It slams into me and I howl like a lunatic banshee.

When I return, breathless and with my hands gripping the sides of his chest, I see a fierce look shining in his eyes. I attempt to get off his body, but he holds on to me tightly.

'Not yet,' he says.

'No?'

'No,' he confirms, his eyes so hot and intense that heat crawls up my back and neck. I hope to hell he can't see it in the dark. To hide, I resort to being flippant. 'Say hello to the world's first ever dick warmer,' I croak.

He drags his thumb over my lower lip. 'Your lips are the color of ripe peaches, Savage.'

I lick my lips self-consciously. 'You're full of shit, Eden.'

He laughs. 'And your skin shimmers in the dark ... like pearls.'

'OK, now you're really taking the piss.'

He smiles. There is a new softness and a languor to his face that makes him so damn foxy I want to eat him with a spoon, but I don't. The earlier cold shoulder from him still kinda hurts.

Still, it's not too long before he has me on my hands and knees. Gripping my buttocks hard he plunges into me all over again.

I drive into her like a man possessed. The room loses its solidity, and drifts away like a cloud. There is only her and me suspended in nothing. My mind spins and old magic circles around us. I lose all sense of time as her essence rushes through me, merging with me and revitalizing everything dead and diseased in my body.

Freezing cold waves still crash around me, but I do not feel the pain. I tighten my hold on her hips and roar like a beast. I know the pain will come back—its retreat is momentary—but the scale of the relief I experience is impossible to describe.

ELEVEN

You can forget so many evenings of sadness
For a morning of tenderness.
—Je sais, Jean Gabin

I wake up on my back with my cheek pressed against Dom's chest, his big palm resting on my belly, my feet entangled with his, a raging thirst, bursting for a pee, and a twenty-four carat bitch of a headache. My head is pounding so hard it hurts to even breathe.

Never again, I swear.

Gingerly, I lift his hand and, easing myself away from his heavy, warm bulk, I sit up at the edge of the bed. Separated from his body I immediately feel cold and hollow. Just the air conditioning turned up too high, I tell myself. I swing my legs to the cold ground. Ouch, my head. In the blue glow of the night light I make my way to the bathroom. Ohhhh ... Peeing hurts, too. With a long sigh I go into the kitchen in search of a glass of water. On the island top I see a black napkin with two painkillers neatly laid out next to a glass of water.

For a second I stare blankly at the sight.

He put it out for me!

I scratch my head. Ouch. I shuffle over to the napkin, pop the pills, down the water, and head back to bed. Very, very gently, because my head has now started throbbing hard enough to break, I slide back under the covers. A powerful arm circles my waist and a sleepy, warm voice murmurs in my hair, 'Sleep, sweet Ella. You'll feel better in the morning.'

Unable to speak, I close my eyes, and after a while I fall into a deep, dreamless sleep.

A sound wakes me up. I open my eyes, and Dom is sitting freshly showered and fully dressed by the bedside. His hair is still damp, and I am suddenly reminded of the first time I saw him. It feels like our first encounter happened a lifetime ago. Another era. He has become so much a part of my life.

'How are you feeling?' he asks.

I push hair out of my face and blink a few times. My eyes feel heavy and my mouth feels wooly. At least the headache is gone, though. 'I'll survive,' I mutter.

'Look, I have to go out, but stay as long as you like. Make yourself some breakfast. How about I take you out to lunch when I get back?'

'Uh, no, I can't stay. I've got to go to my mum's and then I'm meeting my best friend for lunch.'

'Right.' He takes his phone out of his pocket 'What's your mum's number?'

I stare at him, surprised. 'Why?'

He looks up from his phone. 'I'm a paranoid motherfucker. I always need next of kin information.'

Because I'm so startled by his arrogant assumption that I should give him my mother's number after two nights of ... hot sex—I guess that's what it was, there had been no lovemaking between us—I end up giving it to him. Besides, I'm not even properly awake. So this is officially an ambush of sorts.

'Now, your best friend's name and number?'

My eyes widen, but I cave in and give him Anna's number, too.

'Right, I'll get my driver to pick you up and take you wherever you want to go. He'll be waiting for you in the foyer.'

I shake my head. I just woke up and I'm being steamrolled into agreeing to all kinds of things. 'Please don't do that. I'll just call a taxi.'

'No you won't. Brian will take you,' he says, his jaw hardening.

I cover my eyes. It really is too early to fight with anyone, let alone a juggernaut like him. 'OK, fine.'

'I'll pick you up from your place at eight tonight. Wear your red dress.'

I uncover my eyes. 'Ah ... we're going out tonight?'

'It's Saturday. What else would we do?'

His phone must have buzzed in his pocket. He takes it, looks at it, and raises his eyebrow enquiringly at me. I shrug to indicate that he's welcome to take the call. He presses the button and listens to a woman's laughing voice saying something. I immediately turn my eyes away from him and pretend to be very interested in a ray of sunshine that's pouring in through the curtains, which he must have partially opened.

My stomach's churning with a mixture of hurt, shame and fury. What a sick bastard. As if he had to bloody take the call in front of me while I'm lying naked in his bed still smelling of sex with him. I don't let any of my feelings show on my face, though. He wants us to be enemies who fuck? Sure, I can do that. In the end, he'll be the one who's sorry. A voice in my head says, 'In your dreams he'll be the sorry one.'

'Cut it out, Layla,' he says into the phone and cuts the connection.

'What are you looking at?' he asks me.

'The dust motes,' I say softly, relief pouring through my veins. All is forgiven. He was talking to his sister. I feel gooey inside.

He turns his head to look at the particles suspended in the rays of sunlight. 'Why?'

'Because ...' I pause. Oh my God, I am so happy for no reason whatsoever. 'The dust motes are magic. They're around us all the time, but you can only see them in a burst of sunlight.'

'OK.'

'Don't you get it? They're the universe's way of telling us that there's more to life than we can see, hear or touch. You know, like dogs can hear things we can't, bats can feel sounds, and other animals can see ultraviolet light.'

He stares at me. 'And you're a tax collector?'

I shrug.

'I'm going, but before I go ...' He pulls at the sheet that I'm holding fast to my chest.

I clutch the sheet harder and laugh nervously. 'What are you doing?'

'Taking something to remind me of you.'

The sheet slips down my body.

'Open up,' he says, looking down at the triangle between my legs.

I spread my thighs and he inserts his finger into me. Unbelievable, but I'm already so wet that it just glides into me. He takes his finger out and sniffs it. 'That'll do me,' he says.

He kisses me on the mouth and then he's gone.

After the door shuts, I lie unmoving in the quiet of the empty apartment for a few seconds. Then I jump out of bed

and run into the bathroom to see what I look like. I freeze with shock to see the state I'm in. Jesus! I've honestly never seen myself look more unattractive.

I shower, get back into my clothes and go downstairs. A man in a black jacket gets up from one of the sofas by the plate-glass windows.

'Miss Savage?'

'You're Brian?'

He smiles and nods. 'Where can I take you?'

I give him my address and he takes me home in a beautiful dark blue Bentley. As I get out of the back seat, the parking attendant who admired Dom's Maserati passes me.

'Does this one belong to the same guy?' he asks.

'Mmm,' I say, and, smiling like a cat who got the cream, run into my building.

My flat seems poor and cramped after his luxurious apartment. I quickly eat a bowl of cereal then take the Tube to my parents' home. My mother looks at me strangely.

'Are you all right, dear?'

'Yeah, why?'

'You just seem a bit pink. As if you're coming down with something.'

I cough. 'I'm fine, Mum.'

'Come through. I'll make us a cuppa.'

We have tea together, and I try my best to pay attention to my mother's chatter, but it's very hard going, and after a while I tell her I have to go meet Anna.

Anna and I meet in Starbucks. She peers at me closely. 'What's wrong with you?' she asks.

'Nothing's wrong with me,' I say with a sigh.

'You look like you're catching the flu or something,' she insists.

'OK. I slept with a man.'

'What the fuck?' she screams, so loudly the people at the next table give us a disapproving stare.

'Speak up, won't you? I don't think the people in the next street heard you,' I whisper fiercely.

'Tell me everything,' she orders, and takes a massive bite of her egg sandwich.

'There's not much to tell. He's just a guy. It's just a sex thing.'

'When do *you* do a sex thing?' she asks with her mouth full.

I grin at her. 'When he looks like a Greek god.'

'Who *is* this guy?'

'Someone we're meant to be investigating.'

Her mouth drops open and I see partially chewed egg and bread and something green. She swallows hurriedly and says, 'Jesus, Ella. Is this like the invasion of the body snatchers? You're sleeping with a tax dodger? You HATE tax cheats.'

I bite my lip. 'I don't know, Anna, I'm so confused. Everything I believed in for so long now seems like a badly thought out illusion. I can't explain it. All I know is I just have to be with him. He has something that pulls me to him.'

'Wow!'

'I know. Can you believe it? Me saying something like that?'

She shakes her head. 'So, it's serious?'

'No. There's no chance of that happening. He doesn't want anything more than sex from me.'

'What?' Her brow is furrowed.

'Yeah. He has walls like an impenetrable nuclear bunker. I think he's had some terrible tragedy happen to him. The first time we met, I walked in on him when he wasn't expecting me to, and he looked totally tormented. I have never seen anybody suffering in that way.'

'Not another fucking loser, like that psycho Michael.'

'He's not a loser. He's just had some kind of tragedy that he hasn't got over.'

'Oh no. You're going to fall for this guy, aren't you?'

'I won't.'

'You won't? You're already more than halfway there.'

'I'm not,' I insist firmly.

She sighs. 'Is the sex at least good?'

'Fan-fucking-tastic,' I say with a large grin.

TWELVE

Dom

She opens the door and my eyes widen.

I told my secretary, 'A red dress with a slit at the back.'

'How much do you want to spend?' she asked.

'Get her something spectacular that I'll enjoy taking off,' I said, and I never gave it a second thought after that. Until now!

Spectacular would be an understatement. She looks fucking unreal!

An innocent, but almost secret smile slips onto her face, and suddenly, for just a sliver of time, the past becomes the present. It is as if I have known her forever. Something in my gut catches, and I grab the tax investigator's hand and yank her hard. She tumbles into my arms in a delectable rush of soft flesh, blonde curls, and rising perfume.

Our bodies touching from chest to thigh, I curl my fingers into her silky hair and crush her mouth under mine. It parts. She tastes of chocolate. I plunder, I brand, I claim. Mine. This one's mine. Blood pounds into my dick. I want to walk her backwards into her flat, push her up against the wall, and shove my hard, hungry cock into her like on that first night.

I pull my mouth away, furious with my own lack of control.

She blinks up at me, dazed, panting, her spine tense. 'What's the matter?' she whispers.

I say the first thing that comes into my head. 'You taste of chocolate.'

'And that's a ... bad thing?'

'Ella ...' I begin, but there's nothing to say. I can't promise her anything. Give her anything. There is nothing for sweet Ella. Just these crazy moments until they, too, are gone. I shake my head. 'We'll be late. Let's go.'

She backs away from me. Her eyes are confused and hurt. 'Where are we going?' Her voice is pseudo breezy.

'My mate Justin is having a party.' My voice is distant. I hate the way it sounds, but it's too late to take it back.

She nods. 'That'll be nice.'

'You look beautiful.'

'Thank you,' she says sadly.

I'm fucking lame, I am.

I don't allow that strange 'episode' to spoil my night. I've always known that something is wrong, but I also know that it is neither of our faults. I'll just live for the moment, and let the future take care of itself.

The party is already in full swing when we arrive. Dom parks the car, and we walk toward the house. He doesn't hold my hand, or anything like that, but he keeps my body close to his so that it's clear to anybody looking that I'm with him.

The smell of a barbecue is coming from the garden, and Justin's living room has been turned into a giant disco with flashing lights. As we enter the room the DJ spins 'Feel This

Moment' by Pitbull and Christina Aguilera, and it's as if they're singing to me.

'Ask for money and get advice,' Pitbull raps.

I turn toward Dom. 'I love Pitbull.'

'Yeah?'

'Yeah. You wanna dance?' I ask.

He looks down at me and suddenly grins. 'Why the fuck not?'

He pulls me to the middle of the floor, and, man, can he jive. I look into his sexy eyes and just for that moment I'm the luckiest girl alive. I laugh, feeling so happy. Oh, if only this moment could last and last ...

Justin is wearing a thick gold chain with a medallion and his shirt open down to his waist, and a couple of gangsta type gold rings, but he's cool. He raises his eyebrow at me. 'Now, why didn't I think of that?' he says. 'Wanna reduce your tax bill? Just get yourself a hot tax collector girlfriend!'

I just smile. This is a thin ice lake he's trying to get me to skate on.

'So, how much of a rebate are you givin' him?'

I shrug. 'Nothing.'

'Why not?'

'Tax cheats annoy her,' Dom says dryly.

'No kidding? Why?'

I shrug casually. 'I don't know. I guess it started when I was a kid. Some of the women on the estate sold Avon cosmetics in their spare time and never bothered to declare their earnings, so they always had extra to spend on nice things, and my mum and dad had everything taxed at source so we never, ever had enough.'

'Shouldn't that have made you decide to become an Avon lady?' Justin asks with a humorless laugh.

I search desperately for some kind of argument that will justify my views, but I can't find one, because within Justin's little joke gleams the real truth. A thing that has been polished by years of denial. My views about taxes have been shaped almost entirely by resentment and jealousy. I was jealous because my friends' mothers could afford better things for their families, and my mum couldn't.

Now, when I think about it, I realize, 'Good luck to them.' It wasn't as though they walked away with millions. They were just trying to make their families' lives a little better. If the government can afford a trillion to bail out banks, the little amounts they ferreted away couldn't have made any difference at all.

Unexpectedly, Dom comes to my rescue. He slips his hand around my waist. 'Ella couldn't be an Avon lady because she embodies a life of simple dignity, sacrifice and service.'

I stare at him, surprised.

Dom's cheeks slowly start to expand with a warm, radiant smile.

And I let out a long, inward sigh. He understands me.

Afterwards, we drink lots of cocktails, dance, and watch a fire-eater perform while we eat grilled jumbo prawns with a lime and garlic dressing. It's late when a fantastically handsome guy turns up. The photos I've seen of him on the net haven't done him a shred of justice. He's obviously very popular with the girls, because immediately there's a bevy of them around him. He looks over to us, catches my gaze, and a strange expression crosses his eyes. It passes in a flash. He comes up to us.

'When did the Inland Revenue start hiring ex-beauty queens to collect their taxes for them?' he asks with an irresistible sparkle in his laughing blue eyes.

Dom sighs heavily. 'Ella, meet my brother, Shane. Shane, Ella Savage.'

I hold out my hand, but he grabs it, and, pulling me toward him, envelops me in a bear hug. I'm so startled by his infectious warmth that I burst out laughing. He holds me around my waist and whispers into my ear, 'Has my brother managed to bring you over to the dark side?'

I giggle.

'We have chocolates,' he whispers darkly.

Dom reaches out, catches my wrist and tugs me firmly toward him. 'Haven't you got a bit of skirt you have to chase?' he asks his brother.

'Nope,' Shane says, and helps himself to a prawn from my plate. I realize I really like him. He must be the life of every party. He's such fun. As if on cue, a tanned blonde in a tight, hot-pink dress and seven-inch heels comes up to us.

'Hey, Dom,' she greets politely, smiles at me uninterestedly, and then bats her eyelashes at Shane. 'You said I could have the first dance.'

'And I meant it,' he says, and, taking her hand, leads her towards the music. A few steps away he stops and turns back to me. 'You should come for lunch tomorrow. My ma makes a wicked Sunday lunch.' Then he's pulled away by the blonde. His departure leaves the air around us tense.

I sneak a look at Dom, and he's staring at me, his eyes wiped of all expression. 'Yeah, maybe you *should* come. Meet the rest of the family.'

'Maybe it's too early,' I say, giving him a chance to back out.

His eyes twinkle. 'We're gypsies, Ella. We're not subtle, and we don't do tact. We say what we mean, and we do what we say.'

I chew on my lip. 'Maybe we should wait until after Monday. Your family might hate me after my meeting with your accountant.'

'I don't care what happens on Monday. I could be dead by Monday,' he says flatly.

Before I can answer, there's the sound of a loud crash. Both of us turn to look. From where we're standing, I see Justin pointing his finger and arguing loudly with someone whose body language is just as aggressive. Beside him, on the patio floor, is an overturned chair.

'Shit, the Barberry brothers,' Dom says, jumping to his feet. 'Come on,' he urges and we walk quickly toward the brewing quarrel. The men are arguing bitterly, their aggression quickly filling the air with tension. I can't properly make out what they are fighting about with all the onlookers shouting at the same time. As we arrive, it transpires that one of the Barberry brothers has insulted one of Justin's mates.

'I'll fucking kill you,' Justin is shouting to the Barberry brother who's supposed to have thrown the insult. There are four of them, and they all look as though they're spoiling for a fight.

Dom looks at me. 'Stay here,' he orders, and he strides toward the men.

I can see that the situation is quickly getting out of hand. And sure enough, seconds later someone throws a punch, and then it's a free-for-all. Everyone's swinging punches, chairs are being smashed, and more men are joining the melee. I stare at them in disbelief. I've never been to a party that's erupted into a steaming fight before. And it's a proper brawl, as well.

From the corner of my eye I see Shane wading in, coming to his brother's rescue. Not that Dom seems to be needing any help. He's roaring and going for it like a mad man. It's incredible how this party has disintegrated into this mess in the space of just a few seconds.

To my surprise, the other partygoers aren't trying to intervene and stop the fight, but are either watching it as though it's part of the entertainment, or clapping and cheering on Justin and the Eden brothers against the Barberrys. There are four Barberry brothers against three, which seems unfair to me.

I see one of the Barberry brothers try to sneak in behind Dom and punch him from the back. Without thinking, moving purely on instinct, I pick up a wine bottle and, rushing forward, smash it over his head. There's a loud clunk. The man turns back with a growl and sinks slowly to the ground.

Ooops! In the movies, bottles that come into violent contact with human heads always shatter to smithereens. I look up from his prone body and meet Dom's eyes. There's a trickle of blood coming from his eyebrow, and he's staring at me with his mouth slightly open. I drop the bottle.

'He was going to hit you from the back. And that would have been unfair,' I say mechanically.

He grins suddenly, and it's like the sun has come out from behind a dark cloud.

'Behind you!' I scream.

Dom whirls around in time to face another fierce-looking Barberry brother. With my hand over my mouth, I watch Dom lay into him. As the man clutches his side and stumbles away, Shane walks up to Dom. The left side of his face is swollen.

'You OK?' he asks, as if it's the most normal thing in the world to turn up for a party and get into a massive punch-up.

'Yeah. You?'

He smiles. 'Always.'

Justin comes up to them and claps them both on the back in an almost congratulatory manner. He's laughing. This *is* normal for them! Dom leaves them and comes up to me. His eyes are dark and devouring. He looks at me as if I'm ... hmm ... well, food.

He grabs my hand and starts pulling me away. I run to keep up with his long strides.

'Where are we going?' I ask breathlessly.

'Somewhere I can ravish you.'

I grin. 'Dom, do you think he'll be all right?'

'Who?'

'The guy I hit with the bottle.'

'Are you kidding? It's gonna take far more than a bottle to down a Barberry boy,' he says.

And I laugh.

And so does he, as we run to the car.

We climb into it in a rush, and, like children who have been promised a trip to the ice cream parlor, we can hardly sit still with excitement. I smile a secret smile. It's clear that the rush of adrenalin and testosterone has fueled his sexual appetite and I'm going to reap the benefit. Dom drives us to a quiet country lane. And there, under a half-moon, he lays me across the back seat and buries himself all the way inside me in one hard slam, then works it until we're both an exhausted, satisfied, beautiful, sweaty mess. He reaches below, finds his trousers, rummages in one of the pockets and produces a gold bracelet.

'Here,' he says and capturing my hand fixes it on my wrist.

I bite my lip.

'What?' he asks.

'Did you steal it or something?' I ask with a grin.

'Why would you think that?'

'I don't know. Bracelets usually come in a box.'

'I can get you a box if you want.'

I shake my head slightly and gently touch the jewels on the pretty bracelet.

'Sapphires,' he says.

It's not big or flash and there is no great declaration that he bought them because they match my eyes or anything romantic like that, but I almost want to cry with happiness.

'It's beautiful. Thank you,' I choke

'You're welcome. Wear it all the time,' he says casually.

And my heart soars. 'I will.'

For a long time, we lie naked and as precious as the stars shining brightly in the night sky.

THIRTEEN

Dom

'**Y**ou wouldn't have any sisters for me, would you?' Shane teases Ella, a seductive smile spread across his face.

We're at my ma's for Sunday lunch. I don't know what I expected when I sprang Ella, the tax collector, on my family, but they've surprised me with the genuine warmth of their welcome. Never once has she been made to feel that anything might be amiss. Of course, Shane has to make a bigger ass of himself than usual.

'Afraid not,' Ella says with a grin. 'But I do have a brother if you're interested.'

'Ah, I'll let you know if I start batting for the other side,' Shane says with a laugh.

I know Shane's banter means nothing, but what the fuck! I feel jealousy pour through me. I place my hand possessively on her curvaceous bottom and throw my younger brother a 'back the hell off' glare.

With a brotherly pat on my shoulder and a mischievous glint in his eyes, he moves away.

Ella goes to join the women in the kitchen, and Jake comes over to me.

'So, that's Ella Savage,' he says quietly, a strange look in his eyes.

'Yeah,' I reply, my tone neutral but forbidding any further intrusions.

'She's beautiful.'

'I know.'

He raises his glass. 'Here's to you.' And for a moment there's a tinge of sadness in his face. Then Shane joins us.

'Hoi,' he says. 'What are you guys drinking to?'

'To Dom,' Jake says simply.

Shane grins wolfishly. 'And the *very* gorgeous Ella.'

I stare at him warningly, even though I know he's only yanking my chain. We all raise our glasses and drink. And I wonder if it has been a mistake to bring Ella to meet my family. They're ready for her, but I'm not.

I *love* Dom's family. And I don't say that facetiously. They're so kind, and I can feel how genuine their welcome is in every word and gesture. I especially warm to Layla. A laughing woman-child, she's the baby of the family. She throws her arms around me and kisses my cheeks as though we're long-lost sisters. It's immediately obvious that everyone loves her to death and is very protective of her.

Her husband, BJ, is another matter, though. He's the largest man I've ever met, with a hugely muscled chest and bulging arms. His eyes are so black it's impossible to know what he's thinking. He doesn't say much—his entire world seems to be made of his wife and their little boy. A highly energetic little thing who crawls around at frightening speed.

Jake, Dom's oldest brother, is the most mysterious of them all. I wouldn't want to mess with him. It seems as if he

regards all the people gathered in that house as his personal responsibility. Almost as if he's the alpha and this is his pack. His wife, Lily, is exotically beautiful and friendly, but not overly so. She's more reserved. His daughter is precocious, a cute little sweetheart whom I instantly fall in love with. We get on like a house on fire. Considering she's just three years old, I consider that a great victory.

I get a more muted reception from Dom's mum: outwardly kind and friendly, but sometimes I catch her looking at me warily. I guess I can't blame her. I'm the dreaded tax investigator. In some ways their kindness makes me feel like an impostor. Someone who's come to hurt one of them while enjoying their hospitality.

Shane was right—his mother's roast is wicked!

And thanks to Shane and Layla, lunch is a great laugh. I look at Dom, and realize I've never seen him as relaxed as he is with his family. He catches my eyes and smiles at me. A real, genuine smile.

After the meal, I join the women in the kitchen. Layla opens the freezer and brings out a tub of gin and tonic ice cream.

She looks at me and shakes her head. 'When I was pregnant I never had any cravings because I was so worried about my baby, but since I gave birth, I can't stop eating this stuff. I have it made specially. It's really delicious. Want some?'

'Uh, no,' I refuse politely.

'Just have a little taste,' she insists, coming to me with the spoon.

'No, really. I couldn't. I'm so full.'

'OK. But if you change your mind, I keep a tub in Dom's house, too,' she offers with a smile.

'Thanks. I'll keep that in mind.'

While Layla stuffs the spoon of ice cream into her mouth, Lily pops her head behind Layla's and shakes it as if warning me never to try Layla's ice cream. Hiding a smile, I turn to Dom's mother. 'Can I do anything to help, Mrs. Eden?'

'No, child. Everything's already done. We all just come in here so my daughter can eat her ice cream.' She looks out of the window and then back at me. 'It's such a beautiful afternoon, I think we'll have coffee out on the terrace.'

I smile at her. How lucky this family is. I think of my poor parents stuck in their dark, poky flat and feel a little sad for them. And then Rob is in my head, saying how life is unfair. One child born with a golden spoon in its mouth, and another born starving.

'I really liked your family,' I tell Dom as we make our way back to London.

He glances at me. 'Yeah, I think they really liked you too.'

'I especially liked Layla. She's so sweet and childlike.'

'Hmm ... Don't be fooled. Underneath all that sweetness are nerves and determination made of solid steel.'

'Really?'

'Absolutely. She's very special.'

'You're really lucky to have them all.'

He doesn't turn to look at me. 'I know.'

There's silence for a few seconds, then he says, 'You never talk about your family.'

'I didn't think you'd be interested.'

His head swings around. 'Tell me about them.'

'Well, we're four: my parents, my brother and me. My parents live in London. My father took early retirement because he's plagued by all kinds of diseases, and my mother's his full-time caregiver. My brother's just graduated from uni and is now traveling around Asia with his girlfriend.'

He nods. 'Are you a close family?'

'I'm close to my parents, but my brother and I don't get on.'

'Why?'

'I don't like the way he treats Mum and Dad. They have so little, and he's constantly asking them for money.'

'Do they survive on their pension alone?'

'Not really. I help them with bits and pieces, groceries and stuff.'

His eyes swivel around. 'On your salary?'

I shrug. 'I manage.'

And again he looks at me as if he's seeing me for the first time.

FOURTEEN

I have exactly three opportunities to trip up Nigel Broadstreet. Not because he sucks at his job—at full flow he is brilliant in a totally slippery way—but because of the things I have seen and heard while I've been with Dom.

However, I don't take them.

I just sit back and let Rob get more and more frustrated and lose more and more ground while Nigel puts forth more and more 'evidence' to support his claim that it was all an honest clerical mistake. No matter what Rob says or does, Nigel is impossible to faze. He is as cool as someone on a deckchair on the *Titanic* the day before the disaster, who had a helicopter ride off the ship that evening. Smooth. Confident. Secure. Unshakeable.

Watching Nigel in action isn't like watching a cheetah kill. There's no dazzling speed, claws, teeth, clouds of disturbed dust, or flying fur. It's more like watching a python wrapped around a goat. Every time the goat exhales, the python squeezes tighter until the last breath is gone. At which point the python, at its own leisure, swallows the goat whole.

As we leave the restaurant I pretend to be disappointed with the outcome even though I'm actually feeling very satisfied. It is rare that someone gets the better of Rob, and he's such a jumped-up, pompous ass that the pathetic side of me quite secretly enjoys seeing him brought down a peg.

In the car he fumes impotently. 'I hate these oily bastards. I'd love to investigate his accountancy firm. I'm sure there are more than a few skeletons rattling in there.'

Wisely, I say nothing.

As soon as I'm out of Rob's sight, I text Dom.

You might want to give your accountant a huge bonus this Christmas. X

I chat for a bit with the receptionist. She tells me her dog swallowed her ring so she has to dig through its poo with a stick. I make the appropriate noises of sympathy mixed with revulsion. When I leave her I take the lift upstairs and go straight to my desk.

I sit down and pull up the Integrated Compliance Environment (ICE) desktop interface. I bring up the original search request I made for Lady Marmalade. Scanning through the form, I notice that, under 'Reason for Request and Any Additional Information', I've input all his brothers as additional associated persons that I wanted researched. Even BJ's name is there.

Leaning back, I gaze at the entry.

Every name on the list means something to me now. They're real people. They live, they breathe, they have hopes and dreams, they love their families, and they hurt when I go after them. I remember how emotionlessly I had compiled the list. How proud I used to be of the impressive responsibility I had, to make a decision on whether to challenge a declared tax return, and at what level that challenge should be made. How powerful it used to make me feel.

I was a different person then.

My mobile pings. I pick it up and look at it.

Want to celebrate with me?

I type back:

Obviously.

The answering ping is immediate.

Pick you up at 6. Wear a bikini under your clothes. Or don't.

Still smiling, I click out of the form and pull up the ICE Feedback Form. I complete it and click 'Send Form'. There. Case closed.

I sit for a while with my hands in my lap and then I open a fresh Word document and begin to type into it.

We drive out to his country house, which takes us about two hours. We turn off a main road and drive for another couple of minutes on a much narrower country lane before we come upon a rather nondescript steel gate, which he opens with the touch of a button on his key fob.

We then travel through about a mile of woods, which Dom tells me he has turned into a bee, bird and deer sanctuary. And as we drive slowly through, I start to see colorful birds everywhere.

'Oh my God,' I cry with delight, when Dom points out two sweet little deer hidden among the trees They do not scamper away, even at the monstrous sound of the V8 engine, but they gaze back at us, their large, moist eyes totally unafraid.

'Are they tame enough to be petted?' I ask, turning my head to stare at them.

'They come up to the house looking for food in the mornings. You can hand feed them then.'

'Really?'

'Yes, really,' he says and there is an indulgent look in his eyes. He obviously cares very much for his deer.

The sun is setting, but the air is still deliciously warm, and I'm almost struck dumb by the unspoilt beauty of the woods, and the thought that one man owns all this while people like me cannot even afford to buy a matchbox apartment. But I don't think these thoughts with the resentment I would have felt in the past. Instead, it is with a confused sadness. Is the world really just an unfair place where people have been arbitrarily made poor or rich by the accident of their birth? And does that mean that there is nothing I can do to make it a better place?

As we drive up to the house, I have to gasp. It is so beautiful. With two stately stone pillars and a frontage utterly covered in ivy, it is like an enchanted mansion straight out of a fairy tale.

Dom turns to me. 'Like it?'

'Like it? Dom, it's absolutely fabulous,' I enthuse. I turn to him. 'Does it remain empty while you are in London?'

'No, I have a housekeeper, and her husband doubles as the gardener. They stay the nights in the house when I'm not around, but when I'm here they live in that lodge there.' He points to a small cottage covered in wisteria and climbing roses. Nothing could be more English than that pretty little country home.

'Right,' I say, my eyes going back to the dreamy main house.

Dom parks the car and we cross the gravel and go up the stone steps. He pushes open the beautiful old doors.

'Don't you lock your doors?' I ask, surprised.

'Only in London.'

Inside are powder blue walls with white trims, gleaming oak floors, palladium windows with beautiful window seats, and a charming mixture of antique furniture and pastel furnishings. It is airy and elegant. There's a wingback chair next to a bay window and a book on a little round table next to it. I can almost see myself sitting in that chair reading and leaving the book there on the table.

I turn away from the sight. Disturbed. Why, I care not to think about.

He takes me through to a dining room with gold damask wallpaper and black and white curtains. It leads on to a large, shabby-chic style French kitchen with sandstone tiles. There's a cute breakfast table in a sunny corner.

'Want a drink?' he asks.

'I'll have some tea.'

He fills a kettle and sticks it on.

I sit on one of the chairs by the counter. 'Dom, I need to ask you a question. It's rather important to me, so please answer it as honestly as you can.'

He leans his hip against the island and glances at me warily. 'OK.'

'You think you shouldn't pay tax because the very richest are not paying theirs. But what would happen if everybody did that?'

He looks at me seriously. 'I wish everybody wouldn't pay. That would make this entire corrupt merry-go-round grind to a sudden halt. They can't imprison everybody and we'd then have to come up with something different. Not this corrupt system that has slowly concentrated half the world's wealth into the hands of one percent of the population and allowed eighty-five fucking people to amass as much as three and a half billion people combined!'

He pauses to let his words sink into my psyche.

Is he serious? My mind boggles. 'Eighty-five individuals own half the world's wealth! How is that even possible?'

'Not only is it possible, but the study concluded that soon the wealthiest one percent will own more than the rest of the world's population put together!'

I nibble the pad of my right thumb and reflect on his claim. It doesn't sound right. Too unbelievable. 'Where are you getting your figures from?'

He crosses his arms and narrows his eyes. 'It's public information, Ella. You can find it on the websites of the BBC, or *Forbes*, or the *New York Times*, or anywhere really.'

I scowl. How can this information be public knowledge and there still be programs on TV like *Benefit Street* where the poorest, neediest people are put to shame because they receive pitifully meager handouts from the government?

At that moment it occurs to me that not only have I watched these programs myself, but that I, too, have been hoodwinked into despising those poor people while the real culprits remained invisible to my rage and condemnation. What a clever sleight of hand by the one percent indeed!

The kettle boils and he pushes himself away from the counter, drops a tea bag into a mug and fills it with hot water. He looks at me. 'Milk? Sugar? Lemon?'

'Black, two sugars,' I say automatically.

He drops the cubes into the drink and brings the mug to me.

I smile up at him. 'You made me tea.'

He frowns and seems surprised. 'Actually, it's my first time, too. I don't believe I've ever made tea for anyone before.'

I put the mug down and reach into the purse slung across my body. 'I want to show you something,' I say. Unzipping it, I take out a folded piece of paper and give it to him. He takes it from me and unfolds it. I watch his eyes scan down my letter.

Then he looks up and smiles at me. It is a rich smile. 'You know, when we're at school, we're really only taught one thing that the system considers important. Every school in the world has different curricula and different subjects, but all schools have this one agenda in common.'

'What's that?' I ask curiously.

'Schools tame children and teach them obedience.'

'Obedience?' I say slowly, tasting the word.

'Obedience to the bell, the teacher, the rules, the grading system, the uniform, the time-keeping. It's how the few control the many.' He re-folds my letter. 'This letter of resignation is your first act of disobedience. And for that I congratulate you.'

I look up at him, fascinated and intrigued. Never could I have imagined at first sight of this arrogant, cock-sure man that there was such hidden depth to him. 'Will the system ever get changed, Dom?'

He shrugs. 'I don't know, Ella. It's hard to fight it because it *is* us. *We* are the ones who are making this system work, with our apathy, our compliance, and our obedience.' He smiles and shakes my letter at me. 'But every time someone writes a letter like this, it gives me hope that one day, maybe not in my lifetime, but one day the world will be different.'

There's a sound at the kitchen door, and a middle-aged woman comes through. She has badly dyed blonde hair and a big smile on her face.

'Hello, Mr. Eden,' she greets cheerfully.

'Hey, Mrs. B. Come and say hello to Ella. Ella, this is my housekeeper, Mrs. Bienkowski.'

'Hi, Mrs. B. It's a pleasure to meet you.'

Mrs. B turns out to be a warm, bustling character. As soon as Dom disappears into his study to make some calls, she takes me upstairs to a huge master bedroom with floral curtains, cream carpets, and a massive bed full of pillows. She shows me how everything in the bathroom works and then she asks if I have any allergies. I tell her no and she tells me dinner will be at eight.

That evening we set off on one of the walking trails. The air is clean and there's no noise of traffic—only the sounds of birds in the trees. Everywhere there are feeding posts. A red squirrel races up a tree. At a water fountain a pair of courting pigeons are kissing and flirting with each other.

A feeling of peace like I've never experienced growing up and living in London steals into my body. I take large breaths of fresh air. We hardly speak because words are not necessary, and I think I'm too stunned by how much my life has changed. How much fuller and richer it is. How much I love him. There, I've said it. I love Dominic Eden.

I know he has promised me nothing, but oh, how I do love this man.

How could I not? He came into my life like a tornado. Inconvenient. Unwanted. Destructive. He overturns everything I thought I believed in and fills me with the kind of passion I never knew existed. So yes, I do love this complicated, damaged, rich, strange, kind, beautiful man.

I stop and he stops too, and looks down at me. In the last rays that filter through the trees and catch his face, he is beautiful beyond any prince I could have dreamed of as a child. I entwine my arms around his powerful neck, he dips his head and we kiss. The kiss is different. It is different because of me, because of where we are, and because of him, too. When he raises his head, his eyes are dark and enquiring.

I just smile mysteriously and carry on walking.

When we arrive back at the house, we eat in that country dining room with the black and white curtains. Mrs. B has lit candles. In their yellow glow Dom looks impossibly mysterious and romantic. When he smiles, my heart actually lurches. I truly cannot believe my luck. Here I am jobless, but so incredibly, unbelievably happy.

We have coffee out on the long terrace overlooking lush green lawns.

'Until you find another job, I want to take care of you,' he says suddenly.

'Thank you,' I say softly. 'But I'll be OK. I have a little bit put away for a rainy day.'

He touches my hand. 'Ella, it's not a rainy day while I'm around.'

Something in his statement jars, but I don't dwell on it. I'm living for the moment. The future is far off and could even be beautiful.

'I didn't mean to say rainy day. Honestly, I have savings I can dig into,' I say with a smile. I don't tell him that it is a pitifully small amount.

He looks at me intently. 'But I want to help, Ella. It will give me great pleasure.'

'How about I'll ask if I need help?'

He looks at me with a flash of irritation and I just laugh. He's cute even when he's annoyed.

Eventually, Mrs. B comes to say goodnight. We watch her toddle off down the path and disappear from sight when she turns at the side of the house. I lean back and breathe in the night-scented air.

'How quiet it is here,' I say.

'Mmmm' He turns his head to look at me. 'It won't be so quiet when I get a hold of you.'

I laugh, the sound rolling into the dark night.

He crooks a finger at me.

I point to my chest and widen my eyes as if to say, me?

He smiles slowly. 'Yeah, you with the gorgeous ass.'

I make a big production of sensuously uncrossing my legs and stretching my body out. I slink out of the recliner and glance at him from under my lashes. While keeping an eye on me, he is taking an ice cube out of his glass. Gosh. He really is one super-tasty dish. I actually can't wait to get to his skin. Can't wait for him to touch me, kiss me, take me. It's never been like this for me. Ever since I met him it as if I am in a dream world where only he and I exist.

I take my shoes off and the grass is springy and cool under my feet. When in an animal sanctuary... So I leave my independent, strong self in my handbag and getting on my hands and knees on the sweet-smelling grass, I slowly, and I mean slowly, cccccccraaaaaawl to him. Yup, that's right. I will meet him animal to animal. Tonight is going to be a wild ride or my name is not Ella Savage.

I reach him purring like a tiger and angling my mouth I suck at the ice cube. Melted ice runs down my chin.

He puts his hand on my head and smiles. 'I don't like your pussy lower than my mouth.'

'No?'

'Fuck no.'

He grabs my hand and pulls me up. We run into the darkness of the garden.

'Where are we going?'

'Do you trust me?'

'Of course.'

'Good. Because it's time to face the truth.'

'What truth?' I ask breathlessly.

'There's a heated swimming pool at the bottom of the garden.'

I laugh. 'You're mad.'

'Totally.'

And I see it. A frosted glass structure. From the outside I can see many lights flickering in it. He opens the door and we are in. Lit purely by candles, hundreds of them, it is incredibly beautiful, with the wavy light reflecting on the water. It is also very warm. Like being in a tropical country. The candles are scented and the perfume is unfamiliar to me, but exotic, the way I imagine some jungle flower in the tropics to smell like.

'Wow! It's really hot in here,' I say.

He doesn't answer. He gets on with stripping me down to my bikini. I squeal when he picks me up and throws me into the deliciously warm water. I float on my back and watch him get naked before he plunges in.

He swims to me, wraps his arms around my body, and kisses me passionately. I have never kissed anybody while I am in water. It is a sensual, sinuous experience. When he lifts his head I am no longer in the middle of the pool, but have been brought close to an edge.

'Feel me,' he says.

My hands curl around his cock. 'Done,' I say.

And then I am slowly, with water sluicing down my body, rising out of the pool. Fuck! He's strong. I feel the hardness of the tiles by the side of the pool under my buttocks and thighs.

'I want to kiss your clit now...'

I spread my legs out eagerly. I've never known a man who is so crazy about eating my pussy as he is.

His lips move forward and kiss the front of my bikini bottom. Looking up at my face, he pulls on my hips to bring me even closer.

'Move the fucking material.'

Now that is what is called a fucking command. I pull the triangular piece of cloth slowly across to one side and expose my pussy to his eyes and lips. I put my hand on his shoulders to steady myself and press my naked pussy against his face.

'Lie back,' he orders.

With my legs still in the warm water I lie down on my back. I feel the cool tiles on my back and his cheeks brush against my thighs as he moves between them. My legs move up and across his shoulders. And so he licks. Long languorous, thorough licks. The same dedication with which way a dog would groom itself clean. Earnestly.

There's a job to be done here.

With each lick he goes deeper and deeper inside. One finger touches my hard clit.

'Oh!' I grab his head and spread my legs wider still. His tongue slips inside my pussy. Just a bit. Wow! It is enough to carry me home. I moan when he uses his finger to gently spread open my swollen lips.

'So pink. So sweet,' he murmurs.

One finger slides inside as his tongue continues to lick. I push against the finger. It slides farther inside. My eyes close and my body arches. His finger moves in and out of my wet, wet pussy. He covers my clit with his mouth and sucks.

My hand is clenched on the tiny material that I am holding back. My body tenses and I begin to moan. He begins to rub his whole face in my pussy. The action is so dirty I explode right there and then. Gushing onto his chin and listening to him slurp my juices greedily.

I come up on my elbows. Breathing heavily and craving cock! 'I think I'm going to need a very big cock deep inside me.'

He grabs the sides of my bikini and yanks them down my legs. 'I agree.' He presses his palms on the edge of the pool and pulls himself out. Then he lays a towel beside me and I quickly get on my hands and knees, push my bottom up and wait.

His huge erection slides in slowly. The fit is tight and the sensation of being stretched and filled is wonderful. Then he holds still and my pussy calls him. I move against him, rocking my body, calling his sperm. This is the first time we are doing it bareback. Nothing between us, flesh to flesh. He reaches forward and starts massaging my clit. Little slow circles as I impale myself repeatedly on him. His stiff cock goes in and out of me like a piston.

'I'm nearly there,' I say, and he grabs my hips and rams into me. I gasp at the rough, hard slam. He fucks like savage, jerking me like a doll. I feel his shaft become harder and bigger and then he sprays his load deep inside me. In seconds I am adding my own cum to his. It's a beautiful moment. We climaxed together. Without planning. Without trying. It just happened naturally.

He withdraws his throbbing cock and some of our warm cum gushes out of me, and drips down the inside of my thighs. He runs his fingers up and down my spine. We say nothing. We just enjoy the orgasmic high until we slip into warm water.

Like dolphins we glide and chase. Our bodies wet and slippery, we fuck in the water. I look deep into his eyes as I climax. He doesn't know it, but that is my body saying, I love you.

I don't know what lies in the future, and I don't care. I am just happy seizing the moment.

FIFTEEN

I return home the next day, still enchanted by the feel of deer eating directly from my outstretched palm, to find my answering machine blinking. One message at twelve thirty a.m. Who the hell left a message after midnight?

I press play and the message is blank. Well, it's not exactly blank—I can hear someone breathing. Frowning, I replay it. Yes, for at least thirty seconds someone held a phone to their ear and breathed into it. A chill runs up my spine. I dial 1471 and an automated voice says, 'Caller withheld their number.'

'Fuck you, Michael,' I whisper into the stillness of my flat.

I stand for a few moments looking at the phone. Then I pick up the receiver and call my mother.

'Hi, Mum,' I say brightly.

'Ella,' she says. 'Guess who I saw?'

'Who?'

'Your ex, Michael.'

I grip the phone harder. My mum doesn't know how much trouble I had with Michael. I never told her how crazy it all got because I didn't want to worry her. She only knows that he had become a pest and she was instructed to entertain neither phone calls nor any attempts from him to make contact.

I feel my heart rate increase. 'Oh?' I say as casually as I can. 'Where did you see him then?'

'I bumped into him at the supermarket.'

I frown. 'Which supermarket?'

'Morrisons.'

'You mean the small one near you?'

'Mmm.'

'Why was he shopping there? He doesn't live nearby,' I say, thinking aloud.

'I have no idea. He never said.'

'What did he say, then?'

'Not much. He was very friendly, though. He invited your dad and me for dinner. Obviously I said no. And then he went on his way.' My mother pauses. 'He didn't ask about you or anything like that.'

'When was this?'

'Day before yesterday. I wanted to tell you yesterday, but I forgot. I haven't done anything wrong, have I? I couldn't be rude.'

'Of course you didn't do anything wrong, Mum. But if you see him again, even accidentally, let me know, OK?'

'OK. When are you coming over?'

'This weekend?'

'That'll be nice. Why don't you stay the night?'

'Um ... I probably won't. But I'll definitely come over on Saturday. We can do some shopping and then I'll take you and Dad out for lunch.'

'All right, love. Do you want to speak to your dad?'

'What's he doing?'

'What do you think he's doing?'

'Oh, if he's watching TV don't bother him. I'll see you both at the weekend,' I say quickly.

'Goodbye, love.'

'Speak later, Mum.'

I put the phone down and call Anna's office number.

'How was it last night?' she says with barely suppressed curiosity.

'Er ... it was great.'

'Great?' she explodes dramatically. 'That's all I get?'

'I'll tell you all about it in one minute. Anna, has Michael tried to contact you?'

'Michael? I'm the last person that spineless, useless pig will call after the ear bashing I gave him the last time he tried to get *me* to pity *him*.'

'Right,' I say distractedly. Just the thought of having Michael in my life at this moment when everything is so wonderful and dreamlike gives me the shivers. I couldn't go through all that again.

'Why are you asking' Anna queries quietly.

'I think he called here last night, and Mum said she met him at the supermarket. I'm sure it's just a coincidence, but I just wanted to make sure he hasn't tried to contact you as well.'

'Coincidence? My ass! I'd call the pig right now if I were you and warn him that the injunction is still active. He's not allowed to come anywhere near you, or your family members.'

'Can I call you back Anna?'

'Sure. I'm here bored out of my mind. I'd love to hear about how you sucked Mr. Eden's fine, non-tax-paying cock.'

'Speak to you soon,' I say with a small laugh and cut the connection.

Right. Anna is right. The brightest thing to do is to face it head on and nip it in the bud. I dial Michael's number. Amazing how it's branded into my memory. I shudder at the thought that I'm again calling him.

The sound of his phone ringing echoes in my ear.

But he doesn't pick up, so I leave a coldly brutal message telling him to stay away from me, my mother, my workplace and all my friends. I remind him about the court injunction and tell him that if he ever calls me in the middle of the night again I'll get the police involved. Again!

I know he definitely won't want a repeat of what happened the last time.

I stand outside Rob's door holding my envelope, a tight ball of nervousness in the pit of my stomach. Well, you don't have to fear him after today. I knock on the wood

'Come,' he calls.

I open it and as I enter he looks up from some papers. There is slight frown on his face. 'What is it?' he asks impatiently.

I walk quickly to his desk and place my envelope down on his table.

He narrows his eyes. 'What's this?'

'It's my letter of resignation.'

His eyes pop open. For a second he actually looks panicked. 'What?' he erupts.

'I ... er ... I'm leaving HMRC.'

He stares at me with a shocked expression while I fidget uncomfortably. I certainly never expected this reaction. I've always suspected he secretly doesn't like me.

'Why?' he asks finally.

I look down at a spot on the blue carpet. 'We've actually had this conversation before, you know, about the unfairness of taxation. All this time, I thought I was making things better, but it turns out I'm not. I'm just perpetuating a system that is intrinsically wrong.'

'I see. So when did this change of heart come about?'

I shrug. I really don't want to discuss Dom with him especially since he dislikes him so intensely. 'It doesn't matter,' I say. 'I just came in here today to give you my letter in person and thank you for everything you've taught me. I won't be coming back after today. I've got some leave accrued to me and I'll just use it up as part of my notice.'

'Don't be stupid, Ella. No matter where you go there will always be unfair practices. At least here you know that you'll have a good pension scheme to take care of you.'

'Look, Sir. It's really kind of you to think of my future and everything, but I just can't stay.'

'But you're one of our rising stars. You have a real talent,' he says.

I look up, surprised by the compliment. I don't think I've ever had one from him. 'Thank you, Sir, for saying that. Er... it ... um ... means a lot to me, but my mind's made up. I just can't work here anymore.'

He frowns. 'Where will you go?'

I shrug again. 'I don't know yet. I'll probably find something temporary first and see how it goes.'

He holds my letter out to me. 'I'm not going to accept your resignation. It seems to me you are acting on an impulse. You should take some time to think about this more clearly.'

I don't take the letter from him. 'No, I have thought about it carefully.'

'You're throwing away a really good career on a whim. I always saw you as one of the managers here.'

He did! Really? Who would have guessed by the horrible way he treated me?

'It's not a whim, Sir.'

'Why don't you have dinner with me tonight?'

My eyes widen with shock. Wow, Rob has always been so distant and cold with me that I can't think of a more uncomfortable way to spend an evening. Besides I have absolutely nothing in common with him. I shake my head.

'It's not a date,' he says dryly.

I flush bright red with embarrassment. See, why I can't have dinner with a brute like him? 'I know that, Sir. Of course, it's not a date. I realize that you just want to try and talk me into staying, but really there's just no point. I've made up my mind.'

He stands. 'I think you're making a mistake.'

I smile awkwardly. It never crossed my mind that he would try to stop me from leaving that he even considered me such a valuable member of his team. Having said that, I suppose I was pretty useful to him. I did all the legwork so he could go out there and achieve all his monthly quotas.

'Why don't you take the leave that you are owed to relax and reflect on your decision? And if for any reason you change your mind you can always come back.'

I shake my head and start backing away. 'No, my mind's made. Thank you, Sir, for everything.'

'Wait, Ella.'

Holding the door open I turn around and find he is only a few feet away from me. 'At least finish the bloody week,' he says angrily. 'You're going to leave everybody in the shit leaving like this.'

I'll be glad to see the back of him. I shake my head, and say resolutely, 'Goodbye, Sir.' Then I close the door, happy that I have made the right decision.

Three weeks later ...

SIXTEEN

Dom

My mother always has her children driving over to her other childrens' houses delivering homemade food. I'm sure she does it because she thinks it will mean we see more of each other. Maybe she's right. I suppose I would see less of them without these errands she makes us all run for her. This week I have a box of Shane's favorite—lemon cupcakes—sitting on the passenger seat of my car.

I turn off the engine, grab the cakes, and, locking the door, cross the courtyard toward his apartment. My brother is a funny guy. It's easy to misunderstand him and think he's a pushover or a shallow playboy, but that's just a façade he employs since it's so convenient and effective. The opposite is true.

He's actually very deep. Deeper than me, anyway. Me, I'm a simple guy. Neanderthal simple. Especially when it comes to women. My woman is my woman and mine alone. Shane's more complicated. He doesn't go out there all guns blazing to keep his woman.

Like that time with Lily. It was Shane who was first interested in her, but he took her to a party at Jake's house, and Jake and Lily immediately hooked up. I know that Jake and Lily are mad about each other and all that, but the ease with which Shane allowed Jake to take his woman shocked me. I mean, I don't know what I would have done. I love my brother, but I might have had to punch him real hard. I know I definitely wouldn't have behaved like it was nothing, like I was some sort of wuss.

It bothered me so much that I asked Shane how he could be so cool about something like that. He shrugged and said, 'I can get a woman any time. Sometimes I open my kitchen drawer and one pops out. But I can never replace Jake. I'd give my life for him. He's family.'

And suddenly I remembered being fourteen again. My father had just been killed, and Jake had taken his place, so he was never in the house. It seemed to me then that my whole family was falling apart, and for some weird reason I became furious with my mother, as it was her fault that my father had stolen money from a gangster and had his throat cut.

Rebelliously, I began to act out. I cut school and would never come home until late, and when I did come home I wouldn't speak to anyone. I was rude and sullen. I stole alcohol from the supermarket and got drunk. And when I was drunk, all I wanted to do was fight. I fought with everybody in those days.

Shane had just turned ten, then. One night I came home late, nearly midnight. Layla was asleep, Jake was out, of course, and only my mother and Shane were home. I walked into the house and heard a strange crooning sound coming from the living room. So I stopped and tiptoed to the door, and what I saw changed me forever.

My mother's head was in my brother's lap. She was weeping quietly, and he was gently stroking her cheek and kind of singing to her in a strange, reedy voice.

'Don't you worry, Ma. Don't you worry. Everything will work out perfectly. Jake and I'll take care of you. Dom will come around. He always does. Don't you worry, Ma. Don't you worry.'

I didn't show myself. I walked backwards out of the door. I went to an illegal, open-all-night pub and got totally smashed. I felt so ashamed. Shane had taken on the role that I should have. Jake was doing his bit, and I was slacking. No one had asked me to change my ways. Everybody was just waiting for me to come to my senses.

I woke up the next morning with an almighty hangover, and totally changed. I pulled my weight, and I've never forgotten the strength of character that Shane showed at the tender age of ten. I know it's all still there. He's playing the part of the devil-may-care playboy, but one day the real Shane will come through and reveal himself.

I open the entrance door to the block of apartments. It's a Sunday night—the night porter is nowhere to be seen, and the reception area's deserted. I get into the lift and hit the button for Shane's floor. The doors open, I get out of the lift, walk down the short corridor, and knock on his door. He opens it in a stained T-shirt and ripped jeans.

'You OK?' he says.

'Yeah, good,' I reply and hold out the box of cakes.

'Thanks.' He takes the box, immediately opens it, and, selecting a cupcake, bites into it. 'Delicious,' he says, and holds the open box out to me.

'Nah,' I decline, and he shrugs and leads the way to his living room.

We get into the room, and to my surprise my niece and nephew are playing there. They squeal with delight when they see me.

'Where are their parents?' I ask.

'Mummy and Daddy and Uncle BJ and Aunty Layla have all gone to dinner,' Liliana announces importantly.

I look at Shane curiously. 'Are they here on their own with you?'

'What're you looking so surprised for?'

I cross my arms. 'They trust you to take care of their kids?'

He seems amused. 'Yeah.'

I feel vaguely miffed. 'How come they never ask me to babysit?'

'They love their kids, Dom,' he says with a perfectly straight face.

I scowl. 'What the fuck is that supposed to mean?'

He raises both his hands in mock surrender. 'Hold your fire. Just kidding. It's probably because you don't know the first thing about babies.'

'How much is there to know?'

He grins. 'Can you change a diaper?'

Changing diapers! Of course not. 'Can you?' I ask, genuinely surprised. See what I mean about my brother being a dark horse.

He shrugs carelessly. 'Sure.'

'When did you learn to do that?'

'Had a girlfriend who had a kid,' he explains casually.

'How difficult is it?'

He pops the last bit of cake into his mouth and says, 'Piece of cake.'

'So why won't they trust me to babysit?'

He puts the box of cakes down on a cabinet and turns to me. There's a curious expression on his face. 'Do you want to?'

I look down at the kids and hesitate.

Shane begins to smile. That 'stupid, see, I knew you couldn't do it' smile.

It gets my back up. 'Yeah, I do,' I say nonchalantly.

'OK, I'll let you get on with it then.'

'Wait a minute. Where are you going?'

He looks at his watch. 'If I leave now, I could take Tanya out to dinner.'

I frown. 'You're going to leave them both here with me? Alone?'

'That's the plan. Unless you think … you can't cope.'

I look at the children. They're sitting on the floor like two little angels. They stare back at me with big, curious eyes. Of

course I can do it. What can possibly go wrong? If Shane can
...

'No, go ahead,' I tell Shane. 'Have fun. I can manage.'

But Shane has me figured pretty good. He's already pulling his T-shirt over his head and striding toward his bedroom. He comes back into the room in a clean T-shirt. My brother is so good-looking he doesn't even need to run a fucking brush through his hair.

'Right then,' he says cheerfully. 'All their stuff is in the spare bedroom. In an hour's time, warm the milk already prepared in the bottles and just give it to them.'

I nod slowly.

'You sure about this?'

'Have fun, Shane.'

'Laters,' he says to the kids, and, winking at me, goes out of the door.

I look at the kids. 'It's just us now,' I say, and walk to the window, where I watch Shane get into his car and roar off.

Inside the apartment Tommy gives a great big howl.

I rush to his side. 'What?'

'I pinched him,' Liliana confesses calmly.

'What did you do that for?'

'He poked me in the heart,' she says tearfully, pointing to the middle of her chest. 'And it hurt.'

'He's just a baby, Liliana. He didn't really mean it,' I explain reasonably.

'Yes, he did,' she insists as I pick Tommy up while he carries on with his meltdown. I realize immediately that there's a very bad smell coming from him. Holding him at arm's length, I then put him back on the floor.

Liliana is looking up at me with enormous accusing eyes, and I experience a rush of panic. I shouldn't have let Shane leave. I brush my face with my hand while Tommy continues to bawl inconsolably.

'Fuck it,' I mutter, and pick him up again. I hold him the way I see everybody else holding babies. The way Shane does. With his little stiff body close to mine—but he only screams even harder. I put him back on the floor.

'Do you want some ice cream?' I offer desperately.

Tommy stops crying instantly, and, standing up, gazes at me with tear-stained, hopeful eyes. His mouth is still quivering, just in case I don't come through with my offer. 'I cream,' he shouts happily.

'Yes, ice cream,' I repeat brightly.

'He's not allowed to have any,' Liliana forbids in an eerily grown-up voice.

At that, Tommy throws himself to the ground and howls his head off in frustration. 'I waaaaant i cream. I WAAAAANT I CREAM,' he hollers.

'Why is he not allowed ice cream?' I demand.

The little madam has her chubby arms crossed over her chest and is glaring up at me. 'Because we are *both* not allowed.'

'Why not?'

'There's sugar in it and sugar is bad for children.'

'Well, he's damn well having some,' I mutter.

'I'm telling,' she warns.

'Yeah, you do that,' I say, and, picking Tommy up by the armpits, begin to stride toward the kitchen with her following behind. If she's not careful she's getting Layla's disgusting gin and tonic ice cream.

There's a highchair pushed up against a wall. I drag it to the table and secure Tommy into it. The smell from his diaper is making me gag. I move away from him and open the freezer door. One scoop isn't going to kill them. Triumphantly, I pull out a tub of cookies and cream flavor and show it to Tommy.

'Mmmm,' I say in an exaggerated way and put it down on the counter.

Tommy cackles with delight.

I turn and look at Liliana. 'This is your last chance.'

She blinks, and I know I've got her.

'I won't tell if you won't,' I cajole softly. I know it's wrong to bribe her like this, but what the hell. This is an emergency.

She grins suddenly, and I see Jake in her little face. That same gorgeous smile. Something inside me knots up. I feel a wave of deep love for her.

'I cream,' Tommy demands, banging the tray.

'Right,' I say, and fill Tommy's bowl with three scoops of ice cream, because one just seems so mean.

I pull a chair out and raise my eyebrows at Liliana. Very primly, she walks over to the chair and slides in.

I put a bowl down in front of her. 'Do you know how to change a diaper, Liliana?'

She shakes her head solemnly. 'No, but Mummy knows how. We can call Mummy.'

I pick up the ice cream tub and start scooping it out. 'No. No, let's not.'

'Daddy knows how, too. We can call him,' is her next brilliant suggestion.

I put the tub of ice cream down. 'I know what,' I say in an unnaturally high voice. 'Shall we learn it together on the Internet after you finish eating your ice cream?'

She starts bouncing up and down. 'OK.'

I get my phone out and dial up YouTube—how to get a diaper on a baby in less than one minute. I put my phone on the table and we watch the video together while Tommy spreads ice cream all over his face, clothes, and chair.

When it's over, I look across at Liliana. 'You ready?'

I pull a couple of kitchen towels, and as I'm walking toward Tommy, he manages to spin his bowl and it flies in the air and crashes dramatically to the ground, breaking and spilling ice cream everywhere. Christ! Liliana covers her mouth with both her hands. Over her hands, her eyes are round and full of an 'oh, oh, look what you've let happen now' expression.

'Want i cream,' Tommy bawls.

Jesus. This is turning out to be much harder than it looked.

Liliana uncovers her mouth. 'Uncle Shane always uses Tommy's plastic bowl.'

'Great. Thanks for the early tip,' I mutter.

I stop for a moment. I need to think. And I can't think with all this noise. These kids are doing my head in. First: stop that kid from howling. He wants ice cream. She says plastic bowl. Right.

Ice cream.

Plastic bowl.

I open the cupboard and find a green plastic bowl. I show the kid the bowl and he stops howling. I toss a couple of scoops into it and plonk it in front of him. He sticks his spoon into it and shovels it into his mouth.

'He'll be sick,' a small, knowing voice says.

'No he won't,' I snarl.

'You shouted at me, Uncle Dom.' Her lower lip starts trembling.

Oh no. Oh no. 'No I didn't,' I deny, while plastering a big, fake smile on my face.

'Yes, you did,' she wails and scrunches up her face.

For fuck's sake! I start walking toward her. 'That was just a joke, sweetie. I wasn't shouting. Look, do you want more ice cream?'

She sniffs and nods.

I grab the tub and put four generous scoops into her bowl. I look at her, and she stares at me with her spoon lifted meaningfully above her bowl.

'More?' I ask incredulously. This is the drama queen who claimed sugar is bad for children.

She nods vigorously.

I don't believe this. I throw another couple of scoops in.

'Thank you, Uncle Dom,' she says solemnly, and drops her spoon into the ice cream. While they're eating, I pick up the broken pieces from the floor. The ice cream is melting fast, but I manage to mop up the largest blobs with paper towels. However, I can see that I'm going to have to settle them in the other room and come back to clean this mess.

SEVENTEEN

Dom

After they've eaten, I clean Tommy's face and hands, pick him up, and, with Liliana following behind, carry him to the spare room. It's a surprise to see it done up colorfully with two cots in it. They must stay with Shane often.

I put Tommy on his back on the table with the plastic mat spread on its surface.

Liliana wrinkles her nose. 'Tommy stinks.'

'You bet he does.'

There's a pile of nappies, and I take one and unfold it, and place it on the table. I undo the straps on the sides of Tommy's diaper and lift the front flap away from his tummy. The sight and stench of the kid's shit just makes me want to gag. I mean, seriously gag. I actually start to retch. And I would have been sick too if I'd not very quickly re-closed the diaper and taped it back on.

'That's not how you change it,' Liliana says.

'I know that,' I say, turning my head to the side and taking deep breaths of clean air. I pick up my phone and dial Ella's number.

She answers on the third ring. 'Hey, sexy,' she breathes into the phone.

Not feeling sexy right now. 'How do you feel about changing a very smelly diaper?'

'Um ... Is this a trick question?'

'No.'

'It sounds like one.'

'Look, I need to change a diaper, and I can't get past the gag reflex.'

She begins to chuckle. 'I'll be right over. Where are you?'

'I'm at Shane's apartment. I'll text you the address.'

My phone rings again. It's Lily. Oh fuck! 'Hey, Lily,' I say too brightly.

'Hey, Dom. Shane called to tell us you've taken over. How's it going?' she asks casually, but I can hear the thread of panic in her voice.

'Great.'

'Yeah?'

'Yeah,' I insist confidently.

'Er ... Can I speak to my daughter, please?'

'Sure,' I say, and, looking at Liliana, put my finger on my lips to warn her not to say anything about the ice cream.

She nods conspiratorially. I smile at her approvingly and show her the thumbs-up signal.

She takes the phone, listens for a moment, then says, 'Yeah, but Uncle Dom gave us ice cream. Tommy had some, but I didn't have any.'

I stare at the little lying rat in shock. What a bare-faced liar! She drops me in the shit and saves her own skin. Even I wouldn't have lied like that at her age. Hell, her belly is still stuffed full of undigested ice cream.

'And, Mummy'—she looks up at me before continuing sanctimoniously—'Tommy's diaper is full of poop, but Uncle Dom doesn't know how to change nappies. He called someone to come and help him.' She listens for a bit more then she says, 'Nope. Nope. OK, Mummy. I love you too, too much too.' The little minx then hands the phone back to me. 'Mummy wants to speak to you.'

I bet she fucking does. You little rat, you. I glare at her as I snatch the phone from her.

'Hi, Lily.'

'Is Ella coming round, Dom?' Lily asks crisply.

Bloody hell. She's sharp. 'Yeah,' I admit.

'Oh! Good ... er ... when?'

'Fifteen minutes tops.'

'That's fine, then. We'll be back in an hour's time. Is that OK?'

'Yeah, that's just fantastic.'

'See you later. Oh, and, Dom ... Don't give my daughter any more ice cream,' she says, and I can fucking hear the laughter in her voice.

'Not a drop,' I say, and kill the call.

'Is my Mummy mad at you?' Liliana asks innocently.

Un-fucking-believable. 'What do you think, you little troublemaker, you?' I ask as my phone goes again. I glance down. It's Layla. I groan. Now what?

'Hey, Layla.'

'Dom, where's my son right now?'

I turn around to where I saw him last, and to my horror he is nowhere to be seen. I feel a flash of panic. The flat is eerily silent.

'Oh fuck,' I curse.

Layla's voice is deliberately calm. 'He'll be in the kitchen, Dom.' I start running toward the kitchen. Layla is right. He is. He's sitting by the bowl of cat food. And ... Oh! Damn! He's fucking scooping up handfuls and *eating* it.

'I found him,' I say, lifting him up with my other hand.

'What's he doing?' Layla asks.

'Nothing,' I say, as I stuff him into the highchair.

'What did you call for, Layla?' I ask, while I try to hook pieces of cat biscuit out of Tommy's mouth.

'Just to tell you to put the cat bowl up where Tommy can't reach it.'

'Yeah. I'll definitely do that.'

'Call me if you're unclear about anything, OK?'

'Right, will do.'

'Bye.'

I press the disconnect button and throw my phone on the table. Jesus, kids and their crap. How do people put up with this shit? I clean his mouth out while he tries his best to swallow the brown mush down. I wipe his hands.

'Uncle Shane doesn't allow Tommy in the kitchen because he likes eating the cat's food,' Little Miss Perfect says.

'Yeah?' I have a new respect for Shane. I had no idea kids were such a handful.

'You have to watch him or he'll drink out of the toilet, too,' Liliana chirps, nodding her head sagely.

I turn to look at her. She's enjoying this. Well, she's not going to win. A fighter can't be afraid of anything.

I pick up the cat bowl from the floor and put it on the counter. Then I lift Tommy up and stalk into the living room. The truth is, I feel quite distraught. I don't know if cat food will make the kid sick. I put him on the floor. I want to Google the effects of eating cat food, and I realize my phone is still in the kitchen. I go to get it, and come back to find Liliana standing in the middle of the room with her hands on her hips.

'Tommy is sucking the cat's tail,' she announces in what can only be described as a passive-aggressive tone.

'What the hell?' I turn to look at Tommy, and indeed he's sucking on its tail. I run to him, pick him up, and try to shoo the cat away, but it hisses at me and refuses to move. I drop Tommy onto the sofa. There's a toy train on the table and I give it to him. He takes it with a squeal of delight. How much longer before Ella gets here? I really can't handle this for many more minutes. I run my hands through my hair.

'I'm bored,' Liliana says.

I rub my hands together with fake enthusiasm. 'So, what shall we do until Aunty Ella comes, huh?'

Liliana shrugs. 'Shall we play hide and seek?'

'Nope. Let's not do that. How about we watch some TV?'

'OK,' she says agreeably.

'Lee Jaw,' Tommy says.

'What?'

'Little Lucien,' Liliana translates.

I switch on the TV, find the video, and press play. Both kids settle on the floor. The doorbell goes. Oh! Thank God. I rush to open the door and by God Ella is a sight for sore eyes.

'Hey, sexy,' I say looking her up and down. To my horror, I see Tommy shoot out of the front door past my legs. Honestly, I'm way too shocked to do anything, but Ella catches him by the scruff of his T-shirt.

She smiles at me. 'When they run away from you, they're not really running away. They just want to be caught.'

'Oh, boy, am I glad to see you.'

I pull her in and close the door. 'Listen, Ella. Tommy ate a bit of cat food before I could get to him.'

To my relief she grins. 'It won't hurt him. Most things won't. Kids are made to be as tough as old boots. To ensure the survival of the human race and all that.'

'Really?'

'Yeah. My brother took a dead cockroach from the mouth of a cat and ate it. My mother never recovered, but he was perfectly fine.'

I sigh with relief. 'Christ was tested in the desert by Satan. I've been tested by my nephew.'

EIGHTEEN

I walk into the kitchen and catch Dom on his hands and knees wiping a wet sponge on the floor in circles, an action that is only serving to smear melted ice cream all over the floor. I stand there looking at him, at his endearing helplessness, and falling in love all over again. I don't know how grating an undomesticated male can eventually become, but right now, it's like watching puppies fall asleep on the lip of their food bowls. Cute, cute, cute.

He looks up, sees me, and sudden panic flares in his eyes.

'Where's Tommy?' he asks urgently.

'Relax. He's *inside* his playpen with a bottle of milk.'

I hear him exhale with relief.

'And Little Miss Perfect?'

I bite back a smile. 'Watching a cartoon.'

'Is it normal for a three-year-old kid to talk like her?'

'She is a bit precocious, but kids nowadays are more advanced than we were.'

'Right,' he mutters.

I smile at him.

'Thank you,' he says.

I start walking toward him. 'Need some help?'

'Nah, I think I've nearly got it all,' he says, looking down at the mess.

I go over to the cupboard under the sink, and, opening it, find some cloths and a bottle of floor cleaner. I find a bowl and fill it from the hot water tap. I squirt a little cleaner into the bowl and walk over to him. I take the sponge out of his hand and replace it with a wet cloth. I toss the sponge across the room into the sink and squat beside him. I wink and begin to clean the floor. He copies my actions exactly.

'So you got the diaper on, huh?' he asks casually.

'Yeah.' I dip the cloth into the bowl of warm water and rinse it.

'Any problems?'

'Nope.'

'Hmmm ... Good.'

There is silence for a few minutes.

'What do you think they feed that kid?' he asks.

I hide my amusement as I wring milky water out of the cloth. 'I don't know. Maybe dead cats.'

'I never imagined a baby could stink like that,' he says in an awed voice. He actually shudders.

I push the bowl over to him. 'I'll have to be sure not to fart in bed, then.'

He stops swirling the cloth in the water. 'Let's make a deal. Any time you eat a dead cat for dinner, and you think you're gonna fart in bed, just let me know, and I'll put a sick bowl by my side,' he says very seriously.

I laugh so hard at the thought of him puking his guts into a bowl that I fall over backwards. He sits on his heels looking down at me. 'Have I ever told you, Ella Savage, you are one delicious woman?'

'Is it because I'm covered in ice cream?' I giggle.

He bends down and kisses my nose. 'Even before that. Well before that,' he growls.

We're interrupted by an incoherent scream of rage coming from the living room. Dom freezes.

'Go on,' I say. 'I'll finish up here and join you.'

'No, you go. I'll finish up here and join *you*.'

I try not to chuckle. 'Are you afraid of them, Dominic Eden?'

'Terrified,' he says.

I kiss his nose and go into the living room. Tommy is upset because Liliana has changed the channel.

'Right,' I say. 'No more TV. How about we read a book?'

Both are happy with that, so I take Tommy out of the playpen, and together we choose a book and cuddle up on the sofa to read it. By the time Dom comes in, both kids are leaning on either side of me and we are more than halfway through the book.

He stops at the entrance and watches for a minute before he comes in and sits down with us. After reading the book, we play with the kids.

It's a game where Dom has to say, 'Fe fi fo fum, I smell the blood of a half-gypsy girl and the blood of a full-gypsy boy.'

Total panic ensues, with Dom taking on the persona of a zombie-like creature and chasing the kids, and them dodging his flailing arms while they squeal, scream, and laugh hysterically. As soon as their parents arrive, Liliana dashes to the door and lunges at her father.

'Tommy broke a bowl, Daddy,' Liliana says, as soon as she is high up in her father's arms.

'I smell ice cream,' her father says with a straight face.

She covers her mouth. 'Tommy ate ice cream.'

'And you didn't?'

She shakes her head vigorously.

Jake looks at me. 'My daughter is such a liar.'

'You can say that again,' Dom mutters.

'Why does my son smell of cat food, Uncle Dom?' Layla asks.

Dom coughs.

'Because Uncle Dom let Tommy eat cat food,' Liliana says.

'How much?' Layla wonders.

'Maybe one mouthful,' Dom admits sheepishly.

Layla grins. 'Actually, I think you coped brilliantly. Much better than I thought. What are you doing next Sunday?'

Dom actually takes a backward step, and everybody laughs. Even BJ joins in at the terror on Dom's face.

After they've gone, Dom closes the door and turns to me. 'Do you want to have sex in my brother's flat?'

'No, I don't. But you can take me to dinner and then have sex with me at my place. You won't believe what I'm wearing underneath these boring old clothes.'

His eyes brighten. 'What are you wearing?'

'It's a surprise.'

'Let's go,' he says, and bundles me quickly out of the apartment.

NINETEEN

'**I**'ll go feed the parking meter,' I offer, opening my bag and getting my coin purse out.

'No, stay in the car. I'll do it,' Dom says.

I shake my head. 'Dom, it's just there across the road. I'll do it,' I insist, and, opening the passenger door, get out.

I cross the road, put enough coins into the machine for two hours of parking time, and get a receipt. When I look up, I see that he has got out of the car and has his forearms resting on the roof as he stands looking at me. A breeze blows at his hair and he smoothes it down. He is so gorgeous I still get butterflies in my tummy just looking at him.

I grin at him and step onto the road. There's a loud blare from someone's horn, and I wake up from my little dream world where only Dom and I exist. I turn my head and see a white van coming, so I quickly step back onto the pavement.

The van passes, and Dom comes back into my sight, no longer casually resting his forearms on the roof of his car, but standing with his hands at his sides and staring at me in disbelief. His face is white and his mouth is hanging open.

'What?' I mouth, shaking my head.

A car goes past. The road becomes empty and I run across it.

'What?' I ask again.

He shakes his head slowly, blankly. 'Nothing.'

'You're as white as a sheet.'

He looks at me strangely. 'Am I?'

'Yes.'

'I thought that car was going to hit you.'

I laugh. It's not really a proper laugh. I'm disturbed by the sudden change in him. His expression and demeanor are so bizarre and out of character. We were laughing two minutes ago. 'Well, it didn't,' I say.

'I know. I saw that,' he says robotically.

'Dom, it wasn't even a near miss. I had plenty of time.'

'I know,' he says again.

I take his hand, and I'm shocked to find it trembling.

'What's the matter, Dom?' I ask urgently.

'Nothing. Let's go to dinner.'

I give him the parking receipt and he displays it on the dashboard and locks the car. Then we walk to the restaurant and sit opposite each other. I look at him and he looks away.

'Dom, what the hell is going on?'

He turns to me. 'Leave it alone. Please.'

Because I can see that he is so extremely affected, I drop it quietly.

The waitress comes and he orders a triple whiskey. My eyebrows rise involuntarily, but I say nothing. When the drinks come, he downs his in one go and calls for another.

We order our food. It comes and we eat. All the while, we talk in a wooden manner. He tells me Lily is pregnant. She just found out today. Shane has started dating a magician called Tanya. Jake is sending their mother on holiday to Spain. And I tell him my mother has invited us to dinner on Saturday. He nods. He smiles. But his face is a mask.

Dessert menus are flourished. He wants nothing. So I follow his lead. He refuses coffee. And then I know he doesn't want to spend any more time with me.

He's pushing me away.

And it hurts like mad. Why? What have I done? How can he just shut me out for no reason like this? I start to feel angry, but I'm unable to express my anger. Some part of me knows that whatever it is, it's serious. It's eating him up. The bill gets paid.

'Come, I'll take you home,' he says, getting to his feet.

I nod and pick up my purse. Yes, he definitely wants to get rid of me. We walk to the car in silence. We drive in silence. Outside my apartment, I turn toward him.

'I'll call you tomorrow,' I say quietly.

'Yeah, OK.'

He bends and kisses me lightly on the cheek. 'Goodnight.'

He's dismissing me as if I'm some woman he doesn't give a shit about. I feel utterly abandoned. I peer into his closed face. 'Have I done something wrong, Dom?'

He shakes his head. 'No, it's not you.' And then he grips the steering wheel. 'It's not you,' he says again. As if in those three words lies the solution to what is eating him.

'Goodnight,' I say.

'Goodnight, Ella,' he says softly.

I get out of the car, sad and confused. He waits until I get into the door of my apartment building before he drives off. I lean against the wall of the foyer and listen to his car blast off into the night before I slowly climb the stairs up to my flat. I let myself in. There is a lamp burning in the living room. I walk to the sofa and sink heavily into it. It feels as if my whole world has just collapsed.

I'm in love with a man I cannot understand. A man who is closed off to me. The only time he's real with me is when we're in bed, but tonight, for no reason that I can see, he has rejected even that from me.

I *know* we have something.

It feels so real, but is it enough?

381

I go into my bedroom and sit in front of my dressing table. My face looks dazed and lost and I feel like crying, but I don't. I tell myself that I am strong. I can be strong for him and for me.

One day he will tell me what's wrong.

One day I will make his demons go away. Until that day, I will be here waiting and loving him. I cleanse my face, get into my pajamas, and finish my toilette. Then I go back into the living room and listen to music.

I listen to Heart singing 'Stairway to Heaven'. And the sadness of the song makes me tear up. The song ends, and my phone buzzes. A message from Dom. I am so desperate to open the message that I drop the phone. I pick it up and click on the text.

Are you still up?

My hands shake as I type in my one word reply: Yes. And click send. I cover my mouth and wait. The phone sounds again almost immediately.

Don't go 2 bed. Coming round in 10 minutes.

I stare at it. And suddenly it's as if I've been told I've won the lottery. I leap up from the sofa and run to the bedroom. I get out of my PJs and slip into a sexy nightie. It's see-through with a plunging neckline and little pearl buttons. I light some scented beeswax candles. I slick on nude lip gloss. Standing in front of the mirror, I brush my hair and dab perfume onto my wrists.

Once I'm satisfied with my appearance, I go back to the living room and because I gave him a key to my flat last week I arrange myself in a sexy pose on the sofa. I hear his key in the door and hurriedly fluff my hair. The door opens. He stands for a moment in the doorway and sways slightly. Then he comes in and, closing the door, leans against it. I stare at him. He is dead drunk!

'Hey there, tiger,' he drawls.

'Hey, you,' I say cautiously.

He starts walking toward me, stumbles once, rights himself, and continues on his journey to me.

'You drove here like this?' I ask incredulously.

He nods.

'God! Dom. You can barely stand. You could have killed yourself. Or someone else.'

'I didn't,' he mutters, 'kill anyone, if that's what you're worried about.'

I stand. 'I'll make some coffee for you,' I say, heading toward the kitchen. I love him, but I'm not going to condone drunk driving. As I pass him, his hand shoots out and he pulls me into his hard body.

'I spent a lot of time and money to get into this state. I don't want to sober up just yet, thanks,' he says.

I look into his eyes. There's no real focus in them. If I'm going to find out anything, now is the best time. 'OK. Come sit with me and let's talk.'

He shakes his head slowly. 'I didn't get this way to sit and talk with you.'

'What do you want to do, Dom?'

'What I always want to do when I'm around you, Ella.'

A chill comes into my body. Here. Cold, clear proof that I am nothing but a good fuck. I'm in love with the guy, and all he wants from me is sex.

'Is that all you want from me?'

He frowns and peers at me. 'Awww, Ella. We have this. Isn't this good?'

I don't answer him.

'C'mon, babe. Don't kick a man when he's down.'

'Are you down?'

He breathes out. 'Like you wouldn't believe.'

'What's wrong? Tell me, please?'

'You don't want to know.'

I stare at him with frustration. 'But I do.'

'Trust me, you don't want to know.'

I look up at him, confused and intrigued. What on earth could it be that I wouldn't want to know?

He frowns again. 'I can't talk about it yet,' he says and slips his forefinger into my cleavage. He gazes into my eyes. 'You're so beautiful,' he whispers.

In the candlelight, his eyes glimmer. The air is snatched from my throat. I suck in a breath. Strains of music surround us. It's so sweet and intoxicating, it should have been magic, but it's not. An air of barely suppressed grief hangs around him. He sighs heavily, and a deep worry line etches itself between his eyebrows.

My heart feels heavy.

'There are all kinds of memories hiding in the curves of your breasts,' he murmurs. His eyes flutter shut and then snap open. He is maudlin. Vulnerable.

His other hand comes up and cups my breast. He rolls my nipple between his fingers and I feel the familiar itching between my legs start. His eyes darken as he thrusts his knee between my thighs. I push my sex against the hard muscles and feel his cock pressing against my hip, straining to get to my wet heat.

'Oh, Ella,' he groans, and, lifting me up, clumsily carries me to my bed.

He drops me on the bed, and, with haphazard urgency, removes his shoes and clothes. He lands on the bed heavily and immediately rolls onto his back.

'Ride me. I want to watch your face when that hot little pussy of yours stretches wide for my cock,' he growls.

I clamber over him and sit on his thighs.

He pops the two little pearl buttons on my nightie. My breasts spill out and he slides his hands over the flesh and massages them.

'You really are so ripe and beautiful,' he mutters to himself.

I arch my back to push my breasts into his hands.

'Get naked,' he orders.

I pull my nightie over my head and fling it to the floor.

He takes a deep, satisfied breath, curls his hands around my midriff, and pulls me down for a kiss. I spread myself flat over his hardness as his mouth claims mine. He smells of alcohol and something broken. I don't know him, and he won't allow me in. The thought is extraordinarily painful. A lone finger strokes the swollen lips of my vulva as the kiss goes on. It makes me melt into him until he digs his fingers into my hips. I pull away from his mouth and stare down at him.

'Come, sit on my face,' he invites.

I knee-walk along his body and turn to face his feet. Hovering over his face, I slither and snake my body like a belly dancer so he can see what a gooey puddle my pussy has become.

'So eager, so wanton,' he growls.

Cupping the globes of my bottom as I gyrate teasingly above him, he lifts his face and extends his tongue. It flicks my clit and I whimper with the velvet heat. He pulls me lower and lets his tongue worm its way through the damp undergrowth.

As soon as he tastes my syrup, he pulls me all the way down, and I helpfully spread my thighs as wide as I can. I reach down and let the tip of my tongue flick and tickle his cock. He shudders under me and glues my vulva to his face. I feel my juices flow out of me and drip into his mouth.

Down his throat they go.

Fisting the base of his shaft, I take the meaty pillar deeper into my mouth, curling my tongue around it. I bob up and down, my eyes shut. The rest of the world melts into nothing. There is only his mouth on my pussy and his cock in my mouth.

My orgasm comes suddenly, without warning. I push my palms into the mattress and climax hard with his cock buried deep in my throat, my nipples throbbing and tingling, and my whole body singing.

In all the rush and uproar, it occurs to me that I am hopelessly addicted to him. That I've been addicted from that first fix, when he threw me against a wall and shoved his cock into me without asking my permission.

A drop of slippery liquid touches the roof of my mouth. Ah! I start to suck really hard, as if I'm milking him. He comes in a thick, frothy spray, which I swallow willingly. Strange, how I adore my own sense of complete and utter submission to this man. I wriggle my hips.

'Don't you dare move,' he warns.

I don't. Very gently, I keep sucking the semi-hard flesh in my mouth. I work on it until it starts to stretch and grow and become rock hard. I take his cock out of my mouth, and, crawling down his body, poise my pussy over his erection.

'I want to hear the animal noises you make,' he says.

I hold onto the base of his shaft while he groans with pleasure as his erect cock slowly fills me up. Once all of him is inside me, I ride him with rhythmic, languid thrusts, and animal sounds fill the bedroom until we come, gripping each other so hard he leaves marks on my skin.

'I don't want to sleep the whole night,' he whispers fiercely.

'Why?' I whisper back.

'Just this one night I don't want to close my eyes. All I want to do is make— Fuck all night.'

'OK,' I say, but we do fall asleep. Curled up against each other like two puppies in a basket. And we sleep soundly until the wee hours of the morning when a large hand crashes into my ribs and shocks me awake.

I sit up and see Dom thrashing his legs and moving his hands restlessly.

I switch on my bedside lamp and start shaking him and urgently calling his name. His eyes fly open. They are wild with horror. They fasten on me and widen with shock.

He rises off the pillows and grabs my upper arms, but I have the impression that I've become part of the nightmare that he's still locked into. 'I thought you were dead,' he says in a strange voice.

'I'm not,' I say.

At the sound of my voice he suddenly lets go of my arms. He falls back on the pillows and covers his eyes with his forearm.

'Oh! God!' he howls. The sound comes from somewhere so deep and pained that I become frozen with fear.

A few seconds pass before I shuffle closer. 'Tell me, please, Dom. Just tell me what's wrong?' I beg.

He puts his arm down and looks at me. 'You're a good person, Ella. But I just can't do this anymore. It's a lie. All of it is a lie.'

He vaults off the bed and begins to dress.

'You're going to leave now?' I ask in disbelief.

'I'm sorry,' he says, and, without looking at me, walks out of my door.

I sit there stunned. I have no idea what the hell has just happened. Has he just fucking broken up with me?

Bang, bang, my baby shot me down!

TWENTY

I stand at the window in a daze and listen to his car come to life with such an explosive sound that it makes me jump. I don't go back to bed after he speeds off. Maybe because I cannot believe that he will not come back.

We were going so good. It seems incredible that he would raze the city and salt the earth just like that. Over nothing. Nothing earth-shattering has happened. I stepped onto the road without looking, but it wasn't like I was in any real danger. It would be a stretch of the imagination to even think so.

It doesn't make sense. Nothing makes sense.

Unless it is in some way connected to that terrible grief that lives deep inside him. The one I accidentally glimpsed when I went back into the restaurant for Rob's umbrella that first day. When I found him so curled up with pain that he reminded me of a wounded beast. The kind of suffering that is so blind and raw that approach is dangerous and any attempt to help would be suicidal.

I pace the flat incessantly, stopping only to throw a double vodka down my throat. I find myself back at the window looking down at the deserted street, as if in disbelief. We've never spent a night apart ever since the first night I spent at his house. After two hours of waiting, I finally admit to myself that he's not coming back. Not tonight, anyway.

I go and sit dry-eyed in front of the television. I recognize that I'm watching a movie, but beyond that I don't register anything. All I can see before my eyes is the moment he ripped my chest open with a knife by saying, 'I just can't do this anymore.'

Do what? I haven't pushed or tried to get from him anything that he didn't want to give. I switch off the TV and put on my CD player. Whitney Houston's 'I Will Always Love You' comes on. It grates on my nerves. I switch it off with a grunt. The flat becomes horribly silent.

I rush to fill it with sound. I pick Vangelis. It's Dom's favorite. Beautiful, dramatic music fills the air, but for some reason the only thing I want to listen to is 'Stairway to Heaven'. The wistful longing and mysterious lyrics suit my mood. I listen to Heart's rendition of the song.

In my condition it seems to me that the arrangement of music is in timeless layers that open up like a flower to reveal a yearning, fragile soul calling for something almost forgotten.

When Heart's version ends, I move on to Dolly Parton's. As soon as I've listened to her, I put on Led Zepplin's original version. Then I go back to Heart's version. Obsessively, I open my laptop and look at street performers singing the song. Again and again I return to Heart's version. I listen and I listen. As if the solution to my problem is hidden in the song.

But there is no solution.

I am the woman who thought that everything that glitters is gold. The one who was building a stairway to heaven, but, as Dom once told me, my stairway is whispering in the wind.

When dawn breaks in the sky I am still listening to music.

Dom doesn't call even in the morning.

I go to work, a wreck. I open the door to my office and look at my desk with dread. I hate this temporary job I took last week where I have to field on-line complaints all day about packages that have not arrived, are delayed, lost, or damaged. My job is to calmly absorb their frustration and send them on the relevant department.

The dreary drudgery of it has to be seen to be believed. At least when I was at HMRC I felt I was doing something good. There was always that feeling that I counted for something.

Here, I'm a cog in the wheel.

I truly count for nothing. Perhaps I should have listened to Dom. Perhaps I should have taken his offer of money and waited until I found a better job. But I couldn't bring myself to do that. I was too proud. And now I think, Thank God I didn't take his money.

No matter how bad this job is, at least it pays my bills.

I sit at my desk and jump every time my phone rings. Sometimes I stare at it as if I can metaphysically make him call me. I wait and wait. Until lunchtime, until I can bear it no more. I pick up my phone and call Jake.

'Hey, Ella,' he says. His tone is surprised and cautious.

'Hello, Jake. I ... uh ... Can I talk to you ... um ... alone?'

'Of course,' he says immediately, and his tone tells me what I suspected. He knows exactly what's wrong with Dom.

'Thank you, Jake.'

'No problem. We're in the country tonight. Want to come over for dinner? I can send a car.'

'No, no. No need for that, I'll borrow a friend's car. And I won't disturb you at dinnertime. I'll come just before that.'

'All right, see you about six thirty.'

'That'll be great. Thank you.'

'You know how to get to mine, right?'

'Yes. I'll see you then.'

'See you later.'

'Jake?'

'Yeah?'

'I really appreciate this.'

I hear him draw in a sharp breath. 'That's OK, Ella. I'm always happy to help.'

I park Anna's company car next to Lily's Mercedes-Benz and walk up to the front door. Smoothing down my hair, I ring on the doorbell. Lily opens the door with a smile.

'Hello,' she greets.

'Hey,' I say awkwardly.

She opens the door wider. 'Come on in,' she invites.

I step into her home. Lily is one of those women who have it all. Happiness, beauty, love, wealth.

She's wearing a long, halter-neck dress that comes to her ankles. It's one of those dresses that you know cost an arm and a leg. Once, a dress like that would have sent me to my computer to see if her husband's tax records matched that level of expenditure, but those days are gone. It feels as if the notion that I was a tax officer at Her Majesty's Revenue Customs was another life, or just a dream of mine.

I smile at her. 'Congratulations. I heard you're pregnant.'

She rubs her belly and smiles contentedly. 'Yes, thank you, Ella. And how have you been keeping?'

'Good,' I say.

'Jake's expecting you. He's in his den. Do you want to come through and have a drink before you see him?'

'No. No, thank you,' I refuse politely.

Liliana runs in from one of the reception rooms, screaming, 'Aunty Ella, Aunty Ella.'

She is wearing a pink skirt and a T-shirt that states in bold letters 'My Mother Thinks She's The Boss'. I go down on my haunches. 'My, my, look how much you've grown since I last saw you.'

'That was yesterday,' she says scornfully.

'Dear me. Yes, that was yesterday.'

'My poo was blue today,' she declares suddenly.

'Oh,' I exclaim.

'Lil,' her mother reprimands, 'what did I tell you about telling the whole world about the color of your poo?'

'Aunty Ella is not the whole world,' Liliana argues with impeccable logic. She turns her adorable face toward me. 'My poo was made of icing.'

I straighten and look at Lily.

'She went to a birthday party yesterday and ate too much blue icing from a Thomas the Tank Engine cake,' Lily explains

Even though I was distraught, it made me giggle. How utterly sweet.

'Where's Uncle Dom?' Liliana demands.

The laughter dies in my throat. 'I ... I have no idea.' Voicing the thought saddens me greatly. Far more than I would have expected.

'Lil, Aunty Ella has come to see Daddy. Say bye-bye now.' She looks at me with an encouraging smile. 'Go on, Ella. It's just at the end of the corridor.'

'See you later, Liliana,' I call as I start walking down it.

'Can I go and sit with Daddy and Aunty Ella?' I hear Liliana ask her mother plaintively.

'No, you can't.'

'Why not?' the minx demands.

I don't hear Lily's answer because I'm already too far away, or they've moved into one of the other rooms. It hits me then: I'm not part of this family, and it looks like I never will be. I stand for a moment outside the door at the end of the corridor. Taking a deep breath, I knock.

It is opened almost immediately.

'Come in,' Jake invites cordially.

He is wearing a black T-shirt and gray jeans, and I must admit, just being in his presence makes me nervous. He is as big and intimidating as Dom, but there are absolutely no buttons to push. No weakness. No secret sadness to exploit. He is one of those smoothly impenetrable and guarded people. It was always clear to me that he is the boss of his family. He guards them as ferociously as a mother lion guards her newborn babies.

Woe betide *anyone* who tries to hurt them.

'Thanks,' I say quietly, and step into a large, wood-paneled room. It has soft rugs, a heavy wooden desk at one end of the room, and a nest of expensive leather couches at the other end. There is an air of old world opulence about it all. Here, one can feel safe and cultured. The outside world never intrudes. Here, Jake is King. From here, he controls his empire.

He gestures toward the sofas.

I move over to them. My legs feel like jelly and my skin is tingling with nervous energy. Stop it, I tell myself. *You have nothing to fear.* I am on the same side as Jake. I don't want to hurt Dom. I love him. It is perfectly obvious that he is in terrible pain, and I just want to help him.

'I was just about to have a drink. Would you like to join me?' he says.

I start to shake my head and then decide that I actually do need something strong to calm me. 'I'll have whatever you're having.'

'I'm having a whiskey,' he says, and I nod.

He moves toward a drinks trolley. With his back to me he pours two fingers of whiskey into two glasses and comes toward me. As he crosses the room, he passes the last rays of evening light coming from the window. They hit the side of his face and I am struck by how handsome all the Eden brothers are.

I take the glass and bring it to my lips. The whiskey is strong and hits my empty stomach like liquid fire.

Jake doesn't say anything, simply watches me with a deliberately bland expression. I know that his first and most natural instinct is to protect his brother. These gypsies stick together. For them, blood will always be thicker than water. He will help me, but only if it means it will also benefit his brother.

Fuck it. I decide to take the bull by the horns.

'Last night Dom had a nightmare. When I woke him up he thought I was dead. And then he... he ... said he couldn't continue our relationship anymore and walked out of my flat. I haven't spoken to or seen him since. Can you tell me anything that would help me understand what's going on, Jake? I ... I'm ... really ... um ... in love with your brother.'

An expression of pity crosses his face. He takes a gulp of whiskey and turns his face away from mine. Seconds pass in silence. He appears to be looking into a distant past. At something that saddens him very much.

He turns to me. 'When Dom was seventeen years old, he fell in love with a girl. She was sixteen. A laughing, wild, rebellious gypsy girl. Her name was Vivien. He thought they were soul mates because they were both so crazy and so alike. They could finish each other's sentences. He wanted to marry her straightaway, but I forced him to wait until he was eighteen.

'"You have your whole life ahead of you. What's the hurry?" I told him. The truth was, I disapproved of her. She was bad for him. Too wild. She took too many risks. She egged him on, dared him to new and dangerous adventures. The kind of things that could land him in prison. Together, they reminded me of Bonnie and Clyde. I hoped, I prayed it would not last.

'But I was wrong. The love he had for her didn't die. It just became stronger. They became inseparable. After his eighteenth birthday, very reluctantly, I started to make plans. Everything was ready. In one month they would have been married, but then she did something no one had ever dreamed she would. I don't know how she did it, but she stowed away on a smugglers' boat that Dom was on.

'It was night and the sea was rough. Something happened on that boat. She fell overboard and was swept away.'

TWENTY-ONE

Dom

With the swiftness of a gull, Vivien went over. She rushed to her fate, so near to me that I know I could have caught her if only I'd put my hand out.

Her hopeless, terror-stricken, doomed face, I saw for merely a moment, but it would be forever etched in my soul. The wide, laughing mouth had become a dark hole in her white face, and her beautiful, dancing eyes were huge with shock. Legs wheeling. Arms flailing. Desperate .... Oh God! How desperately she had looked for something to hold on to, anything, other than salty, gray air and diagonally flashing rain.

The cast iron rule was:

If you fall overboard that's your fucking funeral. *The boat stops for NOTHING.*

One look at Preston and Dallas and I knew: they had absolutely no intention of stopping. Hardly surprising since the pair were certifiable psychopaths. It was the reason Jake wouldn't have anything to do with them. But me, I had to be the big I AM. I had to work with the most dangerous thugs in Britain to prove what a tough guy I was.

So ...

They wouldn't stop. I couldn't overpower them—both carried guns. The choice was simple to make. I didn't think. I didn't hesitate. Not for one second. In a flash I pulled out a lifejacket from under the canopy and, with it clutched in my hand, I vaulted over the side of the vessel into the roiling sea, as far away from the pull of the boat as possible.

I hit the water, and sank quickly into a pitch-black abyss full of bubbles. Using my arms to counteract the downward pull, I fought and kicked my way back up, and burst onto the surface with a great gasp. I knew when I jumped overboard that the sea was choppy and treacherous, but in the light of a three-quarter moon it looked as if I was in the middle of a mass of boiling black oil.

Fortunately, it was late July and, though the water was cold, it wasn't paralyzing. At a guess I would say it was just over fifty degrees Fahrenheit. In that temperature a man could survive for a good few hours before hypothermia set in. That is, if he was wearing a lifejacket or had something to hold on to.

I was wearing my GPS tracker, and I knew that either Preston or Dallas would radio Jake to let him know what had happened, and he would come for me. But it could be hours. I could survive, but what about Vivien? She was small, and the shock of falling into the water would have caused her to swallow a lot of salt water. I looked around frantically.

Until you've been alone in the middle of an endless stretch of water, you don't know how truly small and insignificant you are. I was like cork bobbing on an unforgiving, restless landscape that contained absolutely nothing, not one fucking thing. It had swallowed everything.

She was nowhere to be seen.

I screamed for her over the sound of the boat's engine, but there was no reply. Telling myself that she wasn't scared of water, she was a good swimmer, and she was young with a robust constitution, I hooked my hand through one of the armholes of the lifejacket and began to swim strongly toward the area where she'd fallen.

But the truth was I was petrified. I'd never been more afraid in my life. My body was pumping with adrenalin. The raw panic surging through me was tempered only by incredulity that *this* was actually happening to *me*.

In my head my father was saying, *Don't thrash about, lad. Keep still. Float. And don't fuckin' stretch your hand out—it cools the body. Use your legs. Conserve your heat. Conserve your heat. Conserve your heat* … But my hands and legs were moving about wildly. There was no thought of conserving heat.

The sound of the boat died away and I stopped swimming. Treading water, I shouted out to her, and listened. Nothing. *Where the fuck is she?* My heart was beating so hard I felt it bang in my ears. I knew if I didn't get to her soon, she would die.

I turned round and round, scanning the dark, restless water, hoping, praying. And then, with a surge of excitement, I saw her. She had just colored her hair—the most horrendous orange you ever saw—and I hated it, but it was glowing and floating like seaweed in the moonlight.

Jesus!

She was floating face down! Like a doll being tossed about in the waves.

Fuck me, Vivien! You were planning to go down without a word.

Kicking quickly and powerfully, I swam up to her and threw my arm in a bear hug across her lifeless body. It frightened me how totally unaware of me she was. Grabbing her biceps, I spun her around so she was facing upwards. Still holding on to her body, I swam under her and emerged on the other side of her head, so her back was lying on my chest.

Her eyes were closed, her skin was cold and bluish, and her head lolled. I squeezed her with both forearms in the way you would if someone had swallowed something that was blocking their airways. To my horror, I had crushed her so hard I heard a crack. I prayed I had not broken a rib. *A broken rib won't matter if she's dead*, a voice in my head said.

I was suddenly engulfed by the most horrendous fear.

I don't know how I did it with the waves bashing us on all sides, and the plumes of spray that hit us in the face, but I managed to grab her tight, pinch her nose with my other hand, and blow into her mouth while pressing the heel of my hand on her diaphragm thirty times, twice a second. I kept on doing it until she coughed, vomited a load of salt water out, and started gulping summer air.

I felt a surge of fierce joy. Quickly inflating the lifejacket, I began to massage her shivering body, keeping her skin as close to mine as possible. She came back to life slowly. The first thing she did was fucking apologize.

It made me so angry. 'Shut up, Vivien. Don't you dare apologize. We said we'd never say sorry to each other. We're the wild ones, remember?'

'I can't believe we're going to end up as shark food,' she said. There was no fear in her voice. Maybe she was in shock.

'These waters are too cold for sharks,' I replied, rubbing her arms furiously. I knew we were a long way from being saved.

'So this is how my life ends,' she said in a voice full of wonder.

It hit me in the chest like a kick from a horse. 'You're not fucking dying. Stop being so fucking dramatic.'

She turned her head slightly and looked at me sadly. 'I feel so stupid. This is the stupidest thing I've done. I can't believe I'm going to die because of my own stupidity,' she whispered. And then the thought occurred to her. 'Oh my God, Dom. I've been so selfish. You're going to die too.'

'Neither of us is going to die. Jake will be here soon.'

'What if he doesn't come? He doesn't like me, you know,' she said.

'Stop talking nonsense. Why wouldn't he like you?'

'You're such a fool, Dom.'

'He'll come.'

'What if he doesn't make it in time?'

'He'll make it in time,' I said, a wave slapping salt water into my mouth.

'I'm sorry, baby.'

I could feel the rage in my guts. 'Stop apologizing. I'd do the same again given half the chance.'

'If I die, will you marry someone else?'

'I'll never marry anyone else, Vivien.'

'I couldn't bear it if you do.'

'Look, I fucking won't, OK?'

'You promise?'

'I promise.'

'I'll come back and haunt you if you do.'

'You're not going to fucking die, so this is a stupid discussion.'

'But if I do. Don't fall in love with anyone else.'

'You won't,' I said through clenched teeth.

She didn't speak anymore, and for more than an hour both of us were mostly silent. We spoke only to check that we were both still alive. I kept glancing at my watch every few minutes. Time had never moved so slowly. After what seemed like interminable hours my legs felt like dead weights and I was struggling to move them.

By then, Vivien was also no longer shivering. There was a strange lethargy about her. I knew that at that rate she was not going to last. I turned her over so her chest was pressed to mine. It was harder work for me, but I didn't know what else to do to warm her up.

'Don't move unless you have to. Don't even kick your legs. Stay still and conserve your energy,' I told her.

'I'm afraid, Dom. I'm afraid I'll die.' Her voice was quivering with emotion.

'No, you fucking won't. I won't allow it.'

'My wedding dress. You'll never see me in my wedding dress,' she moaned into my neck.

The dank taste of the ocean was in my mouth. 'I'll fucking see you in your wedding dress if I have to bury you in it,' I growled.

She giggled. It was a weak, lazy sound. She was slipping away. I could feel it as strongly as I knew my hands had become so numb I could no longer feel them.

'It doesn't hurt like I thought it would. I'm not scared anymore. It's almost peaceful, actually. Just like falling into something soft and dark.'

I held her tighter still. 'Vivien, you have to fight it. Stay with me.'

'Hey, baby! Look at those lights. They're beauuuuuutiful.'

'What lights?'

'Can you not see them?'

'No.'

'Oh, I pity you. They are sooooo beautiful.'

I gazed down at her face. It was animated in a way it had not been since I'd found her floating face down. I became terrified.

'Vivien, look at me,' I shouted, but she was so entranced by the vision in front of her that she refused to turn in my direction. I grabbed her chin and turned her face toward me. Her eyes were glassy and empty. They seemed unable to focus on me. She made a small, incoherent sound of displeasure or irritation.

'The lights. I want to see the lights,' she mumbled pleadingly.

I released her chin and she turned away immediately to gaze with fascination at the lights only she could see. I looked around desperately at the empty blackness stretching out in all directions around us. And I prayed. And I prayed.

It felt like we had been in the water forever.

My legs were getting tired of treading water, and I could see that she had given up the desire to fight the cold. Not even the lights could interest her anymore. Her eyes were closing. Her body, having imposed increasingly drastic measures to keep functioning, was finally starting to shut down. Her heartbeat was becoming weaker and weaker. If I didn't do something soon it would stop completely. Then only her brain would be alive. And then even that would die. I *had* to pull her out of her slump.

I shook her and she opened her eyes weakly.

'Listen,' I said with fake excitement. 'Jake's coming. I can hear the engine of his boat.'

She seemed to listen. 'I don't hear it,' she mumbled groggily.

'There's too much water in your ears,' I lied.

She smiled weakly, only half-conscious. 'I'm so happy. He can take me back to my mother,' she said, and I smiled back, but my smile became a grimace of horror when her heart stopped and she died from the sheer relief of thinking that she had been rescued.

I couldn't believe it.

I'd heard of people dying from the relief of thinking they'd been rescued, but I had never thought that it would happen to her. I held her body tightly against mine. It was impossible that she was gone. I couldn't comprehend that something as alive as she could ever succumb to something as ordinary as death. Or that as fierce and possessive as my love was, I couldn't keep her. I had held on so tightly, with every ounce of my being, and yet she had slipped away, like sand from a clenched fist.

So I shook her limp body. I rubbed her arms and legs. I gave her mouth-to-mouth resuscitation, but Vivien was gone.

The pain and horror of losing her was unbearable. Words couldn't enter into my pain. I began to scream. I screamed and screamed like a madman. I cursed, I swore, I sobbed until no sounds would come out of my mouth.

I kissed her cold, blue lips.

'Oh, Vivien!'

In my head she was wearing a red rose in her hair and whispering, 'You're my gypsy hero. You'll always be my gypsy hero.'

'Oh, Vivien!'

Once there was a way to get back home again...
—https://www.youtube.com/watch?v=LjOlofG72ZE

TWENTY-TWO

'When we pulled their waterlogged bodies out of the water, Dom was nearly as blue as Vivien. He never uttered a single sound, not pain, not grief, not relief. His fingers were so tightly clenched around her corpse it was ages before we could prize them away from her cold flesh. He stared vacantly into the distance. When I called him, he turned slowly and looked at me as if he didn't recognize me. As if we were not flesh and blood.'

Jake stops speaking, and I see him shudder with the terrible memory.

'I brought him to my house and put him in my bed. He slept for three hours. Then came the profuse diarrhea brought on by the seawater he'd ingested, and the uncontrollable muscle tremors. He became very ill, and Shane and I took care of him. He even missed her funeral. They buried her in her wedding dress, apparently in accordance with her wishes. She had told her mother that if she should die before her wedding she was to be buried in her dress.'

As Jake speaks, a numbing cold is creeping into my body, and I hug myself and force myself to listen to his words.

'Dom was so ill that for a while we even thought he was going to die. But he didn't. His body grew stronger, even if his head was totally fucked. For weeks he had such severe nightmares that he would move bedroom furniture around in his sleep and wake up screaming on the floor. He was like a madman. He blamed himself. He couldn't look at a picture of her without getting into an uncontrollable rage. I gathered up all the photos of her and hid them.

'Then one day I came back and he was making himself an omelet. "Want one?" he asked, and I knew it was going to be all right. We ate together and he thanked me for everything I'd done. Then he left.'

Jake looks at me with somber, sad eyes. 'Ever since then there has been no other woman in his life. One-night stands, casual flings. No woman, no matter how hard they tried, and believe me when I tell you a lot tried, and very hard too, could get close to him. Until you.'

Jake pauses and takes a sip of whiskey while watching me intently from above the rim of his glass.

I drop my eyes. Some part of me feels a flash of joy at his last sentence, but it's muted. I think I'm in shock.

'Don't give up on him so quickly. He's come so far because of you,' Jake says, as if he's trying to sell me the idea of staying in a relationship with Dom. As if he needs to.

I look up at him suddenly and his eyes slide away. Not immediately, but he can't hold my gaze! I watch him take another sip before he raises his eyes to me. I stare at him. He looks back without flinching this time, but that moment he couldn't hold my gaze has given him away.

'There's more, isn't there?' I ask.

He sighs. It's actually a sound of relief. As if a burden is about to be lifted from his shoulders.

He nods, stands, and walks over to his desk. He unlocks the last drawer and takes a photo album out. He turns the pages to somewhere in the middle and walks back to me carrying the open album. He stands over me and holds the book out to me.

I take it from him. It's one of those fancy albums with tracing paper between the pages holding the photos. I take the end of the tracing paper page and turn it, and pretty much just stare at the picture. It's a photo taken outside some kind of temple. The sun is shining brightly. I'm wearing a pink tie-dyed T-shirt and a long flowery skirt. It looks like it's been taken in a foreign land. India, perhaps. Asia, definitely.

But I've never been to Asia.

All these impressions hit me in seconds. I raise my eyes upwards and Jake is looking down at me, his eyes full of pity.

'That's her?' I ask in a shocked whisper.

'That's Vivien.'

'Oh my God!' I cry. The girl in the photo looks exactly like me. The similarity is uncanny. Except for her hair color, I am her twin.

'I'm sorry,' Jake says softly.

Suddenly *everything* makes sense. Everything! It explains why the whole family had behaved so strangely when Dom introduced me. I'd thought it was because Dom was dating a tax inspector, but now I know. Ah! That would nicely explain away the uneasy, quickly hidden expression on his mother's face whenever she thought I wasn't looking.

A thought seeds itself into my head.

'Did you already know what I looked like when we met?'

'Yes, Shane had warned us all.'

I nod slowly, taking the information in. 'Did Shane know Vivien?'

He frowns. 'Of course. Dom was going to marry her.'

'I see.' Some part of my rational brain makes the observation that only Shane in this family is truly impenetrable. His classically handsome face had betrayed nothing when he had met me for the first time at the party. Nothing but an open friendliness and an irresistible charm.

'Right,' I say slowly. My whole life is falling apart around me. 'So, Dom went out with me because I reminded him of his dead fiancée.'

'I'm sure the fact that you look like her has something to do with it, but you're totally different in every way.'

I look at him with disbelieving eyes.

'Everything about you is different. She was selfish, tempestuous, controlling and impulsive, and you are careful, kind, considerate and deep.'

Oh my God. The way he describes me makes me sound so boring. I cover my eyes with the palms of my hands. What a fucking mess!

Jake comes over and goes down on his haunches in front of me. Startled, I uncover my eyes. Jake at close quarters is an intimidating experience. It's like being too close to a live wire. Part of me wants to move away.

As if he knows that I am uncomfortable, he fixes me with his mesmerizing eyes and moves in for the kill. 'Remember, when I said Vivien was no good for him, I truly meant it. You are the perfect match. You balance him and bring out the best in him. You make him happy.'

'But he wants her. She is his true soul mate. I'm just a poor imitation.' It hurts like hell to voice the thought. I feel the tears start welling up in my eyes.

'Ella, listen to me. He was eighteen. She was his first love. Do you remember what you were like when you were eighteen? If he had married her, it would have been a disaster, and they would have ended up hating each other and getting divorced. But because she died, she has become his dancing queen, young and sweet, only seventeen. A great, lost love. But he has suffered enough. She's gone, and you're here.'

'I'm nothing to him.'

'You have no idea what you've done for him. The demons had completely taken over when you came into his life. You broke them up with your softness.'

I stare at him wordlessly. How much I want to believe him, but my heart feels like it's breaking into pieces. He never wanted me. He was trying to replace her. When he was touching me, he was really touching her.

'He never really wanted me,' I sob. 'The whole time he was pretending I was her.'

He reaches out a hand and touches my cheek. His hand is warm and gentle. And it makes me want to lean into it for the comfort it holds.

'Ah, Ella. You're not a man. I am. Take it from me. My brother wanted Vivien the way a boy wants a girl. He wants you with the passion with which a man wants a woman. Let him discover that. Give him a chance. There's a lot of Dom that you've not seen yet.' He smiles tenderly and removes his hand.

I stare at him through a film of tears. The kindness and softness that he's showing has surprised me. He always looks so unreachable and aloof.

'But he doesn't want to be with me anymore,' I say softly.

'If you believed that you wouldn't be here now.'

I sniff. 'So what do I do? Wait for him to come to me?'

He shrugs. 'I won't tell you what to do, but if I were you I wouldn't let anything stand in the way of something I wanted. I'd go and fight for it until it was mine or I had died trying. The journey has just begun and the destination could be a very beautiful place.'

He stands, and walks away from me toward his desk. He comes back with a box of tissues. I pull out a couple and wipe my face. Then I stand.

'I should be going,' I say.

'I'll walk you to your car.'

'There's no need.'

'I want to,' he says with a gentle smile.

I turn toward him. 'Thank you, Jake.'

'I'll always be here for you. Don't give your ear to the devil.'

To love too much is to lick honey from the point of a knife.

TWENTY-THREE

I think I was OK while I was in Jake's house. While I was saying goodbye to Lily and Liliana. I was even OK when Jake closed the car door for me and waved me away.

It hits me when I'm on the motorway.

Suddenly my windpipe feels like it is full of concrete. I can't breathe. I swerve into the hard shoulder. Horns blare. I screech to a stop. I feel as if I'm suffocating. I open the car door and stumble out. I lurch to the edge of the road and collapse holding my throat. I take shallow breaths.

On my hands and knees, I pant until I feel my airways open. Cars whoosh past at great speed. Somebody thinks to stop his car up ahead. A man runs toward me. I hold my hand up, the palm facing him to tell him not to come forward. He stops a few yards away.

'Are you OK?'

I nod.

'Do you want me to call an ambulance?'

I shake my head.

'You sure?'

I nod and smile weakly at him.

'Want me to wait with you?'

I shake my head again, touched by the kindness of this stranger.

He raises his hand in some kind of acknowledgment and, turning around, starts to walk away.

'Hey,' I call out.

He turns back.

'Thank you.'

'It's all right,' he says, and with a backward wave returns to his car. I watch him drive away. I sit by the side of the road, and, with the engine of my car still running, I burst into a flood of tears. When it's all over, I get back into my car and drive home. There, I stand in the shower and let the water wash away my pain. I wrap myself in a robe and call Anna. I tell her everything.

'I'm coming over,' she says. 'Put some shot glasses in the freezer.'

'Oh, Anna,' I sigh, tears filling my eyes.

'We need to get drunk. It's been ages.'

She arrives at my doorstep with two bottles of her father's homemade gooseberry vodka. She gets the cold glasses out of the freezer and pours us a shot each. The sweet, sharp taste is like summer in a glass.

I down another shot and put the glass on the coffee table with a thump. One bottle is rolling on the floor and this bottle is almost half empty.

Anna claps her hands excitedly. 'I know what. You should become the coffee beans,' she slurs.

I frown blearily. 'The coffee beans?'

'You know. From the story on the Internet about the grandmother, the broccoli.' She stops, her eyes narrowed. 'No, wait. It wasn't broccoli. It was carrots. Yeah, that's right, the carrots, the eggs and the coffee beans.'

'I don't know the story.'

She sits straighter. 'This woman gets cheated on—'

'That's not my situation,' I protest immediately.

She waves her hand airily. 'Just wait for the end, will ya?'

'Go on.'

'She goes to her grandmother and asks for her advice. The grandmother puts three pots of water on the stove. Into one pot she puts broccoli.'

'Carrots,' I correct.

She nods sagely. 'I was just checking to see if you were listening.'

'Yeah, right.'

'Now that we've established that you're paying attention, we'll carry on. And in the other two pots she puts the other two ingredients.'

'Eggs and coffee beans.'

'Exactly.'

I sigh. Even though I am so drunk, I can't get Dom out of my head.

'She lets all the ingredients boil for twenty minutes.'

'Why twenty minutes?'

'Do you want to hear this story or not?'

'Go on,' I say, and reach for the bottle again.

'She takes all the ingredients out, and basically shows her granddaughter that the carrots went in strong and hard and came out soft and malleable. The eggs went in soft and came out hardened. Only the coffee beans elevated themselves to another level, released their fragrance and flavor, and changed the water. So all three objects faced the same suffering and adversity, but each reacted differently. When the situation gets hot, you have to decide which are you.'

I put the bottle down. 'I feel like the carrots at the moment.'

'That's today. What will you be tomorrow and the day after?'

I drop my forehead into my palm. 'Oh, Anna. My life is such a mess. I thought I was in such a good place—and now look at me! My world was like a bubble waiting to pop.'

'Hey, look on the bright side. At least she's dead.'

'What?' I gasp.

'Yeah. At least she's not around to disturb your fragile peace of mind with cruel physical comparisons.'

'What do you mean?'

'I mean I have a raging aversion to *all* my boyfriend's exes. Like, seriously detest, abhor, and hate them. I get so jealous that I can't stop pouring over their Facebook photos to examine their tans, their smiles, their outfits, in the hope of finding faults so that later I can subtly criticize them while in conversation with my boyfriend.'

She stops and picks at her nail polish.

'In fact, one or two I've hated so much I even fantasized about breaking into their houses and stabbing them while they slept in their beds.'

'Really?' I ask, shocked.

'Absolutely. It's petty and childish, but I can't help it. It's like an addiction because I'm so insecure. I feel as if I'm in competition with them. I'd much rather a dead girlfriend who looks like me.'

'No, I'd rather have an ex who's alive. I can't even consider pouring over her Facebook pictures to subtly criticize her because she's been put on some kind of pedestal. I mean how do you compete against a dead woman?' I ask garrulously.

'God! I hate exes. Alive or dead, they're just trouble. Talking about exes, I forgot to ask before, have you heard from your stalker?'

I shrug. 'I think I frightened him off.'

'No more midnight phone calls?'

'No more,' I mumble. The room has started to spin. 'I need to pee and to get to bed,' I say, and stand up unsteadily.

She stands and we use the bathroom together. Then she helps me to bed.

'Sleep next to me,' I tell her.

She smiles down at me. There's a strange, pitying look on her face as she stands over me.

TWENTY-FOUR

I, stalker

I stand over her and a thrill runs through me.

I am in her space, her bedroom! How strange that hatred, in its intensity and viscosity, should be so similar to passion. Look at her! Sleeping the gentle sleep of angels. So beautiful. So innocent. Bitch!

I take a step closer. My shoes are soft-soled and make no sound. It is a warm night and a window is open. Gentle breezes make the curtains flutter. Otherwise, everything is perfectly still. It is dark, but my eyes are accustomed to the dark. I have embraced the dark, made it my friend, taken it and its terrible secrets into my heart.

I bend down so that I am only a few inches from her skin.

How sweet and divine she smells. And yet, she destroyed me without a second thought. I still remember the first time I saw her waltzing across a room and thought, wow! She's hot. I didn't know she was a half-woman, half-serpent. But I was a man then.

She changed me, made me into the thing I am now, a shell. I loved her for so long. But there is nothing in my life now except this all-consuming obsession I have for her. Look at her throat. The seductive curve begs you to kiss it, wrap your fingers possessively around it, and squeeze it, until her eyes fly open and watch you in horror even as her pussy curls helplessly around your rock-hard dick.

Very gently, I blow into her slightly parted lips. My stale vapors enter her pink mouth. I will contaminate you yet further, my sweet.

'Mmm...' she murmurs.

I freeze.

She moves away from my warm breath. Even in sleep she is moving away from me. I guess she only wants a big man. I have seen her with him. He holds her possessively. He would make a formidable enemy, but I will not be confronting him. I will just be taking her away from him.

Why? Because she is mine.

Let him be broken, the way I was, when he took her away from me. I've taken care of all the other men who have sniffed around her like wild animals. It was easy because she didn't want them. She wants this one. I have followed her up to his house in the woods, which he never locks, and watched from the window as he fucked her. It made me sick to my stomach. I threw up in the bushes. I thought she was something special.

Cheap hussy was mewling like a kitten for his dick.

I feel my cock harden. So. My body still wants the little bitch. I shall have her. I shall tie her up and have her until my body feels the disgust and abhorrence my mind feels for her. I would take her today, if not for the other woman sleeping in her bed. My opportunity will come again. One of these days she will be alone again. And I will strike then.

I straighten, and, turning my head, look at my own visage. How curious. It is a pale and glowing mask in the moonlight. Looking back at me is the almost demonic face of a man possessed by rage and hatred.

Vengeance will be mine.

I stand there for a long time. Only when I have had my fill of my complete power over her vulnerable form do I turn around and leave the way I had come.

Through the front door.

TWENTY-FIVE

Dom

The wound is the place where the light enters you.

—Rumi

I knock at the semi-detached house and Vivien's mother opens the door. The past ten years have not been kind to her.

'Hello, Mirela.'

'Hello, Dom,' she says with a smile, and moves back to let me in.

I go into the living room and look around me. Nothing seems to have changed. Everything is spotless. The kitsch decorations, the fans on the walls, the patterned carpet, the net curtains, the ornate figurines, and the bohemian crystal vases filled with plastic flowers. She gestures for me to sit.

I sit on an armchair with a crocheted lace antimacassar. The cushion is old and lumpy. I feel a sense of guilt. I should have come earlier. I should have given them some financial help. I know Jake gave money, but I should have done something too.

She takes a seat opposite me. There is a low coffee table with an oval lacy doily-like thing between us. On it she has set a crystal bowl filled with sugared almonds, a tray with a teapot and cups, and a plate covered with a napkin. She smiles at me mistily and begins pouring the tea. She doesn't ask how I like my tea. She pours exactly the right amount of milk and drops in a cube of sugar. She hands it over to me.

'Thank you,' I say, accepting the dainty china.

She lifts the napkin off the plate and reveals thinly sliced rectangles of marble cake. She picks up the plate and holds it out to me. 'Your favorite,' she says.

Something heavy lodges in my heart. I've been so selfish. I take a slice and hold it awkwardly in my fingers

'How have you been?' she asks, pouring herself a cup of tea.

'I've been all right.'

She looks up. 'I'm so glad to hear that. I've been waiting for you to come for ten years.'

My eyes widen with shock. 'Why?'

'I knew you'd come when the pain was gone.'

I draw a sharp breath. 'The pain is not gone.'

She half smiles. 'I'm sorry. Of course. The pain never goes. But it lessens. That's what I meant to say. When the pain lessened.' She drops a couple of cubes of sugar into her tea and stirs it with a teaspoon. I watch her lift it to her lips and sip at it delicately. She puts the cup and saucer back on the coffee table.

'Eat, eat,' she encourages.

I bite into the slice of cake. The smell and taste of it roll the years back. It is as if I am eighteen again. It is an old ritual, the two of us having tea and cake while I wait for Vivien to come out of her bedroom, all dolled up, and ready to paint the town red. I gaze into her eyes and wonder if she has traveled back with me, but she hasn't. She doesn't need to. She is still trapped there. She has not moved on. Everything in this house is exactly like it was when I was last here a decade ago. In this world of lace and plastic flowers, I could maybe turn my head toward the corridor and maybe, just maybe Vivien will walk through.

The knowledge is like a flash of lightning that lights up a black sky with white light. Vivien is not Ella. They are as different as oranges and oysters. Only in appearance are they alike. In temperament and personality no two women could be more unlike than Vivien and Ella. And that streak of lightning makes something else crystal clear.

I'm in love with Ella.

I loved Vivien, and a sad part of me will always love her, but it is Ella now and not Vivien that I think of every day. That I take to bed. That I crave. That I miss when we are not together. That I want to call and tell when something happens to me. That I want to share my life with.

Vivien's mother looks at me sadly. 'When I lost my daughter, I lost a son, too. You were the best thing that ever happened to my Viv. It was my greatest dream to see you both married. I've missed you greatly, Dom.'

'I'm sorry I didn't come round before today, Mirela. I always enjoyed our little chats.'

She smiles happily. 'Me too. You're like a son to me, Dom. You must come and see me again.'

'I will.'

'I've thought of you a lot. I know you've made a great success of your life. The ladies at the church.' She smiles shyly. 'I listen to their gossip.'

'Mirela,' I begin and then I pause.

'What is it, Dom?' she prompts.

'When Vivien was dying in the water, I made her a promise. I told her I would never love anyone else.'

'Oh, Dom. Have you let that promise keep you from finding happiness all these years?'

I link my fingers together and say nothing.

She leans forward. 'Listen to me. She was afraid, and she was clinging on to you. I love my daughter, but she was a minx to make you promise such a thing. She's gone, and you are here. You've wasted ten years. Don't waste another moment. If there is one thing I learned from losing Vivien, it is to appreciate every moment you have with the people you love.' Her lips curl up in a bitter smile. 'You don't know how long you have with them.'

'I still feel guilty. I could have saved her.' I exhale my breath slowly. 'If we hadn't argued. If I hadn't told her Jake was coming.'

She starts shaking her head in distress. 'Don't do that, dear boy. There was nothing you could have done to stop it. God knows, you tried. It was simply her time.'

'She was too young to die.'

'About four months after Viv passed, I dreamed of her. In my dream she was eleven or twelve years old, before she started dyeing her hair in all those atrocious colors. She was running in a field and she was laughing. Her mouth was stained with the juice of berries. She ran up to me and said, "Look what I found, Mum." And then I woke up and I cried for hours.'

She pulls a handkerchief that she has tucked into her bra out from the neckline of her blouse and wipes her eyes.

'But as the weeks and months went by, I took comfort from that dream. I think she wanted me to know she wasn't blue and lying in a satin-lined box as she was in my waking hours. She wasn't still. She wasn't dead. She was alive. Somewhere in another dimension that I can't access, she still exists. She has never appeared again in my dreams, but she doesn't need to. I understood what she was saying to me.'

'She's never come to me,' I say.

'Perhaps you are only allowed to go to the people you can no longer damage,' she says softly.

'I found someone,' I blurt out suddenly, but even as the words exit my mouth I want to un-utter them. I am shocked at myself. What madness possessed me to tell Viv's grieving mother *that*?

She swallows hard. 'I'm so glad,' she croaks.

Angry with myself, I apologize. 'I'm so sorry. That was unforgivably insensitive of me. I don't know what came over me.'

She shakes her head and, reaching out a work-worn hand, grips my knee. 'No, I'm glad for you. You're a good man. You deserve to be happy.'

I cover her hand with mine.

'You know that song by Pitball?' she asks.

I smile slightly. 'Pitbull?'

'Yes, yes, the man with the bald head.'

'You listen to Pitbull?' I ask, surprised.

'My granddaughter does.'

'Marko has a daughter now?'

'He has three children. Two boys and a girl. They're my life. Anyway, Pitbull sings a song called "Give Me Everything Tonight". He says, "What I promise tonight, I cannot promise tomorrow." That's truly life. You might not get tomorrow. So whatever you want to do, go do it tonight.'

And from her flow precious memories. If not for the intervention of the cruel hand of fate, she would have been my mother-in-law. I squeeze her hand and feel a great love for this kind and generous woman. We are connected forever by having loved the same person, and by the grief of having lost her.

'When you remember Vivien, remember that she was always laughing, always wanting to have fun. She wouldn't want to be the barbed wire wrapped around your heart.'

I nodded. 'I know.'

I press a thick wad of money into her reluctant hand and kiss her powdered cheek goodbye. She stands at the door and gazes wistfully at me. I walk up to her wooden gate. I even open it. Then something pulls at me. I turn around and walk back to her. She looks at me enquiringly.

'I want to show you something, but I don't want to upset you,' I say.

'Yes, show me,' she says immediately.

I take my phone out and scroll to the picture of Ella. I hold the phone out to her. 'This is Ella, my girlfriend.'

She gazes at the phone for a long time. When she looks up, her eyes are swimming with tears. 'She's beautiful, Dom. Will you bring her to dinner one day soon?'

I nod, and it's impossible for me to talk because I'm so choked up.

'God knew he shouldn't have taken her away from you,' she says, giving me back the phone.

I take the phone from her and walk away, my heart finally free.

Where, O death, is your victory:
where, O death, is your sting?
—1 Corinthians 15: 55

TWENTY-SIX

Dom

I turn the car around and drive to the cemetery where Vivien was laid to rest. It's a sunny day and the cemetery looks pretty with brightly colored petunias bordering it. I park and go up to a rickety iron gate. I'm not sure exactly where her grave is, but I remember my mother once mentioning that hers is a plot in the east end of the cemetery, and that there's an oak tree nearby.

I take one of the small paths that radiate out to a serpentine perimeter path to lead visitors around the outer graves, some of which are centuries old. It's hard to imagine that these people walked this earth hundreds of years ago.

They are mostly overgrown, unkempt and crumbling, but one of the ancient, ornate altar tombs catches my attention, and I find myself wandering to it, and reading the worn inscription. Herein lies Arthur Anderson-Black.

Resting in the arms of God forever,
loved forever, missed desperately.
Flying with the angels, your memory
will never die. Our beloved father,
brother and uncle. We will never forget you.
Rest in peace till we meet again.
1830–1875

I think of the mourners who erected the tombstone for him three hundred years ago. Their remains have joined his under the clay soil. But did they meet again? I've never walked around a cemetery on my own before, and it is an oddly surreal experience. Walking among the dead makes you appreciate the impermanence of life and the permanence of death like nothing else can. All these people once lived and walked and talked and did their thing as if they would live forever. This house is mine, this land is mine, and now they are all just gone forever.

The saddest headstones are the ones erected by grieving parents. They are the most poignant. A simple epitaph on a new grave touched me deeply.

> Beneath this simple stone
> that marks her resting place
> our precious darling sleeps
> alone in the Lord's long embrace.
> May 2001–December 2001

As I stroll along the path I remember what my mother once told me. When the fruit is ripe and ready, it will leave the branch easily. I was the branch that Vivien was torn away from. I wasn't ready. She still had too much to live for. Without realizing it I have fallen into a kind of melancholy, contemplative mood, and it is a shock to see a hilarious marble tombstone.

Is This Headstone Tax Deductible?

It makes me smile. I take my phone out and take a photo for Ella. The tax inspector in her will appreciate it.

The curved outer path meets an axial pathway that takes me to a central chapel, and a small custodian's lodge that was designed to be used for burial services. The path meanders, and I pass a newly dug grave awaiting its occupant.

I walk over to the manicured grass and spot the oak tree in the distance. I begin to walk toward it. I no longer look at the gravestones on either side of me. As if I'm guided by an invisible hand, I move forward with sure steps until I'm standing in front of Vivien's grave. My breath escapes in a long sigh. Ah, Vivien. Her grave is a custom memorial in polished black granite with a carved weeping angel holding a rose. The setting sun makes the stone glow red.

Vivien Jessica Finch
Goodnight, dear heart,
goodnight, goodnight
Oct, 10, 1987–Jul, 24, 2004

I kneel down and touch the smooth stone. How she would have hated this place. This peace. This quiet. This impenetrable air of mourning and stillness. The impulsive, impetuous Vivien with roses in her hair, the one who could never sit still for a moment is not here. I laugh. The sound is loud and strange among the silent tombstones. It disturbs the peace. Perhaps no one has laughed here in centuries.

A strong breeze rushes at my face. I look up, surprised. And suddenly I hear Vivien saying, 'I'll come back and haunt you.'

'You never did come back to haunt me, did you?' I whisper into the wind.

And I remember her laughing. How she used to laugh. She was wild and beautiful, but never vindictive.

I wonder where she is now.

'Wherever you are, Vivien, remember I truly loved you,' I say, and, in the trees, a lone bird calls. I stay a little while longer, but I am restless. For I stand there, a living, breathing mortal, with hot blood flowing in my veins. One day I'll join them in their repose and their silence, but not yet. I have a life and it's calling me. I walk away and never look back.

As soon as I get into my car, I call Ella. She picks up on the first ring.

'Ella,' I say.

And she starts to weep.

And suddenly I can't wait to see her. 'Where are you?' I ask.

'On the way home,' she sobs.

'Go home and wait for me. I'm taking you out to dinner. I'll be there in less than an hour. Wear something sexy,' I say, joy pouring through my living blood.

I stuff my phone into my pocket and, feeling light-hearted enough to fly, I run up the three flights of stairs. I let myself into my flat and, pressing my palms to my face, I go to the mirror. Wow! Look at me glow.

Undressing quickly, I step into the shower. I fly out in five minutes and do my hair. Putting a tiny amount of gel into the ends of my hair I blow dry it, and leave it as a mass of tumbling curls on my back and shoulders.

Then I sit on the bed and paint my toenails bright fuchsia. I wait ten minutes for them to dry. When they are, I pull on strawberry-flavored, edible panties, carefully stick edible, chocolate-flavored arrow tattoos on my belly and thighs. All arrows point towards my hoo-ha, which has already started humming with anticipation.

Oh, and there are watermelon-flavored pasties for my nipples.

Just thinking of Dom licking everything off makes a shiver run down my back. Smiling happily, I slip into a white

dress with secret mesh panels on the bodice and back. It molds to my body then flares out from mid-thigh to my ankles.

With butterflies in my tummy, I step into strappy silver shoes. My toenails, bright and glossy, peep out as I walk three times into a cloud of perfume I have sprayed above my head. Sitting at the dressing table, I apply fuchsia lipstick and a layer of mascara, and I'm ready. I look at the time. Still ten minutes to go. The doorbell rings. He's early. He's eager. I grin at my reflection.

Way to go, girl.

I don't walk to answer the door, I run. I open the door and my smile dies on my lips. I recognized him straightaway, even with the unkempt beard and mustache, but why on earth is he dressed like that? And what the hell is he doing here? What's that supermarket trolley doing out in the corridor? But before I can say or do anything he reaches out, and stabs me in the hand with something sharp that he was holding concealed.

It acts so quickly I don't even feel myself hit the floor.

TWENTY-SEVEN

I, stalker

'Do not run away; let go. Do not seek, for it will come
when least expected.'

—Bruce Lee

Quickly, I push the trolley into her apartment and close the
door. Using the tattered blankets inside the trolley, I bundle
her up in them. Then I turn the trolley on its side, and pull out
all the assorted bits and pieces inside it: old newspapers,
empty tins, plastic bottles, some boxes. I drag the trolley so it's
facing her body and kind of roll and push her body into it.

Excellent ... She fits even better than I thought.

Grunting, I try to pull the trolley upright, but it is too
heavy. I let it drop back down. Slight change of plans.
Straightening, I walk over to a small, painted cabinet and take
out a phone directory. I lift the trolley slightly and push the
thick book into the gap. Now I have more leverage. Using both
hands I give the trolley another great heave. My second
attempt is successful.

Panting slightly, I throw the other odds and ends on top
of her body and stand back to look at the end effect critically.
Yes, no one would suspect that it is anything other than the

trolley of a homeless man filled with everything he possesses. There's a mirror on her wall and I go and look at myself.

Good. I look like a tramp—unwashed, unshaven, dirty. It took me weeks to perfect this look. Because of her, I've spent every waking moment planning and learning. Yes, I learned to pick locks, to gather intel, to bug, to follow, to immerse myself into my disguises, to pretend to be Melanie, someone who likes and makes light-hearted comments on all her pathetic little posts on Facebook.

Carefully, I push the trolley into the lift. Thank God! It's working.

As I push her through the foyer, I see the big man go running up the stairs. And I smile. Too late! I push her out into the evening air and down the street. Not one person looks me in the eye or suspects anything. By the time I get to my basement flat it's nearly dark. I glance around. There's not a soul about.

I go down the steps and open the front door of the place I have rented. I go back up and overturn the trolley. I pull her body out and carry her down to my flat, her feet dragging against every step it takes to get to my front door. I drop her inert body just inside my house and, running up the stairs, I push the trolley down the steps and leave it in my garden. Then I go back into my house and close my front door.

There, there now. All done.

It is destiny that she should fall into my hands like an apple from a tree.

I drag her to a wall and prop her into a sitting position against it. The harsh illumination from the bare single light bulb makes her skin glow. Up close, she is even more beautiful. It's obvious that she doesn't belong in these surroundings. Her perfume wafts up to my nostrils. I breathe it in deeply. I haven't smelt a woman for a long time. Not one as fine as her, anyway. My hand moves to her breasts, but I can't bring myself to touch her. No, I won't steal it when she's asleep. I'm not lustful and unchaste. She'll be bound, naked and wide-awake, when I defile her.

She must witness the moment I force myself on her, and bring her to ruin.

I secure her hands behind her back with plastic ties. Next, her legs. Rolling her onto her side, I look at her. Her face is angelic. It's almost an abomination to see her silky golden curls tumble onto the dirty carpet. I used to dream of them spread over my thighs as she swallowed my cock.

Bitch ruined my life.

I spit in the dirt near her head and move away from her.

In that first moment of consciousness, when it's still dark behind my eyelids, there is only the sensation of a throbbing pain in my temples. The sensations that follow on are much stranger. An unfamiliar feeling of stiffness and constriction. Something scratchy against my cheek. The smell of damp and dirt. My eyes snap open in alarm. My hands and legs are tightly bound, and I'm lying on my side on a filthy carpet. My mind goes blank. What the hell is happening? I blink, and lift my head from the rough bristles.

'You're awake,' a man's voice says.

And it all comes flooding back.

Oh God!

My blood runs cold. A pair of jeans-clad legs and badly stained sneakers come into view. I raise my frightened eyes all the way up to his face. Oh, dear Jesus! My mouth opens.

'Surprise!' he says.

My voice is hoarse; a shocked whisper. 'What are you doing?'

Rob's cold, mean eyes regard me steadily, pitilessly.

'What do you want from me?' I cry desperately.

The question seems to infuriate him. His eyes flash, but he controls himself. 'What do you think I want?' he asks menacingly.

I stare at him with startled, terrified eyes.

'I know you like big cocks. I've watched you take it all into your dirty cunt. All of it being stuffed into Ella Savage's greedy, greedy cunt,' he says in a sing-song voice.'

'Please, Sir,' I say automatically, my mind and eyes unable to believe the transformation of the man I knew for more than a year to this dirty, crazed man and the hateful words that are pouring from his mouth. How could he have hidden this from me? From all of us?

His eyes widen mockingly. 'You don't have to beg, Ella. You're a dirty bitch but I'll fuck you.'

I shake my head to clear it, but it causes a flash of pain to stab at my temples. I'm too confused to be able to comprehend my situation. I look at him pleadingly. 'Why are you doing this? I haven't done anything bad to you.'

'You know,' he says evenly. 'You are the most self-absorbed bitch I have ever had the misfortune to meet. I was *in love* with you, you shameless slut.'

'What?' It is like being in the twilight zone. Nothing makes sense. Rob was in love with me!

'Unbelievable! She didn't even notice,' he notes in wonder.

'How was I to know?' I cry defensively. 'You were always rude and cold to me.'

'If I had not been rude and cold would you have loved me back?'

Oh, my God. Oh, my God. I'll never be able to reason with him. 'Maybe.'

He walks up to me and viciously kicks me in the stomach. The wind is knocked out of me. I gasp for breath and automatically curl myself protectively, but there are no more blows. I need a strategy. I need to keep him from getting angrier. I need to calm him down.

'That's for lying. No more lies.' He stands over me. 'Have I made myself clear?'

Unable to speak I nod.

'You haven't answered the question.'

I turn my face and look him in the eye. 'No.'

He explodes with laughter, a bitter sound that rings around the empty flat. 'I thought so. Too good for me, are you?'

'No,' I try to explain. 'You were my boss. I never even thought about you like that.'

He turns his back to me, his palms clasped over his head, before suddenly swiveling around to face me, grotesquely angry. 'You didn't think of me like that,' he shouts. 'Do you know that I've been taking care of you and protecting you from the moment you appeared for the interview all round-eyed and dewy faced. You were never good enough for the job, too weak and indecisive, but I took you in, taught you everything, and gave you a chance. And what do you do? At the first opportunity you turn your back on me for that stinking gypsy brute.'

He spits on the ground.

'By the time I came back from the toilet it was already too late, wasn't it? You were itching for his dick. All the way back to the office in the car, I could smell your arousal. Disgusting.'

My mind scrambles around wildly. I have to pacify him. 'It's not like that,' I tell him, my voice trembling with emotion. 'I didn't turn my back on you. I quit my job because I found out we were wrong about everything. We've all been manipulated and tricked into demonizing the wrong sections of society. The real cheats, the truly rich, are always going be out of our reach, and all we are doing is squeezing the ordinary person.'

He narrows his eyes. 'How convenient! As soon as you landed yourself a loaded boyfriend, you're no longer interested in protecting the poor, taxpaying public anymore, and become more concerned with not demonizing the section of society he belongs to.'

I exhale in frustration. 'You don't understand. I truly believed we were helping the ordinary hard-working British public, preventing them from having their pockets picked by people who didn't pay their proper taxes, but he showed me that I was wrong.'

He pushes out his jaw aggressively. 'I can't believe I wasted all that time on you. You're just a stupid bitch.'

'I'm sorry. I'm really sorry. I honestly didn't mean to hurt you,' I cry out.

He stares at me, his face hard. 'It's great that you're sorry, but it doesn't change a damn thing for me. I've got nothing because of you. Did you know I was happily married? She used to make steak and kidney pies for me on Sundays. And then you came, batted your eyelashes, made me want you, and ruined everything.' He runs his hands through his hair distractedly. 'I've done things for you. I even took care of Michael for you'

'You did what?' I gasp.

'Yes, I broke into his house and made those phone calls so you could actually have the necessary proof and get your restraining order.'

My mouth drops open. 'He never stalked me, did he?'

'He didn't have the brains to be a stalker,' he scoffed. 'That was me. It was always me. I was always loyal to you.'

'Where is Michael now? Have you done something to him?'

'Of course not. I'm not a killer. Well, I wasn't. You are the only one capable of driving me to murder.'

He squats next to me. His crotch is so close to my face I can smell his odor: an unwashed, stale, cheesy smell. He flicks open a switchblade and brings it close to my face. It catches the light and inspires dread. Averting my gaze from it, I realize that he's just trying to frighten me, but I can't help the terror that floods my entire body. He's a man who has driven himself to the edge of madness. And he's holding a knife.

'Look at you. You thought you could say sorry and all would be forgiven.' Reaching out a hand he puts it on my bare knee.

I flinch. 'Please. Please don't,' I beg.

His eyes are cold. 'Don't worry. I don't have a big cock. I will fit beautifully in your ass.'

I shake my head with terror.

He bends closer, his eyes widening menacingly. 'Don't you like it up the ass? Didn't the slimy gypsy stuff his dick up your bottom?'

'I'm sorry. I'm so sorry. I didn't mean to hurt you,' I cry.

'No, I'm sure you didn't mean it. However, you did. And now you can compensate me for my suffering,' he says, and slowly runs his hand up the inside of my thigh.

I squeeze my legs shut and trap his hand. He laughs, an ugly sound. He wrenches his hand out from between my thighs and continues upwards on the fronts of my thighs. His progress is relentless. His fingers have already reached the edible panties that I wore especially for Dom. I stare at him desperately. His fingers suddenly pinch my pussy lips together and I jump with horror.

At that, lust filters into his eyes. With both hands, he tears my skirt right to my waist. He sees the chocolate arrows and a light comes into his eyes.

'My, my, what do we have here?'

He bends his head and licks an arrow.

I start screaming, but he suddenly slaps me so hard my jaw feels like it has been dislocated. Stinging tears fill my eyes.

He grabs my panties.

My head and jaw are throbbing so bad I can hardly open my mouth. 'Wait,' I cry, a sharp pain shuddering through my face.

His hand stills.

'Yes, my thoughtless actions brought you terrible pain. But are you better than me if you rape me?'

His eyes flicker. 'I'll pay for my sins. But now it's your turn. Don't worry I'm kind enough to use butter.'

I draw in a shocked breath.

'I don't want to tear you. I want to use you many times before I discard you.'

'And after you've raped me, what will you do? Kill me? And then what?'

He takes his hand off my thigh. 'Don't you get it? The only thing left for me is the satisfaction of knowing you will get what you deserve.'

He turns me roughly onto my front.

'Pleeeeease,' I beg.

He hooks his fingers into the top of my flimsy, edible panties. At that moment there is a massive bang and the door of the dingy flat flies open and hits the wall hard. Both Rob and I freeze. Dom charges through the door followed by Jake. Even through the fear and shock my brain notes that they look so big and ferocious compared to Rob. Before I know it, I feel the cold, sharp end of Rob's knife pressing into the skin of my throat.

'Don't come any closer, or I'll slit this bitch's throat from ear to ear,' he threatens with a tremor of panic in his voice.

Both Dom and Jake take a step back, Dom with both his hands raised, the palms showing.

Jake is the first to speak. 'If you hurt her, we will kill you. If you let her go now, you have my word we'll do nothing to you. We won't go to the police. We're gypsies—we settle everything on our own. I'll even give you money.'

'Money,' Rob spits. 'You think you can buy me? This is *my* bitch.'

I see Dom start, his face reddens, and his hands clench so hard the muscles of his shoulders bulge.

'Listen,' Jake says. 'If you think you're going to walk out of here alive after touching one hair on her head you're mad.'

My breathing is shallow. Rob's painfully firm grip on my shoulder has not eased at all.

I feel Rob's body become tense. In the end he is a coward.

'You'll gain nothing by taking a life and surrendering your own. Make no mistake. If you harm her, we'll kill you with our bare hands.'

Rob's grip eases a fraction.

'Let her go. We won't hurt you,' Jake adds persuasively.

'You'll not keep your word. I know how this works.'

Dom is as still as a statue.

'No. My word is my honor,' Jake says.

Rob's face crumples. Suddenly, he erupts with the hysterical laughter of a madman. Nobody reacts. Both Dom and Jake remain stony-faced. As suddenly as he had begun laughing, he stops. 'All right. Prove it,' he says, and throws the knife on the ground.

No sooner does the knife hit the ground than Dom rushes forward with an incoherent cry of rage and starts kicking the shit out of Rob. In his uncontrollable frenzy, strings of curses stream out of his snarling mouth. 'You fucking ugly cunt. You think you're so big? Let's see how big you are without your blade. Fucking piece of chicken shit.'

Jake grabs Dom by the front of his shirt and pushes him back.

'Look at her face. He fucking hit her. I want to kill the fucking cunt,' Dom roars.

'No, you fucking don't,' Jake growls. 'Take your woman out of this hellhole and leave me with him.'

Dom's face is tight and tense, and his hands are clenched into fists. He takes a great shuddering breath as he fights to control his natural instinct.

Jake lets go of his shirt. 'Go home, Dom.'

Dom turns toward me, his face immediately softening. Taking his jacket off, he covers my half-naked body with it. While Rob cowers on the ground and Jake stands over him, Dom takes the knife from the floor and cuts the ties around my hands and ankles. Then he takes me into his arms and hugs me tightly.

'Come on,' he says in my ear.

I pull away from him. He stands and pulls me up. My legs are shaking. He puts his arm around my back, and leads me out of that hellhole.

TWENTY-EIGHT

Jake

I wait for the door to close then I walk over to the man curled up and writhing on the floor. I stop in front of him and he looks up at me with bulging eyes.

'Please, I beg you. Don't hurt me. I'll do whatever you ask,' he whines like the coward that he is.

I yank him up, struggling, cowering and screaming like a stuck pig, and pin him against the wall, until he suddenly realizes I am not going to hurt him, yet. I let go of him so he falls to the floor. He lands in a heap, but quickly scrambles into a sitting position against the wall. I fix my eyes on his bloodied face. His left eye is beginning to swell, his cheek is grazed and there is a cut on his lip which is bleeding.

The knife is beside us. His bulging eyes stray to it, and I don't try to kick it out of the way or reach for it. Instead I smile coldly and instantly his mouth begins to tremble uncontrollably.

'You gave your word,' he grovels.

Calmly I reach down and pick up the knife.

'What are you doing?' he cries in panic. He is so terrified he is trying to crawl sideways up the wall.

I move close enough to hear his heart thumping in its cage and say nothing. Simply watch the terror behind his pupils. Taking my time, I bring the knife to his throat and point it so the tip nicks his throat. He freezes. A drop of blood appears on his skin.

'Please, please, don't kill me. I wasn't going to hurt her. I just wanted to frighten her, teach her a lesson. I love her,' he begs pathetically.

I frown. 'You don't love her. You can't. You're a rat. She's a woman. Rats don't love human beings.'

'Yes, yes, I'm rat. You're right. I don't love her,' he agrees immediately, shaking his head wildly, snot running from his nose and into his mouth.

'So we both understand this clearly. Whose woman is Ella?'

'Your brother's,' he utters immediately

I inhale the stench of his urine. A dark stain is spreading over his crotch. I raise my eyes back to his blubbering face and feel nothing. Not even hatred. He could be a discarded bottle top on the floor of one of my clubs. A bit of waste. A nuisance. I have to pay someone to clean it up, dispose of it.

'Good. I'm glad we agree. Now. You made a mistake when you took my brother's woman, because that involves me and a whole world of trouble for you,' I tell him.

Sheer panic leeches into his face. It's been a long, long time since I brought a man to such fear. It's irritating that I have to do this. I don't want to be like this. But men like him force me to return to this unpleasant business.

My voice is emotionless and flat. 'My brother isn't a killer. Sure, you got his blood boiling, but a kicking within an inch of your life is as far as it would have gone. Me, I can kill in cold blood. I could kill you right now without breaking into a sweat. As painless as swatting a fly.'

His head jerks.

I continue as if we are having a polite conversation. 'There are so many ways I could end it for you. Slit an artery and watch you bleed out on this floor. My favorite, actually. Or stab you repeatedly, slicing through every vital organ. A bit messy, but it has its uses. Or many non-fatal cuts to make you suffer a long, slow painful death. So far no one has pissed me off enough to make me resort to this method yet.'

He shudders visibly.

'I would probably be doing the world a favor to kill you, but looks like you're the luckiest man alive tonight. We arrived here before you had a chance to really fuck it up for yourself. So I'm going to make this one exception. I'm going to let you live. I am going to walk out of here and you are going back to wherever you presently call home. Once you get there you have twenty-four hours to put your affairs into order and leave London. For-fucking-ever!'

I nod slowly.

'I don't care where you go or how you get there. Take a flight, take a boat, take a train, but in twenty-fours if you are still anywhere within 100 miles of my brother, *his* woman, her family or me, you will have a sea burial. There are two men outside. They will follow you home. Don't mind them. They won't harm you. Their job is to escort you home safely.'

I stop and pause. 'Do you understand me?'

He nods so violently his head bangs against the wall.

He reaches out a hand towards my leg, 'Thank—.'

My voice is like a whiplash. For the first time I actually feel enough raw fury to end his life. 'Don't even fucking go there,' I tell him.

He shrinks and begins coughing and spluttering.

'Good.' I stand and look down at him for a few seconds longer, and then I turn away and open the door. I take the stone steps two at a time and see the car with my back-up pair, Eddy and Mace inside. Eddie lifts his hand. I nod. As I step onto the pavement my phone rings. It's Lily.

'Hey, baby,' I say into the phone. And there is nothing but love in my voice.

TWENTY-NINE

Dom opens the passenger door to a blue Mercedes-Benz sedan and I slide in. I want to ask whose car it is, but I don't. I feel too numb and cold to actually care. Some part of me is still in that disgusting flat, still with Rob. Yes, I was so afraid of him.

I turn to Dom urgently.

'What will Jake do to Rob?'

'I hope he kills that miserable fucking coward,' he rages.

'I don't want him to be killed,' I whisper.

He turns on me. 'Why do you care so much? Fucking hell, Ella, he had a knife to your throat and he'd already torn your skirt.' He clenches his jaw. 'God knows what he would have done if we'd not come when we did!'

'I don't want his blood on my conscience, Dom. Please,' I say with a sob.

His face softens. He grabs my forearms and pulls me toward him. 'Listen. Jake is honorable in the old-fashioned way. In the gypsy way. But he'll arrange it so that pathetic pussy never comes near you again.'

I start to cry softly. 'Just take me home, please.'

'Hey. Don't cry, baby. You're safe now,' he cajoles, and pulls me tight against his chest, careful not to hurt my throbbing jaw.

'Just take me home,' I whisper tearfully into the hollow of his throat.

He takes me home and parks outside the entrance.

'You'll get a ticket,' I warn automatically.

'It doesn't matter,' he says, and, getting out of the car, helps me out. Together we walk up the three flights of stairs. When we get upstairs, I realize that I have no keys. I look up at him. My head is spinning, my jaw is throbbing and I can't think properly.

'I don't have my keys,' I wail as if it's the end of the world.

'It's OK, Ella. I have mine,' he says gently.

He lets me in. I stand in the hallway of my little home. The first thing I see is the phone book on the floor. I can't understand why it is there. I look around me. Everything is the same, and yet everything is different. It has been invaded by a man who hates me. The thought makes me feel almost ill. I press my lips together to stop from breaking into tears again.

'I need to take a shower,' I say in a trembling voice, and start walking toward the bathroom. Dom catches me and tugs me back so I'm pressed up against his body.

He takes my chin in his hand.

'I feel so dirty,' I say.

'You're not dirty, Ella. We got to you before anything really bad could happen.'

I frown. 'How did you find me so quickly?'

He curls his hand around my wrist and lifts it up to my eye level.

'What?' I ask, confused.

'This is a chipped bracelet.'

'What?' I say, confused.

'Told you I was a paranoid motherfucker.'

'You gave me a bracelet with a tracking chip and you never told me about it?' I ask incredulously.

'Yeah,' he says, totally unfazed.

 447

I pull slightly away from him. 'And you've been tracking me all this time?'

'Not really. The chip is in there, but while you were safe there was no need to track you.'

'I can't believe you gave me a chipped bracelet, like I'm your pet or something.'

'You're my woman. I protect what's mine,' he says forcefully.

I shake my head in disbelief. I want to be angry, but I'm all emotioned out. I look at the bracelet that he gave me two weeks ago. Gold with little square pieces of sapphire set into it. It's a bloody tracking device. Still, I can't complain, it certainly came in handy today.

'I know about Vivien,' I say softly. My heart feels as if it's a heavy rock.

'I know. Jake told me.'

I sniff and look at the pulse beating steadily in his throat. 'I saw a picture of her,' I say, trying to be casual, and failing miserably.

He puts his finger under my chin and lifts it until I'm forced to look into his gorgeous eyes. They are filled with soft lights, the pupils so large they are almost the size of his irises. 'Yeah, you look like her. And yeah, I admit, in the beginning I confused my lust for you with a love lost tragically. I thought you'd make the pain go away for a while. I thought I was temporarily re-creating an old magic. I didn't know you were a thief. That you'd steal my heart, weave yourself into my soul, and make me fall deeper in love with you than I've ever done with anyone else.'

My mouth drops open. 'You ... love me?'

'Yes.' He beams.

I shake my head in disbelief. 'You love *me*?'

'Yes, I love you, Ella Savage. I fucking love you.'

'Since when?' I ask, almost unable to believe what he is telling me.

448

'I don't know. All I know is that I love, love, love you.' He picks me up and twirls me around. 'And I'm never letting you go.'

I look down at him seriously. 'Maybe you just think you love me because I look like Vivien?'

'Oh, my darling, darling Ella. You've no idea. I'm so in love with you, I feel high, as if I've dropped an ecstasy tablet.'

'But how do you know it's really me you want and not her?' I insist.

'No two women could be more different than you and Vivien. It's you I want to wake up to in the morning. It's your skin I crave, and it's your laughter I yearn to hear on the phone.'

'Oh, Dom. I feel so confused. I don't know what's happening anymore. First, I find out about Vivien, then I get kidnapped, then I think I'm going to be sodomized and raped, and then I get rescued, and now you're telling me you love me! I'm thinking I'm going to wake up soon!'

'Want me to pinch you?' His eyes light up. 'Or, better still, I can fuck you awake? Did I see a chocolate arrow on your thigh just now?'

I have a sudden image of Rob, his long, hot tongue slowly licking the other chocolate arrow from my thigh. I shudder. 'I need a shower.'

His face hardens. 'Did he do anything to you?'

'No,' I deny immediately. 'Of course not.'

'Then how come there's only one chocolate arrow?' he demands aggressively.

Suddenly tears come back to my eyes. 'Please, Dom. Leave him alone. If he is diseased, I infected him.'

'Did he do anything to you? I'll fucking kill the sick bastard if he did,' he declares furiously.

I take both his hands in my palms and look deep into his eyes. 'No, Dom. He didn't do anything to me. After everything that's happened, I just feel unclean. I need to wash my body and my hair.'

'All right,' he says. 'Want me to come with you?'

'No. Why don't you pour yourself a drink? I'll be out soon.'

I go into the bathroom and take all my clothes off and stand under the hot shower. I rub at the chocolate arrow vigorously. Then I see the watermelon pasties run pink into the plughole and I start to cry. I don't know why I'm crying. Maybe it's the tension. I hear a noise, and the door to the shower is open and one hot, fully erect alpha is standing there.

'Don't cry, Ella' he says softly. 'You're safe now.'

'I know,' I sniff.

And he puts out a hand and touches my midriff where a huge bruise has formed. 'He hurt you,' he whispers in a shocked voice.

'It actually doesn't hurt.' And it's true.

He comes into the shower, and the cubicle is so small the practical solution is for me to climb onto his body and curl my legs around him while he holds on to my buttocks and fucks me. Hard. Oh, so hard. It's what I need. I feel the tension, fear and doubt wash away. We come together under the cascading water. He kisses me gently and I cling on to my hero. God, he's so gorgeous.

'This weekend I'm taking you riding. You'll love it.'

'Why? Because Vivien loved it?'

He smiles, a beautiful, pure smile. 'No, because it's horses. You cannot *not* love my horses.'

'OK.' I grin.

'Do you love me?' he asks.

'Oh, Hell!' I say. 'Isn't that as obvious as fuck?'

'Yeah, it is, but I just like to hear it rolling off your tongue,' he says with a mischievous, awesome, sexy grin.

And we both laugh.

I can be your hero, baby
https://www.youtube.com/watch?v=koJlIGDImiU

EPILOGUE

SIX MONTHS LATER

I lift the stick and see the thin blue line. And a bubble of laughter comes up and erupts in my mouth. Oh, my God. Oh, my God. I put the stick on the edge of the sink, wash my hands, and walking on air, go back into the bedroom.

'Come here, woman,' Dom says from the bed.

I don't go to him. I just stand there and admire him. His swarthy skin contrasting darkly against the white sheet. His chest and arms muscular. His smile white and beautiful. A thought. I can't believe he is really mine. I wake up every morning and I just can't believe my luck. Nobody gets this lucky, surely?

He raises his body up slightly, his smile disappearing. 'What's wrong?'

I smile happily. 'Nothing. Absolutely nothing.'

'So what're you standing there for? I'm hungry for pussy juice.'

I laugh and go forward. He reaches out and pulls me into bed and I tumble into his warm, hard body.

'What's this?' I say with widened eyes.

'That, Mrs. Eden is called your husband's fucking erect cock.'

While I am still laughing, he rolls me over on my back. I feel a finger slide into me. I stop laughing. 'Oh, Dom,' I sigh.

A long time later, when we are both exhausted and lying on our side facing each other, he says, 'I did warn you I was hungry.'

'Mmmm,' I say sleepily.

'It's Sunday. Let's stay in bed and fuck and eat junk food all day.'

'I can't I promised my mother I'd help her pack.'

He is immediately on his elbow looking down at me, a frown line between his eyebrows. 'Pack? Pack what?'

'Her stuff. Remember they are moving in a week's time.'

'Fucking hell, Ella. My wife doesn't pack. That's what movers are for. Shit, you could ruin your back doing things like that.'

'I have called the company you told me to call. They are packing all the big things. I'm just helping Mum to package some of her decorative items in bubble wrap.'

I touch his face wonderingly. 'Thank you for taking care of my parents. My Mum thinks she died and went to heaven. Not even in her wildest dreams did she think she could ever own a house, let alone something so beautiful as the one you bought them. And my father is a whole different man. Who knew that all he needed was hormone therapy?'

'I'm the one who has to thank them for giving you to me,' he says lovingly.

'Talking about that. You might be in a position of giving someone away too in about twenty odd years.'

He suddenly rolls me over and pins me under him. 'You're still speaking English, right?'

I burst out laughing. 'Yes, I am.'

He frowns. 'It's not going to be able to crawl as fast as Tommy, or speak like Liliana is it?'

I laugh even more. 'I don't know it might.'

'Oh shit,' he curses.

'Stop making a joke of everything, you big fucking hulk, you. Aren't you happy?'

He looks down at me, blue eyes full of laughter. 'Yes, I'm so happy I could fuck you all over again.'

I grin up happily at him.

'I love you, Ella.'

A warm feeling of such love and joy gushes into me I have to gasp. 'I love you too, Dominic Eden. I love you so much I could fuck you all over again.

'Go on then,' he challenges cheekily, as his mouth comes down to claim me.

EIGHTEEN MONTHS LATER

I place Adam on the changing mat.

'Right,' I say confidently. 'Let's do this.'

He gurgles up at me. I take a deep breath and blow it out.

'Right,' I say again. 'We're doing it without Mummy.'

This time he blows a bubble. I look down on the changing mat.

Wipes. Check.

Fresh clean diaper. Check.

Diaper rash cream. Check.

Plastic bag for disposing of soiled diaper. Check.

If I'm really fast I won't get more than a lungful of stench. Adam kicks his legs and hands encouragingly. I unfold a diaper and put it close by.

454

Gently, I take his shoes and socks off. He seems happy enough at this stage, and so am I. I unbutton his little suit and expose the diaper. I pull his little legs out of the suit.

I take a deep breath of clean air and, holding it in my lungs, I pull both the Velcro tabs at the same time, and, detaching the diaper from his tummy, reveal the extent of the damage.

Fuck! Not good.

I grab his ankles in my hand, pull his bottom upwards, and, using the diaper, wipe away the worst of the brown mess before smoothly sliding the diaper out. I fold it on itself and fix it with the sticky tapes. As fast as I can, I clean the area with the baby wipes, making sure to get into all the folds. I dump the wipes into the plastic bag with the soiled diaper and tie it tightly.

I let out the breath I was holding in a sudden burst.

Adam grabs his toes with his hands and watches the great big gulps of air I take.

'And then what happened?' I say to him.

He claps his hands and coos.

'Mummy's the first best thing that ever happened to me, and you're the second best thing that ever happened to me,' I tell him.

He lets out a little squeal.

'I know, but Mummy has to come first. Without Mummy there would be no Adam. You see how all this works, huh?'

I carry on talking more nonsense while I apply diaper cream, and then I lift his little bottom up again and slide the new diaper under him. I pull it over and snap the Velcro bits down. I dress him again in the same clothes. I tickle the soles of his feet and he cackles with laughter, his big blue eyes sparkling with innocence.

'You wait until you become a daddy. Then we'll see how you get on with changing dirty nappies.'

I wipe my hands and, picking him up, hold him close to my chest. After a big kiss and hug, we go downstairs. He can have a bottle of lovely warm milk while I have my glass of whiskey.

I've fucking earned it.

I open the door and see Dom coming down carrying Adam. My face breaks into a happy grin. No matter how many times I see the two of them together the joy that fills my heart never lessens. I love them both so much sometimes it feels as if my heart will burst with happiness.

'Hello,' I say.

'Ah, Mummy's home,' Dom says with a grin.

'Hello darling,' I say going closer to them. Adam is so crazy about his Dad he will not come to me or anyone else when his father is around, but he does make an excited squawk and wave his little arms at me. I walk up to them and standing on tip- toes kiss first Dom and then my beautiful son.

I touch Adam's diaper. 'Does he need changing?'

'All done.'

My eyebrows rise. 'You changed his diaper?'

'Of course.'

I hide a smile. 'Any ... um ... problems?'

'No,' he says casually.

'Well done,' I say with a huge smile.

'Although, you really should stop feeding our son dead cats.'

I laugh.

'And what have you been up to?' he asks.

I lift up my bag of shopping. 'I got you your favourite.'

His eyes twinkle. 'Chocolate arrows?'

I pretend to be serious. 'No.'

'Watermelon pasties.'

'Be serious, you,' I reprimand with mock seriousness.

'If it's not watermelon pasties I give up. I don't know. What?'

'Edible panties.'

He grins cheekily. After thousands and thousands of grins. After all this time my tummy still flutters with the incredulous thought, and this man is mine?

'Wonderful,' he says, eyes twinkling. 'It's been ages since I ate one of those delicious things.'

'You ate one two weeks ago,' I remind.

'That's way too long, Ella, my love. Way too long.'

THE END

BEAUTIFUL
BEAST
A BAD BOY ROMANCE
GEORGIA LE CARRE

Beautiful Beast

Published by Georgia Le Carre
Copyright © 2015 by Georgia Le Carre

Cover Designer: http://www.kevindoesart.com/
Editor: Caryl Milton & IS Creations
Proofreader: http:// http://nicolarheadediting.com/

ISBN: 978-1-910575-20-8

BEAUTIFUL BEAST

Georgia Le Carre

Dedication

To my darling husband,
I couldn't do without you.

One

'My milkshake brings all the girls to the yard.'

I stand at the bar, my hand loosely curled around a bottle of ice-cold beer, and try to imagine a hundred years passing inside these glittering walls. And in a flash I am connected to every sad, twisted fucker inside that cavernous former theater. In a century we're all going to be nothing but a fistful of dust. But today ... Hot blood throbs in my cock and I am still king of my empire of dirt.

I cast my eyes around—and everything is exactly as it should be.

Cool air filters out of vents in the ceiling, loud music beats on my skin like morning rain in the tropics, and roving spotlights pick up waitresses in fluffy white tutus. With their tight little butts on show, they glide around as perky as fucking swans.

Sometimes the spotlights stop to lick one of the scantily clad, insanely glamorous dancers sprinkled around the place like magic dust. They are the candy in my sweet shop. Because ... Hidden in the cool shadows of the booths where the spotlights never go, soulless men in dark suits and bulging wallets wait with buckets of champagne and an insatiable taste for pussy. Not that they can actually have any while they're in here, obviously, but hey, they can jerk off to the memory until their dicks drop off.

Yup, all is well in Eden.

I pick up my beer, bring it to my lips, and notice something that *isn't* exactly as it should be.

Martin, my manager, is escorting one of the dancers out of one of the VIP rooms. His lips are compressed into a thin line of fury, and she looks shit-scared as she struggles to keep up in her seven-inch-high transparent, plastic shoes. They have red lights inside the wedges that flash every time she takes a tottering step. Fuck, my four-year-old niece wears trainers that flash. I have never seen her before, so she must be new.

A row of beautiful girls preening by the bar exchanges knowing looks. One or two giggle heartlessly when a discreet, black exit door draped with thick, red velvet curtains swallows the pair. Beyond is Martin's office where the hiring and firing is done.

I take a sip of cold beer, my eyes swinging back in the direction of the VIP room they have just vacated. In an impressive show of clockwork precision, the housemother, Brianna, is already slipping into it. You can tell by her purposeful air and the veiled expression on her carefully made-up face that she is on a clean-up mission.

She emerges a few minutes later, smiling serenely, and nods to one of the girls loitering by the bar. The girl immediately starts walking toward her. They meet by the mirrored pillars, exchange a few words before the girl makes for the VIP room, and Brianna continues, unruffled, on her journey.

Problem solved.

The music changes and AronChupa's quirky track 'I'm an Albatraoz' fills the charmed air. One of the club's favorite dancers, Melanie, a sleek black girl in a skin-tight catsuit with geometric patterns, struts energetically onto the stage. The effect of her appearance is instantaneous: the atmosphere in the club becomes electric. The stage lights are switched off, and Melanie disappears. All that remains is the collection of fluorescent patterns on her costume working their way strongly up a pole. It is a marvelous sight and the audience erupts in a collective roar of approval.

I place my drink down and turn back to watch the curtained door. I don't tend to interfere in the day-to-day running of my club. Why would I? Any fool can see that between Martin and Brianna they run a very tight ship. And yet something about flashing shoes has my interest piqued.

Perhaps it is because I can always tell an innocent with one look, and she is as green as they come. I wouldn't be surprised if this is her first attempt at strip dancing. But mostly because I can never let an injustice pass. It used to get me into all kinds of trouble when I was a kid, but it's in my DNA; I just can't look the other way.

Less than five minutes later she tumbles back into the club. Her ridiculous wedges are still flashing, but tears are streaming down her face. Martin has cracked the whip. She has been fired. She lurches toward a side door that leads to the changing rooms. I walk quickly to the door nearest to me and enter my pass code. The door opens into the passage she has entered.

'Oh!' she exclaims when she sees me. In the bright lights of the corridor, her face, under its thick make-up, has a washed out hue, and her eyes are glassy and distraught.

'Come with me,' I say, and she silently follows me upstairs to my office. I hold the door open and let her precede me. Closing the door, I then walk toward my liquor cabinet.

'Would you like a drink?' I throw over my shoulder.

'No thank you, Mr. Eden,' she replies meekly.

I turn my head and meet her eyes. She is actually a stunner. 'Call me Shane,' I tell her softly.

She frowns with confusion.

'Have a seat,' I invite and pour two stiff measures of brandy.

Walking over to her, I hold out a glass. She accepts it with a murmur of thanks and I notice the sudden change in her body language. She thinks I am coming on to her. Unsure about my intentions, she has reverted to her usual routine. Sweet, really.

I have occasionally dated girls from the club if they're totally irresistible and they get my 'have cock will travel' rules, but generally I prefer not to. It's bad business all round. I move to my desk and, leaning my butt against the edge, cross my arms over my chest and smile at her.

She smiles back tremulously, her eyes moist with invitation. In a practiced gesture of seduction, she looks down and bats her waterlogged eyelashes coquettishly.

'What's your name?' I ask her.

'Bubbles.'

I hide a smile. 'Right, Bubbles. Want to tell me what happened?'

She turns bright red. 'Martin fired me,' she confesses painfully.

'Why?'

'I ... I ... let a customer ... uh ... touch me,' she reveals.

'You must have known you're not allowed to. Why did you do it?'

She looks up at me, her eyes large and begging. 'I swear I didn't want to. I told him no, but he said if I didn't allow him to he would call for another girl. I've only been here for a week and I've hardly made enough to cover my house fees. He was the first man who asked me for a private dance. I didn't want to break the rules, honestly I didn't, but at the same time I didn't want to lose my best chance to make some money, especially after he told me that everyone did it.'

She opens her left palm in an appealing gesture. 'So I told him I needed to go to the toilet and I went out into the club and asked Nikki for advice, since she's the best earner in the club.'

Her face becomes bitter. 'She told me I'd be stupid to let such a high flyer escape. And that any of the other girls would have touched him without a second thought. "It's totally harmless. Just touch him from the outside of his clothes and no one will be the wiser," she said.'

I frown. 'Were you not told there are cameras inside every booth?'

'Yes,' she admits sadly. 'And Martin has just taken me to his office and made me watch myself act like a fool. But Nikki convinced me that the cameras are just there for show. That there is no film in them and no one actually monitors them. I know I did wrong, but I truly believed her. She is the star of this club. Nobody makes more money than her. I'm a nobody; I've just started working in this club and I'm no competition to anybody, so I never thought that she would play such a dirty trick on me. How wrong I was.' Her voice is filled with regret.

She leans forward suddenly, her face intense. 'I felt I had no choice. She told me that if I don't start earning money soon I will be thrown out because I was taking the place of a girl who could be earning big money for the club. I really didn't know what else to do.' Her face fills with sadness. 'I have commitments. My mother, my babies. I have twins in Brazil. My mother is taking care of them. I need to send money back. They need me to survive.'

She is so young, it never occurred to me that she is a mother. 'How old are you?'

'Nineteen.'

I nod and gaze at her. She lacks confidence, but Brianna did not make a mistake taking her on, and Nikki had good reason to try to eliminate her. She has something very special, and one day she will be a valuable asset to this club and great competition to Nikki.

I put my brandy down. 'I'll give you another chance, but if you ever break any of my club's rules again, you're out and, as per industry practice, your name will be circulated to all the other clubs.'

She clasps her hands together, her eyes shining with gratitude. 'Thank you. Thank you so much, Shane. I promise on my two children's lives I'll never let you down.'

'Good.'

As if unable to contain her excitement she bounces out of her chair like a puppy.

'Go home, Bubbles. I'll have a word with Martin later.'

She comes close enough for me to feel the heat coming off her body and, tipping forward in her flashing wedges, plants a feather-light kiss on my cheek. I cock an eyebrow and she lets her heels drop back to the ground and, slowly, licks her thickly glossed lips. Yes, Bubbles definitely has something.

A ripe, tight, eager pussy. Very predictably, my cock is interested, but my cock is always full of bad fucking ideas. Girls like Bubbles, they look like they're figuring on a cheap thrill with a hot, hard dick for the night, but that's like watching a snake slither up to you and thinking, Awww ... look, it wants a little cuddle. Take it from me, they don't even give you a chance to take the condom off before they're making wedding plans in their heads. Me, I like a little bit of Angela, Pamela, Sandra and Rita.

I pull a fifty from my shirt pocket and hold it between my index and forefinger. 'Take a taxi home tonight,' I tell her.

Disappointment flashes in her chocolate eyes, but she takes the hint and deftly plucks the note from my fingers. The same action has been performed ever since man first invented currency, and its primal nature tugs at something in me. Have I really done Bubbles a favor today? She's naïve and innocent now, but one day she will learn all the things that strippers learn about men, and their greed, and their lust, and their ugliness. She will learn to exploit those qualities and she will make lots of money, but will that really be a good thing?

'Don't do anything the little voice inside you tells you not to,' I tell her.

She nods slowly. 'You are a very beautiful man. Not just your face and body, but your heart too,' she whispers. She pauses for a moment. 'I promise you will never regret this decision.'

Then she walks out of my office and closes the door quietly behind her.

Two

SHANE

The early bird gets the worm, but the second mouse gets
the cheese.

—Steven
Wright

I hear her shoes clatter down the wooden stairs as I light a
cigarette and take a deep drag. Walking over to the large one-
way mirror, I look down at my club. My eyes look for and
immediately find Nikki. She is sparkling like a diamond.
Sitting next to a man, her pose provocative, she raises
perfectly manicured fingers and over the thin material of her
gown, sensuously rubs her nipple. Her mark—I can tell
straight away he's got a cock full of bad fucking ideas too—
stares, transfixed.

You have to hand it to her, she's good, she's real good.

She even had me fooled once.

With girls like Bubbles you see them coming. But when
Nikki approaches you, you don't even see the snake, you just
see the grass moving. Nikki is poisonous even when her legs
are splayed wide open and she is moaning, in that crazy
Russian accent of hers, 'It's so deep, baby. Oh yes, fuck me,
baby. Fuck me hard. Show this nasty pussy who its owner is.'

She crashed a vase into a mirror when I ended it. Good
thing I'm an old hand at ducking. Sometimes, I still catch her
watching me with a strange mixture of frustrated lust and
venom, but she refuses to leave. Why, I don't know. Any club
would welcome her with open arms. I could have fired her, but
why spoil a good thing? She's the club's highest earner.

I am suddenly distracted by a flash of white that appears in my peripheral vision. My eyes shift to follow it. A girl in a shimmery white dress is moving across the floor in the direction of the toilets. Her walk is slow and sexy, effortless, and her bone structure is very fine and delicate. In the dog world she would be a Saluki bred by the Bedouin to race across the desert sand during a hunt. A dog considered too fine to be called simply a dog.

Her skin is very pale and her hair is raven black. It pours thickly down her back like an oil slick. Normally, I would have been put off by the combination of pale skin and long black hair. It reminds me too much of the chalk-white, black-wig-wearing female demons in the Japanese horror flicks that my sister and I used to secretly watch until the early morning hours when we were really young, but something about this woman ...

I exhale smoke.

A strobe light catches her face and my eyes widen.

Whoa! She is far more stunning than I had imagined. In the blue light she looks almost unreal, like a creature from a fairy tale. So pure she cannot be tainted by vulgarity or coarseness even when she is surrounded by it. The quality is so rare I don't feel her call in my cock where most women make their presence felt, but deep in my gut. A tendril of excitement twists up my spine.

I want that woman.

Badly.

I kill my cigarette in an ashtray on my desk and leave my office. I take the stairs two at a time, stride down the corridor, and enter the club. Cool air from the vents above hits my face. Dillon Francis and DJ Snake's track 'Get Low' is playing. I position myself by the Chinese bar with its blue and white porcelain tiles.

An acquaintance grasps my hand and pumps it. 'Hey, Shane, how you doing? Let me buy you a drink?'

'Thanks,' I say with a smile, 'but I've got one coming.'

He wants to talk, but I turn away from him and watch the door that leads from the toilets. My drink arrives and I take a gulp. The door opens. A woman comes out. The door shuts again. I am holding my breath. I let it go in a rush. Why am I behaving like this? My skin prickles, as if it knows something I don't.

The door opens once more and she walks out. Her stride is still a slow sway, but up close she is even more breathtaking. And again I have the impression that she does not belong in this place. As if she is a shimmering water queen risen from a river, able to transform boredom into a feast of the senses.

As she gets closer I have the impression of something exotic. It could be her nose or the straightness of her eyebrows. But blood from distant lands flows in her veins. Her lips are full and painted some spicy color, a mixture of turmeric and chili. Her eyes are elongated and look straight ahead.

She would have passed by without noticing me if I had not shot out an arm and grasped her delicate wrist. Her reaction is strange because it is so deliberate. She stops walking and lets her gaze swing slowly from my hand wrapped around hers up to my eyes. This close, her irises are light green and liquid, the pupils flaring. They are almost ethereal. I have the weird sensation that I am waking her up from a dream. It is disconcerting.

Inside the circle of my fingers, her bones are as fragile as a bird's. I stare into her deeply mesmerizing eyes. They make me want to know everything about her. About what has made her so fragile and otherworldly. They make me want to possess her.

'And who would you be?' I ask, flashing her my most charming smile.

She stares up at me for a few seconds longer. Then she frowns. 'I'm probably not what you think I am.'

What surprises me is that she did not mean her answer to be provocative or flirtatious. That instantly makes her the most interesting woman I have ever met. My cock is pulsing and crushing against my jeans like crazy, so, naturally, I promise myself that I am going to fuck her. I'll be damned, I can't remember the last time a woman had me this strong. I widen my grin. 'What do you think I think you are?'

Her lips move and words quiver out. 'A random pick-up.'

'Wrong. I think you're the most beautiful woman in this club, and I'd like to take you out.'

'Where would you take me?' she asks curiously.

'The woods.' My answer irritates me. *Bravo, Shane. You sound like a fucking serial killer.*

But the first flicker of interest appears in her eyes. 'The woods?'

'Yes. I have an old chateau in France. It is very beautiful this time of the year. At night the fireflies come out.'

She inhales with surprise. 'Fireflies?'

'A sight to behold, they are. I never tire of watching them as they blink around the garden. There used to be more, but there are fewer and fewer of them now.'

'I have never seen fireflies. They seem more like the stuff of myths. How magical to see them for real.'

'Then you must come to Saumur.'

'Saumur,' she murmurs, tasting the name on her tongue.

'I promise you'll love it. There are crickets and bull frogs and wild boar, and occasionally a peacock looking for a mate will wander into the grounds.'

Her mouth parts with wonder. 'Really?'

'Scout's honor.'

'Will I have to sleep with you to see all this?'

I am still holding her hand. I stroke the silky skin on the inside of her wrist with my thumb. 'Not if you don't want to,' I say.

She smiles slowly, sexily. When she smiles she's as beautiful as a field of fireflies.

'We can just be friends?' she asks cautiously.

My eyebrows shoot up. That's a new one for the books. I honestly don't think anyone has *ever* said that to me. 'We can be whatever you want us to be.'

She leans closer, her eyes suddenly alight with mischief. 'Are you wearing mascara?'

I laugh. 'No.'

'You have very fancy eyelashes,' she says solemnly.

'I could say the same about you.' I swear I have never had such a weird conversation with a woman before.

'But I'm wearing mascara,' she says with a grin.

'Do you have a name, mascara-wearing babe?'

'My name is Elizabeth Dilshaw, but everyone calls me Snow,' she says as she gently tugs her wrist out of my grasp.

I don't want to but I let go. 'Really? Snow?'

'Yes. I was born in India where almost everyone is dark-skinned, so when I was born so fair and with such a full head of midnight-black hair, all the nurses started calling me Snow White. The name stuck and I became known as Snow.'

I smile broadly. She did step out of a fairy tale, after all. 'Skin as white as snow, lips as red as blood, and hair as black as ebony.'

'And you are?'

'Shane.'

'Yes, I think I'd like to see the fireflies and have you as my friend,' she says softly.

Izzy Azalea and Rita Ora's 'Black Widow' is playing. There are people brushing past us; I can smell their perfume and cologne. They serve as a backdrop for her. Someone calls my name, but I don't turn to look. 'Can I get you a drink?'

She bends her head and shakes it, and her beautiful hair moves like a silky curtain around her face. 'No, I'm with ... friends. I have to go back to our table.'

I take my phone out of my pocket. 'What's your phone number?'

She lifts her head and tells it to me and I key her number into my phone. Not taking my eyes off her, I press the call button. A bird starts chirping from inside her bag.

'Now you have my number too,' I tell her.

'Yes, now I have your number,' she says slowly.

The moment is strange, surreal even. Full of undercurrents and deeper meanings, it doesn't belong in the middle of a club relentlessly dedicated to the pursuit of the pleasures of the flesh. All the clever words and witty remarks have deserted me. I don't want to let her go.

My phone vibrates in my pocket. I ignore it. 'I'll call you tomorrow,' I say.

She nods slowly. 'Yeah, maybe you will.'

For some odd reason her voice is sad. As if this promise has been made before and never kept, even though I cannot even imagine a scenario where a man takes her number and does not call. She is impossibly intriguing. I resist the temptation to reassure her that I will call.

'Well, then. Nice to have met you,' she says and, turning, begins to walk away.

'Snow,' I call.

She turns around, one charcoal eyebrow raised.

'I will call you,' I promise. It has never happened to me before. I have never cared to reassure anybody that I will call. If I felt like calling the next day, I called. If I didn't, well ... c'est la fucking vie.

One side of her mouth lifts, and then she turns away and carries on in her path, again an incorruptible fairy tale creature. When she disappears from my sight I can't stop smiling. I take a triumphant sip of my drink before tilting my body slightly so I have a view of her table.

And that moment is like that video of John Newman's track, 'Love Me Again'. Do you know it? Where a boy and a girl meet in a dreary club. They escape from her wannabe gangster boyfriend and run out of the back doors. Hand in hand, full of hope and excitement, thinking they have outrun the bad guys, they get out of a narrow alleyway and dash straight into an oncoming vehicle. The video ends abruptly on a black screen.

I guess you are supposed to infer that they die.

Snow's table is Lenny the Gent's table.

The fairy tale takes an unexpected and unwelcome turn. Lenny 'the Gent' is not the wannabe variety but a real gangster. What they used to call a mobster. They call him the Gent because he is always so fucking polite. He would say 'please' or 'do you mind' before he hacked off your face. The Gent is surrounded by beautiful, giggling women vying for his attention, but he gazes at Snow's approach with the kind of hunger that makes me sick to my stomach.

Fucking hell. Straight into an oncoming vehicle!

Snow is Lenny's woman.

When she reaches his table, he stretches out his hand. For a second she hesitates then she opens her bag and gives him her phone. He pockets it, and taking another phone out of his pocket gives that to her. She puts it into her bag and sits down beside him, and he places his hand on her thigh.

I try to make out her expression, but her face is as smooth as a statue. Like a man in a daze I start walking toward her. My mind is blank. Fortunately, I collide with a waitress.

'Sorry. It was my fault,' she apologizes.

'Don't worry about it,' I tell her, my hypnotic trance broken.

I stop where I am standing and look at Snow. She is staring vacantly into her drink, her numb face the perfect frame for her empty eyes. The emptiness is total. I recognize its significance instantly. Her frozen body and expression are an instinct to survive. She has locked herself away in a place where she cannot be corrupted by the baseness and degradation around her.

A nearly naked woman is writhing her flesh close to Lenny the Gent's face, but, like mine, his eyes are glued on Snow.

There is only one way this thing is going to end. Badly. But I don't care. I have always gone where angels fear to tread. The blood expands in the veins of my forearms.

Snow will be mine.

The second mouse will get the cheese.

Three

SNOW

Better keep yourself clean and bright;
you are the window through which you must see the
world.

—Lucien Bernard Shaw

'**A**re you ready to go?' Lenny asks. As if it is ever my decision to stay or go.

I turn my head in his direction and feel like a deer that has stepped out of cover. It stops and stands, motionless, nose to the air, watching, smelling, ready to flee at the least sound. A million years of evolution has taught it how to sniff out danger.

He looks back at me, his eyes totally blank. It is the thing that I find most unnerving about him: how dead his eyes can be at certain moments. Then he smiles and his face fills with human emotions and I forget that momentary disquiet.

'Yes, I'm ready to go,' I reply.

'I'll be coming up with you tonight,' he says, watching me for my reaction.

I become cold inside. The deer would have bolted, but I don't. My face cracks into a smile. 'Of course,' I say quietly.

He stands and holds out his hand. I take it. At the next two tables men are standing up—his minders. We walk out of the club followed by them.

What a mistake it was to talk to that impossibly gorgeous man, to flirt with him and pretend that I could ever go out with one such as him. Shane. Beautiful name. But it was stupid and careless to walk back with some of his warmth still wrapped around my wrist and his cocky smile lighting my eyes.

Lenny knew straight away. He sees everything. Eyes like a hawk. I am his possession. He doesn't use me too often, usually twice a week, sometimes thrice, but I am his, just as much as the hammock he uses only in the summer is. He will sleep with me tonight because he wants to exercise that ownership over my body.

He is actually furious.

We get into the rear of his Rolls-Royce and he leans back and runs his hand along my inner thigh. I inhale sharply. It is an involuntary gesture and his hand freezes. My gaze swings nervously to his eyes. With a cold, hard smile on his face, he moves his hand relentlessly upwards.

I suppose it is my fault, really. If I had not allowed the other man into my head. If I had not come back thinking of fireflies. If I had just been a little better hidden, he would not be doing this now.

'Open your legs,' he instructs.

I part them slightly. His fingers pull away the material of my panties and brush at the seam of my core. I flinch inwardly. Outwardly, my face is calm. I stare straight ahead as if nothing is happening.

'Dry,' he murmurs. 'You're always so damn dry.'

I swallow hard. 'I have lubricant at home.' My voice sounds suddenly panicked. I don't know where the instinctive horror of him comes from. He has never hurt me—at least, not yet. Perhaps, the revulsion comes from the frightening emptiness in his eyes, or the smooth hairless skin on his back. Like a reptile.

'Hmmm.' He takes his hand away and I close my legs with relief.

The car stops outside my building and we get out. In the lift, I know he is watching me steadily, but I cannot look at him. Here the lights are too bright, God knows what he will see. The lift doors open and we step out onto plush maroon carpet. We walk down the corridor and he opens the door with his own key. It is a small one-bedroom apartment. I live here. He pays the rent and all the bills.

I put my purse on the sideboard and head for the little table that serves as my bar. If I'm going to have sex I will need a very stiff drink.

'Would you like a nightcap?' I ask politely.

'Yeah, pour me whatever you're having.'

I require a drink where I can put lots of alcohol into the mix and no one will be the wiser. 'I'm having vodka and orange juice,' I throw over my shoulder.

'That'll do me,' he says, and slumps onto the sofa.

I've noticed recently that he's changing right before my eyes. His moods are becoming darker and more frequent. With my back to him I prepare our drinks. Mine is three-quarters vodka and a quarter orange juice. I carry our drinks over to the sofa and hand him his. I sit next to him and take a gulp. Heavens, it is strong.

'I have some of your favorite caviar. I'll go and get it,' I say, attempting to stand.

His hand shoots out and clamps around my wrist. My shocked eyes fly to his face.

His thin, cruel mouth twitches. 'I'm not hungry ... for that.'

'Oh, OK,' I mumble anxiously, and take another gulp of my drink. I steal a glance at him and he is watching me with the kind of coldness that chills me to the bone.

'Will you need to finish all of that before you can do anything?' he asks, lighting a cigarette.

I nod and push the ashtray toward him.

He looks at me through swirls of smoke. 'Go on then. Fucking finish half a bottle of vodka before I fuck you,' he says. His words are vicious, but his tone excruciatingly courteous.

So I do. I drink the whole thing and it seeps into my limbs and deadens them. My head gets fucked and I no longer care about anything. I put the glass down carefully and look at him expressionlessly. 'I'm ready,' I tell him.

He stands and, pulling me up, carries my limp body to the bedroom. As bedrooms go it is unremarkable. All the furniture came with the apartment and I have not added anything to it. But it is clean. Very clean. I couldn't bear it if it was not.

He helps me undress and when I am naked he lays me on the bed. He doesn't undress fully. Just his trousers and his underpants. His legs are oddly stick-like compared to his upper half, which is thickly muscled and bull-like. His penis is dark red, erect and ready. The sight gives me a twinge of distaste, but I damp it down quickly.

I know he's not a good man, but I owe him my life.

I stare up at him dumbly as he opens the first drawer and takes out a condom packet. He rips it open and rolls it on himself. Then he reaches into the drawer again and takes out a tube of KY jelly. I watch him with detachment as he unscrews the tube, chucks the top carelessly behind the bedside cabinet, and squeezes a couple of inches of gel onto his finger. He places the tube back on the cabinet surface, and comes up to me. His finger is gentle as it slides in, but the jelly is cold, and my muscles contract in rejection.

'Shhh ... relax,' he urges, thrusting his finger deeper into me.

Don't worry, Snow, the way he tells it, it will not be a long tale of the night. Just a little story. A quick in and out. I turn my face to the side, and he climbs onto the bed and lets his mouth crawl from my neck down to my breasts.

'You're so fucking beautiful. So fucking beautiful. Anybody tries to take you away from me, I'll fucking kill him,' he mutters as he pushes deep into me.

I don't make any sound. I start to feel that familiar feeling of being almost weightless. I know it is actually happening to me, but it feels removed as if it is happening to someone else and I am just watching.

As his body slaps against mine, my mind floats away to my childhood days. I am six years old again. My hair is in two long plaits that reach my waist and there are jasmine flowers woven into them. I can smell their strong fragrance. My nanny, Chitra, and I are standing barefoot at the entrance of an Indian temple.

Together we start ringing the big temple bell. We do so because the priest has given us special permission to help. The bell is made of different types of metal. The sound echoes into the distance to welcome the god and goddess.

Chitra and I walk into the temple together with all the other devotees. We stand with our hands clasped and watch the stone statue of the goddess being washed and dressed. A flame is waved around her then brought to us. We hold our cupped hands a few inches above the flame and touch our warm palms to our faces.

The priest, his mouth stained red with beetle juice, smiles indulgently at me, as he offers me half a coconut filled with a small banana and some flowers.

Chitra and I fall to our knees and let our foreheads touch the cool tiles. While she prays, I turn my face to look at her earnest eyes and think how beautiful she is and how much I love her. I love her more than I love anybody else in the whole wide world.

Then we stand and she bends and kisses me. She never lets her lips touch my skin; instead she presses her nose on my cheek and inhales audibly. When she moves her face away, her breath rushes against my skin. That is her way of kissing.

Lenny climaxes, as he always does, with a shrill scream.

His mouth is too close to my ear and the horrible sound startles me out of my dream. Suddenly, I feel the length of his body on mine, all the rough hairs on his legs and belly scratching my skin. He rests on his elbows and looks down at me with heavy-lidded, blank eyes. I stare back at him wordlessly.

'Poor Snow,' he says. For some inexplicable reason, his pity breaks the protective numbness.

'Don't,' I whisper, and I feel my eyes fill with tears. They roll down the sides of my cheeks 'Please don't.'

'For fuck's sake. I'm sorry, OK? Don't cry. Just fucking don't cry again, OK?'

But I cannot stop. So he pulls out of me, takes the condom off, ties it, drops it to the side of the bed, and holds me while I cry. He cannot fix me, he knows that, but he is the only one who knows.

He alone knows what happened to me that night in that hotel room.

Four

SNOW

He gets out of bed and, standing over me, regards my naked, trembling body. What he is thinking I don't know, but with a sigh he walks away after a while, and comes back with a cream blanket. He covers me with it and, moving to the other side of the bed, props himself up on three pillows and lights a cigarette.

We don't talk while he smokes.

Under the blanket my body gradually warms. I start to feel safe and peaceful again. We have a strange relationship, Lenny and I. But then again I don't know what normal is. My parents had a strange love–hate relationship too. My father loved my mother and she despised him. I don't despise Lenny. I … am grateful to him. I don't think of the future. Lenny is forty-two. When he found me I was nineteen. I am now twenty.

He kills the cigarette and turns to me. 'You all right?'

'Yeah,' I say softly.

'Want me to stay the night?'

'No,' I mumble.

'I'll call you tomorrow, OK?'

'OK.'

'Do you need any money?'

'No.'

He reaches for his pants and takes a wad of notes out and puts it on the bedside cabinet. 'Here. Go buy yourself something nice to wear tomorrow.'

I don't say anything, not even thank you.

He vaults out of the bed, gets dressed quickly, then comes over to my curled body. He kisses my hair. 'I'll see myself out. Goodnight, Snow.'

'Goodnight, Lenny,' I whisper.

After the door closes behind him I stay still a few minutes longer. My limbs feel heavy and lethargic, but I know from experience that sleep will never come while I have that dirty, sticky feeling between my legs. I force myself to my feet and into the bathroom. I run the shower and stand under the warm cascade.

Water is good. Water cleans.

I shampoo my hair even though I washed it earlier in the evening, and soap every inch of my body. I realize that I am sadder tonight than usual. Is it the loss of Saumur? Or is it the loss of Shane? I let the water wash away the sadness bleeding out. I only have to do what has proven to work for a year now. Just hold on for tonight. It is always better in the morning light. I have come so far.

I can be like the reindeer moss. Its patience is legendary. Its survival skills are second to none. You can keep it in the dark, freeze it, dry it to a crisp, but it won't give up and die. It simply lies dormant waiting for better conditions. That day will come when conditions will improve for me. Until then I will wait patiently.

By the time I switch off the shower and get out, my fingers are so wrinkled they are like little prunes. I dry myself quickly and, wrapping another towel around my head, I dress in striped pink and yellow cotton pajamas.

I hook up the hair dryer and direct it at my hair before I pad barefoot through my darkened living room. I see my purse lying exactly where I left it. I open it and take out the phone Lenny gave me. It is exactly the same as the one I handed over to him, but when I switch it on it has only one number keyed into it. His.

I feel that strange sense of hopelessness and anxiety try to seep into my body again. But before the feeling can swamp me I put on Vivaldi's *Four Seasons* and return to my bedroom. I find, screw back the cap of the lubricant and put it away. Using a tissue I pick up the used condom and flush it down the toilet.

Then I go back into the bedroom and sweep the wad of money into the drawer. I shut it with a click, straighten and look around the spotless room. I can still smell the stench of our coupling and Lenny's cigarette. After cleaning out the ashtrays and returning them to their proper places I open some windows.

Cool night air blows in as I stand at the window and look out at the night scene below. A foraging fox trots along the wall that separates my building from the next. It is carrying something in its mouth, probably from the rubbish bins. The woman living in the ground floor flat is always complaining about foxes getting into her bins and the foul smell of the excrement they leave behind.

As if it has felt my gaze, it suddenly turns and looks at me. Its eyes are shining brightly, and I am suddenly struck by its wild beauty. It lives and dies in dirt, but it is full of intelligence and the joy of its own creation. It doesn't compare its existence with other creatures, bemoan its foxiness, or try to be like another. It is simply content to be a fox. It is free.

That is more than I am.

I watch it until it disappears then I turn away and look at my alarm clock. It is nearly four in the morning. I should really get some sleep.

I switch off the light and lie on my bed staring at the ceiling.

Even though I try to keep my mind blank, a face floats into my head. Such beautiful eyes. So blue and so bright. I liked him as well. Something delightfully cheeky and cocky about him. I imagine him to be fun and sexy. I circle my wrist the way he did. He had such massive, strong hands. When he held my wrist I actually didn't want him to let go. I stroke my skin the way he did silkily, as if he was already making love to me.

'Shane,' I whisper into the darkness.

He was gorgeous, but I will never see him again. I feel a ribbon of sadness curl around my heart and I take a deep breath. No, I shouldn't allow myself to get silly. He was not just gorgeous. He was too gorgeous. Too young. Too carefree.

It's not a lost opportunity. He just wanted to have some fun. You can't trust a man you find in a strip-dancing club. Anyway, I am too mangled and broken for him. He wouldn't have the patience to put up with my drama. In the end he would shatter my heart. I try to convince myself that it is a very good thing that his number is gone. A blessing in disguise that I will never see those beautiful blue eyes again.

For almost an hour I try to fall asleep. But sleep refuses to come.

Maybe I should take a pill. I go into the bathroom and take one of my little pills. After a while I feel relaxed and floaty. Nothing matters anymore. I no longer feel sad that I will never again see Shane, or Saumur, or the magical fireflies.

Five

SNOW

When I wake up, the sun is filtering in through the gap I left in the curtains. I sit up and hug my knees. What shall I do today? Last month, for the first time since Lenny installed me in this apartment, I woke up and thought, I have nothing to do. I need a job. I need to meet new people.

But Lenny doesn't like me to meet people. He says I am a bad judge of character. 'Look what happened to you the last time you made a friend,' he points out.

But, more and more, I feel I am fading away within these walls.

After I have brushed my teeth and dressed, I sit in the kitchen and have a bowl of cereal. The apartment is so still I can hear the sound of my teeth crunching the flakes of corn.

The letter flap clatters and I leave my bowl and run to the front door. I pick up three envelopes from the floor. A bill, a menu/leaflet from a local Chinese takeaway, and a letter from one of the boutiques where Lenny has opened an account for me.

The letter I am waiting for did not arrive.

With a heavy heart I put the bill aside for Lenny to give to his secretary, and I open the letter from the boutique. There is a sale this weekend and they are writing to invite me to arrive an hour earlier and join the champagne pre-sale party. I throw the invitation away with the leaflet.

Then I sit down to finish the rest of my solitary breakfast.

When I have washed the bowl and spoon and put away the breakfast things, I walk over to the drawer that I swept the money into last night. I take out the wad and count it. Two hundred pounds. Wow! My tears must have moved him.

He is not usually so generous with cash. He prefers to open accounts for me in different shops that he pays for at the end of the month. I don't know what limits I have in those stores but I haven't yet come across one, even though once, in a state of deep depression, I unthinkingly picked up a dress worth three thousand. However, my credit card has only a two hundred and fifty pound limit.

I keep aside forty pounds. The rest I neatly arrange so that all the heads face upwards. Then I get down to the side of the mattress and gently unpick the slash I have sewn up. I add the new notes to the growing brick of money. It makes me happy to see it. I have more than half of what I need. Quickly, I sew it back up so it is almost impossible to tell that my mattress is my piggy bank.

Afterwards, I do what I do every day.

I set about thoroughly cleaning the apartment. I vacuum, I brush, I wipe, I wash, I shine and finally I walk around plumping and smoothing the cushions on the sofas so that there is not a single wrinkle in any of them.

The doorbell rings and I look out of the peephole and see the girl from the local florist holding a large bunch of long-stemmed red roses. I open the door and thank her for the flowers. I close the door and I put my nose to them. There is no scent. I take them into the kitchen and remove the wrapping.

There is no card. Cards are not necessary.

I get a bouquet every time Lenny fucks me.

I put them in water and carry the vase to the coffee table in the living room. They are not what I would have chosen, but they brighten up the place. Later I will pop by the florist on my way back from lunch and get myself a fragrant mix of gardenia, honeysuckle and sweet pea.

I glance at the clock. It is lunchtime. So I get into my jeans and a gray sweatshirt with a hood and go out into the bright sunshine. Usually I buy myself a sandwich and go down to the park and eat it on one of the benches. But today I feel more lost and homesick than I normally do, so I walk down the road, and turn into a little side road.

At the end of it is a small Indian restaurant. I open the nondescript door and enter it. It is a small place with grand ideas borrowed from India before colonial times. Checkerboard black and inky blue floor tiles, fans hanging from a dark-lacquered oak ceiling, an aged brass bar in one corner, cut-glass wall lamps, hunting trophies from the days of the Majarajahs and bitter chocolate, leather love booths and banquettes.

Muted classical Indian music is playing in the background. The smell of cardamom, spices and curry fill the air and I breathe in the familiar scent. The restaurant is deserted. It almost always is at lunchtime. I used to worry that the business was going to go bust, but Raja, the solitary waiter they have working during the lunch shift, assured me that they get very busy at night.

Raja pops his head up from whatever he was doing below the bar, and smiles broadly at me. 'Hello,' he calls cheerfully.

I smile back and take a seat in my usual corner.

'How are you today?' Raja asks when he brings my bottle of mineral water, a basket of poppadoms, and a silver container with condiments and pickles.

'I'm fine, thank you. How are things?' I say.

He nods. 'Very good. Busy tonight. We have a big birthday party.'

'Oh! That's good.'

'Yes, the boss is very happy.'

I smile.

He holds on to the menu in his hand. 'Same as usual?' he asks.

'I think so.'

'OK. Two minutes and I will bring your food,' he says as he walks away.

I go into the women's toilet and wash my hands. When I return to my table, I break a piece of poppadom and, after spooning a tiny amount of sweet mango chutney on it, place it on my tongue. And as it does every time that I do this, the scent and taste take me back in time.

I think of our cook, her wrinkled, cinnamon hand holding out a freshly fried poppadom. But back home we called them appalam. They were hot and, because they were fried in new oil, they did not have any aftertaste. I chew the poppadom slowly. But something is different today. I can't ignore the aftertaste.

It is the beautiful man from last night.

I can't stop thinking about him, and he has infected me with a sense of restlessness and dissatisfaction. I suppose it is to be expected. I lead such an uneventful and dull life, meeting him was like touching a live wire. He invigorated my entire system. And that voice—deep, sexy, cheeky.

I start thinking about him.

He was different from everybody else at the club. Tall with broad shoulders, he alone wore a scruffy T-shirt, worn jeans, and the cockiest grin I've ever seen. A man like him did not need any adornment. He stood alone at the bar. How strange that no dancers tried to accost him. Perhaps it was because he is poor. But he owns a chateau in France so that can't be it. Perhaps he exaggerated. Maybe it's just a run-down farmhouse. Even so I would have liked to have seen the fireflies.

I take a sip of mineral water.

I should stop thinking of him. He is gone. I have no way of contacting him, and he has no way of contacting me. I lean back with that feeling I cannot shake no matter how many times I have tried since last night: I have lost something irreplaceable. Which is madness, really. Of course I haven't lost anything important. That was lost a year ago.

At that moment the door opens and I look up at the intrusion. I have begun to think of this deserted restaurant at lunchtime almost as my own personal space. The door pushes farther in and I freeze with shock.

Impossible! How can it be? What the hell is he doing here?

Inside my body, my hearts starts dancing like a wild thing.

In the daylight Shane's eyes are so bright they are sparkling blue jewels in his face. His mouth is full and sensual, his jaw classically chiseled, and his hair thick and glossy. My eyes pour down his body. He is carrying a motorbike helmet and wearing a blue T-shirt and faded black jeans low on his lean hips. I guess he is what they mean when they say someone is rocking muscles.

I have two seconds before he sees me.

Six

SHANE

I spot her straightaway. She is tucked up in one of the dark brown booths and staring at me with saucer eyes. Her hair is up in a ponytail and her face is devoid of any make-up. She looks even more vulnerable and childlike than she did last night. There is something in her eyes, something that hides and feeds on her.

I know I shouldn't be here.

She's broken. I can see that a mile off. Injured people cling. They are needy. I'm not the kind of guy she needs. Someone like me, I take what I want and I walk. I've never looked back. Never promised anyone anything. My way or no way. But she poses a challenge. A threat. And a promise. And I cannot walk away from her. This is just something I have to do.

I go up to her table and sit opposite her.

'What are you doing here?' she gasps.

I grin. 'Having lunch with you?'

'How did you know I'd be here?' Her voice is breathy. It gets under my skin. Everything about this woman gets under my skin.

'I paid someone to follow you last night, Snow.'

She inhales sharply. 'Why?'

'Because I promised you a trip to Saumur and I didn't know how else to contact you.'

It's amazing the effect my words have on her. Saumur and the fireflies shimmer like a magical promise on her lovely face.

'If you had me followed then you must know that I'm with some—'

I place my finger on her lips to silence the rest of her words. She could have moved back, but she didn't. Her lips are so warm and soft, it sends my dick rigid against the zipper of my jeans. Jesus. I have it bad for her. Her eyes close, but they hold closed for a second longer than it takes to blink. Why, she's savoring my touch. I stare at her. Her eyes open. The green is a few shades darker.

She blushes.

And suddenly I know: she is a sexual innocent.

She must be the most sexually unaware woman I've ever met. She's with Lenny, and it is clear that in exchange for the use of her body he is giving her some kind of protection, or perhaps it is some kind of a financial arrangement, but it is clear that she has never been touched by a real man. I think about her screaming my name while my cock is deep inside her and immediately my cock, already straining uncomfortably, starts throbbing painfully.

I clear my throat. 'Do you still want to see the fireflies?'

She takes a deep and shuddering breath.

SNOW

I shouldn't involve him in my mess. I know how cold and wicked Lenny can be, but my head nods and he removes his finger.

'Would you like to go on Friday night? I'll bring you back by Sunday.'

'I ... I can't do it at the weekends.' In spite of myself, my voice becomes sad. 'Actually, I can't leave the country at any time. He ... er ... expects me to be around all the time.'

There is a slight tightening of his jaw, but his eyes are expressionless. 'Lenny is busy this weekend.'

 493

My jaw sags. 'You know Lenny?' I breathe, taken by surprise.

'It's a small world, Snow.'

'Then you must know what he is.'

'Yeah, I know what he is,' he says, but he appears unimpressed.

I lean forward. 'He's a gangster. He's killed men before,' I say fiercely.

There is no change in his voice. 'I know.'

I drop back to the chocolate chair back. 'Are you not afraid of him?'

He shakes his head slowly, never taking his dirty, cocky, arrogant gaze off me.

I stare deep into his eyes. The flecks inside them are almost violet. I feel transfixed by them. as if he has a strange power over me. 'Who are you?' I whisper.

'Good afternoon, sir. Can I get you anything?' Raja asks.

His voice startles me and I jump.

Shane doesn't look at Raja. 'What's good to eat here?' he asks me.

'The Neer dosa with chicken curry, I think,' I say awkwardly.

'Is that what you're having?'

I nod.

He glances up briefly at Raja. 'I'll have two portions of that and a bottle of beer.'

Raja shuffles away, his eyes brimming with curiosity. From now on, Raja will never look at me in the same way again.

'I'm not a gangster, if that's what you're asking,' Shane says.

'So, what are you?'

He shrugs carelessly. 'I'm just a regular guy. I own some businesses.'

'And how do you know Lenny?'

'My brother used to do business with him.'

'Is your brother a gangster?'

'He used to be.'

'And you? Were you one too?' I ask.

'No.'

'What are you doing here?'

He grins irresistibly. 'I'm doing what the fireflies do when they flash. I'm sweet-talking you.'

Raja comes with the beer and a glass, and Shane ignores the glass and takes a mouthful straight from the bottle. 'So: are you on for Friday?'

'I don't think you understand. Lenny will kill you if he finds out.'

'I don't think you understand. Lenny is sorted.'

'How?' I demand.

'Let's just say he's had an offer he just can't refuse.'

'What kind of an offer? I thought you said you weren't a gangster.'

'I'm not. But I know people Lenny wants to trade with. As to what kind of an offer, you're better off not knowing Lenny's business.'

I frown. 'You're not going to get him into trouble, are you?'

His jaw tightens. 'Lenny's old enough and ugly enough to dig himself into trouble without any help from me.'

'But it's not some kind of trap you're luring him into?' I insist.

His face softens. 'It's not a trap. It's just business.'

And immediately I know. He is telling the truth. I hardly know Shane but I trust him. 'OK, I believe you.'

'Good.'

'What time Friday?' I ask.

He throws his head back and laughs, a triumphant, satisfied laugh, and my gaze travels helplessly down his strong, brown throat. He's special. I know then that we are not going to be just friends, even though this is exactly the kind of man my mother warned me to avoid at all cost. *Men who are too beautiful have too much choice. And a man with too much temptation is like a pig in shit. It will roll around in it all day long.*

Our food arrives, and Shane watches me ignore the fork and knife as I tear the crêpe-thin Neer dosa with the fingers of my right hand, then dip it into the creamy chicken curry, bringing it to my mouth.

'Does it taste better like that?' he asks with a crooked smile.

'Actually, yes,' I admit. 'You can wash your hands in the men's toilet.'

'No need,' he says, spreading his fingers out in front of him. He has beautiful hands. They are large and masculine, the nails square. 'I've eaten things off the floor and survived.'

I watch him rip the delicate white dosa, dunk it in the curry and put it into his mouth. He chews thoughtfully then raises one impressed eyebrow. 'It's good,' he pronounces.

I smile. 'I think so. It's a dish from Mangalore.'

'Do you come here often?'

'Yes, as often as I can.'

He looks around at the deserted restaurant. 'Is it always this dead?'

'Yes, every time I have been here. Most of their business is at night. But, to be honest, I like it like this. It's got vellichor.'

He takes a pull of his beer. 'Vellichor?'

'A place that is usually busy but is now deserted. You know, like that strange wistfulness you get in used bookshops. The dusty cries of all those forsaken books waiting for new owners.'

His lips twist. 'And you *like* that?'

I shrug. 'It suits me—my frame of mind.'

'You're a very strange girl, Snow Dilshaw. But I like you.'

God knows why, but I flush all over.

'Tell me about yourself,' he invites, finishing the first plate and pulling the second plate toward him.

'What do you want to know?'

'Everything. Start with where you are from.'

'I grew up in India. My mother is English and my father is Eurasian.'

He makes a rolling gesture with his left hand. 'Must have been an amazing childhood.'

I shrug. 'It was different.'

'Tell me what it was like,' he asks.

'My father was an industrialist, a very successful one. He traveled a lot, and since my mother insisted on accompanying him everywhere, my two older siblings and I were left in the care of our many servants. Until I was almost five years old I actually thought my nanny, Chitra, was my mother. She did everything for me. I even crept into her room and slept in her bed when my parents were away.'

He raises his eyebrows in shocked disbelief. 'Wow, you thought your nanny was your mother?'

'Yes, I did. I loved her deeply.'

Shane stares at me with such shock and curiosity it is obvious that he must come from a very close-knit family where there is no doubt who the mother is.

'That's sad,' he says.

'Yes, finding out that the beautiful, perfumed, blonde woman with the chilly eyes and milky pearls that whispered against her silk blouses was my real mother was very confusing. Of course, I was in awe of her. Everybody was. In a land where everyone was dark-haired and mostly dark-skinned, she seemed to be very special. No matter where we went everybody stared at her.

'I remember once the two of us were waiting to be picked up by our driver outside a shop and there was a street procession passing in front of us. Basically all manner of society was being presented, schoolchildren, teachers, soldiers ... One of the groups was singing, blind beggars holding onto each other for support. But as they passed us one of them broke years of professional disguise to swivel his supposedly blind eyes and stare at my mother.'

Shane frowns.

'So even though I could see clearly that she was very special, I never took pride in being her daughter. I guess even as a small child I already perceived a lack of love in her. Sometimes it even seemed she could hardly bear to be in the same room as me.'

'I'm sorry. That must have been terrible,' Shane says softly.

'I don't know that it was. I think growing up in a fatalistic society just makes you accept the unacceptable more easily. Once I asked Chitra why my mother loved me so little. She looked at me with her great, big, sad eyes and said, 'She might be an enemy from a past birth.'

Shane's eyes fly open. 'Wow! That's some heavy shit.'

'Not really. Chitra is a Hindu and she believes in reincarnation. According to her even though you have no recollection of your past lives, your spirit recognizes your enemies and your lovers from other lifetimes, and reacts accordingly.'

'What about your siblings though? Was it the same for them?'

'If I was my mother's enemy from a past life then my brother, Josh, was a great love. When I was six I heard her tell him, "I dreamt of you every night when you were inside me." There was just nothing he could do wrong. Once he stood on the dining table and holding his little penis sprayed the whole room with his pee. It even hit our cook and she had to run to her quarters and bathe. But when my mother was told about it, she only pretended to scold him. He ran off to his bedroom to sulk. I still remember how my mother had gone upstairs and sat in his room for ages to cajole him into coming downstairs for dinner.'

'Let me guess, he turned into a nasty little boy who pulled your hair and made you cry.'

I smiled. 'Pulled my hair? He took it a few steps further. He set it on fire. It was the only time I saw my father lose control. He put the fire out with his bare hands and afterwards he tore a branch from a tree and whipped my brother with it until my mother came running out of the house screaming hysterically and threw herself over my brother's body. I can still picture my father standing over them panting and wild-eyed. But enough about me, what about you? Tell me about you,' I urge.

'We are gypsies. My mother is from a Romany gypsy family and my father is an Irish traveler.'

'Oh wow! That's really interesting. You must have had some childhood too.'

'I did. I had a wonderful childhood. At least, until my father died. Then it all kind of fell apart for a while.'

'I'm sorry,' I say.

'It was a long time ago,' he says, and quickly changes the subject back to me. 'So, when and how did you end up in England?'

'I ran away from home when I was nineteen,' I say shortly.

His eyes fill with curiosity. 'How old are you now?'

'Twenty.'

He frowns. 'You've only been in this country for one year.'

I nod.

'How did you get mixed up with Lenny?'

I shake my head. 'I can't talk about it.'

He stares at me, his eyes unreadable ice chips, and I drop my gaze

'But you are with him willingly.'

I nod.

'I want you to memorize my phone number and address.'

He tells it to me and makes me repeat it.

'If at all you need me, just call me or come directly to my home. There's a spare key under the mat. Ring the supervisor's bell and tell him your name and he will let you in. OK?'

'OK.'

Seven

SNOW

When I hear the letter flap clatter back to its closed position the next morning, I run to the door to find two letters on the floor. One is a utility bill. The other I hold in both hands, my stomach clenched with excitement. With shaking hands, I tear it open and my eyes graze the first paragraph.

Oh my God! They accepted me!

I hug the letter quietly to the middle of my chest and feel a tiny fountain of joy bubbling inside me. The reindeer moss sees the water and knows things are about to improve.

If only there was someone I could tell my happy news to, but there is no one. I have no friends in England, and I have cut all ties with everyone in India. Of course, I can't tell Lenny because he wouldn't approve at all.

When I pass the mirror, I look at my reflection and almost don't recognize the woman standing there looking back at me. Why, I look so alive. And then I am full of defiance. Why shouldn't I celebrate my good news with someone?

I pull on a light summer coat and run out of my apartment. I skip down the flight of steps and onto the pavement. I think about taking a taxi, and then I decide that, from now on, I'm going to save every penny. I am closer than ever to my goal.

I walk down to the Tube station in a happy daze. In the carriage I smile to myself. A woman catches my eyes and, instead of looking away, smiles back. I grin at her. She smiles again then looks away.

Shane, it seems, is only nine stops away from me.

The magazine seller outside the station points me in the right direction, and I happily float towards where he indicated. Shane's building isn't quite as exclusive or as nice as Lenny's, but I didn't expect it to be.

I know Shane doesn't have much money.

He drives a motorbike, and when I asked him outright how he knew Lenny he vaguely mentioned running a few businesses. In fact, I imagine his chateau, if it is not a farmhouse, to be a bit of a run-down job, but I don't care. He is my friend.

I stand outside his apartment block with my finger hovering over his bell and have a moment of doubt. He did tell me to come whenever I felt like it and that he is almost always around before lunch. *What if he's not in, or he has a woman friend over?* The thought is slightly sickening. With an odd flutter in my tummy, I ring the bell.

Shane's voice comes through the speaker. He sounds aggressively surprised.

'What are you doing here, Snow?' he demands.

'You said I could visit if … if … I wanted to,' I stammer.

The buzzer sounds and I push the door open. I cross the foyer toward the lift, but all my earlier enthusiasm has evaporated to nothing. He didn't sound happy to hear from me at all. I get into the lift and press the button for his floor. When the floor indicator passes the first floor, I hit my forehead with the heel of my hand.

Idiot!

This is not India where people just drop in on each other without calling ahead. I remember now, how it used to enrage my mother when my father's Indian relatives would simply turn up and call at the gate whenever they felt like seeing my father. It was their custom, but not hers.

And Shane is British, like my mother. I should have called first.

Suddenly, I feel tearful. The little fountain stops bubbling and reindeer moss withdraws into itself again. Oh God! I've ruined everything. The lift door opens at his floor and I rush to press the button to close the door. For good measure, I hit the button marked G a few times too. Hurry up and close, I pray, but as the doors start to shut, a huge male hand curls at the edge of one of the closing doors.

'Whoa,' Shane says appearing fully at the entrance of the lift. 'What the fuck? Were you going back down?'

I shrink back. 'I'm sorry. I should have called first. It was rude of me. I forgot. These English customs; I'm not used to them. You might have guests, or you might be busy.'

He stares at me incredulously for a second. 'You came to visit me?' he asks.

I nod miserably.

He holds the door of the lift open, and reaching in pulls me out by my wrist. I bite my lip to keep from crying, but the tears are already stinging at the backs of my eyes. I can't believe I am now going to cry, to add to my humiliation. I swallow hard and start blinking the tears back. Oh God, he's going to think I am the biggest cry-baby in the world.

For a moment he seems frozen with astonishment. Then he reaches out suddenly and pulls me towards his hard body.

'I don't have guests and I'm not busy,' he says into my hair.

Like a fool, I start crying in earnest. 'I don't know why I'm crying. I have no reason to cry. I'm such a colossal idiot,' I babble.

'I love it that you dropped by,' he says softly.

'Really?' I sniff.

'Abso-fucking-lutely.'

The little fountain in my heart starts bubbling again.

'I'm sorry if I sounded unwelcoming,' he says softly. 'I didn't know what to think. You took me by surprise. I was not expecting you, and I automatically thought something bad had happened to you.'

I wipe my eyes with the backs of my hands. 'No, I'm sorry. I don't know what's wrong with me. Crying like a fool for no reason.'

'Forget it,' he says kindly.

'OK,' I agree, smiling gratefully.

'Come on,' he says and takes me to his apartment.

The first thing I notice are the toys scattered on the floor.

His smile is mocking. 'In case you're wondering, they're not mine. They're my niece's and nephew's. I'm babysitting for the next two hours.'

I listen, and the apartment is pretty silent. 'Where are they?'

'Sleeping, thank God.'

I chuckle. 'How old are they?'

'Liliana is four going on thirty-four, and Tommy is a three-year-old who, uniquely, channels monkeys. He climbed the cupboard the other day to reach for a packet of sweets.'

'Oh,' I say with a laugh.

'They'll be awake in an hour and you can meet them then.'

He wants me to stay and meet the children. 'I'd love to,' I say shyly. 'So, they are called Liliana and Tommy.'

'Well, he's still called Tommy,' he says dryly, 'but, she decided last week that she no longer wants to be known as Liliana, but Margarite Hum Loo.'

I laugh. 'Margarite Hum Loo?'

'Yes, and you can't shorten it and call her Margarite either. It has to be the full whack or nothing.'

I smile. 'Why that name?'

'No idea. You can ask her yourself when she wakes up.'

'I will,' I say still chuckling.

'I'm just about to make myself a meal. Join me?'

'Thanks, but I'm not hungry.'

'You'll regret it.'

Laughing, I follow him to his kitchen. It is done up in warm tones of honey and yellow.

'What will you have to drink? Milk? Juice? Water?'

'Juice will be nice.'

'Orange, apple, or—Liliana's favorite—mango crush.'

'I'll try the mango crush then.'

He takes a glass out of a cupboard and pours a thick orange-red liquid into it.

A cat comes to rub its face on my legs. 'You have a cat,' I exclaim, surprised.

'Yup. That's Suki,' he says, scooping rice into an opaque plastic cup. He pours it into a silver colander.

'Do you need some help?' I offer.

'Let's get the rules clear right from the start. This kitchen is my domain,' he states.

'Good, because I can't cook to save my life,' I say.

Sipping my drink, I watch him rinse the rice under the tap, drain it, and pour it into a pot. He pours bottled water onto it, salts it, puts a lid on it, and leaves it to cook.

'You sounded happy when you rang my bell,' he says, fishing out a live lobster from a pail of water with ice cubes floating in it.

'I was,' I say distractedly as I stare at the lobster. Its claws are tied, but all its little legs are waving frantically. 'I mean, I am. I received some good news this morning.'

He picks up a big knife and puts the lobster on the chopping board. 'Yeah?'

My eyes widen with horror. 'You're not going to kill that lobster and eat it, are you?'

His hands still. He looks up at me. 'Yes, why?'

I puff air out of my lips. 'I mean, it's alive. Wouldn't you feel bad to eat something you've killed with your own hands?'

He rubs his jaw with the edge of the fist that is holding the knife. 'Don't you eat lobster?'

'Yes,' I admit uncomfortably, 'but I couldn't eat it if I saw it alive a few minutes before.'

He laughs. 'We all have to die, Snow. This guy has had a good life at the bottom of the ocean, and I'm giving him a quick death. I wish my death could be so quick.'

'I just can't get my head around it.'

He grins. 'That's because you're a hypocrite, Snow. You'll eat it after someone else kills it for you, arranges it neatly on a Styrofoam tray, pulls a bit of cling film over it, and sticks it on a supermarket shelf.'

'Afraid so.'

'Right. Look away now. I'm about to say his last rites.'

I turn my head and hear a crack then a squelching noise before the knife hits the chopping board. I turn back, and the lobster has been neatly halved lengthwise. Some of its legs are still waving. Then they all slowly stop. Something about its still body makes me remember when I wanted revenge so bad I wanted to kill, and not just a lobster, but human beings. When I could have killed with a song in my heart.

'Shane?'

He looks up at the different tone in my voice. 'What?'

'Could you kill a human being?'

His eyes narrow, and he looks dangerous.

'If he's hurt you—I mean really, really hurt you, or someone you loved ...'

He doesn't hesitate. His voice rings strong and sure in that kitchen, with the rice boiling and the dead lobster lying on the wooden board. 'Yes. I'd kill for those I love.'

I nod slowly, and for a few seconds we gaze at each other. His eyes burn with fierce intensity. No more is said, but I suddenly feel safe, safer than I have ever felt with Lenny. My muscles are singing with renewed vigor, and I feel as if I could do anything, be anything.

Eight

SNOW

'**W**hat made you decide to pay me a surprise visit?' he asks, as he begins the task of scooping up and discarding the yellow-green tomalley from the two halves of the lobster.

'I'm really sorry; I realize now I should have called. It's not the done thing in England to turn up unannounced at someone's door.'

He lifts a lemon from a fruit bowl on the kitchen table, washes it under the tap, and cuts it into wedges. 'It's done, but usually by people selling things you don't want, and suspicious girlfriends trying to catch their boyfriends in compromising situations,' he says dryly.

'You can add a new category to your list. Foreign-born women who have just received great news.'

He looks up from the lobster, his eyebrows raised expectantly. 'You have great news?'

I nod excitedly.

'Spit it out then.'

'OK, here it is,' I say with a happy grin. 'My greatest dream for as long as I can remember was to become a pre-school teacher. To give back to other children what my nanny gave me. To instill in them a thirst for knowledge. But my mother did not want me to become a teacher. In her opinion, it was a badly paid, thankless job, and, no matter what I did, I could never change those children's lives one iota. I guess that's the real reason I ran away to England. I knew if I wanted to chase my dream, I had to leave India ... and, since I had a British passport, I came here.

'But here, in England, all teaching colleges require you to have work experience before they will accept you. Soooo ... I applied to do some voluntary work at some local schools, and this morning a letter arrived from one of them to tell me that I've been selected.'

'Am I looking at the happiest teacher-in-training ever?' he asks, his blue eyes crinkling up.

'Pre-school teacher-in-training,' I correct. 'I only ever wanted to teach small children.'

'I think you'll make a brilliant pre-school teacher.'

'You mean it?'

'Of course. How could you fail to be when you are so enthusiastic and eager? When you see education as passing down the magic,' he says, placing a cast-iron griddle pan on the stove and switching it on.

As we carry on talking, he drizzles the two halves with olive oil and seasons them—salt, pepper. I watch his beautiful hands take a pinch of paprika and, hovering over the lobster, he rubs his fingers together. A sumptuous, exotic red mist settles like crimson dust upon the gray flesh of the crustacean. Out of nowhere, a thought snakes into my head. How great it would be to have those big, powerful hands on my body.

With a pair of scissors, he snips off a sprig of parsley from a pot growing on the windowpane, chops it finely, and drops it into an earthenware bowl. He uses the heel of his hand to break up a garlic bulb, and chops four of its cloves. That goes into a blue earthenware bowl with two thick sticks of butter and a sprinkle of chili flakes.

He pours a little olive oil onto the hot pan and places the lobster halves flash side down. The flesh sizzles. Very quickly, he flips them over and pours cognac in two quick strips over the seared flesh. Two long blue flames leap up angrily from the pan.

'Wow! Impressive,' I say.

'You think that's impressive? Wait till you see what else these hands can do,' he teases.

My face flames as bright as the lobster shells.

The rice cooker pings at the same time that he takes the lobsters off the fire.

He turns to me. 'Would you like some?'

My mouth is salivating with all the delicious smells, but I shake my head resolutely. I saw that lobster alive. Hypocrite or not, I couldn't. I'd be eating the moment of its death.

'Last chance,' he offers.

'Thanks, but no,' I say firmly.

He opens the rice cooker and spoons the rice onto an enormous, white, square plate. He takes the lobster halves and lays them on the rice. Carefully, he spoons the melted butter mixture over his meal.

He looks up at me. 'So, you're just going to watch me eat?'

'Yes. If you don't mind.'

'Hmm ... Want a double chocolate chip cookie instead? They're very good.'

I hesitate. 'Um.'

'Her majesty, Lady Margarite Hum Loo baked them.'

I smile. 'She did?'

'She's an awesome baker,' he says persuasively.

'In that case, OK.'

He opens a tin and brings it to me. They are in the shapes of animals.

I take a cat. 'Thank you.' I bite into it. 'It's actually delicious,' I say, surprised.

'Bring the whole tin with you,' he says, and leads the way to his dining table, which has been set for one.

He raises an eyebrow. 'How about a glass of Pinot Blanc?'

I shake my head, fascinated by the care he has taken to cook his own meal. Only a true gourmet would go to such great pains to prepare a feast for one, but he seems unaware of how unusual his behavior is.

He fishes a bottle of wine from a bucket of ice, and pours himself a glass of wheat-colored liquid. Then he sits down and lifts his knife and fork. I watch him cut out a piece of lobster and, in a sensual act of pure pleasure, slip it into his mouth, and suddenly I'm salivating like Pavlov's dog. My cookie seems to be a childish indulgence when I watch him savor every mouthful. As if each mouthful was a unique work of art that he has been given the privilege of experiencing.

I watch him eat, and it is a joy to do so. We talk and we laugh. He is easy and funny. There are only two or three bites left on his plate when there is a shrill scream from somewhere in the apartment.

'Good timing, kids,' Shane says good-naturedly, and stands up.

'Shall I wait for you here?' I ask.

'No, you don't want to miss this,' he says with a laugh.

I follow him to the entrance of a room painted in bright colors with two cots and lots of toys.

'It was *not* an accident!' a beautiful, blue-eyed little girl with her hands on her hips screams furiously at a boy who has his arms crossed.

'What's going on here?' Shane asks calmly.

'He,' she fumes, throwing a fierce glance toward her cousin before bringing it back again to Shane, 'banged me on the head with his train while I was sleeping.'

Shane moves into the room. 'Let me see that head,' he says.

She touches the top of her head gingerly and cries pitifully, 'I've been treating him happy and he just wants to kill me.' She takes a shuddering breath, and, opening out one palm beseechingly toward him, demands. 'Why? Why?'

Shane gets to his haunches in front of her. 'Of course, he doesn't want to kill you, sweetie. He's your cousin.'

'Yes, he does. Yes, he does,' she insists, striking the sides of her little body violently. She points at Tommy dramatically. 'He just wants me to die out here.'

Shane busies himself with gently feeling the top of her head. 'Now, why on earth would Tommy want to kill you?'

She thinks for a minute. 'So he can have all my toys,' she says triumphantly.

Shane shakes his head. 'He's a boy. He doesn't want your dolls and cookery set.'

She appears to lose interest in Tommy's motive. 'Is there an egg on my head?' she asks anxiously, instead.

'Maybe a very small one,' Shane agrees.

'I'm never sleeping with him again. Don't make me, Uncle Shane,' she pleads.

I have to turn my head to hide my smile. How Shane is keeping a straight face is beyond me.

'Why did you bang her with your train while she was sleeping, Tommy?' Shane asks the little boy, who has so far said nothing.

He scrunches his shoulders up to his ears. 'It was an accident. I wanted to kiss her, but the train fell from my hand, and ... and ... banged her head.'

Shane turns to Liliana. 'See? It was an accident. He just wanted to kiss you.'

'I don't believe him. He's a'—she frowns to think of the right expression—'juvenile delinquent.'

Shane's lips twitch. 'Do you know what? I kind of believe him. You're very, very kissable.' And he kisses her on her cheek, twice, loudly. 'Don't you sometimes look at your new baby sister and want to kiss her too?'

She looks at Tommy from the sides of her eyes. 'Yes, Laura's cute,' she admits.

'Can you forgive him?' Shane asks.

She stares mutinously at Shane. 'I'll have to think about it.'

'All right then. Think about it while you have lunch.' He turns his gaze to his nephew. 'Tommy, what do you say when you accidentally hurt someone?'

'Sorry,' he pipes up immediately.

'Good boy. Now, why don't we all go into the kitchen and have some lunch?'

Tommy, relieved that he is not going to be punished, nods eagerly.

'Who's that?' Liliana asks, noticing me for the first time.

'That's Snow. Say hello.'

'Hello, Snow,' she says, wiping her tears, her rage forgotten.

'Hi, what's your name?' I ask with a smile, simply because I want to hear her tell me her new name.

'Margarite Hum Loo,' she replies solemnly.

'That's a pretty name. What does it mean?' I ask equally solemnly.

'It doesn't mean anything. I just like it because it reminds me of a seahorse, or a mermaid, I'm not sure which yet.'

I smile at the purity of her innocence. It's been a long time since I was in the presence of children. It is like bathing my soul in clear, pure spring water. It makes this morning's news even sweeter.

I turn to Tommy. 'Hello, Tommy.'

'Hello,' Tommy says shyly.

'He's a cry-baby. He cries all the time,' Liliana denounces scornfully.

'Excuse me,' Shane interrupts, 'but you used to cry when you were his age too.'

'I only cried for milk; he cries for everything.'

Both Shane and I crack up.

'Are you Uncle Shane's girlfriend?' Liliana demands suddenly.

I look at Shane, but he just looks at me innocently.

I clear my throat. 'I'm Uncle Shane's friend,' I say primly.

'Don't you want to be Uncle Shane's girlfriend?' she asks curiously.

I feel myself flush and Shane grins evilly. 'Answer the child then.'

'Well,' I say.

'I know what. You can marry him if you want and then you can kiss like mummies and daddies.'

Shane bursts out laughing, and even I have to smile.

The next hour is the best fun I've had in years. Shane and I prepare thick homemade fish fingers that Liliana's mother has sent, shelled peas, and mashed potatoes. The kids are a barrel of laughs, but my first impression of Tommy as a helplessly little baby is quickly dispelled. He turns out to be the naughtiest little imp.

After lunch, Shane puts on the Whip/Nae Nae record and Liliana, who knows all the moves, starts dancing. Disgusted with the noise and activity, the cat retreats into the kitchen.

'Again,' Liliana cries when the track ends.

God knows how, but on the third run the bossy boots manages to make both Shane and I join in. I have been out of circulation for so long, I don't know any of the steps, but Shane, like Liliana, knows them all. He looks real good doing it too.

We all stop when the phone rings.

'Can I answer it, Uncle Shane?' Liliana asks.

'Go on. It's probably your daddy anyway.'

She rushes to the phone, picks it up, and says, 'Hello, Margarite Hum Loo speaking.'

'Daddeeeeee,' she squeals. She listens for a while, then asks, 'What time are you coming? OK. Hi, Mummy. Yes, I was very, very good. Tommy wasn't, though. He banged my head really hard. On purpose. I was very brave. There was a very big egg on my head, but it's gone down now.'

I turn toward Shane with widened eyes at the lies she was telling.

'Don't worry, everybody knows what a terrible shit-stirrer she is,' he whispers with a wink.

Her mother must have asked about lunch because she says, 'Yes. Fish fingers, mashed potatoes, and peas.' She swivels her eyes toward me. 'No, but Uncle Shane's girlfriend is here. Yeah. Yeah. I don't know.' She takes a big breath. 'Mummy, did you buy anything nice for me? Yay! OK, see you soon. I love you, Mummy. Bye, bye.' She puts the phone down and skips over to us.

'Mummy and Daddy are coming.'

'I guess I'd better go,' I say.

'You don't have to,' Shane says immediately.

'No, I should go. It's getting late.'

'Are you sure?'

'Yeah, I'm sure,' I say with a smile.

'I'll call you a cab.'

'Thanks, Shane.'

In less than five minutes, the cab calls up that he is waiting downstairs.

'I really enjoyed my time here,' I say.

'Hold on. We'll all come down with you.'

So, all of us pile into the lift and go down. As Shane shuts the door of the taxi, I see a silver Bentley drive into the forecourt. I turn back to watch it, and I see a tall man with very similar coloring to Shane, and a beautiful woman with a slightly Oriental feel to her features get out of the car. The woman is holding a baby in her arms and Liliana is jumping up and down with excitement. As soon as Shane lets go of her little hand, she races to her father and throws herself at him. He catches her, lifts her high into the air, and whirls around while she squeals with delight.

Then the taxi turns into the road and I can no longer see them.

Nine

SNOW

It is nearly 7.00 p.m. and the light that fills my apartment is livid and deep, half storm-purple and half the fiery orange eyes of a hawk. I've been wandering aimlessly within these walls ever since I returned from Shane's house. Hearing myself breathe. Jumping at the sound of the water in the pipes.

Feeling something. Dread and excitement.

A hot, damp wind pushes in through the window and I stop and gaze at my surroundings as if seeing it all for the first time. Everything is still and silent and bland. There are no cherished paintings, family photographs, or lovingly collected little objects of beauty. The walls are magnolia, the furniture is plain and brown, and it is all as clinically clean as an ICU unit in a hospital.

Which is strange considering that this place has been my salvation, my solace, and my sanctuary. My hiding place from the world outside. The world that is always waiting to hurt me. I listen to the silence, and it feels heavy and oppressive.

I turn my thoughts to little Liliana, the shit-stirrer.

'Margarite Hum Loo,' I whisper, and just saying her made-up name aloud in the stillness makes me chuckle.

I try to imagine her in her own home with her parents. It is clear that they adore her. The image that comes to my mind seems warm, bright, full of laughter, and infused with the smell of Liliana and her mother baking a new batch of cookies.

I think of Shane. Of course, he will not be at home now. He will probably be in Eden. I try to picture him walking around, talking, laughing, and I feel sad that I am not part of his life. I realize I miss his mischievous sense of humor, his handsome face, his wolfish grin, and his warm, sparkling eyes.

But I stop myself short. I cannot be part of his life. No matter what it looked like this afternoon, he is a playboy through and through. I saw that a mile off. No one that good-looking can be trusted. This is just a flirtation for him. Soon he will be gone. Looking for greener pastures.

My thoughts inevitably return to my mother. She would be so disapproving if she ever met Shane. Not that she ever will, of course. She always wanted her children to marry into money.

'What can you do with good looks?' she used to say. 'You can't eat them. They won't pay the bills. All they are is endless trouble. Finding phone numbers in their pockets, going through their credit card bills, and worrying every time they're a little late home.'

So my sister, Catherine, married into money.

When she was twenty-three she met Kishore, a nondescript guy with curly hair. He was thirty and from a 'good' and powerful Indian family. They fell in love over a plate of marsala tosai, she signed a six-page harshly worded pre-nup contract, and they got married in one of the biggest society weddings in Calcutta. Political figures and Bollywood celebrities attended the glittering occasion.

Now she has given him three kids, he cheats on her all the time, sometimes even openly, but she won't leave. She won't give up the mansion, the servants, the swimming pool, the invitations to all the best parties, and the overseas shopping trips.

My brother, on the other hand, has told my mother in no uncertain terms that he will marry only for love. It is the only time that we agree on an important issue.

My brother and I don't get on. From the time we were children, he didn't want me around. I never understood why he resented me so much. He had everything. He was the favorite of both my parents and got absolutely everything he ever wanted.

Even when Papa lost all his money and all that was left was the house, which fortunately he had transferred into my mother's name, and the money he had stashed away in her account, I was immediately pulled out of Calcutta International school. It was decided however, that there was enough money to pay Josh's school fees and eventually to send him to America to finish the last part of his education.

Our very large house was sold. Some of the proceeds went toward Josh's education fund, and some was put toward buying a smaller house. When Josh flew away, I was left in the house with my parents, the cook, the gardener, and a cleaning lady who came in daily. All my fine school friends had dropped away one by one. They were either too busy, or had left the country to finish their education. Papa locked himself into a room and let the TV blare. Without my brother and with the loss of her grand lifestyle, my mother became a very unhappy woman.

For a long time after our slide into disgrace, staff from my father's offices and factory used to come to the front gate pleading for their unpaid wages. Once, I asked my mother why we didn't just pay them at least something.

'Elizabeth,' she said tight-lipped. 'If you had your way, you'd have us all begging in the streets with them, wouldn't you?'

As time passed, Papa's unpaid staff grew more and more desperate. They started shaking the gates and shouting insults. My mother used to stand at the window behind the curtain, and look down at them as the gardener chased them away by hitting their fingers with a broomstick and scolding them.

In fear of their anger, my mother arbitrarily decided she did not want me to finish my education, even at the local school. I was very upset, but I didn't want to go against her, since things were already so fraught at home. So I sat in my swing and read. Tons of books. I read the classics. I read translated works. I read Indian poets. But my life seemed meaningless. I felt like a prisoner. Trapped and without a future. I wanted to live.

I don't know what made me decide one day to run away. Perhaps because I could not see my mother ever allowing me to pursue my dream of being a pre-school teacher. I opened Papa's safe—I had known the combination since I was fifteen—and stole the money I needed. My passport was ready from the time I was first sent to international school. I took a taxi to the airport and got on a plane.

I was nineteen when I arrived in London. It was autumn and the air was chilly, but I remember I was so excited and so filled with adrenalin I did not feel the cold. In my T-shirt, I traveled to Victoria Station. From there it was easy. I got into the Tube station, bought a ticket, and took the Victoria Line, then got off two stops up at Oxford Circus.

Central London's Oxford Circus was a shock. The bustle, the energy. I could not believe it. The world seemed a big, beautiful, bright place, and I was so happy. I walked to the YHA hostel. I had checked them out on the Internet and I knew they had beds for £18.00. It was a lot in rupees, but I expected to find a job as soon as possible.

The YHA was a fun place decorated with brilliant jewel colors. It looked more like a kindergarten than a budget hostel. And I loved it. There were two beds in my room. They had bright apple green pillowcases and duvet covers. One was already taken. I put my bag on the other and thought I would burst with excitement.

There was free Wi-Fi, so I went down to the Internet room. It had purple beanbags, which I thought made the place look funny and warm. I sat down at the computer and sent Papa an email telling him that I was in London. I apologized for taking the money from the safe, but I promised him that I would pay the whole thing back as soon as I got myself a job. I told him I loved him and my mother and then I signed off.

When I went back to my room, my new roommate was already there.

'G'day,' she called. I had never heard the greeting before. Later, I would learn that it was short for 'Good day'.

Suddenly, that old flicker of discomfort is back. And so is that sensation of gnawing apprehension. I sigh deeply and close my eyes. Her face is so vivid that it could all have happened yesterday. I know I'll never forget her as long as I live. *I'm fine. I'm fine now. I survived.*

I go to the kitchen and switch on the kettle. I don't want to remember any more. Not today. I don't want to have to take those pills. I want tomorrow to be a fun adventure. I want to see the fireflies. I want to run away from here. From Lenny and the sickening, unspoken agreement that I have to pay his kindness back with my body for as long as he wants. Which could be forever. I put a tea bag into a mug.

The phone rings. I stand in front of it and let it ring twice more before taking the call.

'Hello, sweetheart,' Lenny says.

'Hello, Lenny.'

'How are you?'

'I'm fine.'

'Good. Look, I've got business over in Amsterdam tomorrow, so I'll pick you up and take you to dinner tonight.'

'Uh. Not tonight, Lenny. I'm really very tired.'

There is a malevolent silence. 'Oh yeah? What have you been up to all day?' His voice was deadpan, cut from rock.

'Nothing. I cleaned the flat, had lunch at a cafe, and then I went shopping. You know how shopping always exhausts me.'

'Did you get something nice?'

'Yes, I did.'

'What?' There, there's the reptile lazily sunning itself on a warm stone suddenly striking. He's caught me out. When his secretary goes through all the boutique accounts and the credit card bill, there will be no purchases with today's date. He will know I lied. I haven't lied to him before.

'A red dress,' I say. And then quickly add, 'I used the money you gave me the other night.'

'Good. Wear it when I take you out on Monday night. I'll be back by then, and we'll do dinner somewhere nice.'

I grip the phone hard and keep my voice light. 'That'll be nice.'

'All right. Call you when I get back.'

'Have a good trip.'

I switch off the phone. I'm playing with fire. Things are unraveling too fast. I almost got caught there. Lenny is unpredictable, his violence legendary. A ruthless, wild raptor. If he even scents another male trespassing on his territory, I will see the incandescent, uncontrollable fury that I have only glimpsed so far.

Once, a drunk man touched my bottom in a club. It could have been an accident, but I jumped because it had startled me. Lenny saw my reaction and he turned and calmly nodded to one of his henchman. The big brute immediately went forward and kicked the shit out of him right in the middle of the club.

I was so shocked I froze, but when I got control of my limbs I turned to Lenny and cried, 'Stop him! Stop him!'

And Lenny clicked his fingers and his other henchman stopped the assault.

I looked at the man, bleeding and groaning, and then I looked at Lenny, and there was absolutely no expression on his face. It was nothing to him. And I was afraid. For the first time I became afraid of Lenny. And I knew he had not done that to punish the man, but to frighten me.

521

I don't love Lenny. I never have. I just let him use my body because I didn't know what else to do. I was so broken, and he had taken care of me. I had no one else. When he put his hand on my thigh that night, I couldn't bring myself to stop him. And then, before I knew it, he was on top of me and we were having sex.

But it has to stop.

Even if it means my dream of becoming a pre-school teacher is delayed, I have to take back control of my own life and find a job to support myself so I am no longer beholden to him. Perhaps I could rent a room cheaply. Better that than let him use my body anymore. I wasn't strong enough before, but I know I'm ready now. I know I have to act soon. But there is a tight feeling of apprehension in my body that sets my teeth on edge. Secretly, I am afraid of Lenny.

I go into the kitchen, butter a slice of brown bread, and put together an open tomato and cheese sandwich. As I cut the little cherry tomatoes, I think of Shane cooking, the passion with which he prepared his meal, the enjoyment he took from every bite, and it occurs to me that I live without tasting life. My whole existence is a meal without salt.

I walk to the dining table with my sandwich and my cup of tea. I lift up a slice of tomato, put it in my mouth, and let the fresh zest of its juice burst into my taste buds. I wait for the flakes of sea salt to melt on my tongue. Next, I take a bite of bread and cheese. The cheese tastes milky and smooth as I roll it slowly together with the nutty, rich taste of the buttered bread. I savor it the way Shane relished his meal. With my eyes closed, my meal is no longer a humble sandwich, but a complex of things of many scents, flavors and textures.

I can see that just by being on the outside edges of my life, Shane is already subtly changing me. Yes, there is a lot of terrible pain trapped inside my body, but when I am with him, it hides away, as if it is afraid of him. It is afraid he will banish it away forever.

That evening I listen to music and go to bed early, but I am too excited about my trip with Shane to sleep.

Finally, just when I have fallen asleep, I am awakened by the sound of a key in my door. I freeze with fear. Then I hear the familiar sound of Lenny's footsteps. He comes into the bedroom and silently walks over to the bed. He stands over my prone body and watches me. I keep my breathing even and deep, and pray that he will not wake me up.

To my relief, after a few minutes he quietly slips out of the flat.

After I hear the door shut, I sit up then go over to the window. From the darkness of my window, I watch him walk to his car. The driver opens the back door and Lenny gets into it. Feeling unnerved, I return to bed. It has been a long time since he did that. He used to do that a lot when he first found me, when I was almost mad with grief and horror. I wonder why he did that today.

Does he on some level sense that another man has strayed into his territory?

Ten

SNOW

Shane comes to collect me at 9.00 p.m. because that is when Lenny's plane takes off and there will be no more calls from him after that. A man in a peaked cap opens the back door of a blue Mercedes and I slide in. Shane introduces him as the driver of the family's company car.

'Mostly only my brothers use this car. I can get anywhere faster on my bike,' he says.

'We're not going to Heathrow Airport?' I ask when I notice the car going on a different route.

'No, we're flying out of Luton,' Shane says.

'Oh,' I say, and settle back against the plush seat while Shane gives the man instructions to bring his car to the airport on Sunday. I don't listen. A ball of anxiety sits at the base of my stomach. I feel as if I am cheating on Lenny, even though I don't love Lenny and he cheats on me all the time, and anyway, I am not going to do anything with Shane. Shane and I are friends, and we are just going to see the fireflies.

At the airport I am in for a shock. We are walking toward a private plane!

'Wow! Whose plane is that?' I ask, astonished.

'My brother bought it about two years ago for the family's use.'

'Is he the ex-gangster?'

'Yeah. Jake was a gangster, but don't judge him too harshly. He had no choice. He did it for us. It was a great sacrifice for a man who wanted to be a vet.'

'You love him very much, don't you?'

'We're blood. I'd give my life for him.'

 524

And his eyes shine with sincerity.

Then the pilot is introducing himself to me and we are walking up the steps into the jet. It is another world. The inside of it is beautiful, with heavy, wooden doors, red, luxurious carpets, and huge cream seats facing each other with tables in between. There are fresh flowers everywhere and it smells of perfume. Farther along, closer to the cockpit, there are two single beds with furry slippers tucked at one end. The table we are invited to occupy has a white tablecloth spread over it and is set as if in a fancy restaurant.

We sit and the smiling air stewardess pops open a bottle of champagne.

I can't help being wide-eyed with wonder. 'Oh my God, how amazing,' I gasp. 'This is exactly what I imagined it must be like to be a film star.'

He laughs softly, his handsome face indulgent, and we clink glasses then drink.

Fruit and tiny little canapés are served on a mirrored platter.

It takes us an hour and forty minutes to arrive in Cannes, a town so exclusive that there is no commercial airport and only private jets are authorized to land. There are no queues, Immigration and Passport Control, or baggage to worry about. Instead, our passports are checked by two policemen, and then we step onto the runway.

'Welcome to France,' Shane says.

I marvel at how easy and smooth travel is for the rich. 'I can't believe we're actually in another country.'

'Come on. We've got dinner reservations,' he says, and leads me to a waiting car.

Full of excitement, I look around me as the palm-tree-lined boulevards swish by as we get into the town. I gaze in awe at all the beautiful old buildings. In twenty minutes I am ushered into one of Cannes' famous seafront restaurants, Le

Palais Oriental. It is brightly decorated with blue seats, white tables, and mirrors on the ceilings.

The place is in full swing, heaving with belly dancers and huge groups of noisy party-goers. We are greeted by a friendly Moroccan waiter who shows us to our table. The tables are low, and Shane has to sit with his knees spread far apart. He catches my grin and acknowledges the funny side. I love that he is able to laugh at himself. There is something so endearing about a man like that. My father couldn't. My brother will never be able to, and Lenny will tear your head off before he'd even contemplate doing such a thing.

Shane and I order tagine of lamb with prunes and couscous, which our cheeky waiter claims is terrific because it is cooked on the bosoms of angels.

We drink mint tea and watch the dazzlingly graceful belly dancers as they advance, retreat as they snake their arms sinuously in the air, and shimmy their hips so hard and fast their luxurious costumes swim about their feet. I feel an instant affinity with them—the colorful costumes, the sun-drenched skin, and the bells on their bra tops remind me of the beautiful Indian dancers of my childhood.

Like those Indian dancers, they twist their bodies into shapes that express joy, laughter, sadness, grace, lust. This story is one of entrapment and beauty. One woman wears a veil and over it her dusky black eyes flash enticingly. Not only her body, but her eyes speak.

I look around me and there are different reactions to them. To some, these women are cheap meat, but there are others who see what I do. All dancers are dreamers. There is no such thing as a sinful dancer.

'I've never seen a belly dance in the flesh,' I tell Shane.

'Do you like it?' he asks.

'It's simply beautiful,' I say, watching a woman in a blue costume. Her personality and her sensuality flow through the timeless moves her body makes.

'I agree.'

I turn to look at Shane. He is watching me. 'The one in the blue costume is so seductive.'

'Yes, she's so seductive,' he says softly, but he does not turn to look at her.

When the lamb comes, it is succulent, and the couscous could indeed have been cooked on the bosom of an angel. We eat our food and drink our wine, and slowly the beat of the Arabic music makes me tingle, and my body moves in tune with it.

'Do you want to dance?'

I shake my head. 'Perhaps I could dance under a moonless sky, or if I was on my own and no one could see me.'

'Great: Moonless Sky is my chosen Red Indian name,' he says cheekily.

'Forget it,' I say.

'Never say never.'

We leave the restaurant late, our bellies full and the scent of adventure beckoning us as we drive to Shane's chateau. In thirty minutes we arrive at a set of arched black iron gates. We drive up a road for a few minutes in total darkness and then, suddenly, we have reached our destination.

Saumur.

My mouth drops open with astonishment. This is no farmhouse or dilapidated chateau! How is it possible that Shane could own something so magnificent? Built from pink stone and trimmed in white, it rises from the ground in a truly imposing and majestic structure.

'Wow,' I exclaim opening the car door. 'But this is a palace!'

'How astute of you. It used to belong to an Iraqi prince, so it's architecturally more royal palace than chateau.'

The gravel crunches under my feet as we walk up to the chateau. He unlocks the tall door and switches on the light and it is breathtaking. I look around in awe. My father was very rich once, but, even then, our mansion house was nothing like this. I have to seriously re-evaluate Shane's financial worth. And to think I had been expecting a ruined chateau or a farmhouse! God, it never crossed my mind that he could afford such extraordinary splendor. This pile must be worth millions and millions of pounds.

'All this belongs to you?'

'Yes,' he says staring curiously at me.

'You're so young. How could you be so rich?'

'I have my brother to thank. He started us off early. He got us into the property market, investing in Internet start-ups, bought us all citizenships in Monaco, and put us into every tax saving scheme available.'

I look around in wonder. 'It's absolutely stunning, Shane. You're so lucky.'

'Come, I'll show you the best part of the house.' He winks at me. 'Just in case you want a midnight swim.'

Stunned by the grandeur of the place, I follow him through the rooms with their high ceilings and the lovely marble floors. In the main salon there are stupendous art deco chandeliers and superb antiques. He leads me toward the pool, which has been uniquely situated in the center of the property.

I gasp when we reach it.

It is like suddenly finding yourself in a different world—the sumptuous, luxurious, precious, lost world of an Oriental potentate. Lit by softly glowing lamps, it must be seen to be believed. Massive and round, it is surrounded by tall double Corinthian marble columns that form a veranda around the pool. The stone columns are slightly submerged, giving the illusion that they are rising from the water.

The roof is covered in wisteria, throwing the reflection of the columns and dripping plants into the still water. There are white orchids growing in large bronze pots and loungers with cream cushions.

Made speechless by the unrivaled luxury and beauty, I walk toward the edge of the pool. There are rose petals floating in the water.

I hear him come up behind me. I turn around and look up at him. 'Wow,' I whisper.

His eyes are hidden by shadows. There is a slight tension in his body. 'Feel like a midnight swim?'

I am suddenly wary. 'I didn't bring a swimsuit.'

'There are swimsuits in the changing room, I believe,' he counters.

'I didn't come here to sleep with you,' I say, and my words hang between us. Both of us know that's a lie.

'Pity. Still, I'm only inviting you for a swim.'

I bite my lower lip. 'OK, let's swim.'

In the changing rooms, I find some plain black bikinis. I get into one and, after slipping on a toweling robe, nervously go back out to the pool. The air is warm and scented with the smell of the countryside. His back is to me and he is naked, but for a pair of briefs. He turns slightly when he hears my approach, and smiles.

And he takes my breath away—he's the sexiest, most delicious thing I've *ever* seen. I gape at him like a silly teenager with a crush. The air changes between us. I feel goosebumps scatter quickly on my skin like millions of insect legs. A shiver goes through me, and between my legs a strange throbbing begins.

I breathe in deeply. What the hell am I doing?

I force my eyes away from him. If I'm planning to sleep with him, I should have drunk more alcohol at the restaurant.

'Could I ... er ... have a drink?'

He turns fully then. Tattoos. Muscles. Ripped body. And a beast of a cock, barely held in check by his swimming trunks. All as if carved from glowing marble. There is no fear or shame in his face. He is the most self-assured, beautiful thing I have ever seen. Powerful male sexuality radiates from every pore of his impressive form. My mouth feels dry and my body does something it has never done before.

It aches for him.

Eleven

SHANE

She stands in the glow of the lamps with absolutely no idea of just how fucking beautiful she is. She looks like she's made of porcelain, or fairy dust. I want to go up to her, strip her naked, and ravish her right there on the cold tiles, but I can see that she is so nervous, her knuckles show white where she is hanging on so tightly to the edges of her robe's front.

'Sure, you can have a drink. What do you want?' I say, ignoring my raging hard-on, and sauntering over to the concealed bar to the left of me. She trails behind.

'Vodka and orange juice,' she says.

I pick up a bottle of Grey Goose and a tall glass. 'Say when,' I tell her, and begin to pour.

I am nearly halfway up the glass and she is still staring at it. I carry on pouring, my eyes on her face.

'When,' she says.

I stop pouring and put the bottle on the bar. She lifts her eyes to mine. What kind of strange, sexy creature have I got standing in front of me? No woman has captivated my interest like she has.

'You can fill it to the top with orange juice now,' she says.

I don't move. 'You'll drown if you drink this much alcohol before you get into the water,' I say softly.

'Oh! I guess I should have asked you to stop pouring earlier.'

'What's the matter, Snow?'

'Nothing's the matter.' She bites her lower lip. It is sweet, glossy, and plush. A whore's mouth in an angel's face. I picture her lips on my abdomen and going lower still. My cock

531

hammers and heat churns in my balls. Fuck, my dick is begging me to throw her against the nearest wall.

'Is this what you have to do before you let Lenny touch you?'

Her eyes fly open, and she takes a step back from me as if I have struck her. 'You have no right. You know nothing. Do you hear me? Nothing!' she cries and then she begins to run.

My reflexes are fast, propelled by the hellfire of lust burning in my blood. I catch her easily and spin her around to face me. She gasps, sharp and sudden, and looks up at me with startled, wide eyes. Her robe is gaping open, and I can see the soft curve of her breasts as they rise and fall with her agitation. Hell! I want to fuck her senseless. I can feel myself pulsing.

'I'm sorry. I shouldn't have said that,' I apologize. My voice is tight with frustration.

'No, I'm sorry. It's my fault. I overreacted. I'm just nervous. You're the only friend I have. I don't want to fight with you.' Her voice is wobbly.

I let go of her forearms and flash her a good imitation of a grin. 'So, let's not fight then. How about a swim?' I say, and, turning away from her, dive cleanly into the pool. With slow strokes I swim away from her. I'd need to do fifty laps to burn off this sexual frustration.

When I reach the other end, I turn back to look at her, and she is sitting at the edge with her legs moving languidly back and forth in the water. In these surroundings she is like a fantasy figure, a figment of my imagination. I experience a strange sense of possession. The urge to mate with her is primal, strong and rabid. If I was an animal, my fur would be bristling, my tail out and wagging stiffly, and my ears erect.

The drive to mount a woman, possess her and claim her as mine is an unfamiliar one. Sure, I could write a whole fucking encyclopedia about the impulse to mount a woman, but to possess and claim her? I exhale the breath I am holding and, swimming back to her, grab her feet. They are small and soft.

She giggles. 'That's ticklish.'

'Are you coming in, Miss Dilshaw?'

She doesn't stand and take off her robe the way any other woman with a body as dazzling as hers would have. Instead, she slips it off her shoulders awkwardly while still sitting, and pushes it off her hips and thighs just before she slides into the water. I catch her in my arms.

Her body is narrow and slippery. She gazes up at me, her lips slightly parted, and her eyes so dilated they are almost black. And it's clear I'm not the only one who fucking wants it bad. She wants it too.

'You can let go of me now,' she whispers.

'Give me one good reason I should.'

'Because I want you to,' she says.

'Liar,' I counter softly. 'Here's what I think you want. I think you're aching for the taste of my cock.'

'Mighty sure of yourself, aren't you?' she scoffs, although bright red is crawling up her neck and into her cheeks.

'Shall we put it to a test?'

She looks alarmed. 'What do you mean?'

I move my head closer and she jerks back.

'What's the matter? Don't trust yourself to resist even a little kiss?' I taunt.

'I trust myself,' she says, and, holding her chin high, closes her eyes like a schoolgirl expecting her first kiss. This is unfamiliar territory! It's been a long, long time since any woman behaved in such a virginal way. If I wasn't bursting out of my trunks to get to her, I would have found it funny.

I pull her toward me, bend my head and touch my lips lightly to hers. Her reaction is explosive. She moans, her hands snake around my neck to twine in my hair, and she practically melts into me. The water laps around us as her mouth opens and her nipples are like little pebbles burning against my chest.

I kiss her full and hard, my tongue pushing into the warm softness of her mouth. And there is not a damn thing tentative about the way she sucks on my tongue. She looks like a little spring flower, but she kisses with the kind of wild, reckless passion that blows my mind. She does it with the kind of desperation of someone starving.

I wrap my hands around her waist and push her upwards. Water cascades down her beautiful body, as I lift her onto the edge of the pool and place her firmly on her butt. I haul myself out. Getting on my haunches, I untie her bikini top. It falls away easily.

'Shane,' she whispers, my name catching in her throat.

Her breasts are small and perfectly formed, the areolae, shy rose buds. She gazes up at me, her eyes enormous, the eyelashes wet, and her delicious mouth swollen and red. My lips brush the side of her neck and she leans her head to the side and offers me her throat. It is a call to mate as much as it is when a female wolf lifts her rear and exposes her vulva to tell her alpha that she is in heat. My tongue trails down the silky skin. I've done this a thousand times before, but this time my movements are jerky with urgency.

I lay her on the cool tiles and wrap my lips around her nipple. She groans and closes her eyes. My hand slides down her body and moves toward her bikini bottom. I hook my fingers into it and suddenly she starts struggling under me. I lift my head in surprise.

Her hands move to cover her breasts.

'I'm so sorry,' she says.

I feel a surge of searing temper. This is fucking bullshit. I'm too old to play these cock-tease games. I grab her wrists and pull them apart and hold them high over her head so her breasts are exposed to me. She does nothing to stop me. Then I look deep into her frightened and excited eyes.

'Well, I'm fucking not,' I grate. I don't hide the feral hunger in my eyes as I let my gaze roam her whole body, lingering lustfully on her breast, as if I own it all. And in my mind I do. She will be mine if it's the fucking last thing I do. 'I will have you, Snow Dilshaw. Fucking count on it. Not tonight, but you will be mine. And you know it too. You just like dragging things out. But you're wetter than you've ever been, aren't you?'

She says nothing, just stares up at me.

So, I slip my fingers in that last scrap of cloth between her and me, and brush my fingers between the soft lips. They are fucking soaking. I smile. I take my fingers out and suck them. Her eyes widen with surprise.

What is it about her? She is like no other woman I have been with. Even at a time like this, I can't be angry with her. All I want to do is wrap her in my arms and tell her it's going to be all right.

I stand and pull her to her feet. I pick up her discarded robe and tie it around her waist. And the strangest thing happens to me. I had a raging hard-on and yet at that moment I could have been belting little Liliana into her coat. I feel only a fierce sense of protectiveness toward her. Anybody touches her or tries to hurt a single hair on her head and I'll break their fucking backs.

The day will come when *I* will yank her hair and she won't be afraid of what comes next. She will just call my name, and tighten her muscles around my cock as I thrust it deep inside her. She's mine. She just doesn't know it yet.

'Come on, I'll show you to your room,' I say.

I need to put some space between us. I don't completely trust myself with her. I need to be level headed.

Because this one's a keeper.

Twelve

SNOW

I wake up, confused by the faded splendor of my surroundings. And then I remember where I am ... and what happened last night. And I touch my lips wonderingly. No one has ever kissed me like that. So dominant and possessive, as if he owned me. And I have never felt so alive, almost high. Like that time I was buzzing from drinking too much cough medicine. Heat and lust had pooled between my legs and I longed for him and yet I stopped him.

I think of Lenny saying, 'Before I'm finished with any man who touches you, he'll be wishing I had killed him.'

The thought makes me turn and bury my head in the soft, fragrant pillow, away from the wrongness of what I am doing. Sharp guilt slashes through me. It makes a bright new wound. I am betraying Lenny who has never been anything but kind to me when I was broken, and, to make matters worse, I am endangering Shane.

Lenny will have him for breakfast. Shane is a playboy; Lenny is a psychopath. Right now, just lying in this stupendous bed alone, I am cheating on Lenny and implicating Shane. Last night ... Oh God, if he knew.

Oh God.

Show some freaking spirit, Snow.

I sit up suddenly, with a new resolve. No, I won't betray one whole year of kindness for one stolen night of dark pleasure. In my own way I care about Lenny and I'll never forget what he did for me. I won't do this to Lenny. I will leave him in a good way. A way that I can be proud of. Without betraying him. Without anyone getting hurt.

I feel empowered by my new resolve. I won't have sex with Shane. I'm not some slut who can't control herself. Today, I will be very careful not to get into any kind of situations where we are both half naked again.

Today, I will be more guarded.

But the resolution makes me feel trapped. The future stretches bleak and pointless. Excruciating, actually. What about what I want? A wretched knot of nerves deep inside me shudders painfully. *Don't think about it now, Snow.*

I square my shoulders and, kicking away the fragrant sheets, leave the splendid room fit for an Oriental potentate. I wash in a fabulous green-veined marble bathroom. Water plinks from the polished gold taps onto the ancient stone.

There are glass jars of sweet-smelling salts and I drop in handfuls and watch them bubble and fizz. The air fills with their perfume. The longing for the unattainable feels only like a faint ache. I am used to that feeling. I brush my teeth as the bath fills. I undress and slip into the warm, silky water.

'Ahh ...'

I lean my head back and sigh. I don't allow myself to think of anything. When the water cools, I step out of the bath, dry myself on a soft lemon-scented towel, and pull on an apple green T-shirt and a pair of skinny jeans. I stop and look at myself in the gilded mirror. The color of my top makes my eyes look good.

I make the bed before closing my bedroom door and going downstairs.

As I walk down the grand steps, I try to imagine what it must be like to actually live here. There can be only one word to describe it: magnificent. I wonder who else lives in this vast property. Someone must be cleaning the house, the pool, the grounds. Whoever they are, they are doing an admirable job. There isn't a speck of dust to be seen anywhere.

As I get to the bottom of the stairs, an unsmiling woman appears in the archway leading to the other end of the house.

She has salt and pepper hair that is neatly tied into a bun at the back of her head, and she is wearing a black dress and heavy shoes with gleaming buckles that I associate with Victorian times.

'Bonjour, mademoiselle,' she greets. Her voice is as somber as her attire, and her lips have barely moved.

I am pretty certain she is saying 'Good morning,' and that the reply should be 'Bonjour, madam,' but I'd be stuck after that. The extent of my French is 'Bonjour,' 'Bonne nuit' and 'Merci.' 'Sorry, I don't speak French,' I admit with an apologetic shrug and smile.

'Ah, oui. Monsieur Eden est à l'extérieur,' she says formally, and points in the direction of the pool.

'Oh, merci,' I say.

'Je vous en prie,' she replies, which I presume must be 'You're welcome' to my 'Thank you.'

I smile politely.

She nods again gravely, and retreats into the shadows behind the arch.

I walk out to the pool. In the daylight, it has lost its magical appeal. It seems newer and more nouveau riche, but it is stunningly beautiful all the same. I go beyond the submerged pillars and see Shane working shirtless in the garden. His body is magnificent in the morning sun. I walk up to him.

I shade my eyes and call out, 'Good morning.'

He turns to look at me, and I find myself inhaling sharply. Damn, the man is edible.

'Mornin',' he says, and wipes the sweat from his brow with the back of his hand. He sticks the shovel he was using into the ground and takes a few steps toward me. I swallow hard. Dear me!

As he approaches, I see everything I did not see in the soft lighting of the pool. His chest is a mass of glistening, rippling muscles, and his shoulders are covered in beautiful tattoos. Sweat is running off his body in rivulets. My heart swells and I feel almost intoxicated, but I try to appear unaffected. He stops about a foot away from me and I can actually smell him, and he smells damn good. Wow! Who would have thought that sweat could smell so tantalizing? Oh, God. I can't believe I'm crushing on him like a schoolgirl.

'Um ... what are you doing?' I babble.

'I'm planting some rose bushes,' he says.

'Mmm ...' I say, my eyes sliding hurriedly away from his body and finding about five pots of rose bushes on the ground. And all my high and mighty resolutions crumble to dust. I want to feel his velvety skin on mine and to taste his tongue again.

'Don't you have a gardener?' I ask because my skin is sizzling and I can think of nothing else to say.

'I do, but I like working with the land,' he says.

'Oh, OK,' I say, my gaze following a drop of sweat as it travels down between his taut pectorals. *I could lick that off him.* The air between us buzzes with desire. *Mine.* The undeniable truth is: To hell with it all. I want this man with a burning need. I want to rest my chin on his hard chest and watch him sleep. And when I feel like it, I want to kiss him awake.

'Are you going to stand there all day staring at me?' he teases.

I flush all over. I am so distracted by his big, golden body, it is embarrassing. 'I'm sure I wouldn't be the first one,' I mutter, taking a step back.

'Give me ten minutes to finish up here.' He raises one glorious eyebrow. *God, how good-looking is this guy?* 'Want to have that swim or maybe walk around the garden before breakfast?'

'OK,' I say unsteadily, and am turning away when his hand catches my arm.

I look up into his face. His eyes are crinkled up against the sun and flame blue in his tanned face. 'You look beautiful this morning. I could stand here all morning staring at you,' he says softly.

I can't help it: the heat creeps up from my throat and up to my cheeks. Suddenly, the desire in my head is out in the open, in the darkening of his eyes, in the tightening of his jaw.

'Now, on your way, before I throw you on the ground and show the rabbits how it's done.'

I stumble away quickly. When I am halfway to the house, I turn around and see him standing where I had left him, just staring at me. After that, I don't turn around anymore.

Once past the house, I decide not to swim but to explore the gardens. An elderly man in faded clothes and a battered hat is trimming some bushes in the far corner of the property. He lifts his hand to me in a wave, and I return the greeting absent-mindedly. I guide my feet out beyond the garden, which is haphazardly crammed with all kinds of flowering plants.

There are butterflies and birds aplenty, but it is not the kind of properly manicured garden I would have expected for a house like this. Still, it has a charm all its own. The type of charm that sinking rusty old tram cars in the ocean produces after ten years. That's when it becomes a gloriously colorful reef and the home of hundreds of diverse schools of fish.

As I walk through the garden, I sense the true elegance of allowing nature to take its own course. It is like being in a lost, secret garden. In some places the weeds are taking over, but, even then, there is rich beauty to it. Bushes and creepers have been deliberately allowed to become overgrown to help bury the vulgarity of superfluous statues and stone arches. A sort of balancing of scales.

I like it, but it makes me wonder why someone would buy a stupendously beautiful, but totally nouveau riche chateau like Saumur and allow the grounds to go their own wild way like this.

A fat, ash-gray cat with yellow eyes comes and meows by my feet. I reach down and tickle her behind her ears. She rubs her head against my legs before wandering away to curl up on an old, sunlit bench.

As I venture farther, I realize that some of the property is thickly planted with bushes and low-hanging trees, but that a great part of it is pure meadow. Not far away I can see a wide expanse of water glistening in the sun. There is a Moroccan style tent by the edge of the water. Inside there is a bed with lots of jewel-bright red and green cushions.

For a while I sit at the edge of the water and look out at the glinting surface. It is serene and peaceful, but my mind is in turmoil. I have never wanted anybody the way I want Shane, but I am not a free agent ... yet. Lenny is still in the picture, and it would be wrong and ugly of me to betray him, and ... yet, I want Shane. The desire is so strong I don't think I will be able to resist it for much longer.

But, as I sit motionless and contemplate the silent beauty of the water, a profound transformation takes place in me. There are no mobile phones, no police sirens, no car horns, no emails, no birthdays to forget, no queues, no terrorists, no wars. All the stress, noise, fears and distractions that form part of my everyday life seem to belong to a different world.

The sun warms my skin and reflects off the water, and still beauty and peace in the air trigger ancient genes that humans must share with all the other creatures we have evolved with. My body relaxes, my pulse slows, my body feels charged, and I feel as if I have come home.

I hear my name being called and turn around to see Shane walking toward me. Freshly showered, he has changed into a clean T-shirt and blue jeans. His hair is still wet. With the sun behind him, I can't see the expression on his face.

I stand and brush my bottom with my hands. 'The lake is beautiful,' I say.

'Well, I like it.'

'Why have you allowed the place to go to seed like this?'

He looks down at me. 'I bought this place only because I heard of the sightings nearby of fireflies. And then I set about making the environment irresistible to them. They love moisture, tall grasses and low-hanging trees that they can hide in during the day, and an abundance of insects, slugs, and snails.'

'Will we see them tonight?'

'I'll be very disappointed if we don't. We'll come out after dinner. They're usually around about nine-ish.'

'You really love them, don't you?'

He grins. 'My madness is I have no time for things that have no soul.'

'Actually,' I admit, 'I like it wild and overgrown too.'

'Then you'll definitely like the owner of this place.'

'Is he the one who's built like a god?' I ask cheekily. Being cheeky with a man is something I would never have done before I met him. I'm the boring one. Never say boo to a cat.

'That's the one,' he says, and something in his eyes lights up.

I laugh, and in that moment I'm not the girl with the terrible past. I'm just a girl flirting with an irresistibly sexy man.

Thirteen

SNOW

We have breakfast at a rickety wooden table under the shade of a massive old oak tree. There are croissants, pastries, cold country butter, homemade jams, and slices of watermelon. An unsmiling Madam Chevalier pours thick, strong coffee into small cups for us. It is too bitter for me, but Shane has no trouble downing his. I decide to stick with orange juice. When she goes back into the house, I whisper to Shane, 'Is she in a bad mood?'

'Nope. She's always like that,' he says unconcernedly, and bites cleanly into a croissant.

'Really? Why?'

He shrugs. 'Fuck knows. Probably disapproves of what I'm doing to the grounds.'

I stare at him. 'And you don't mind?'

'Snow,' he explains patiently, 'this woman cooks using a recipe book that is one hundred years old. As far as I'm concerned, she can be as sour as she likes. Don't judge until you try her Soupe à l'Oignon Gratinée.'

I shake my head. 'I don't care how good a cook she is; I don't think I could ever live with disapproving staff.'

He grins roguishly. 'Here's something you might not yet have picked up: Madam secretly likes me.'

'Shane Eden, you are incorrigible.'

'I'll take that as a compliment,' he says with a low chuckle.

543

After breakfast, the elderly man I had seen pruning the bushes ambles toward us with a hearty smile plastered to his ruddy face. Shane introduces us, then tells me that Monsieur Chevalier is taking us to Cannes' indoor market. He is a much friendlier chap than his wife, and, because he doesn't speak a word of English and Shane's French seems to be pretty basic, he compensates with a lot of nodding and grinning. We get into his beat-up truck and he drives us to Forville Market.

It is a large red-brown building that oddly reminds me of the Red Fort in Delhi. Inside, it is vast and cool. Vibrant with shoppers and a seemingly inexhaustible array of produce, it is a treat for the senses. There are stalls dedicated just to mushrooms! All kinds, shapes, colors, and scents. Other stalls specialize in dried meats, fruit, flowers, vegetables, cheese, wine, olives, pastries, bread, spices, honey. And everything looks so fresh and clearly locally produced. It is the opposite of the sterile environment of the supermarket where everything is sanitized, homogenized, and sold under a plastic covering.

Shane buys the ingredients for our dinner: a rack of lamb, baguette sticks, onions, vegetables, pineapple. The sellers all seem to know and like him. One asks about the fireflies and says he wants to bring his son to see them during the week. He tells Shane mournfully that the fireflies have stopped coming to his land. He blames the pesticides.

When we get outside, Monsieur Chevalier packs everything into the back of his truck. The plan is for him to drop us off at Le Suquet, a quirky, hilly town overlooking a harbor, before setting off to Saumur to deposit the market produce with his wife.

Le Suquet is the old part of the city so it is full of quaint, narrow streets full of old-fashioned shops. It is charming, and I fall in love with it, but it is here that I notice that women simply can't stop staring at Shane. Everywhere we go, he gets ogled at. And I mean really ogled at. When we stop at a little café with tables spilling out into the sideway and order pissaladière, a beautifully simple and delicious pizza with onion, olives, and anchovies, the waitress actually totally ignores me, and flirts outrageously with Shane.

'Are you a model?' she asks him in English.

He says something to her in French, which makes her glance at me, shrug, and start taking the order.

'Well,' I say when she walks away, 'she certainly thinks you're God's gift.'

He crosses his arms. 'Says the woman who's got most of the population of Le Suquet staring at her like zombies with working dicks.'

I snort. 'Zombies with working dicks? Excuse me? There were girls walking backwards after they passed us just to keep admiring the other side of you.'

'Well, darling, while you were looking at the women walking backwards, I've had to endure the painful sight of men blatantly stripping you with their fucking eyes.'

I lean back. 'You're serious?'

'Damn right I am. It's fucking annoying.'

My eyes widen. Can it really be that Shane Eden is jealous? The thought is like a bolt of lightning in my heart. 'Are you jealous?' I ask incredulously.

'Yes,' he admits gloomily.

'I love it when you look all brooding and moody. It's kinda sexy.'

He perks up. 'Did I just hear you describe me as sexy?'

'Yeah, I think I might have.'

'Well, that's what's called progress.' His voice is warm and full of laughter.

'By the way, what did you tell the waitress just now that made her look at me?' I say casually, taking a sip of my perfectly chilled rosé.

'I told her I was gay but that she was welcome to you.'

I almost choke on my drink. 'What?' I burst out.

He laughs.

'You don't care if people think you're gay?'

'Nope. It's extremely useful in certain circumstances.'

'Couldn't you have just told her you weren't interested?'

'Girls like her don't give up easy; she'd have been slipping her phone number into my hand as we left. And that would have just made you get all jealous and pissed off.'

'I'm not jealous,' I deny.

'Oh, you're jealous all right, Elizabeth Snow Dilshaw. You're the kind of woman who would try to make a man wear a chastity belt.'

His statement surprises me. He hardly knows me. 'What makes you say that?' I ask curiously.

His eyes are like mirrors, giving nothing away. 'Experience,' he says cryptically.

'Well, you're wrong. I have never been jealous in my life. Not with Lenny, and certainly not with you. In fact, I found it amusing that all those women were looking at you.'

'That's really great to know, because they don't make chastity belts in my size.' He grins. 'Too large.'

'I wouldn't have cared if the waitress had slipped you her number,' I say.

There is mischief in his face as he reaches out, grasps my wrist, and strokes it with what seems to be a seductive promise. It is intimate, delicious, and wonderful. Pleasure ripples over my skin, sizzles into my muscles, and instantly I feel strong desire swirl inside me like dead leaves picked up by the wind and helplessly drawn into another's world.

The expression in Shane's eyes changes, becomes so lust-drenched that I am undone by the look. I lick my lips. And we find ourselves lost in our own world. We stare at each other hungrily. Desire shimmering between us like some invisible magic. My blood heats up and I feel wetness pooling between my legs. God, it never crossed my mind that I could be so sexually aroused while sitting in a restaurant just looking at a man.

The waitress comes with the food, and, standing over us, clears her throat loudly.

I snatch my hand away. She plonks the pizza in the middle of the table, slaps a small plate in front of each of us, and stalks off.

I giggle at Shane.

'I told you what she's like,' he says.

We both laugh.

The pizza is beautifully simple and delicious. Once Shane has paid our bill, we walk out and start walking uphill. It is hot, and the hill is steep, but we get to the top. We stand outside the majestic old church, Notre-Dame d'Espérance, and look down at the stunning view over the bay.

'Want to go into the church?' Shane asks.

'OK.'

We pass through the old doors, and inside it feels like we have entered a different world. Even the air is cold enough to make me shiver. The stone walls give the impression of damp chill, and the air is hushed and still. Our footsteps echo. Afternoon sunlight falls dustily from high stained-glass windows into the dim interior and lays in milky shapes of color on the floor. It is deserted except for a woman with a black shawl on her head, bowed in prayer in one of the front pews. She does not turn to look at us. I look at the vast, high-ceilinged space in awe.

'Vellichor much?' Shane whispers next to me.

I glance up at him. 'No, I love it. This is far better than any used bookshop.'

He looks at me strangely. 'Are you messing with me?'

'No, I'm serious. Ever since this place was built, people have been coming here bringing all their pain, sadness, hopes, gratitude, and joy. The stones have absorbed it. Hundreds of years of human emotion. Can you not feel it?'

He stands very still for a few moments, then looks down at me. 'Nope.'

'Shame,' I whisper, and move forward.

He follows me. 'Have you never been to a church before?'

'No. My mother is a non-practicing Christian so she never took us to church. However, I begged and harassed my nanny until she gave in and took me to the temple with her in secret.'

'How old were you then?'

'My first trip was when I was five.'

'Are you a Hindu then?'

'No. As a child I didn't go to the temple to pray. I just loved my nanny so much, I couldn't bear to be parted from her for any length of time. Plus, I enjoyed the trip because it was colorful and the priest allowed me to ring the bell.'

We find ourselves at a side altar with burning candles, and Shane turns to me. 'Do you want to light a candle?'

'What does it signify?'

'It's a symbol of your prayer that carries on burning even after you are gone.'

I remember Chitra lighting oil lamps and asking her why she was lighting them, and I still recall her answer. Sweet Chitra. I miss her so. *'It is a way of asking for something from God. The fire lifts your prayer up to God,'* she said.

I look up at Shane. 'Yes, I'd like to leave a prayer here.'

He drops a note into the donation box slot and takes two candles out. He passes one to me, and we stand side by side and light our candles solemnly. I watch Shane place his in its holder, and I close my eyes and pray. I pray like I've never prayed. I pray to any god, Hindu or Christian, who will listen. I ask the stones to absorb my prayer and keep it safe after I am gone and even when the candle burns out. I pray for a bright, silent intercession from the heavens that my actions harm neither Lenny nor Shane.

I open my eyes and see another candle about to sputter out. It seems to grasp desperately for its last breaths of life. I cannot watch it die. I look up at Shane. He is watching me avidly. 'Can we buy another candle?'

His eyebrows rise, but he puts another note into the box and takes another candle out and gives it to me. I light the candle using the fire of the prayer that is about to sputter out, and plant it next to it. I watch the new flame take over and then I turn to Shane and smile. 'Shall we go?'

We go out into the afternoon air. It is warm and full of the smell of the sea.

'Feel like an ice cream?' he asks.

'Lead the way, sir.'

'Step this way, madam, for the best ice cream ever,' he says when we reach a sweet little shop with a green and yellow signboard and cast iron metal tables and chairs outside. There is a bell at the door that chimes prettily when we enter the shop. It is obviously a mom and pop business. The ice cream counter curves around the entire shop in the shape of a U. A man with a walrus mustache is standing behind it. He knows Shane, and talks to him in French.

'You can have as many flavors as you want in a cone,' Shane tells me.

There are so many unusual flavors it is difficult to choose, but in the end I decide on four different types of chocolate: Ecuadorean dark chocolate, Mexican chocolate with cinnamon, Rocky Road, and white chocolate with ginger. Shane has salted Turkish pistachio, grape nut and black raspberry. Shane pays for our ice creams, the man gives us napkins, and we carry our treasures out into the sunshine to sit at one of the tables outside. I carefully lick the white chocolate ginger bit first. It is delicious.

'Good?' he asks.

'Very,' I say looking up at him through my lashes.

'Are you flirting with me, little rabbit?' he asks, his lips covered in ice cream.

I remember how they felt and tasted last night, and feel a rush of something through my body—what, I do not know, but it is exciting. I like that about him. The way he makes me feel so alive. 'Maybe,' I say boldly.

His grin is wolfish, his eyes full of light. 'Works every time,' he says.

'What?'

He takes a lick of his ice cream. 'Feed a girl ice cream and she gets an appetite for love.'

'I said maybe,' I remind pointedly.

He chuckles and looks at me with lazy eyes, his whole body relaxed. 'Maybe, definitely, what's the difference?'

The sun is warm on my skin, I am with the most dazzling man on earth, and suddenly I feel bold. I lean forward and lick his ice cream. 'This is maybe,' I say softly. Then I stretch forward and, going close to his face, lick his lips. 'And this is definitely.' I lean back and try to look nonchalant. 'See the difference now?'

Something flashes in his eyes. Suddenly he doesn't seem so tame and friendly anymore. It's like waking a sleeping tiger; I can't tear my eyes away from him.

He smiles slowly, invitingly. 'I'm a bit of a slow learner. Would you mind if I run through that again?' he asks.

My heart begins to race. I can't believe I started this. What on earth was I thinking of? And yet, I can't back off now. 'No,' I say huskily.

'So this, then, is maybe,' he says, and, bending down, kisses me, his lips gentle, but persuasive and insistent.

I try to keep my head, I really do, but, by God, the blood is drumming in my ears and all kinds of winged insects are fluttering in my stomach. The man can really kiss! He lifts his head. I gape at him stupidly. His eyes are heavy-lidded.

'Now, let's try definitely.'

He takes my lips again, but this time his mouth is more sensuous, more—far more seductive, urging mine to open. His tongue slips in. Waves of dangerous pleasure sweep through my body and stir my blood awake. I begin to respond to him. *Oh God!* I think dazedly, my whole body feeling like it is blazing with need. I want him inside me!

He ends the kiss, and I feel his face move away from me.

'I think I got the difference now,' he drawls, his eyes languorous.

His hand reaches out and straightens mine so my ice cream cone is no longer tilted at an almost horizontal angle. I look at my hand as if it is separate from me. There is a puddle of melted ice cream on the sidewalk. I turn back to face him. His face is deliberately neutral. He stretches like a sun-warmed cat.

'We should be getting back,' he says, and stands.

We walk down the hill in a kind of pregnant, expectant silence. Neither acknowledges it, but both of us know. This is just the beginning. There is no denying this thing burning between us.

Monsieur Chevalier is leaning against an old wall, smoking a cigarette and waiting for us. He drives us back to Saumur in good spirits. The men talk in their own way with hand gestures and half-understood French, and I hang my head out of the car and breathe in the scent of France.

Who knows if I will ever come back here again?

Fourteen

SNOW

We agree to meet in the great Salon at seven. I have an hour to soak in the bath and dress. I get into a two-piece dark grey cocktail dress. It has a high scoop neckline with cut-in shoulders. The crop top is encrusted with floral beading with a keyhole opening at the back and a scalloped trim along the midriff. The short flaring skirt is layered with organza fabric and stops just below the knee. I slip into beaded high heels and pull my hair into a knot at the nape of my neck. I line my eyes, brush the mascara wand a couple of times over my eyelashes and color my lips a deep red.

The effect is sophisticated and sleek.

Feeling nervous and excited I go down to the salon. Shane is already there. He must have heard my footsteps on the marble floors because he is standing by the window, a glass of some amber liquid in his hand, looking at the entrance. I stand at the doorway for a second. Both of us drink in the sight of the other. This is the first time I have seen him dress up and he is, well, there is no other way to describe it, breathtakingly, extraordinarily handsome.

'Will you walk into my parlor, said the Spider to the Fly,' he says.

'Oh no, no, said the little Fly, 'for I've often heard it said, they never, never wake again, who sleep upon your bed!'

He walks up to me. 'I promise I'll eat you and you'll live to see the day,' he murmurs, his breath whispering into me.

I find myself blushing. He touches my cheek and my throat feels suddenly parched.

'What will you have to drink, pretty little fly? Vodka and Orange?'

'No,' I say. 'I'll have a glass of wine.'

'We're having a Beaujolais with our starter. Want a glass of that? Or would you prefer champagne?'

'The Beaujolais sounds lovely.'

'Make yourself comfortable,' he says and disappears out of the room. I walk to the window he had been standing at and look out. It faces the side I have not explored. An open meadow borders a forest. I wonder if that is where the wild boars live.

I hear him come up to me and I turn around to face him. He holds out my drink.

'Thank you,' I say softly.

He lifts his glass. 'Here's to the fireflies.'

I lift mine. 'The fireflies,' I repeat, looking into his eyes and knowing that we are not drinking to the fireflies.

First course is Madam's famous Soupe à l'Oignon Gratinée made to a century's old recipe. As the dish with a thick golden crust is put in front of me, Shane explains the laborious technique that Madam used to make it.

'Baguette toasts, half an inch thick, are spread with butter and layered with grated Emmental cheese, sautéed yellow onions, and tomato purée. Over this construct she gently pours salted water. The dish is then simmered for thirty minutes and baked uncovered for an hour at 350 degrees.'

'No wonder it looks almost like a cake,' I say.

'Bon appétit,' he says.

'Bon appétit,' I reply and dip my spoon into it. The inside is so thick and thoroughly amalgamated it is impossible to

discern the cheese from the onion or the bread. I put it into my mouth and catch Shane looking at me.

He raises his eyebrows and waits for my verdict.

I exhale and widen my eyes. 'It's to die for.'

He grins, happy, wholesome, irresistible. 'That's exactly what I think.'

When the soup bowls are cleared away, Madam serves pineapple tartare, finely diced raw pineapple mixed with salt and a hint of chili. It is the perfect palate cleanser after the richness of the starter.

Outside it gets dark and Madam lights candles. I notice that no lights have been turned on anywhere in the house.

'Is there no electricity this evening?' I ask.

'Lights affect the fireflies. It interferes with their mating process so we keep it to a minimum during this season.'

In the flickering candlelight the dressed up Shane seems like the perfect host, sophisticated, charming, and urbane. A beast that can only be admired from afar. I almost wish for the Shane in the T-shirt and jeans that was just good fun.

A spruced up Monsieur Chauband wheels in the main course. 'Gigot d'Agneau Pleureur,' he announces proudly.

'It translates as a crying lamb gigot because the meat is cooked in an oven, slowly, on a grill, with sebago potatoes and vegetables placed on a rack underneath it. The meat's juices, the tears, fall on the vegetables and cook them,' Shane explains.

I bite into a piece of meat and it is tender and succulent.

'Tell me about your father. You never talk about him,' Shane invites as he pours red wine into fresh glasses from a bottle of Merlot that Monsieur brought in.

I pick up my glass and take a sip. The wine is robust and fragrant. 'I told you a lot about my family and my childhood, but you told me nothing about your family or your childhood. What was it like being from two different types of gypsies?'

He spears a capsicum on his fork. 'I actually know very little about my Romany heritage. My mother doesn't speak much about her family. All I know is when she fell in love with my father, she had to elope because my grandfather was so furious with her. Not only had she chosen someone outside the clan, but she had chosen a well known gambler. On the day she got married he disowned her. She could never again go to see her family. Even when her sister died a few years ago her family were forbidden to tell her.' A shadow of sadness crosses his face. 'I know my mother misses her family very much, but there is nothing anyone can do while he is still alive.'

'That's so vindictive. Didn't you say your father has already passed away?'

'My father was murdered, Snow.'

My eyes widen in shock. 'Your father was murdered? How horrible!'

His face tightens with an old anger that cannot be forgotten. 'Yes, he made the stupid mistake of stealing from his boss. Unfortunately he was not just any boss, but a mean gangster. So Jake, being the oldest, was forced to go and work for the man who slit our father's throat from ear to ear, and pay off the debt.'

'Oh my God,' I gasp.

'Yes, it was a very traumatic time for us, our family fell apart after my father's death. For a very long time Jake was lost to us. He put food on the table and paid all our bills, but everyday he became colder and more unreachable. I think he hated himself and what he was being forced to do. My poor mother used to cry at night when she thought no one could hear, and my brother Dom became an angry rebellious stranger. Only my sister Layla, because she was so young, remained mostly unaffected by our tragedy.'

He pauses and takes a sip of wine.

'Then one day for no reason, Dom turned over a new leaf and that made my mother a bit happier, but things really turned for the better when Jake was nineteen. That was when he fought back and took over the organization. Once he had done that he streamlined everything, moved away from all the illegal aspects of the business, and concentrated all his attention on gambling dens and strip clubs. He started to make a lot of money, and I mean really a lot.' He pauses and smiles, a clean, gorgeous, heart-throbbing smile. 'That's when he got both Dom and me in to act.'

'So you got into strip clubs and gambling dens too?'

'Not gambling dens. Not even Jake does that anymore. Our family invests mostly in property and aspects of the entertainment sector: restaurants, gentlemen's clubs, and normal clubs.'

'Hmmm ... so you must meet a lot of beautiful girls.'

'Yes, I do,' he says with a cheeky grin. 'But when you own a candy store you don't actually eat all the sweets in it.'

'This reminds me of a joke,' I say so lightly, it trips off my tongue.

'Yeah?'

'A woman treats her husband to a strip club on his birthday. At the club the doorman says, "Hey, Jim. How are you?" The wife looks at Jim and asks, "How does he know you?" "I play football with him," he tells her. Inside the bartender asks, "The usual, Jim?" Jim turns to his wife, "Before you say anything, dear, he's on the darts team." Next a stripper comes up to them and touching herself sexily says, "Hi, Jim. Do you want your special again?" In a fit of rage the wife storms out dragging Jim with her and jumps into a taxi. And the taxi driver says, "What's up with you, Jimmy Boy? You picked up an ugly one this time." Jim's wife gave him a very nice funeral though.

Shane throws his head back and laughs and I do too, a little, but when the laughter dies down, he looks at me teasingly. 'You won't have to give a nice funeral, Snow.'

'Don't worry, I'm not holding it against you, but I could tell the moment I laid eyes on you that you're a playboy.'

He fixes his gaze on me. 'I'm not going to pretend I'm some saint. I'm a man and I have needs, and sure, there are always women willing to satisfy them, but I happen to want you.'

'So that's what I've become. Part of the horde of women always willing to satisfy your needs.'

He stares at me curiously. 'Don't you think we'd be real good together?'

'I have not thought about it,' I lie.

'I think we'd be earth-shatteringly good together,' he says softly.

My heart thumps in my chest.

'You know you want me too.'

I open my mouth to protest and he raises his hand. 'There's no reason to be ashamed of your body's urges, Snow. When you're ninety you're never going to think oh hell, I wish I hadn't slept with that Shane guy. You're going to regret every opportunity you didn't take.'

'So sex with you has become an opportunity, has it?' I scoff.

'Don't knock it until you try it, sweetheart.'

'Just because you're handsome—'

'First I'm sexy, now I'm handsome too ...' he says, a playful glint in his eye.

'In an obvious playboy sort of way, of course,' I say.

'Of course. What other way is there?' he drawls.

Before I can respond, Madam Chaumbond appears at the door, her demeanor, formal. 'Etait-il bon?' she asks, her voice carrying over the vast space.

Shane turns to me. 'Madam would like to know if you enjoyed your food.'

'It was incredible,' I say sincerely.

He turns to her and translates.

And in the small smile of satisfaction that she permits herself, I realize that Shane is right. She does have a soft spot for him. It was there all along in the big portions, the care with which she served him, the details she lavished on the food.

'Bon,' she says with a dignified nod, and withdraws, her black clothes swallowed by the shadows that have lengthened around and inside Saumur.

Shane picks up his wine glass and turns to me, his eyes glittering. 'Are you ready to go into the forest with the big, bad wolf, Snow?'

'You've got your fairy tales mixed up, but yeah, I'm ready.'

Fifteen

SNOW

The air is fragrant with the smell of flowers. Carrying torchlights we set off for the dark forest. It feels cooler under the canopy of leaves.

'It will rain later tonight,' Shane says.

'How do you know?'

He glances at me. 'The weather forecast.'

'Right,' I say embarrassed. I got caught up in the idea that we were in a magical place far away from civilization. Besides, there are, after all, people who can tell it is going to rain by the 'feel' of the air or by looking at animal behavior or observing the sky.

We take a path that is so narrow it will only accept one person at a time. I follow Shane's broad back until we come upon a clearing with a spooky log cabin. It's exactly how I had imagined the witch's hut that Hansel and Gretel found in the forest would look.

Shane opens the wooden door and we are standing in a rectangular room roughly about fourteen feet by ten with a wooden board floor. The planks make a creaking sound as Shane walks on them. A large blackened stone fireplace is set into the back wall. A fire is lit, but it is low with bits of charred wood and plenty of ashes.

'What's up with that?' I ask shining my torch towards a huge black cauldron hanging to one side of the fireplace.

He grins. 'Authenticity. You can't have a witches hut and no cauldron.'

'Right,' I say with a smile and shine my torch all around the room. There is a single bed with a blue and yellow bedspread at one end, and a small wooden table and four chairs in the middle. The wooden shelves have stuff on them, an axe, nets, knives, tin boxes, bowls, worn books, mortar and pestle, wooden spikes, dark gunny sacks. I guess they are a hunter's utensils.

Shane opens a box of candles and lights some. There are windows, but their shutters are closed. Strands of mushrooms are drying from a string hung across the firewood. There is the smell of earth and burning wood. In another corner there are bunches of herbs hanging from the ceiling. There is a large rocking chair next to the fireplace. It has an old cushion on it.

'Monsieur Chevalier uses this cabin a lot during the truffle hunting season,' he explains with a smile. 'I think it gives him a break from Madam.'

I chuckle quietly.

He takes a brown bottle from a shelf and hands it to me. 'Mosquito repellent made of herbs.'

I rub it on my hands and legs and it smells pleasantly of lavender.

He snatches a couple of blankets and a basket and we set off again. We reach another clearing where there is a round flat surface with a green plastic covering. Shane flicks the covering off it and reveals a round bench with a flat round mattress and lots of cushions on it.

'Go on. Climb aboard,' he urges.

I get on the mattress and lie back. The sky is alive with stars. He switches off the torches and lies next to me. I can hear sounds in the forest, foraging animals, insects, and I can hear him breathing next to me. My whole body tingles with hyper awareness. He turns his head and looks at me. His eyes are gleaming in the dark. I inhale suddenly.

We're going to have sex in the forest.

And then it happens. A tiny light comes on close to my head. Startled, I gasp and jerk my head around. Why, it is a firefly. The little creature flashes and then goes dark. And then flashes again. Magical.

'Look Shane,' I whisper in wonder.

'Look, mate. This one's taken, go flash elsewhere,' he tells the firefly.

I laugh, a laugh of sheer joy and enchantment and reach up with my cupped hands.

It darts away.

'Oh,' I say disappointed, but I realize that others are dancing into view. They glow and flicker in trees and in the air, and slowly they light up the whole forest like a Christmas tree giving enough light that I can make out Shane's features. Between the blades of the tall grasses and dandelions, hundreds of lights twinkle as if all the stars in the sky have fallen to earth.

'It's the most beautiful thing I've seen. I'll never forget this night as long as I live,' I whisper in an awed voice. 'Thank you, for bringing me here.'

'The show's not over yet, honey. I've still got a bit of flashing to do myself,' he says lazily.

The words die in my throat when I see his shadowy face loom over me before warm soft lips are kissing me.

SHANE

We Irish believe in faeries. The Irish fairy is not like Peter Pan's Tinker Bell. An Irish fairy can take any form she wishes, but prefers the human form. Our elders claim that they are beautiful, powerful and impossible to resist, which really, is a crying shame, because most Irish faeries love to bring misfortune and bad luck to the mortals who come near them.

At that moment in the glow of the fireflies, Snow looked like an Irish fairy.

Beautiful, powerful and impossible to resist.

And I don't resist. The air is laden with sexual longing, I have a raging hard on, and her white skin and luscious black hair are spread out before me like an irresistible siren's call. Come misfortune, treacherous rocks, and bad luck. I'll deal with you later. Her mouth is warm and sweet, scented with honeyed apricots she ate earlier. Her top has a metal hook, a hole and four little buttons at the back. All in a row. Piece of cake to undo.

I pull her towards me so she is lying on her side and unbutton them. I slide my hand in and stroke her silky back.

SNOW

The fireflies are still twinkling and shining around us, but I cannot look at their magic. I can only look at the beauty of Shane's face. My blouse whispers as he tugs it off.

I smell him, his cologne, his sweat, his desire. It is all male. I can't help but look at his cock. It is so massive, so thick, and the tip is already dripping.

'My God! You are so big,' I whisper.

'Yeah, and it's all going into you. Every last fucking inch.'

Between my thighs I am wet and aching for the feel of his hard cock deep inside me.

In a daze I reach out a hand and curl it around the thick shaft and I open my mouth. Because it's him. Because I want that liquid that's dripping from the tip. He puts his hands on my shoulders and I wrap my mouth around the shaft and slide down the smooth shaft. His hands are strong and aggressive. Nothing like Lenny.

He strips me quickly until I am buck naked. He pulls back and looks at me with hunger in his eyes. His fingertips slide over my body, possessively. It feels good. I want him to know that it feels good so I moan.

He stops. 'I'm nearly ready to explode, but first I will take care of you,' he says assertively.

He slips his hand down my hips and opens my legs, but my body knows what it wants. I lift my hips and offer my wet pussy to him.

He sinks a thick finger into me. I gasp with pleasure.

'You're so swollen and wet,' he says, his eyes dark with desire.

The smell of my own desire floods my senses making me flush with excitement.

His huge cock pushes against me before slowly, inexorably pushing in. For a moment it hurts so much it feels as if I am tearing apart and I claw at his shoulder. But this pain is different from any other kind of pain I've endured. It's a ... good pain.

'You're too tight. The pain will pass,' he tells me. His face is rough with a mixture of lust and concern.'

'I know,' I gasp.

'Want me to stop?'

'No,' I growl. I want him inside. My body is not too tight to take him. I grasp his firm buttocks and pull him hard towards me. His cock breaks me open. The shock of the pain steals my breath and makes me freeze as he slides in.

He goes so deep I can't catch my next breath. He pulls back and thrusts in. Again. And again. I groan. His large hands grip my hips and of their own accord they move back and forth. Shane's mastery and technique is evident in every move and touch and soon I start to relish the pounding my pussy is taking and the pain has transformed into warmth and pleasure. Pure, real pleasure. My eyes widen with surprise. I never thought sex could be like this.

'Oh Shane,' I beg. 'Don't stop.'

He answers by grabbing both my wrists and putting them high above my head. He looks down at my breasts with hunger. I feel them bounce and jiggle as he continues to thrust into me. I feel helpless. He controls everything. I am his to do whatever the hell he wants to do to me.

Then he is swooping down and taking my nipple in his mouth. Lenny has taken my nipples in his mouth more times than I can remember, but it never ever felt like this. My body arches with pleasure. His tongue flicks the tips. All the while he is thrusting deep into me.

And then it comes. The promise that began from the moment Shane held my wrist when we first met.

The orgasm.

The thing I have never experienced. And it blows my mind. I cry out his name. I am so shocked by the experience I don't even realize that he had been holding on for me, and as soon as he sees me climax, he pumps me so hard the platform bed we are lying on starts to shake with every hard slam.

He doesn't scream like Lenny when he climaxes, he roars and carries on thrusting through it until that last thrust when he holds himself, throbbing and pulsating deep inside me. Breathing hard he looks down on me. I lie limp under him, my thighs trembling and my toes curled.

I am his.

I feel sore and tender, but I don't want him to pull out of me. I want more. I want a repeat. I want another climax. It felt so good.

'I want more,' I whisper, without any shame whatsoever.

His eyes flare. 'You can't handle more, Snow,' he mutters.

'I can,' I insist.

He kisses my forehead and tries to pull out of me, but I grab his buttocks. 'Don't,' I plead.

He smiles. 'Aww, sweet Snow. Don't fret, I'll give you a different kind of more,' he teases gently.

He pulls out of me, removes the condom, while I lay with my legs open and wait. He comes back and puts his head between my thighs and begins to suck my clit. The shock of his hot mouth between my legs is like an electric bolt.

I start to crest again and dig my heel into the bed, my muscles stretching, my neck arching uncontrollably.

Sixteen

SNOW

'You want me again?'

I wake up and look straight into Shane's sleeping face. Curiously, I watch him slumbering He looks so young. One could fall in love with a face like this. Last night is like a dream. I remember it in a daze. My head swims to think of how wanton I have been. Me saying, 'You want me again?

Three times, I asked him that. That makes a total of six times.

A secret smile is curved on my mouth when his long, sooty lashes lift. We stare at each other, the smile dying on my lips. Passion flames deep inside me. His gaze moves from my eyes to the curve of my cheeks and lingers on my mouth, now provocatively parted. An invitation.

Breathlessly I watch fire leap into the blue depths.

He rolls his body over mine. Resting on his elbows his mouth comes down on my own I wind my arms around his neck and pull him even closer. His fingers rake through my hair, forcing back my head. My mouth opens in hungry response as our lips touch. The kiss seems endless. As if neither of us can satisfy our need for each other. I feel my body sizzle with need.

He lays on his side, tugs the sheet off me, and lets his eyes rove down my body. Trembling and impatient I slowly open my legs. Another invitation.

'Fuck, Snow. You intoxicate me,' he says hoarsely.

My mouth is dry with heady excitement. 'Do I?' I whisper throatily.

'I took one look at you and all I wanted to do was possess you. It didn't even matter that you were with Lenny. I couldn't walk away and leave you. I just had to have you. Any risk was worth it.'

'You've got me now.'

'Yeah, I've got you.'

I watch dreamily as his head moves down my body trailing a velvety hot tongue on my skin, fluttery, half formed kisses, or whispers, hard to say what they are really. My body lifts off the bed to meet those whispery, whiskery things. But it all changes when he buries his mouth in my throbbing pussy.

He devours me as if he is starving.

Squirming with intolerable pleasure, I reach for the edges of my pillow on either side of me and grab them tightly. His tongue runs down my slit all the way underneath me until I feel the tip touch my anus. I freeze with shock. No one has ever put his tongue there before. I have a sudden lightning thought – Oh God! If my mother knew she'd be horrified.

And suddenly a flash. I remember the tearing, piercing pain. No, not again. The thought is terrifying and my legs struggle to close, to stop him, but he forcefully keeps them open with his powerful hands. I raise my head and shoulders in a panic.

He lifts his head and looks at me.

'I got to have all of you, Snow. Every last inch. I'll lick what I want and fuck what I want.' His voice is calm. His expression is as unshakable as a granite hill.

I open my mouth and nothing comes out.

'I won't hurt you,' he says quietly.

Instantly all the fear falls away from me like an unwanted coat and a strange excitement shivers up my spine. I don't want him to stop. I like the idea of being totally at his mercy and submitting to his power.

 567

He pushes my thighs closer to my body so that he has total access to everything, and he returns to his task of claiming every last inch of me. Holding my cheeks firmly open, he presses his tongue against the ring of muscles. I groan, half with embarrassment, half with electric pleasure. He pushes again.

As his tongue pushes in, his finger enters my wet sex. I writhe with pleasure. Very gently he withdraws the finger and pushes that slick, honey coated finger into my ass. He raises his head and looks into my wide eyes.

'Do you trust me?'

I nod.

'I'm going to fill your sweet little asshole with my cock.'

Another lifetime ago I would have protested. Would have said, 'Never.' But not now. Now I want it. I *need* it. I nod again.

He smiles and reaches for a bottle of pure pomegranate oil sitting on the bedside cabinet that he told me he used for sunburn. He unscrews the top, flips it to the surface of the cabinet and, holding it over my exposed pussy, tips the bottle. A thin red stream of oil hits me and he uses his other hand to smear it all over the quivering flesh of my sex.

The movement is sensuous and slow, like a massage, as if he is anointing my sex. It reminds me of the dedication with which the priests bathed their deities. With reverence. As if what lies between my legs is precious beyond compare. He dips a different finger, his middle finger, into my pussy and uses that to insert into my oily anus. One by one he uses all his fingers until that entire region feels like a hot mess of saliva, my own juices, and oil.

I sigh with the incredible sensations.

He introduces his thumb. It is thicker, but I am so relaxed and so open to anything he wants to do to me, it slips in easily. He drives his thumb in and out of me. My neck arches. I am ready.

He gets on his knees and I see his cock, massive, twitching and throbbing, wanting in. I feel no fear. The lower half of me is like an uncovered bowl. Exposed and waiting to be filled. He reaches for a condom, rolls it onto himself, grabs me under my thighs and with one swift thrust slams deep into my dripping pussy.

I shudder with pleasure as my muscles clench around him like a closing fist. My blood rages through me. He pulls out and fills me again and again. Plowing in so deep I cry out with each thrust. When I think I am about to break apart he pulls out of me and rests the tip of his cock against the tight muscles that he has worked so long to loosen.

He locks eyes with me.

The head of his cock presses hard against the ring of oily muscles and slowly, slowly he starts to enter me. His thumb had been pleasure but this, this was sheer pain. I wince and grip the pillow. 'You're too big,' I groan.

'Breathe deeply and relax your muscles. Do what your body doesn't want you to do,' he instructs.

I frown.

'It's telling you to push out. Pull me in.'

I take a deep breath and will myself to relax, my quivering, tense legs becoming limp.

When I exhale he senses the give in my body and seizes the opportunity to gain another inch into me.

I cry out at the knife-like pain of the intrusion, and he stops and waits for my body to adjust to his girth. I take another deep breath and as I exhale again, the massive shaft lodged inside me takes another inch of me.

Every time I exhale and he feels my muscles relax, he takes that lull to force his way in again. I gasp with the sensation, but he just keeps going, deeper and deeper into my body until his balls are touching my skin. His cock is firmly wedged all the way inside my bowels.

Then he stops and smiles. The slow smile of a conqueror. He's got what he wanted.

There are tears in my eyes, but it doesn't hurt anymore. Just feels tight and stretched. I close my eyes.

And he begins to thrust his cock in and out of my ass. Part of me hates the sensation and another part of me wants more. But the more he rams in and out, the more the strange, dark pleasure takes over my body.

'Harder,' I hear myself cry. 'Fuck me harder.'

He pumps faster and I feel as if I am drowning in sensations. My skin feels alive. Another part of my brain is shocked at my own salaciousness. My whole body is alive with nerves that I never knew existed. I even feel his cock pulsing inside me.

Staring at him boldly, I clench my muscles with all my might and he groans. It is a powerful feeling that I can affect him this deeply. His movements become more frantic. And then I feel it, his cock swelling inside me. As hard as I can, I milk that cock. And he responds by throwing his head back and roaring while jerking and spurting and spitting inside me.

He pulls out of me and lays me back on the bed. I watch him take his condom off and then he turns to me and, hunkering over me aggressively, impales two fingers into my pussy. I gasp and he jams them as deep as they will go.

My body stretches into a bow as he rhythmically pumps his fingers in and out of my wetness. He is doing it so hard I can hear the squelch of my juices. I watch his brown hand go in and out of me in a daze of sensations. His other hand moves lightly over my clit, his face submerged in concentration as if he is an artist working on a masterpiece.

'Squirt for me, pretty pussy,' he says.

'Shane,' I call. My voice sounds broken. And then a wail, a shocking animal-like sound comes from deep inside me as I fall over the edge into the abyss of pure pleasure. He holds me as I clench, shudder and gush over his fingers. I open my eyes and he is gazing down at me possessively. He bends down and licks the tears from my eyes.

'Sleep for a bit now, Snow,' he says, and there is an almost hypnotic quality to his voice and, closing my tired eyes, I fall into a tranquil, dreamless sleep.

❦❦❦❦❦

I wake up to the sound of people talking. I sit up naked and look around me. The sheets are soiled with oil and stains of our coupling. Wrapping myself with the top sheet, I walk over to the window. Shane is below. He has been working in the garden again. His body is glistening with sweat. I watch him quietly talking to Monsieur Chevalier.

Suddenly he looks up and sees me. For a while we simply look at each other. Then he waves.

'Wait for me. I'm coming up,' he says, and starts striding towards the swimming pool. I turn away from the window and face the doors. He bursts through the double doors like a force of nature or an untamed tiger. Wicked eyelashes and curving, wet, seriously sexy muscles. His mother built him beautiful and then he went and added all those gorgeous tattoos too.

'You're awake,' he says.

'Yes,' I reply shyly.

He walks up to me and pulls at the sheet. At first I hold on to it and then I stop resisting. The sheet comes off in his hands and I stand naked in the afternoon light.

'You're perfect,' he whispers thickly, his eyes smoldering with need.

Seventeen

SHANE

I watch the way the light falls on her pale and fine-boned body and marvel at her fine beauty. Her limbs are as delicate as a porcelain doll. Even when I fuck her I sometimes feel myself hold back in case I hurt her. I see the stains of what I did to her earlier on her inner thighs, and I become a slave to the pull of desire for her. I can't help it. I just want to fuck her over and over again. She's like no other. With her nothing is enough.

I run my palms over her nipples and see them become thick with arousal.

'Are you wet?' I ask her.

She bites her lip and nods. 'Shane.'

'Snow.'

'What are we doing?'

'I don't know what you are doing but I'm ruining you for any other man.'

I bend and, putting my hands under her knees and back, I lift her nude body into my arms and carry her to the connecting bathroom. I set her down in the shower. I take off my jeans and step out of them. Her eyes are wide as she stares at my erect dick. It is almost purple with need.

Why I need her cunt so much is a fucking mystery to me. With every other woman I immediately lost a little bit of my desire for her as soon as I fucked her. And every time we'd fuck I'd lose more and more until I wanted her no more. But not with this one. With this one, I cannot get enough. It is like pouring oil on fire. The more I get the more I want. I stand immobile. I have never enjoyed a woman's eyes on me like I do hers. When she watches me, I actually feel a high.

When her gaze leaves my erect cock and rises up to meet my eyes, I step into the shower. I switch it on and warm water cascades on us. I take the bar of soap from the metal holder and I hold it out to her.

'Soap yourself up for me. Show me,' I instruct.

She takes the soap and runs the bar across her chest, under her arms, around her neck then—God, would believe, shyly—between her legs. Soap suds slide down her inner legs. She raises her arms and bends her elbows to do her back. She does the crack of her ass. Then she does her thighs and legs. She picks up her foot to do it and reveals the delicate, pink folds of her sex. I stare at them transfixed. She puts the foot down. Raises the other. Shows me another eyeful. Water rains down on my cock, making it bounce. It is so fucking hard it is tingling.

I bend down and take her nipples between my teeth. Water runs into my mouth, changing the normal sensation of having a woman's nipple in my mouth. I've been in the shower with hundreds of women. I've taken all their nipples in my mouth. But when I take hers I don't feel that it is a simple exchange of pleasure: I make you come and you make me come.

No, I feel like eating her alive, consuming her. I feel like going on my knees and fucking feasting on her pussy for days. I feel like never letting anyone else have her. I feel like keeping her forever. I feel like she is mine. And yet of all the women I have been with she is the least mine. In fact, she belongs to someone else. Fucking Lenny.

It is a kind of frustration that makes me bite her breast. She gasps. I lift my head.

'Why did you do that?'

'Did you not like it?'

'I don't know.'

I take the nipple back into my mouth and suck hard enough to cause her pain. She makes a small cry.

I lift my head. 'Do you want me to stop?'

'No,' she whispers, her eyes wide and dilated.

I take her other nipple in my mouth and suck it gently. After pain, pleasure. She moans. I turn her around so she is facing the tiled wall. Very firmly I tilt her hips upwards. Then I get on my haunches. I turn her body to watch me. I grab the flesh of her cheeks and blow on her sex. She shivers with anticipation. I bury my face between her cheeks and ... I feast. This time I can't help it. I suck, I lick, and I bite the plump flesh. Even her pitiful whimpers don't stop me. I ravish her like I have never ravished another. I suck until she shudders in ecstasy.

My cock is hot and hungry. I feel the blood surging urgently through it.

I pull her out of the shower and position her in front of the sink.

'I want you to watch me fuck you in the mirror. Hands on the sink, legs spread, ass sticking out,' I tell her as I open a drawer and take out a condom. While she stands gripping the sink hard, legs apart, and pushing her cute little ass as high as it will go, I open a drawer and find a bit of rubber.

'Play with your clit,' I tell her.

She takes her right hand off the sink and starts moving it in circles. Her back arches even more causing her ass to go higher and her whole sweet pussy to hang between her legs. My favorite pose for a woman.

Perfect. Just fucking perfect.

I grab her hips and slide into her. I slide so far in her eyes widen in the mirror. I fuck her hard from the back, our wet bodies slapping, our eyes locked on each other in the mirror. The sound of the two of us echoes through the bathroom like an erotic sexual symphony. Our wet flesh slapping, the sink creaking, her groans, my grunts and finally her strange animal-like cry as she comes hard on my dick. Whoa. There's no holding back after that. I explode deep inside her. I don't immediately slide out of her, I stroke her hair and, pushing it away from the back of her neck, kiss it.

I look up and her eyes are sparkling, her cheeks flushed, her mouth slightly open and panting. 'Another last one for the road?' I ask, hopefully.

And she giggles like a fucking kid.

SNOW

Lunch is served outside. There is the scent of citrus in the gentle summer breeze. We have pan-fried duck confit served with potatoes roasted in duck fat and bowls of tomato salad. The duck is extraordinarily succulent and tasty. Shane tells me the preparation of the meat takes Madam up to thirty-six hours.

Afterwards, Madam serves me chocolate soufflé with a cherry on top of it and brings a cheese board for Shane. I break through the chocolate crust and spoon the soft creamy chocolate filling into my mouth.

'Mmmm ... very, very delicious. Want to taste?' I ask.

He moves his face closer. The crisp male cologne on his skin mingles with the scent of the dark chocolate and makes me feel almost drunk. Swallowing hard, I feed him a spoonful. He catches my wrist, chews, and swallows. He bends and slides his tongue along my collarbone. My eyes widen.

His bright eyes flash. 'You're right, very, very delicious,' he murmurs.

And though he has done all kinds of things to me and we are lovers, heat rushes up my neck.

And those sinful, sinful lips that have been on every inch of my body, twist with amusement. 'You're blushing.'

To my horror I flush even more.

 575

He chuckles. 'Do you know you blushed through our entire first time?'

'How could you tell? We did it in the pitch dark,' I retort.

'Snow,' he says caressing my name like a kiss. 'You were at least two shades darker.'

'And you ... you ... panted through our entire first time,' I lie.

'Sometimes you make me feel so cheap,' he says with a sexy grin.

'I doubt any woman could make you feel cheap,' I reply.

He moves closer to me and for a heart stopping moment he hovers over my mouth. A pulse throbs at his throat and sexual energy glimmers off him like a heatwave. His fingers seek the hem of my skirt and push it upwards.

'You are a strange combination, Snow. Enormous, butter-wouldn't-melt eyes and a slutty mouth built for suckin' cock,' he says, lust thickening his voice. 'All I want to do is fuck you all the fucking time.'

And to my shock I actually feel like standing up, wrapping my thighs around his hips and impaling myself on his big, hard cock. Wet lust quickly flowers between my legs at the thought.

But he pulls away from me with a frown. 'What do you want to do this afternoon, Snow? Go back into town? I could take you around the sights if you want. Or take you shopping.'

There is so little time left of our weekend together. I may never see him again. I don't want to waste these last few hours in town and certainly not shopping. 'I want to stay here. I want to swim with you, and then ... I want to end up in your bed.'

His strong hand reaches down and curls around my wrist and he pulls me up. We run up the grand curving staircase up to his bedroom where he flings me on his bed, rips off my clothes, and thrusts into me urgently, as if he can't wait another second.

'Your pussy fits around my dick like a fucking glove,' he growls.

He does not stop all afternoon until sweat runs down his curving muscles and I am so exhausted and sore I have to beg him to stop.

Eighteen

SNOW

We arrive in London at ten past nine and clear Customs as simply and easily as we had in France. We reach the car park quickly and come to a stop in front of a muscular red Camarro with white racing stripes on the bonnet. I know hardly anything about cars, but this one is one of those fire-breathers specially built for dangerous speeds.

'Is this *your* car?' I ask incredulously.

'If it's not, then we're about to become car thieves,' he says, holding open the passenger door for me.

'Very impressive,' I say, sliding into its plush black leather interior.

'She's a babe,' he says closing my door.

Shane is very quiet in the car on the way to my house and in the tense silence I start to feel a knot of apprehension in my belly. All this while, seduced by the magic of Saumur, I had let myself totally forget Lenny, but now I am afraid that even though Shane said he had arranged it that Lenny will not call during the weekend, what if he did? I hate the thought of having to tell a whole pile of lies. But more than any of that is the sinking feeling that France was just a dream. It's over.

This is reality. This is real life.

But I simply don't want to go back to how it was before. I don't want to feel Lenny's body on top of me, using me to relieve his sexual urges. I feel sick even thinking about it. I am not the woman who left for Saumur. I've changed, and significantly.

We reach my apartment and I look down at my hands clenched hard in my lap. The silence is unbearable and I am dying to ask him if I will see him again, but what if this is it? If this is all our liaison is supposed to be?

'You can turn on your phone now,' he says, his voice empty and hard in silence.

I nod and look at him.

He seems so distant. Is he eager to get rid of me? Could it be that this was all an elaborate ploy just to sleep with me? Surely someone who looks like he does, doesn't need to go to these unnecessary lengths. And yet he is so cold and unreachable it is as if he can't wait to get rid of me. I feel tears start pricking the back of my eyes. I won't cry in front of him again. I always knew he was conquering the world one pussy at a time so I shouldn't be so hurt and I'm not so broken that I don't have my pride still.

'OK, thanks,' I say quickly and reach for the door handle.

His large hand curls round my arm. I turn to look at him and he says, 'Oh Fuck.' And pulls me into his arm. 'Don't cry, Snow. Just go back to your apartment and he'll call in the next thirty minutes. Just be normal and all will be well.'

I look up at him with confused eyes. 'How do you know when he will call?'

He runs an agitated hand through his hair. 'Because I arranged for two prostitutes to keep him busy until you were safely home.'

My mouth drops open. 'You did what?'

'It was the only way I could be sure he would not call while you were away. It was the only way I knew to keep you safe.'

I take a deep breath. 'You did that for me?'

He turns away from me and, staring ahead, grips the steering wheel. 'It's no big deal, Snow. Just go. And answer his damn call and ... be as normal as you can, OK?'

'OK,' I whisper and, getting out, I slam the door closed and run into my apartment building without ever looking back. As I get through my front door I hear his car blast away, the tires screeching madly around the corner.

SHANE

I take my foot off the gas as I come up to the next red light. Fuck. My fingers drum on the dashboard. I rest my elbow on the window of my car and squeeze my temples. I always knew she was something special. I turn my eyes and catch the gaze of a man in a seven series BMW. He shakes his head with distaste because I am unconsciously revving my thunderous V8 engine impatiently and it is annoying him.

'What the fuck are you looking at?' I snarl, and the little coward immediately stares straight ahead.

The light turns yellow and I hammer the gas pedal and fly off the mark. Up ahead I see a U-turn sign. I could take it. But that would be madness. Gritting my teeth I keep my foot on the accelerator. I pass it. I can't believe how angry and resentful I feel. Soon I hit the motorway. For twenty minutes I drive. I know he will have called by now.

I hit the music and Lana Del Ray's Summertime Sadness comes on.

My car eats up the miles and in my head I see only the expression on her face when I left her. I have just given her back to him. What the hell was I fucking thinking of? I feel bitter, as if I have been cheated. What I really want to do is drive back to her place right now and take back what is *mine*. Fuck the consequences. But a sane inner voice stops me. *It is you who made these arrangements. This is the safe way. This way you get the girl and keep Lenny off both your backs.*

My mind turns to her in the forest.

How sweetly she gave herself to me. I could have done anything to her and she would have let me. And the way she had looked at me with those big, green eyes full of trust and innocence when I took her little ass and made it mine. And then I think of that ugly fuck, Lenny, touching her. And I feel fire burn in my belly.

Fuck it.

I'm not fucking giving her up to him. Not even for one day. Fuck the safe way. Change of plan, asshole. She's mine. She was mine from the moment I laid eyes on her.

SNOW

I close the door and the house is as silent as tomb. I take my little suitcase into my bedroom. The flowers I bought on Wednesday are dead. I put the suitcase on the bed and go back out to the living room. I sit on the sofa and put my mobile phone beside me and wait.

When the phone rings I jump. I take a deep breath and wait for the third ring before I pick it up.

'Hello.' He sounds like he is drunk or high. I've seen him take cocaine from the dining room table before. He's even offered it to me, but I didn't want to and he said, 'You're right. Maybe you shouldn't. Your head's fucked enough as it is.'

'Hello,' I say. My voice is beautifully normal. It appears I am just as capable of deceit as Lenny is. Still, Lenny never promised me fidelity. That was never in the cards.

'How are you, luv?'

For some reason that endearment grates on my nerves. I'm not his luv and I never will be. 'I'm fine,' I reply.

'Good. I'll be back tomorrow morning. Don't forget I'm taking my girl out to a fancy restaurant tomorrow night.'

I feel a stab in my chest. I'm not his girl. He's been with two prostitutes. Not that I care or ever cared. I just don't want to sleep with him anymore. I don't want to go out with him. I don't want him to touch me. Ever again. I hear myself say, 'OK.'

'Right, I'll call you when I touch down. Goodnight, Snow.'

'Goodnight, Lenny.'

I kill the call and lay the phone down on the table. Tomorrow night looms on the horizon. What on earth am I going to do? Oh God! I cover my face with my hands. What a mess.

My phone rings again making me jump. I pick it up and look at the screen.

Number withheld.

My heart starts beating fast in my chest. I accept the call.

'Hello,' I say cautiously.

'Will you have dinner with me tomorrow night?'

My heart soars with joy. He called. He called. It isn't over. Then reality hits. My heart sinks like a heavy stone inside my body. 'I can't go. I've already agreed to meet Lenny for dinner.'

'Yeah? Well, poor old Lenny won't be able to make it for dinner with you tomorrow. He will be otherwise tied up.'

I feel a wild rush of joy flash through every cell and nerve in my body. It comes out as a mad giggle even as I wonder what exactly he means by tied up. More prostitutes? More business deals that Lenny simply can't say no to?

'Snow,' he calls softly.

'Yes,' I whisper, gripping the phone hard.

For a few seconds he is quiet. 'Wear something pretty tomorrow.'

'I will,' I say, and I am smiling from ear to ear.

'Goodnight, Snow.'

'Goodnight, Shane.'

Oh my God. We're having dinner tomorrow.

I place the phone on the table and, jumping up to my feet, do a totally mad dance around the coffee table.

'Yes. Yes. Yes.'

It seemed as if he couldn't wait for me to get out of his car so I thought he didn't want me anymore. But he *does* want me.

I stop suddenly. And what of the next day? What will I tell Lenny when he wants to have dinner with me on Tuesday? Or Wednesday? How long can Shane keep him busy? How will I escape from Lenny?

Monday passes with interminable slowness. Lenny gets into Heathrow at nearly midday and calls me from the back of his car. He sounds upbeat, but ends the phone call by saying that something has come up and he won't be able to make dinner today.

'That's OK,' I say quickly. 'I need an early night anyway.'

'Why?' he asks immediately, his voice suddenly different.

But I am a better liar than I could ever have imagined. 'I didn't sleep very well last night.'

'Nightmares?' he asks quietly.

And instantly I feel like a bitch. What I am doing is so wrong. I am cheating on someone who has only ever been good to me. I have to do something about my situation, and fast. I close my eyes and, taking a deep breath, I lie. 'No, not nightmares. I think I ate something that didn't agree with me. I kept going to the toilet.'

'Ah well, in that case it's for the best that we are not doing dinner today. Rain check for tomorrow?'

'Tomorrow,' I repeat softly, guiltily.

Nineteen

SNOW

More than an hour before Shane is due to pick me up I start panicking. I don't know why I am more nervous today than I was even when he was taking me away to France. Then I had no expectations. Now my feelings are involved. I really, really like Shane.

I practically pull nearly all my clothes out of my wardrobe, and still feel that nothing I have is suitable for tonight. Everything is either too short, too long, too tight or just too meh. I want to look perfect for Shane.

A bath, I think. A bath always calms me right down. I chuck a soap bomb into the water and wait for it to fizzle out before I pour a good one fifth of a bottle of oil into it. I lie in it and take deep calming breaths, but even that doesn't relax me. The turmoil is inside my tummy.

Impatiently, I wash my hair and get out of the bath. I wave the hair dryer at my head and brush it until it is as sleek as the coat of a black panther. Wrapped in a towel, I go back into the bedroom and stand in front of the clothes strewn all over my bed.

Red. I'll wear red. I slip into red, satin and lace matching underwear. I hook on suspenders and carefully pull on sheer nearly black stockings.

I look in the mirror. Not bad.

I put all the other clothes back into the wardrobe and slip into my red dress. It is a fitted, tailored thing with buttons all the way down the front that makes it look like I am wearing a long, tight jacket that comes to the middle of my thighs.

Because it has long sleeves I will only need to carry a light coat for when it gets colder.

I paint my lips in a similar shade to the dress and carefully pull the mascara wand a couple of times over my eyelashes. Then I sit on the bed and pull on shiny black, patent leather boots. I find a little red clip in a drawer and I slide it into my hair. Finally, I dab perfume at my pulse points.

I find my red purse and put my lipstick, my credit card, a wad of tissue, a couple of mints, and as I always do, my little pill container with a few of my pills in them. That done, I kill the rest of the time by pacing the floor restlessly.

When Shane arrives he calls me on my mobile and waits for me downstairs. I go down and for a second he does not see me. He is leaning against the glass, his hands jammed into the pockets of his black jeans and he's staring at the floor. He looks remote and preoccupied. As if the weight of the whole world is on his shoulders. I start walking towards him. He looks up and straightens, stares at me with such an odd expression that I stop walking, my stomach sinking, and I ask, 'What is it?'

He shakes his head and a small smile lifts the corners of his lips. 'Everything's good. You look amazing.'

Shane takes me to a restaurant called Lady Marmalade. It is only when we get there that I realize that Lenny has taken me there before. I debate whether to tell him and I decide that I will, but later, when we are seated, I will casually mention it then. It's not like it is important.

We walk in through the doors and a man in a navy suit rushes out to greet Shane. He claps his hand on Shane's back in a familiar manner and Shane calls him as Mario. There is only one word to describe the man's behavior: effusive. His eyes turn to me and quickly travel down my body the way Italian waiters do, half-professional, half-over-the-top-leering. With great enthusiasm he shows us to a table in the middle of the restaurant. Almost immediately, waiters start dancing around us, flicking napkins open, flourishing menus.

I am still studying my menu when a tall, broad man strides up to us.

'Hey,' the man says to Shane, his face lit up with genuine pleasure. He looks very much like Shane, but he is a little older, and while Shane's looks are more classically handsome, this man is more aggressive looking with a strong, stubborn jaw.

Shane looks up and smiles at him. 'What the hell are you doing here?'

'Bloody cheek,' the man says with a laugh. 'I'm on my way out actually.'

Shane turns towards me. 'Snow, meet my brother, Dom. Dom, meet Snow.'

Dom turns to me with a smile which freezes on his face. He frowns as he tries to remember. I recognize him at the same time he remembers me. I've seen him once before. Then it suddenly comes to me. He owns this restaurant. He came to say hello to us when I was here with Lenny, but it was months ago, and I was so spaced out on my pills then that I did not really take note.

'Hello, Snow,' he says. His voice has lost all its humor and cheer.

'Hi,' I say awkwardly. I look at Shane and he is staring quizzically at me.

'I've been here before with Lenny,' I explain quietly, my heart sinking.

Shane nods slowly, his eyes betraying a spasm of fury, then he squashes it down and turns to his brother.

'Look,' Dom says tightly, 'it's none of my business, but—'

'Then don't fucking get involved,' Shane cuts in. His voice is cold and clipped.

I stare at him in shock. I have never seen him as anything but cheeky and charming, but Dom doesn't appear to take any offence at his brother's openly hostile tone.

'I'll talk to you tomorrow,' he says quietly. There are deep worry lines on his forehead. Unlike my brother who can't even stand to be in the same room as me he must love Shane very much to care so deeply that his brother is going out with Lenny's girl.

'Sure. I'll call you,' Shane says distantly.

His brother turns towards me. 'Goodnight. Enjoy your meal,' he says formally.

'Thank you,' I whisper.

He turns away and takes two steps before turning back to look at Shane. 'I'll be waiting for your call.'

Shane nods.

His brother walks away and Shane turns back to me. 'I suppose you've lost your appetite.' His voice crackles with aggression, but his gaze is innocuous.

I nod slowly.

The expression on his face changes and he looks at me wistfully. 'Why didn't you tell me?'

Seeing the look of disappointment in his eyes as if I have betrayed him, is unbearable. Tears sting the backs of my eyes. I feel as if I have ruined everything. Unable to look into his eyes I gaze down at my clenched fists. 'I'm sorry,' I tell my hands. 'I was going to. Really I was. I just didn't want to spoil our evening.'

I look up and he is leaning back against the chair and looking at me expressionlessly.

Mario appears at Shane's elbow, his large smile quickly faltering at the tension he finds between us. 'Something to drink perhaps?' he suggests uneasily.

Shane doesn't look at him. 'Can you give us a minute, Mario?'

'Certainly,' Mario says, and with an expansive gesture, backs off.

Shane sighs. 'Do you want to stay, Snow?'

'Are you going to carry on being angry?' I ask anxiously.

His mouth twists ruefully. 'I'm not angry now.'

'It sure looks like it to me,' I say miserably.

He reaches a hand out and gently traces his knuckle along my jaw line. 'My poor Snow. Did you have fun here with Lenny?' he asks.

'No.' My voice is strangled.

'No tequila shots upstairs?'

I shake my head.

Shane laughs suddenly. 'Then you haven't really been to Lady Marmalade at all,' he declares, and raises his hand. Mario must have been hanging around watching because he materializes at our side like a genie out of a bottle.

'Give us the works, Mario,' he says.

Mario raises his hand like the conductor of an orchestra and says, 'Bravo.'

So the evening begins. A bottle of champagne is popped and glasses filled. Shane is funny and cheeky and sexy all at once. We eat the insanely good food and then he takes me upstairs where there is a bar and a dance floor. We do tequila shots at the bar and then Shane whirls me off to dance. We join the conga line of someone else's party and I laugh until my stomach aches.

'If I die tomorrow, I'll die happy,' I tell him.

He pulls me towards him. 'I won't. Not while you're with him. Even dead I don't want him to have you. He doesn't deserve you,' he growls.

I stare up at him, shocked by the passion in his voice.

Mario gives me a little box of chocolate truffles as we are leaving. 'I noticed that you liked them. Have them for later,' he says with a nod and a wink.

'Thank you,' I say, surprised and touched by the gift.

In the car, Shane tells me that we will be dropping by Eden.

'We'll have a quick drink there. There's something I have to do at the office.'

We are nearly there when my phone goes. I freeze with fear.

Shane stops the car at the side of the road and switches off the music.

'Take the call,' he says tautly.

'What if he is calling me from my apartment?'

'He's not.'

'How do you know?'

'Just trust me.'

He takes my purse from my lap, pulls my phone out and gives it to me.

I click accept and Lenny says, 'Did I wake you?'

'No,' I say, and even to my own ears my voice sounds shaky.

'Are you all right?'

'Yes. Yes, I'm fine.'

'Where are you?'

Paranoia grips me. I swallow hard and try to keep my voice neutral and casual. 'In my bedroom.'

'Are you just about to go to bed?'

'Yes.'

There is a pause, then he says, 'I have a surprise for you.'

'Oh.'

'I'll give it to you tomorrow night.'

'All right.'

'Sweet dreams and don't let the bed bugs bite.'

'Thanks. And goodnight, Lenny.'

'Goodnight, luv.'

I disconnect the call and put the phone back into my purse. Shane starts the car and drives on. He doesn't say anything. The atmosphere in the car is so tense I feel it pressing down on me.

Twenty

SNOW

Inside Eden, the manager comes forward to help me with my coat, but Shane forestalls him, lifting my coat away from my body and tossing it carelessly on the counter. He places his hand on the small of my back in an unmistakable gesture of ownership and leads me into the club.

Flushed and tense with nerves, I let him guide me into the club. Music throbs around us and I am conscious of almost everyone staring at me because I am with Shane. Some of those looks are filled with malice and envy. Their faces swim before me. I force my spine straight and hold my head up high.

A blonde woman dressed in a powder blue suit hurries towards us. Her face is wreathed with a friendly smile that encompasses both of us. 'Hello,' she greets.

'Briana, meet Snow, my girlfriend. Snow, this is Briana, the housemother of this club.'

'Hi,' I say, taking her cool hand and feeling suddenly shy. I feel as if I am floating on cloud nine. I can't believe that Shane introduced me as his girlfriend. It feels strange and fantastically wonderful.

She turns to Shane. 'She's simply gorgeous.'

Shane moves closer and slides his arm around my waist. He looks down at me, his eyes gleaming with triumphant ownership. 'Yes, she is rather ravishing, isn't she?' he murmurs.

'Would you like to stay and have a drink?' Brianna asks.

'I'm actually here to pick something up from the office.' He turns to look at me. 'Would you like to stay for one drink?'

'OK.'

'Come on,' Brianna says and leads us to a booth in the corner. We sit down and a waitress comes with a bottle of champagne and fills our glasses. When she is gone we clink glasses.

'To us,' Shane says.

'Is there an us?' I ask softly.

'Yes, there is an us,' he says, and his voice is terse, almost brutal.

'To us,' I whisper.

He raises his glass to his lips and watches me over the rim with a dark, brooding look. A muscle twitches in his cheek. The atmosphere between us grows tense again and I feel myself start to tremble. I have never seen Shane angry. I don't know why he is, but I know he is seething under the surface. It all started when Lenny called.

'Come here,' he says with an edge to his voice.

I put the glass down on the table and, licking my lips nervously, shift closer to him leaving six inches between us. He ruthlessly jerks me sideways towards him so I tumble off the seat with a surprised gasp and land in an ungainly fashion in his lap. My hands searching for balance are both gripping his body. He puts his hands on my hip and thigh and pulls me closer to him so my body is molded to his and my thigh is pressed against his erection.

'I want you like hell,' he whispers into my neck. 'I want to fuck you, right here, right now.'

'No, please, Shane,' I protest, even though I am already embarrassingly wet at the thought. It is amazing how he can arouse me with a look, a touch, a suggestion. 'Can't we wait till we get to your place?'

'I'm sick of waiting. I'll have you now and you'll fucking enjoy every minute of it,' he says, his face hard.

I shake my head, staring at him with a jumble of excitement and horror. My body seems to be flaming with heat and my heart is beating so fast I feel it like a flutter in my chest. 'We are in a public place,' I whisper.

'Snow?' His eyes are as hungry as a wolf in the night.

'Yes,' I say.

'That wasn't a request.'

'This is madness. There are cameras, aren't there?' I cry.

'They get turned off when I get into a booth.' His face is dark with desire. A horrible thought enters my head. Does he bring all his women here and have sex with them here? Is that why there are no cameras here?

'No,' he says violently. 'I don't fucking don't do this with all the others.'

He kisses me then, so brutally I taste the salt of blood on my tongue. Shocked by the intensity of his mouth, I automatically try to push him away.

'Don't fight me, Snow,' he grates harshly. 'I need this.'

I look into his eyes and I see that he is telling the truth. For whatever reason he needs to take me here in this public place where anyone could come by and see me taken like some cheap slut. The fight goes out of me. I lie in his arms while his fingers snake into my dress and push aside my panties. There is nothing I can do.

He is going to make me climax here.

SHANE

Her eyes are wide open with surprise and affront, but she's practically vibrating with excitement and anticipation. Like biting into a ripe summer cherry, my fingers sink effortlessly into her tight, little pussy. The sound of her helpless whimper turns my blood to fire. I feel the kind of feral hunger that makes me insane with need. My cock pulses hard, right on the edge of something.

If I don't get into her soon I will fucking explode.

 593

I want to lay her on the table, tear her clothing off and bury myself so deep inside her that it obliterates the memory of that sick bastard. She doesn't know, but I still see him in her eyes. She still thinks of him. She doesn't want to 'hurt' him. She feels 'grateful' to him. And the worse part of all: she feels 'guilty' when she's with me as if she still belongs to that sicko. I hate that. Fucking hell, she's mine.

'Open your eyes,' I tell her. My voice throbs with fury.

Her eyes fly open, large and guileless. When she is aroused her eyes become brilliant and shiny. I had a cat once with eyes like that. Beautiful.

Staring into her fabulous eyes I add another finger. Her pale legs tremble open further. She gasps, her body arching slightly.

'Have you ever been finger-fucked in a club, Snow?'

She shakes her head.

With a little laugh I realize that I don't need to fuck her, I just want to lay claim to her. Make her submit sexually to me anywhere, anytime. I need to dominate her and get it through her head that she belongs to me, mind, body and soul and I won't tolerate even the ghost of Lenny's memory.

Every time I see him in her eyes, I'm going to fuck her until he is completely gone. My other hand roves possessively over her body. I unbutton the first two buttons of her dress and slide my hand inside it. I run my palm caressingly over her nipples. Through the thin silky material of her bra, they are like small stones under my palm. I push up the bra cup and pinch her nipple. She groans softly.

Using my thumb, I gather the slickness from the tender pink folds and begin to relentlessly circle her clit. She rocks with sudden hunger.

'I love your body, little rabbit,' I tell her, thrusting my hand harder and harder as she starts to quake, her exposed breast jiggling.

She buries her head into my neck. 'I'm going to come, Shane,' she gasps. It is almost a plea. Asking my permission to come. I like that. It's fucking horny. I pump her even more furiously and her poor little pussy clenches around my fingers. Then she goes over the edge beautifully.

I let her hide, her body shuddering, and her muscles locked around my fingers. I hear her heart thudding hard against mine.

'I don't ever want you to go back to Lenny,' I state harshly.

She pulls away from my neck and stares up at me, her face a confused oval of white. 'I can't do that. I owe—'

'Owe? What do you owe, Snow?' I ask, my voice is a vicious snarl.

She shakes her head and tries to wriggle away from me, but I grip her hips hard.

'I'm the man with my fingers buried inside your pussy, and that's the way it's going to be every night from now on,' I tell her thickly. And, staring insolently at her, I begin to move my fingers in and out of her in a show of my total control of her body.

She stares at me helplessly, her eyes darkening again with spiraling excitement.

'What do you owe him, Snow?' I ask softly.

'I can't tell you,' she says hoarsely.

'Why not, Snow?'

She bites her lip with consternation and mounting arousal.

'Are you afraid of him?'

'No, not really, but I can't talk about it. It's too dreadful to talk about.'

'Sweet Snow,' I groan. 'You're too fucking sweet to be true.' And, bending my head, I kiss her hungrily. Her fingers cling to my shoulders and suddenly I have the ugly searing thought. Did she cling to him? Did she ever come alive under his hand and his mouth? My tongue pushes into her mouth roughly, my teeth hurting her soft flesh. I hook her tongue, bring it into my mouth, and suck it so hard she whimpers and tries to fight back, her clenched fist striking my forearms, then grabbing my hand and trying to pull it out of her pussy.

I pull my mouth away and her rage dissolves at the expression on my face. So full of lust it startles her. We stare at each other as I continue to pleasure her. She comes with a strangled cry of submission. I caress the delicate bones in the curve of her spine.

'You're never seeing Lenny again,' I say firmly, and slipping my fingers out of her, I pull her bra cup over her breast, button her top and pull her dress over her thighs.

She drops her eyes. 'I'll come back with you tonight, but I'll have to see him again. I have to explain.'

'No, you fucking won't. I'll take the fight to him. I knew what I was doing when I decided to hunt you. I knew there'd be consequences to pay. And I'm ready to pay them.'

She licks her swollen mouth nervously. Unshed tears glimmer in the depths. 'Lenny is dangerous, Shane. I can't let you confront him. Please, I'm begging you. I know how to handle him. He won't hurt me.'

'No fucking way. I wouldn't trust him with you for a minute. I'll rot in hell before I let that psychopath anywhere near you again.'

She looks at me desperately. 'Maybe we can run away together.'

I laugh mirthlessly. 'Run? I come from a long line of bare-knuckle fighters, Snow. We don't fucking run. We fight for what we want. I'm not scared of him. If I was, you'd be in his bed now. I want you and I'll fucking fight to the death for you.'

'Oh, Shane. I'm so sorry. I never meant to get you into such a rotten mess,' she cries.

'Fuck, Snow,' I say in wonder. 'You didn't get me into this mess. I'm my own man. *I* got me into this rotten mess and I'm not one tiny bit sorry. I'll fight anyone for you.' I touch her lovely, sad face. 'He should never have had you in the first place. He's got no soul, Snow.'

She hugs herself as if she's cold and stares at me intensely. 'You don't understand. He'll let you win a bare-knuckle fight. He'll even clap you on the back, congratulate you, and tell you the best man won. But he's a vindictive man, Shane. He never forgets. When you think it's all fine, he'll send his attack dogs.'

I smile. 'Ah, Snow. You didn't think I was going to challenge him to a bare-knuckle fight, did you? You only do that when you're fighting a man. He's not a real man. He has no honor. You'll just have to trust me when I say I *do* know men like him. I know exactly what makes them tick and exactly how to approach them. And he's not the only one with attack dogs.'

She stares at me. 'You have a plan?'

I nod. 'I have a plan.'

'What is it?'

'The less you know the better.'

'Is your plan dangerous?'

'Not to me it's not. I'm pretty sure I've got it all covered.'

She looks scared. 'Promise?'

God, she's so beautiful she takes my breath away. I smile slowly. 'Promise.'

She smiles back tremulously.

'Listen, I've got to go upstairs and get something, and then I'm taking you home. Want to come up with me or wait here for me?'

She smiles shyly. 'You've made a mess between my legs. I need to go freshen up. I'll just nip into the Ladies while you're up.'

'Don't clean too hard. I plan on making one hell of a bigger mess when we get home.'

'I like it when you make a mess,' she says and, leaning forward, kisses me lightly on the tip of my nose. It's sweet.

'Go anywhere you want inside the club, but don't walk out of it. It's dangerous for a woman outside.'

'I have no intention of going out,' she says with a heartbreaking smile.

Twenty-One

SNOW

I am washing my hands when the woman walks in. She stands next to me and looks at herself. I cannot help but stare. Blonde, and well over six feet tall in her high, white shoes she's unbelievably beautiful. Her eyes are deep blue and she is wearing flash eyelashes, the tips of which she has dusted with silver. It has a very dramatic effect when she blinks. To my surprise she smiles warmly at me and I smile back.

'Hi,' she says. 'I saw you come in with the boss.' Her accent is quite strong, possibly Russian.

'Yes,' I say shyly. It's going to take some time before I get used to thinking of Shane as my boyfriend.

'I'm Nikki,' she introduces.

'You can call me Snow.'

'Snow. Beautiful name for beauty.'

'Oh, thank you, but you're the real beauty here.'

She waves my compliment away modestly. 'It's all make-up. You should see me in the morning.'

'I don't believe that for an instant,' I tell her. And that's the truth. She would be beautiful without any make up. She's perfect in every way. Tall, blonde, big breasts, stunning.

Haven't I seen you here before?' she asks opening her little clutch purse.

'Not really,' I say awkwardly.

She takes her lip gloss and unscrews it. 'Yes, I have. I never forget a face. In this business you need to have a good memory.' She smiles. 'You know, which customer likes which move ...' She lets the sentence hang and applies a layer of gloss onto her bee stung lips and then turns to look at me again.

'It's been nice meeting you. Maybe I'll see you around,' I say.

She narrows her eyes at me. 'Ah, I remember now. You're Lenny's woman.' And she smiles happily. 'I knew I had seen you before. Lenny is a good customer of mine,' she says with a knowing wink. 'But between you and me you've done well to dump him for Shane. Lenny's very generous and all, but Shane's brilliant in bed, isn't he?'

I freeze. 'I beg your pardon.'

'Oh don't worry. I'm not jealous or anything. We finished ages ago. I know all about his,' she makes air quotation marks, 'have cock will travel' rules. He's had at least twenty women since we broke up.'

'What?'

She widens her eyes. 'Oh, I didn't mean to shock you or anything. I didn't know you thought it was serious. Take it as a friendly warning, dahling, it's never serious with Shane. He's a total manwhore with a frisky donkey dick, but that's what makes him so good in bed. Look, don't worry about it. Just enjoy it while it lasts. Just don't let him break your little heart. Good luck, sweetie.'

I think of Shane. The way we made love. *Have cock will travel!*

My throat clogs. I'm so fucking pathetic. *You don't eat all the candy from the candy shop.* Again and again I make the same mistake. I trust the wrong people. He doesn't eat all the candy just the best pieces.

But he told me I was his. I belonged to him.

The air suddenly feels chilled. Her words are like frost covering my heart. Gooseflesh crawls on my skin. I feel cold. So cold. Even colder than when I stumbled out of that hotel room.

God, how stupid I've been. Of course a man as beautiful as he is will have loads of women after him. Of course he is a player. Look how he chased me even after he saw me with Lenny. I can't believe I never saw it until now.

There is no puzzle to put together. A child could have worked it out. I was just too idiotic, too unhappy to see it. And there I was besotted, thinking he was the other half of my soul. He is just a courteous, charming player. Disgust crawls over my skin. I feel humiliated and used, again. All I want to do is run away.

Malicious amusement at my naivety glints in her eyes. Unshed tears scorch the backs of my eyes. I won't give her the satisfaction.

'Leave me alone now,' I say. My voice is strangely detached.

I drop my eyes to my hands. They are still wet. I need to dry them. I walk over to the hand drier and hold my hands inside the machine. Hard jets of air blow on them. I hear the door open and close and I crumple. For a second I stand where I am with my back to the door, the poison spreading into my body, and then I walk to it and stand just inside it. Afraid to open the door.

Oh, my poor heart. It still wants to believe.

But the cold truth was undeniable. She is right. I always knew he was a playboy, but I could not help myself, and after a while I started to believe in him. But if this stunning creature couldn't keep him, what hope have I?

I have let Shane break my heart.

I open the door and the beautiful night creatures are going about their fun and laughter. Nothing has changed for them, but for me it feels as if I am dying. I start walking towards the entrance. I can make out Nikki. Her face is turned towards me, her claws sheathed, but her eyes filled with dark interest. I feel every cliché: the ground dropping out beneath my feet, my whole world shattering before my eyes, and our life together vanishing in a cloud of smoke.

My stomach twists and I start hurrying to the door. As I get closer, my feet speed up even more. Soon I am running. People are turning to stare, but I don't care anymore. I just want to be out of this ugly place with its ugly, ugly people doing ugly, ugly things to each other. Tears soak my eyelashes and run down my face.

He's just a habit. A very bad habit. But even the worst habits can be broken. I will survive. I survived the hotel room. This is nothing.

But tears keep pouring down my face.

I run out of the club and suddenly find myself in the deserted parking lot. The night is so sultry it is almost muggy, but I feel cold and numb. My life seems like a dream that I'm walking through with my eyes closed. Making mistake after mistake after mistake. Ignoring every clue.

I look around me in confusion. How will I get home? I have no money. My hands are shaking. I bow my head to think and when I lift it, suddenly, and bewilderingly, I am surrounded by men. Where did they come from? Who are they?

I peer at them and they look like they are part of a stag night party because one of them is wearing a pair of felt antlers. He comes up to me and touches me. I freeze. Another touches my hand.

'Come on, love. Give us a kiss.'

One of them takes a note out of his pocket. 'Go on love, he's getting married tomorrow.'

Another one says, 'Come guys. Leave her alone. She's scared shitless.'

'Fuck off, Larry. It's just a bit of fun,' says the guy who took the note out of his pocket. And the rest of them laugh.

Somewhere in my head I realize that they think I am one of the strippers. That they are not going to hurt me. They just want to buy a kiss for the groom, but a kind of paralysis has swept over me and my whole body is in lockdown. I cannot move a muscle.

Only my eyes swivel over them in terror. And then the fear comes.

I am so exposed. So utterly vulnerable. They could take me. There are six. I want to scream. I want to run. But my body does nothing. I can't understand what is happening to my body. I am frozen I have become petrified. Like those tree fossils from millions of years ago. It is incomprehensible and terrifying.

My purse has fallen on the floor and all the contents have fallen out. One of the guys comes really close to me. 'What's wrong, sugar? Are you all right? We're not going to hurt you.'

His breath reeks of alcohol.

I look at him wordlessly.

'Hey, look at that. She can't move.'

He starts to laugh. Tears start rolling down my face. Daringly he touches my breast. And yet I can do nothing. He sniggers. 'Shit, this chick is like a statue. We could take her home with us.'

The other guys crowd around me curiously. It is exactly like it was before. I was frozen and tears were escaping fast from my eyes and no one cared. They just went on doing whatever they wanted to me.

Suddenly there is a great roar and wind whooshes by me. I stare in shock as Shane punches the guy with the antlers and kicks the guy who wanted to take me home, to the ground. I have never seen the primal animal inside him, and I stare transfixed.

He is so achingly beautiful. Like an animal. No rules. Perfectly unfettered, free to extract whatever punishment he wants. There is no pretense, no nod to what is socially acceptable. He just surrenders to the beast inside him.

In the commotion the other men are screaming, 'What the fuck?'

'Hey, we didn't mean her any harm.'

'We didn't fucking do nothing,' is the cowardly defense to Shane's fury and fists.

Two of them turn and run away. The bouncers appear and Shane is putting his arm around me.

He bends his knees and looks into my face. I just stare at him. He is white about the mouth. His hand is bleeding. He cups my face with his hands.

'Are you all right?' he asks. His voice confuses me. It is strange and different. As if he is speaking a different language.

I take a shuddering breath and open my mouth to say, yes, but no words will come out. I close my mouth.

'It's OK. It's OK. I'm here,' he says and crushes me to his chest. I am trembling so hard he pulls back and looks at me worriedly.

I know the bouncers are all around me, but I don't see them. I know Shane is holding me, but I can't feel it. Some one is picking up my things from the ground and putting them back into my purse. Shane gives his car keys to someone who brings the car right next to us. Shane opens the car door and puts me in it. We drive back to his home in complete silence. Once we get there he comes around and lifts me bodily from the car.

'I can walk,' I croak.

'It'll be faster this way,' he says. In the lift I feel his eyes staring down at me, but I keep my head bent.

Inside the apartment he lays me on the couch and goes to the liquor cabinet. He pours us both brandies. A super large one for him, which he throws down his throat, and a smaller one that he brings to me. I take it and curve my hands around the cold glass. He sits opposite me. His face is still pale under his tan.

'Do you want a hot drink?' he asks.

I shake my head.

'Drink up,' he instructs.

I take a gulp and the alcohol runs through my body like fire.

'Finish it,' he says.

I do it and he leans forward and takes the glass from my hand.

I look up at him to say thank you and my breath is stolen from me at the strange unfathomable expression on his face. 'Why did you leave the club?' he asks.

'I went to the Ladies and met Nikki.' My voice is emotionless. Truly I don't feel any of the emotion I felt before. I just feel like a shell.

His face crumples. 'Oh, Snow. What do you want from me? I've never pretended with you. You knew what I was. I chased pussy. But, every one of those girls knew exactly where they stood with me from day one. I never cheated on anyone and certainly not her. Yes, I slept with her, but she was never anything to me and she knew that.'

'It was just a shock. I guess I am more jealous than what I thought.'

He looks at me curiously. 'What actually happened outside the club?'

'I'm really tired, Shane. Can we please talk about it in the morning?'

'OK, let's get you in bed.'

And the truth is, the trauma with Nikki and what happened outside the club has actually utterly exhausted me. I feel numb. The whole night is like a dream. My eye lids are so heavy they close even as my head touches the pillow. The last thing I remember before I fall into a deep sleep is his large, strong hand curling around mine.

He whispers something in my ear, but I don't catch it.

Twenty-two

SNOW

One year before ...

'Either the well was very deep, or she fell very slowly, for she had plenty of time as she went down to look about her and to wonder what was going to happen next.'
—Lewis Carroll, *Alice in Wonderland*

Kim, my new roommate in the YHA hostel, was not strictly beautiful, but she was attractive, with bright laughing eyes, dark shiny hair and, as I said before, had the biggest grin I'd ever seen in my life. And I warmed to her instantly.

'And I'm Snow,' I said.

'Cool name. So where're you from then?' she asked.

'India.'

She looked me up and down. 'No kidding. I thought Indians were brown.'

'Mostly. There are fair Indians up north, but in my case my mother is English and my father half-Portuguese.'

'So you ... like just arrived.'

'Today,' I said.

'And you've never been to this part of the world before?'

'First time,' I said with a huge smile.

'Excellent. I'm from Australia. I'll show you everything. I know all the happening, fun places. I presume you don't have much money.'

'Afraid so.'

'No problem. Part time work is so easy to get. You'll have to apply for a National Insurance number first, and that will take like six weeks to come through.'

My eyes widen. 'Six weeks!' I exclaim.

'But,' she grins, 'in the meantime you can just work illegally.'

'Really? Doing what?'

'Anything. Waitressing, bar tending, dancing in clubs, babysitting anything that gives you cash in hand. You're so gorgeous you could even make mega bucks as an escort.'

'An escort?'

'Yeah, all these lonely businessmen come to London to do business, and they pay hundreds of pounds for someone to sit with them and keep them company while they eat their dinner.'

'Don't they expect you to sleep with them after that?'

'No, you can say no, if you don't want to. It's up to you.'

I shake my head. 'No, that doesn't sound like me. I'm too shy to do something like that.'

'I've done it before. It's really, really good money.'

'You have?' I asked, shocked.

'Sure,' she said airily. 'I didn't sleep with a whole bunch of them. Finally, this really handsome American guy booked me and I'd have paid to sleep with him. So I did and he gave me $500.00. And you know the best part? When you go back to your own country nobody will ever know. Want to try? We can do it together.'

I frowned. 'Sounds like fun, but that's just not me.'

'Right. Let's cross that off the list. Can you do secretarial work?'

I bite my lip. 'No.'

'No sweat. You can wait tables, right?'

'I've never done it before, but I'm a fast learner.'

'That's the spirit. We'll register you with a catering employment agency tomorrow and see how that goes, ok?'

'OK,' I agreed happily. 'Besides, I'm not afraid of working hard in a restaurant kitchen, doing washing up or something like that.'

'Great, we'll do that tomorrow. Let's hit the town tonight.'

'Tonight? No, I just arrived. You go on ahead. I might just have an early night. And anyway, I'm afraid to waste the little money I have on a night on the town.'

'Oh, come on, don't be a spoilsport. We have to celebrate your arrival tonight because it's ladies' night. You won't have to spend a penny. The taxi and everything else will be my treat. I'll take you to this amazing place in Earls Court. It's jam-packed with Australian surfer-type blond boys. I promise, they'll love you.'

'Are you sure?'

'Absolutely.'

I looked at her gratefully. 'Thank you so much, Kim. I was a bit scared of how I was going to cope, but now you've made it all so easy and such fun.'

She grinned good-naturedly. 'Don't thank me. I'm using you as bait. In order to get to you they're going to have to buy me some free drinks too.'

'You don't need me to attract a man, Kim,' I said sincerely. 'You're really attractive.'

'Yeah, I'm not ugly, but I'm no beauty. I know that.'

'You are beautiful in my eyes. You have a beautiful soul,' I said, and she smiled back at me.

That night we got ready. I didn't have anything sexy enough so Kim lent me her pink mini-dress. It was made of Lycra and clung to every curve. I stood in front of the mirror uncertainly.

'You look amazing,' she said.

'You don't think I look too slutty?'

'You couldn't look slutty if you tried, babe,' she said. 'You have more class in your little finger than Kim Kardashian has in her whole body.'

She got into a backless orange dress, which set off her dark hair. I helped her put a fake tattoo on her back. Then we were both ready. She looked me up and down.

'You look great. Really great.'

'So do you.'

'Thanks, Snow.'

And so we went out. First we went to a pub. We had many offers, but Kim was very protective of me. Whenever it seemed someone was getting too familiar, she pulled me away. I had two glasses of white wine and I was already feeling a bit tipsy.

'I hate to be a killjoy, but I really have to get back,' I said.

'No, no, you'll sober up after we eat some food. The real fun hasn't even started yet. You have to come to this club. It's so awesome. Even celebrities go there.'

'Can't we go tomorrow?'

'No, we're out now. Remember, ladies' night. Come on. It'll be fun. I promise. Please, please?'

'All right,' I relented.

She started jumping on the spot. 'Thank you.'

So we left the pub and went down the road to a kebab shop. Kim had a burger and I got myself a chicken kebab. Kim insisted on paying for everything.

'My treat, remember?' she said.

We sat on high chairs facing the glass windows and ate our meals. And as men passed on the street, they looked in and gawked at us. We laughed back at them and I swear that at that moment I never had the slightest inkling of what awaited just a few hours away. Not a clue. All I felt was a sense of freedom. I was in England and I was doing what I wanted to do. I knew I had made the right decision to leave India. My new life in England stretched out full of excitement and promise.

After we ate, we took a taxi. From the outside, the club did not look glamorous at all. It was tucked away on one of the small streets off Earl's Court road, but I couldn't find my way back there when I tried many months later.

There were two bouncers standing outside. As Kim had said, it was free for women that night so we sailed through. By then it was half past eleven. It was in the basement so we went down some stone steps into a small cramped area that was lit by red lights. A bored woman taking money off some guys barely glanced at us as we went through a black door into the club.

There was a dancing area and a few people were rubbing up each other, but mostly people were in dark corners making out.

'Come on,' Kim said, pulling me by the hand to the bar. As my eyes got used to the dark, I realized that the place was mostly full of men. There was no one our age. Both the men and women seemed to be decades older. And there were definitely no celebrities. The place could be described in one word. Seedy.

I looked at Kim, surprised. 'This is it?'

She tapped her nose. 'They come incognito. Wait until a bit later. For the meantime look at that guy checking you out.' A man with grey in his hair was staring at me. When he saw me looking back at him he smiled and nodded. And I don't know why I felt the hairs at the back of my neck rise in fear. I turned back quickly to Kim.

'Listen, Kim. I don't like it in here. I don't want to stay.'

'Just give it five minutes,' she pleaded. 'It's really good.'

'OK, five minutes,' I said.

At that moment she saw someone she knew. She waved at him and he started to come over. He was more our age and I relaxed a little.

'Hey, Andrew,' she greeted and threw herself at him. He kissed her on both cheeks and then looked at me. 'And who have you got here?'

'This is Snow. Are you going to buy us a drink?'

'Of course. What are you girls drinking?'

'A double gin and tonic,' Kim said.

'Orange juice,' I said reluctantly. I really wanted to leave, but I felt too frightened to find my own way back to the hostel so late at night. I knew I had too little money to take a taxi back. Back home I would have been driven to the club and the driver would be waiting outside to pick me up.

The drinks appeared on the bar next to Kim; she took them and passed mine to me. As I sipped my drink, Kim and Andrew carried on talking about people I didn't know. I was starting to feel really, really tired. In fact, I was getting so tired that I couldn't keep my eyes open.

'Can we go home, Kim?' I asked.

'What's the matter with you?' Kim queried, a frown on her forehead. 'Are you all right?'

'No, I feel dizzy. Maybe I'm jetlagged, and with the alcohol ...' I mumbled.

I felt as if I had no legs. Nothing to hold me up. As if my head was free-floating. In fact, my whole body seemed to be 'gone.'

I tried to widen my eyes and focus on Kim, but it felt as if I was detached from my body and physical surroundings. It was like being in a dream or a nightmare. Everything is fluid and strange. You move differently. I saw her grab my arm without really feeling anything. Neither fear or panic. There was no emotion at all. I felt Andrew and Kim grab my body and start helping me out of the club.

I couldn't walk.

'She just needs a bit of fresh air,' she told the bouncers. I could feel my legs hitting the concrete steps, but I felt no pain.

'You all right, love?' the bouncer asked.

611

I wanted to tell him that I had not drunk a lot, but the effort was too much. But even then I did not panic. If only I had made a real effort to tell him, everything would have been different. I was watching with great detachment as Andrew and Kim walked me down the sidewalk. We came to a car. Andrew opened it and together they put me inside. Both of them got into the front.

I remember dry heaving.

'Is she all right?' Andrew said.

Kim turned to me. 'Don't worry. We'll take care of you,' she said, but her voice was echoing.

When she turned and talked with Andrew, their voices felt like they were coming from very far away or from underwater. Then I blacked out. When I came to again, Andrew was pulling me out of the car and carrying me. The sidewalk was wet. I felt the drizzle fall on my face. I tried to talk. I wanted to know where Kim was, but I could not open my mouth. I had no control of any part of my body. I felt a shaft of fear then. It crawled into my head on all fours.

'Don't try to talk. It's OK. Everything is going to be OK,' he whispered.

But I remember thinking that he looked nervous.

Then I blacked out again.

When I came around, I still couldn't move a single muscle and I was in that dreadful hotel room.

Twenty-three

SHANE

I wake up suddenly with a jerk and freeze. Moonlight is filtering in through the curtains. Everything is still .... and wrong. Immediately I turn my head and look to the pillow beside me. It is empty. I jack-knife to a sitting position and listen. There is an intermittent scratching noise coming from the bathroom. I leap out of bed and rush towards the sound. There is no light coming from under the door. I rap on it. The scratching stops, but there is no answer.

'Snow,' I call. 'Are you in there?'

There is no answer. I can feel my heart hammering in my chest.

'If you don't open this door I'm fucking breaking it down,' I say. My voice has a thread of panic running through it.

Still she doesn't answer.

Dread is like an icy claw around my heart. I stand back and start kicking the door. After three kicks it smashes open. I switch on the light and find her naked and cowering in a corner. Her fists are covering her mouth. Above her fist, her eyes are large and wild. Her hair is messy and strands fall over her face. She stares at me without any recognition. As if she is not even looking at me.

What the fuck! It is an incredible shock to see her reduced to something so feral, but another part of my brain takes over. Calmly, it deduces where the sound has come from. She has been scratching the side of the bathtub with her fingernails.

I take a step forward and she presses her back into the tiles, a look of sheer terror on her face.

I lift my hand. 'It's just me, Snow. Shane.'

She stares at me without comprehension.

I very slowly get on my haunches, and when it looks like that that action does not spook her, I get on my hands and knees and start a half-shuffle, half-crawl towards her. 'It's me,' I urge softly. 'I'm not going to hurt you.' I stop a foot away from her.

'What are you doing here, Snow?' I ask in a conversational tone, as if I was asking her to pass the salt.

'I feel cold. So cold,' she says, and indeed her teeth are chattering.

'Here, let me warm you,' I say without making any move towards her.

'No,' she whispers. 'Nobody can warm me. I saw them again tonight.'

'Saw who?'

'The bastards who did this to me.'

'What did they do, Snow?' I ask, the blood in my veins turning to ice.

'This,' she says, and opens her thighs. She makes a fist with her small hand and is about to hit her own exposed sex when I grab it and stop her. I stare at her.

'No,' I say. 'You can't hurt that. That's mine.'

She doesn't fight.

'That's yours?' she asks in a small voice.

'That's mine, Snow. I don't care what happened before this, but that is now mine.'

'I was a virgin and they didn't even use a condom,' she sobs.

'Oh Snow,' I say, and feel tears start prickling my own eyes. The sensation is novel. I haven't cried since the day I found out they slit my father's throat. I blink the tears away quickly and gather her into my arms. At first she thrashes and hits out instinctively, but I hold her tight.

'I got you,' I tell her. I got you, babe. No one will ever hurt you again.'

'Something terrible happened to me in that hotel room, and I cannot tell you about it because it was too horrible.' Her body shakes with emotion.

I hold her tightly. 'It's not your fault this happened to you. Nothing you did made you responsible for your assault. Shhhh ... Shhh ... Shhhh' I whisper in her ear until her struggles cease and she is limp in my arms.

I slip one hand under her knees and the other around her back and carry her back to my bed. I lay her down, and when I try to disengage myself she clings desperately to me, so I sit on the bed and hold her. After a while she starts sobbing.

'Break open, Snow. Cry all you want. You deserve compassion from yourself. You are always being compassionate to others. Now be compassionate to yourself. You deserve this moment of grace. You're OK. You'll always be ok. You have nothing to be ashamed of. This world is a better place because you are in it.'

Then falteringly, with great shame in her beautiful eyes, she tells me what happened.

And my blood boils.

Twenty-four

SNOW

The first thing I saw when I came to that night was the ceiling. It was off-white and sort of fuzzy around the edges and I couldn't understand why. And then it came back to me that I had been very unwell. And Kim and Andrew must have brought me here because they couldn't take me to the YHA. My mouth felt numb, strange, and I was freezing cold. I realized almost immediately that I was so cold because I was completely naked.

That was when I heard voices. Men's voices.

I tried to move my head to find the owners of the voices, but I couldn't. My entire body was frozen. Not even my little finger could lift away from the bed. Desperately, I swung my eyes around. I was in a hotel room, not a good one, but not a grubby one either. It was one of those family rooms with a double bed and a single in it. I was lying on the double. The curtains were pulled shut, and I could see many bottles of alcohol on a desk in the corner of the room, and the men in different stages of undress were actually crowding around it and snorting lines from the table.

There were six of them. They had different accents. The only impression I had was that they were all excited. I could sense it in their voices and the air. It was like they were at a party. One, I could tell by his accent, was German. I'm not one hundred percent sure, but it was possible one of the men was Middle Eastern. Three were definitely European, but I was certain that none of them were English. There was an Indian man too.

When I first spotted him, I had the ridiculous idea that I could plead with him. Tell him I, too, was from India. Ask him for mercy.

Then they were on top of me until it felt as if they were thrusting hot metal rods. Burning. Burning. But I couldn't scream. I couldn't do a thing. Not one thing. They pinched my nipples. They were animals. Licking. Biting. Hurting. Their faces were alive with lust.

The whole time I could hear them talking to me; calling me a dirty little bitch. You like this don't you. You want more. Take that, slut. Give it to the bitch. Fill her up. I was like a life-size doll that they could bend, twist, flip, and pull according to their wishes.

Months later when more and more memories came back and I researched it on the net, I found other women with the same story to tell. I pieced their memories with mine and a picture emerged. Strangers went onto the dark net and paid to gang rape a woman in a hotel in London. I even remembered that one of them said he had flown into London for the express purpose of raping a drugged woman. The others had presumably included it as part of their holiday experience.

For hours they used my body. Every orifice. Even though I could not move a single muscle I felt it all. Tears continuously flowed out of my eyes, but they didn't care. They just carried on one at a time, two at a time, three at a time. For hours and hours. I was a human toilet.

I thought the night would never end.

But I won't carry on with any more gory details, you can use your imagination.

I don't know exactly when they left, but when I came back from the darkness I was alone. I wanted to get up and run away. I was afraid they would come back but I could not move. I didn't give up. I just kept on trying to move my finger. I knew Andrew or Kim had spiked my drink and it would wear away.

An hour or so later, I could move my fingers and my mouth. With all my strength I waved my fingers and, slowly, movement came back to me. I was so frightened and so filled with adrenaline that I did not feel any pain at all then. When I sat up, I saw that my entire body was blue-black with bruises and bite marks, and there was quite a lot of blood between my thighs.

When I tried to stand I fell over. My legs felt like they did not belong to me. They were like jelly. The whole time I was terrified the men would come back. I started to crawl and pull myself along the carpet. I dragged my body to the door, but my hands were almost useless. Crying with frustration, I finally managed to open the door and I was in the corridor. It was empty and silent. At the end of the corridor I could see a lift.

I had gone beyond fear. My mind was blank. All I had to do was reach the lift doors and someone would help me. The carpet burned my legs and elbows, but I felt no pain. Unable to see clearly, I pressed both the buttons on the consul. When the lift doors opened I saw a man standing inside it. He looked down at me with a frown. There were other people around him, but my vision was strangely blurred and I could only see his face.

For a brief moment I was afraid again. There was something about him that frightened me. I opened my mouth to scream, but no sound came out.

I fainted at his feet.

That man was Lenny.

Twenty-five

SHANE

For a seed to achieve its greatest expression, it must come completely undone. The shell cracks, its insides come out and everything changes. To someone who doesn't understand growth, it would look like complete destruction.

—Cynthia Occelli

'Lenny?' I repeat in disbelief. I am in such a rage that it is difficult to keep my voice from shaking.

'Yes, Lenny,' she says quietly. 'The hotel belonged to him. He was on his way up to the suite he keeps for himself on the top floor.'

I frown, but I don't share my thoughts about Lenny. 'So Lenny took you to the police?'

She shakes her head. 'No, he took me to his suite and when I woke up I didn't want to go to the police. I was in a state of shock.' She makes a small noise. 'To be honest I think I was a little mad. And I was so sick from the drugs they had given me.'

'Didn't he take you to the hospital?'

'No, he brought a doctor to the suite. The doctor cleaned me up and prescribed some pills.' She stops and says, 'I think I need one now. Could you please get it for me?'

I go out to the living room and look in her purse. The pills are in a transparent plastic tub with a white screw top. There is no label on the tub. I unscrew it, take one pill out, and slip it into my trouser pocket. Then I fill a glass with water and take it and the container of pills to her. I shake one out and hold it out to her.

'It doesn't have the label. What is it?'

She puts the pill on her tongue and swallows it down with water. 'I don't know what it is, but it helps me.'

I take the glass and put it on the bedside table.

'So,' I say. 'You never went to the police.'

'No. Lenny said it would have been too late anyway. They would all have left the country by then. Plus, I can't remember their faces clearly. They blur in my mind. Once, I hated them and I wanted them to be punished. I used to pray that something horrible would happen to them, but I don't think about them anymore.'

I look at her swollen face. 'They never used a condom. Have you had yourself tested for any diseases?'

She shakes her head. 'Lenny always uses a condom and that is why I am very careful with you too.'

I don't feel the kind of burning anger that I would have expected to feel. Inside, I am cold as ice. I want Snow, and I want revenge. And I will have both.

'Do you understand now why I am indebted to Lenny? I was so broken and he fixed me. I couldn't go home. I was too ashamed. And I couldn't hold down a job. He gave me money and protection. And all he asked for in return, when I was a little better, was … a bit of comfort.'

'Fuck it. You don't owe him anything, Snow. He abused you.'

She shakes her head. 'No, no, you don't understand. There is an Old English word, *bereafian*. It means to deprive of, take away, seize, rob. That is what happened to me. I was seized and robbed. But not of my purse or money. I suffered shocking loss. Indescribable. It was so horrific that when I dragged myself out of that room I was like a dead person. I fell unconscious at his feet. He picked me up and took care of me, but I can't even remember that time properly anymore. It is a blur.'

She frowns trying to remember.

'It's as if there is opaque heavy glass between me and those images of me scrabbling around the floor like a spider, hissing, furious, ... helpless. I stopped eating. All I really remember is outside it rained and rained and my rage was like a dully burning metal inside me. The agony was so total, time stopped rushing forward. There was no future. For months I never went outside. If not for my pills and Lenny, I would not have survived. Can you believe I bathed only when Lenny marched me to the shower and turned on the tap?'

She looks at me beseechingly.

'He was patient with me for months. I was like a mad woman. I slept all day with the curtains drawn. Everything terrified me. I couldn't even walk down to the corner shop. He saw me through it all without ever giving up on me. The first time I felt human again was in spring when I was walking on the pavement and I saw an earthworm writhing on the concrete.'

She smiles mistily.

'I crouched down and Citra's face came into my mind. "When you see a worm on a pavement, remember that it is having a bad day. Pick it up and put it on some grass or soil." So I carefully picked it up and carried it in my cupped hands all the way to the park. I left it on the grass, and the simple act of how it had burrowed into the cool earth still made sense when the rest of the world did not. I felt then that there was order in the world. I was having a bad day, but I would find grass and earth again. One day.'

'He should have taken you to a proper doctor and had you examined and treated. Instead he caged you, manipulated you and used you.'

'It's not like that, Shane. It was not his decision. I didn't want to see anyone. Not even a doctor. I was too ashamed. I didn't want another person seeing or touching me. He brought me medicine.'

'I am almost certain that what he gave you is not proper medicine. The bottle doesn't even have a pharmacy label on it. Knowing him it's bound to be something that helped to make you even more dependant on him. And then he locked you away in an apartment and did not allow any other man to touch you, while he availed himself to any number of whores he wanted. How did you ever think he was helping you?'

Twenty-six

LENNY

Come on. The lift doors opened, and this exotic, raven-haired, green-eyed beauty literarily crawled up to my feet and gave herself to me. I didn't ask for it. I didn't arrange for her to be kidnapped and raped and thrown to grovel at my feet.

I mean, what would you have done?

Taken her to the police and walked away?

No fucking way. I'm no Good Samaritan.

Besides, I didn't want the police crawling all over my hotel, minding my business for me. The way I saw it, she was like a gift from heaven. Yeah, of course she was covered in bruises. Jesus, the bastards sure worked her good. Six, she told me later. But even with her entire body covered in bruises she was a raving beauty.

So I took her back. I patched her up. You have to understand she was no walk in the park. She was bloody, fucking hard work. Those first few months were no joke. She wandered around mute and half-crazy. She used to try to scrub herself clean, scratching her skin like an animal until it was raw and bleeding. And then there were the nightmares, the waking up in the middle of the night screaming in agony as if she had a wound in her body and her soul was pouring out, the shaking, the crying, the catatonic trances.

But the funny thing is, I never thought to throw in the towel. She had been given to me. And in this shitty life it's not often that you are given anything that special. You have to fucking fight for every last inch, let alone a jewel like her.

My father used to say, you give a donkey a page from a fine book and it will eat it, you give a child the same page and it will scribble all over it, you give a learned man that page and he will read it. I always knew she was a page. The donkeys had tried to eat her. I knew I could never read her. But I could scribble on her for a while.

It took time before I could scribble on her. Months.

But the day came when I could part those white thighs and enter her. Fucking her was different than with any other woman. I can't explain it. When I fucked her it was like fucking a child or a dumb animal. Not that I have ever fucked either. Just what I imagine it could be like. She never responds because she doesn't enjoy sex. She never climaxes and I never try to make her enjoy it. You see, I kind of like that she gets no pleasure from it. It's kinda virginal and pure. Like in the olden days, when they grinned and bore it. That kind of woman doesn't exist anymore.

Now every fucking bitch is shoving a ten-inch vibrator up her wet cunt every chance she gets. No class at all. And I'm all about class. It's perverse, yet it excites me to think she doesn't want me in her body, but she allows me to because she's grateful. Because she belongs to me. The way your pet belongs to you. You can do anything because you're the master.

I enjoy being the owner of such an exquisitely beautiful human. I'd buy her a collar and take her out to town to show her off if I could. Maybe one day I will. I'll take her to one of those kinky places where the men come bringing their women on leashes. And the women have to crawl on their hands and knees like dogs. The problem with those clubs is that you have to share. And I don't think I could do that. Mine is the only dick that's going up that girl.

Everywhere we go I see men looking at her hungrily, but I don't see any interest in her eyes. Sometimes though, not often, maybe once or twice, I feel her wanting to fly away. She gets that look in her eyes, and those times I remind her again of that day I found her. I deliberately make her cry.

I make her realize that she's irreparably damaged and she needs me. I'm the one who took care of her. I'm the only one she can trust. In the beginning I used to tell her that no other man would have her once they knew she was so defiled. I mean six men in one session. No man wants that.

But don't ever make the mistake of thinking I don't care about her. When I don't see her for a few days I start to miss her. I miss her distant smile. I miss the taste of her skin. I miss her vacant eyes while I am pounding away into her dry little pussy. I miss the smell of her hair. I miss the way her tears roll down her cheeks.

Yeah, I'm missing my little pet right now.

Twenty-seven

SNOW

The sound of a woman's voice wakes me up. I sit up. There is a toweling robe laid on the bed for me and I slip it on and go to the door. I open it a crack and hear a peal of laughter. She comes into view and I realize that she must be a relative. She has exactly the same coloring as Shane, tall with long dark hair. She is visibly pregnant. Since she can't be much older than me, she must be his sister, Layla.

'Well, where is she then?' the woman demands. 'I'm dying to meet her.'

'Asleep, but she won't be for much longer if you carry on laughing like a demented hyena,' Shane says.

I open the door and step outside. 'Good morning,' I say awkwardly.

'You're up,' Shane says with a smile.

'Yeah,' I say. I feel embarrassed and strange. After last night I don't know how Shane feels about me anymore.

All I know is that I was awful. Enough to put the most ardent suitor off. I vaguely remember falling asleep in his arms after taking my pill.

'So you're, Snow. I'm Layla, Shane's sister.'

'Hi,' I say with a small wave.

'I hope he hasn't told you anything horrid about me, because I have far worse secrets about him,' she says and, coming up to me, envelops me in a huge hug. She is definitely not the typical reserved, stiff upper-lipped, English person. In fact, she is very much like an Indian, who has no real concept of personal space. I, of course, immediately warm towards her.

'I've brought you some clothes. They're not new, but they are clean. I brought all stretchy stuff so it'll be like free size. Of course, you'll have to fold up the jeans.'

'Thank you. I'll just change into them and join you,' I say, taking the bag she is holding out to me.

'I'll be in the kitchen having a bit of ice cream,' she says.

I look at Shane and he raises his eyebrows as if to say, are you OK?

I nod and, looking at Layla, say, 'Great I'll see you guys in the kitchen.' I go back to the room and close the door, but not all the way. I hear Layla say with a laugh, 'I thought you were never going out with any girl with white skin and black hair.'

'And I thought you were never going out with BJ,' he retorts.

I don't catch her answer as they disappear into the kitchen.

I dress in the T-shirt and skinny jeans that she brought. The jeans are too long so I fold them at the top. I quickly brush my teeth with the brand new toothbrush Shane has left by the sink. I comb my fingers through my hair and make for the kitchen.

Layla is sitting at the counter eating ice cream and talking animatedly about her son. She turns towards me. 'Would you like to have some ice cream?'

'Layla,' Shane says pointedly. 'Snow is not weird. She doesn't want ice cream for breakfast, besides, don't you have somewhere else to go?' he asks.

Layla slides off the seat with a sigh. 'I don't have anywhere to go to, but all right I'll go.' She grins at me. 'I'll grill you at my mum's house at Sunday lunch.'

'Oh, for God's sake, Layla,' Shane says exasperatedly.

'Byeeeee,' she says, and walks out of the kitchen. We hear the front door close behind her.

'How do you feel this morning?' Shane asks.

'Yeah, fine,' I say uncomfortably.

'Good. What do you want to have for breakfast?'

'Shane?'

'Yes.' He appears solicitous. A stranger.

I dig my fingernails into my palm. Wow! It's been a long time since I did that. The pain of my fingernails dulls the other pain. The pain of thinking he regrets ever hooking up with me. Lenny accidentally revealed once that other men wouldn't want me after they knew about what had happened to me, and I grew up in India where the shame of being raped actually causes women to be killed. He always claimed he didn't care, but other men might not be able to take it. Some men are simply not strong enough to cope with such horror. Some marriages even break up after a rape.

'I'm ... sorry about last night. I haven't had a flashback in months. It must have been the shock of what happened outside the club that triggered it.'

'Don't apologize for last night,' he says harshly, striding towards me and stopping a foot away from me. 'You have nothing to apologize for.'

'Erm ... OK,' I say, taken aback by the sudden fury in his voice. 'Er ... Thanks for asking your sister to bring me these clothes. I'll just pop back to my apartment and get some of my clothes later this afternoon ... if you still want me to stay, that is,' I say uncertainly, my gaze searching his face for clues of reluctance or a change of mind.

His eyes are like frozen blue orbs and his words as sharp as razors. 'I've *not* changed my mind, and you're never going back there again. I've thrown away your red dress. From now on I pay for everything that goes on your back.'

'Oh,' I exclaim, stunned by the intensity of his words. The more I know him the more I realize that beneath the easygoing charm and humor lurks a much darker beast.

His expression warms suddenly, confusing me. 'Now, do you want blueberry pancakes, scrambled eggs and smoked salmon, a banana smoothie, waffles, warm brioche with butter and cherry-plum jam, or a full English for breakfast?'

'Oh!' I exclaim, overwhelmed by the choice. 'I usually just have toast or cereal.'

He smiles. 'Yeah, I've got that too.'

I pause. Why should I have the same old boring thing? 'Actually, the brioche with butter and cherry-plum jam sounds really good.'

His eyes twinkle. 'It's one of my favorites too. Sit and talk to me while I get it.'

'Can I help?'

'Nope,' he says immediately.

So I sit at the able while he moves about preparing our breakfast. Soon the entire kitchen fills with the lovely yeasty aroma of toasting brioche and hot coffee. He brings the food to the table and I realize just how hungry I am.

I watch Shane's large, capable hands tear apart the soft loaf and the steam rise from the middle of the bread. I watch him spread the jam on the pastry, not across the whole half, but just a corner. And on top of the jam a shaving of cold butter. Then I watch his strong white teeth bite into the piece and his sensual enjoyment of the complex tastes in his mouth, cold, warm, sweet, starchy, buttery, plummy.

As I watch him, I feel the thaw inside me. Ever since that horrible day I could not connect with anyone. I was frozen inside. I just felt utterly alone. Kim's betrayal made the whole world frightening. I knew I could trust no one. Everyone wanted something from me. Even Lenny.

For the first time today I feel something deep and real.

I feel love. Great love for the man sitting next to me.

After we eat, I look at him. Somehow I have to explain away last night. I can't just leave it like that.

'About last night.'

He lifts his head and looks at me expressionlessly.

 629

'I know I was downright pathetic in the bathroom yesterday, but I guess I'm not a very strong person. I—'

'Not a very strong person? What the hell are you talking about? Fucking hell, Snow. You're one of the strongest women I know. You were strong even when your whole world was crumbling beneath your feet.'

He shakes his head.

'You came to England on your own in search of a dream. That's brave enough to start with. And then you endured an ordeal at *nineteen* that could have sent a grown woman mad. And the best part, you survived it all on your own, without any professional help, any proper medication or counseling to lessen the pain, and under the manipulative and insidious influence of a total psychopath.

'That, in my book, makes you an incredibly strong person. Strength doesn't always mean a woman never cries or has a breakdown, or a woman who never gives an inch to man because that could be interpreted as her being weak. But it definitely means a woman who quietly rebuilds her life after it is shattered through no fault of her own. You're a fucking warrior, Snow.'

Twenty-eight

SNOW

That day, Shane takes me shopping for some clothes. He seems very familiar with the art of taking a woman shopping. I quickly buy some cosmetics, a bottle of perfume, a pair of jeans, a couple of T-shirts, underwear, and tights.

'Right, you need something jazzy for tonight,' he says, and takes me to a boutique where the two assistants seem to know him very well.

He makes me try on three different dresses and buys them all.

'Have you got something for her to put her lipstick into?' he asks the girls.

They come back with three different evening bags and he nods approvingly. Afterwards, we have lunch in a cozy little café nearby, then drop by a shoe shop to get shoes for all three dresses.

'Tired?' he asks.

'A little.'

'Come on, I'll take you home and you can have a little nap. I've got errands to run.'

He drops me back to the apartment then goes out. I plan to clean the place, but someone has come in while we were out and cleaned the place thoroughly. I try to read a book, but I am too wound up. Despite everything Shane says about Lenny, I know I still owe him an explanation. No matter what anybody says, Lenny took care of me.

I sit down and write a letter to him. I tell him that I have fallen in love with someone else. I tell him that I will always care for him and be grateful for what he did for me. I tell him that one day we'll be friends. And then I tear the letter to shreds and throw it away. I know what is bothering me.

There is no happy ending to this story. Lenny is going to be furious with me. And he's going to want to know who has taken his possession away from him.

I sit on the couch and feel shivery, and frightened for Shane. What if Lenny hurts Shane? I know Shane can use his fists, I saw that in the car park, but this is different. Shane is too sweet to take on a ruthless gangster like Lenny. I see it in the eyes of all the people we meet, how wary they are of him. They wouldn't be afraid if there was nothing to fear.

By the time Shane comes back I am in a real state. I have convinced myself that Lenny is going to kill him. That I should never have started seeing Shane in the first place. Tears are pouring down my face. When he walks through the door he immediately comes to my side

'What's wrong?' he asks.

'He'll kill you, Shane. I know Lenny. He'll kill you,' I babble hysterically.

He sits back on his heels and looks at me. He reaches out a hand and strokes my wet cheeks. 'Do you really have so little faith in me?'

'You don't understand. I know him. I know what he is capable of.'

'Then rest easy that you don't know what I am capable of.' And something lurks in his eyes.

'Are you going to hurt him?'

'That's up to him.'

I cover my face with my hands. I can't help feeling so guilty. That all of this is my fault.

'I should have walked away from Lenny first. And then come to you. How stupid I've been,' I sob.

He pulls my hands away from my face. 'I couldn't have waited that long. This is not your fault. I chased you. You were minding your own business. I knew what I was getting into.'

'Nobody's going to get hurt?'

'Unless someone fucking asks for it,' he says.

'Promise?'

He smiles a little sadly. 'Promise. Now go put on one of your new dresses. I'm taking you out on the town.'

I slip on a knee-length black dress with diamante straps, a tight bodice and a flaring skirt and go out to meet him in the living room.

He smiles softly. 'Beautiful. Just beautiful,' he says with great satisfaction in his voice.

We go out to dinner at Layla's husband's restaurant. Again we are treated as if we are VIPs. Nothing is too much trouble. The food is excellent and Shane is courteous and attentive, but he seems distant and preoccupied. And I realize that since my meltdown last night we haven't had sex.

I start to wonder if Lenny was right. Knowing I have been gang raped would put even the most persistent man off. I start looking for little signs of change in his behavior. Is he looking at that woman? Why is he not reaching for my hand? Did he just avoid my eyes?

Then why is he helping me? Is it because he is just a nice guy and he doesn't want to hurt my feelings? The more I think about it, the clearer it becomes that ever since last night he is definitely more distant. He has hardly touched me all day and all throughout our meal.

A woman comes up to him.

'Shane,' she coos.

'Bella,' he replies coldly.

'You were going to call me,' she says, one beautifully plucked eyebrow raised.

I feel a burning in my gut. What a cheek? I am sitting here and she is hitting on my man. That brings me up short.

Maybe he is not my man. And the thought brings tearing pain. For a year I felt no pain at all no matter what someone did or said, and now the ability to feel something more than just baffled sorrow at what happened to me that day in the hotel room is back. My body is responding to external stimulai again.

Shane shrugs his wide shoulders in a gesture of casual disdain. 'I figured that if I didn't call back you'd get the message.'

She turns to me. 'Don't gloat too much honey. He'll do the same to you one day.' Her voice is acid.

I feel the blood drain from my face.

'Sharpen your claws elsewhere, Bella,' he says menacingly, rising to his feet. A gesture meant to dominate by his sheer height and presence.

'Fuck you both,' she spits, and flounces away.

Shane resumes his seat. 'Sorry about that,' he says, his eyes seeking mine.

'It's OK,' I say lightly, but Bella's words are burned into my mind.

⋐⦿⦾⦿⋑

After dinner, Shane takes me to a club called Gibran.

'I've got to see someone quickly,' he tells me.

There is a long queue outside, but he leads me to the front and the bouncers come forward quickly.

'Good evening, Mr. Eden,' they greet politely, unhooking the red ropes, and standing back respectfully.

Inside we are whisked past the entrance ticket queue by a small middle-eastern man. 'This way, Mr. Eden,' he says, and leads us through the doors.

He looks up to Shane. 'How are your brothers doing?'

'Good, thank you. How's the family?' Shane replies.

'Very well, thank you.'

Hard rock music pulsates around us. Shane keeps a firm hand on the small of my back as we make our way through a sea of heaving, sweating bodies until we come to a VIP area. A group of people are sitting in a booth with low couches. There are brass lamps on the table.

My eyes are immediately drawn to a powerfully built man. He has shoulder length hair and eyes that are so light blue they look like chips of ice. He has a nasty scar that starts just under his eye and it zigzags down one side of his face. He is wearing a black vest that shows off an enormous tattoo of a fierce cobra with its hood and mouth open. It begins at the top of his muscular shoulder, its long body twisting around the length of his arm and hand, and its tail ending at the base of his wrist.

He looks menacing, very menacing.

He is leaning back on the low couches, but looking as relaxed as an animal about to strike. When he sees Shane, his mouth twists slightly. He makes a movement with his fingers and two half-naked girls entwined around him on either side stand and move away. His disregard for them as human beings is so blatantly callous it takes my breath away.

Shane pulls me forward and the man's eyes flick over to me quickly.

His eyes are both stunning and scary. I find myself instinctively moving close to Shane. Shane looks down on me, and smiles reassuringly. The man sits forward, the movement so quick, that again I am reminded of a striking cobra. When he stands he is as tall as Shane, but he vibrates with a kind of dangerous energy. They bump fists, only it looks nothing like any fist bump I have seen. This one bristles with their combined energies. If Shane is white magic, this man is black magic. The difference is that stark.

'Will you have a drink?' he drawls. His voice is deep and his accent reminds me of Nikki, the nasty blonde I met in the ladies' toilet at Eden.

'Thanks, Zane, but I can't stay,' Shane says. 'Just checking to see that everything is going forward as planned.'

'Everything's good to go.'

'Good. Thanks, man. I owe you one.'

Zane smiles and nods slowly, and that slow nod makes me shiver. I can tell that the day will come when he will arrive to collect for whatever favor it is he is doing for Shane.

We walk away, my heart fluttering with tension.

As soon as we are out of earshot I tug Shane's sleeve. 'I don't like that man.'

Shane stops abruptly, leans down and takes my face in his hands. 'Listen to me, Snow. I trust Zane with my life, and so must you if anything happens to me. I brought you here so you could see him and he could see you. You will be financially well off and he will protect you from Lenny.'

My heart crashes with horror and I cannot stop the fear in my voice. 'Are you expecting something to happen to you?'

'No, this is a contingency plan.'

I frown. 'What about Jake? Why am I not going to him?'

'I don't want Dom or Jake to get involved. But especially Jake. He has been taking care of us for his whole life and that's enough. He has a family of his own now and it is time he put them first. No, Zane will sort it out. He is being well compensated for anything he does.'

'You're scaring me, Shane.'

'Don't be scared. I'm just writing my will. Not because I expect to die tomorrow, but because if I should, I want to go to my grave knowing that those I ... care about are protected.'

'Why did you choose Zane?'

'Because he is more, far more dangerous than Lenny.'

'And he's a friend of yours?'

'As friendly as you can get with the Russian mafia,' he says dryly.

'Shit, Shane. I thought you said you were not a gangster.'

'I'm not. But like I said, I know people.'

Thirty

SNOW

https://www.youtube.com/watch?v=k3Fa4lOQfbA

When we get back to Shane's apartment I am feeling tense and unsure of myself. Shane has showed no signs of wanting me sexually. As if all the passion has cooled since my meltdown.

'Nightcap?' he offers, walking into the sitting room.

'OK,' I say, following him in.

'What do you want?' he asks.

'Whatever you're having is fine.'

'I'm having Cognac.'

'Great.' I perch at the edge of the sofa and watch him pour our cognac.

He comes over and holds out my glass and then sits next to me, but not too close. There is a good three inches between my thigh and his knee. He leans back into the seat. I lick my lips and turn back to look at him.

'I don't have to stay here, you know. I feel strong enough to make it on my own now. I could get a room ...'

He frowns. 'What on earth are you talking about?'

I shrug. 'Well, ever since last night you are different. You're friendly and protective and kind, but it's as if you don't want me anymore, sexually, I mean.'

He stares at me incredulously. 'What?' he explodes. 'You think I don't want you?'

I bite my lip. 'It's not like what it was in France, is it?'

He sits forward and shakes his head in wonder. 'What a crazy thing to think?' It's not like France because I didn't want to rush you. Can't you tell I'm fucking fighting with myself to keep my hands off you because I don't know if you are ready after last night?'

'I'm ready now,' I whisper.

He smiles slowly, his eyes glinting. The old Shane is back. 'Prove it by doing a strip dance.'

'You own a strip club. I'd have thought you'd be bored with that by now,' I say with a smile. In truth I want to shout with joy. He still wants me.

'I want to see *you* dance.'

'Now?' I ask with my eyebrows daringly lifted.

'Can't think of a better time.'

'OK.'

He stands and walks to his music system and chooses something.

'What song have you chosen?'

'*Je T'aime ... Moi Non Plus* by Serge Gainsbourgh and Jane Birkin.'

'God, isn't that like a really old number? My mother used to listen to it,' I say, surprised.

He grins at me. 'My grandfather had a thing for Bridgette Bardot and Jane Birkin. I've got all kinds of boyhood fantasies around this song.'

I laugh. 'Do you know what the title actually means?'

'It translates as, 'I love you ... Me neither.'

'Interesting,' I say.

'That's what couples in the throes of lovemaking say to each other,' he says with a wink.

'Right. I'll be back in a minute,' I say crisply, and taking my glass of cognac with me and swaying my hips with attitude, walk to the bedroom. I close the door and go to his wardrobe. I pull out a white shirt. Quickly, I undress. I leave my panties on, but take off my bra. I put on his shirt and leave it unbuttoned to the waist. I don't do the last two end buttons either. Then I roll up the sleeves until my wrists show. Keeping my high heels on, I choose a blue striped tie and knot it loosely around the collar of Shane's shirt. I put on my new super shiny lip gloss. Then I look around the drawers and find a cap. I arrange it at an angle on my head and look in the mirror.

The look is just what I wanted. A little bit 'je ne sais quoi.'

I finish my glass of cognac, Dutch courage and all that, and walk out to the living room door and pop my head around the doorframe. He presses the remote on his hand and the music comes on. The old fashioned guitar cords of rhythm and bass guitars and snare drums fills the spaces between us.

'Je t'aime, Je, t'aime,' whispers in her breathy and ethereal voice, so high it is almost the unbroken voice of a little choirboy. But extremely erotic all the same.

I drape myself around the doorframe and, raising my leg slowly, caress the door with my foot. I step into the room and teasingly lift one edge of his shirt exposing the top of one thigh and a glimpse of my black lace panties. He doesn't know my sex is already wet. I catch his eyes and he is staring at me, mesmerized, and that gives me the confidence to go on.

I tug at the tie and it comes off. Holding it in my hand, I twirl it before flinging it at him. He catches it mid-air.

I face away from him and, swaying my hips, let the shirt drop off one shoulder, exposing bare flesh. I drop the other end and the shirt falls to my mid back. I turn my head back and look at him and smile.

The look on his face, the lust in his eyes, is priceless.

Very slowly and still gyrating, I let the shirt fall farther still, until it is skimming the top of my bottom. I play with the material seductively before dropping it lower still. Right on the fleshiest part, I rub the material in a sawing motion. Then slowly I drop it further until my entire ass is exposed. I quickly unbutton the shirt and slip it completely off. Holding it at arm's-length away, I allow it to dangle on one finger before letting it drop to the floor.

I gyrate the top half of my body in a large circle, like the belly dancers in France, so that all my hair falls forward and covers my breasts. Then I turn around and shimmy my hips as I walk towards him.

I put one leg on the sofa arm and immediately his eyes move to my pussy. He can see that the crotch of my panties is soaking wet. I put my hands around my neck and lift my hair so that my breasts are on display. The tips are hard and ready. Then I let my hair fall back into place again.

The heavy breathing noises of simulated sex start on the track.

I lick my glossed lips and he crooks a finger at me.

Instead of going to him, I make a pointing hand and slowly shake my finger at him while smiling regretfully.

He laughs, a deep sexy sound.

Lowering my hands, I begin caressing myself. Running them over my neck, circling my bare breasts, cupping the soft mounds of my bosom, and massaging them while my head is thrown back. I feel the ache in my nipples and rub my fingers lightly over the hardened swollen buds.

A sigh of pleasure escapes my mouth.

My hand roams lower and lower until it reaches the top of my panties. I linger tantalizingly before slowly letting my fingers slip behind the elastic. I look up to see his reaction. His gaze is transfixed on my fingers and he has a massive hard on. I move my finger in a circular motion. My breath hitches and becomes uneven.

'Aaaa ...' I gasp.

I move to the coffee table and sit perkily on it. I am only three feet away from him. I place both hands on my knees, and I draw them up and spread them so he can see just how wet the material of my panties are. Leaving my legs suspended

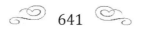

641

open, I lean back on one hand while the other slips over the crotch of my panties.

'Oooo ...' I coo, my voice as breathy as Jane Birkin's.

Hooking a finger into the side, I push the material out of the way and expose the glistening pink folds beneath. I let my clit protrude for a whole three seconds, or at least until his gaze comes up to meet mine. His eyes are dark with lust. There never was anything for me to worry about. He really, really, really still wants me.

He pushes forward suddenly and, grabbing my arm, pulls me forward, and with hair flying and legs flailing, I tumble into his arms. My cap slides down and falls in my lap.

'Hey,' I protest. 'I'm not finished.'

'Sorry. Time's up. I can't wait anymore,' he says, his right hand ripping my panties.

He steps out of his pants and pulls his briefs off in a hurry. He lowers his head onto the couch and, holding me by the waist, lifts me up and over his face. He maneuvers my crotch over his mouth and slowly lowers my wet pussy over his extended waiting tongue. The hot, velvety tongue penetrates my flesh, and I cry out with pleasure and squirm. Holding me tight, he pumps in and out of me a few times.

'Oh, mon amour,' Jane Birkin whispers and sighs.

Ah, the pleasure. My head rolls back with how good a tongue fuck feels. I have never had one. His tongue probes every inch of my pussy. Then he moves me back a little and licks my clit. I place both my palms over his head and just close my eyes, enjoying the erotic sensation. I moan deliriously when he clamps his mouth around my clit and sucks it until my muscles start contracting.

I explode in a terrific rush. As I climax, he moves me again and fills my pussy with his tongue and I come hard on it.

'Oh my God,' I breathe, as he carries on slurping at my dripping pussy.

He wraps his hands around my ribcage and starts to move my body down his. I realize that he is about to lower me onto his cock.

'We need a condom,' I whisper urgently.

He stills, his expression unreadable, then nods and, putting me aside, goes to get one. When he comes back he rolls it onto his shaft and looks at me.

'Open your legs and show me again,' he says.

I obey and he inserts a finger into it. Instantly, my muscles clench around it. He takes his finger out and holds it in front of my mouth.

'Suck it,' he says.

I open my mouth and suck his fingers, tasting the musky sweetness of my own juices. He sits down and, putting his hands around my waist, lifts me onto his lap. He lets my body hover over his cock. I hold it steady and he lowers me onto it. Slowly he travels deeper and deeper into my body.

'You belong to me now,' he says harshly. 'I'm going so deep into your body that you'll never even be able to think of another man inside you.'

And he does. He goes so deep I never thought anyone could go that far. My body breaks out in goose pimples and I move restlessly, lifting myself away from the relentless impaling, but he tightens his hold on my body and, keeping me tightly in place, carries on pushing me down onto his massive shaft.

'That's enough now,' I groan.

'No, you can take more,' he insists. 'Suck me in.'

So I let him go deeper and deeper into me until I can bear it no more and I cry out.

'You're mine,' he says, and pushes that last tiny bit deeper into me. And at that moment I feel him tense, his nostrils flaring as he climaxes hard, so hard he leaves fingerprints on my waist.

'I claim you as mine,' he growls gutturally in my ear.

Thirty-one

SHANE

I am jerked awake by the sound of the doorbell. I look at my watch. It's nearly two o'clock in the morning. Snow, too exhausted to fully awaken, stirs beside me and mumbles something.

'Go back to sleep,' I whisper, and vault out of bed.

I pull on my jeans and, with my heart hammering, I sprint to the door. I did not expect retaliation so soon. I'm not ready. I switch on the security video camera and see Jake standing there. For a second I blink. What the fuck is he doing here at this time? And then I know. I buzz him into the building and run my fingers through my hair. I really didn't want to deal with this now. I hear a soft rap on the door and I open it.

My brother comes in and he looks as fresh as a fucking daisy.

'Want a whiskey?' I offer.

'Yeah,' he says, and leads the way to the living room.

I pour us both large doubles. I down mine in one and move towards him with his.

'Is it true?' he asks.

'Is what true?'

'You're going with Lenny's girl.'

I sigh. 'Who told you?'

His mouth twists. 'Would you believe, one of your dancers?'

'Good old Nikki,' I say.

'Do you know I didn't believe it? You're going out with Lenny's girl.'

'Stop fucking calling her Lenny's girl. She's not his girl. She's mine.'

My brother stands and paces the floor. He seems barely able to keep his cool.

He turns suddenly to me. 'I never expected this from you. From a hothead like Dom, maybe. But you! You're too smart to pull a stunt like this. For God's sake, Shane. What are you thinking?'

'It's done now,' I say quietly.

'No, it's not. Walk away and I'll work something out with him.'

'No,' I say firmly. I have never said no to my brother. My respect, loyalty and love for him is so great I would truly lay down my life for him.

He frowns. 'Is she worth it?'

'Yes.'

He stares at me with disbelief 'Do you even realize what this means? You take his woman and you are declaring war. He's not going to ask you to put your hands up for a bare-knuckle fight. He's going to hire someone to knock you off when you least expect it.'

'I'm prepared to die for her,' I say seriously.

His eyes flash angrily. 'You're prepared to die for her?' he rages. 'What the hell, Shane? You're a fucking kid. You haven't even lived yet and you're prepared to die for her? No woman is worth that.'

'Would you die for Lily?' I ask quietly.

He starts and then he closes his eyes in defeat. 'How long have you known her?'

'A few days.'

'Right,' he says sarcastically.

'I know what I want, Jake.'

He sighs tiredly. 'All right, Shane. Leave it with me. I'll sort it out somehow.'

'I don't want you or Dom to get involved.'

He stares at me in surprise.

'This is my shit and I'll sort it out.'

I see a flash of temper in his eyes. 'Now you're really behaving like a kid. You can't handle Lenny on your own, Shane. He's a fucking snake. He'll clap you on the back and sincerely congratulate you for winning his girl and then bash your head in with a hammer two days later.'

'I have a plan.'

His eyes betray his disbelief that I could actually have a workable plan. I guess I'll be his snot-nosed kid brother forever.

'What's the plan?' he asks slowly.

'I've already said. I'm not involving you or Dom in this.'

He stands in frustration. 'Now you're being ridiculous. We're a family. When we fight as a family we're stronger.'

'Not this time. This time I go it alone.'

'Why? What are you trying to prove?' he asks with barely controlled impatience.

'Jake, ever since Dad died, you've been fighting all our battles for us. You put your own life on hold to keep this family together. Don't think I don't know how you used to come home and cut that cross into your own body. You did loathsome things so we could all eat. But now you have a family of your own. And for the first time you're happy. And I'd rather die than take that away from you.'

He sits down suddenly and gazes down at the floor. 'I can't let you deal with him on your own, Shane. You don't know what he's capable of. I do.' He looks up into my eyes. 'I used to work with him. And I know you can't take Lenny's girl and walk away unscathed.'

'He doesn't love her, Jake.'

'I know he doesn't love her, Shane. He's a psychopath. He doesn't love anyone but himself. But it's a pride thing. He'll take great pleasure in hunting you down and parading her on his arm in all the places where he's known.'

'Jake, you have to trust me when I say I know what I'm doing.'

'Oh, fuck,' he says, and runs both his hands through his hair. 'At least tell me what you're planning. I promise not to interfere.'

I look at him incredulously. 'You're not going to interfere? That's a laugh. You can as much stop yourself from getting involved as I can give her back to him.'

He gives a long sigh. 'Just remember I'm here for you. No matter what.' He sighs again. 'And whatever you are planning to do you better do it fast. Word gets around.'

No ... do not go around bragging, no ...
That you've stolen my heart
And I've nothing more to give...
-*The loser*, Enrique Iglesias

https://www.youtube.com/watch?v=tLcfAnN2QgY&list=RDG
MEMYvZjTda73N9ELoQo2TnYngVMtLcfAnN2QgY

Thirty-two

SNOW

After I hear Jake's words to Shane, I creep back to bed and, turning on my side, breathe deeply and evenly until I hear the front door close and Shane comes back into the room minutes later. He stands for a good few minutes looking down at me, but I just pretend to be sleeping. Finally, he goes to his side of the bed and quietly slips in.

For a long time he doesn't sleep. He just lays on his back staring at the wall. I can feel him thinking. Planning whatever it is that he is arranging. He never touches me. A last I hear his breath become even and he sleeps, but I never fall asleep again.

When morning comes, I carefully burrow under the cover and gently lick his sleeping cock. I am so gentle I do not startle him awake. I awaken him gently. His hand moves down and strokes my hair as his cock hardens with surprising rapidity. I take the beautiful, porcelain-smooth thing into my mouth, and let it slide along my tongue.

Oh! Shane.

It must have been delectable for him too, because he groans. A low, long sound of pure pleasure. He puts his hands around my head, gently forcing his cock to the back of my throat. His cock pulses and throbs in my mouth as if holding back from spilling its hot milk down my throat. I let him hold me there. If only he would hold me there forever. A few drops of pre-cum touch the back of my throat and I swallow them eagerly.

I drank my lover.

Let him be part of me. The action, the swallowing movement of my mouth excites him, and he begins to pull me up and down his shaft until his body clenches and he explodes. The force of his orgasm bursts inside my mouth, thick spurts of semen pouring into my throat. This I will take with me.

And I will remember this morning forever.

He pulls me up his naked, warm body and kisses me deeply. He rolls me onto my back and touches my naked pussy. He smiles slowly.

'You're wet,' he accuses.

'And what are you going to do about it then, big boy?' I ask.

'I'm going to eat you,' he says, and goes down on me.

My climax when it comes is bitter-sweet. Sweet because my whole body arches and strains with waves of pure bliss that feel as if they will go on forever. Bitter because they stop. And when they stop I lie drained and almost tearful.

Everything must come to an end.

But the pain of letting go is almost too much to bear. When you find something so beautiful you can't be expected not to cry when you are told you can't have it. Tears swim in my eyes. I blink them away.

He comes up my body and rests on his elbows. 'Hey, are you OK?' His eyes are concerned.

'Yeah, it was a really good orgasm,' I say, and I even manage to smile up at him.

He grins. 'How good was it?'

'Like a box of chocolates and a newborn German Sheppard puppy called Ghengis?'

'Really? As good as all that,' he teases.

'Yes, as good as that.'

He kisses the tip of my nose. 'Oh, Snow. There is just no one like you.'

'That's true,' I say, and kiss the tip of his nose. Against my thigh I feel his cock grow again.

'Really? You can't be wanting it again,' I say with a laugh.

'I'm fucking starving for you. But first, a trip to the toilet is in order. I don't want to be peeing inside you.'

'Ugh, you're disgusting.'

He gets off me laughing and disappears into the toilet. I watch his nude body walk away from me avidly. I will remember this.

When he comes back he sheaths his cock and pushes deep into me. I cry out. Not with pain or pleasure, but with gratitude. I will have this until the day I die. For the first time in my life I understood women who never remarried after they lost their love. Nobody else is good enough. Once you get that one person who is right for you, you will never again want anybody else.

Maybe I will marry. Actually, of course I will marry, my mother will make sure that I do, but I will never, never, never love like this again. Never.

And when we come we lock eyes with each other. It is beautiful.

'I'm yours,' I whisper, wrapping my legs around him tightly.

'Like you won't believe,' he whispers back.

Our bodies entwined, we lie there. It's hard to look into his eyes. They are so blue, so sincere, so awesome. I want to tell him. I want to tell him that I love him like I have never and will never love again, but I realize that my declaration would be neither here nor there.

So many women must have expressed that sentiment. So what if I do too. No, I won't. It will be my little secret. No one will ever know. Not him, not my mother or my father, or anyone. Maybe I will tell my grandchildren one day. If I have them. If I am not contaminated with HIV or even full-blown AIDS.

'Listen,' he says. 'I've got a full day today. Can you entertain yourself for a few hours?'

I smile. Can he see how much love I have for him? 'Sure, I'll clean the flat or something.'

'No, don't do that. I've got a woman coming in to do that. She'll come around about two this afternoon.'

'I'll read a book,' I say quietly.

'Good girl.' He pauses. 'Only thing, don't leave the apartment will you?' If you need anything just call me and I'll arrange for it to be brought to you.'

'I don't need anything, Shane.'

We get out of bed and use the bathroom together. It should have been mundane, a little domestic scene, but it is not. It is special. And it makes me think. How stupid we human beings are. We think that just because we do something all the time it is not special. It is. Just think that tomorrow is the last time you will ever brush your teeth with the one you love. See what I mean now?

So we brush our teeth and use the toilet. And he doesn't appreciate it, because for him it is just another boring task, and he thinks he will do it tomorrow with me too.

When he says, 'What do you want to have for breakfast?'

I know exactly what I want. 'I'll make breakfast,' I say.

He smiles. 'You don't cook.'

'You'll eat my burnt toast and like it,' I say with mock severity.

A strange look crosses his face, but I don't ask that thing that all lovers who are confident of their place in a relationship ask. 'What? What are you thinking of?

Instead, I go into the kitchen. I know exactly what I am recreating. I switch on the oven. 220 degree Fahrenheit. I take the cherry plum jam out of the fridge and put a few spoonfuls on two plates. I take the plates to the top of the oven and I put them there so they will be at room temperature when we have it.

I open the oven door and a blast of hot air hits me in the face. Perfect. I put the brioche rolls onto the metal tray and slide them in. I squeeze oranges and pour the juice into two glasses. I place the container of unsalted butter on the table and set it with knifes and spoons and forks. And the whole time Shane sits at the table and watches me with slightly raised eyebrows.

I take the brioches out of the oven, place them on the table, and sit next to him.

Shane looks at me. 'Thank you.'

'Bon appétit,' I say.

I watch him tear into the brioche. I watch the steam rise from the inside. I watch him cut a small bit of cold butter and lay it on the corner of the brioche that he has already spooned the cherry plum jam on. I greedily watch him put it into his mouth. I close my eyes because I know exactly how it feels and tastes in his mouth. Cold butter, hot pastry, warm jam.

I will remember this forever.

We eat and we drink and then it is time for him to leave. He doesn't kiss me deeply the way people who say goodbye do. He thinks he will be back in a few hours. He thinks I will be here when he comes home. He doesn't know I love him too much to allow him to ever risk his life for me.

I walk him to the door and kiss him goodbye as if I am kissing him before he goes to work. He walks out to the lift. I stand and watch him. The doors of the lift open. He goes in.

And my heart breaks.

I take a shuddering breath and suddenly he is coming out of the lift. He walks up to me, takes me in his arms and kisses me as if he will die without me, his tongue finding its way into my mouth. Entangling with mine. Pulling mine into his mouth. Sucking my tongue.

When he pulls away I am trembling.

'I'll finish that when I come back,' he says dragging his thumb along my lower lip.

I sigh and lay my head on his chest. I hear his heart beating. A steady fast rhythm. I will miss that.

'See you later,' I say.

'Alligator,' he says.

Then he walks into the lift and does not come out again.

I close the door and I go to sit at the kitchen table. I look at the breakfast things around me, the crumbs, the smeared jam, the knife slicked with butter, and my heart feels so heavy. I go into his study and I look around. Once I asked him why he lived in this apartment when he could afford something better. He said this was only a place to sleep in. He mostly lived in the country.

I sit at his desk and write him a letter. It is short. Goodbyes are best short. Besides, there is not much to say. Whatever it was, it's over now. Our time has run out. Soon the wind will blow me away. There is nothing else I can do. I touch my finger to my lips and lay it on the letter. There is a photo album on one of the shelves. I take it down and I turn the pages. His family are all there. I smile to look at their happy faces. How lucky they are.

I come upon one where he is alone. It is a recent one. He is on a boat looking like a film star. His hair wind-tossed, his beautiful body is tanned and relaxed and I wonder who took the picture. Carefully I take the photo out and, without bending it, I slip it into my purse.

Then I go into the bedroom. With my heart weeping, I stand there, memorizing the lingering smell of us, the sun falling on our tangled sheets. I'll dream of this little piece of heaven forever.

With a loud sob I run out of the apartment.

I take a taxi to my street and ask the driver to drop me off at the corner. Cautiously, I walk towards my apartment building. I look up at the windows and they are all shut, the curtains drawn close. Exactly how I left them. I cross the street and go into the building and up the stairs. The door opens behind me and I whirl around nervously, but it is only the woman from the floor above me. She nods and moves to the lift. I take the stairs.

The corridor is deserted.

I go to my door and listen. There is no sound inside. Very quietly I let myself in and stand for a moment. It is silent and still. Vellichor. Once I would have appreciated it. Now, I want nothing to do with it.

I walk into the middle of my apartment and look around at my scrupulously clean home. Everything in its place. Except for the smashed vase and the flowers scattered everywhere. So he has been here. And he is not happy.

I take a deep breath and steel myself.

Quickly, Snow.

Ignoring the mess, I hurry to the bedroom and unpick the mattress. I take out the money and stuff it into my bag. I don't take anything else. I am already at the door when I hear my phone ringing. I walk to it.

Lenny.

While it is still ringing, I take a piece of notepaper from a drawer and write on it. I thank him for everything he has done for me, but I tell him I have to return to India, back to my family. I say goodbye and I end it by saying.

Please don't ever try to contact me again.

I stand at the door and take one last look. The walls seem full of my grief. Other than that, there is nothing of me in here. Then I walk out of that place forever.

I take a taxi to Heathrow airport and buy the next trip to India, which is a noon Air India flight.

655

'You have a stop in New Delhi,' the woman tells me.

'That's fine,' I tell her.

At the check-in counter, the staff appears surprised and almost suspicious that I have no luggage. But I guess I don't look like a terrorist so they let me pass. I go through passport control and sit down on one of the seats. I feel numb.

On the flight I don't sleep. I close my eyes and think of Shane. I imagine him coming home and finding me gone. I imagine him calling one of his other women. I imagine, I imagine, I imagine. When the air stewardess comes around with the food trolley I have a raging headache. She gives me a couple of painkillers.

I take them and lie back in terrible pain.

Thirty-three

SHANE

We have a bitter north-westerly wind coming off the sea today.
The cat is curled up and I'm about to do the same for the afternoon.

I knew she was gone even before I got to the flat. I guess I knew from the moment she did not answer the phone. I open the door and the sound of silence is deafening. A pressing sensation of heaviness lodges itself in my chest. I walk to the kitchen table and there is a letter there. I leave it where it is and go out onto the balcony. I sit on a chair and, lifting my legs up, rest my crossed ankles on the railing.

I light a cigarette and take a long drag. Warm smoke fills my lungs. I blow the smoke out slowly. I don't think. I just smoke. When I'm done, I kill the cigarette and go back into the kitchen.

I pick up her letter and read it. Her writing is delicate and neat. Just like her.

Hey Shane,

Before I go, I wanted to say it was fun while it lasted, and that I really enjoyed myself with you. You're the most beautiful man I've ever met.

I want to thank you for trying to help me, but more important than that, I want to thank you for bringing me back from the dead. If you had not come into my life ... I

don't even want to think. You were like a lone star shining brightly on a dark night.

Anyway, I am returning to India today. In the end, that is my home. I will be safe there.

Take good care of yourself and thank you again, for everything. I'll never forget what you did for me.

Best,
Snow

p.s.
Nothing was a lie. I meant every word I said to you. Every breathless word.

I let the letter flutter down to the table surface, and go into my bedroom. I sit on the bed and, taking her pillow, bury my face in it. I inhale deeply and let the smell of her hair fill my brain. I should have known last night that she was not asleep. I was too caught up in my plan.

How can she go to India? She has no money.

And then a reluctant smile comes to my lips. She *had* money put away. Good girl. And though it cuts like a knife that she has gone, I am glad that she is out of harm's way. The best place for her at this moment is to be far away.

I put the pillow down and look at my watch. In three hours I have a meeting with Lenny. I'll get her back. This is just temporary.

Whatever it takes.

Beware...
Beware...
Of my hunger
And my anger
- Mahmoud Darwish

Thirty-four

SHANE

He sits behind his desk, a cigarette between his lips, and squints at me. Cigarette smoke rises between us. His hand moves and the sickening gleam of white makes me think of him touching her body, and in a flash, before I can stop my thoughts, they have run on like stallions in heat. Him on top of her. Her on her hands and knees, and him pushing into her pussy. His ugly fingers digging into her little bottom as he slams into her. My gut twists with the kind of raw, tearing jealousy I have never experienced before. I want to fucking shatter the smug bastard's jaw.

He looks at me expressionlessly. 'What do you want, Eden?'

'You already know what I want,' I say coldly.

He laughs, a short bark of disbelief. 'You're one cocky cunt. You think you can come in here and ask for my woman and I'll just hand her over to you? What do you think she is? A cheap bottle of whiskey that I can pass on to you? Huh?'

'She's not your woman,' I say calmly.

'If she's not my woman, then what the fuck are you doing here asking for my blessing to keep on fucking her?'

'I'm here because you're a cunt, Lenny.'

His eyes flash, but his voice is polite. 'You're Jake's kin so I'll ignore that insult, but I suggest you stop right there. This is going to get ugly real soon and before you know it, it'll be outright war.'

I push my chest out. 'She doesn't love you.'

'My jacket doesn't love me. But it's mine and I use it whenever I please.'

His sneering tone and his choice of words are calculated to infuriate me. I unclench my hands. He will not get to me.

'Well, she is not a jacket. She's a woman, and she can decide who she wants to be with.'

'Let me tell you why she belongs to me,' he says conversationally, as if he is telling an amusing little anecdote. 'When she crawled up to me and begged me to help her, her entire body was covered in bruises and bite marks. There were grip marks on her cheeks where they held her face and fucked her mouth. They had filled her belly with their semen. When she vomited I saw it. Globs of it.'

My face whitens and he sees it.

'Awww ... I've upset the pretty boy. Well fuck you. Her anus was bleeding. She used to scream when she went to the toilet. Her cunt was so swollen she couldn't walk straight for days. She was like a mute child for weeks. I took care of her. I ran the bath and fucking bathed her, asshole.'

He stops and tilts his face upwards.

'She'd wake up in the middle of the night screaming and thrashing, reliving it all. Sometimes she didn't recognize me. She was half mad. One day she ran down the street in the middle of winter stark naked. I ran out after her, tackled her to the ground, and brought her back. I won't tell you the rest of the stuff I went through with her. She was a broken bird. Totally helpless. I could have done anything I wanted with her, but I never touched her for months. So don't come here with all your youth and arrogance and pretend you know how to take better care of her just because you fucked her a few times. Because you fucking don't. You don't know what we've gone through together.'

He laughs bitterly.

'For the first time in my life I felt pity for another creature. She moved something in me. They say that everyone, even the worst killer, has a divine spark in him. She touched that spark. She made me good.'

661

For some strange reason I actually believe he is telling the truth. That at some level he cares for her. 'If you truly care for her then give her your blessing. Let her be happy.'

'With you?'

'Yes, with me.'

He leers. 'Why? Because you like the taste of her pussy? Eh?'

My jaw clenches. 'Don't talk about her like that.'

'Look at you. You think you've got it all figured out. You think it's a fucking song taking care of her? Are you ready for the flashbacks? Are you ready to be sitting in the middle of a classy restaurant as she freezes up like a fucking statue, or worse for her to start screaming her head off for no goddamn reason? Are you ready to chase her naked body down the road in the dead winter? Are you ready for her to start sobbing while you're fucking her?'

The desire to sock him one hard, so hard he'll never be able to talk again, is so strong I have to clench my fists and force myself to stand still. I take a deep calming breath. I will not let him rile me. No matter what, I have one objective and I'm not going to let anything stand in the way.

'I'm not here for relationship advice, Lenny.'

'You're a young punk. What do you know about relationships? Do you think I don't know about you? Tell me, what's the longest a relationship has lasted with you?'

'She's different. In exactly the same way she touched that spark in you, she touched something in me too.'

He laughs with suppressed fury. 'Yeah, I'm sure you believe that too.'

'It doesn't matter what you think,' I say quietly. 'I'm not here to convince you of anything. I'm here for the videotapes.'

'What videotapes?' he asks, but I see the furtive gleam in his eyes that he is unable to hide fast enough.

'The videotapes that show every occupant in the lift getting off on the second floor of your hotel.'

'What makes you think such videotapes exists?' he asks slyly.

I look at him steadily. 'You forget we know the same people. Everybody knows you have surveillance in your lift.'

He looks at me calmly. 'The tapes are my property. As is Snow.'

'You should have handed those tapes over to the police. It's an obstruction of justice.'

His eyes turn mean. 'Are you threatening me, boy?'

'No, I have less incentive to give the tapes over to the police than you have. I want those men.'

His eyes glitter. 'Revenge. Yes, I thought about it. But it seemed like a wasted effort when I already had the bird in my hand. In a way I owed them thanks.'

'Just give me the fucking tapes. You got no use for them.'

He shakes his head. 'You have a lot of balls coming here asking for this, asking for that. Who the fuck do you think you are?'

I'm done playing with this fuck. There is only one way to deal with a psychopath. And it's not by expecting empathy or giving it. The only way is to yank their greed chain. 'You know the sweet deal you cut in Amsterdam?'

His eyes are suddenly sharp.

'That's my deal. You get any ideas about not playing along and I'll pull the rug from under you. The Russians will be down by two million euros and guess who they'll be coming after? How many breaths do you think you can take before they catch up?'

Lenny smiles tightly and nods. 'Well played, boy. And you did all this for her.'

'Yes.'

'And you want my blessing?'

'No, I don't need your blessing, Lenny. I know what you are. You saw a broken bird and you didn't take it to a vet so that it he could properly heal it, or even attempt to punish the sickos who hurt it. You just took it into your home and caged it, and hoped that it could never fly free again. And you made sure she had no friends so she had no support system outside of you. So don't give me your bullshit about how much you loved her. You did nothing for her that was not totally selfish.'

'She'll be so easy to break.'

I walk up to his desk and plant my palms on the edge. I bend my body menacingly over him. 'Try it,' I say softly. 'Just fucking try it and I'll fucking burn down everything you ever built and see you in hell.'

His color changes, but he looks at me scornfully. 'Do you imagine that I am afraid of you?'

'You should be. I'll tell you this just once: she's mine now. You get in my way and I'll break your damn neck with my own hands.'

He pushes his twisted face towards me. 'You're a fucking fool, Shane. You walk out of here and you're a dead man.'

I stare at him cold-eyed. 'From the moment I stop breathing, you become a walking time bomb. You want war, Lenny, I'll give you war. Or you could simply give me the tapes and I'll call us quits. You have your plum deal and I get my revenge.'

'And the woman?'

'Is mine,' I state flatly.

'And if I say no?' His voice is calculating, probing.

'Then it's war and we both lose. I don't get the girl. You don't get your hands on those lovely millions and we both have some very pissed of Russians, but I figure they'll be more pissed off with you than me.'

'Get out of my office,' he shouts angrily. A vein has popped into existence on his forehead.

'I'm not leaving without the tapes.'

He flies up in temper and stomps over to his safe, opens it, and extracts two videotapes. They are held together with a rubber band. He deliberately chucks it on his desk in such a way that it slides on the surface and falls to the floor together with his pen. I bend down and pick both items up. Calmly, I return the pen to the surface of the table.

I meet his furious eyes. 'Obviously, my guys will be crosschecking with your staff about the records of all the occupants of that floor on that day, and they won't be expecting a frosty reception.'

'You got your tapes. Now fuck off,' he snarls.

'I'll see you around,' I say as I exit his office. Outside, his minders give me dirty looks.

Thirty-five

SNOW

Fifteen hours later, I arrive in Calcutta.

With a heavy heart, I change some money and walk out of the gleaming new Chandra Bose airport. Outside, I get into a taxi. The driver is a smiling, jolly man.

'No bags?' he asks in English.

'No,' I tell him. 'No bags.'

I give him my address and he starts the car. He tries to engage me in conversation with inquisitive questions, but I give him monosyllabic answers, and after a while he gets the message and begins to sing to himself.

I stare out of the window at the dusty billboards, the trees I have missed, the throngs of people, and the vehicles that honk for no good reason at all, and I remember my mother's unkind comment while I was growing up.

She said that Calcutta is like a giant mechanic's shop. A grimy and greasy place where there is no such thing as pure white. And maybe she is right. I can see that there is no building or anyone dressed in brilliant white, but perhaps white is overrated. The heart of this city beats as strongly, or even more strongly than London.

The taxi driver stops his noisy car outside the gates of my family home, and I pay him before getting out of the cab. He drives away and I walk up to the gates. They are locked.

I stand there, my fingers gripping the metal bars as I look into the compound. The year I have been away is like a fantasy I created in my head. Nothing has really changed. What happened in the hotel room was just a nightmare. Lenny is part of that nightmare. And Shane, he is just an impossible dream.

Of course, I could never have a man like him. I just conjured him up.

I look at the green, perfectly manicured lawn, the perfectly straight flowerbeds, and as I am standing there blankly, Kupu, the gardener, comes into the garden with a hose pipe. At first he doesn't see me. Then he looks up and does a double take. His jaw drops open in surprise and then he starts running towards me.

'Snow, Snow,' he shouts happily.

And for a moment my sad heart lifts. I love Kupu. This is my real family. Kupu, Chitra, and Vijaya, our cook. I have missed them. With shaking hands, he unlocks the padlock from a set of keys dangling from his tattered belt.

He opens the gate and I walk through.

He puts his palms together in a prayer gesture. His rheumy eyes are wet.

'How've you been?' I ask in Tamil.

'I'm so glad you've come home. It's not been the same without you,' he replies sadly.

'How is Papa and Mummy?'

'Your papa is lonely. He's lost a lot of weight, but he won't go to the doctor. He spends all his time in his room watching TV.' He drops his voice to a whisper. 'Your brother is home.'

I sigh. 'Thank you for the warning.' I touch his skinny, wrinkled arm. 'I'll see you later, OK?'

His hands come out to grasp my hand tightly. 'All right, child. Don't worry, God sees everything.'

And I just want to burst into tears. God didn't see anything. He let it all happen.

I turn away and walk up the short driveway to the portico of the house. My father's car is in the garage. I open the intricately carved, heavy Balinese doors, and I am standing in the cool interior of my family home. But for the emptiness inside me, it is like I have never left. I walk further into the room and my brother pops his head around the side of the couch, sees me, and raises himself onto his elbow.

'Well, well, the prodigal daughter returns,' he says sarcastically.

I walk closer. He is flipping through a sports magazine and eating monkey nuts. He puts the magazine down. 'Are you back for good?'

I nod.

'Why?'

I shrug. 'Just wanted to.'

His eyes glint with malice. 'The streets of London are not paved with gold after all, eh?'

'They are paved with the same gold as the streets of Kansas City,' I retort.

He looks at me with irritation. 'That was not my fault. Americans are just stupid.'

'Really, all Americans?'

'Yes, they are *all* as stupid as you are,' he says, cracking a nut and lifting the pod over his mouth, letting them fall in.

My brother will never change. He will always be peeing on other people's heads. I watch him chew. 'Where's Papa?'

'Where do you think?'

There is no point in talking to my brother. The longer I stay the more likely it is that we will end up in a huge argument. I turn away from him and start walking towards the stairs.

'Hey, you never said, what happened to your big dreams of becoming a teacher in England?'

'Who told you that?'

'Mother, obviously.'

'I see.'

'So you couldn't make it there then, not even as a pre-school teacher,' he notes gleefully.

'No, I could not make it there,' I say dully.

'You shouldn't have bothered to come back here. There's absolutely fuck all to do. And don't start making plans to set up here forever either. I'm in the process of persuading Mother to sell this house and buy a smaller one for the three of us. I want to use the remainder of the money to set me up in a business.'

I go up the stairs and knock on my father's door. Even from outside I can hear the TV turned up loud.

'Who is it?' my father growls impatiently.

I open the door and enter his room.

His bad tempered scowling face freezes for a second. Then he stands up and exclaims in shock, 'Snow?'

Kupu is right. My father has lost a lot of weight. His face is sunken in and his shirt is hanging off him. 'Yeah, it's me, Papa.'

He fumbles around the low table in front of him for the TV remote. He mutes it and turns towards me eagerly. 'When did you come?'

'I just arrived.'

'But why didn't you let us know? Who picked you up from the airport? Does your mother know?'

'I took a taxi from the airport, Dad, and no, Mum doesn't know. It was a spur of the moment decision to come home.'

'Are you all right?' he asks worriedly.

'Yes, I'm fine.'

'Are you sure?' he insists, frowning. 'I ... I mean, we ... have been so worried about you.'

'Yes, Papa. As you can see I am just fine.'

He nods a few times. 'Come in. Come in. Come and sit down with me. Are you tired? Do you want something to eat? Vijaya can make something for you.'

I go and sit down next to him. 'No, I'm not tired. I slept on the plane and I am not hungry. Are you all right?'

'Yes, I am all right.' He looks at me and sighs. 'You left a child and you have come back a woman. It is a man, isn't it?'

'Yes,' I whisper.

His eyes narrow. 'Are you pregnant?'

I shake my head.

'Are you sure?'

'Yes, I'm very sure.'

'Thank God. Oh, thank God for that,' he says with relief.

I find my eyes filling with tears.

'Don't worry, Snow. *I* will find you a good husband. You are young and beautiful. Many boys from good families will come for you. Don't ever tell anyone about this man who cheated you. You know how it is. People will talk. The less they know the better.'

'Oh, Papa. No one cheated me. And I don't want you to find me a good husband. I promise I just need to stay here for a while and then I will get my own place and be out of your hair.'

'Your own place? Out of my hair? What is this Western nonsense? You are my daughter and you will stay with us for as long as you are unmarried.'

'Oh, Papa,' I sigh.

He grabs my hand. 'This is your home. As long as I am alive you have a home here. Nobody can kick you out.' My father exhales loudly.

'I've missed you, Papa.'

He nods slowly. 'I've made a mess of everything, Snow. A horrible mess. Do you know that you could recognize and follow my voice from the time you were born? You would turn your big, green eyes and stare at me. But I didn't have time for you. I was too busy. And for what? I lost it all anyway. Now I sit here in this little room and turn the TV up too loud and pretend to be bad-tempered so no one will come in. I'm an old fool.'

'You're not an old fool, Papa,' I say sadly.

'Yes, I am. No one will know my regrets, except me. Now go and see your mother. She will be very happy to see that you have come home.'

'I'll see you at dinner, OK?'

'Yes, yes,' he says softly.

I stand up and kiss him.

I leave my father's room and as I am closing the door I see my mother coming down the corridor. She is dressed in a housecoat. She stops mid-step. Her eyes widen.

'Hello, Mum.'

She recovers herself and walks up to me. A year has made no difference to her. She is as beautiful and as distant as ever.

'You look different,' she tells me. She stares at me. 'Something happened to you ...'

I drop my eyes.

'Something bad,' she says.

I inhale a quick breath and meet her inquisitive gaze. 'Yes, but I'm fine now.'

'Tell me what happened to you,' she says sternly.

I shake my head. 'Oh, Mum. You know what happened to me.' In spite of myself my voice breaks.

'I warned you, but you've always been too wild, too rebellious, too clever for your own good.' Her tone is cold and unforgiving.

And then I see it in her face. She is not sorry for me. She is glad that I have been punished. I have acted impulsively and I have been punished.

'Is it OK for me to live here for a while?' I ask softly.

'Of course. Where else would you go?'

'Thanks, Mum.'

'I'll go and tell Vijaya to lay an extra place for you for dinner. Why don't you go and have a shower and freshen up? You can fill me in later. It's been so long since I've been in London.'

And then she walks away. I turn to watch her go. *What have I ever done to you to make you hate me so?*

I know my time here will be short. I have a little money still and I must find a way to go to the city and find a job there. I *will* make it on my own. I *can* make it on my own. I *will* become a pre-school teacher.

I think of Shane. He seems to belong to a different world. I wonder what he is doing now, and immediately I feel a tearing pain in my chest. I take his photo out and look at it. *Are you well? Are you safe, my darling?* I trace his jaw line with my finger. I stroke his body and the tears come hard.

Oh, Shane, Shane, Shane.

Thirty-six

JAKE

I enter the smoky back room of the Chili Club, and Lenny is sitting behind his desk. I close the door and he rises and comes forward.

'How are ya?' he asks, pumps my hand and gestures to a chair. His friendliness doesn't disarm me or take me off my guard. Lenny and I go back many years. I know him well. He is nicest before he sticks a knife in your back.

'Good. You?'

He turns the corners of his mouth downwards. 'Can't complain.'

I sit, lean back, and watch him take his seat behind the desk. He opens a silver cigarette box and holds it out to me. Technically, I've stopped smoking. But I still indulge once in a while. I reach out and take one. He flips open a black lighter. I lean forward and wait for the tip of my cigarette to burn cherry bright.

'Thanks,' I say and leaning back, inhale deeply.

He lights his own cigarette and sits back, making his chair tip back. I watch him inhale and exhale. His eyes find mine through the haze of smoke.

'Like old times, eh?' he says.

'Like old times,' I repeat. My voice is easy.

'What do you want, Jake?' he asks slyly.

'My brother came to see you?'

'Yeah,' he says. 'We came to an agreement.'

I don't show it, but deep inside I feel a flare of pride and joy. I came here thinking I'd have to bargain, threaten, and even murder if necessary, but Shane's got it all covered. My baby brother's grown up. He fought his own battle and won. How the fuck did he do it though?

I take a lungful of hot smoke. 'Right. So we're good.'

He jerks his head backwards as if even the thought of war between my family and him would never occur to him. 'You know me. I don't keep grudges.'

And I know why too. Because Lenny always settles the score until he's satisfied that he has had his pound of flesh. 'Yeah, you're a straight guy, Lenny.'

'I'd never harm your family, Jake.'

I fix him with a stare. 'No, you're too clever for that.'

He flicks ash into the ashtray. 'War between us is good for no one. The Mafia learned that the hard way, eh?'

'He's young, I hope he didn't give too much away,' I say.

He barks out a laugh, short and sharp. 'Too much? Shane? You don't give him enough credit.'

I say nothing. I drag another lungful of smoke and exhale it slowly. Suddenly I feel worried. What has Shane got himself into? What could he possibly have done that Lenny is so pleased with himself. I expected to find him spitting blood.

I frown. 'What exactly did you agree to with him?'

'Relax, Jake. He's a chip off the old block. He didn't have to give too much away. It was no big deal. I was happy to give her up. She's damaged goods. I was keeping her as an act of charity.' He looks at me craftily. 'He helped set me up with a juicy deal.'

He glances at his cigarette tip. 'And the little punk introduced me to two of the best whores I've ever had. I'm flying them both over for this weekend. One of the fucking bitches is double-jointed. She can suck her own pussy.'

He stops to catch my gaze, and there is something chilling about his eyes. 'They put up a good show. I could give you their phone numbers if you want?'

There is a sour taste in my mouth. Amazing to think this was my life for so long. It wasn't me then, and it's certainly not me now. I grind the cigarette butt in the ashtray on the table. 'Thanks, but I'll pass.'

Lenny watches me with his empty eyes. I know he is hiding something. That bullshit about keeping Snow as an act of charity, my four-year old daughter could see through that one. Shane has something on him, but I don't need to know how far Shane has gone. Shane did what he had to do. All I need to know is that Lenny has not been left with a grudge. And I am satisfied that no retaliation is due. I stand up.

'See you around, Lenny.'

'Give my regards to Snow,' he says.

I turn around and stare at him.

He smiles slowly. 'Bad joke,' he says.

I open the door and walk out of his property never to return.

Thirty-seven

SHANE

I stand outside the gates to her parents' house. There is a bell, but before I can ring it, a skeletal man in an old shirt and stained baggy trousers starts crossing the garden and comes towards me. His face is full of wrinkles and he has only a few yellowing sticks for teeth. He stands a foot away from the gate and peers worriedly at me.

'Snow. Is Snow home?' I ask with a friendly smile.

And suddenly his face splits into two with a happy greeting. Nodding vigorously, he unlocks the gate and lets me in. I wait while he relocks the gate, and when he makes a beckoning gesture with his right hand, I follow him. He opens the front door, kicks off his rubber slippers and looks pointedly at my shoes.

'Of course,' I say, and take off my shoes.

He points to a sofa. I sit and he quickly disappears. I look around me. It reminds me of a Balinese interior with beautiful hardwood furniture and two fans tuning lazily on the ceiling. I walk to the window and look out ... and I immediately see her.

She is in the garden sitting on a covered swing reading a book. I turn away to go to her and find a blonde woman in her early to mid forties standing at the entrance of the room. She is beautiful in a hard sort of way, and even though no two women could be less alike, I know immediately that this is Snow's mother. She has the chilly, stern air of a school mistress. Her eyes sweep over me disparagingly. Oh fuck! T-shirt and jeans. *Not a good look, Shane, my boy.* She would have warmed better to a sharp suit and a Rolex watch.

She comes forward. 'You are looking for my daughter, I believe,' she says in such a strong British accent that she must take great pride in it to keep it so strong after all these years of living in a foreign country.

'Hello, Mrs. Dilshaw.'

She inclines her head to acknowledge my guess. 'I'm afraid I have no idea who you are.'

'I'm Shane Eden.'

'Have a seat, Mr. Eden.'

I walk to the settee I just vacated. She perches daintily on the one opposite mine. 'May I ask what you want of my daughter?'

I smile. 'I guess you could say that I've come to ask your daughter out.'

Her eyes become hostile. 'Didn't my daughter run away from you?'

'No. She misunderstood the situation. I've come to explain.'

'I'm afraid that won't be possible, Mr. Eden.'

I frown. 'Why not?'

'This is not London, Mr. Eden. We have different customs here. Certain ... niceties have to be observed. Reputations are so easily ruined. Snow's father is in the process of negotiating a marriage for her. I'm sure you'll appreciate how confusing it will be for her to have your presence here now. I'm sorry you have had a fruitless journey, but I'm afraid you won't be able to see my daughter.'

'I totally understand. Thank you for being so frank with me,' I say and stand.

She stands too, but with surprise etched in her eyes. I don't think she expected such an easy victory.

I start walking to the front door and she follows.

The thin man is sitting on the front steps. When he sees me he stands up and runs towards the gate. I slip on my shoes.

'Goodbye, Mrs. Dilshaw,' I call over my shoulder and start walking towards the gate. The old man lets me out. I step outside and he immediately padlocks the gate. The mother is still waiting at the front door. I wave at her. She does not wave back. I thank the old man and I start walking down the road.

I walk on until I reach the edge of wall to their property. Then, praying for an absence of guard dogs, I climb over their neighbor's wall and drop into their garden. I run along the wall that separates the two properties until I am about halfway down, where I estimate Snow's back garden to be on the other side.

I put my hands on the top of the wall, pull myself up and over, and drop into the springy, perfectly manicured grass of Mrs. Dilshaw's garden. Twenty feet away I can see Snow gently rocking on the covered swing. There is an open book in her lap, but she is staring at a far away spot on the horizon. She is wearing some kind of breezy Indian costume with a long soft-green top and trousers in the same material. Her hair is down her back in a one long plait.

She looks vulnerable and lost.

I stand watching her with an ache in my chest, and I remember a National Geographic documentary of two elephants reuniting after a separation of twenty years. Since they did not know how the elephants would react, they let them meet in a barn with a thick metal gate between them. The younger strong elephant put its trunk through the gaps in the bar and stroked and hugged the other elephant, but such was their desire to get closer that they bent solid metal.

That is what I felt like at that moment.

I could bend metal to get to her. To hug and press her body to mine and never let go. I want to carry her off to my hotel room and claim her all over again, but I don't do that. Her mother's words are still fresh in my mind. For her sake I must be mindful that the culture here is different. I am a foreigner. A white man. I don't want to embarrass her. I don't know what she has told them about me. I take a few more steps towards her, but she doesn't see me. She is totally lost in her own world.

'Hello stranger,' I call out.

She nearly jumps out of her skin, the book falling to the grass, her hands rushing up to clutch her chest. Our eyes meet. Hers are as round and shining as a startled cat's. Then a look of such wild joy rushes into them that the desire to throw her on the grass and take her is almost unbearable.

Her mouth opens. 'What ... Why ...Why are you here?' she stammers.

I take a step towards her. 'Guess.'

She shakes her head as if in disbelief. 'How did you find me?'

I shrug and go closer still. 'I saw your passport while we were in France remember? Besides, Elizabeth Dilshaw is not a hard name to find in India.'

'But how did you get in here?'

'I scaled your neighbor's wall and jumped into your compound.'

'You did what?'

'What's so surprising about that?' I grin. 'Technically speaking, I've climbed mountains and crossed seas to get to you.'

She doesn't smile. 'You can't fight Lenny. I don't want you to, Shane.'

'I'm not starting a war with Lenny.'

'But he will hurt you if he finds out.'

'Lenny's taken care of,' I say shortly.

Her eyes narrow suspiciously. 'What do you mean?'

I shrug casually. 'He's given us his blessing.'

She stares at me. 'That can't be. Lenny would never give his blessing to us.'

'You have my word that it is true.'

She frowns. 'How can that be? I know him. I've seen him in action. Even Jake warned you how vindictive he can be.'

'Tsk, tsk, you been listening at doors again,' I say lightly.

'Did you do something to him?' she asks urgently.

I walk up to her and get down on my haunches in front of her. I take her soft small hands in mine. 'I didn't hurt him if that is what you are asking. Let's just say that he and I have an understanding.'

She frowns. 'You make it sound so easy. It couldn't have been. The Lenny I know is very vindictive. He enjoys hurting people.'

'Lenny is a psychopath. Like a reptile he's motivated by self-interest at all times. He had something I wanted, but then I had something he wanted more than the thing he had that I wanted. So we made our exchange. Besides, he knows a war with the Edens would have left blood on the floor, most probably his.'

'So what do we do now?' Her voice is so soft I almost do not hear. I see her body tremble through the thin material of her outfit, and I remember again how she trembled with trepidation every time she wanted me in Saumur. I smile inwardly.

'You had a dream. You have to follow it. Come back to England with me.'

'Just leave. Just like that?'

I grin. 'We can kiss first.'

She looks around nervously. There is no one around, but she shakes her head. 'That would be a bad idea.'

'I met your mother by the way.'

'What? When?'

I grin. 'Before I dropped over the wall. I tried the gate/front door route, but your mother gave me my marching orders.' I change my voice to a falsetto. 'This is not London, Mr. Eden. Certain niceties have to be observed.'

She giggles.

'She also informed me that your father is in the process of arranging a suitable wedding for you. Obviously, no one had informed her that you are mine.'

'What? My father is doing no such thing,' she says crisply.

'Mr. Eden,' a stern voice calls from the French windows.

I wink at Snow. 'I have to go, but will you come see me later at the Oberoi Grand?'

'Yeah, I'll come to see you,' she says with a sultry look in her eyes.

And my fucking randy cock dances excitedly.

'You're not going to jump over the wall again, are you?' she asks.

'I think I'll brave your mother one more time. See you later,' I say, grinning at her.

'Alligator,' she says.

I turn. 'Coming, Mrs. Dilshaw,' I say, and start walking. As I get closer I can see how furious she is.

'How dare you?' she rasps.

'Sorry, but you'd have done the same if you had travelled thousands of miles to see someone.'

'Get out of my house.'

I smile widely. I'm in a good mood. So I'll be generous. 'I have a funny feeling, Mrs. Dilshaw, we're going to be seeing a bit more of each other than you're expecting, so it might be a good idea to keep it civil. Good day, Ma'am,' I say, and walk out through the front door again.

My heart is soaring.

Thirty-eight

SNOW

I've been to The Oberoi grand a few times. It is one of the oldest heritage luxury hotels in Calcutta. As soon as you walk in from the crowded street, you enter a different world. Back to a time when the Indian Maharajas did 'posh' far better than the English. There are framed prints of birds and bejeweled, turbaned men on the walls. The reception floors are gleaming black marble with little diagonal white marble squares, and the dark wood paneling in the lobby is carried right through to the elevators and all the way to the toilet seat covers.

The door is held open for me by a uniformed doorlady. She is genuinely courteous and friendly. I walk up to the lobby and they call Shane's suite for me. They probably think I am a prostitute, but I don't care. With an impeccably polite smile, the receptionist passes the phone to me.

'Hi,' I say into the receiver.

'Stay there. I'll come down,' he says.

'No, I'll come up. I know my way to the deluxe suite.'

I get into the lift and go up to his floor. I knock on the door and it opens after the first rap.

Before I can say anything he pulls me in and, fisting his hand in my hair, swoops down on my lips. I gasp with shock and his tongue enters my mouth. His other hand comes around my waist and slams me into his hard body. He sweeps his tongue through my mouth. The raw animal desire radiating out of him makes the blood pound in my veins. From the first day I have been helpless in its wake.

Never taking his mouth away from mine, he walks me backwards towards the bed and we fall in a tangle. Our clothes come off haphazardly. The sound of zips, something tearing, something else whispering, and our hearts booming, fill my starving senses. Then we are naked. I hear the sound of the foil. And then he fills the aching, empty hole inside me with his beautiful, big cock.

'Ahhhh ...'

The orgasm when it comes lasts and lasts. With white dots before my closed eyelids. I slump against the headboard, exhausted.

'I was so hungry for your flesh I couldn't wait to fuck you again,' he growls.

'The insides of my thighs ... they are trembling ... for more,' I whisper.

'Tell the insides of your thighs I haven't even begun.'

Hours we are in that bed. I am aware of all the places his hands have been, my ankles, the soles of my feet ... the insides of my wrist ... the delicate skin at the nape of my neck.

And then his phone rings. 'Aren't you going to answer that?'

'No,' he says, and carries on kissing all the small bones of my spine.

But his mobile rings again. And again. He stops with a frown and answers it.

He sits up. 'Yeah.'

He turns slightly away from me. 'I'll be there in a couple of days. Why?' He listens again and sighs, his shoulders sagging. 'Fuck. Right. Yeah. Tell Ma I'll be there.'

He ends his call and turns to me. 'Look, I wanted to meet your parents properly and all, but we have to go back tonight. My mother's father is on his deathbed and he wants to see the whole family before he passes on. My mother wants me there.'

I sit up and touch his throat. He is so perfect I could weep. 'You go ahead. I'll join you in a couple of days. There's something I must do first.'

He looks at me. 'No, Snow. I don't want to leave without you.'

'I promise I will leave the day after tomorrow. I have to go and see Chitra.'

He looks at me curiously. 'Why?'

'I don't know why. I just know I have to go and see her before I leave.'

'Where is she?'

'Kupu knows where she lives. He will take me.'

'Is it far away or dangerous?'

'No.'

'Regardless, I'll arrange for someone to go with you and Kupu. You're not travelling around on your own.'

'OK, but you don't know anyone here,' I say with a grimace.

'Listen. You know me.'

'Yeah. I know all about you.' I smile gratefully.

'When was the last time you saw her?' he asks curiously.

'I haven't seen her since I was ten. Something happened and one day she was no longer there.'

'All right, go and see her. I'll arrange a ticket back for you for the day after tomorrow. Don't let me down.'

'I'll never let you down.'

'Chitra's poor, isn't she?'

'Very,' I say sadly.

'Would you like to give her some money?'

Immediately my eyes fill with tears. 'Yes,' I say, swallowing hard, unable to believe that he would be so generous to someone he had never met.

'Oh, sweet Snow. What a soft-hearted thing you are.'

'Thank you, Shane. You have no idea what this means to me.'

'Here's what I want you to do. I want you to go see her and give her enough to change her life. Buy her a little house or something. You decide what is best for her, OK?'

I stare at him in astonishment. 'You'd do that for a total stranger?'

'You're my baby and you love her. So she becomes part of my family.'

OMG! He called me his baby! I feel so happy I think my head is going to burst. And I almost blurt it out that I love him then, but I don't. I just don't have the guts.

'You're leaving tonight?'

'Yeah. My brother's secretary has already booked me a flight.'

I nod. 'Go and meet the old devil.'

'I really wanted you to come.'

'I know, but I'll be there the day after tomorrow.'

'I will arrange for you to be picked up at Heathrow and brought to my grandfather's place. Have you got a mobile phone?'

'I haven't got around to getting a new one yet.'

'I'm going to transfer some money into your account tomorrow. Get a mobile phone immediately so you can call me, and more importantly I can call you anytime I want,' he says with a grin.

'OK, I will.'

We make love one more time. My body tingles, and then it is time for me to go. It feels strange to let him go again. At the door, I lay my cheek against his chest. I can hear his heart pounding, and wish I could stay there forever just listening to its steady beat.

'Hey,' he says softly. 'It's only two days. Nothing can keep us apart again.'

Thirty-nine

SNOW

To my horror, Kupu takes me to the slums in the outskirts of the city.

'Chitra lives here?' I ask in disbelief.

'Yes, Snow,' he says as if living in this rubbish heap is normal. 'She lives here now.'

I am almost speechless with shock when we go down a dusty mud path filled on either side with corrugated iron roofed huts. Kupu stops outside one of the shanty huts and calls out for Chitra.

She shuffles out wearing an old sari and is holding a dirty, folded-up cloth pressed to her mouth. Her gaze falls on Kupu and then flutters over to me. For a few seconds her eyes squint and her head cranes forward with disbelief. Then her eyes widen and she stares at me as if she is seeing a ghost.

We look at each other. Then she screams with joy from behind the cloth pressed to her and almost trips over the doorway in her rush to hug me. Tears pour down her face.

I hug her tightly and join her in her tears. She is happy to see me, but I am horribly saddened and frightened to see the state of her. She is a shadow of her former self. Her eyes are deeply sunken and her body is a bag of bones. That she is very ill is clear. I can hardly believe this is *my* Chitra. Wiping her tears with the ends of her sari she bade us to enter her tiny hut.

I look around at the bare, pitiful surroundings. There is only one plastic chair, a little stove, some cooking utensils, and some cardboard boxes with her belongings in one corner.

It is like an oven in this small space and I actually feel claustrophobic and oppressed. To think that Chitra spends her whole life here is unthinkable to me.

'What's wrong with you, Chitra?' I ask.

'I have tuberculosis,' she says, suddenly breaking in a hacking cough that causes her to double over with its intensity.

'But tuberculosis is curable. Why are you like this?' I ask when the coughing fit is over.

'I've been treated for lung problems for more than a year now, but because the doctors have been making wrong diagnoses and prescription errors, they have made the disease stronger rather than curing it. Now my doctors keep changing the drugs, but nothing seems to work. The only thing they have not yet attempted to do is surgery to remove the infected parts of the lungs, but I can't afford it and anyway I am so weak now I don't think I can even survive it. Because of all the wrong diagnoses I have hearing loss, terrible joint pain, you cannot imagine how they ache at night.'

That afternoon I call Shane on my new mobile and tell him exactly how I want his money for Chitra to be spent. I want her to have the best doctors in India to perform her surgery, and when she is better I want her to come and stay with us for a while. He says he will get someone to immediately start making the arrangements for her surgery and treatment. In less than an hour he calls back to give me the address of a private hospital to take Chitra to recuperate.

We admit her there and I breathe a sigh of relief. It is air-conditioned and clean and modern. The nurses there immediately take over. I stand at reception and cry from pure release of the fear and tension I had been holding ever since I saw the state Chitra was in.

I tell Chitra that I have to go to London, but I will be back for her.

She hangs on to my arm pitifully. 'Go, my beloved daughter. I will always love you,' she says, and both of us burst into tears.

When I tell my mother my plan to join Shane in London, a massive argument errupts. For the first time ever in my life my father takes my side.

'Just let her go,' he says.

'Did you actually see the man she's going to?' my mother snaps.

'No, but I trust Snow,' my father says quietly.

'Well, I saw him and he looks like the worst kind of player.' She turns to me and demands. 'What is he? Irish?'

'He's a gypsy.'

She clasps her hands and shakes her head in disbelief. 'Oh my God! I can't believe it. He's a gypsy! They're the worst. They're just a bunch of thieves. What does he do?'

'He's in business.'

'Business? What business? Stealing manhole covers during the night and selling them for scrap?'

'Mum, please leave it. Even if he is poor, and he is not, I'm going to him.'

'He'll get you pregnant, break your heart, and he'll leave, and then you'll come running here with his bastard baby in tow.' She turns angrily to my father. 'Is that what you want for her?'

'I want Snow to be happy,' my father says stoically.

I look at my father and he quickly winks at me. My eyes widen with surprise. I swiftly look at my mother and thank God she missed the wink.

'I'm talking to two brick walls here,' she bursts out. 'He *won't* make her happy. She's infatuated with his looks and superficial charm. It won't last.'

'I don't believe that it won't last.' He turns to look at me. 'Snow is special. It's hard to leave her.'

I smile at my father. And he smiles back.

'Well, don't turn around and say I didn't warn you,' she huffs.

My mother is so furious with me she refuses to come with me to the airport.

Shane had led me to believe that someone holding a placard would be picking me up at Heathrow airport. So it is a great shock to see him standing there with a massive bunch of flowers and an even bigger pink teddy bear. I don't run into his arms. I stop so suddenly the person behind bangs into me, and I stare at the sight he makes. All at once he is cute, ridiculously edible, and heart-stoppingly gorgeous.

He crooks his finger at me so I rush to him and hug him while he holds the big bear and flowers at the sides of his body.

'A teddy bear?' I ask.

'It's Layla's idea,' he confesses sheepishly.

I laugh. 'Your sister thought you should buy me a teddy bear?'

'Yup, I get it.' He spots a little girl standing nearby and he holds the bear out to her. 'Want this?' he asks.

The girl nods big-eyed and immediately takes it.

Her mother says, 'Oh, that's so kind of you. Thank you.'

'No problem,' he says and turns to me. 'God, I've missed you. I actually can't wait to get inside you.'

And that is what he does. We get into the car and, halfway to his grandfather's home, we stop on a small country lane where he rips my panties off and gets inside me ... perfection!

His grandfather's home is a small bungalow with tarmac outside, and chintz curtains, lace covered armchairs, and a patterned carpet inside. His grandmother is a grey woman who has the cowed, beaten eyes of someone who has spent some of her teenage life and her entire adult life with a bully. A woman who lives like a silent ghost, terrified of provoking her husband's rage, just for the crime of existing.

She is in the kitchen making a famous Romany dish that Shane tells me is called Jimmy Grey. Beefsteak, liver, chicken and pork, onions and swede, shallow fried in animal fat.

As a race, the Romany gypsies are proud people. They eat, sleep, grieve, and celebrate only with their own kind. Jealously guarding themselves from infiltration by non-gypsies, they neither trust nor like the ways of others. Perhaps their mistrust of other races comes from centuries of persecution and hatred they have suffered no matter where they go. As soon as I am brought into her presence, I feel that instant wariness and mistrust.

I am a gorger, a non gypsy.

So I hold back too, and just watch the large personalities around me set about preparing for the death of one of theirs. After introducing me around to a whole bunch of uncles, aunties and cousins, Shane takes me into the bedroom.

Death is already in the room, in the smell and the odd stillness. There are fresh wild flowers in a vase by the bedside, and candles have been lit even though it is in the middle of the afternoon The old man must have been large in his day, for even after more than a year of cancer eating through him he is still a big, strongly built man.

Under his bushy grey eyebrows he has fierce black eyes that alight on me. Shane brings me closer and he stares at me with his black eyes. I want to say something, but I am almost hypnotized by his strange stare. Silently, without having uttered a single word, he turns his face away after about a minute.

'Come on,' Shane whispers in my ear and we exit the room.

I exhale the breath I was holding. 'That was weird,' I say.

'Yeah, who knows what is going through his head? Come on. I want you to meet my mother.'

Shane's mother is outside drying clothes on a washing line.

'Ma,' Shane calls, and she turns and looks at us. There are clothes pegs in her mouth. She takes them out and holds them in her hand as we walk up to her.

'Hello, Snow,' she says, her eyes sliding over me. She is not overly friendly, but she is different from her mother and father. She has kindness in her eyes, and a deep love for her family.

'Hello, Mrs. Eden. I'm sorry about your father,' I say.

'Don't be sorry, my dear. It'll be good for my mother. She'll finally be free.'

'If he was such a horrible man in life, why did your mother rush her whole family here?' I ask Shane curiously.

'Gypsies are superstitious people. The belief is that people can come back from the dead to wreak revenge on the living. So when someone is dying, their families, friends, acquaintances and even enemies come to them to ask for forgiveness and settle any strife, for fear of the mulo, a type of undead.

That afternoon Mickey passes away. The funeral is a massive affair. More than a thousand people travel from all over Britain to come to the old man's funeral. He was a great boxer in his time and was highly regarded.

The dead man is dressed in his best attire, his gold watch, and his favorite pipe are put into the coffin with him.

Part of the tradition is to have the body at home, and have mourners and relatives pay their respects by coming to the house, so a marquee is erected. A skip is hired and left outside the house to light a bonfire in. People come and go all hours of the night. There is a lot of cooking, drinking, toasting to the dead man, and singing. The entire affair is characterized by abundance, public mourning, and solemn ritual.

It all ends with a massive procession of hundreds of people walking the five mile walk to the cemetery. The convoy includes the horse drawn carriage that carries Mickey, eight cars, lorries carrying wreaths and floral tributes. They celebrate the life of Mickey. Children, even Lilliana and Tommy, ride up front in a horse drawn cart alongside the hearse.

After the funeral, all of Mickey's possessions are brought out and burned. It is a form of destroying all material tied to the dead.

That night in the hotel, we are both lying on the bed, tired. Shane turns to me and says, 'I don't want to use condoms anymore. I want us both to take our tests.'

I don't look at him. 'OK,' I say quietly.

Forty

SNOW

Three days later, after Chitra has been successfully operated on, the letters drop through the letter flap. I pick them up and take them to Shane. He is working on his laptop, but he looks up when I come into the room holding the envelopes in my hand. For a second I imagine I see dread in his face, but then it is gone in a flash. He closes his laptop and grins. 'Do you want to go first or shall I?'

'You,' I say, a knot in my stomach.

He walks over to me and takes the envelope I am holding. He tears it open and glances at it. He looks up at me. 'I'm clear.'

'Oh, good,' I choke. 'Right,' I say and, taking a deep breath, I tear my envelope. My hands are shaking so much I can't even take the letter out. His hand covers mine. 'It doesn't matter either way. Whatever it is we'll deal with it, OK?'

'OK,' I whisper.

I pull the letter out of the envelope and unfold it. I let my eyes skim it. My eyes start to tear up. I'm in the clear. I look up and his face is a picture. He is pretending as if he doesn't care either way. And suddenly I am so full of joy and happiness I want to play. I want to say, 'No, all is not well,' but I find I can't even do that to him. It's too much. So I just shake my head.

His eyes widen. 'What?' he gasps.

I stare at his reaction. My God! He has been terrified about the results. Probably even more than me. My mouth opens to tell him it is just a little joke, but the penny drops for him and he snatches the paper out of my hand and reads it. He looks up, his eyes totally blank.

I start walking backwards. 'It was just a joke. I just wanted to see your expression. Come on. It's funny,' I say cajolingly.

He lunges forward, grabs me by my thighs and, hauling me up, throws me over his shoulder like I am a sack of something unprecious.

'I'm sorry, I'm sorry,' I say, but by now I am laughing so much. *I'm clear. I'm clear.*

He takes me to the bedroom and throws me on the bed.

'Hey,' I protest.

He reaches forward and unbuttons my jeans and pulls the zip down. Then he grabs the material at the heels and yanks so hard my jeans come off in one swift movement.

'I don't know what you're so angry about. It was just a joke,' I giggle.

He throws my jeans behind him and hooks his fingers into the tops of my panties. They come off real easy.

'Come on, Shane,' I coax.

Silently he pulls my T-shirt over my head and, while I am slightly raised off the bed, unhooks my bra and flings that away too.

'Awww ... baby, don't be so evil,' I whisper.

With a totally granite face he undresses, his cock stiff enough to be a coat stand, and crawls on the bed. The violet specks in his eyes are glowing as he grazes his thumb across my lower lip. Delicious.

'Now why would I be evil? This is a fucking celebration. We're both in the clear, my darling.'

'Exactly,' I whisper.

He curls his hands around my ribs. His lips brush my ear. 'Flip over, Princess.'

Something about his voice makes me look again at him, but he smiles innocently. I get on my stomach and he presses his long body against mine and slides his cock in. My body arches with pleasure.

It is the first time. It is our first time.

His arm comes around my body and I thrust my breast eagerly into it. He rams into me hard. Really hard. It's what he's wanted to do for a long time. Come inside my body. And he's going for it.

It is raw, uncivilized, brutal and beautiful.

And when, finally, he gets to spurt his seed deep inside me, it is with a kind of sigh. A sound of deep satisfaction. As if something long desired had been achieved. For some seconds he remains inside me, throbbing. Then he withdraws and I feel his fingers enter me. Not to arouse me, but to smear his seed all around my sex even between my ass cheeks. He takes great pleasure in it. He even bites my ass. Then he turns me around.

'Your turn,' he says.

And I smile, because my turn means the world is about to turn upside down. And upside down it goes. He massages my wet flesh. I moan. He sucks my clit. It doesn't take long before I jerk violently and climax. Does he stop? No. Of course not. His fingers milk me. Again and again. Until I shriek and spasm uncontrollably.

Does he stop then?

Noooooo ...

Emotion wells up inside me, a humbling, breaking typhoon. I'm free. I'm actually disease free. I don't have to worry about infecting him ever again. Tears slide down my cheeks. He licks them. The way a dog would. I like dogs. They are loyal creatures.

'You're mine,' he says and kisses, licks, sucks and strokes every inch of me. Every crevice has its day. We do everything. He tastes my skin as if tasting it for the first time. He holds my thighs and drinks from my pussy. And then he comes inside me. Again. We go at it for hours.

It is afternoon when I cry. 'No more, Shane. No more. I can't take anymore.'

'Yes, you can,' he says.

And he is right. I can.

Trembling and breathless I climax again. I flop on my back, exhausted and limp. Shane lies beside me, our fingers entwined. For a while neither of us speak. I look up at the ceiling. 'What if I get pregnant, Shane?'

'Don't worry. We'll just get an abortion,' he says.

My head whips around. 'What?'

He turns his head to face me. 'What's wrong?'

For a moment I can't believe what I am hearing and then I start punching his arm. 'You bastard,' I accuse, laughing.

He grabs both my hands and pulls me on top of him. We are both sweaty and our bodies slip.

He doesn't laugh. 'Do you know how sad and destroyed I was when you shook your head earlier? I felt as if you had stabbed me in the heart with a knife.'

Immediately I am contrite. 'I'm sorry. I shouldn't have done that. It was no joking matter. I think I was so relieved I kind of lost of my senses. I thought it would be funny. I see now how wrong I was. Will you forgive me?'

'There's nothing to forgive. Remember what the most famous person in your land of birth said, Love does not measure. It just gives.'

'Mother Theresa,' I whisper.

'I love you, Snow. You'll never know how happy I am that your tests came back negative.'

My head swings around. 'What?'

'Yeah, I'm in love with you. Can you fucking believe that?'

I stare at him. 'It's not another retaliation joke, is it?'

'No, it's not a joke. But I was kinda hoping you might return the sentiment. A bit.'

697

I start laughing with joy. 'I love you, Shane Eden. I love you so much, I thought I'd die when we parted. I used to dream about you telling me you loved me, but I never believed that it would happen,' I reply.

'You know what you make me feel like? You make me want to dance in the kitchen with you. And go out with you to used bookshops and rescue the oldest, saddest books in them. Or go to the market and buy up all the lobsters in it and set them free in the ocean.'

My eyes start filling with tears of happiness.

'Do you know that poem by Pablo Neruda, If You Forget Me?'

I shake my head.

'It reads, if little by little you stop loving me, I shall stop loving you little by little.' He traces my cheekbone with his finger. 'Not for me. Nothing you do or say can ever make me forget you and nothing can extinguish my love for you. My love is a guest of eternity. I'm never ever letting go.'

Dizzy with happiness, I get on one elbow and, resting my head on my palm, I circle his nipple with a finger. 'So when did you realize that you loved me then?'

'I always felt really possessive of you. From the first moment I saw that slime ball touch your thigh in my club, I felt something, a burning anger, deep inside as if he was stepping into my territory. I think it made me a bit schizophrenic. Sometimes I worried about hurting you and sometimes I was rougher than I should have been. And when I dropped you off after the holiday I was like a bear with a sore head. I drove straight to my mum's house and I was in such a fowl mood my mother actually chased me out of her house.'

I giggle.

'You can laugh, but you don't know how I burned with jealousy. Fuck, even thinking about it now makes me feel uneasy. I didn't sleep that night. Short of going up to him and bashing his head in, I did everything in my power to make sure he would be kept up so late, he wouldn't get it into his head to take an early flight and turn up at your place that night. But I couldn't sleep. I realized that I didn't feel good when you were out of my sight. I wanted to protect you. In my head you were already mine, you just didn't know it yet.'

'Really?'

'Yeah,' he says with his trademark mischievous grin.

'But when did you realize you *loved* me?' I probe.

'I think it was when I saw you surrounded by those idiots outside the club. Oh, my God. I have never felt such a mad rage in my entire life. I knew I could have killed them. And then when I looked into your face. I was so frightened that somehow I was too late, they had hurt you. You couldn't speak. You couldn't move. Jesus, I've got goose bumps now just thinking about it.'

He touches my face. 'You just looked so broken and I didn't know what to do. That was when I knew I loved you, and I would have done anything for you. Anything to wipe that look from your face.'

I frown thinking of that night. 'I don't know what happened to me that day. I just froze. I couldn't move a single muscle.'

'Fuck don't tell me that, Snow. I won't be able to let you go anywhere without me. It terrifies me to think that you are that defenseless.'

'I'm not defenseless. I think I was already in a state because of the shock Nikki gave me, and then them ... Anyway, it doesn't matter. Nothing happened.'

'Yeah, and nothing fucking will. I'm getting you a bodyguard.'

I jump up in horror. 'What? No way. I'll feel silly.'

'Hmmm ...' he says absently, and I can hear all the wheels in his head turning away.

'I'm serious, Shane. I'm not having a man following me around as if I'm some celebrity. It's just ridiculous.'

'Then you won't fucking go anywhere without me then,' he says flatly.

'Oh, darling. I'm not going to let them ruin my life any more. I'm not afraid. Not anymore. Every day, ever since you came into my life, I have become stronger and stronger. My greatest regret is that I never went to the police and at least attempted to punish them. It's not revenge although that would be sweet. It's just that I know all of them will do it again to other young girls like me. They enjoyed it too much not to. My memories are all jumbled. Who knows, my evidence could have saved someone from what I suffered?'

Forty-one

SNOW

The day of our wedding dawns bright and cold. It is such a mad rush, the process of getting ready, but finally I am. Nobody allows me to see the mirror until my ensemble is complete, down to my satin covered shoes and my bridal bouquet.

'Oh, Snow,' Layla says in an awed voice. 'You look like a fairy tale princess.'

I look at myself in the mirror and my mouth drops open in astonishment. I *do* look like a fairy tale princess!

The dress is everything I ever dreamed of. It has an illusion sweetheart neckline, a ball gown silhouette, and lace sleeves that are longer than my fingers, giving it the impression of a medieval costume. There are delicate lace details on the edges of the sleeves and a stunning appliqué on the bodice. On my head sits a glittering tiara made of stars.

I have to blink to stop myself from crying with happiness. I can't believe I am getting married to Shane. It's like a dream. It's just too perfect.

'No, no, no,' cries Lily. 'Don't you dare cry and ruin all the make-up artist's work.'

That makes me laugh.

There is a knock on the door. Layla runs to open it and my father comes into the bedroom. His eyes are filled with pride. At that moment I am suddenly painfully aware that my father, who is twenty-five years older than my mother, won't be on this earth much longer. He kisses me gently on the cheek.

'I haven't been a good father to you, but I'm so proud of you,' he says gruffly. There is regret etched on his face.

'No, Papa. You've been wonderful. I wouldn't exchange you for all the world.' And it's true, no matter how distant we have remained through the years, I have loved him. I truly, truly love him. As I look into his shining eyes I suddenly remember being a small girl sitting in his lap and him whispering in my ear. 'You're my princess,' and then my mother coming into the room, and my father putting me away as unobstructively as possible.

As the image recedes, there is a commotion at the door and my mother comes in. Automatically my father takes a step back, almost guiltily. And I see what I have never seen before. The unconscious pattern of our relationships. All of us afraid to show affection to anyone but my mother.

My mother takes a deep breath. 'You look wonderful, Snow,' she says.

And I smile at her. As if she really means it. As if she really loves me. I know she thinks the dress is too big and not elegant enough, but I don't care. It doesn't matter. I love her, anyway. I just have to remember what Shane said, 'Love does not measure. It only gives.'

'You look beautiful too, Mum.' And she does, in a cream suit with her trademark pearl necklace around her throat.

'Thank you, my dear,' she says politely.

'Well, I guess we better get going,' my father chips in.

I turn to him, beaming. 'Yes, we should.'

In the car, with the fragrance of my bridal bouquet enveloping us, my father turns to me. 'She does love you in her own way, you know?' he says.

'I know, Papa. I know,' I say and squeeze his hand.

'You have a heart of gold, Snow. A heart of gold,' he mutters. 'To everyone else you may look like a grown woman, but to me you will always be in pigtails and asking me what God eats, or why mice are not striped like tigers?'

We arrive at the castle and an assortment of people are waiting outside; the planner, photographer, and some other organizers. Little Liliana is one of the flower girls. Dressed in a black and white printed dress with a flower crown and carrying a miniature green wreath, she looks utterly adorable. She grins and waves at me. And Tommy, the ring bearer, is all dressed like a mini man, and trying very hard to look up someone's skirt.

As we walk to the entrance, we pass lovely moss-covered animal topiaries. Pigs, bears and rabbits. We enter the impressive doorway and walk down a dark stone corridor.

My father turns to me. 'Are you ready?'

I nod silently, speechless. They open the great doors and the little girls go ahead, strewing rose petals.

Everyone turns to look at me, but I walk down the aisle in a daze, my eyes searching for Shane. I see his dark head almost straight away. He has turned and is looking at me. Through my veil our eyes meet. And my breath is snatched away.

He is so incredibly handsome.

My feet stumble and I cling automatically to my father's arm. He glances at me anxiously, and Shane makes a slight movement as if he is about to leave his position and come to me, but I recover, and we carry on down the aisle under Shane's watchful gaze.

My father lifts my veil and kisses me on my forehead. Shane breaks tradition and hugs my father as if they are old friends. My father nods, overcome with emotion and turns again to me. He hugs me tightly and then pulls away. As he is turning away, I call him as if I am a little girl again, 'Daddy?'

He twists around, tears in his eyes, and I hug him again. 'I love you,' I whisper in his ear.

And he says, 'I hope you know I've always loved you the best.'

And I whisper back, 'Yes, I know that.'

Then I am given to Shane. He holds out his hand and grins irrepressibly at me, as if he too can't believe his luck.

The words of the service sound like they are coming from the bottom of the sea. I repeat them carefully. It is truly like a dream. I just cannot believe that I am marrying Shane. As if in slow motion, I am holding out my hand and Shane's strong fingers are slipping the ring onto my finger. I look up at him.

'You may kiss the bride,' the priest says.

Shane bends his mouth and, as his lips touch mine, all the hundreds of guests fire their cap guns at the same time. The reverberating sound startles me. I gasp and a laughing Shane gathers me in his arms and takes my mouth in a long, deep kiss.

'God, I love you, Snow,' he says, looking into my eyes.

The organ music reaches a crescendo triumphantly.

'Let's go,' Layla says to me after we have posed for photos in the castle and on the lawns, 'Time to change.'

'Change? Into what?'

'It's a surprise,' she says with wink.

We go into one of the smaller rooms next to the great hall where the reception will be held, and there is a deep red and gold traditional Indian bridal costume hanging on a hanger. I turn around and look at Layla. 'I'm wearing an Indian costume?'

She laughs gaily. 'We all are. It was Shane's idea.'

I laugh in disbelief. 'Really?'

'Yes,' she says excitedly.

'OK,' I say, getting into the groove of an Indian wedding. I think of Chitra sitting out there in the crowd. She'll be so tickled.

Layla and Lily quickly help me out of my wedding gown and into the Indian costume. The hairdresser gets to work next, taking down the tiara, and putting gold pins in my hair, and stringing a forehead decoration into the mix.

Red and gold bangles are slid up my arms. An Indian make-up artist from Hounslow uses eyeliner to enhance my eyes, making them appear dramatic. Gold antique jewelry is loaded onto my body: necklaces, forearm decorations, rings, chains. I am surprised by my reflection. I have never seen myself look so flushed and excited before. I am so happy I want to weep with joy.

Layla appears beside me. She looks gorgeous in a lovely blue lehenga. She smiles. 'You look absolutely lovely. I wish I had done an Indian version for my wedding too.'

I just laugh.

'One last hug,' Layla says and we do a quick A line hug, since her pregnancy is showing even more now.

We leave the little changing room, and outside I am surprised to see that the others have changed into Indian costumes too. They look beautiful in their bright lehengas, saris, and salwar keemezes.

Feeling suddenly shy, I follow Layla through the crowded hall. People keep stopping us to congratulate and compliment me. Just outside the room where the reception will be held, Shane is waiting for me in a Sherwani. He looks so dashing it takes my breath away. Jake and Dom are also wearing Kurtas, and they stand beside Shane and smile at me. I smile back and feel so touched that they have all made such an effort to embrace me into their family. Shane comes up to me. He takes my hand and exhales slowly.

'I always had a fantasy of bedding an Indian princess,' he tells me with a grin.

I glance at the main table and see my mother. She looks stiff and uncomfortable. My father catches my eye and waves. I release my fingers from Shane's. He looks down at me.

'I'll only be a minute,' I say.

'Hurry back,' he says.

I walk over to my mother. She alone has refused to wear Indian attire.

My father stands. 'You look absolutely beautiful, my darling.'

'Thank you, Papa,' I say and kiss his cheek.

He squeezes my hand and, leaning forward, whispers, 'I'm so proud of you.'

I turn to my mother. She knows she is being watched so she stands and smiles at me. 'Yes, you look very ... nice,' she says.

I know she is surprised by the wealth she has witnessed today. When Shane came in his T-shirt and jeans she assumed he was a poor gypsy boy. Now she can see how wrong she was.

'You've done very well,' she says stiffly.

'I married Shane because I love him, Mother. I would have married him even if he had nothing.'

'It's good then that Shane has a bit of money, isn't it? I was thinking of sending your brother to England. Give him a fresh start. Maybe your husband can help him find a job or set him up in a business.'

I feel a twinge of sadness then. Even now, on my big day, my mother cannot just be happy for me, but uses the occasion to try and help my brother. And then I think of Shane saying, 'Love does not measure. It just gives.' I love my mother, and if there is anything I can do to make her happy, I will.

'I'll ask Shane,' I say softly.

And she beams happily.

The food was prepared by one of Dom's chefs and it is fabulous. There are speeches from Jake, my father, Dom, and Layla's husband, BJ. Then Shane stands up to make his.

He thanks the ushers, the bridesmaids, and all the people who have attended. 'If I forgot anybody, what can I say?' he says.

Then he turns to me. 'There is no Romeo or Juliet that ever was, is, or ever will be, that could ever compare to what is you and me. There is no sonnet or song that has been written that comes close to describing my level of fucking smitten. You are not just the love of my life, but the fabric, the reason, and the basis for my life. And when time has passed and everyone else sees you as old and gray, I will still see you as you are this day. So I'll finish by saying that we'll be moving to a new home soon, so do not come around because we'll be banging and screwing at every opportunity we get. Thank you all for coming.'

The crowd loves him. I look for Shane's mother and she is smiling. I swivel my gaze towards my mother and she is grimacing. I meet her eyes and suddenly I don't care that she disapproves of me, or that I would never be good enough for her. I look towards Shane and guess what? He is gazing at me with stars in his eyes. *You can't spoil my day, Mum. Never again.*

'Are you ready for your first dance, Mrs. Elizabeth Snow Eden?'

I am just about to say yes, when Layla hits the stem of her glass to indicate that she wants the floor.

And Shane groans. 'Oh shit.'

Layla stands and raises her hand. 'Well, normally, the sister of the groom never speaks, but I just have to repay the favor my brother paid during my wedding when he stood up and gave some friendly advice to my husband.'

She looks sideways at her brother and then proceeds to tell everybody two of Shane's most embarrassing alcohol-soaked stories.

One involves him getting so drunk when he was sixteen, he ended up losing his keys, climbing up the drainpipes and jumping in through his upstairs bedroom window, only to find that he was in the next door neighbor's bedroom.

'The widow was glowing the next day,' she says to whistles, catcalls, and a thunderous applause of approval.

Layla then suggests that I sew our front door keys to his clothes.

The other story also involves a younger Shane getting so drunk that he falls into a patch of rosebushes and gets scratched to bits. He goes home and carefully applies plasters all over his face and falls into bed. In the morning, their mother finds about ten plasters in the shape of his face on the mirror. The crowd roars with laughter and Layla advises me to plant thornless roses in my garden.

And with that, she ends with the words, 'Jokes aside, you're both so incredibly lucky. At the end of this ceremony, Shane, you get to go home with a wife who is warm, caring, beguiling, and who radiates beauty and grace from every pore. And, Snow, you will go home tonight having gained a lovely dress and a gorgeous ring.'

That brings a smile even to Shane's sour lips.

Afterwards, Robbie Williams' *She's The One* comes on, and Shane takes me by the hand and leads me to the dance floor.

'Do you know what I love most of you?' he whispers.

I shake my head.

'Your lips.'

'So soft and delicious. I once dreamed of licking them.'

As we whirl and dip, I feel as if I am floating on air. There'll never be another day like this. Never.

And then suddenly the disco lights come on and bangra music starts, professional dancers fill the floor, and Shane lifts his hands and starts doing the bangra! I cover my cheeks with my hands and laugh. My goodness! He really doesn't do things by half. And then I join in as well. Layla, BJ, Jake, Lily, Liliana, Dom and Ella all hit the floor. And all of them have some 'moves' they have learnt.

My heart feels as if it will burst with joy at this beautiful, beautiful family I have fallen into. All those years when I yearned to be in a happy family are suddenly here. Shane catches me in a totally non-bangra move and, laughing, I realize there'll be many days like this. Many more.

Forty-two

SNOW

Christmas Eve

I hear the key in the door and I run to it. Standing on tiptoes, 'I,' I say, and kiss his forehead, 'love' I say, and kiss his nose, 'you,' I say, and I kiss his right eye, 'Shane,' I say, and kiss his left eye, 'Eden,' I say and kiss his lips. It was meant to be a peck, but he deepens it and kisses me passionately. I pull away and look at him in surprise.

'Is that the I-want-to-take-you-to-bed kiss?' I ask with a smile.

'It wasn't a bedroom kiss. I have something for you,' he says very seriously.

My eyebrows rise. 'What is it?'

He takes my hand and leads me to his study. He sits me down at his desk and opens his laptop screen. He turns the machine towards him and taps a few keys, then rotates it back to face me.

'What is it?' I ask curiously.

'Your Christmas present,' he says quietly, and walks out.

There is an arrow pointing to the left in the middle of the screen. I click on it and my eyes widen and my hands fly up to cover my open mouth.

In a panic I hit the arrow, the video stops playing, and I close my eyes. My heart is pounding and my breath is coming out sharp and fast. For a few seconds I do nothing, just stare at the frozen screen.

The frame shows a man, his eyes horrified and his mouth open wide in a scream of white hot pain. He has been tied up to some kind of wooden contraption, and behind him a black man with the biggest penis I have ever seen in my life is sodomizing him. To their right there is another man standing by and watching impassively. My eyes return to the man screaming. *I recognize you.* He was not screaming then. He was laughing, taunting … lusty. 'Give it to her, give the bitch some cock.'

To my surprise a smile comes to my lips. *Give the bitch some cock.*

My hand moves seemingly of its own accord and my finger presses the arrow.

The images start moving. My smile stays, then widens cruelly. *Now you know what it feels like to be totally helpless.*

I watch the coward slobber and scream and beg. Snot runs down into his mouth.

Tsk, tsk, even I didn't cry like that.

When the black man is finished, the other man takes over. He doesn't use his cock though. He uses a frighteningly big dildo. I peer closer. The dildo is studded. A mad giggle escapes my lips.

The man shakes his head and begs for mercy. *Well, well.*

They untie him and make him sign a letter. I cannot see what he is putting his scribble to, but he signs it with a shaking hand.

Then they beat him so mercilessly I hear the sound of bone crunching.

Ah well, Karma. It's a bitch.

I sit through another five little clips. Two of the faces I cannot remember, and that bothers me. Just imagine if I had been in a shop or some other public place and they had come in, I would have had no idea they were rapists. I would have spoken to the bastards normally. Why, they even looked like decent blokes.

At the end there is a template copy of the letters all the men have signed.

Dear Friends and Family,

Last summer, five other sickening perverts and I met in London to gang rape a drugged, innocent nineteen-year old girl in a hotel room.

I am sending you this letter so you know the real me.

Yours sincerely,

Then the video cuts to the impassive man saying that the letter and a copy of the recording have been hand-delivered to the men's families, and an email sent to every single person, even takeaway addresses on their phones and email list.

I close the screen and feel a strange sense of lightness. In this unfair, cruel world where the poor and the helpless always get trodden on, Shane found my justice for me. With a sigh of contentment I get up and go into the kitchen.

Shane is standing by the kitchen sink looking out of the window. When he hears me, he turns and looks at me. For a moment I do not recognize him. It is shocking that someone as beautiful as he is could ever be so cruel. I feel the same way I felt when I saw a lion killing a poor impala. How could such a beautiful beast do that? And then he smiles at me and I recognize him. He is *my* beautiful beast.

'Are you OK?' he asks.

I nod. 'Thank you for the black roses,' I say quietly.

'It was a pleasure.'

I walk up to him. We are accomplices. We are now bonded by revenge and blood. 'How did you find them?'

'Lenny had the surveillance tapes the whole time.'

I gasp with the stab of pain. 'I trusted him,' I whisper.

'I know, but you were so traumatized you would have believed anything.'

'I'm a fucking bad judge of character, aren't I? Again and again I trust scum,' I say bitterly.

'No, you're not. You're beautiful. If only the whole world would be as innocent and trusting as you, then it would be an unrecognizable, beautiful place.'

I look up at him. Sometimes I still can't believe he is really mine. 'Oh, Shane. You did all that for me. Have I ever told you you're my hero?'

He grins. 'A gypsy hero? Does such a beast even exist?'

'Yes, it does. I caught one.'

He laughs. 'Let's have a drink. Let's drink to those men's poor wives and children.'

So we drink ourselves silly and then I say in a slurred, slutty voice, 'I have a present for you too.'

And he grins. 'Oh yeah?'

'It's in the bedroom. I'll just go and get it.'

'I'll be waiting right here,' he says, plumping the cushions behind him and settling down.

I go into the bedroom and quickly undress. Naked, I get into high heels and wrap a big red ribbon around myself and tie a huge bow at my waist. Then I walk out to the living room.

'Here's your present,' I say.

And I swear I see forever in his eyes.

SHANE

Christmas Day

Liliana is sitting on my lap and telling me tales tall enough to make any full-blooded gypsy proud.

'Santa came to my house, you know,' she says importantly, 'because I've been a very, very, very good girl.' She drops her voice to a hoarse whisper. 'I saw him.'

I keep my face straight. 'You saw him?'

'Yup.' Her eyes are huge.

'When?'

She fingers a bow on her dress. 'Last night. I saw him eat two cookies and drink half of the milk that I put out for him.'

'Wow,' I say in an impressed voice. 'Did he say anything to you?'

'No,' she says shaking her head vigorously. 'I was hiding behind the door.'

'Why didn't you show yourself?'

'I didn't want to frighten him, Uncle Shane,' she says as if that is the most obvious thing in the world.

'Anyway,' she carries on, 'he left three presents. Two for me because I've been so good, and one for Laura because she's just a little baby and babies just need milk.'

'Right.'

She cups her hand over my ear and whispers, 'Don't tell anyone, Uncle Shane, but I woke up early and sneaked downstairs when everybody was still sleeping, and opened all my presents.' She claps her hands. 'And then I closed them all back.'

'So you know exactly what you've got for Christmas?' I ask, amazed that she actually did that. Even I never did something like that at her age.

She nods happily.

'So what will you do when you open your presents later and everybody looks at you?'

'Pretend to be surprised and happy,' she says coolly.

I have to laugh. 'Show me your surprised and happy face,' I ask.

She opens up her eyes, drops her jaw, and smacks her cheeks with her palms while managing to look like she is grinning. 'Yeah, that'll work.'

She makes her face normal again. 'Did Santa leave you presents?'

'He gave me mine early this year.'

She crosses her little arms over her chest. 'What did he give you?'

'He gave me a wife.'

She frowns and looks at me as if I am stupid. 'Auntie Snow is not a present. A present is like a real thing. Like a toy or a doll.'

'That's true. Maybe he's left one under the tree for me.'

She slips off my lap. 'I'll go and look for you, OK?'

'OK, but don't peek.'

She shakes her head solemnly. 'No, I only peek at my own presents.'

At the front door, I hear Layla, BJ's and Tommy's voices wishing my mother a merry Christmas. Liliana forgets about looking for a present for me, and rushes off to the front door. Jake returns from the garage where my mother keeps her fridge, carrying two bottles of whiskey. It has started snowing and there are snowflakes on his hair and shoulders. He sets the bottles on the table.

'What time will Dom be here?' he asks.

I look at my watch. 'Anytime now.'

At that moment BJ and Layla come through the door. BJ is holding a baby carrier. The room fills with the sound of us wishing each other a merry Christmas. A pink-nosed Layla kisses both Jake and I and then disappears off to the kitchen to see what the women are up to.

BJ leaves the baby carrier on the floor by the chair next to me and collapses into the chair. 'Where's the fucking alcohol?' he asks.

I laugh and Jake pours out whiskey for us all. Before we can take a sip, Dom and Ella arrive. Ella is carrying their little boy, Alex. Jake pours another glass. Again the room fills with sounds of Christmas greetings.

'You guys started without me,' Dom complains, as Ella goes out with Adam.

'Nope,' Jake says and pushes a glass into his hand.

We raise our glasses. 'May it always be this good,' Jake says.

And we drink. Life is good.

Just before lunch, Snow comes up to me. 'I've got a surprise present for you,' she says, her eyes shining.

'I thought I got mine last night?' I tease.

'This is better.'

I raise my eyebrows. 'Better than the one I got last night?'

'Much,' she says, her eyes sparkling.

She puts her hand out, I take it, and let her lead me. She pulls me upstairs to my mother's guest bedroom.

'Are you ready?'

I guide her hand to my crotch. 'Is that ready enough for you?'

She gasps and says sternly, 'It's not that kind of present.'

'Well, then it can't be better than last night's.'

'Shane?' she whispers.

'Yes'

'Don't spoil it.'

I put my hands up in surrender.

She opens the door and we enter ... and a male German shepherd puppy is sitting inside a large metal cage.'

'Merry Christmas,' she shouts.

I turn my head to look at her. 'This is my present?'

'Yes, isn't he wonderful?' she enthuses ignoring my unenthusiastic tone.

'So my present is a dog from your favorite breed?' I ask.

'Yes,' she says blithely, and goes to open the cage door. The dog immediately jumps all over her excitedly. And I can see that she is dying to pick him up, but she doesn't.

'Have you any suggestions for a name for him?' she asks instead.

I shrug.

'You could call him Ghengis ... if you want to,' she suggests.

I turn away from her and say, 'Ghengis.'

The dog immediately looks at me with its bright, intelligent eyes.

I turn to her. 'How strange. He seems to answer to that name.'

She bites her lip. 'I might have called him by that name once or twice,' she admits.

'So, how long have you had him?'

'I've been keeping him here secretly for the last two weeks. I wanted to house train him before I gave him to you. I know the apartment is too small for him, but we'll be moving to our new house in two months, right? And Chitra will be coming to stay with us so she can help take care of him too.'

'Right.'

'See how perfect it is?'

I smile. 'How old is he?'

'They're not sure because he was abandoned, but he's about four months. Look what he can do, though,' she says scooping the bundle of excited fur up in her arms. She takes a treat out of her pants pocket and holds it in front of his nose.

'Off,' she says and the puppy stills.

'Look in my eyes,' she says firmly, and the puppy immediately ignores the treat and looks into her eyes.

'Take,' she orders, and the puppy immediately gobbles down the treat.

'Good boy,' she approves. She brushes her chin against his head and looks at me. 'You can teach him so many other things.'

I grin. God I love this woman so much I could eat her. She just solved my biggest problem. Here is the bodyguard that I was looking for. I will train him myself. This dog will go everywhere she goes and be her protector when I am not around.

SHANE

Christmas Night

I get back from the toilet and there is a dark shadow on my side of the bed. I go closer and it raises its head and gives a low growl.

'What the fuck?' I swear.

I hear a giggle from Snow's side of the bed.

I switch on the light and Snow has her head buried under the cover, trying to stop herself from laughing, but her shoulders are shaking silently. On my side of the bed, Genghis has his teeth bared and his eyes are downright frosty. It looks quite comical. Then Snow pops her head out of the blanket and she is laughing behind her hands.

Suddenly I freeze with the realization of how precious this moment is. I wish that I could hold it for a hundred years. My four-month-old, usurper puppy trying to claim my woman for himself, and my woman giggling like the most beautiful, carefree child.

But I know the puppy will become a loyal dog, the giggling beauty will become a woman who will have my children, the dog will die, and the woman will become old, wrinkled and frail.

And then we'll all become a fistful of dust.

But today ... my cock is throbbing with hot blood and I am king of my empire of dirt.

I chase the dog away, rip open my dressing gown, and claim the woman. A big cock wrapped up in a ribbon and a bow is extremely difficult to resist.

The dog is too young to know: the second mouse always gets the cheese.

The End.

I **LOVE** hearing from my readers so by all means come and say hello here:
https://www.facebook.com/georgia.lecarre

or

Click on the link below to receive news of my latest releases, great giveaways, and exclusive content.
http://bit.ly/1oe9WdE